PLAYER MANAGER 2

All rights reserved. No part of this publication may be reproduced, stored in a retrieval system, or transmitted in any form or by any means electronic, mechanical, photocopying, recording, or otherwise without prior written permission from Podium Publishing.

This is a work of fiction. Names, characters, places, and incidents are either products of the author's imagination or used fictitiously. Any resemblance to actual events, locales, or persons, living, dead, or undead, is entirely coincidental.

Copyright © 2023 by Ted Steel

Cover design by Damonza

ISBN: 978-1-0394-4584-0

Published in 2023 by Podium Publishing
www.podiumaudio.com

PLAYER MANAGER 2

TED STEEL

Podium

THE STORY SO FAR

Max Best has been cursed with the ability to see the attributes of football players and to manage football matches. He gains experience points by watching live games and can spend XP to upgrade his skills. He has had enough minor success as an amateur manager and scout to impress a handful of football insiders. But he still works in a call centre and has turned months of grinding into exactly one hundred pounds.

PLAYER MANAGER 2

*"In order to write about life,
first you must live it."*

—*Ernest Hemingway*

1
SCOUTING MAX BEST

After watching sixth-tier Chester compete like tigers against fifth-tier Oldham in a VIP box where two former players were the kings of the jungle, I made a decision. The fastest, surest way to get what I wanted—financial security and a job as a football manager—was to become a player. Once inside a football club, I'd be able to take over. I'd be a parasite, but one of those benevolent ones, like the one that makes you find cats amazing.

Footballers train, what, ten minutes a day? So I could still be a scout. I could still be an agent. There would still be opportunities to manage youth teams and the like.

My days of working in the call centre were numbered.

The next few days were a blast. A riot. Mike Dean and I, partners in crime, called and texted each other like lovestruck teenagers. We cooked up a heist plot that could easily have been turned into a three-part BBC special.

The intended victim, I suppose, was Ian Evans, the Chester FC manager. The loot? His approval for the signing of a certain Max Best.

In a couple of weeks, once my ankle was more or less fully healed, I would turn up for my trial, impress Evans, sign for Chester, and get paid at least 350 pounds a week. The exact number of pounds was the cause of rather a lot of bickering, but MD and I both agreed that 350 was the absolute floor. Once I was a Chester player, I'd be able to start sticking my nose into everyone's business. Start rebuilding the club in my own image, from the inside. Not powerful, exactly, but not powerless.

The one possible flaw in the plan was what if I turned up to the trial and was shit?

So that's what we were on the phone for: scheming and plotting ways to make sure my trial was plain sailing. And mate, we spent more time laughing at our solutions than we did thinking of problems. Because for once in my life, the solutions were undeniably perfect.

You might be thinking, *But bro. We've seen you play. Jackie has seen you play. We know you're good enough for Chester.*

Well, maybe. I'd only played about twenty minutes of football since being cursed, and that was five-a-side against some CA 1 guys. (CA, I believed, stood for Current Ability, measured out of 200.) And if we want to get paranoid, most of my good play said as much about Raffi Brown, my footballing soulmate, as it did about me.

Being cautious—and this was my one shot at getting a playing contract at Chester until Evans was gone—I couldn't assume that the curse had turned me into Soccer-Man. Sure, I was objectively stronger than before, but I'd also felt really weird when I'd taken to the pitch. Acing the test *wasn't* a sure thing.

So. I went through my known strengths and weaknesses and thought about what drills that ruled in or out. We'd try to show my good qualities in the trial and hide the bad ones.

At the very start of the process, I took a piece of paper and created a player profile. At the top I wrote *Max Best*. I focused on the attributes I'd unlocked, since those were what I had the most points of comparison for.

Acceleration and Pace
I was never very fast, but I wasn't slow, either. Obviously most professional athletes would absolutely bang me in any kind of race. But I allowed myself to imagine I was faster than Ziggy, so I gave myself a 5 in both the speed attributes.

Bravery
Absolutely a 1. I didn't think of myself as a coward. I would definitely probably maybe run into a burning house to save a supermodel. It wasn't about being a coward, it was about priorities. Have you seen these defenders who do a tackle and the ball bounces towards a striker and the defender sort of wriggles like a worm to do a header? With his head two inches above the ground and a boot flying towards both ball and head at speed? It's fucking mental. You really have to be tonto to do that. Me? Forget it. I liked having my nose on the *front* of my face.

Dribbling and Finishing
I wasn't sure how to rate these. Obviously, both should have been 1. But James Yalley had a 6 in dribbling, and if he was better at running with the ball than me then I'd honestly just quit my job in the call centre and try to get a worse job in a worse call centre. I mean, seriously, that's how low I would feel. And finishing? I was feeling pretty sharp in the five-a-side match. I dared to dream and gave myself a 5.

Handling
What am I, a goalkeeper? Next!

Jumping
What am I, a flea? Next!

But seriously. This was one of my absolute, most critical flaws as a player. For a start, ninety-nine percent of the football I'd ever played was indoor football, futsal, or five-a-side, and you just don't do many headers in those games. In some matches, headers are banned! Plus, why are you jumping? Because someone sent you a bad pass, basically. If you have to jump, someone's made a mistake. And that's always annoyed me. Plus, I didn't like it. What can I say? I didn't like jumping. I just didn't. Jump for a header? No. Jump out of a plane? Veto. Jump for joy? No. One hundred percent of the world's joy is on ground level. I hated jumping so much I didn't even wear jumpers.

Heading
Weirdly, I was always quite good at headers. I wouldn't *jump* for a header, but if the ball was kicked *right* onto my forehead, I would redirect the shit out of it. Put me up against a real defender, though, and I wouldn't even bother competing. So I could give myself a heading rating of 10 knowing it would never actually come into play.

Passing
With this one I got a bit arrogant. A bit uppity. Because if you asked me, I was an unbelievable passer of a football. The more the trial was based around passing, the better. In my mind, I was already the best at passing in the entire sixth-tier of English football. 15 out of 20, yo. Nuff said.

Stamina, Strength, Tackling, and Teamwork
1, 1, 1, 1. You might be thinking, *But you can lift weights, bro*, and yeah, maybe the curse had beefed my rating there. And maybe it had also given me mad stamina. But was I going to let that come into the trial? Fat chance. I had spent most of my life as weak as a baby.

But teamwork, bro. You're all about teamwork. You had a whole arc where you ruined your career for the sake of teamwork. Yeah, I believed in teamwork. For other people.

Technique
My general level here was pretty high. Above average. Controlling a pass, hitting a volley or half-volley. Yep. I was pretty confident about it. But also, Supercoach Jackie had done that drill where he'd smacked balls at me and I'd dealt with everything. My skill was kind of undeniable. I gave myself a 10, though I suspected it might have been higher.

Other Attributes
What other things had the curse mentioned? Influence. Not relevant to the trial. There was OFF, which I still thought was something about offside. Again, that was unlikely to come up. Especially if I was designing the drills! Flair, creativity. Yep, I'd score well there. But Ian Evans didn't want such players, so there was no point showing that.

And set pieces. That was the ace I was keeping up my sleeve. I used to be able to take a good corner, but I hadn't taken one for at least five years. If things were going badly, I'd try to whip in some dead balls. If I could hit a good corner, Ian Evans might want me around. But again, it had been *so* long since I'd taken one, I couldn't be sure I still had it.

So this was me:

MAX BEST		
Born MYOB	(Age 22)	English
Acceleration 5		
	Handling 1	Stamina 1
	Heading 10	Strength 1
		Tackling 1
	Jumping 1	Teamwork 1
Bravery 1		Technique 10

	Pace 5	preferred foot R
	Passing 15	
Dribbling 6		
Finishing 5		
CA 1	PA 1	
Player/Manager		

And now, my absolute priority in life was to let my ankle heal. Keeping still, foot raised. No six-hour drives. No walking dogs.

I imagined my ankle as having its own health bar, like in a video game. In the days after the injury, it would have been fully red. Danger! Zero percent! After getting it checked by Livia, there would have been a few pixels of green. Now I had to get it to at least seventy percent health.

Why the rush? Because Raffi was waiting for *his* trial, and even worse, his wife Shona was waiting. And because Henri Lyons was waiting—he wanted a deal in place for January 1st so he could escape his purgatory in Darlington. And because I wanted to get out of the call centre racket.

So I didn't do any scouting for Chester. I didn't go to Hough End on a Sunday morning. I postponed the double date, but I did do one Culture Club session with Emma. (I chose the movie *Knives Out*. She liked Captain America's sweater and wondered if the writer had mixed up two subgenres in order to disguise his lack of mastery of either.)

I worked. I went home. I rested. I didn't hoard my money to get my agent license—I used my spare hundred pounds to eat healthier. Blueberries. Kale. Broccoli. My Nutribullet got used! I was thankful I hadn't sold it.

And while I ate anti-inflammatory foods, I devoured content: *Welcome to Wrexham*, *All or Nothing*, a bunch of YouTube channels. MD sent me a few books he owned that were on my list, including *Moneyball* and *Inverting the Pyramid*.

And I stayed home some more. And I rested some more.

Quick detour to tell you about Ziggy. Ryan Ziggs, as no one was calling him.

After scoring his wondergoal (which video replays showed he'd sliced, *sideways*, onto a defender's head) Ziggy had played the first half of the next match but was replaced by one of the strikers back from suspension. The next match, he'd been on the bench. The match after that, he hadn't been in the squad. He was now FC United's fifth-choice striker.

Ziggy was depressed, but I wasn't worried—as his CA kept improving, he'd start to get named in squads and then start getting minutes again. Also, he was paying me! Thirty-five pounds every week. Cash!

And finally, a quick word about the curse. After a week of aggressive rest, I'd started to pop to Platt Lane and Hough End to do some light experience point accumulation. Just a bit here and there, using the crutches all the time even if I didn't really *really* need them.

By the time of my trial, I'd collected 360 XP, which was pretty feeble, but in my head I was grinding by not grinding. When the calendar hit November 1, I'd been expecting a new perk to be available. Shocktober finally left the store, but it wasn't replaced. That wasn't unusual—sometimes the perks only appeared halfway through the month. Maybe there wouldn't even be one in November because I was carrying a debt. Or maybe the curse was waiting to see how my trial went. Maybe if I got a pro contract it would start giving me playing perks. That'd be fun. Anyway, the World Cup was due to kick off on November 20, and I would have been astonished if that wasn't the theme for November's perk.

Regardless, I had no plans to spend any XP until I saw what the monthly perk was. So really, all my focus was on impressing Ian Evans.

XP balance: 946

Debt repaid: 106/3,000

Sunday, November 6.

The day of my trial. Raffi Brown's, too. Shona was pleased that I wasn't full of shit, but incredibly apprehensive for her family's future.

Henri Lyons was coming "to watch," though of course the real reason was to let him meet Ian Evans. If they hit it off, I could help Henri escape his ordeal at Darlington. He hadn't played a single minute of football since I'd met him, and since Darlington were doing well in the league without him, the situation wasn't likely to change.

After losing in the FA Cup, still high on adrenaline, Chester had won their next league game, but came crashing down, losing their match the day before my trial. 3–0. At home. Bad news for me—Evans was likely to be in a grumpy mood. Or maybe it was good news. Perhaps he'd be more interested in freshening up the team. MD had told me that the best thing about Evans was that he liked a smaller squad, so there was budget to bring in a few free transfers.

Okay. I've set the scene. The criminals have arranged the heist. They've got men on the inside. They've synchronized their watches. Nothing can possibly go wrong!

2

IAN EVANS

Raffi picked me up and we drove to Chester. He was excited; I was nervous. I was a *bag* of nerves. There was so much riding on this one morning!

We arrived at Chester's training ground—a business park owned by a credit card company—and I got changed. Raffi hadn't been joking about his boxing training—when he took his shirt off, I saw a phenomenal set of abs. Way to make a dude feel puny, bro.

The place was so strange. It was soulless. Even the shittest football ground had a kind of residual life force to it. This . . . thing . . . was a wide, flat, two-story building full of offices, and out the back a couple of grass pitches and a couple of low-quality artificial ones. The pitches were obviously intended for use by the staff of the credit card company. I wondered if any of those guys had talent. If I ended up signing for Chester, it'd be easy to go and scout them. Maybe I could get a fancy credit card, too. I bet credit card companies had *really* attractive receptionists.

Don't get ahead of yourself, Max! Thinking about the prize was fruitless. I had to focus on the process.

And the process was do things you know you're good at, and nothing else.

I took one deep breath, left the building, and listened as my boots clattered—stupendous volume—across the concrete paving stones. As soon as my studs sank into the grass, all my nerves evaporated. I knew everything would be okay. MD was already in place, and he threw a ball towards me. I let it roll onto my right foot and did a couple of kickups. Absolutely no pain. Green green green! As long as I avoided really hard shots, I'd be laughing.

I jogged around a bit, getting closer to the halfway line as I did. There was already a little gaggle of people there. My ankle felt fine; all that resting had paid off.

The first thing I did was introduce myself to Ian Evans. I'd only ever seen him from far away, so he always had quite an insubstantial quality. He was abstract. He was the *notion* of Ian Evans. But up close, he was substantial. Concrete. Formidable. He was the same height as me, but broader, chunkier, more powerful, more menacing. His features were bigger than normal, like a CGI artist's vision of an orc, or one of the blue people from *Avatar*. The nose was broad. The cheeks and mouth hewn by years of football management into a permanent grimace. The eyes blue, watchful, sharp. His hair had started to recede, but at some point it had screamed "No surrender!" and where it remained, it was magnificent.

His presence was titanic. He dominated the scene to an unbelievable degree.

He gave me a firm handshake—not obnoxious, not macho—and regarded me with a look that showed he had not heard of me. He didn't know about the under-fourteens incident. I had a clean slate. But by God, I'd have to work hard to impress him. Well, my dude, I got you covered; the hard work had started two weeks ago.

I shook hands with one of his first-team coaches. Vimsy, they called him. Was he in line to be the next manager? I was dubious; he didn't have anywhere near the charisma of his boss.

Chester's head physio, Dean, was there. He—loudly, as we'd planned—told me off for not going to get a check-up on my injuries. I promised him that I had taken it easy.

Then came what we in Manchester like to call the *coup de grâce*—the arrival of my "old friend" Henri Lyons. There was another round of greetings and handshakes.

Ian Evans gave MD a long, hard look. He understood that he was being played, but he didn't mind it. Clubs weren't supposed to negotiate with players from other clubs. It was called tapping up and was illegal. The fact that the best striker in the league had turned up "to watch his friend's trial"—well, it was the kind of scam Evans had seen and done countless times.

"As everyone knows," MD declared when everyone was ready, "Max had a bit of an ankle injury recently, so the plan is for him to show some moves and give us an idea of his skills. Raffi's in peak condition so we can ask a bit more of him! Dean, would you mind getting us some raw physical data?"

The physio made us do some very tiny drills. Some things were almost like a medical—stability tests, resistance tests. Then long runs up and down the pitch—apparently, football people liked to judge the way players ran, as though they were horses. Finally, some short sprints, then some sprints with little turns at the end. My goal during the whole thing had been to match Raffi. To keep up with him, or be only slightly behind. I matched him easily, but found he was already blowing hard. Me? Fresh as a daisy.

Next we did some basic ball work. I floated some crosses in for Raffi to head into the goal. When it was my turn to score the headers, Dean went nuts. Pretend nuts, you understand. He was doing what MD had told him. "Max, you can't head the ball! Not without a mask. No chance. And no tackling, either. Doctor's orders!"

"Gosh," I said. "That's a shame. How are we going to check Raffi's crossing ability?"

Vimsy was about to say something, but Evans stopped him. He wasn't enjoying the performance, exactly, but he appreciated it.

"Oh, I have an idea!" said Henri. "My boots are in my car. I could help out? I've been known to score the odd header." He gave us his most dashing smile, and fuck, I finally understood the phrase "he swept me off my feet."

"What do you think, Ian?" said MD.

This was the moment. If Evans had the slightest interest in signing Henri, we'd find out. If he wasn't interested, we'd find out. It was such a low-stakes way to do it that everyone could save face if the answer was no. "I think it's a great idea," said Evans. "I've always admired Monsieur Lyons." Henri zoomed away to his car and was back in seconds, ready to play.

So that was that, then. If Evans wanted Henri Lyons, there really wasn't much jeopardy left in the day. MD would tell Evans he'd have to sign me first, then Henri would come. And if he was going to sign *me*, they might as well sign the clearly superior Raffi, too. A good deal for the club. A coup. Fresh faces, fresh blood. And in Lyons, a bona fide goal machine.

This was the greatest criminal enterprise of all time. If this was a movie, it would be the kind where they plan the crime and carry it off smoothly. No alarms, no surprises. Ah . . . bliss.

Raffi spent a few minutes doing head-high crosses for Henri to crash into the goal. Henri's heading was thrilling. Poetry in motion. Evans was purring.

Great. So we'd done heading. We'd done pace. Next up was passing.

We had two wire men set up. Wire men. I don't know what the manufacturers call them. Imagine a piece of metal in the shape of a man that you can use as an opponent in training sessions. We stood two of them a yard apart and did a drill where two of us tried to pass the ball through the gap while getting farther and farther apart.

I easily beat Raffi, then I easily beat Henri.

Henri beat Raffi.

Then I crushed them both again.

Smasho and Nice One turned up. MD had invited them—at my suggestion—to pretend to be shocked at how good I was. It was all part of the scene. It was all scripted. They were happy to oblige, since we'd openly confessed that the plan was for me to help out with the youth teams.

I was about to launch into the next phase of the heist when things went sour. The twist. This *wasn't* the everything-goes-smoothly movie. It was the casino-manager-knew-you-were-coming-and-prepared-accordingly movie.

Ian Evans whistled at us to stop. We trudged over to find out why, while Vimsy dashed onto the pitch to remove the wire men and cones we'd laid out. "Lads," he said. "When MD said I should come and watch some potential signings get put through their paces, I said sure, why not. And it's been . . . amusing watching you fannying around. But we lost three–nil yesterday, so I cancelled the team's day off." He whistled again, and the entire Chester FC first team squad burst out of the building and jogged onto the pitch. They surrounded us, like police circling the criminals near the end of the film. Caught red-handed. Not such a foolproof plan after all. Evans continued. "So why not kill two birds with one stone? Let's have a quick game. Two twenty-five-minute halves. Extra session for this shower of shite who call themselves professional players. And a trial for a couple of lads who think they can do better. To hell with this farce. If you want to catch my eye, catch my eye by playing. Mister Lyons, you're exempt. I know all about you. I'd have you in my team any day of the week and twice on Sundays." He fixed his underperforming team with his heat vision. "The rest of you, you'll run the miles you should have run yesterday. You'll press and harry and get stuck in like you should have YESTERDAY."

Physio Dean stepped forward, genuinely flustered. "Ian! Raffi Brown is fair game, if he wants to play, but Max can't join a proper match. His ankle's not fully healed—you can tell from how softly he kicks the ball—and we haven't checked his eye socket. It could be fractured!"

Evans didn't look at him. He stared right into my soul, stepped in front of me, loomed over me somehow even though our eyes were level. "If he wants to play for Chester, he'll play right here, right now." He gave MD a quick blast of angry energy, then turned back to me. He pushed me in the chest. "So what's it going to be, Maxy No-Thumbs?"

Oh my shitting God.

He knew.

He knew who I was. Somehow he'd known what I was plotting. Every minute that he'd watched me dick around was a minute when he was taking the piss out of me. And now he was all up in my face, giving me verbals, giving me shit, pressing my buttons.

Well, what I did was simple. I took a deep breath, and very calmly and with full emotional control explained that I'd be happy to play but wouldn't challenge for headers or tackles because that would be all a bit silly, wouldn't it?

Hang on, I'm not sure that's right. Let me think . . . Ah, yes. It didn't happen like that. It *actually* went a little bit like this:

He pushed me in the chest. "So what's it going to be, Maxy No-Thumbs?"

I pushed myself into his hand so that he'd have to back off. This elderly man. He didn't budge. He was made of fucking *iron*. "I'm up for it. I'm down for it. I'll play anywhere, anytime." I'd tried to break into a Vegas casino and been caught. This caper was over. The only thing to do in such a situation . . . is raise the stakes. "But let's make it interesting. You manage the first team. Four-four-two maybe. And I'll manage the rest. Your reserves and my mates. An amateur. A striker who hasn't played for months. And a guy with no fucking thumbs." I was right in his grille now, pointing both thumbs into my face. It was hot. It was sweaty. The fan fiction would be epic.

His sneering face sneered even more. "Player-manager, is it?" He laughed. It sounded like he was scraping burnt flesh from a cheap pan. "You're on. Saddle up, cowboy."

"Yippee ki-yay," I said, backing away with my arms spread wide.

I was going to shove 4-4-2 so far up Ian Evans's arse it'd have to be removed by a team of surgeons working round the clock.

This wasn't a trial anymore. This was a tribulation.

3
MAX'S MISFITS

Ian Evans gave me ten minutes to organise my team. Before we formed a loose huddle on our half of the pitch, my guys grabbed luminous yellow bibs. As Raffi went to grab his, Shona called out to him, "Why you playing a match?" He smiled at her as if to say, "It's okay, honey. This is part of the plan." You can't spell smile without *lie*.

Henri picked up a bib, too. He wanted to play!

"No way," I said.

"Max," he said. But instead of finishing the sentence, he pulled the bib on. He twisted left and right to allow me to admire his form.

"Dude," I said.

"Max," he said, and this time he pushed his finger onto my lips. The international gesture for "hush, babes." Fucking French people! If Henri got injured, his club would go ballistic. I would never be able to step foot in Darlington ever again. I would have to spend half my income on bodyguards. My search history would be filled with "Darlington mafia," "are Peaky Blinders from Darlington," and so on.

As he jogged away, I tried tearing some of my hair out. "Argh!" I said, then smiled at Shona, as if to say, "Still the plan." She gave me a Look.

Magnus Evergreen arrived. You remember him. He was the player/coach/physio with the cleanest aura in Chester. I guessed that Dean had called him as backup in case things got feisty and more medical staff were needed. Yeah, well. I wasn't planning on getting injured. Not again. "Magnus!" I called.

He pottered over, his huge arms swinging low. "Max Best," he said, offering me a handshake.

"Yeah yeah yeah. We'll bond over a chai tea latte and a ceremonial exchange of friendship bracelets. But later, yeah? I need a sub. Get changed and grab a bib."

He gave me a placid look and held out his wrist. It was covered in bracelets and ornaments and shit. "Do you craft your own?"

"No!" I said, pushing his arm down. "Sorry. I'm stressed off my tits. Would you please help me out? I urgently need a guy on the bench. I'm not fit, my bro hasn't played much. *Neither* of my bros have. I'd kill for some tactical flexibility."

He looked worried. "Okay," he said. "But you shouldn't joke about killing. It darkens the soul."

Now, this might sound absolutely bonkers to you, but even in the eye of a footballing hurricane his words resonated with me. "Can you . . . lighten a soul?"

"You can try."

"Mate!" I said. "I want to fucking talk to you. At length. About all this shit. But now I need a spare left back. Do you feel me?"

"Okay," he said, and he walked towards the credit card building. In fucking slow motion! And while I gnashed my teeth, he turned and said, "I've been learning about breathwork. And I have a lot of thoughts about slowmadism."

I jabbed a thumb at him and jiggled it around. Good for you, buddy!

That reminded me. Maxy No-Thumbs. Rage flooded me again. But it was a cold rage. For once in my life, I had sight of the bigger picture, and that was making Henri Lyons look good. If this trial finished with Ian Evans telling MD to try to sign Henri, then that would be a good day. Raffi, sorry to say, was secondary. It was possible he was already tainted by his connection to me. Still, if it was a choice between Raffi looking good and me looking good, I'd be choosing Raffi all day long. My career at Chester was stuck on the launch pad. All because I'd tried to deceive the manager. Really, people are so sensitive sometimes. So, priorities, in order: 1. Henri. 2. Raffi. 3. Winning the game. 4. My playing career.

I rubbed my temples. Time was already running out. What did I need to do? Talk to Mike Dean about all this? No. We'd been outplayed. How, though? I raged again, but this time it was hot, violent rage.

I stomped over to Dean, the physio, and gave him a blast of attention. He'd been the one leaking all our plans to Ian Evans. "Dean, mate. Thanks for this. Appreciate it. If there's a loose bit of bone in here," I pointed to my skull, "and it gets jabbed into my fucking brain, don't feel bad about it. I'm sure you did what you thought was right."

He spluttered at me, but I'd gone super cold again on my way back to the huddle.

Time! Running out!

I opened the tactics screens. Chester FC were playing 4-4-2. Diarmuid Dubhlainn, also known as Aff, was their dangerman on the left of midfield. Sam Topps was their captain, their pitbull in the centre of midfield. Not as limited as he appeared to the naked eye—he had decent technical qualities.

My screen showed some things I already knew. Ben "Cavvers" Cavanagh, Chester's reserve goalkeeper, was on my team. I was quite happy with that since according to the curse he was slightly better than the first team keeper. I also had Carl Carlile, a talented and flexible defender who routinely stank the place out. There was something undermining his performances—a big shame because he potentially had a good career ahead of him. I also had Magnus Evergreen—he was listed as a sub. He could play anywhere in defence or midfield, and he was by far the weirdest player I'd ever scouted. He had that minus 2 potential ability (PA), but now his CA was written in red—it had fallen from 23 to 22! WTF was with this guy?

I also noted with some dismay that Henri's CA had gone red. Dropping to 54 meant he was still easily the best player on the pitch, but drops were bad. My mantra was: number goes up!

I shook it all off. Not the time! The default tactic was 4-4-2, of course, and the curse had put most players in good positions. I was on the left of midfield, which didn't feel like where I needed to be. I quickly used what I knew about the players to rejig the team, putting myself in the centre of midfield next to Raffi, with Henri ahead of us. I imagined a powerful triangle of likeminded players getting a grip on the game and dominating it.

Since no one on the touchline could hear us, I didn't even pretend to give instructions. The players knew what I wanted. I had two new formations I could try, but doing so would give me a splitting headache and this wasn't the right day for that.

What else?

I bit my nail while I thought about what I could do. Something occurred to me, and I disabled the match clock from my vision. Behind it were two buttons—Bench Boost and Triple Captain. A slight boost to any subs that came on, plus my captain's influence score being multiplied. Those abilities were only supposed to work once per season, but this match (Chester FC versus Max's Misfits) counted as being played in a brand-new season. I was really using these perks in a way that wasn't what the designers could have intended. And I loved it.

"Raffi, mate," I said. "You know the way I get a bit weird?"

"Yes," said Raffi, with nowhere near enough hesitation.

"Er . . . well, bit of a mad superstition thing here. Can you just pretend to be fiddling with your laces or doing something with your baby when the match starts? And then come right on for Magnus. You'll be off for thirty seconds, tops."

He sighed. "I'm not even going to fight this," he said as he loped away.

Magnus Evergreen came on. When he realised he was going to start, his whole posture changed. He became visibly less weird. More serious. He saw me gawping. "What?" he said. "I know my job."

"It's just for a minute," I said. "You won't be annoyed?"

"I know my job," he said.

So that was an early activation for Bench Boost. Now for Triple Captain. It was based on an attribute I couldn't see—influence. Who was the best choice for captain? Raffi was a lead-by-example type. Henri was a lead-by-scoring-goals type. I didn't know the rest of the team very well. So I took a risk and gave myself the C. (The team sheet now read *Max Best (C)* and I liked it.)

Vimsy stepped onto the pitch with a ball. The match ball. He was going to referee. Not exactly neutral, but what was I going to do? Zap through a portal and come back with Uriah Rennie? I wished.

What else? I thought. *What else, what else?*

I checked through every screen. Virtually every option on both teams was on its default setting. All normal. Nothing out of the ordinary . . .

Until some impulse to look in every last nook made me check Chester FC's tackling settings. Their tackling intensity was set to hard. Because this was a friendly, my options were limited to easy.

So.

There was at least one advantage to being a dinosaur!

Or maybe Ian Evans had his own version of the curse. I'd started to pick up little hints here and there. Insinuations that certain managers had inexplicable powers. José Mourinho's players used to be amazed at how he'd predict what would happen in certain matches. He'd design his entire tactical plan around one incident that he *couldn*'t have known would happen. And then it would happen. Pep Guardiola would often get plaudits for moving players into new positions. Well, I knew the trick now, didn't I? The trick was to have access to a cosmic database of where players could play!

So what if Evans was inflexible *by design*? Could he have a curse that let him gain XP when he didn't change tactics? And was he able to spend the XP buying motivation?

Yeah yeah yeah. Food for thought.

Right now, all that mattered was that I'd set up the team the best I could. The irony was that if my guys pulled through and helped me win, helped me get a contract, then that would hasten their exit out of the club. Almost all of them were easily upgradeable.

And as for me . . .

I felt lean. Mobile. Agile. Invincible.

I was going to put on the greatest performance by a Max since Maximus Decimus Meridius in the movie *Gladiator*.

I glared at Ian Evans. An emperor I wouldn't mind usurping.

Get ready to be entertained, *mate*.

We kicked off. Henri passed the ball to me. I played it to our left back. Absolutely beautiful. Five seconds in and almost everyone who mattered had touched the ball and completed our passes. The match ratings didn't change—every player on the pitch currently had a 6/10 rating. So the curse wasn't impressed by my 100% pass completion rate. Fine. Be like that.

The match settled into the normal patterns you get when two teams play 4-4-2 against each other. A lot of huffing and puffing and cul-de-sacs ending in long passes. Raffi came on during the first break and joined me in the centre.

I strolled around, dividing my mental runtime between the action on the pitch and the high-level manager view. The ratings of the players on the first team started to creep up—a few 7s here and there. Ours didn't.

It was early days, but it seemed like we would be in for a struggle unless something changed.

What was it that people like Magnus Evergreen had on posters in their hallways? *Be the change you want to see in the world*. Was that it?

Anyway, I decided it was time for the party to start.

"Yes, Raffi," I said, moving into position to receive a pass from him. I took a touch and looked forward—Henri pointed to where he wanted the through ball. I took a swing, one beautiful seven-iron of a pass coming right up! But my foot hit fresh air. While I'd been daydreaming about backspin, Sam Topps had whizzed past and nipped the ball from my toes. By the time I realised what had happened, he was ten yards away.

Nothing came of that break, but my match rating dipped to 5. Wow.

My next involvement came when a Chester player hit a back pass to his goalie, who booted it upfield. It was curving and spinning in my general direction, so I got into position to take it on my chest. Once I had it under control I'd move left or right depending on what the sitch was. I glanced right to see how that part of the pitch was shaping up, and in those microseconds, fucking Sam Topps appeared out of nowhere, jumped for the ball, and headed it away from me.

Oh, I thought.

Well, fine. I increased my workrate, running close to my teammates when they had the ball so that I could get involved in the game. I longed to create chances for Henri. A quick hat-trick for him would do everyone the world of good. But every time I got the ball, I felt Sam Topps storming towards me. Once I hit a pass that he blocked; it went out harmlessly for a throw-in. Another time he barged me off the ball before I could sort my feet out. The third time, I finally got my body working and was able to drift past him. But no sooner had I eased past Topps than another Chester player zoomed off with the ball. The ball that had been in my possession mere seconds earlier.

With me out of position and Raffi darting forward to help me attack, we were suddenly short at the back. Chester's midfield passed it left to Aff, who skinned Carlile and crossed to where there were a superabundance of Chester players waiting to knock it into the net.

1–0.

I went down on my haunches.

You're a human being. You've had that dream where you're trying to run but you can't. Imagine that dream, but it's really happening, and it's costing you a life on Easy Street.

This was too fast. Bewilderingly fast. If you think a speed attribute of 5 is slow then Chester were generally a slow team. From the side of the pitch, from the stands, watching as a fan or a scout, they seemed lethargic. Glacial at times. But on the pitch, in the middle of it all, the players were like electrons whizzing around faster than the eye could see. Maybe this was why older players took up golf. In that sport, faster, younger men didn't steal the ball every time you were about to do something beautiful with it. Of course, I didn't have advancing years as an excuse.

"Max," said Raffi, coming over to check on me while the teams reset. "You okay? You hurt?"

"Nah," I said. "It's just too fast."

"I feel ya." Raffi was more or less holding his own, though, with a match rating of 6. Mine was down to 4.

So that was that. I was, officially, dogshit.

How had I come to believe my own hype? How had I come to believe that me being half-decent was even possible? Because of fucking Jackie Reaper, that's how. Him and his moronic pep talks. I grunted with frustration and trudged off the pitch. Magnus Evergreen, a player with spindly legs and minus PA, would do a better job than me. Mark this side quest as FAILED.

4

TWO TOUCH

Football glossary: *Two touch. A type of game (usually a training sesh) in which players are only allowed to touch the ball twice. Controlling the ball counts as one touch, and the subsequent pass or shot is the second touch. Once another player has touched the ball, your touches are reset. Two-touch sessions develop technique and speed of thought.*

I allowed myself a moment to enjoy the sensation of my ambitions crumbling around me. It was like the moment after a video game boss fight where the thousand-year-old temple starts collapsing and you're supposed to sprint out. But I just stood there, defeated, and let my hubris entomb me.

Crash! I'd tried to take a shortcut into the heart of a world I knew almost nothing about and I'd been mugged, beaten, and left for dead. Wasn't that supposed to happen in chapter one?

Bang! Fifteen yards to my right stood Ian Evans, snarling. He'd outwitted me so completely I barely registered on his radar anymore. His Crush the Rebellion quest was marked COMPLETED, and now he was raging at his underperforming players. Shouting at a lazy fullback or a midfielder who'd missed a tackle was mother's milk to him.

Wallop! Between us, a discreet few yards back, was MD (looking pale), Physio Dean (fuming), Shona (proud/fierce/worried), and Smasho and Nice One (happy, unhappy, respectively).

So, I thought.

What the fuck, I thought.

The most likely explanation for what had just happened was that I was *exactly* as good at football as I'd always known.

But I *was* stronger and fitter than ever, so the curse had done *something*. And that's when I had one of the worst moments of my life. Because the answer was so obvious! So clearly true. The curse *had* given me the body of a good footballer, but something was stopping me from using it. What? Simple. My shitty, broken brain. Riddled with a neurological disorder inherited from my mother. Yes! And what that meant, beyond the obvious, was that it wasn't only my mum who was showing symptoms unusually early.

I was, too.

Fuck. My brain, my actual brain, was turning into Swiss cheese. What were the symptoms of my family's condition? 1. Personality change. Tick. Max Best, sexy beast? Since when? 2. Less control over emotions. Tick. That would explain why I was so prone to anger. And why I'd burst into tears because some fourteen-year-old thought I was cool. 3. Memory loss. I mean, maybe. There was the whole *Champion Manager* thing. What if Mum had been the one who remembered it properly, and I was the one who'd forgotten? And there were little things. Jackie had said a phrase I liked but he swore he'd learned it from me. I couldn't remember ever saying it. And I'd forgotten that I needed to raise five hundred pounds to get my license. Sure, there was a lot going on in my life, but seriously. That should have been at the forefront of my mind.

I was mashing my lips with my fingers. It was something to do.

On the pitch, the first team were suffocating us. There was clear blue water between their match ratings and ours. Aff was routinely roasting Carlile. Magnus was playing better than me, but only to a 6/10 standard. Henri was not in the game—we couldn't get the ball to him. He seemed to be enjoying his battle with the centre back, though. Raffi was looking good visually—he moved well, and his two-footedness got him out of jams over and over again. But his match rating was flitting between a 5 and a 6.

I made some tweaks. Short passing on this player, mixed passing on that one. I tried Raffi as a playmaker. I tried going long ball for a minute. Vimsy didn't give us an offside decision and I thought about scrapping the offside trap. (But it seemed like an honest mistake and not part of some plan to destroy me. The reserves were his mates, as well as the first team, and annoying Henri Lyons by giving bad decisions on purpose would have been counterproductive.) Every change I made lowered our average rating. Every change back allowed the giant snake that was Ian Evans to squeeze even more life out of us.

Huh. So this was how it was supposed to work. Open a wound and press until it hurt.

Archaic, brutal . . . effective.

While the match clock ticked over, my thoughts bouncing between my various and many failures, Smasho and Nice One came for a chat. Really not the time, dudes!

"All right, Max?" said Nice One.

"I've had better days," I said.

"You went in two-footed on Deano, there," said Smasho, who was practically dripping with glee.

"Deano? You mean Judas."

Nice One shook his head. "Max, be fair. You've asked him to get involved in some weird shenanigans and he's tried to score some brownie points with Ian by letting him in on the plot. Ian's going to be here a lot longer than you. It's human nature." So they didn't know about the plan to let Evans go at the end of the season. That was interesting—I wondered if Physio Dean did. If Spectrum knew then presumably everyone on the coaching staff knew. My mind began fizzing. What if Evans had allowed the trial to go ahead as part of a plot to usurp Mike Dean? If Evans wanted to stay on, the best way would be to get the Supporters' Trust to fire MD. Who would then be replaced by an ally of Evans. Yes, that would work. And it would be easy to get rid of MD—especially if he was wasting his time on a moron like me. Nice One was watching my face carefully. Seeing me go through round after round of calculations, he said, "Careful, now. If you want to play here, you really need to try to get on with people."

"Me?" I said, with an unpleasant kind of scoff. "Play here? Didn't you watch?"

Nice One looked at Smasho, who frowned. The latter said, "Yeah. You look decent. What's the problem?"

And here I was back to this lunacy! Again! You didn't need a curse to see how bad I was. Come *on*! I liked the guys, so I put a lid on my temper. "I was pretty awful," I said. Understatement of the month. On the pitch, Carlile was being smashed in his battle against Aff. I tried setting Carlile to mark his opponent. See if that helped.

Nice One shook his head. "I can't tell if you're joking. You've got nice balance, you're two-footed, you move great."

"I missed every pass, I was beaten in every duel, I was all over the shop. When you were on the pitch did you ever think you were stuck in quicksand while the rest of the game went on around you?"

Nice One nodded. "Yeah. Loads. So? Also, me and Smasho had some common sense. We never tried to be player-manager. Smasho, who's the last player-manager you can remember?"

"Ooh," he said, rubbing his neck. "Kenny Dalglish isn't it? In the late eighties."

"Yeah, managing one of the greatest club sides ever known. Players who knew the game inside and out. Not saying it was easy but it's as easy as it gets, I reckon. On the pitch, I mean. Off the pitch . . . yeah. But since then? Nothing. Oh, maybe Wayne Rooney at Derby, but he didn't play much. Stuck to managing ninety-nine percent of the time. Now, Max, let me see if I understand what's going on here. You want a playing contract so you can help out around the club. That's a bit arse-about-face, but we'll let it go. You've got your mate there in midfield and Henri Lyons as potential clients. You thought the best way to show them off was to try to pull the wool over Ian Evans's eyes."

"No, that was just for me. The other two can stand or fail on their own." I set Raffi to try long shots. Maybe he'd get lucky. Or a shot would rebound and Henri could score.

"Right. Great. I'm sure you can explain that in a way Ian Evans will understand. So you've got caught out and now to prove yourself you've got to play a match. You've just come back from injury and you might have a big hole in your nut. You ran your mouth off and now you have to *manage* this team, too. You've never played at this level, you've never managed at this level, and after ten minutes you've subbed yourself off because you weren't up to speed in the game. You're beating yourself up because you think you should be instantly world-class at everything. How'm I doing?"

I didn't know where to look, so I chose one of his shoes. "Yeah," I said. "That sounds about right." He'd helped me calm about eighty percent of the way down. Maybe I didn't have holes in my brain. Maybe I was simply asking too much too soon.

Nice One bit his lip and shook his head at me. "Smasho, promise to keep this to yourself."

"What?"

"Max's stupidity."

"You'll need a lot more than my silence to keep *that* a secret."

"Benny looks up to him," pleaded Nice One. "If he finds out Max is actually clueless, it'll be like the tooth fairy and Santa all over again."

I held my hands up. "All right," I said. "All right. I get it. I've been an idiot. Now what?"

Smasho made an annoyed noise. "Now get out there and ease yourself into the match. Ian's been doing this for forty years, and he was a good player, too. You finish the game strong and he'll give you a fair crack of the whip. No one will remember the start."

Nice One nodded. "Seriously. We've all been through days like this. Every division is another step up. You'll feel like this every time you play at a higher level."

Smasho added, "And cut this player-manager shit out, too."

He was right. Trying to do two intensely demanding things at a higher level than I'd ever done . . . was dumb. And since this counted as a training session, I wasn't even getting XP.

"Nope," I said.

"At least change the formation," said Nice One, flapping his arms at the pitch. "You're matching them up with worse players. I mean . . ."

"I can't," I lied. "Four-four-two's the best setup for this group." The truth was, if there *was* something wrong with my brain, it was possible that unlocking new areas of the curse was accelerating my degeneration. Buying a new formation didn't lead to a headache, but *using* a new formation did. What if those headaches were tiny black holes appearing inside my skull? I could still play, though. That wouldn't add to my brain rot. "But you guys are legends. Tell me, what can I do to play better? What I normally do isn't working."

Smasho laughed. "Yeah. It *would* work if you played in a veteran's league. In Italy. Taking everything nice and slow. Get the ball, look around, puff on your cigar, play a pass sideways. But this is England." He looked at his mate. "Isn't it?"

Nice One looked left and right. This was their first time at this particular training venue. "*Might* be Wales."

Smasho slammed a fist into a palm. "This is England or Wales. Footy here's fast and furious. If you want time on the ball you've got to earn it. You don't know how to do that. That's fine, mate. You'd normally learn that in the youth teams, right? You coming in at your age, it's going to be hard. I'm not saying you can't do it, but it'll take more than ten minutes, yeah?"

Nice One stepped in. "Max, there's a reason teams do two-touch training sessions all the time. If a match is going badly, you go two touch for a bit. Get the ball moving around, get some confidence back. One touch, control. Two touch, pass. Get out there and play two touch for the rest of the half."

I nodded. It made sense. Don't dwell on the ball. Pass it before Sam Topps could even react. "Yeah," I said, as Raffi tried to line up a long shot but had the ball taken away from him. "Yeah. But that'll still be too slow . . ." I turned to the pitch and ordered Carlile to sub off. I moved Magnus to right back, hoping he'd be able to deal with Aff a bit better. "I'll start with one touch," I told the legends as I jogged into the midfield.

"We were just trying to help!" yelled Nice One. He seemed genuinely annoyed, but I didn't have time to wonder why.

The match continued to be bewildering, but now I only looked at the manager screens during breaks in play. There's a throw-in? Check the match ratings. Someone's rating dipped? Wait till the *next* break to try to see why. Compartmentalising the roles helped.

So instead of scanning the whole ocean every three seconds like a fucking submarine, I was only checking my immediate passing options. Where was Raffi? Where was the right midfielder? Who was free at the back? I kept scanning and scanning and whenever the ball came anywhere near me, I deflected the ball to whoever was open.

A booming goal kick came my way. I didn't want to head it, so I blocked Sam Topps's path and used the bony bit of my shoulder to direct the ball to a teammate.

There was a scrappy bit of play in midfield, Raffi competing with his man. The ball broke loose and I was on it like a flash. Topps sprinted towards me, but I'd already played a soft toe-poked pass ten yards forward to Henri. Good, but the move broke down.

A long pass to Aff and the Irishman was driving at Magnus. The hippie kept retreating, kept retreating, didn't make it easy. I sprinted over to help. Aff tried a smart cut-back move that would have taken two of us out of the game. But I read it. I jabbed the ball away from him straight to Magnus. He played it back to me first time, and, adding some distance between us, I played it to him—again, first time. Boop boop boooop. This little pinball move enraged Sam Topps, who hadn't laid a finger on me since I'd returned. He sprinted as Magnus played yet another first-time pass to me.

I started my passing motion—another pass to Magnus! Topps was on me, ready to intercept, to tackle, to do *something*. But I chose none of the above. I let the ball go through my legs, turned, and sprinted. Topps was gone-zo, and now we had the numbers. We had the momentum. I played the ball to Raffi and kept running. He threatened to shoot—had I forgotten to stop him taking long shots?—and a couple of defenders moved to block the shot. Instead, he passed to me and I played an instant pass into Henri's path.

But he hadn't anticipated it. He was out of practice, and we hadn't come close to such a moment of quality yet in the game. He raised a hand in apology. As the goalie collected the ball, I checked the match ratings. Raffi and I were both on 6. Aff had dipped from an 8 to a 7.

This was working. I smelled blood, mate.

I strode around the pitch. When I moved out of my defined area, the formation graphic changed. I, personally, wasn't limited to the formation, then. I could play as a third striker. I could be a defensive midfielder (DM) or a central attacking midfielder (CAM). I could set a formation and then tweak it—as long as I was tweaking myself. It was a lot easier than asking a player's grandmother to shout at them like I'd done with Future.

Future. Now *there* was a thought . . . He'd made a big step up in difficulty and breezed through it by playing as a defensive midfielder.

While I was out of position in the DM slot, the ball came to me. I did a crazy angled pass into Raffi, then burst forward. He held the ball and waited for me to get level with him. The return pass was slightly overhit, so I took it on my left foot. A bit annoying to break the one-touch streak, but I called "Henri, go!" and shaped to hit a left-footed cross. A defender threw his leg at the space where the ball would travel. Really, these guys never learn! I breezed past him and was dribbling now. Forward, forward, waiting for someone to try to stop me. The plan was to attract another defender and then offload the ball to the guy on the left.

But the defenders kept backing off. Backing away. And there I was, feeling fresh, feeling whole, with the ball as pretty as a picture. So why not? I cocked my left leg and twatted the ball towards the right of the goal. It flew straight as an arrow . . . left chemtrails . . . past the goalie's despairing leap . . . and crashed against the crossbar. There was a smattering of applause. Not from Evans, I assumed. I didn't look, though. I'd gone internal.

I checked the match clock. Twenty-four minutes. Nearly halftime. We could win this. I subbed Henri off and took his position as striker. For the second half, he'd have the Bench Boost bonus. That was interesting—so did I, presumably. Huh. Thanks to the tips from the legends and the boost from the Boost, I'd done all right. Do what you can and nothing else. Don't overreach. Keep it simple. Take what help is on offer. Yes, mate.

While I waited for halftime, I thought about my brain. What evidence was there that the degeneration had already started? None, really. I'd talk to one of the specialists at my mum's care home. See about getting myself checked out. But I was moving normally. I was competing with players in the sixth tier *and* Ian Evans. Yes, it was hard. Yes, I had a lot to learn.

But fuck. If I didn't give this match everything I had, how would I be able to look Benny in the eye and demand it from him? If I couldn't walk the walk, why should any player listen to me?

Vimsy blew for halftime.

As I walked towards our side of the pitch, I changed the formation to 4-4-2 diamond.

Yeah, a big headache for me coming up.

And a fucking migraine for Ian Evans and his minions.

By the time I crossed the halfway line I was grinning like a maniac.

5
DIAMOND GEEZER

Thirty minutes until the end of my trial.

You're caught in a snare. You need something sharp to cut your way out.

Your friends need to show off, but they're looking a bit drab. A bit dowdy. You need to dress them up and there's no time to lose.

You've got to pay your rent and you need to sell something fast.

There's one answer to all these problems.

Diamonds are hard; they cut. Diamonds are beautiful; they pimp. Diamonds are my favourite colour—the colour of money.

Diamonds are a Best's best friend.

"Vimsy, mate. How long's the break?"

"Five."

Five minutes to think through what I needed for the second half. Not long.

Still, I was on a high. It was like I'd just been given the all-clear after a terminal diagnosis. I felt euphoric. It must have seemed, from the outside, like mania. Mike Dean gave me a worried look. I wanted to talk to him, to explain that everything would be all right. But there was no time. I gave him a cheerful smile. It was the best I could do.

Shona was built different. She shuffled in front of me so that I'd have to stop and chat. I patted baby Serina on the head. So warm! Why were baby heads so warm?

"Max," said Shona. "I'm stressed, Max. Things don't seem to be going well."

"Stress is the time before you make a decision," I said, because I'm profound like that.

"Stress is the time before I give you a slap." She pinched her nose. She'd always had this conflict when it came to me. I was the only one who believed in her husband, but also, I was a damned fool. And it was clear I'd done something wrong here today. The waves of absolute certainty and belief that were emanating from me seemed to seep into her, though. She sighed. "Do we need to win this match or what? Is it all about personal performance? What are the victory conditions here, Max?"

I looked at her husband. He was deep in conversation with Henri and the other striker. Possibly talking about his new role as a CAM and what runs he should expect them to make. His CA was green. This session had improved him by two points. I speculated that since he'd been at an academy as a young player, his CA had previously been 10 or 20 or whatever, and that getting back to his previous best would be much quicker for him than for someone like Ziggy who had to do it for the first time. "He's already won. I know I ask a lot of you, but trust me. It's happening. That's a million-pound player right there."

Baby Serina gurgled.

"That's right!" I said. "Group hug!" I raised my arms.

Shona wanted to be mad at me, but she relented and stepped into the hug zone. Once it was over, she said, out of nowhere, "Carl is a nice boy."

"He is?" I said. But I didn't have time to think about it.

Twenty-eight minutes left.

I jogged towards the Chester FC club legends. As I went, I heard a strange voice. Physio Dean. I'd completely deleted him from my database of people who existed. A metaphorical one, you understand. Not the one given to me by the curse.

I shrugged at him to show I hadn't heard.

"Max," he repeated. "No headers!"

Well. That meant another quick recalibration. I'd basically decided never to talk to him again, and from his side, I'd shown him up in front of everyone. And here he was, looking out for me. Why can't pricks be consistent in their prickness? I gave him a tiny nod, but no smile. Fine. No headers.

Twenty-seven minutes left.

And finally, since I was over that side of the pitch anyway, I dished out a couple of tiny hugs for Smasho and Nice One. They seemed taken aback. "Guys, I needed that pep talk. Thanks a billion. One touch. Keep it simple. I feel much better. Thanks." I tried to move away, but this interaction wasn't over.

Nice One said, "Are you pulling our leg?"

"What?"

"We said play *two* touch. One touch is much, much harder."

I thought about that. "I'm just boinking the ball in the direction of a teammate. I'm not good enough for two touch, I know that for sure. I need a lot—a *lot*—of training to get up to this level." I glanced at my team. They were drinking, chatting, taking in calories. "Listen. You're right about the player-manager thing. I have to do it because I said I would, but in the second half I'm going to focus on playing and let the team get on with their jobs." Two heads nodded vigorously. Max seeing sense at last! "If you want to shout out some things I'm missing, I'd love that."

"Yes! Finally, my management career can begin!" said Smasho, rubbing his palms together. "Twenty years late, but that's by the by. Against four-four-two you play three-five-two and overrun the midfield. I learned that from Benny."

"Interesting," I said, with a tiny smile. "But we're doing four-four-two diamond and letting them have the centre. All right?"

"Max, that's crazy," said Nice One as I walked away. "Smasho, tell him that's crazy. Er . . . isn't it?"

"I don't know," I heard Smasho say. "Everyone always said I'd be a shit manager. Especially you."

Tactics corner:

You remember 4-4-2, right? Four guys at the back, four guys in front of them in the same vertical lines, two strikers. Loads of advantages, not many disadvantages. It's the default formation in England, and presumably the world. And with good reason. It's solid and players know what to do just by looking at the guys around them.

Four-four-two diamond is almost identical. We're just going to move the two guys in the very centre and make one of them go forward and the other guy go back.

4-4-2 DIAMOND

Note that you'll see some managers use a diamond formation with the left and right midfielders very narrow. The curse gave me this version, with the dudes still nice and wide.

So what do I get?

Two things on a strategic level: 1) The creation of an attacking triangle. 2) The creation of a defensive triangle.

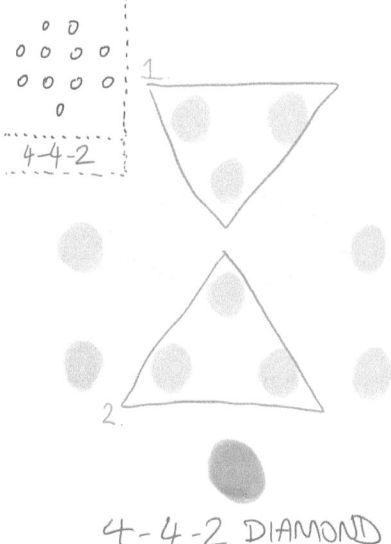

4-4-2 DIAMOND

Now, you might not have studied architecture to the same depth as me, but I've watched more than three YouTube videos on the subject. And there's one thing all architects agree on—triangles are strong. In theory, triangle one would help us create more chances and triangle two would make us better defensively. Yes, please!

The downside to the diamond is obvious—you give up the heart of the pitch. But do hearts beat diamonds?

My experience from beating Man City was that if you're playing a better team, they're going to win the midfield battle anyway. So can you create other points of strength? Can you gain more than you lose?

I didn't really think Sam Topps and the other Chester central midfielder (CM) had the attributes to do us a lot of damage, but we'd soon find out.

So that's the strategic stuff. What about the personal elements?

Well, I certainly hoped it would be good for Raffi. Playing further forward, he was much more likely to get goals and assists. The position wasn't his preference, but he only needed a couple of good moments to seem impressive.

And since Raffi was decent in the air, we'd have the option of sending some direct balls. With three people to aim at, something was bound to come from one or two headers. That was a bit of a plan B, though. I felt confident we'd be able to play some nice football in this setup. I made sure all the players were set to short passing and that no one was on long shots. I wanted to pass the ball forward, then have high-quality shots from inside the penalty area. That was plan A.

As for me, playing in the DM slot seemed like it would give me lots of people to play one-touch passes to. And if I did find myself with a bit of time and space, I could play a longer pass to Raffi—it would be just like passing the ball between the wire men. Piece of cake. The kind of long pass I dream about. Literally.

Also, from the DM slot I could shuffle across and help our right-back deal with Aff. I wasn't normally motivated to do defensive work, but with the tactical overviews I understood where the danger was. Stopping Aff was crucial for my team, and I was happy to put a shift in.

So that's the whos and the wheres and the whys.

I checked what Ian Evans was up to. He was still ripping into his team. Motivational halftime team talk! Normally my instinct was to do the opposite of my rival, but today I felt like channelling my inner football dinosaur. I did my customary look over the shoulder to see if Mr. Yalley was going to appear. Then, with shining eyes and a beating heart, I told my players what I needed.

Twenty-six minutes left.

"Guys," I said, as they regarded me with curse-inflated respect. "You know what I want tactically. But there's something beyond that."

Henri interrupted me, the absolute menace. "Max, I notice you've given a hug to almost everyone in the crowd."

"That's not a crowd. That's just some people who are nearby."

He made a strange, unconscious motion that I later realised was him trying to flick a scarf further round his neck. "Nevertheless. I want a hug."

"Mon amigo. I'm busy. I'm about to give the fucking motivational speech of a lifetime."

"Max, you substituted me for a *defender*. Do you know how that feels? It feels bad. I am bereft. I am bereft and I need a hug. Okay?"

I gave the prick a microcuddle and was about to launch into the talk when I glanced at him. He seemed genuinely happy, which made me burst out laughing. "Jesus wept. Right, my dudes. Listen."

The team were in various states of readiness. Some were lying down, some were on their haunches, some were standing.

"You guys saw in the first ten minutes that I've never played at this level before. I don't have a clue what it means to be a pro. I've seen football documentaries, I've heard interviews. I know in a roundabout way what it means to be a reserve team player. You are unappreciated. Undervalued. You're not in the first team. You train but you don't play. The crowd don't sing your songs. Some of you might break into the first team in the next few weeks. But most of you, it's going to be a long winter. Yeah? So let me give you a gift. It's the gift of *vengeance*. You come with me, men, and we'll fucking murder that mob in the second half. You give me twenty-five minutes of sprints and concentration and quality, and we'll leave them fucking hung, drawn, and quartered. They all played yesterday; they're shattered. Their confidence is smashed. Their form is shit. You're not in the first team? Why the fuck not? You're miles better. Ben!"

I turned to the goalie. "You're fucking quality, mate. These clowns aren't going to get a sniff this half, but if they do, you'll be there. Fucking Octoman, the eight-armed goalie. Okay?" He smashed his gloves together. "Magnus. I love everything you're doing. This isn't the right time but holy shit if I come back to Chester and find you haven't been taking your footy seriously, I'll be pissed. You've got something. Okay? Carl. I don't know what's going on with you, but I know you can keep fucking Aff quiet for twenty-five minutes. I *know* you can. So let me ask you a simple question." I moved closer to him so that I could get a good read on his face. "Are you an American or an American't?" He frowned and said he was half-English, so I repeated the question, but louder. He finally understood and shouted "AmeriCAN!"

I swept my gaze across the others. The guys who didn't have outstanding PAs. The guys I would cut and replace, given half a chance. I'd never see them again, so I went all-out. "Dudes. It's going to be a long, cold winter. You're going to freeze your arse off at home and then freeze your arse off on the bench. I'm offering you twenty-five minutes of glory. Twenty-five minutes of sticking it to Ian, sticking it to the guys who are in your spots." I got quiet. "All I'm asking . . . all I need . . . is twenty-five minutes of *sprints* and *concentration* and *quality*. Twenty-five minutes." I pointed at one of them. "Are you with me?"

He went, "Yeah!"

I pointed to another one. "Are you with me?"

He went, "Yes, Max!" Then I stood tall and shouted it and they all stood tall and responded.

Half the team marched back to their positions doing that clenched-fist thing Benny had done in the under-fourteens match. Ready to fight. Ready to scrap. Ready to prove their worth.

You want to make this a test of motivation, Ian? I'll give you more motivation than you can fucking handle.

Twenty-five minutes left.

The second half kicked off, and once again I was confused as to why the teams hadn't swapped sides at halftime. (Later, I asked Nice One and he told me it was because Ian wanted to micromanage Aff. Huh. Made sense. I dropped that into my bag of tricks.)

There were two minutes of huffing and puffing before I touched the ball. I played a simple pass to Carl, who played a simple pass forward. One more pass inside and Raffi was on the ball in a dangerous area. Nothing came of it, but I liked what I'd seen. "Yes, men!"

Now, perhaps I should mention one slight trick I was playing on Ian Evans. Like with the Man City false midfield strategy, during breaks in play I was resetting the formation to a basic 4-4-2, and only when the game got going did I switch it to the diamond version. Evans didn't spot what we were up to. To be fair, I'd proven myself to be an idiot, so he wouldn't have been on the lookout for any clever moves.

Apart from that, I let the game happen and focused on my own performance. One-touch pass, one-touch pass, cover the right back, hit a long clearance. I barely looked at the management screens. The less I looked at them, the better I played. But the less I looked at them, the more the half-time motivation seemed to ebb away. I got the feeling being a player-manager would always come with this kind of trade-off. Sigh.

Still, with me in the DM role, we were stopping loads of attacks and I was collecting a lot of loose balls that normally Sam Topps would have competed for. So the first team virtually stopped putting pressure on us, and we slowly started to turn the screw. That said, Raffi was not a natural fit in his new position, and his match rating dipped to 5. I thought about swapping places with him—he'd be as good as me in the DM slot and I'd probably be much more suited to the CAM role. I had a bit more imagination when it came to forward play. I'd definitely give Henri some chances to score. But if I moved forward and made the job look easy, that'd be bad for Raffi.

So I kept things as they were and in a break, called out, "Raff! Two touch! Use the width!" Basically, keep things simple, like I was doing, and instead of trying to play difficult passes to the strikers, he should look to pass out wide.

He nodded.

Twenty minutes left.

My suggestion worked . . . great. In the next five minutes, Raffi became the fulcrum of the team. One of the fullbacks or I would pass to him. He'd take a touch and pass it to the side of the pitch where a midfielder had made a run. The wide players started to put crosses in, and suddenly Henri came alive. He shoved his opponent to get a little head start. He did a spin move that bought him a yard of space. He repeated the move but then instantly doubled back. And once we started to feed him, he became more aggressive with his running. He was a whirlwind of dynamic forward play. Sprint, stop, recover, sprint, stop, recover. His combination of physicality, intelligence, and hard work made him a fucking nightmare at this level.

It didn't take him long to score.

Raffi played a pass to the left, and the left midfielder chose to pass to Henri's feet. He held the ball up and rolled it back to Raffi. Raffi shaped to pass it out wide like he had been doing, and even my eyes were drawn to the right wing. But Raffi rolled the ball vertically, towards the penalty spot, two yards in front of Henri's unorthodox sideways sprint. The finish was clinical and my sort-of-clients gave each other a big smile and a sloppy high five.

I called them over to me. "Guys, that was embarrassing," I said. They gave me a blank look. They'd just combined to score a nice goal! "Jesus. The goal was quality. I'm talking about this." I mimed a shitty high five. "Raffi, you held your hand up like this, sort of twisted away. Henri, you didn't look where you were slapping so you just caught the side of his little finger. Next time, I want to hear the slap from fucking Scotland, yeah? Put some fucking effort into it. Some technique."

Raffi snorted and turned away, taking the congratulations of some teammates. Henri nodded so hard he risked straining his neck. "Yes, Max! I love a manager who cares about the important details. The angle of the slap in the celebration. Yes, Max!"

I laughed. "Your movement off the ball is incredible. The finish was perfection. What's left for you to improve?"

He stopped nodding. "You make a good point. So you will send me to slap school?"

"You betcha."

"And what about you? Is this good for your career if Raffi and I steal the show?"

"Absolutely."

"Then I will score again. And I will put my heart and soul into the hand slap, Max. I will make you proud."

Now, this was such a minor (and silly) moment that it barely warrants inclusion in this story. But I can't help but think that something I said was what caused Henri to do what he did next.

Fifteen minutes left.

The game was running along the lines I'd established. The first team would hoik the ball towards us and one of the defenders would head it away. I'd pick it up and play a first-time pass to someone, and then we'd be attacking. Sam Topps had actually given up on trying to get close to me, and he was sort of looking a bit lost in the centre of the pitch. So I did something I had told the under-fourteens to do, and passed the ball back to the goalie to keep him involved.

Now, I didn't know it at the time, but Ben Cavanagh was a smart cookie. And when I passed it to him, he saw an opportunity upfield. He absolutely leathered the ball—it almost looked like a miskick except it zipped about seventy yards to where Henri could chase it.

And there was a coming-together, a tussle, and suddenly the centre back was booting Henri up the arse.

I wish I didn't have to say this so often, but I lost my shit.

I sprinted forward and even though I'd started farther away than most players, I was one of the first on the scene.

The centre back was called Glenn Ryder. He was six foot three and formidable. I gripped his shirt with each hand and pushed him backwards. Away from my client. The one who wasn't supposed to be there. "No," I said. "No. No. No!"

I'd pushed him back about five metres when people started grabbing me. I vaguely heard some shouts from Physio Dean, but almost all of my attention was focused on this Ryder guy. Tunnel vision. Focus like the tip of an arrowhead. In that tiny diamond of awareness, his confused expression peeped back at me.

And then Henri's voice. Calming. "Max," he said. "Max."

"What?" I demanded.

"Max," he said, as he coaxed my fingers away from Ryder's jersey.

"What?" I said with slightly less heat. But then, enraged again, I said, "He kicked you!"

"Oui," said Henri, and by now he had separated me from the defender. But strangely, he was pulling the three of us away in the same direction. "Oui, Max. But you see, I kicked him first."

That stopped all my aggression. "You . . . what?"

Henri stood beside Ryder with his arm around him. He grinned at me. "I've been kicking him the whole match." He turned. "Haven't I?"

"Yeah, you dick," said Ryder, delighted.

What the devil was going on? I put my hands on my head, ran them through my hair. "The fuck?" I said, eloquently.

Henri took his arm from his opponent's shoulder and curled both hands into fists. He held them out, theatrically, towards me. "Max. We're competing. We're professionals. We're trying to get the upper hand. This isn't the Chester Knights, now. It's two no-good sons of bitches trying to *heke* out an advantage. This is football."

I stared in dismay at Glenn Ryder. "And you like this?"

"Yeah," he said. "It's not often you get to compete against someone of his level."

Clearly, I wasn't about to understand the psychology of these dudes. I pinched my nose and sighed. I moved a bit closer to the pair of nutjobs. "Listen here, you twats. Cut this neanderthal shit out. You can explain it to me later. I need to send this guy back to Darlington in one piece. There's like, thirteen minutes left. Can you give me thirteen minutes of fucking Teletubbies football? Please?"

Ryder's eyebrows shot up. "Henri, lad. Who is this guy to you?"

"He's my agent."

"Oh. Oh!" Ryder checked me out. "No shit? Why is your agent better than you?"

"Max!" complained Henri. "He is winding me up! I will boot him up the *harse*!"

I pointed at them sternly. "No more kicking. I swear to God. Cut it out."

Both men held up their palms in surrender. No more kicking.

Vimsy had given us a free kick. Like me, he hadn't seen Henri's provocation and had only seen Ryder's retaliation.

I'm not sure what made Ian Evans lock back onto me as his primary target. It might have been me pushing his strongest defender away like he was a helium balloon. Or it might have been what I did with the free kick.

Either way, the next thirteen minutes had a clear dynamic. It was Max Best versus Ian Evans, all in, all out, and we both had aces up our sleeves.

6

AND AGAIN

Football glossary: And again! A shout from one participant to another meaning "Do that one more time, please, would you, good sir?" or "Please complete the action that I have started." For example, a coach might use this phrase to encourage a player to repeat a certain sprint. Or player one may pass the ball to player two and shout "And again!" as a request for the ball to be returned to player one.

Thirteen minutes until the end of my trial.

Since I'd set myself as the set piece taker, no-one tried to claim the ball. I stood over it, thirty-five yards from the goal, watching with mild annoyance as half my defenders went into the attacking box, and two midfielders went back into defence. The default idea in football is that a manager sends all his beefy boys up front where they might score a header, and keeps a couple of shorter, faster players in defence in case of counterattacks. I didn't necessarily want to challenge this orthodoxy, certainly not right now, but I wanted to be in control. I fiddled with the tactics page until I found that my only option for set pieces like this (and corners) was to tell players to either go forward or stay back.

I set Raffi to go back, then as he jogged towards our goal, I sent him forward again. He didn't blink—he simply turned back and headed for the penalty box.

What I really wanted was to micromanage the guys and put them in very specific places. That didn't seem possible—maybe with a future perk!—but I waved and shouted and told them to overload the far post.

The standard play here was that I would send a fast, curving, high pass into the mixer, AKA the danger zone, and one of my dudes would head the ball into the net. And if I kicked the ball well enough, even if no one touched it, my pass would arc into the goal. The goalkeeper would have little chance to stop it because he needed to position himself to deal with any headers.

Really, the free kick couldn't have been in a more delicious position. It was hard not to drool on the ball. You know, like the alien in *Alien*.

The goalie had placed a two-man wall, but it seemed pointless to me. At this distance I had pretty much the whole goal to aim for.

I took three steps back, added another half a step for luck, then approached the ball and struck it with equal parts sweetness and savagery on its bottom right curve. A firm but pleasurable spanking, more than enough to send it on its way to the top-left corner of the net with just a hint of spin to take it even farther away from the goalie.

Not that he moved. Almost nobody did.

I couldn't remember ever hitting the ball as perfectly. The thrill of the contact and the *blish!* as the ball struck the net made me chuckle. I turned away and started to jog back to my own half.

Vimsy blew his whistle several times. He was holding his arm up. I shrugged at him. *What?*

"Obstruction," he said, with a somewhat unpleasant smile. "It's an indirect free kick. You'll have to take it again."

I eyed him. I couldn't get a read on his personality. Was he disallowing the goal to wind me up? Was he doing it to please Ian? Glenn Ryder had kicked Henri, and kicking someone resulted in a direct free kick—one where you could shoot directly at goal. It was possible Vimsy had blown his whistle when Henri and Glenn started grappling with each other (before the kick). It was also possible he was just being a dick.

"Fine," I said. "Raffi," I called. My dude came over. I whispered to him and he nodded. When it came to football he always understood me at light speed.

He stood over the ball while I fixed a loose shoelace. Vimsy blew his whistle. He was ready. I wasn't. Raffi rolled the ball under his foot and when I stood up I got mad at him. "Get to the fucking far post!" I yelled.

"But Max," he said.

"Fuck off," I said, pointing to where I wanted him to go.

Hurt, he loped off. Not exactly heading away at top speed. I shook my head at him.

With a big inhalation of breath, I took three and a bit steps back and looked at the far post where all my targets were. I approached the ball and struck it with equal parts sweetness and savagery on its bottom right curve. Firm but pleasurable, top-left, hint of spin. Controlled, pasted.

I wheeled away, delighted, while Raffi came sprinting at me with the biggest smile I'd ever seen on him. I gave him a huge hug. "Yes, Max!" he said. "Fucking banger!"

On the touchline, Ian Evans shouted, "Vimsy, what the fuck?"

We turned to look at the coach-turned-referee. He raised his hand as if to signal that the kick was indirect, but then a beatific smile split his face. He pointed to the centre spot and whistled. Goal! Two–one! Max's Misfits were ahead!

Raffi and I bounced around, laughing. His match rating hit 8, and mine 7. Not bad after such a disastrous start!

I heard Shona yelling and we went over to see what was up. "Raffi. Max. What was that? What is happening?"

Smasho and Nice One had moved closer, as had MD MD, Physio Dean, and even Ian Evans. Everyone wanted an explanation.

"It was an indirect free kick," I said. "So Raffi rolled the ball forward. And I shot. Simple."

"What was all that yelling at him, then?"

"Distraction," I said. "The other team could have taken the ball at any time after Raffi touched it. Instead, that's your husband's second assist of the match."

"Genius!" said Nice One. "I haven't seen that move in years."

"Max," said Smasho, who was taking his role of assistant to the manager seriously. "You're winning now, so are you going to stick with four-four-two diamond or go more defensive?"

Diamond. The cat was out of the bag. I glanced at Ian Evans—all the recent weirdness, all the times Raffi and I popped up in odd positions, it all clicked into place for him. My deception had worked incredibly well. His scowl deepened and he stormed away, shouting instructions to his team.

I called out something noncommittal to Smasho while Raffi and I jogged back into position. As I went, I tried to listen in on Ian's commands. No such luck. Fortunately, the curse was whispering in my ear.

Eleven minutes left.

Now that Ian knew, I didn't bother trying to hide our diamond shape. The match restarted and I strolled around the DM slot. I allowed myself the luxury of checking out the tactics screens mid-match.

He'd matched our diamond shape! I was astonished—this was the first tactical change I'd ever seen him make.

That had me worried for a moment. We were back to having the same formations, but my team had worse players. Not a good recipe. While I mentally bit my nails, I realised that Sam Topps had been set as the first team's CAM. That made absolutely no sense. Of the four players playing in central midfield, he was the least suited to the attacking role. Huh. I continued wandering around, not trying to get involved in the game, just thinking. Trying to strategise while being in the trenches was the biggest problem of being a player-manager. Generals haven't fought on the frontlines for thousands of years. (I guess. I watch more architecture videos than history ones.)

But as I strolled towards the right back position in case I needed to help our current defender (I was rotating Magnus and Carl) I realised that Topps wasn't really playing as the CAM. He was marking me! I checked the tactics screens, and sure enough, he was listed as marking Max Best.

I laughed.

This gave me the chance to use one of my earliest tactical innovations—one I'd never actually tried. Perhaps you remember when I was controlling the FC United reserve team and had Gribbin as the playmaker? Neil, the FCU first team manager had set a dude to mark him, and my first impulse had been to move Gribbin to the wing and have two opposition players in one slot. I hadn't done it because I didn't want to annoy Neil. Today I had no such qualms.

In fact, I went one step further—I switched Magnus to the DM position and went to right back myself. I even assigned myself to mark Aff. So now Topps was marking me, and I was marking Aff. I was basically forcing Chester to play with ten men. So I just kind of stood there, trying not to mess up the offside trap, while Aff and Topps scratched their heads.

To hammer this advantage home, I set the team to play down the left and even switched Henri to be the left-sided of the two strikers.

This delightful situation went on for about ninety seconds before Ian started raging at Topps. Topps gave his boss an earful back, and Ian threw his hands up and cancelled the mark-Max-Best plot. I instantly went back to DM.

Smirking.

Eight minutes left.

During a break, Ian called Glenn Ryder over and gave him some instructions. Ryder passed it on, and suddenly the next phase of the match started.

Chester's first team began booting the ball high into the air in my general direction. An artillery bombardment! With me defenceless. No headers!

On the tactics screen I saw that Evans had set the tactics to long ball and play through centre.

Fine. As soon as I spotted it, I swapped with Raffi, who won most of his headers, killing the plan dead.

As always, my response to Ian's changes was almost instantaneous, but *he* took time to react. And when he did react, it took even more time to get his new message through to his players. The curse was definitely a blessing in that regard.

So now I was in the CAM slot and in theory I should have been having the time of my life. But the first time the ball came to me, I got stuck in traffic. Too late, I realised I'd forgotten to do the half-turn thing. So annoying!

"And again!" I shouted not long after, and got the ball in the identical position. This time I was on the half-turn and the angled approach did feel much better. But when I tried to slide a pass through to a striker, I hit it tamely to the first defender. The angles were all wrong! I punched my palm. "Fuck!"

Finally, a long pass towards Henri was partially cleared by a defender. The first team's DM and I competed for the ball. I held him off with my newfound strength, but as I tried to turn with the ball he held onto my shirt and leaned into me. Not enough to pull me down, but enough to stop me doing anything constructive. It's not how I'd ever played football, but Vimsy didn't call a foul and I wasn't sure what to do except judo-throw the guy to the ground.

Someone ran off with the ball.

I glared at the guy. "Were you told to do that?"

He looked confused. "Do what?" But then his game face was back on, watching the action unfold, checking he was in the right position. To him, what he'd done was as natural as breathing. To me, it had been stressful to the point I was starting to get angry. I don't like fighting. I didn't tell Old Nick I wanted to star in WrestleMania.

Interesting. Lots to think about.

But with me having a stinker in the CAM role, I had to change something. My match rating had dropped to 6. Magnus was struggling against Aff. Carl was talking to Shona—apparently besotted by the baby. One option was to finish the match with my other new formation, 4-3-3, but I didn't want to deal with that level of headache. So I switched back to 4-4-2 and swapped places with the right midfielder. I'd be stood right in front of Ian Evans, so I'd be able to hear his instructions and maybe counter them. Also, if I got the ball and did something dramatic, he might tell Aff to stop making forward runs and help the fullback deal with me. And if Aff stopped attacking, the first team would lose their main threat.

It was an idle thought, really. There were only about five minutes left, and I was happy for the team to keep attacking down the other side of the pitch. I was starting to feel fatigued. I felt like I had maybe one more sprint in my legs. One more clearheaded decision.

But when you set a team to attack down the left, that is just a tendency, and soon enough the ball was passed to Raffi. He fizzed the ball towards me and kept running after it. This extra sprint cost him a good chunk of his remaining energy—he was blowing, too—but it gave me so many options. He was such a generous player!

I shaped to pass back to him and shouted, "And again!" The signal that I'd pass back to him and then run down the line.

Of course, if you were the defender in that situation, you'd have to suspect that I was going to do the opposite of what I said. Especially after my free kick trickery.

But when someone shouts "and again" and starts the passing motion, it's like creating a black hole. Ninety-nine percent of defenders will get sucked in ninety-nine percent of the time.

Instead of passing it back to Raffi with my right foot, I used my left to nutmeg the defender, and then I was away. I was sprinting down the line, one touch to push the ball about four yards ahead of me, giving me enough time to check where the strikers were. Henri was still the left-sided striker, which meant he was going to attack the far post. Perfect.

I whipped the ball towards him, head-height, and he soared and powered it down past the goalie.

For a second, he froze up there at the top of his leap. That was the poster. That was the cover. That was the statue.

And he landed, gathered his feet, and ran towards me. He stopped and concentrated on the high five. It was still pretty bad. He looked at me. I shook my head. "Putain," he said.

Three minutes left.

It was nearly over. I was right—as soon as I'd appeared in front of Ian, he'd told Aff to stop making forward runs. The tactics screen had Aff with a backwards arrow on him. Pointing towards me. Unbelievably defensive. Using your sharpest sword as a shield. Bonkers.

I was happy to let the rest of the game play out, but my team weren't done with me. A few neat passes and Raffi had time and space to drive forward. I knew what he wanted, and I had no choice but to give it to him. I strolled, I strolled, I sprinted, and I got onto the end of Raffi's pass a yard ahead of my opponent. He launched himself in a heroic attempt to make a block, but I'd already crossed the ball. I sensed the goalkeeper would try to get to the ball before Henri could head it, so this time I hit it low and hard. Henri adjusted his feet—he needed to slow down a little—and side-footed the ball into the empty goal.

A hat-trick for the Frenchman, and his shithousery had won the free kick that led to our other goal. His match rating hit 10. Hair flowing, teeth gleaming, he looked around to see where I was.

I was where I'd ended up after hitting the cross. I was finished, physically and mentally. Match rating 8. One goal and two assists, yes, but a shockingly bad start. Eight seemed fair. Henri bounded over and I put my palms out flat so he could strike them from above. He messed that up, too, but he didn't care. He threw his arms around me, then opened them to let Raffi in. Raffi was on 8 out of 10, too. It seemed a fraction low, but again, he'd had several bad patches.

"What do you think, Max?" said Henri, speaking fast, breathing heavily. "Have we time for another?"

"No," I said. I left the hug so I could turn properly. Ian Evans had gone, and the first team were either on their way to the dressing rooms or were gathering the corner flags. "He's ended the game early."

"Thank shit for that," said Raffi. "My legs are jelly." He slumped to the ground and put his hands on his head.

Henri laughed and knelt down next to him—he started massaging Raffi's calves. "Too much upper body work, Raffi Brown. Don't forget your cardio."

"Ah, that's the spot. Oh, shit. Yes." Raffi groaned. I was starting to get jealous. My legs were screaming, too. Who was going to massage me? Livia? Could I work out her phone number from her Disney+ password? Some of the first team players walked past and gave us pats on the shoulder and things like that. Some of the reserves were wandering around in a kind of trance, unable to believe what they'd just accomplished. They'd banged the first team 4–1. But the doubt in Raffi's voice brought me all the way back down to planet Earth. "Max," he said. "Why do I get the feeling that winning wasn't the right thing to do?"

"Henri," I said. "What do you think of Raffi here? Think he can make it as a pro?"

"Is that a joke? Of course."

"If I die, will you help him find a club?"

Henri flopped on the ground next to Raffi, hands pressed into the grass. Massage time was over. "Oui. But what are you planning to die from?"

I joined them on the ground. I desperately needed a shower, but the building was so far away. I just wanted to sleep. "My next header could be my last," I said.

And for some reason, that was really funny.

When the last chuckle faded, I sat up. "Raffi, mate. It's pro football. If they didn't want us to win, they shouldn't have challenged us. Maybe I messed things up doing it the way I did. Got their backs up. That's on me. So the question is, are you going to give me another chance? Find another club. Get you another trial. Do all this again?"

"This?" said Raffi. "Again? Yes, Max. We just beat a proper team. Yes, I want to do this again."

"And again," said Henri.

He helped us up and we leaned on him all the way back to the changing rooms.

7
BETAMAX

The changing room, the showers, my first time with professional players, seen, heard, and smelt through a gauzy Instagram filter. Hazy, distant, weak. There was banter, joking, one-upmanship, but even though I felt disembodied the banter seemed lacking. Forced. This nineteen-man squad had been divided into winners and losers, and the losers had just beaten the winners. No one knew how to act.

Some of the reserves tried to chat with me. With most of them, I only had the energy to summon up basic platitudes or to deflect their queries. But when Ben Cavanagh came over, I imagined an action replay of the long pass he'd hit towards Henri, and I told him it was my personal highlight of the match. He gave me a weird look. I looked for Magnus Evergreen and once again encouraged him to keep training as a player. I didn't understand his negative PA, but I did know that his CA had increased by one point during the match, and I felt in my bones that he was a useful and flexible instrument that any manager would want in his toolkit. And yeah, if he could give a massage, that was always useful.

When I left on my wobbly legs, Henri hadn't come out of the shower. I got the feeling he'd still be in there while we were driving past Manchester airport. I asked someone to tell him I said bye.

I stumbled out into the cold morning air—how was it still morning?—and felt the first proper wave of nausea. I dropped my bag and leant forward.

"What is it, Max?" Physio Dean asked. Treating everyone, as per his oath. Even me.

"Feel sick."

"Did you eat this morning?"

"A bit." I tried to keep my voice neutral. "I hadn't planned to play a whole match."

"Yeah, well," he said, and it was briefly awkward. But he shook it off. "Here," he said, handing me a sachet of something. "Get this in you."

I tried to rip open the packet but was too weak and too uncoordinated. Dean did it for me and I chugged whatever it was. Some weird powder. Tasted of strawberry. He put his hand in the box and took out another sachet. He looked at me and added two more. "Take another one in twenty minutes. You're going to drive back to Manchester? If you aren't going to eat within the next hour, get those other two down you."

"What is it?"

"High-glycaemic carbs, protein, electrolytes. Marathon runners swear by it. Try to drink a lot, too."

"Have you got any ibuprofen?"

He gave me a sharp look. "What do you need those for? Tell me all your symptoms."

"I'll take three fat ones, thanks."

There was a brief battle of wills which I won by not fighting. With a shake of the head, he found a packet of painkillers and handed it over.

"Thanks."

"Don't play again until you get assessed," he said.

No energy to tell him to get stuffed. "Aight."

Next it was MD MD. I couldn't read his expression, but he wasn't pale anymore. His job wasn't at risk. I mumbled that I needed to get home and recover and we could chat later. Then it was Smasho and Nice One. They saw I was in a state and helped me walk to the car park. My calves were going from burning to threatening to turn inside out.

"What are you going to tell Benny?" I said.

Nice One laughed. "If he tidies his room, I'll let him watch the video."

"Video?"

"I filmed some of it." He tapped on his phone and then turned it sideways. It was pretty shaky, a finger blocked the screen sometimes, and the luminous bibs made the footage look even more amateur. But it was the first time I'd seen myself on tape since the curse. Nice One tutted. "Ah, not that one. That's from when you played attacking midfield. Room for improvement in that position, Max! I know someone who made it look easy. Didn't I, Smasho? Ah, here we go." He found the right clip. Raffi came up behind me and watched along. We saw

Raffi take the ball, glide across the midfield, and play a pass to some guy. The guy did a ludicrous body swerve and then was sprinting away so fast that Nice One couldn't match the movement. By the time he found the player again, a goal had been scored.

"Who's that?" I said.

Everyone laughed. They thought I was joking. Just in time, I laughed, too.

But then I took the phone from Nice One and watched the clip again. That was me! Fuck. I looked . . . amazing. I watched it again.

"Yeah, yeah," said Nice One. "We've seen it now. Go to the next clip."

I swiped and saw a very similar scene—the events of our fourth goal—but this time with much better camera work. When it had actually happened, the first team's left back had seemed to be competing hard against me. It'd felt like if I made the slightest mistake, he would eat my lunch. But on the tape, I'd completely left him for dead, and despite striking the ball powerfully across my body, I still looked fluid and symmetrical. The guy in the video could have performed the whole act on a balance beam.

For the first time, I saw the player Jackie Reaper had lost his shit over.

"Next time," I said, reluctantly handing the phone back, "film Henri, not me. Benny could learn a lot from him."

"Maybe he won't have to watch videos to see him play, eh Max?" said Smasho. He was a former player. He could put two and two together just as well as anyone.

I tried to keep a poker face, but there's a reason people don't play poker immediately after running a marathon. "Henri Lyons is under contract at Darlington," I said. With that came the first pang of headache, so I said it was time to leave.

Shona drove. I was in the passenger seat. Raffi was in the back with Serina.

Raffi, normally taciturn and watchful, chatted away the whole time, full of vim and vigour. He reenacted our goals, described interesting things he'd seen, and asked me why I'd made the changes I had. I told him the truth, more or less, and that got him chatting even more.

After half an hour I asked Shona to pull in somewhere so I could walk around a bit. The pain in my legs was more urgent than the need to get home. We ended up in the same services where I'd had it out with Jackie Reaper, and since we were there, we decided to get lunch. Raffi ate tons. I tried to force a burger down my throat. The headache and nausea were in a fight for my attention. At one point, Raffi took Serina to the bathroom and while they were gone, Shona patted me on the hand.

It was such an odd gesture that for a while all I could do was stare at her wedding ring. So young, so serious.

"Max," she said. "I've never seen Raffi this happy. I want to thank you for that." The hand vanished. "I've got a confession to make." She looked left and right and lowered her head, forcing me to do the same. "I've been looking for other agents."

She stared at me, waiting for a response. "Okay," I said.

"You're not mad?"

I shrugged. "You're just doing the best for your family." Plus I had a six-month break clause.

"Yeah," she said. "It's just that, to be honest, you're so obviously an amateur. And it was taking so long." Fair and fair. "I told Raffi, it's not enough that he likes playing with you. But er . . ." That was interesting. I'm pretty sure that was the first time I'd ever heard her use a filler word. "But I think after this morning, there's no going back. If you need to bring him to other clubs, go ahead." She took a deep breath. "I'll be patient." She grinned. That had cost her. "Raffi told me you'd started him on a training plan. Can we get into that a bit more? More detail? More serious?"

"Wait wait wait," I said. "Why tell me this? You could have just . . . not."

"I think it's good to be honest, Max. For both our sakes. I don't want that weighing on me, and your next clients might just leave without telling you why."

"Huh. Okay. Hit me."

"What?"

"Tell me everything I did wrong."

"We don't have that much time, Max."

I laughed. "Top five, then."

The hand reappeared as she counted points on her fingers. "You're abrasive sometimes. You rile people up. Sometimes good, sometimes bad. You don't explain yourself. You think you know best. You don't communicate well enough or often enough. And the whole Max Best thing," she said, waving her hand as though she was throwing confetti over me. "It's unpolished. Sloppy sometimes. I wrote to a real agent and got an email back. With a proper header at the top, Max. The personal touch is fine to a point but when it comes to, you know, my family's future, a slick logo is reassuring. Do you know what I mean?"

I nodded, agreeing. "Absolutely. You know I'm learning as I go?" She did. "And I can't afford all that sort of stuff. So I'm grateful for your trust. I know I'm a bit . . . unprofessional sometimes. But there's one thing you'll get from me you won't get from Mister Glossy Web Two-Point-Oh Man. And that's an unshakeable belief in Raffi. I *will* get him where he needs to go."

Shona leaned back and finished her coffee. "I know, Max. I know. But you need a logo. A website. Business cards."

I pushed my plate away. I was done with chewing. I'd chug the last two sachets of NASA powder in the car. "Who was the agent?"

"Excuse me?"

"Who wrote to you?"

She took her phone out and tapped it. "Bradley Rymarquis," she said, incorrectly pronouncing the name with a French twist. "I saw him on TV. Do you know him?"

"Never heard of him."

And oh, man, I wish it had stayed that way.

On the way back to Manchester, I got a text.

Jackie: Fucking hell, Max.

I wondered who had talked to him, which version of the morning's events he was responding to. I didn't reply.

It was a tough night, a long night, but the next morning I felt fine. I went to work and didn't feel like pursuing conversations about religion. So I cycled through other topics: logos, brands, trust. Basically treating the bank's customers like my own personal focus group. My brand colours would be red, white, and black, like Manchester United. Or blue and white, like Chester. And the logo would be a head with an angel on one side and a devil on the other. Or just the letters M and

B. I finished the day in third place in the stats, and apart from a few mind-numbing moments, I'd quite enjoyed myself.

After work, I went to Ardwick Powerleagues to grind.

But I also had a new mission—learning to play football.

Sure, I suddenly had the body of a footballer. I could run, dribble, pass, take a free kick, and backheel-nutmeg a goalkeeper. Great. But playing football against pros meant being in a lot of situations I'd never experienced before. Opponents grappling me. People running into my back while I was trying to control a pass. I didn't know how to be part of an offside trap. I didn't know where to stand on throw-ins. Dozens and dozens of small details.

So many new problems.

So few solutions.

Even someone like Benny, a fourteen-year-old academy kid, would have had hundreds of hours more training than me. He was explicitly being taught about half-turns and using his body and what to do in situation X, and he was implicitly learning much more simply from playing with and against good players. Me? I'd only ever played with and against CA 1 guys. I'd never had a minute of coaching, except what Jackie Reaper had told me.

So while I picked up 90 XP (and paid 10 towards my debt) I was also looking for situations like the ones I'd struggled with, to see how other players dealt with them. But it became clear that I wasn't going to find answers at a Powerleague. The situations I struggled with didn't occur in five-a-side matches, and even if they did, both players in the situation would be shit and their solutions meaningless.

With a sigh I drained my thermos and went back to my car.

I needed to watch players who were better than me.

A good way to do that would have been to go and scout a sixth-tier match. One of Chester's rivals. But Inga didn't call me, and MD brushed me off when I texted him. "Talk soon" was all he wrote.

So that seemed like that, when it came to Chester. The thought of having to start again at a new club used to exhaust me, but now I didn't care. I'd make some calls, Raffi and I would turn up for a trial, boss the game, and I wouldn't piss anyone off. Easy!

And as for Henri, now that I'd seen him up close, I was sure there'd be dozens of clubs who would want to sign him, even with his bad boy reputation. Now, technically, Henri wasn't my client. He kept verbally hiring and firing me, but the one thing I knew was that I'd be his agent if I could engineer a move for him. Which was possible—probable even—but not certain.

The only certainty in my footballing life, really, was that Ziggy was paying me to be his agent. So I looked at the Tuesday night fixtures and saw that FC United were playing at home. I drove there, bought a ticket, and enjoyed the match from the terraces.

I could have asked for someone to let me in for free, but who knew what that would lead to? I wanted to drop in unannounced, be anonymous, and see how things were going.

What I saw was that Ziggy wasn't in the matchday squad, but he did go through the warm-ups before the game, and I saw his latest profile.

	BARRETT GRAVES	
Born 13.1.1999	(Age 23)	English
Acceleration 4		
	Handling 1	Stamina 5
	Heading 6	Strength 6
		Tackling 3
	Jumping 7	Teamwork 16
Bravery 4		Technique 6
	Pace 4	preferred foot R
	Passing 6	
Dribbling 3		
Finishing 17		
CA 16	PA 58	
Striker		

Hey, now!

His CA had improved by five points! That was fascinating. Because of injuries and suspensions, he'd played one whole match, and then he'd played the first half of the next one. Long before he was ready. It made sense that this baptism of fire had led to a big jump in his current ability. He'd learned how far short of the required level he was, and like me he'd found himself in situations he didn't have solutions for. He probably spent the next few days mentally replaying those moments, wondering what he could have done differently. And since he was training more or less full-time, he could ask Jackie and the other coaches for help. Try out his solutions in practice matches.

Yes, training was essential. But a few minutes on the pitch would go a very long way in a player's development. It's like with muscles— you have to give them a shock so they will grow.

The question for Ziggy now was, could he ride that match and a half all the way to CA 30, where he'd start to really compete for regular game time? Or would his progress stall at a certain point?

And would attributes like passing and stamina keep improving if his CA stayed flat? I read through the profile again and smiled at his jumping score. Wasn't that his second improvement there? Had that happened because I'd told him to focus on that, or would it have happened anyway?

Ziggy was the closest thing I had to a guinea pig. A test subject. I'd have to keep a much closer eye on him.

XP balance: 1,126

Debt repaid: 126/3,000

After the match, I surprised Ziggy by meeting him outside the dressing room. (A steward let me in. My natural charm helped, but mostly it was the photo of us signing the FC United contract.) Ziggy was very happy to see me, and we went to the pub. Both drinking alcohol-free drinks. Model pros.

While a table of women very studiously *didn't* look at us (except when *we* weren't looking at *them*), I told him all about Chester and he told me about FC United. Two old veterans exchanging war stories.

While I described Ian Evans, Ziggy picked up his phone and tapped at it.

"He might not be there for long," said Ziggy. "Chester lost again tonight." He showed me the phone. Two–nil.

I was briefly interested in the fact that I hadn't even thought to look. Chester was a dead battery. "Oh?" I said.

"Darlington are top of the league. That's good for you, right?"

"Yeah," I said. If they didn't need Henri Lyons, I could become his agent. If they needed him, he didn't need me.

"Chester are sixteenth."

"Okay," I said, not giving a shit. "FCU are near the top, right?"

"We're eighth," he said. "We would be fifth, but we had a three-point deduction because we had too many loan players in one game. You're only allowed five but somehow there were six."

"Loans," I said, wagging my finger. "That's what Henri needs. We find a club who'll pay his wages from January to the end of the season. Darlington won't get a transfer fee, but they won't have to pay his wages."

"That'll work," said Ziggy, with the confidence of an industry insider. I wasn't so sure. There was a chance Henri had pissed off people in Darlington so much that they would keep him around just out of spite.

I sat back and took a proper look at Ziggy. He was looking more solid every time I saw him. "Ziggy, mate. Are you having fun?"

"Now?"

"Being a footballer."

Shy grin. The old Ziggy. "A bit. I want to play, but . . ."

"But it's still fucking top, yeah?" I thought about what it meant to be a footballer. A lot of attention from women. The ones on the next table were glancing at us a lot, now. Permission to approach. "How's Lula?"

"That's over."

"Oh. What happened?"

"How's Beth?" he said.

I smiled. That was his way of saying "Next, please."

We were just debating whether to stay and have another alc-free beer when my phone rang. Mike Dean. Managing director of a club tumbling down the league table. Bizarrely, when Ziggy saw who it was, he started filming me. The phone's camera lens was right in my face.

"Max," said MD. "Hope you're well. Ian Evans and I would like to meet you tomorrow evening. Have a chat. Do some business, maybe."

"Will I book us a table in that curry place?"

"The meeting would take place in Chester, Max."

He was being strange. Distant. Professional. I guessed that the moment Ian Evans had sprung his trap had made MD realise how precarious his position was. Possibly he'd decided to stick to counting money and stay away from the football side of things. "So I'll work the whole day, drive to Chester, chat with you guys, then drive home again?"

"Yes, Max."

"And that will be worth my while, will it?"

"Yes, Max."

"Fine. See you tomorrow." I ended the call, then looked up at Ziggy. "Huh."

Ziggy turned the camera back on himself and said in a dramatic voice, "You're done with Chester. But they're not done with you."

I nodded a few times. "Early night, then." I gripped the phone and talked right into the mic. "By the way, Ziggy."

"Yeah?"

"Keep bouncing on your bed."

He blushed and jabbed at the phone. It wouldn't respond. "How did you know?"

"I saw you jumping in the warm-up. You're like a flea. Boing! Gravity barely applies to you anymore."

"Max," he said. He stopped the video and smashed the delete button. But he was delighted I'd noticed his hard work. "It's not the bed. It's my niece's trampoline." He glanced at the table with the women, then back at me. "Do you think I just deleted a historically important clip? The call to set up the meeting where they offer you . . . what?"

"One of three things. They want Henri, they want Raffi, they want me."

"Or all three!"

I laughed. "I wouldn't bet on it." I clicked my fingers. "That reminds me!" I dug out my wallet and took out the betting slip from when I'd bet on Ziggy to score. "Nearly won five hundred quid on you."

Ziggy held the paper like it was the *Magna Carta*. "Max," he said. "You really believe in me."

"Of course I do, mate."

"Can I keep this?"

I laughed again. "The fuckers are never going to pay up. So sure. You keep it."

"You should film the meeting tomorrow. You versus Ian Evans, round two. I'd love to see it."

I pressed the tip of my finger down into the table. "If there's one thing I can guarantee you, it's that this meeting will not be confrontational."

Ziggy gave me a blank stare. "Right. The kind of nonconfrontation that people stay up till 2 a.m. to watch. Live from Madison Square Garden."

"Mate," I said.

"Mate," he said. And I saw him glance at the betting slip and then at the ladies. It was the perfect prop to get a conversation going. But he folded it up and slipped it with infinite care into his wallet. It was not an icebreaker. It was something more.

"Right, I'm off," I said.

"Me too," he said. "Let me know how it goes. Can you at least send round-by-round scores?"

"It's not going to be like thaaat," I said with a hint of a whine.

And, true to my word, the following evening I behaved beautifully. For almost five minutes.

8

A PRISONER'S DILEMMA

Moneyball—What Do Footballers Earn?
On average, a player in tier five (Wrexham, Oldham, Altrincham, etc.) can expect to earn around £700 per week. In tier six (Darlington, Chester, etc.) this drops to around £300–400 per week, which is below the average national wage in the UK (£550 per week).

The average League Two (tier four) player earns £1,000 a week. Enough to buy 1,200 bananas from a grocer in London.

The average League One (tier three) player earns £2,000 a week. Enough to buy 2,400 bananas or 470 banana smoothies from a famous high street location.

The average Championship (tier two) player earns £14,000 a week, which as you know could buy 17,000 bananas or 438 tubes of Ole Henriksen banana face primer.

The average Premier League player earns £64,000 a week. Enough to buy 77,000 bananas, or half of *Comedian*, a piece of art which comprises a browning banana taped to a gallery wall. Or if you prefer food to art, it would buy you the world's most expensive banana split, which is prepared and served to you atop Mount Kilimanjaro while a cellist plays Bach.

Wednesday, November 9.
The outskirts of Chester. The UK headquarters of a small but international credit card company.

I was in the temporary office of Chester FC's seventy-two-year-old manager, Ian Evans. There was this weird sense of being in a police interrogation room. The main piece of furniture was a desk; one whole wall was a window. Unlike a real police room, this window wasn't a one-way mirror. It was a real window looking out onto the pitches outside. To the left, some Chester players were doing a light session, and to the right there was a game going on. I guessed it was some of the employees from the offices—part of me wanted to pop outside briefly and scout them all. It would help me get a scouting achievement. I *suspected* the next one would trigger when I'd scouted 2,500 players, but the achievement system was so weird I didn't really give it much thought.

But the main reason I got interrogation room vibes was because I'd been left alone in there, made to wait by two older, male authority figures. Pretty much a standard scene in every police show. Maybe they were watching me, right now, on a camera feed. They'd wait for me to start sweating, then barge in and do good cop/bad cop on me.

They'd left a prop—a football-themed flipchart. Every sheet had a pitch outline, so coaches could scribble formations without having to draw the markings every time. I needed that! I wondered if it came in small sizes. What shop sold this stuff? One of the millions of things I didn't know.

I picked up a marker from the flipchart's little tray and put the cap back on properly. No sense in letting the pen dry out.

The topmost sheet had an analysis of Chester's squad with the heading *Week 45 Squad Overview.* Each position on the pitch had the nicknames of every first team option, ranked in order. Some names appeared two or three times depending on how flexible those players were. Some names were followed by numbers in brackets—I guessed the length of their current injury. In the goalkeeper position there were three names. The second was Ben Cavanagh (Cavvers), who I suspected was actually the best goalie. In the right back position there were another three names. And as a fourth option, someone had added, in a different colour and different handwriting, the name Magnus. So someone had been paying attention on Sunday!

I glanced at the door. It was pretty weird that they'd left me alone in here. But that was *their* problem. I was feeling nosy. If they updated this chart once a week, then the page behind this one would be the week forty-four squad, the one from before my trial. I flipped it over—very nosy!—and grinned. I turned another sheet, and *there* was the week forty-four squad. I went back to the intermediate sheet.

Its title was *January*, and there was only one name in each position—basically, Chester's strongest lineup. Aff on the left of midfield and Carl at right back. But it had Henri as one of the strikers, Raffi in centre mid, and me as the right mid. One potential future version of Chester FC. If they played their cards right!

I thought about what was best from my point of view—to let Ian and MD know that I knew that they wanted all three of us, or to pretend I hadn't seen it.

I decided to change it back to how I'd found it, and went to pee. When I got back, Mike Dean and Ian Evans were waiting to give me a quick handshake. I wasn't sure if they knew I'd seen the January wish list, and I suddenly felt excited.

The prisoner's dilemma is a famous thought experiment where two prisoners have to make a decision based on inadequate information. A prisoner, and this will be annoyingly simplistic to some people, can choose to cooperate with the other prisoner—or betray him. The catch is they don't know what the other prisoner will choose, and choosing wrong is catastrophic. The optimal outcome is when both prisoners cooperate.

Was this a prisoner's dilemma kind of situation? Chester FC wanted things. I wanted things. My clients wanted things. There was a very simple version of this meeting where we would talk through our wants until we reached a compromise that satisfied every single party.

But that wasn't the dynamic. Ian Evans was hostile to me but wanted Henri. MD's job was to get the players Ian wanted for as little money as possible while not burning bridges with the child prodigy (me), who the *next* manager might want to work with. And that's where the most thrilling part of this particular social dynamic came in. I controlled the destinies of three players—what if I wasn't the *prisoner*? What if I was the *jailor*?

This was a high-stakes game where every player had their own goals, information, and even their own rule books. Absolute chaos. I loved it.

MD was behind the desk. Making Ian sit somewhere less alpha in his own office. Bit of a show of power there! I was proud of him. Ian was on a hard-backed chair by the wall, facing me. I adjusted my chair so that I was angled more towards Ian, House of Commons style. Adversarial.

"Thanks for coming, Max," said MD. He was doing his "distant businessman" thing again.

"Yep," I said.

"Where shall we start?" he said. Already trying to get information from me!

"Why ask *me*?" I said, pretending to be fascinated by the ornaments on Ian's desk. "I have no idea what this is all about. As far as I know, you're going to ask me to give you twenty quid for parking in your spot that time."

MD shuffled some papers with a tiny grin. The guy who'd let his hair down in front of Charlie's Angels was still in there! "Okay. Let's start with Henri Lyons." He passed a document over to me. "A standard loan contract. From January 1st to the end of the season. This isn't binding, you understand. There's still a lot of work to do. This is just to show how committed we are." I flipped through it. Seemed extremely boilerplate. It was also incredibly meaningless. MD might as well have handed me a post-it that said *IOU a trillion pounds lol*. "So the main questions are, will his club let him leave in January? And can we afford his wages? And if we can't, will Darlington accept a percentage?"

"That's a lot of questions, Mike."

He tried to give me his serious look, but it had no effect. "Okay, Max. Why don't you start by telling us his salary and we'll take things from there?"

I forced my eyebrows up my forehead. "You want me to tell you my client's most private information? What am I, one of Mark Zuckerberg's horcruxes?"

"Er . . . I don't know what that means," said MD. He was getting annoyed by my attitude. "How much does he earn, Max?"

"How much can you pay him, Mike?"

"That's . . . that's not . . ."

"It's the same discussion. One of us is going to have to make the first move." In the prisoner's dilemma, the guy who betrays his friend is set free. "Fortunately, it's in my interest to get Henri a move, and he loves Chester. So tell me the maximum you can pay, and then the absolute absolute maximum."

"Max," said MD, like I was a child.

I experienced a pang of annoyance so strong it made me question if I wanted to be doing this agent shit. But then I went right back to enjoying it. Negotiating a three-person transfer wasn't something that happened very often. "Mike! I should be talking to clubs in League Two. You've got a chance to get a deadly striker for pennies on the dollar. What the fuck am I saying? He should be playing in League One! Three divisions away! It's insane you even have a shot at this. And Jesus. Imagine if he likes it and wants to stay next season? Imagine if he signs a long-term contract. A top striker for free. You're welcome. Tell me your budget and your real budget."

"Max," started MD, so I picked up the sample contract and threw it against a filing cabinet. From there, it slid into a rectangular wastepaper basket.

"Next," I said.

"Christ," mumbled Ian Evans. The first thing he'd said. He rearranged himself and looked away from both MD and me. The new posture made him look like an Easter Island statue. It suited him.

"What's next, Mike?" I said.

MD was rubbing his temples. He didn't like this style of negotiating. The weird thing was, I kind of did. It was a bit manic, but I felt like I was just about holding my own. And I'd talked myself into a position where I truly believed Henri should have been talking to bigger clubs. "Eight hundred a week," he said.

"I'm sorry. Are you saying eight hundred pounds a week? For Henri Lyons?"

"That's already smashing our pay structure."

I scanned their faces but saw no signs of deception. I was a bit dismayed. Eight hundred a week was *shit*. It was dentist money. Call centre manager money. All I could think to say was, "Oh."

"So, Max, how much is he on?"

I shook my head. "Enough to never wear the same scarf twice." The truth was I didn't know. Now that Chester had made a move, I could ask Henri. But I was sure he'd be on over a thousand a week. Possibly as much as £1,500. I clicked a hole punch together a few times, then shook my head again. "Honestly, I don't think I can work with that. I'm . . . genuinely not trying to be a dick. He's Darlington's record signing." I clicked the hole punch again. "I'll try, though."

MD looked at Ian Evans, who did some kind of gesture. I didn't see it—I was still processing the revelation of the true extent of Chester's poverty. There were Premier League players who paid people £800 a week to tell them what to watch on Netflix. Probably.

"Okay," said MD. "Can we talk about Raffi Brown?"

"Yes."

"We like him. He's got promise."

"I swear to god, Mike, if you offer five pounds and a bag of crisps, I'm going home."

MD hesitated, then picked up another contract. He handed it over. "We know he's got a job and a kid. Our offer is actually on the high side given his inexperience and his . . . past."

I dropped the contract, unopened, on the table in front of me. It made a soft slapping sound and I glanced from man to man. "Raffi works in a casino keeping the peace. He's a model employee. His bosses love him. I'm not taking him away from that if it means someone brings up his 'past' every time he gets a yellow fucking card, every time someone loses a sock."

"They won't." The first meaningful contribution from Ian Evans. I stared at him, waiting for him to elaborate. "They won't," he repeated. He had this way of saying things that made it sound like he was reading from carved stone tablets.

It seemed like a promise, so I moved on. I opened the contract and skimmed it. Long story short, they were offering £450 a week. About what you'd get on a supermarket checkout. Weirdly, the starting date of the contract was January 2. Transfers could be made on January 1. But Raffi wasn't registered to another team, so he could start right away. Why such a strange date?

I took a deep breath. Zen master. "We're not a million miles away. I want a three-year contract. Five hundred a week the first year. Goal and assist bonus. Seven fifty the second. A thousand the third. Eight-hundred-thousand-pound release clause."

MD threw his arms wide. "Max! What are you talking about? You know we can't pay that. I just told you."

"He won't be here in the third season. This is your incentive to make sure he plays. If he plays, he'll reach his potential. If he reaches his potential, someone will buy him."

"For eight hundred thousand pounds?"

"Yep. When it happens, that'll be cheap. You'll be annoyed. But we . . . But *you* can use that money to invest in the club."

Ian spoke again. "While you take your ten percent of his new wage at his new club."

He was trying to goad me, but in such a clumsy way it was like he'd never done it before. "Yes, Ian. That's right. Perhaps you'd like me to take my eight-hundred-thousand-pound asset and give it to a *rival* club, for free?"

Ian went, "Tsch," and folded his arms. So I tossed the contract against the filing cabinet and heard it slink into the bin.

MD sprang to his feet and retrieved it. "Jesus, Max! We like Raffi. We want him. Just . . . let me crunch the numbers."

"What's this January second shit?" I asked. "You could sign him tomorrow." *If you really wanted him.*

"We're a small club, Max. Image is important. Reputation. When you sign a player mid-January no one bats an eye. Sign one in November and people talk."

Gibberish. Nonsense. There was something oppressive in the atmosphere. Something off. I got the feeling I was back to being a prisoner, no longer the jailor. It was one thing to make a mistake that would tie Henri up at Chester for six months, but quite another to make the wrong decisions on behalf of Raffi and his family. I stood and walked around the room. If I was being fanciful, I'd say I was hoping to walk into a cloud of weirdness and find out if it was coming from Ian or MD. "Are we done?" I said. I needed more information to help me process the information I already had. Otherwise, I'd be taking wild stabs in the dark.

MD frowned and slid the Raffi contract to one side. There was another one underneath. MD pushed it towards me, wordlessly.

I skimmed it while standing. Max Best. Player. "Shirt number seventy-seven," I said, even though I'd tried to stay quiet. That was just so unexpected.

"Seven is taken," said MD, with a slight smile. "That's the best we could do. Er . . . yeah, the best. Seventy-seven Best. Could do well in the club shop."

I kept skimming all the way through to the end where the important bits were. Three hundred fifty pounds a week. That was a piss-take. But what really stood out was the date. If I signed this, I would become a Chester player on January 3.

I glanced at Ian, and the crevices on his face all twitched. Our relationship had started with me trying to scam him, and this was his revenge. Every single facial nook and cranny was in on the plot. We'd been acting out some version of the prisoner's dilemma, except he'd smashed the betray button before I'd even arrived.

I thought about how I'd been left alone in this room with the flipchart, and how I'd "discovered" that they wanted to sign me and my two clients. Me "discovering" that was fundamental to the plot, I was sure, but it was so subtle. It was about making me feel like I was in charge. Making me complacent. Most people would have sat in a chair and not touched anything until the others arrived. Whoever planned this evening *knew* I'd look. So who was behind it? MD had the brains for it, but not the balls. Which meant . . .

"Mike," I said, "could you excuse us, please? Ian and I would like to have a little chat."

9

CHANGE

MD fucked off with good grace.

I stood, picked up the marker pen, and went to the window.

I watched the match for a few moments. I was partly giving MD time to get out of earshot, and partly giving myself time to gather my thoughts. Discussing the contract dates would be explosive and would surely end my time in Chester. Before doing that, I decided to try to *talk* to Ian Evans, to get to know him a bit, to see if there was an alternate path. To get him to change his decision from "betray" to "cooperate."

Outside, a light drizzle had arrived. Most people hated weather like this, but I loved it. The pitch got slick, the ball zipped around, you needed more technique to control the ball. And when the match was over and you had a hot shower and used your fluffy towel and put on your dry socks—mate. What more do you want?

Oh, not much. Just money, status, and respect.

Honestly, though, right then, I would have settled for a good old-fashioned kickabout. Make some runs, make some passes, make some friends.

I sighed, looked back at my foe, and had the strangest feeling that the room had gotten smaller.

Ian Evans. Footballing dinosaur. You always think they're going extinct, but the game keeps producing more of them. I tried to imagine him as a kid, kicking pigskin balls around cobbled streets, wearing clogs or whatever they had in those days. Him trying to do mad skillz, yelling "Stanley Matthews" as he dribbled past two players, the absolute, unbridled joy of winning his first little football trophy. His first pro match, his first goal, his first Brylcreem sponsorship, his first day in the manager's dugout. Sixty-five years of nonstop competition. What would it do to a man?

"Ian, mate," I said, "Do you even like football?"

He snorted, still on the hardbacked chair. "What kind of question is that?"

"Look at these guys," I said, pointing to the office workers. "I can't tell from up here, but they're probably all shit. But there they are, putting their bodies on the line. Tackles, freak injuries, shit, even broken fingers trying to save shots. Why do they do it? For the love of the game and all that. For those little moments of joy. A cheeky nutmeg. A nice pass and only you knew how tight the angles were. Giving the keeper the eyes." Making the goalie dive the wrong way with just a glance. "But you." I shook my head and leaned on the glass. "I've never seen joy from you. I've seen shouting and anger and constipation. But I've never seen fun. I've never seen laughter. I've never seen you attack. You're so defensive. So conservative. So reactionary. You can't possibly enjoy what you're doing."

He didn't move an inch. "I enjoy winning."

I smiled. "Yeah. About that. Your last win was under a different *monarch*, so the question still stands: do you even like football?"

He snarled at me silently. Then he levered himself up and joined me at the window. I say joined. We were actually as far away from each other as it was possible to be. "I like football," he said. "What you like . . . isn't football. What you like is data science. It's gifs and think pieces and wanky podcasts."

This threw me for a loop. I had no idea what he was talking about. I glanced over my shoulder—the door was fully closed. Hadn't MD left it a crack open? "What?"

"I like football," he said. "Football. Or as my old man used to call it, soccer. I don't like xG. Expected goals? We've *got* a number that says what team played better. It's called *goals*. I don't like using fancy new German words to describe things we've been doing for years. Gegenpressing? It's called winning the ball back. Moving into the half-space? That's called *moving*."

"You think I'm a football hipster?"

"I don't give a monkey's what you call yourself. It's all tactics and formations and weird graphs with you lot. You play Champion Manager and think you can set up a team." *Nope! Wrong guy!* "You think you can look at some numbers and say who's going to make it." *Well, actually, yeah, but not in the way you mean.*

"Tactics," I said, "yeah. About that." I went to the flipchart and reset it back to the cover. Then I quickly flipped through each squad overview. "First game of the season: four-four-two," I said. I flipped more pages. "Four-four-two, four-four-two. I think I'm getting the pattern. Gosh, there's another one. Wait, four-four-three? No, that extra striker was just a note to buy toilet paper." I was turning the pages so fast the sheets started to rip. The more I saw 4-4-2 the more annoyed I got. I did sort of try to squash the feeling down. A bit. Honest. I was aware that this wasn't going well but I felt imprisoned. I lashed out at my captor. "Ian, mate, why don't you *ever* change formation?"

He clenched his fist and pressed his knuckles against the glass. His head tilted downwards. "You kids. You've been brought up on slick videos with loads of little circles moving around a pretty little pitch. Oh, let's move this circle here and get a *double pivot*. Oh, move *him* here, he can be a tre-quart-is-ta." He punctuated each syllable with dainty finger gestures. "Fucking pompous tripe. Football's easy. Line up solid. Win your battles, win the game."

I sank back onto the window. I was struggling here. Struggling to identify with him. Surely even *he* wasn't *that* ossified. But the room was shrinking. There wasn't enough air. All I could do was fight. "But you were there in the war," I laughed. He bristled; he was born in 1951. "You don't just match up against the enemy. You do feints. Pincers. You probe for opportunities. You think changing formation is a sign of weakness? That makes no sense."

"I change formation, Best. At Barnsley we played four-three-three. At Cambridge we did four-five-one. At Swindon I got promoted with three-five-two and in them days, no one did that. But what you learn after a lifetime in the game is that at this level, simplicity is best. You can get as fancy as you like, but you're always going to end up right back where you started. Four-four-fucking-two."

"Why?"

"These players can't handle owt else, Best. Case in point. One guy we had on trial. Played centre midfield. Couldn't hack it, so he went to DM. But he was playing like a second right back. Didn't have the tactical brain or the discipline to stay in his slot, yeah? Then—this is the same game, mind—he thinks he'll try his hand as attacking midfielder. Can't hack *that*, neither. Keeps fucking bouncing around 'til he finds somewhere he isn't *shit*. But guess what? That's not how you learn a position. That's not how real football works. You wander around like a lost little lamb, you're fucking your team."

"That guy," I said, with a fake look of interest. "What happened to him?"

"What do you mean?"

"You said he went to right mid and sent in two dreamy crosses."

The snarl was back. "I said he went to right mid and the left back *correctly* didn't expect much from him and lost concentration."

"Oh, right," I said. "That was after he scored a free kick from long range that marked him out as . . . so incompetent as to be underestimated?"

"The left back was probably remembering the fact that when things got tough, the lad subbed himself off and had a little cry."

"Yeah, fair point," I said. "But if the left back was more in touch with his emotions, he'd know that having a little cry can be therapeutic." So this conversation was going great. The more aggressive I was, the closer the walls got. I longed to get out on the pitch. Go and have fun! Why was I stuck in here with this crypt keeper? I felt the marker in my hand. A chance to change the flow of the conversation! You can't believe what it cost me, but I tried. Say what you like about me, but don't say I didn't *try*. I went back to the flipchart and flipped to a new page. I smiled away the claustrophobia. "You're playing Banbury next, right? I haven't seen them but I'll bet you a Frenchman they play a defensive four-four-two. So how about . . ." I scribbled the names of Chester players in a 3-5-2 formation, mumbling *Ryder, Aff, Carlile,* and so on as I wrote. "Oh, mate. This is making me feel very special. Yeah, here's a winning team. Even better, though." I crossed out Carl Carlile's name—I had placed him as the right-most of the three central defenders—and wrote it again, slightly farther forward. "Carl as DM. He looked decent on Sunday. Or put Sam Topps there. That'd suit him." I stepped away and checked out my work. It looked great. "There you go. I call this formation the Four-Four-Two Killer."

Evans stared at the diagram until he started shaking. It took me a while to realise this was a real, genuine laugh. It was almost silent. "You want me to play two-six-two? In a professional match? Well, there it is. There it is right there." He sat down in his chair and rearranged things on his desk that I'd moved. His hole punch. His ornaments. A framed photo of a younger Ian Evans with some teenager.

I pointed out the window. "Let's go try it out," I said.

His hands stopped fussing over things. "What?"

"There's two teams twenty metres away. They know who you are; they'll let us mess about. They'll love it. You manage one, I'll do the other. I'll . . ." I was about to say I'd run the 2-6-2 formation, but I couldn't adapt formations yet, and I didn't even have 3-5-2. I needed to go shopping, but I was still waiting for the November perk to drop. "I'll play a basic 4-4-2. The absolute anti-hipster. All I'll do is shuffle players around and give them individual instructions. You try this," I tapped the flipchart. "It's just three-five-two, Ian! The DM can go back if it starts to buckle. But it won't."

He regarded me. "How would I know who to play where?"

I frowned. "By watching them. Actually, you're right. That's not the point of the exercise. I'll tell you who's best for each role."

"You've seen them before?"

"No. Unless they've been touring Manchester. Don't worry, it won't take long."

His eyes narrowed. "This is that thing where you think you're a good scout."

"I am a good scout. I saw Henri Lyons in the warm-up when you played Darlington. Sunday was the first time I'd ever seen him actually play."

He scoffed—again. "He's the best striker in the league. You don't get a medal for that one."

"I saw Raffi playing five-a-side."

"His talent is obvious. And he started in an academy. You're not the first person to think he's got something. You did well to dig him up, though. Fair play."

"My other client is called Ziggy. I saw him at five-a-side, too, basically playing left back. And now he's a striker for FC United."

"He's the lad who scored that goal where he celebrated like he'd won the World Cup?"

"Yeah."

I was waiting for the laughter, but Evans was nodding. "Left back to striker? That's something."

This was the first time he'd said anything vaguely complimentary, and it infuriated me. I exploded. Flapped my arms around like a teenage brat. "Jesus Christ! You're one of the only people in the country who understands every word of what I just said and what it means. If I told a hundred people I found a player and he's got a contract at FC United, a hundred would think it's worthless because they've never heard of the club. If I told them I found a guy playing left back and knew he'd be a striker, they'd shrug. So what? But you get it. So why are you making this so hard?"

"What am I making hard, Best?"

"Everything." I walked over and flopped into the hardbacked chair that Ian had started in.

He turned around and glanced at the pitch where some of his players were doing small drills. Satisfied, he turned back. I realised he loved control; I could never play for him. He ran a hand through his hair. "What do you want, kid?"

I rubbed my face with both hands and leaned forward. "I want a place where I can bring players. A club that will train up the guys I find. I want to be able to use my skills and I want to build something."

He laughed. More of a big scoff. "What rot!" He scoffed again. "You're all about money."

When he said that, I was reminded of the feeling of reading half a Kafka novel. Page after page of people misunderstanding the main character, accusing him of things he hadn't done. The atmosphere Kafka created was one of the most upsetting feelings of my life. To be safe, I hadn't read anything from Central Europe since. Not *Death in Venice*. Not even *Heidi*.

I was all about money. Holy shit. This was going nowhere. Evans wasn't listening and I was no longer interested in trying to find out what made him tick. On with the mystery of the contract offers.

"Wrong," I said, and moved to the flipchart. "Dead wrong." I turned it towards Evans and flipped to a new page. I wrote a big *1, 2,* and *3* on the top half of the sheet. "Let's talk about these dates. January first. Henri Lyons signs for Chester. Yay!" I tapped the *2*. "January second. Raffi Brown is announced. Whoo! January third. Max Best signs. Shrug." I tapped the numbers a few more times. Evans was following my every move. "What if it doesn't go that way? Let's see. January first, Henri Lyons . . . doesn't sign." I crossed out the *1*. "He's forced to see out his contract. Or he finds a different agent. One who gets him an upward move. Wrexham, maybe! He breaks Paul Mullin's record as the player most hugged on camera by Ryan Reynolds. Good for him.

But what next for Chester? Well, maybe they need to find some other striker. Maybe they need a few quid in reserve to afford him." I crossed out the *2*. "Sorry, Raffi, mate. We like you but deal's off. No hard feelings, yeah? January third. Max Best. Who's that? Some football hipster, always blabbing about xG, apparently. Wait, didn't he fucking smash his trial and lead the reserves to victory against the first team? Yeah, but he's a twat." My volume started to rise, and I started to get closer to Evans. "So, January third, nine a.m., Max Best gets a text. *Deal's off. Soz.* Ah, but wait a second, Ian. December third I've handed in my notice. So January third rolls around, I'm fucking unemployed. No income, mate, at the height of winter. Can't afford heating. Can't afford rent. I'm out on the street—in Chester, mind you, because I fucking moved here for my new job!—and the question is, what gets me first: starvation or fucking HYPOTHERMIA?"

"Oh, spare me," he said. "You're not going to die. You'll find some other club to leech off."

That shut me up. Briefly. "What?"

"Leech. A little worm. A bloodsucker. You're a con man and Mike Dean is the perfect mark. You know more about footy than him—you've blinded him with science. You've had a couple of lucky punches and now he wants to give you the keys to the kingdom."

It was strange hearing this version of me. Hard to work out how he'd come to this conclusion. "Right." I was rapidly cooling off. I liked Chester, the club, but their budget was so tiny I wondered if they could match my ambitions. I should have been looking for a club that could afford to bring in ten new first-team players and twenty youth prospects. This whole mess could be chalked up as a valuable life lesson, a funny story, the equivalent of the music executive who passed on The Beatles.

But Evans wasn't done provoking me. "I took this job because Chester needed me. They needed a steady hand on the tiller. Someone to right the ship. Old-school football wisdom. That's what I offer; that's what I'm here for. MD is a good lad, good Chester stock, but he doesn't know his Arsenal from his elbow. This club has suffered from chancers and grifters before. I well remember when Chester City went bust. You get the wrong sort of people inside a club, it's like a cancer. This country is full of clubs rotting away, hollowed out by bloodsuckers. I won't let that happen under my watch. This community has suffered enough. This community deserves better."

The rain intensified—now we could hear it slamming into the glass. I laughed. It was a bit manic. The laughter of a man who wanted to run around and get soaking wet chasing a ball. The laughter of a man not in complete control of himself. "Community? You're joking, right? On my first day here, I volunteered for a session with the Chester Knights and one with the under-fourteens. From what I hear, that's two more sessions than you, your coaching staff, and your entire first team has ever done! Henri fucking Lyons did the same as me. And neither of us fucking work here! So you can get bent with that. Did you know you had a disabled team? Do you know what's happening in the youth teams? Of course you don't. You're running the oldest squad in the league. There's no pathway for young players. That's your gift to the next manager—absolutely zero development. So let me be the one to tell you—your youth system, yes, *your* youth system, is broken. What's happening under your nose, on your shift, is a fucking *debacle*. If you gave the slightest shit you'd be there every Sunday morning. But they've never seen you, mate. Community? Half those kids don't know what you look like. They'd recognise me, though, I promise you that."

"Yeah, yeah. I bet they all follow you on Snapchat. My job is to keep the team in this league. And I'll do that."

"Community," I scoffed again. "I've been to three of your matches. One was fucking epic. That was the only one where your tactics made sense. Playing against a better team, an Ian Evans special. The other two were dull as dishwater. Attendances are in decline. Because nobody wants to watch twenty-three home matches where twenty are nil-nil or one-nil. They don't want to watch Aff tracking back doing his defensive work. They don't want to watch your strikers ten yards ahead of your defenders. If you actually cared about this community, you'd give the fans something to smile about. Take Aff's leash off. Let the attackers attack. You'd at the very least play some kids so the fans could have some fucking hope for next season. Jesus Christ."

"I suppose you think you're the excitement this club needs. Is that it?"

I shook my head. I picked up the Max Best contract and—carefully—placed it in the bin. No more throwing things! I was maturing! "Max Best is no longer available."

"What about the others?"

I glared at him. "I already said I'd do my best to get Henri. At least I know he'd play every game here." I looked at the *2* on the flipchart.

"Raffi, though. I know he's your type of player. Big, strong, handles himself. But he's young. What are you going to do when he has a bad run? He really, really needs a long-term contract, but he also really, really needs to play. Some other club. A younger manager."

"Now, then," said Evans. "Are you saying you'll try to get Henri here even without you and Brown?"

"Yes. I only want Raffi here if you'll do right by him. That means signing him right away so he can get started. He doesn't have time to waste."

"What? Put him straight into the team?"

"No, you pr—" I took a breath. "No, Ian. As you know from your many decades in the industry, that would be bad for his development. I want you to do what's best for Raffi because that's also what's best for Chester."

"So someone buys him."

"Yes. Because when someone buys him, he can train and compete at a higher level and continue improving."

"And there's some condition to all this, is there? Access to the youth programme?"

"No, Ian." I put the marker pen on the little tray and turned the flipchart back to its original position. "If you don't care about it, why should I?"

Evans picked up the picture of him and the kid, and turned away from me. He had a little think. "All right. We'll sign him as soon as he can get out of his job."

I replied in a flat voice. Sort of defeated, I guess. "He works nights sometimes. Can he come and train in the day while he's working his notice?"

Evans thought about it. "He can't do contact work until he signs properly. Insurance. But yeah. He can come and get started. Yeah. Fresh face. Mix things up a bit." He turned away from me again. "Someone will be in touch. Let us know about Lyons."

I went to the door and had this weird certainty that it wouldn't open. For a second I didn't see a handle and panicked. I left without another word to anyone.

Once back in the car, I hit the steering wheel. If Evans was true to his word, which I suspected he was—to a fault—I'd just bagged myself another fifty pounds a week. If I could get Henri to Chester, I'd be in line for at least eighty pounds a week. Factoring in my Ziggy cash, I was looking at 165 pounds a week from my career as an agent. If I could double that, I'd be able to quit my job.

I hit the steering wheel again. The money meant nothing; the evening had been a disaster, and I couldn't blame Ian Evans for it.

I'd messed up from the start. Maxy No-Thumbs. Befriending MD instead of someone who mattered. Trying to trick Ian Evans. Trying to be a player-manager.

It was all stupendously dumb.

I sat there and bathed in my failure. This, I vowed, would be a lesson. A teachable moment. From now on, I'd be straight with everyone. I'd be honest. I'd take the long and winding road that definitely led to my destination instead of trying to double-jump my way up the sheer face of the mountain.

Becoming a pro player was really a good shortcut. A valid one. I'd improve myself as a player and try again. I looked at myself in the rear mirror. My bruise was gone. There was almost certainly no crack in my skull. I was healed. I could get started right away. But I wouldn't do that player-manager shit again. No chance.

I put my keys in the ignition. This drive home would be the end of the beginning. From now on, I'd do things the old-fashioned way. The Max Best way was moronic. It could never work. There were too many people like Ian Evans in the football industry. I had to change. To try to fit in.

The key wouldn't turn. Why not? I looked down at my hand. The key wouldn't turn because I was making absolutely no effort to turn it.

Change? Fit in?

I looked at myself in the mirror again. "Nah," I said, breaking into a cheeky grin. The car door clicked open and slammed shut. The rear door clicked open, my kit bag slid out, and the door slammed shut.

I strode through the building and out the other side. I walked to the side of the pitch where the office workers were aquaplaning. They were all CA 1 PA 1 no-hopers. I dropped my bag, called a few of the red team over and told them I was a new Chester coach just come from Manchester City and if they didn't mind I'd like to practice what I'd learned from Pep on them. They were delighted. A real coach from their local team using tactics from the world's best manager!

The entire red team came over into a huddle while the whites took on some water and did some stretches.

"All right, guys," I said to my team, pushing the rain out of my hair. I slapped my palms together. When was the last time I'd felt this goddamned *free*? "Tactics time. What's got four points, is really solid, and cuts through anything?"

10

CHAT SHIT GET BANGED

Football glossary: Chat shit get banged. In 2011, long before he shot Leicester City to their 5,000-to-1 Premier League victory, non-league striker Jamie Vardy was mocked by fans of a rival team. He tweeted that those who say negative things might well expect to face negative consequences. Though, being Jamie Vardy, he managed to squeeze all this meaning into four words and zero commas.

Beep. "Hi, Max here, how can I help?"

I'd been at work for half an hour, and the time had flown by. I hadn't taken many calls, though, which was strange because the rest of the team seemed pretty busy. Didn't really care—I was having an introspective morning. Evaluating the night before. Comparing the stress of the "little chat" with the fun I had afterwards. The more time passed, the more I thought the entire adventure had been positive.

Getting Raffi a deal was extremely reassuring. There were probably thousands of apparently shit players out there like Ziggy who'd need a visionary coach like Jackie Reaper—there, I said it—to take a risk. But there must have been hundreds of easy-on-the-eye players like Raffi who even the most tiny-armed football dinosaur would want to sign. So I was really much closer to financial freedom than I thought—I just needed to get as much scouting done as possible before January. Finish the transfer window with a whole stable of players. A fleet of players? A Louis Vuitton manbag full of players.

I had a chunk of holiday time stored up. Normally I rolled my days over to the next financial year because sometimes the bank bought them and I much preferred cash to time off. But six or seven free days in November and December could be used very wisely indeed.

I finished a call and glanced up at the stats board. I was currently in sixth place. Relegation form!

Max Best near the bottom of the table? *Got to do better*, I thought. But why? I had an *extremely* valuable skill and it wasn't one valued by this bank. No, it was a skill prized by football clubs. Even after pissing off Ian Evans, he'd given the go-ahead to sign two of my players. So why hadn't I quit this job yet?

Because there was no need to freeze to death. I could find a few new players and then quit in January. Easy. Done. Conversation over. Ding! Next, please.

My thoughts turned to last night's match. I'd switched the lads (Team 1, as the curse called them) to a 4-4-2 diamond formation to get myself a bit more practice at that. My guys were all CA 1 and had fairly bad attributes, but several of them did well in the DM position, which made sense because even just standing there was sort of useful to the team. But no one got more than 5/10 in the central attacking midfielder position. I knew full well how hard it was. It needed a lot of advanced skills: taking the ball under pressure, turning, having the vision to see an opportunity, making good decisions, having the technique to execute your ideas—it was a lot. And if a player lacked even *one* of those abilities, they couldn't really play the CAM role. So I ended up switching to a plain 4-4-2.

Ten minutes after I'd taken over, a player got injured. Not badly, but he lost a point in stamina; I knew it wasn't simply a knock. I stopped the game and asked a player from Team 2 to help him off the pitch and see if there was a physio on the Chester pitch. He looked a bit shy, so I said, "Tell them Max Best sent you." Then we played ten versus ten for a few minutes. The shy guy came back and said there were no physios but the injured guy had managed to get to his car okay.

Now, I didn't mind playing ten versus eleven. As you know, I have experience playing against a numerically superior team. But the guys on Team 1 asked if I could make up the numbers. "Well," I said, pretending to be reluctant, "my boots are right here . . ."

"Hello? Hello?"

I struggled to escape my memory and come back into the here and now. The caller's name and account details were on my screen. It showed me how long he'd been on the line—a crazy long time. Ten times the norm. That meant he'd been bouncing from department to department while minimum-wage drones played pass the parcel. I hated that. It was enough to get me to focus. "Oh, hello. My name's Max. What can I do for you?"

The customer complained about his treatment while I made noises that showed I agreed with him totally. "How many times have you described your problem to people today?"

"Loads!" he said, before telling me all over again.

Sadly, his problem was not something someone in my department was able to solve. Except that it *was*. I'd seen it done, about a year previously. One of the older guys had seen it done, and he'd learned it from someone who'd seen it done, and so the knowledge had survived. Been passed on like a super-rare gene, such as the one that lets people work as hard on day one of a project as the day before the deadline. When I left, this arcane knowledge would leave with me.

I fixed the guy's problem. The customer was delighted.

"Oh, yes, it works now. Thank you!"

"No problem. Sorry it took so long. The first guy you talked to . . . well, for the sake of my career I shouldn't finish that sentence."

"Won't you get in trouble?"

"What for?"

"For doing something another department is supposed to do."

"Nah. I'll probably get a handshake from the CEO. And a big bonus. Right?"

He laughed and we said our goodbyes.

I slipped deep into my memories again. It had been a huge evening for me. Life-changing in a low-key way. On the plus side, I'd placed a client at a club, and taken a step towards organising my first transfer. My first loan deal, anyway. On the negative side, Ian Evans didn't like me, and I'd let that bother me. And it bothered me that it bothered me! And then there was my performance as a player in the credit card match. Was that a positive or a negative?

"Max." The voice was coming from a woman standing approximately three caverns behind me. Eventually, I realised it was my boss, standing right next to me. Once she'd caught my attention, she pressed a button on my phone. "Can you come with me, please?"

Huh. So I was going to get into trouble for doing another department's work, after all. I took my headset off and dropped it on the desk. I followed my boss, walking much slower, tapping on my smartphone. I wanted it to look like I was playing it cool.

She led me to one of the small rooms that were moronically placed near the lifts so people in meetings were constantly distracted by who was coming and going. There was someone already seated. A guy I didn't know. He had a jumble of folders and papers in front of him. *The Max Best Incident*, I thought to myself. So this wasn't about what had happened earlier. What could it be?

I put my phone face-down on the table and took a seat. My boss sat behind me, sort of blocking my path to the door. That got on my nerves. She was trying to Ian Evans me, but she was no Ian Evans.

They got to the point pretty quickly.

"Max," said the guy. "I'm Kieron Dotson from human capital." That was the bank's obnoxious name for HR. "It's come to our attention that you may be . . . let's say *going off-script* in some of your calls."

He waited for me to react. "Okay," I said. Not going to incriminate myself!

"Maybe I'll play one of the tapes. We have quite a lot of these, sadly."

He pressed a button on a tablet.

My voice, slightly tinny: "*Okay that's sorted. Quick question. Are you Ghanaian?*" The customer replied, then I continued. "*Nigerian? Maybe you can help me anyway. Are you a Christian? Oh, cool. What do you think about sportsmen who don't play on Sunday and that kind of thing?*"

The customer took over. "*Well, now, that's a great question. I remember when I was young . . .*"

The HR dude pressed the button again. Silence.

He waited for me to reply, but this time I didn't.

"Max, this is a bank. It's a place of business. It's not a pulpit or a place to proselytise."

"Does that mean preach?"

"Yes."

I laughed. "Did you know how to pronounce that or did you practice?"

He grinned. "I practiced. This is a new situation."

"Well, the good news is I didn't preach to anyone. I asked about what they already believe."

His grin faded and he folded his arms. Defending himself against my charm. "Max, this is serious. This is really very serious."

"In what way?"

"We're a bank. We're not political, religious, whatever. We treat all customers the same. And also, it looks like these conversations started at around the same time your work performance started to slip. I've looked at your stats and you were number one for a long time. Some weeks ago you slipped to second and third, and this week you've been fifth. You've had verbal warnings and today you'll get a written warning."

I'd had verbal warnings? That was an outright lie. I turned to look at my boss. She returned my eye contact. She would double down on the claim. Things would get messy. I shrugged. Ain't no mess like a Max Best mess.

"Sorry, Kieron, are you saying you're giving me a reprimand because I'm a Christian?"

"No, of course not."

But he was! The opportunity hit me like a revelation. My spine straightened. Attention on deck. Yellow alert! Action stations!

If I played this situation right, I wouldn't need to quit.

I placed all my fingertips on the table in front of me and shifted some of my weight onto them. "My reward for connecting with our customers is to be humiliated. I see. Here's the sitch. I coach women's football and half the players are journalism students." That was a lie, though I thought I'd heard one or two of the Met Heads discuss something along those lines. "I'm going to walk out of here and take my recording of this meeting to the *Daily Mail*." I picked up my phone, tapped the screen to show that I was running the default voice recorder app, and turned the phone so the microphone was aimed right at his face. "Yep—I tape everything. I can already see the headlines. Bank Sacks Employee for Being Too Christian! The photo under the headline: me, looking sad, holding up a Bible." I'd have to buy a Bible, but Kieron didn't need to know that. It was unthinkable to him that I wouldn't *actually* be religious. "Honestly, I don't even read the *Mail*, but I'd buy it for that story. It'll play great in the shires. Big topic of conversation in your boss's golf club. And think about *Mail Online*. The comments section! They're rabid at the best of times. Imagine this one.

Would they do it if he was a Muslim? They wouldn't dare. I'm closing my account. Kieron, I'm sorry but there's going to be a note about you in the annual report." I shook my head. "I reckon I'll get twenty grand out of this. I should thank you, I suppose. I'll try to keep your name out of it, Kieron Dotson." I said the last words directly into the microphone, which was a bit mean-spirited but I was enjoying myself. I was freestyling and it was going well—Kieron had gone pale and my boss had turned to stone—but I wished I'd known something like this might happen. I could have bought one of those chains with little symbols on that I could have used as a prop. What was it called? A rosemary?

"Now, wait a minute," said Kieron.

"You know," I said, thoughtfully. "Now that I think about it, I'm pretty sure I never got a verbal warning. Because I would have gone to the papers *then*, wouldn't I? So maybe my boss got confused or something. Unless, wait . . ." I pulled a concerned face. "You don't think she was . . . lying? To get rid of me? Because of my faith? Isn't that . . . against the law?"

Kieron asked her to leave the room. She was more than happy to oblige. As she opened the door, I called out her name and said, "I forgive you."

She fucked off and it was just the two of us. Kieron asked me to stop recording, and I refused. "This will be my testimony," I said. "A record of what it's really like to be a Christian in this spiritual wasteland."

The rest of the meeting lasted approximately thirty seconds. We agreed that I would be given a redundancy package. I tried to get three months of salary, but he wouldn't budge from two months even with the threat of the *Daily Mail* looming over him.

I promised to delete the recording once the money was in my account and finished by writing down the name of my church. "Hope to see you there!" I said. Then I left the room and headed back to my desk. I stopped after a few strides.

My desk?

I didn't work here anymore. Everything I had brought with me was in my pockets. I went straight to the lift, and every floor I descended lifted my spirits.

I was on a street in Manchester City Centre. Just past 10:30 a.m. People were walking around, going to the shops, coming back from this, on their way to that. Everyone was busy. Everyone had somewhere to be. Their next few days, weeks, months, were planned out. Work, rest, play, work, rest, play.

Me?

I was free. I could do anything. Be anything.

Something strange happened to my face. A sort of tugging sensation that started halfway up my cheeks. My muscles being pulled up, up, and away, like the lifting of a theatre curtain, revealing that a giant smile had been there all along.

An attractive businesswoman was walking towards me just as this happened. She got the full blast and she looked away fast, but with a tiny smile of her own.

I had approximately zero seconds to decide what to do. I decided to leave it. Still, though, I stood there for a second and watched her go. If she turned to look back at me, I'd give her another big smile. Just something to help her get through the day.

I pottered around. Women. The city centre was full of women. All kinds of shapes, sizes, ethnicities, all kinds of hopes and dreams and likes and dislikes. I sat on a bench and let them all walk past. Two minutes of doing nothing. Two minutes of daydreaming. When was the last time I'd sat and done *nothing* in the middle of the day? It was peaceful. Restorative.

Daydreams were always welcome, but women could wait. My double date with Henri, Emma, and one of Emma's friends was this Sunday. I'd asked Emma not to bring Gemma, and that had been our first little fight. "Please bring someone well-read and quick-witted," I said. "My mate is a deep thinker. Imagine me but pompous and attention-seeking."

Well, she didn't like the idea that Gemma was dull and stupid, even though that was obviously true. She said something along the lines of "If you want to get in my bed, don't badmouth my friends."

In other words: chat shit don't get banged.

This phase of my life had the potential to be very relaxing. Lots of daytime walks. Time to think and recharge. On the other hand, when my redundancy money landed, even when boosted by all the holiday pay I'd built up, I'd only be able to survive until mid-January. Late January if I went back to noodles as my main source of calories.

No, that wasn't right. The date where I'd run out of cash would be pushed back once the money from Raffi and Henri started rolling in. My priority, then, was to make sure both those deals happened.

So I drew up a little action plan. I'd spend the rest of the day focused on Raffi. Then tomorrow I'd drive to Darlington and talk to the manager there. If he was open to the idea of Henri leaving, great. If not, at least I would know. Saturday I was flexible, and Sunday was the double date with Henri. Maybe I'd have some good news for him.

And even when doing all these things, I'd still have a shitload of time to grind: scouting, jogging, reading, watching the ever-expanding amount of content YouTube was suggesting to me. I remembered a book I'd reserved in the local library—one about climbing the corporate ladder.

I'd pop by and cancel the reservation. I was working full-time in the football industry now!

Another gigantic smile.

It was 2 p.m. and the Browns were both home. Raffi was eating breakfast, which I took to mean he'd be working the night shift at the casino.

Shona spent a while trying to give me scrambled eggs. "No, thanks," I said. "But I'll rub a baby's head for luck. Where is she?"

"Asleep. No loud noises or I'll kick you out." She tilted her head. "What's bitten you?" she asked. "Did you find a woman?"

"Max Best doesn't find women," I said. "Women find Max Best." Raffi snorted, a gross, eggy sound that I was delighted to hear. "Actually," I continued, stifling a yawn, "I was made redundant today."

"That's it," said Shona, waving a spatula at me. "I knew it was something. You look lighter. Doesn't he, Raff?"

Her husband shrugged. "You okay for money?"

"I will be," I said. "Remember when we met, you thought I was a scammer? Well, it's scam o'clock. I need to borrow five hundred pounds. Right away. Er . . . if you have it."

Raffi had just spooned a bunch of egg into his mouth, so I couldn't understand his reply. Shona, though, simply said, "Bank details?"

I whizzed Raffi a text, she took his phone, and shortly after she was typing into her own. "Wait," I said. "Aren't you even going to . . . ?"

"It's done, Max." She turned her phone around and showed me the screen. She'd just sent me the money! From her personal account!

I went into my bank app and saw the deposit. I was overwhelmed. "Jesus, Shona. Holy crap. I mean . . . That's a lot of money to lend someone."

Raffi had finished his mouthful. His wife had just sent a week's wages to a near-stranger and he was totally chill about it. Maybe because he knew where I lived and had a lot of experience dealing with people who didn't like paying debts. But still. It was a big show of faith. He said, "What's this about?"

"Oh. Chester want you. It's happening." Shona leapt for joy—a star jump—silently. Raffi got up, punched the air a few times, and let out a zero-decibel roar. They embraced and spun around. "What are you—? Oh, the baby."

Shona was crying, and waved air into her face to dry her tears. Raffi was clenching and unclenching his fists.

I gave them a little while to process the news. "So, the loan. I need a number from the Football Association for the paperwork. It's five hundred quid to register with them. Shouldn't take long. I'll do it when I get home."

"Here," said Shona, pulling me into the living room and sitting me in front of her laptop. "Do it now."

"Okay," I said, laughing. "Why not?" Half a day could make a difference.

So I applied to be an agent and sent the money. Easy as pie.

And all of a sudden another weight was lifted from my shoulders. "I'll have some egg after all," I said.

"So tell us about the meeting," said Shona, dabbing tissues onto her eyelids.

"The true version or the one where I make myself look good?"

Shona smiled. "I guess we're only going to get the second one."

"Nope," I said. "There isn't a version where I look good. Long story short, they want Henri, but that was always a given. He guarantees they won't get relegated. He's worth any amount of hassle. And they want you, Raffi. You can start training before you officially sign. I'll give you the details later. So the outcome was good. But then, after the meeting—"

"Wait," said Shona. "What about you?"

"Me? Player? Nah," I said. "Not in Chester."

Raffi made a sort of cluck-hiss sound. Shona drummed her fingers on the kitchen table. "Did you run your mouth, Max?"

"A bit," I said. "Only after Raffi was in the bag, though."

Shona poured me some orange juice. "Relax, Max. We're not going to be mad about every little temper tantrum you throw." The Browns smiled at each other. Some inside joke where I was another toddler in their life. Shona sighed and leaned back, clutching a coffee mug in both hands. "I did say, Max. If you wind people up, it'll come back to haunt you."

"Chat shit get banged," said Raffi.

I laughed. "Funny you should say that," I said. "After the meeting, I went out to the pitches where you did your trial and took over one of the teams."

"How did you do that?"

"I told them I'd just moved from Man City to work for Chester."

Raffi nearly drowned in his glass of orange. "Fucking hell, Max! You're shameless."

"Yeah, but that's not even the good bit. Listen . . ."

So I was player-manager again. I stuck to 4-4-2 and went to right mid. It was like Ian Evans—the prick—said. I needed to learn a position. I was strolling around, mostly doing the manager side of the gig, when someone finally passed to me. I played a one-touch pass diagonally backwards. Kept the ball cycling around.

At that point, and I presume this decision is the sole topic of conversation at all sports psychology conferences worldwide, the left back started trash-talking me. *"You afraid of me, yo? Pep didn't teach you how to take me on?"*

Well.

His words electrified me.

I dipped into my screens, set myself as playmaker and aligned the team's passing to the right. The ball started moving in my direction. I waited, waited, then moved into space. The pass came to feet. No pressure on me. I turned easily and started driving at the left back. I barely even bothered with a feint—I approached him, knocked the ball past, and *motored*. This guy had acceleration 4, pace 6. Somehow with one burst I was not only past him but everyone else, too. I was already through on goal. Pushing into the penalty area from the right. Every instinct was screaming at me to smash the ball as hard as I could. But the goalie wasn't the trash-talker or Ian Evans—he was some guy who never did me wrong. He wasn't even a proper goalkeeper; he was a midfielder. So I looked around to see who I could pass to. There was no one for miles! I tensed like I was going to hit a thunderbolt, but as the goalie cringed I stood on the ball, flicked it up, and held it in my hands. "That was a goal," I declared, and gently tossed the ball to the keeper.

He grinned at me.

I grinned back.

I got a few hand slaps on the way back.

I strolled back to the right mid slot. The left back wasn't chirping away at me now. His sledging days were over. But he hadn't fully learned his lesson. Not yet.

I got the ball again and glided in his direction. He backed off, and I decided to have a little fun. I sprinted one inch, slowed down for one foot, then sprinted another inch. My shoulders were swaying left and right, signalling where I might attack, where I might attack, and the dude was desperately trying to balance and rebalance. I did one last burst, serious this time, no jokes, I was going a million miles an hour and his weight was on the wrong side. The guy made a genuinely heroic effort to stop me. Back he went, back, dozens of tiny backwards steps, but then it happened—he keeled over and landed on his arse.

I'd long since stopped moving. I was literally just standing there, stock still, the ball under my feet, two yards in front of him.

There was raucous laughter from the rest of the players. I flicked the ball up into my left hand, and offered my right to my defeated foe. He grasped it and I lifted him to his feet. He gave me a rueful grin.

"I had to do it," I said. "You know how it goes. Chat shit . . ."

"I know how it goes," he said. He put his hands on his hips. "Every time there's a new player, I do this. I don't know why. Never ends well! I never learn my lesson."

"Yeah, well," I said, glancing over at the only brightly lit window on the second floor of the office building. "I wouldn't know anything about that."

11

TRANSITIONS

Football glossary: *Transition. The chaotic period when an attacking team loses the ball and the defending team becomes the attacking team.*

Friday, November 11.

It was a two-and-a-quarter-hour drive to Darlington, made worse by the rush-hour traffic around Leeds. I'd stuffed my phone full of football podcasts, though, so the trip wasn't entirely dead air. Every now and then I'd pause the podcasts and have a little think. Was I right to wait for the World Cup-themed perk, or should I buy things now? A while ago, I'd convinced myself that a perk in the head was better than two in the shop, but somehow I'd reverted to "keep your powder dry" mode.

In ad breaks, I thought about my goals. They were simple: get Henri Lyons a move to another club. Preferably Chester. But anywhere, really.

I also reviewed what I'd learned about Darlington and their manager, David Cutter. After meeting with Raffi and Shona I'd wanted nothing more than to go to Platt Lane and grind with a kebab in my hand, but I'd forced myself to go home and study. A little bit more professionalism would go a long way.

Around 10:27, incredibly on time, I pulled into the training centre's car park. Like Chester with their training ground, Darlington didn't own the Eastbourne Sports Complex. But they seemed a bit more entrenched—there were a lot of signs with the awesome Darlington badge and font.

I announced myself at reception to a teenage girl who, inexplicably, turned bright red when I spoke to her. She made a phone call and I settled into a chair. Half a minute later, David Cutter strode in, wearing a tracksuit. He'd just come in from the training pitches.

Cutter was six feet tall, or just under, and had that suspicious nose a lot of former players have. The kind of nose that begs the question, how many times have I been broken? It was easy to imagine him walking into the dressing room after a match and being annoyed that a physio wanted to, you know, do something about all the blood.

But there was more to him than his rugged, hard-man past. He was interested. Curious. He shook my hand and on the way up a flight of stairs asked me several questions. Meeting me must have been a chore for him, but that's not how it came across. It came across like I was the most fascinating person he'd ever met.

"Please, Max," he said, once we were in his office. "Have a seat. Tea? Coffee?"

"Tea, please." It was all eerily similar to being in Ian Evans's domain. Cutter radiated the same kind of authority, and he kept glancing out at the training sessions that were going on. But this was the morning instead of the evening, the windows here were much smaller, and the room was much bigger. This space had been personalised to a much greater degree, and most importantly, he hadn't kept me waiting.

I didn't sit down. I wandered from ornament to framed photo to signed shirt to weird trophy. At each one I beamed and looked at him. From his position at a little tea station, he told me what they were. "Wedding present from my father-in-law. My first match as a pro. Sideburns were all the rage, then. That Ajax shirt is Michael Laudrup's. Best player I ever played against. Played out of my skin that day. Every one of us wanted his shirt; I got it. Manager of the Month for Lincoln City. My only trophy from the top-four leagues."

"Mr. Cutter," I said, ecstatically happy. "This is top. It's all top. Holy shit, what's this?"

I'd found a couple of cardboard boxes under a desk. They were full of memorabilia. I started taking things out. He put his hand on my arm. When I stopped rummaging, he wandered back to the tea station. "Thing is, Max, life as a manager is transitory. When I started, the life expectancy of a manager was two or three years. Now, it's six months. So I take out one piece every couple of weeks. No more. It's a constant reminder that I'm four bad results from the sack."

"Fuck that," I said. "You're the best manager in the league."

He smiled but was adamant as he stirred the contents of two paper cups. "Nothing lasts forever. Top of the league today, unemployed by Christmas. I've seen it a hundred times."

"Jesus Christ," I said. Now that I'd had a good old mosey, the action outside became the most interesting thing. I took my tea with a big thanks and sipped it by a window. The first team were zipping around doing a complicated drill, and on another pitch it looked like the goalkeepers were doing a session. I was surrounded by football. Honestly, no joke, if I'd died right then and there, I would have died happy. Happy-ish. "I suppose we should talk about Henri. Where is he?" I put my head right to the glass to get a better look.

"He's not here. Called in sick."

I turned and looked at Cutter. Not sure where it all came from, but a lot of information flooded into me. "He's sick on Friday so you can't pick him tomorrow. He's going to start being difficult so he can get a transfer this January."

Cutter snorted into his tea. "*Start* being difficult?"

I wasn't amused. The vibe Cutter gave off was so overwhelmingly positive I felt more on his side than Henri's. "Mr. Cutter," I said.

"Call me Dave."

"Mr. Cutter is a bit too formal," I agreed. "But Dave is too informal. How about Mr. Dave? No? Dave, listen, I didn't know about that. I didn't tell him to do that. That's . . . that's pretty shit." I shook my head. "I just learned last night that Darlington is community owned. New information! Love it. I'm a big fan of fan-owned clubs. So is Henri, to be fair. This is a really unfortunate situation all round, but there's a clean, simple way to end it with minimum acrimony. That's my goal today. Him not turning up for work . . . is shit. Do you want me to call him and get him here?"

He appraised me. "No, Max. Players do this all the time. This is just the beginning. He'll do it more and more until by January he's practically on strike."

There was a long silence.

"Max?"

"Sorry, Dave. I'm . . . a bit depressed. I drove three hours from Manchester to get ten minutes with you and it's already a disaster. It . . . I really thought it would go well. There's a solution that's good for everyone."

"It's not a disaster *yet*," he smiled. "Tell me your proposal."

I pushed my lips together. I had a premonition of how the rest of the meeting would go: badly.

I looked out the window again. "Can we do it out there?"

His eyes popped. "Out there?"

"Yeah. Then at least if you boot me out of the city I'll have learned something."

Cutter laughed. "You want to see the training session? I thought you were an agent."

I shrugged. "I'm all things to all men. Except Ian Evans. Look, this might sound absolutely bonkers, but it looks to me like you've got four goalkeepers in that session."

"Yeah. One is a trialist. We're just having a look at him."

"Right, but only three are doing anything." The trialist was in full kit, it seemed, but just watching.

"So?"

"So there's a spare goalie. Have you ever seen an agent score a free kick?"

He came with me to the car park, asking me questions about myself and my life. I grabbed my little kit bag. I'd started carrying my boots, shinpads, and four different colour tops with me. Then we went to the pitches.

We walked past the first team. They were doing a new drill. I couldn't quite work out the point. Three players would pass to each other in a certain routine, moving from right to left. Then another three would do the exact same from left to right. And so on, and so on. Sometimes they'd celebrate, sometimes they wouldn't. Baffling.

But then we were at the goalie training session. I pulled my boots on while Cutter stopped them doing whatever they were doing. "All right, lads? We've got a top agent here. Max Best. You know and hate at least one of his clients." There was some chuckling and slapping of arms amongst the goalies and the goalkeeping coach. They all knew who he meant. "He was telling me he took two free kicks against Chester's first-choice keeper. Scored them both. He's wondering if he's the new Juninho Paulista or if that keeper is just shit." I nodded. That was exactly what I was wondering, except I'd never heard of Juninho Paulista. "So line up and show him what proper goalies can do. Yeah? Free kicks from increasing distance."

I got to my feet and rolled a ball under my studs. "Wait a second," I said. The goalies were close enough to hear me speak at normal volume. "This ball . . ."

"Those are the official match balls for this league," said Cutter. "Pretty good quality. Pretty true movement."

"The balls at Chester were, I don't know, heavier."

"Yeah," said one of the goalies. Not the one who'd played for the first team when I'd watched Chester versus Darlington. "Teams like Chester train with cheaper balls. Cuts makes us train with the proper match balls."

Cutter nodded. "Little details, Max. It's more expensive, but if you aren't practicing with the balls you use in the games, what are you really practicing?" I think I sort of stood there, gormlessly admiring him like I'd just fallen in love, because he regarded me like I was a plumber who'd put the taps on backwards. "You wanted to take some shots?"

I shook off my tiny moment of affection and lined up a shot while the goalie got ready. First up was Darlington's first choice keeper. Handling 14. I checked his player history and he'd played every game last season. But I was right on the edge of the penalty area with no barriers and the whole goal to aim for. This would be too easy, and this wasn't really why I was here. I thought about what I wanted to say to Cutter.

I took a couple of steps back, then moved forward and hit the ball hard into the top-right corner of the goal.

"Dave," I said, "Henri wants to leave in January."

The first goalie trudged off looking a bit confused. I took another ball and rolled it until it was a few feet behind where the first one had been. The second goalie (handling 12) took a starting position a little more to the right. I stepped up and curled the ball into the top-left of the goal.

"I think there was a big misunderstanding about the interview he did. I think he was trying to pay you a compliment."

Again, I placed the next ball a little bit farther away. The third goalie (handling 9 but high jumping) stepped a bit closer to me. I hit it low to his right. The net swished, and he punched the grass.

"I suppose it doesn't matter, really. Things went sour and he was too stubborn to explain himself. I just hope there's a way to get through this without anyone burning bridges."

I placed the next ball even farther away. The first goalie was back. They'd ignored the trialist, which annoyed me. What was the harm in letting him have a go?

"I'd like to get him a loan deal with Chester."

I thumped the ball into the top-right again.

"Wait wait wait," said Cutter, before I could continue my spiel. He gave some instructions and soon enough a three-man wire wall was brought out, blocking a section of the goal.

The second goalie signalled that he was ready.

"As you might expect, they can't pay a fee, or even his whole salary."

Swish! Over the wall. Top left.

"But Chester are near the bottom of the league and if he's on loan, he can't play against Darlington. And if he's at Chester, he's going to play against King's Lynn and the other teams at the top of the table. So it's a huge advantage to you. Imagine if you beat Chester one week, and then Chester beat King's Lynn the next. That practically hands you the title! That's worth a tiny bit of money, isn't it?"

The third goalie had moved the wall farther to the right and stood slightly closer to the middle of the goal. Why? Well, if there was a timeline where I would need to understand goalies, it wasn't this one.

Dish! Over the wall. The ball clanged against the crossbar close to the left post. Huh. Slight miscalibration there.

I was vaguely aware that more people were watching than at the start. I pushed such thoughts away. I had a mission.

I'd forgotten to push the ball back, so Cutter did it. I was pretty far from goal, now. I turned to stare at Henri's manager.

"I know he's annoying. He's too French for his own good. But he's twenty-seven. He needs to play. Even if you hate him, it's cruel to make him stay. So that's my pitch. Let me take him to Chester. We could get the paperwork done this weekend and you'd never have to think about him ever again. Chester can pay eight hundred a week. That's about sixteen thousand in extra revenue for Darlington this season. And he might just get you the title by accident." I started my motion to hit the free kick, but stopped. "And I was thinking. I'd take out a full-page ad in the local paper. Sort of a fond farewell from Henri to the fans. *We had some good times. Let's remember those, and not my mistakes at the end. Darlington will always be in my heart.* Something like that. Poignant. Classy. Good vibes all round." I shaped to shoot, but paused again. "Maybe plain text above a picture of a pipe. French people go weak at the knees for that." Since I was so far away from goal, I took an extra pace back, approached the ball, and absolutely leathered it.

The goalie threw himself towards the shot and got about 0.1 percent of the way there. Either I had set pieces 20 or these guys were letting me score. I wasn't sure which option I hated more.

I looked down. "I don't know, Dave. It's obviously in my interest for a move to happen. But I can't think how you getting some money for him is worse than him being here and getting more stroppy and disruptive. And Chester's our preference because it's another fan-owned club. If money's the issue, let me know and I'll see about finding a bigger team with deeper pockets."

Someone whistled three times and the entire training area—between fifty and a hundred people—suddenly stopped. Just froze, like a flash mob prank. Like a horror movie. I looked around, bewildered, and turned to ask Cutter what the eff was going on. He put his fingers to his lips. Not frozen in place by some curse then.

Everyone was looking solemn. Ah. I got it. Eleven o'clock on the 11th of November. Remembrance Day. A one-minute silence to honour those who died in the First World War. I started to look around, really analysing the profiles of the players. But then I mentally slapped myself in the face and looked at the ground. I could fucking stand still for one minute, couldn't I?

I could stand still, but I couldn't let myself think about the War. I always remembered the last scene from *Blackadder*, which made me weepy.

In the end the silence lasted *two* minutes, and the atmosphere was somewhat subdued after that.

The goalies were keen to continue our little drill, but I'd lost all appetite for taking free kicks. I waved at them, sort of a vague thank you, and walked away. Cutter followed.

After about twenty paces, I stopped and watched the first team doing their drills. I thought about apologising for forgetting Remembrance Day, but even in my head it sounded absurd. Better to stick to the football.

"Dave, what *is* this?"

He caught up with me and I realised he was giving me a long, hard stare. "What do you think?" he asked.

I flapped my arms like a prize goose. No clue. I watched the moves a while longer. Left . . . right. Right . . . left. Cutter was obviously a forward-thinking manager. There had to be a point to this. I checked the time on my phone and realised that twenty-four hours ago I'd been released from the call centre. This strange new drill was part of my strange new world. And I loved it. I turned to Cutter and slapped myself on the forehead. "Transitions!"

He released a small smile. He'd been quite affected by the two-minute silence. "Got it."

"But how does it work?"

"Group A attacks, group B counterattacks. You're a Man City fan, right?"

"Please," I said.

"United? Ugh. Hate United. But okay, United are getting quite good at this. Some team has the ball. They're in their attacking formation. All spread out, looking for gaps. Casemiro intercepts, passes to Eriksen, and he hits it long to Rashford. Hit pause. What do you see? Chaos. No one is in a predictable slot. So how do you defend that? How do you increase your chances of scoring?" He pointed to the drill.

"This is all about the mentality of switching from attack to defence and back again?" He nodded. We watched the players run left and right a bit more. "But, mate," I said. "Sorry. *Dave* . . . isn't this pretty advanced? This is, like, Premier League stuff. You're in the sixth tier."

He shook his head. "Transitions. The better your opponents are coached, the more it's your only area of opportunity. Coaches in these leagues are defensive. This is how we gain an advantage." He shook his head again and looked around at his players. "But honestly, it's more than that. Some of these guys are electricians. Carpet fitters. This year, the next, might be their only stint as a full-time pro. How do you go from playing footy every day to twice a week? What about when they retire? These guys won't have media jobs at the end. It isn't easy transitioning from playing the game you love every day to . . . that sort of bleak emptiness when it's all over. Or just take status. This year we're top dogs. Most teams we play think we'll win the league. Treat us accordingly. That feeling is addictive. If we get promoted we'll lose almost every week. How do the lads cope with that change?

Maybe it's fanciful but I hope these drills do more than prepare them for matches."

I stuck out my bottom lip and breathed in through my nose. The way he was talking was intoxicating to me. I wondered if this was how Emma felt when I told her why I liked football. To downplay what I assumed were my flushed cheeks, I sort of snorted out a laugh. "Dave. Do you have any interest in a right midfielder who can score a free kick but can't do any of the basics?" I laughed some more.

When I looked at him, though, he wasn't laughing.

12

CHALLENGE

"Max," said Cutter. "You're interested in our drills, yeah? Do you want to have a go from the inside?"

"Absolutely," I said.

He scanned the pattern of the cones and said the transition drills were over and they were now doing a simple one-touch passing drill. "It's about working as a unit. Scanning for options before the pass comes to you. Variety of passing. It's harder than it looks." Again, everything he said was music to my ears.

Cutter stopped the session and brought me inside. Introduced me to the Darlington players, then went over the rules of the drill. The players weren't overly interested in me, as though randos taking part in their sessions was something that happened all the time. Last week, some lad who does skillz on TikTok. This week, an uppity agent. Next week, Lord Lucan.

The drill involved three players in a coned-off square, with four lined up around the edges. One of the edgers passed it in to player one, and he touched it to player two, who touched it to player three, who passed it to someone at the side. You weren't allowed to pass it to the same edge person twice. There were three wire men in a triangle. They cut out a passing option sometimes, but barely made a difference.

"Sixty seconds, big effort!" someone called.

At first, I was really switched on. Not trying to impress or anything like that. Just that he'd said it was harder than it looked so I was waiting for the challenge to kick in. It never did. It was actually pretty remedial. I think even pre-curse Max would have crushed it.

We did a minute, another group did a minute, then we did a minute, and so on. On our third minute, I lost focus and did my part with a faraway look on my face. Cutter blew his whistle and came over. "You okay, Max?"

"What? Oh, yeah." I scratched my head. How could I say this without being a prick? "You said it was hard."

"Too easy for you? You want it harder?"

I was relieved that he was still smiling. "Yes, please," I said. A few of the Darlington players laughed. I ignored them. "Maybe something that replicates a real match a bit more."

Cutter looked at me sideways. "We do that, too, Max. The initial pass gets fired in harder, higher, with spin, but you still have to lay it off first time."

"Oh," I said. "That sounds top. Can we do *that*?"

He looked around at his players, then back at me. This had the odd effect of leaving him looking at me sideways, still, but from the other side. I wasn't sure if he'd learned the sideways glance thing from some former manager, but it seemed to be his thing.

"Okay, lads. You heard the agent. Difficulty setting: legendary."

There were some groans, and my two teammates *tsk*ed and shot me annoyed looks. I smiled back at them, but their reaction was a warning sign. I didn't want a reputation of being a dick. Any of these guys could be a future player, a future client, and any of them might whisper the wrong words in the wrong ears and cost me.

Cutter himself fired the first pass at us. At me. Hard, hip height. I leant back, raised my foot, and cushioned the ball to a teammate. Then I raced forwards and said, "And again!" But he didn't pass back to me. The drill was that he'd pass to the other player. A bit cringe, but this was it! This drill was hard enough to trigger the part of my brain that dealt with challenges. Yes, mate!

I danced around like an energetic puppy. When the ball was fired at me, I had to react with balance and technique *and* know where my teammates were. When they controlled it—a big *when*, by the way—I had to be in position to play the short pass or the final long one.

I was having a great time, but as I mentioned, the other two didn't control every "legendary" incoming pass, and they got more tired and frustrated. And, of course, there was a convenient scapegoat nearby. Could I do something to make them like me? Or at least, resent me less?

Our minute was up and another team had a go. I watched with great interest—the technique attribute really told you a lot about who would control the first pass. The other passes were so simple that even someone with passing 1 would have been able to do them. But instant control of the ball—no-one here could do that reliably. Well . . . except me.

My unit was back on, and we fell into the same pattern. Me controlling the ball in a variety of increasingly outrageous ways, the other two guys turning into brick walls for balls to bounce away from. At least I finally understood the point of the wire men. As well as blocking some angles, the more the players got tired, the more they started to stumble into the obstacles or just be hindered in small ways.

At one point, one of my dudes jogged backwards to control a high, looping pass and fell over the circular base of a wire man.

I sprinted across to the inanimate object and spread my arms wide, aggressively. "What the fuck are you doing, mate?" There was dead silence, so I pressed on. "You fucking do that again, you'll be going home in a fucking ambulance!" More silence. "Oh, yeah? Your mum!"

And I pushed the wire man on both its shoulders. It veered over, but wobbled back to an upright position.

"Fucking prick," I said. After giving the wire man the middle finger, I bent to help my mate up from the ground.

He loved being part of this scene. He grabbed my arm and pulled me away. "Leave it, Max. He's not worth it."

By now, the ice had broken and multiple observers were in hysterics. I played it straight. Acted like I was still steaming at the wire man. Cutter and his main coach were laughing as hard as anyone. It was my turn to receive the ball, and someone kicked it hip-height again. I threw myself into the air and did a violent scissors kick.

The ball exploded from my boot—if it had been allowed to keep going it would have reversed the rotation of Earth. But it travelled about three yards—right onto the face of the wire man who had tripped my buddy. It fell over and in a flash I was looming over it, screaming, "Chat shit get banged!"

That was the end of that drill.

When everyone had finished wetting themselves, Cutter looked at his watch. He let out one last puff of laughter-filled breath, and cranked himself back into an upright position. He blew his whistle and gestured for everyone to come in. A few of the guys stood close to me. I was the cool new boy in school. "Max, we normally do a quick eleven v eleven on Fridays. Before the big Saturday game. Have you got time to stick around? Have a kickabout with us?"

I looked at the lads near me. I recognised some of them from the match I'd seen, but while I knew their attributes, I didn't really know who they were. Didn't know if they'd try to kick the shit out of Henri's agent. Or if they'd go easy on me because I was a civilian. "Do you do first team versus the rest?"

"Yeah, normally." I pulled a face. I wiped it away as soon as I realised I'd done it, but it was too late. Cutter had seen it. He said, "Problem?"

Now, I knew I should just shut my mouth and get on with things. Take whatever was on offer with a smile on my face. Go along to get along, as the Americans say. "You're going to ask me to play with the reserves against the first team and honestly, that would normally be the highlight of my year. But I did that last Sunday, in Chester. If I could choose, I'd take ten minutes playing with the first team over thirty minutes with the reserves."

"What happened to wanting legendary difficulty?"

I tried to do a sheepish grin. "If I have the slightest chance of playing for a real team, even for ten minutes, I'd be crazy not to ask."

Cutter rolled his shoulders. I saw his eyes flick over to where I'd taken the free kicks. "What position do you play?"

"Right mid."

He laughed. "You lucky fucker. Webby has a slight knock. Fine. Ten minutes. I suppose you'd like to take the free kicks?"

"And the corners, please."

"Oh," he said, eyebrows raised as though I'd asked for a second helping of porridge. He checked his watch. Max time was over. "First team, blue bibs," he said. He picked one up and threw it to me. The other lot grabbed yellow ones. I started to move across to the other side of the pitch. Cutter blew his whistle. "Blues attack this way," he said. There was a big rotation of players. I thought back to what Nice One had told me about Ian Evans keeping an eye on Aff. Cutter wanted the blues to attack that way so that I'd be right in front of him.

I didn't have time to get nervous or really think too much about the match. Basically, I'd woken up, driven to Darlington, asked to take a shot against a spare goalie, and now I was . . . what? Having a trial? It wasn't a trial. It was just a kickabout. He'd *said*. But . . . maybe it was?

It was too weird to think about.

All I knew for sure was that I had ten minutes to play with one of the best teams in the division. If I didn't learn anything from the experience, that would be the biggest fail since . . . the meeting with Ian Evans. Two days ago! Time was flying faster than a tornado that hit a clock factory.

The rest of the players and the coaches zipped around picking up the cones and the wire men. The players showed more urgency doing this than they had doing any of the drills. They wanted to play!

While I pottered around waiting for kick-off, I scanned the players I'd be up against. Darlington reserves, in the yellow bibs. My most direct opponent was the reserve left back. No spoilers, but let's call him Chumpy. He had acceleration 8, pace 7, tackling 8. His stamina was low, but the match wouldn't be long enough for that to matter. Also on my side of the pitch was the reserve left mid. Let's call him TIM, short for The Invisible Man. The opposing central midfielder nearest me was one of those Sam Topps clones that abound in this league. Fuck it—I'll just call him Sam Topps. Good stamina, tackling, teamwork; low technique. Typical tier-six player.

The referee was one of the coaches. He brought his whistle to his lips, and so began my second unplanned match in a week.

I strode around for a couple of minutes. I wasn't player-manager, but I did have access to the tactics screens and match overview. My match rating was 6 out of 10. I walked around, taking in the pace of the game, watching where our right back was, trying to keep good distances between me and the players around me.

Chumpy, the reserve left back, followed me around like a stray dog. I checked the screens but he wasn't marking me. He was just going wherever I went. He wanted to be friends. To ask what I wanted for Christmas. To chat about stonks. When no one was looking, he barged into me. Oh. Not friends, then.

I wondered if I could drag him out of position. I ambled towards the centre of the pitch until the formation graphic changed. That was the point where Chumpy decided he'd gone far enough, and he left me there. He went back to his starting point—in line with the centre backs. That was interesting!

I took a few strides to the right, until Chumpy reacquired me. He jogged towards me, so I moved left until I hit the break point. He fucked off again. He was getting mad but didn't know why. I laughed. This alone was worth the fucking months of grinding and suffering! I had access to an all-new, unique-in-the-history-of-the-world way to express my inner prickness. This was peak prick. I stepped right and when he came close, I stepped left.

While I was testing the break points, my team progressed down the left of the pitch. I didn't sprint forward to join the attack. The guys had shown no interest in passing to me yet. They didn't know me, didn't trust me. The reserve goalie rushed off his line to clear the danger.

No, that's not what happened. Was it? In retrospect it seemed impossible. I had been watching the attackers, not the goalie. How fast was the keeper? I checked his attributes. Pace 4. So he *couldn't* have rushed off his line. I'd have to keep an eye on him. Work out what he was up to.

Three minutes gone, and I hadn't touched the ball. That was about to change. The goalie booted the goal kick long and to my side of the pitch. Ugh. I wasn't supposed to do headers, but I hadn't told anyone. That was dumb. Fortunately, the ball was going slightly out of my zone. TIM and my team's right back competed for it. The ball popped up and I played a one-touch pass to a centre back. He moved it along, and the midfield recycled the ball until it came back to me. I stuck out a foot to control it, but when I did, Chumpy was there to take it away from me.

Huh.

Our right back shouted at me to get back, and to be fair I was already jogging that way. I sprinted to cover TIM, and when Chumpy passed to him, I was there. He hadn't expected me to track back.

Well, he'd do something different the next time.

Different. The next time. That's how I needed to think. Make a mistake once, sure. But then improve on that.

I strolled back up the pitch, back to my right-midfield slot, waiting for my next chance. Of course, if I didn't do something spectacular in the next five or six minutes, Cutter might sub me off and put his real right mid on. But I couldn't think like that. The most important thing for me was to learn. Learn something every time I played. That was the challenge I set myself.

There was soon another little scramble that ended with me one-touch passing back to a teammate. My guys seemed to like it when I calmed things down, and they cycled the ball around until the CM played the exact same pass as before. I felt Chumpy sprinting to take it off me like before, so I started the same motion, only I took a step to the right, planted my feet, let him crash into my right shoulder, and quickly flicked the ball down the line and sprinted after it. I pushed it another five yards and looked around.

I was looking to see what the strikers were doing. Had they started their runs yet? I expected I'd have one option at the front and one at the far post. I wanted to play quick passes whenever possible. The Chester trial had taught me not to dwell on the ball.

But what I saw was the solution to the goalkeeper mystery—he was on the edge of the penalty area, ready to sprint out! He saw himself as a sweeper-keeper. If the guy wanted to be a defender, he shouldn't have been born wearing gloves.

So I had a choice. I could pass or—you know what? Fuck it. I'd made my choice as soon as I saw how far out the goalie was. I struck the ball nice and hard, aiming slightly to the right of goal knowing that the natural swerve of the ball would take care of the rest.

The ball is passed wide to Best.

Chumpy tries to pick his pocket. Best spins and the defender is left on the ground.

Best dribbles down the wing.

He looks up . . .

And fires at goal.

It's there!

GOOOOAAAAAAALLLLLLL!

From 40 yards out!

Where was the keeper?

I was dimly aware of some noises from the side of the pitch. They didn't seem like instructions or anything I needed to worry about. My match rating went up to 8. I continued strolling around the pitch while the game recommenced.

My team started passing to me more often now, and after one-touching some replies I realised that Chumpy had stopped charging at me.

Knowing what I could do to him, he was wary. My piece of strength and skill had bought me a little bit of time and space. Good to know. And after a brief interchange with the CMs, I burst forward and controlled a long pass and looked up. The goalie was way back in his six-yard box. Not so keen to leave his zone anymore! So I'd killed two birds with one goal.

I was delighted with myself. But more delight was to come. I realised that this was the fastest I had ever run in my life. I pushed the ball forward twenty yards and accelerated. I caught up to it in an instant. I did it again. Faster, legs! Onward! Giddyup! I wasn't thinking about the match. Superspeed! Yes, please! Superstrength was weird. Becoming a free-kick master overnight was unearned. But being inhumanly fast—there was nothing I didn't like about that.

The byline was approaching like a cliff edge. I stopped the ball and put on the brakes, leaving the ball six or seven yards behind me. The goalie started to move towards it but when I smirked at him, he went back to his near post. I strolled back to the ball and waited for a striker to catch up. Both of them did, mixed in with a mob of defenders. The pass needed to be good. I struck a little angled chip that landed at the left foot of the striker farthest away. He leaned back and struck a half-volley that smacked into the roof of the net.

Two-nil!

Interesting.

I trudged back to my half of the pitch, deep in thought. First, that striker. He was Henri's replacement in the first team. His shot had been on his preferred foot. He had finishing 14 and technique 8. Now, that half-volley looked flawless to me. Although he had leaned back, which in most cases resulted in the ball flying miles too high, it never looked like he would miss. So in that situation, was his finishing important, or his technique? It seemed obvious that it would be his finishing. But if you did the same thing anywhere else on the pitch, it'd be your technique that mattered. Right?

I supposed that after watching enough footy at this level, I'd start to understand the attributes and what they really, really meant. And if I got a manager gig, I'd be able to set up training sessions that would test such things.

I sighed. Superspeed was thrilling. Wonderful. But still not as good as managing. But if I wanted a manager job, the fastest way was through playing.

The game kicked off again. I stood still, arms crossed, still thinking. What about me?

I was fast. Faster than all these guys. That meant, conservatively, I had pace 14. My technique was better than the best Darlington player. So that gave me at least 13 in that one. I couldn't see the set pieces attribute yet, but it seemed like I had a very high score there, too. Jumping and heading I didn't want to test. Dribbling seemed pretty good. I ran as fast with the ball as without it and felt in complete control. And stamina? Even doing the simple versions of the passing drill, the other players had started blowing hard. I could have gone for days.

"Max," came a new voice. I looked around. It was the right back I was playing in front of. "It's Max, innit? What are you doing?"

"Watching," I said.

"You're supposed to be playing."

"Don't worry about it."

"I've never seen a guy fold his arms during a match. Just saying."

I grinned and uncrossed them. His opinion didn't really matter to me. I trusted the curse's judgement more than his, and the curse said I was playing great. But until I got my feet under a manager's desk, outside perceptions still mattered. Still, I could be active the Max Best way. I jogged sideways to the centre of midfield, had a little look around, then ambled back to the right.

The action was slightly biased to the right now. I checked the tactics; Cutter hadn't changed anything. It was just that the team was using me more. Trusting me more. Trying to get me involved. But I wasn't making forward runs. Wasn't trying to attack. Two reasons. One, the Sam Topps clone had come over to help Chumpy. So just by standing still I was creating big gaps elsewhere on the pitch. Second, attacking down the right was no challenge. Chumpy couldn't defend against me if I sprinted past him. Whereas if I stayed close to him, he might show me one of the tricks defenders used.

Unfortunately, after I'd destroyed him twice, he'd become very conservative, focusing on not being humiliated again. So the only thing I was likely to learn from him was where not to get a haircut in Darlington.

With me relatively passive on the right, the next big moment came on the left. Our guy over there did a dribble, nice bit of skill, and was hauled down. I checked the tactics screen and saw that I was set to take all the set pieces. (Set pieces are free kicks and corners. The ball is stationary, and the other team needs to be a certain distance from the ball. Basically, perfect for me, since I could do whatever I wanted and no one could stop me. No one on the other team, anyway.)

I jogged over and placed and re-placed the ball until I was happy with the way it sank into the grass. I waited for our tall defenders to lumber their way up the pitch. The goalie was stood a bit too far to the right, leaving me with a big juicy slice of unguarded net to aim at.

"Is this direct?" I called out, remembering the Chester incident. The referee nodded. The goalie took a big step to my left. I laughed. Lots of people learning lessons today! But not much chance of scoring if I shot from there.

So I stepped up and curled the ball, hard, head height, towards the far post. Basically trying to hit an arc that lots of my team would be able to attack. It was the left-footed striker who got there first—he powered a header just under the crossbar that the goalie did well to tip over the bar. The save drew applause.

But it was a corner, and the Max Best Show continued. I was about to gently clip it into the danger zone but I remembered how much that frustrated me when I saw it on TV. So I took another step back and gave the poor ball another furious smack. It curved wickedly towards the six-yard line, and again one of our guys won the challenge. A defender did just enough to put him off, and the header went a couple of feet over.

The players loved it—they gave me thumbs-up and clapped and said, "Yes, Maxy boy." (How did everyone in the football world come up with the same nicknames?) The curse loved it. My match rating went up to 9.

I wandered back to right mid. I'd shown some of my abilities. I'd earned the right to start *really* showing off. What did Max Best want? To dick around doing nutmegs and shit. What would Ian Evans want? For me to stay in my little zone and be disciplined and boring.

I did it for Henri.

Went into my little box.

The match clock said I'd been playing for fourteen minutes. So Cutter was happy with what he was seeing. After a couple of minutes of tactical discipline, I turned to him. "Dave," I called out. "When the left goes, can I?"

Cutter nodded. "If you've got the stamina."

"What?"

"You've been . . . let's say . . . conserving energy." A few of the coaches around him chuckled.

"Do you want me to score and assist or do you want me to burn calories? Is this WeightWatchers or a football team?"

He laughed. "Keep doing what you're doing. Join the attacks when you can. Overload the far post."

I nodded.

A couple of minutes later, we progressed down the left again, and the winger did his trick again. This time, the defender didn't foul him. What was the point? I'd only send in a deadly free kick. Chumpy looked over his shoulder to check where I was. I was motionless. As soon as he turned away, I started my sprint. The winger was about to cross to the middle when he spotted my run. He took a pause and hit it higher and longer, curving beautifully into the area I was approaching. One of the centre backs moved towards the flight path of the cross. The keeper had spotted my run, too, and rushed out to narrow the angles. I checked my options, leapt higher than the six-foot-three CB, and cushioned the ball sideways, onto a striker's head. I'd taken the goalie out of the equation; my guy almost couldn't miss.

Three-nil, and my match rating hit 10.

That was enough for me. I really shouldn't have been heading the ball. I walked over to Cutter. "Can I tap out?" I said. "Is that all right?"

He gave me a quizzical look. "You okay?"

"Yeah. A physio told me to get checked out before I play again. I feel like I've pushed my luck enough today."

He nodded and sent the real right mid on. "You sure you're okay?"

"Yep. Promise. I'm just being sensible for once in my life. Are the showers open?" I said. "It's a three-hour drive home and all that."

"I'll get someone to unlock it for you. Do you need a towel?"

"No, I brought one. Thanks."

"Why don't you get showered and changed? But don't rush off just yet. I'll buy you lunch. We can talk."

"About Henri?"

"Sure," he said, scratching his nose. "And other things."

13

COMPLAINTS

After my shower, I went for lunch with Cutter. All very civilised. I asked him about his footballing philosophy and how he'd assembled such a good team. He asked about my footballing history, I told him I had none, and he typed my name into some website. When it came up blank, he said "Unbelievable. You just popped up out of nowhere."

He asked me to return the next morning to play in a sort of demonstration match so he could show me to some guys from Darlington's board of directors.

I wasn't against playing, but I complained about the logistics and cost of driving to and from Manchester, especially as I would be going to the northeast on Sunday, too. Cutter said he'd already thought of that, that he'd get me a half-price rate at his mate's Airbnb. I'd save six hours a day and I'd save on petrol, so I booked it for two nights.

My next complaint was about my recent injury and possible hole-in-skull. Cutter said he'd arrange an X-ray, and if that went well, I could do a full medical while I was there. If we moved quickly, I could even be in the squad on Tuesday night! In short, he was keen to remove all obstacles from me agreeing to sign.

He sweetened the deal by saying that if I joined, it'd be easy to convince the board to let Henri go to Chester.

"If I sign," I mused, "can I get involved behind the scenes?"

"Like what?"

"I've got a good eye for a player. I could help find local talent. But most of all I like managing teams. Maybe I could manage a youth team match every now and then."

He laughed like I was joking. "We have coaches, Max!"

"I just mean every now and then. To test out theories. Improve my skills."

"Do you have any coaching badges?"

"No."

"Max! No serious club would let you manage a youth team! The parents would go nuts."

"What about the reserves?"

"Same thing. You need badges. But even if you had some, our reserve team is pretty unique. It's actually a local club that we absorbed. They benefit from our standing and facilities and we get to put some minutes into some legs. It's a great situation. And they've *got* a gaffer. Good lad, he is. No, Max, put such thoughts out of your head. You're too young for that sort of thing anyway. Concentrate on your playing career."

I bit my nails. Signing for Darlington would unlock Henri's move to Chester. Great. And it would gain me some reputation in the world of football. Great. But if I signed a contract till the summer, I'd really struggle to find games to manage at a decent standard. And Cutter didn't seem interested in my ability to find players. So while being plucked from obscurity to play for a famous team seemed like a fantasy move—a real-life Cinderella story, if Cinderella wore size ten football boots—it would also be a bit of a dead end. Virtually no managing for the rest of the season.

I whipped my phone out and brought up the league table. "You're second. Looks like you or King's Lynn will win the league. How many games does a guy have to play to get a winner's medal?"

"Ten," he said instantly. He frowned, but soon relaxed. "You're checking if Henri will get a medal if we win the league?" He tapped on his phone and eventually said, "No. He won't qualify."

"Shame," I said.

"Unless," he said. He pressed his fingertips together. "I was thinking about what you said. About Henri trying to pay me a compliment when he did that interview. The thing is, I was furious at first, along with everyone else. But when I saw him in training, he gave me those sad little eyes and I realised he was just as hurt as me. So I read the interview again and went cold, you know. That was the realisation that we'd done him dirty. There was nothing bad in what he said, unless you went looking for it. The whole thing was just a mania among the supporters and our social media guy lost his head, too. But by the time I'd calmed down, I couldn't do anything about it. We were in a bad patch, then. I had no clout. But now, Max. If you come in, a wizard on the wing, the fans will get excited. They'll be up for anything. They've not seen a player like you for a long time, if ever. If you go to a fan's forum and say Henri's my best mate, I came to Darlo to play with Henri, they'll soon shut up about this interview. So if you want him to stay, I'll start laying the groundwork. What do you say?"

I rubbed the armrest of my chair while I considered it. The material was old, dirty, and itchy, but somehow it felt good.

If Henri stayed at Darlington and got back in the team, he'd score tons of goals and get promoted to the fifth tier—with a winner's medal. In the higher league, he'd play against Wrexham and be in their latest documentary. His career would have an upward trajectory once more. As his talent deserved.

But if I let that happen, I wouldn't be his agent. After all, he wouldn't pay me to keep him where he *was*. Playing alongside him was appealing from a footballing perspective, but I'd be eighty pounds a week better off if I pushed him down the football ladder.

Financially, there was only one option. Ethically, morally, there was quite another. I knew what I should do.

"Let me think about it," I said.

My skull was whole; I sailed through the medical. Unlike Livia, the doctor was not the living embodiment of all that is good and holy, but he was friendly enough. And since I was fully fit, a lot more comprehensive.

Friday night, I found some matches to watch and picked up 70 XP, plus 7 towards my debt.

The next morning, I played the demo match. My opponent finished with a bruised ego, but I finished with a bruised ankle. And shin. And toe. More on that later. For now, let's just say it was wildly successful in showing my abilities.

After, I got invited to watch Darlington's league match from the dugout, but since Henri would be there, I asked for somewhere more discreet. The Blackwell Meadows stadium was the smallest and weirdest one I'd ever been in, but the fans made a decent racket. The VIP lounge was simply a row of normal seats with *reserved* labels stuck on. There were no boxes. The club was in the process of building a different stadium, but that would take years.

Darlington won 2–1, a very scrappy game, and Henri didn't play. At least his CA was stable. His trip to Chester had done him good.

Watching the match earned me 153 XP, with 17 going to my debt.

Afterwards, I negotiated with Cutter and Darlington's equivalent of MD MD, and we came to a verbal agreement on both deals. Henri's was boilerplate, but my first contract as a professional footballer would be on the strange side. Now I just had to make sure Henri didn't mind.

"I won't do anything without his blessing. As luck has it," I said, "I'm meeting him tomorrow for brunch. Double date kind of thing. So if he okays everything, we can get all this signed, sealed, and delivered by tomorrow night."

"We'll be here until 2 p.m.," said Cutter. "The club secretary is going away for a while. Next time we could do it would be in a couple of weeks, I think."

It wasn't exactly a ticking time bomb, this deadline, but two weeks is a long time in English football. There was just enough of a sense of urgency to give me a sleepless night. While I tried in vain to elevate my ankle while balancing ice packs on it, my brain ran through dozens of potential conversation trees. I would have three hours to reshape the world the way I wanted it. More than enough time. Right?

Sunday, November 13.

It was the morning of my half-blind double date with Henri, Emma, and one of Emma's beautiful, intelligent friends. An important day.

Important because it would be the first time I would see Emma in person since the day I met her. She had sort of become my entire world away from football. An essential distraction. Maybe a permanent distraction.

But it was also important because of the decisions that would be made. One decision that had been made beforehand, obviously, was Emma's choice of friend. I was excited to see who she'd brought. I'd daydreamed about a sort of dowdy librarian-type who Henri wouldn't be interested in until she started picking apart his quotes and theories, and in the end they'd have wild, steamy sex in the Enjoyable French Literature section of her workplace—the library's smallest alcove.

I hobbled to the restaurant. Henri had chosen it. The sign read *Holy Focaccia*. A quirky name that fit Henri completely. But when I saw it and had a peek in the windows, I frowned; it was not the hipster paradise I'd been expecting. It looked really down to earth.

The door opened with a *bring*, and I turned into a large, warm, welcoming space. It was packed. Builders, pensioners, teens, hipsters, goths. This place had them all. Good-natured banter here, gentle laughter over there. Waiters and waitresses hustling and bustling without giving off stress vibes.

More stress was not what I wanted. I was stressed enough. Lack of sleep, anxiety at what Henri would think of my plan, the fact that the whole deal would play out in front of Emma. The stakes were high enough. The thought of doing the negotiation in front of an audience was . . . painful.

I really hoped Emma's friend would help the meal get off to a good start.

"Can I help?" Some teenage boy. Competent.

"Looking for my friends," I said.

The kid was as smart as his uniform. "Would that be a table of two models and one French footballer?"

"Are you a Darlington fan?"

"Of course!"

"You're not mad at him?" Him meaning Henri.

"No way. Not here. We love him here. One time he came and helped us with the dishes. No one knows why. And he brought half the squad for his birthday. He's wicked. Are you his friend?"

"Ask me in an hour," I said, ominously.

He led me under a low-hanging lintel into another, bigger, space. This one had a massive window that looked out over a park; there was good foot traffic. The establishment had placed Emma facing the window so that she'd be the first thing every passerby would see. Great salesmanship. My confidence in the place grew a thousandfold.

But then . . .

"Is everything okay?" said the teenager.

"Yes. Just got cramp in my . . . brain."

The others hadn't seen me. It gave me a few seconds to get my face right. Because sitting next to Emma was her best friend Gemma, the one woman I had marked out as unsuitable for the double date. Henri was whip smart. He was a deep-thinker, a warrior-poet, a bon vivant. He needed someone quick-witted who would call him out on his bullshit. Basically, the female version of me. Gemma . . . was not that.

I turned around as though admiring some of the tat hanging on the wall. Once again it was Emma and Gemma at a table with a footballer and his agent. Last time it was Ziggy, and he and Gemma were a great match. But Henri was nothing like Ziggy. Why had Emma done this? I was the only one who had met both Gemma and Henri and in my opinion, they were incompatible. But Emma thought she knew better. She had such a high opinion of her friend that it transcended my petty, rational objections.

I tried to rearrange my face into something ready for a date, but failed. So I finally followed the kid to the table, hung up my coat, and slid onto my seat. Facing Emma. Diagonal from Gemma. Gemma mostly ignored me, giving almost all her attention to Henri.

Henri was to my left. He slapped me on the shoulder. "Max! Good of you to make it!"

I checked my phone. "I'm exactly on time," I said.

Henri frowned. "I meant that I am happy to see you."

Internally, I sighed. We were all on radically different levels of energy, and it was my fault. This was going to be all kinds of awkward. I wanted to explain but with the ladies watching it didn't feel right. "And I'm happy to see all of you," I said.

"Hi, Max," said Emma. I looked at her properly. Some of my misgivings melted away. She was a stone-cold fox. Amazing body, gorgeous face, and her one unusual feature, her nose, was catnip.

But I couldn't summon the energy to match her greeting. I just couldn't. It wasn't in me. "Hi, Emma," I said. "Henri, I see that you've met Gemma."

"I have indeed!" The way he was devouring Gemma with his eyes hinted that Emma had been right. Gemma was basking in the radiance of Henri's admiration. Emma was trying not to be smug. They'd all met some unspecified number of minutes ago and were getting on like a house on fire.

I felt like the only sports hater in a bar full of people watching a big game.

Emma brought me up to speed. They'd arrived twenty minutes early. The ladies had taken the train from Newcastle to Darlington, so it was nice of Henri to choose a place near the station.

Henri said that he had chosen the place because it was unpretentious, healthy, and the portions were big. His expression invited a comparison to himself. Emma giggled. Gemma seemed confused.

"Max," said Emma, leaning forward, inviting me to look down her top. "I joined a WhatsApp group. About football. They've been sending loads of memes about the manager of Man City. Apparently he lost to Brentford so he's a bald fraud. Obviously, I don't get it. Can you explain?"

The three of them stared at me. I got the feeling that Emma had told Henri that I was really sexy when I talked about football. Although the sands of time were running, I couldn't face talking about sports right away. "Can I make a request?" I said. "Can we not talk about football until after the food? I sort of need to gatecrash the brunch to talk to Henri about footy and it'll be super boring for you guys. So . . . let's just talk shit for a while. Is that okay?"

For once, Gemma was enthusiastically on Team Max.

My eggs Benedict went down easy. The Geordies had full Englishes. Henri had something with avocado.

The time went by fairly well. The engine of conversation was mostly stoked by Gemma's outrageous sexual interest in Henri, but both women were enchanted by his accent, and I admired the way he greased the wheels of the interaction with almost imperceptible topic shifts or flirtatious questions.

I turned and looked out the window while I collected my thoughts.

It would be better if I could get over my vague dislike of Gemma. She had never done me any harm, and she was super attractive. I would have been perfectly happy to sit across from her on the Orient Express. Especially if it was a no-talking carriage.

With Henri there was a potentially tricky conversation to come. There wasn't any friction between us now, but the next station was Frictionsville.

And Emma. It was probably immature of me, but her bringing Gemma had really made me hesitate at the ticket office. Did I want to travel to that destination? Would I really let the Emma train leave the station over something so trivial? Of course not. And yet. And yet . . . She'd dismissed my ideas with the same certainty that Ian Evans had. I noticed that my jaw was clenched tight; I tried to relax.

Mercifully, the staff came to take away our brunches and brought more teas and coffees.

It was time to decide Henri's future, and to find out whether I'd feature in it.

14
PIECES OF SILVER

I turned back from the window and plastered a smile on my face. Everything would be all right! It was a cold smile, though. I wasn't sure I believed it.

"Max," said Emma, with the exact right amount of concern. "Are you okay?"

"I will be," I said. "I just need to talk to Henri about football. Bad timing, I know, but . . ." I looked up at the wall clock. Two hours to go. Easy. "It's sort of time sensitive. There's a guy about to go on holiday and he's the only one who can sign certain documents. Is that all right? You guys can tune out. I need to get some things off my chest."

"I'd rather listen," said Emma.

"Henri?"

"I don't mind," he said. "You can speak freely."

"Okay, okay," I said. The moment had come. I rubbed my hair, rubbed my face, slapped my cheeks. "Right. Henri, I've got good news and weird news."

He raised a hand to stop me, then did the most outrageous thing: he shifted on his chair so that he was facing me, one leg tucked under the other, holding his coffee like he was one of the friends from *Friends*. "Max. Do me a favour. I believe we're about to hear a story. Tell it chronologically." He turned to the women. "If you agree?"

Emma pressed her lips together. Amazing lips. Holy shit. "Is this going to be good?" she said.

"Max gives good story," said Henri. "He's a raconteur for the ages." He awarded her one of his most rakish smiles, and she did an oversized, performative look of amazement.

Once they'd finished sparkling at each other, I flapped my arms. "Should I start now, or what?"

"*S'il vous plait*," said Henri, rolling his hand like he was in the court of the Sun King. That nearly made me chuckle. Gemma smouldered.

"Chronologically?" I said. I shook my head. Tried to remember the olden days. "So . . . Friday. I went to Darlington to talk about getting you a move."

"Wait wait wait," said Emma. "Some context, maybe?"

Henri supplied it. "I play football for Darlington Football Club. I am—what was that expression I learned?—*on the outs* because of my misunderstood genius. Max scouted me and correctly understood he was witnessing a generational talent. He begged for the chance to become my agent. I agreed, providing he could get me a move away from Darlington this January. A trivial assignment, but the wise ones always start with small, simple tasks to build up the confidence of their protégés."

"January is a transfer window," I said. "It's when players can move between clubs."

"Is that what you did with your other client?" said Emma. "What was his name?" she said, pretending not to remember, and very definitely not looking at Gemma. "Shaggy?"

"Ziggy," I said. The table vibrated as though Gemma had kicked her friend on the ankle—our silver cutlery rattled. "He didn't have a club, so I could have brought him to any team at any time. Henri is registered to Darlington, so I needed to negotiate with them. Get them to agree to let him go. If they want to be malicious, they could make him see out his contract. It's called rotting in the reserves. The football equivalent of sending him to Coventry."

"Coventry has a team?" said Gemma.

For some reason, I had superhuman patience. Maybe because my showdown with Henri was mere moments away and I needed to save my emotional energy. Or maybe because my stomach was full and Henri was paying for the meal. "Sending someone to Coventry means not talking to them. I don't know why. Maybe there used to be an abbey there, one of those places where you can't speak. So the bishop would send someone to Coventry because they were, you know, annoying as fuck."

"Right," said Emma, trying hard to understand things. She pointed downwards. "Henri plays here. And they don't want him, but they might keep him?"

I laughed. A bit of the old flame flared up inside me. She was so bright! "That's exactly it!"

"Why don't they want him?" said Gemma. "He's gorgeous."

"He already said," I answered. "It's because of his genius for being misunderstood."

Henri doffed an imaginary cap to me.

"It's one thing to get him out of here, though," Emma said. "It's another thing to get someone else to take him. Right? It's like, you can cancel a credit card but you should wait till you have the next one in your wallet."

"Well," I said. "Yeah. I suppose that analogy works."

"Finding someplace else sounds harder," said Gemma. "My friend had a cat and then they got pregnant and wanted to get rid of it. The cat I mean. Deciding to get rid of a pet is easy. Rehoming it is hard."

"Not really," I said. "I mean, you're not wrong about pets. But . . . Henri, can you cover your ears, please?" He pretended to. I leaned closer to the women. "Henri is the best player in the league. There are fifty professional teams in England where he'd walk into the first team." I signalled that he could remove his hands from his ears. "Anyway, I've already arranged that side of it."

"Max!" said Henri. "You didn't tell me! Chester?"

"I *told* you," I said.

"When?"

I blinked a few times. "Er . . ." I pinched my nose. Instead of telling him about my meeting with Ian Evans, I'd gone to coach some randos and next morning, lost my job. "Shit. Well, anyway, it doesn't mean anything if Darlington force you to stay. So I thought I'd tell you on Friday when I went to meet Cutter, but you weren't there. And then it got weird and I worried . . . Look, I just thought it'd be easier to tell you to your face. Which is now."

"Okay, Max. Okay. Go back a step. On Friday you met David Cutter? That's the manager of Darlington," he said to the ladies.

"Yes. And I knew it would go badly," I said.

"Why?"

"*Because you weren't there.*"

"Ah." He looked unrepentant. The little shit.

"Anyway, from his office I was watching the first team squad doing their training and asked if I could take some free kicks on this goalie who wasn't doing anything."

"Why?" said Emma.

I frowned. "Why not?"

"I mean, is that what men do when they meet? Take free kicks? Is that like when dogs sniff each other?"

"It isn't a standard greeting," said Henri. "Not even in England."

I sighed. Telling the story quickly meant going further and further backwards, making it even slower. I picked up a teaspoon and used it to punctuate my sentences. "Last Sunday, I took a couple of free kicks against Chester's goalie and scored them both. I don't have ready access to a professional goalie, so I just wanted to see how good I actually am."

"But you were supposed to be negotiating," said Gemma.

"I did both. Turns out, I'm not bad at free kicks." Henri snorted at my understatement. "And because of that, Cutter was more inclined to listen to me. I felt that he was interested in me as a person from the minute I walked in, but then he was also interested in me as a player. And players rule the roost. Einstein could rock up to a football pitch and say he's got a plan for how to win the league, but if he can't hit a pass between two wire men, no one will give a shit." Henri opened his mouth to say something, then decided against it. "Right, so the first team were doing some drills. Actually, something happened before the drills. It might be important because a similar thing happened when the Queen died. I was smacking free kicks in all over town when they stopped for a two-minute's silence."

"Remembrance Day," said Henri.

"Right."

"That's where I was," he said.

"What?"

"I don't train on November eleventh. I never have. No one has ever noticed. They only cared this time because I was on the outs."

"What do you do?" asked Gemma.

Henri became still. "I pay my respects," he said. "In my own way."

We processed that. Collectively decided not to ask follow-up questions, even though we were burning with curiosity.

"Okay," I said. "So Cutter thinks I might be a decent player, and he thinks I might be, like, a good person because I was sad after the silence." I waited for one of the three to scoff, but no one knew me well enough to realise how far from the truth that was. "I joined the drills the first team were doing. Found them a bit simple, asked to try a harder version."

"Of course you did," mumbled Henri.

"Then Cutter's like, 'Hey, do you want to play a little match?' And I say, 'Yeah. But I'll be on the first team.'"

Henri groaned. "Max."

"What?" said Emma.

"It's just weird," said Henri. "Typically idiosyncratic."

"I'm not an idiot," I said, and Emma laughed. I smiled. I was warming up to her again. "Yeah, so I do pretty well in the game. Okay. Then—"

"Let me stop you right there," said Henri. "Max, you seem to believe that everyone in Darlington hates me. It is not so. I am, in fact, extremely charming. I have friends in the dressing room and in the coaching staff. I got a flurry of messages during and after your little performance." My skin started to crawl. Friends on the staff? How often did they chat? Would Cutter tell them everything? How indiscreet were they? I hadn't factored *friends* into my equations. *Merde.*

Henri scrolled down his recent chats. "Messages like: 'Henri, why is your agent playing right-midfield for the first team?' 'Henri, there's a guy here getting a trial by saying he's your agent.' 'Henri, did you know your agent is better at football than you? Smiley face.'" He shook his head. "Why do I get the feeling I'll be hearing that for as long as you represent me?"

I turned to the ladies. "Don't listen to him. I am the very definition of an amateur. Henri is an actual professional. He scored thirty goals in sixty games in a brutal, defensive league. That's really good."

Henri sat up straight. "Max scored and assisted twice in an hour in a game where he was also managing the team."

"Henri is universally regarded as the best striker in the league!"

"All right, all right," said Gemma, with a flash of actual annoyance. "Get a room!"

Henri grabbed his phone. "One more. Message from a coach. I asked him to describe you as a player." He cleared his throat and read. "Max is an alien. He strolls around not doing anything, seemingly learning the rules of the sport. Then, at the speed of light and with stardust on his boots, he teaches us how to play."

I laughed. My first belly laugh of the day. "It doesn't say that. No one there is so poetic. Show me that message."

Henri slipped his phone away, his expression unreadable. "So you caught the eye. Then what?"

I relaxed. He was exaggerating how many friends he still had at the club—I was sure of it. I briefly described my lunch, my medical, and that the club had helped me find a cheap place to stay.

"So I wake up Saturday morning and now's the first time I start to get a bit excited. Like any kid, I'd always wanted to be a footballer, but as I got older, I knew it would never happen. I'd sort of squashed the dream into the deepest, darkest crevice I could find. But here I am, on the verge of it! I just need to impress in one match!" I paused to watch the second hand swirl around the clockface. It didn't matter. For a moment I was back in that memory. Smiling, excited, about to open the Christmas presents, only joy, no negativity. "And it's even better than that. Darlington are second in the league, joint first really, level on points with King's Lynn. It's fifty-fifty if they'll win the league, right, so I've got the chance to walk into a team and get a winner's medal right away! There are players who never win anything in their whole careers. And the Darlington players are really good. Not quite Henri, but they're all very solid and if I have a bad game or two while I'm learning the ropes it's probably not going to be catastrophic. And they're good pros. I could learn a lot from them. You have to understand that I was buzzing." I watched the clock twirl some more, until the minute hand clicked forward one slot. My tone darkened. "Cutter picks me up and I go to some pitch. Abbey Road Sports Field. As you've seen, Emma, Darlington is very green and leafy, but this thing is a mud bath. Asking me to pass or sprint on that surface is like asking Elton John to play with the piano locked." I sipped my tea. It tasted like chalk juice. "The left back—that's my most direct opponent—is a yob. Neanderthal. Savage. He loves that it's a mud bath because it slows me down to the point where he can catch me and kick me. The guy kicks me, nonstop, for forty-five minutes."

"Oh, no," said Emma. "So you didn't play well?"

"What?" I said. "No, I scored two goals in the first two minutes. The other players, no disrespect, are shit." A few had CA up to 5, and one guy even had PA 20, but he was on my team. There was no one on the opposition who could match me in terms of speed or skill. "The first time I got the ball, I sprinted and shot. The keeper didn't even move. I'm not sure he even had his gloves on yet. The second goal was exactly the same as the first, except with lots of desperate defending that made no difference." My jaw was tightening up again. I clenched and unclenched my fists to try to release some tension. "That's why this ape was kicking me. With the referee ignoring it, and the head honchos from Darlington a few yards away, also doing nothing. I was getting pretty steamed up. This game could lead to all kinds of opportunities, but if this twat breaks my ankle then I get nothing. No deal for my client. No contract for me. And how am I supposed to drive back to Manchester? I was getting *furious* at Cutter and those guys. It wasn't enough that I could score at will. They were judging my reactions. Like, am I man enough to handle the physical side of the game? Will I snap and retaliate? Fucking Stone Age thinking. I thought Cutter was progressive, but turns out he's just a modern version of Ian Evans."

"Who?" said Gemma.

"Chester's manager. I'm *this* close to just throwing my shirt off and walking topless through the streets of Darlington looking for my car . . ."

"Oh, story got *good*," said Emma.

"But I decide to stick it out. I'm not really in a position to turn down a shot at money."

"Why not?" said Henri.

"I lost my job on Thursday," I reminded him.

"Max!" he said. "You didn't tell me that." He looked at Emma. "Did he tell you?"

She shook her head. Worried.

"It's fine," I said. Then hesitated. "Okay, it's not *fine*. I'm freaking out juuust a tiny bit. Trying to make good decisions with a lot going on, you know? I just want to be through all this and on the other side." I blew out some air. "But look, if I get Henri his move, I'll have a bit of breathing space. Okay? So that's why I'm letting this little sadist get his jollies kicking me. Normally, I'd move around the pitch until the guy went back under his little bridge, but one of the things these football cavemen like to see is tactical discipline. That means staying in your little box on the pitch. So I did that." I felt my ankle and grimaced. "Turned it into mincemeat, the twat. I look like a zombie down there. *Again!* But it was worth it. They invite me to the stadium, Cutter and the other decision makers. I've impressed them. And I've negotiated like a boss. They make me a deal. If I sign for Darlington, they'll let you go to Chester."

Emma let out a tiny screamy noise. "You're going to be a player!"

Gemma picked up her phone. She was looking up where Chester was.

Henri's eyes narrowed. There was a long pause while he thought things through. "But if I have the chance to play with you, I'd like to stay in Darlington. Force my way back into the team."

Here we go.

I put my tea down and turned to face him. Emma and Gemma didn't exist for this part and nor did the clock. "Henri, there's too much bad blood. Too many fans who want you out, too stupid to understand you. Cutter doesn't understand you, didn't defend you, practically joined the mob himself. You have to go. You have to leave. You have to look forward." I let that sit. Henri nodded, once. My throat constricted. I hadn't lied . . . exactly. I wished I could be completely honest with him, but I couldn't take the risk. I would get eighty pounds a week if he went to Chester, and I owed money to every Tom, Dick, and Emre I'd met recently. As always, trying to process my own inner turmoil was perceived by others as a deep, authentic emotion. My voice grew softer because it was the only way to physically get the words out. "We know Ian Evans doesn't understand you as a person, but he doesn't pretend to, either. He understands you as a player, though. And if I'm being honest, I've got a selfish interest in you going to Chester. I know you'll be a role model for Raffi. My other client," I added, for Emma's benefit. "And for Benny and Johnny Winger and all the kids. Henri, did I tell you that Chester's medical department draws admiring glances from many in the world of football?" Henri rolled his eyes, but he was happy to hear me making jokes. I was still gutted that I hadn't given him the full menu of options, but it was too late now. Being on the other side of the moment was an enormous relief. Such a relief that it made me sick. My throat tightened again. "Henri, listen. I know I make terrible jokes and I'm not a super slick agent, yet, but I'm deadly serious about helping your career. Chester is a sideways move, but it's the best we can do right now. It's just a blip, as long as we can get you playing. When I've got a bit of a name it'll be easier to get meetings with bigger clubs. League Two. We'll skip tier five and go straight to the fourth. This summer, anything's possible. We'll both be free agents. We can sign at a new club together, like a double act. This generation's Smasho and Nice One. Maybe even win some silverware."

Henri considered all this. "You're right, Max. You're right. And you've given me what I asked of you." He adjusted his scarf. "But why are you selling this so hard? You get a client and start your own career.

I get the move I wanted." He narrowed his eyes. "Why have you been so bleak this morning?"

"Because if I was in your shoes, and my agent ended up playing for the team that wanted to get rid of me, I'd wonder how much that agent really cared about me. Your friendship is worth more than ten percent of your wages." That sounded pretty dubious to my ears, but the others reacted positively. "I just can't get over how weird it is. It feels wrong."

"Maybe you feel guilty about something," said Gemma. Did my eye start twitching?

But Henri wasn't thinking along those lines. "No, Max. You *must* start your career. Do not think I stand in your way. I am delighted for you."

"I'm also selling hard because we need to sign today. Before one p.m." I lied about the time, but that was a lie I was comfortable with. It was just in case Henri tried to be dramatic by refusing to get there until there were only sixty seconds left.

"One p.m.?"

I pointed to the clock. "The dudes from both clubs are sitting next to their fax machines right now. We can sign, and you'll have a medical in Chester on Monday. Start training with them on Tuesday."

"A medical in Chester? That's . . ." His eyes flickered in the direction of his date. ". . . just another day at the office to me."

"I bet," I said.

Henri closed his eyes for a while. Ruminating. Then he said, "Ten percent of my wages from Chester."

"What?"

"You didn't negotiate my deal with Darlington. You have earned ten percent of whatever you negotiated with Chester."

"Oh," I said. "Yeah, I mean, obviously that's fair but I wasn't expecting more."

"Firm contracts make good friends," said Henri.

"What does that mean?" I asked.

Gemma spoke. "It means if you do business with someone, even a friend, get a good, clear contract and later on there won't be any drama."

"Oh, thanks."

Henri sipped his coffee. "So you'll be a Darlington player and I won't. That's a hell of a twist. May I come to watch you play?"

"You'll be playing at the same time as me," I said.

"I'll get five yellow cards so I can miss a game," he said.

I checked his player profile history tab—he'd only been booked three times the previous season. Strange, given how combative he was. "It's a thirty-pound fine every time you get booked, right? I don't have to pay three pounds of that, do I?"

"No, Max. Do not distress yourself." He leant forward. "Max? I am not satisfied. We've cleared up the business and we should all be celebrating. Where's the Max who led the Knights to victory, who stood up to the problematic parents, who stormed the Chester castle? What's wrong, Max? Everything has turned out well, no?"

"In some ways, yes," I said. "There's just one thing." I looked at the clock. Time was wasting. Why not shut my mouth and let things play out the way I'd designed? I glanced at Henri and Emma. If I couldn't open up to them, who could I talk to? "I don't want to play for Darlington."

Henri was silent. He was looking at me the way I sometimes looked at him—a complete failure to understand the other's motivations.

Emma said, "Why not, Max?"

"They won't let me manage the youth teams. That's the main reason I'm becoming a player—to get reputation so I can become a manager. And I'm unhappy with Cutter. He shouldn't have put me through that trial. But most of all, it's not really Darlington. It's football itself." I looked at Emma. "I think I painted you a romantic view of the sport when we met. And I stand by everything I said. I love it. When I'm watching on TV, that is. Or managing. It's different when I play." I took a big spoon from the table and saw myself in it, distorted and upside down. I put it back. "You might find this hard to believe," I said with a tiny smile, "but some people find me quite annoying. And I'm even more annoying as a football player. I've been the most fouled player on every team I've ever played for. And it's worse now. I'm not playing against kids or teenagers; I'm playing against grown men, and they don't like being humiliated. And when they kick me, I stay kicked. I don't want to spend half my life on crutches for slightly more money than I got at the call centre!"

"So don't play like that, Max," said Henri.

"Okay," I said, with a little heat, "and you'll stop having a ninety-minute war with a defender every time you play?"

He acknowledged the point. "Touché."

"Okay, listen everyone," I said, looking at the time. "I'm sorry I wasn't at a hundred percent this morning. But Henri's decision is a weight off my shoulders. A big one. I think I've found a kind of career shortcut. The maximum progress with the minimum risk. With a bit of luck, anyway. Let's go sign these papers. Then I'll tell you my plan and you can tell me if it's insane."

"Your plan?" said Emma, with a quirky little smile, as though she'd been with me from the start watching me try and fail and try again. *Another plan?* Her smile seemed to say. *Go on then,* I imagined her saying with pretend resignation but real enjoyment. *Let's hear it.*

Suddenly, I felt warm. Energy was flooding into me from all around. Emma? My dream woman. Gemma? She was wonderful. Henri? A little prince. When I spoke, for the first time in days I spoke with charisma. This was the man Emma had travelled to see.

"Plan step one. Complete the seduction of a Frenchman." Gemma looked from me to her date, mouth open. "Henri, do you take me as your lawfully wedded agent? Till June 2023 do us part, with an option to extend?"

He grinned. "I do."

"Emma and Gemma. Do you allow me to take you to watch two men unite in a civil ceremony?"

"We do," said Emma. There was another under-the-table kick, and Emma burst out laughing at her friend's horrified expression.

15

THE FAST TRACK

There was a minor logistics issue. Because I'd walked to the restaurant and Henri had arrived in his impractical two-seated Lotus Seven, he would have to drive me to my car, and then I'd go back to the restaurant and drive the ladies to the stadium. Henri, of course, wanted to do it in a more complicated way.

"We will both drive back here and take one woman each. I choose . . . Gemma." Gemma wasn't the giggling type, but that was the closest she came.

"Oh, great," I said. "Why don't we drive to the flamethrower shop and burn down some trees while we're at it?"

Henri *tsk*ed at me. "Max, I care about the planet. I do. But it will survive this extra half-mile trip. And, in case you forgot, this is a date. I bought a sports car to impress women, Max."

So that was absurd, but that's what we did. Emma got in my shitty box-on-wheels while Henri zoomed off with his date in his green fantasy car. I experienced a rare pang of jealousy.

I rubbed my forehead. "Sorry, Emma."

"What for?"

"Just sorry."

When we got to Blackwell Meadows, Henri's car was nowhere to be seen, but when Emma and I were looking for the entrance, he and Gemma appeared from behind us. Odd.

"This way, Max!"

With Gemma dangling from his arm, he led us through the side of the stadium into an office. Cutter and the club secretary were there. They pushed a contract in front of me, and a memorandum of understanding in front of Henri.

"You first, Max," said Cutter.

"Wait, Max," said Henri. "Let me look." He skimmed through my contract, his face turning from red to purple as he went. "No! Do not sign this, Max! It is scandalous."

Cutter looked panicked, but I intervened. I wanted them to talk to each other as little as possible. For now, at least. "Henri, it's okay. I asked for those terms."

"What is it?" said Emma.

"It's . . . ugh!" said Henri.

I stepped in. "I've chosen to be paid by the match instead of weekly. So I get a little bit of a higher fee."

"It's criminal," said Henri. "They are abusing you. It's a zero-hours contract. Even car salesmen have a basic income guarantee."

"No, Henri. Please! Listen. This is a fair deal all round. What if I'm shit? The club isn't locked in. And if I'm good, I'll actually earn more. See here, I've got a good assist and goal bonus. Okay? Calm down. Emma, this kind of thing is known as pay-as-you-play. Henri's worried that if I don't play, I will be broke. So that's why it's good I'm an agent as well. Right? Right, Henri?"

He grunted. "Yes. It is good you feel financially stable enough to sign . . . this."

I patted him on the back, leaned over, hesitated just for a moment, and signed. Five hundred pounds per match. Five hundred for every goal and assist. No one took a photo. The secretary guy scanned it and faxed it to the Football Association (FA), then tapped away on his computer and checked the printer had paper.

Henri read through his own document, shaking his head at my stupidity. His wasn't an actual contract. It was a thing to say that he *would* join Chester on January 1. It was legal enough for both clubs to plan accordingly. He signed it, then sighed. "So that's that."

"That's that," agreed Cutter.

We all shook hands. The secretary gave me some printout. "Welcome to Darlington!" he said. "Er . . . there will be more to come. I'm afraid it will take a while because of my, you know, holiday. But it's all done and dusted. Shirt number seventy-seven, like you asked for. Ask at the office if you need anything in the meantime."

"What's this?" I said, pointing to a section of the paper he'd given me.

"That's your FAN. Football Association number."

I laughed and groaned and raised my head to look directly at the ceiling. "Jesus Christ. I just borrowed five hundred quid to get that. Did I just chuck five hundred quid in the bin?"

"Why did you need five hundred pounds?"

"To get my agent number. My license number. Thingy. This!"

"Ah! Of course," the secretary said. "Well, don't worry, you had to pay that to start the process, but it will be the same number in the end. If I were you, I'd call the FA tomorrow and get them to link your player profile to your agent one. It'll take them thirty seconds."

"Oh!" I said. That was unexpectedly awesome. Bit of a fast-track scenario.

"If you don't mind," he said, "I'll run off. Double-check my packing, you know."

"I'll be off, too," said my new boss. "Training at nine thirty tomorrow, Max. Don't be late or there's a fine. There are fines for everything. Not from me, you understand, from the captain. He uses the money for team nights out and stuff. Talk to him when you see him."

"One thing," I said, and both men stopped on their way out. "Can we take our dates onto the pitch? Show them around a bit?"

"Absolutely," said Cutter. "Your first time, his last time. Spent in attractive company! There's a groundsman somewhere. Just er . . . don't be too . . . *romantic* out there. We're a family club. Okay, Henri?"

"Please," said Henri, with a smile. "As if I'd have my first kiss in a football stadium. I'm the poetic type!"

Cutter eyed him with a hint of sadness, a hint of pride. "You are and all. Listen, Henri." He looked away, then back. "Good luck, yeah?"

"Thank you, Mr. Cutter. You, too."

Henri showed us around the stadium. It didn't take long. The side with the offices was almost like a cricket pavilion and was known as The Clubhouse. There were no seats there, but I guessed a few people would stand along the side of the pitch, leaning against a railing like at a Sunday League game. Opposite was the south stand, a cute little thing with six hundred seats. The east stand was eight steps high and had no inbuilt seating. A thousand people could stand there. It was known as The Tin Shed, according to Henri, and had been rescued from a previous ground.

Henri advised me not to ask the locals about past stadiums because that was a "canister of worms."

Finally, the west terrace was . . . empty. It was just a space, uncovered. Unlike in bigger stadiums, the home and away fans weren't always segregated, but the away fans tended to congregate there. And get drenched.

So this wasn't Old Trafford, or Anfield, or even Wrexham's Racecourse. Far from it. But where there were gaps in the stadium, there were trees, giving the place a kind of serene Scandinavian quality.

We walked all the way around until we got to the south stand, which felt like the main stand although it was technically not the biggest. All the seats were labelled—*Media, Darlo Fans Radio, Home Director, Away Director, Reserved.*

The real star, of course, was the pitch. It was in decent condition—a bit worn here and there. But it'd do. And the jewel in the crown—the goals on either end, with the standing-room-only terraces behind. When I scored, where would the biggest noise come from?

Gemma didn't want to go on the grass in her high heels, but Emma did. We went to the centre circle and stood awkwardly for a while. I felt like I'd done damage to our relationship and didn't know how to repair it.

She spoke first. "Are you mad I brought Gemma?"

"No, of course not."

"Max?"

I looked longingly at the goal. Although I didn't like being kicked to bits, I loved playing football. At its heart, it was simple. Kick the ball past that straight white line and people would admire you and think you had accomplished something. "Okay, yes. It annoyed me. I know it's wrong to feel like that."

"You're allowed to feel how you feel. But talk to me."

I nodded. "Okay. You're right. I said not to choose Gemma. I'd like to think you would value my opinions on things. I'd like my opinions to be valued."

"I do and they are. But you said you'd bring a footballer and . . . well. Gemma. You know? I thought you were joking about all the philosophy and that. Who knew there were two erudite footballers?" We looked over to the side of the pitch where Henri was being Henri and Gemma was being Gemma. "They like each other."

"I know. It was a good choice. I was wrong." I looked over at them again. "What was I thinking? She's so sexy. What man wouldn't want her? I was being a big manbaby. I know that. But really, I'd have liked to have met another of your friends. You've met two of mine. What the—Hey! They're kissing. What was that he said about first kisses?"

"He said he didn't want his first kiss here. What do you think they were doing in his car?"

I slapped myself on the forehead. "The absolute dog."

After the mutual laugh, there was another moment of awkwardness. Of expectation.

"Oh, wait," I said. "No no no. I'm not kissing you now after I've been fucking weird all morning."

Emma pouted. "How about after you score your first goal?"

"Huh," I said. "Huh. Let's walk to a corner flag. So . . . this Tuesday is a friendly against God-knows-who in the backend of wherever. That doesn't count. Saturday is the FA Trophy. It's a cup for non-league teams. Did you finish the Welcome to Wrexham thing? Wrexham got to the final of that, at Wembley."

"Yeah yeah yeah," she said. "Is the match here?"

"Yes."

"Then I'll be here. Which side will you be playing on?"

I laughed. "If I play, both sides. I play on the right and we switch ends at halftime."

"Hmm." She looked around the stadium. "That part looks the warmest. I'll sit there. You score, you kiss me."

"Okay, okay," I said. "I like the way you think. But what do I get if I score a hat trick?"

"Duh," she said. "A hatful of kisses."

We'd arrived at the corner. I moved Emma out of my way—which she didn't seem to mind at all—and rehearsed my run-up from different angles.

"What are you doing?" she said.

"I think I'd like to score direct from a corner."

"What does that mean?"

I took up a left-footed stance with the corner flag to my left and the goal to my right. The imaginary ball was about a foot off the line. I pretended to kick it. "I approach the ball, hit it hard with a lot of curve. It goes two or three yards out at the . . . what do you call it?

Apex? Apogee? Crest? But then it starts to bend back in." I moved close to her, leaned in, and used her arm to show where I was aiming, like I was teaching her to play pool. My face was almost pressed against hers. I spoke very softly. "There are loads of players in the six-yard box, so the goalie isn't completely free to move. He tries to jump to punch the ball away, but one of our dudes is blocking him. Ball zips past. Swish! Crowd goes nuts." I smiled and eased away from her.

"Right," she said, cheeks slightly flushed. She pointed to my damaged ankle. "But aren't you right-footed?"

I poked my tongue out of the corner of my mouth. "You're right. Everyone thinks I'm right-footed." I moved so that the corner flag was to my right and the goal I was aiming at was to my left. "So in that case, I'd approach the ball from this angle, and curl the ball *away* from the goalkeeper and onto the head of one of my players. Yeah. I should stick to that for now. Keep the element of surprise. Good point. I can shoot when the corner is on the opposite side of the pitch. But maybe I do want to show off from the beginning. Huh. Tricky."

"Are you saying you can kick just as well with your left leg?"

I smiled. "No. Of course not." And I did a very exaggerated wink.

"Max!"

I held my hand out and she took it. We started walking back to the dugouts.

"No, Max, really," she said. "When we met you never said you were a player as well. You were all about Ziggy. So . . . So just how good are you?"

"Ha," I said. "That's the question, isn't it? I honestly, honestly, have no idea. But," I said, pausing to look backwards. "But I think I'll be a real problem at set pieces, and I've always been good at crossing. So . . . I'm good enough to get what I want." We started walking again, but once more, I hesitated. "I think."

Henri invited us back to his house to celebrate.

"To *your* house?" I said.

"I buy a house everywhere I play football. First it's a home, then it's an investment."

"Will you buy one in Chester?" asked Gemma.

"If I'm only there for six, seven months, probably not."

I wondered how much money he had made in his career. Seemed like a lot if he was buying houses left, right, and centre. I took one last look at the goals. Was I making a mistake in wanting to be a manager? Players earned far, far more.

Hmm.

We left the stadium and I followed Henri. He kept trying to go fast but had to slow down because I refused to match his speed.

"Are you doing that to wind him up?" asked Emma.

"Hmm? No. But if it does, that's a bonus."

His house was very nice, decorated and furnished in a minimalist style, very tasteful, very classy, but with cosy moments here and there, such as a chunky leather armchair surrounded by lamps and books. It was top.

After the tour, we retired to his spacious kitchen and stood around his central island. Gemma very close to him, Emma close to me.

Henri took four wine glasses down from a cupboard. He opened his wine cooler and took out a white wine. He pulled out the cork. "This is from my family's vineyard," he said, as though it was nothing.

"A family vineyard? How romantic. Can we visit?" said Gemma.

"Alas," said Henri. "I was lying. I know it's not nice to lie to one's friends. Is it, Max?"

He gave me a stern look. My throat was dry. Did he know? "Um . . . is this about me calling you the best player in the league?"

"That was the truest word ever spoken."

"Certainly," I said, thinking that actually, Raffi had a higher ceiling.

"I refer, Max, to when you said the deadline to sign was one p.m. We ended our nice brunch early because of that. The club secretary told me it was actually two p.m."

Ludicrous relief. But I couldn't keep living like this. He'd signed, now, it was all arranged. All settled. I could come completely clean. Almost completely clean.

"Henri, stop. Please." He looked surprised, but lifted up the wine mid-pour. "I need to be straight with you." Gemma made a scoffing noise. I ignored her. "One question. You only thought about staying in Darlington to play on the same team as me. Right?"

"Right."

"Okay." I cleared my throat. "Here's my plan. Let's see if you want to drink to it or not." I took a breath, paused, and said, "I'm going to play for Darlington, win the league, and then quit. And I'm going to do all that by the end of January."

"Emma, would you please check to see if he has a fever?"

Emma pressed the back of her palm to my forehead. She took it away and I unconsciously tried to follow it. "Well," she declared. "He's hot all right."

Henri grinned. "Indeed. But not sick? No? Well, well. I am . . . gosh. I am speechless. I have never been struck dumb by stupidity before, yet here we are."

"Is what he said impossible?" said Gemma.

"No," I said. "It's trivially easy. If I play ten games for Darlington and they win the league, I'll get a winner's medal."

"Ten *league* games," said Henri.

I hesitated. Had I calculated wrong? "May I?" I said, pointing to a nearby MacBook.

"Oh," said Henri, looking worried. "Er . . . not that one." He moved away, then came right back. "Joking. Of course you may."

I opened it and went to Darlington's fixture page. "Ten. Exactly ten league games before the end of January."

"You'd have to play in every game," said Henri, coming round to look at the screen.

"And I will. I'll be so good in every game he'll keep picking me."

"This one, Max, this one," he said, jabbing at the data. "The tenth match is on January thirty-first. The last day of the window. And it kicks off at seven forty-five p.m. You finish at, what, nine thirty, and at nine thirty-five call the FA to cancel your registration with Darlington?"

"Oh!" I said, happily. "You understand it perfectly."

"No, Max! You cannot call from the dressing room to cancel your contract, then walk in with your former teammates to take a shower. It's unprecedented. It's . . . it's almost sick. What about your reputation?"

I shrugged. "It'll be fine. I'll make up some story."

Henri stomped around his kitchen. "Why are we even talking about this? What is the point? I said I don't mind you playing for Darlington! You need to build a career, Max. Burning everything down is not the way. Believe me! And why are you only telling me this now? I'm not a good enough friend to share the secret?"

"You're a good friend, Henri. That's why I couldn't tell you. Because you'd try to stop me." He stopped pacing. Took a swig from the wine bottle and calmed down. Then he realised what he'd done and got a new one from the cooler. "Henri, you don't know how much I want to be a manager. You can't know, because it isn't rational. I know that. But I'm telling you, friend to friend, that my deepest wish is to manage. I want to manage a football team. Now, let's think about the job market. Football managers are fired all the time. Look at the bottom of the National League North. Telford, Buxton, Farsley. They're all in trouble. What they're doing isn't working. Yeah? Would they give me the job? No chance. Now imagine I play ten games for Darlington and score, I don't know, seven goals with eight assists. There are, like, YouTube highlights of me being fast and doing backheel nutmegs and all that shit I do. I'm a million-pound player, maybe. And Farsley sack their manager and I turn up and say, hey! Do you want a player-manager? I'm a million-pound player and I'll do it for minimum wage. What are they going to say?"

"They're going to say no because you're twenty-two and you're a maniac."

"Okay maybe. Maybe not. But there's one team in this league who have already let me manage their disabled team and their youth team. A team slipping down into the danger zone."

Henri scoffed. "Max! You forget that I will be moving there on January first. And I will shoot them up the table." He smiled at Gemma. "Single-handed."

"That's six weeks away," I said. "What if they're in the relegation zone then? What if they only draw the first few games when you're there? And check this out." I gestured on the trackpad to make a section bigger. "Look at this fixture. Saturday, twenty-first January. Darlington are at home to . . ."

"To Chester," he said, eyes wide.

"So what?" said Gemma. "If Henri is playing, Chester will win. No offence."

"None taken," I lied. "But Henri can't play against his parent club. So it'll just be me. Now, Henri. You're one of the top three football experts in this room. What, in your opinion, will happen to a team in relegation trouble if they lose heavily in a performance inspired by a player they could have signed for free?"

He glared at me. "Define heavily."

I looked at the ceiling while keeping his face in my vision. "Eight–nil?"

He slammed the table. "No! No, Max. I forbid it. If I play for Chester, I play for Chester. I cannot allow this."

"Sorry, mate," I said, slouching on his island. "Not much you can do about it, though." I stood straight again, but my smirk was crooked. "Look. If Ian Evans is sacked, I'll apply for the job. No biggie. Mike Dean will snap me up—he knows I'm a tactical wizard and by then he'll have seen I'm a top player. And then you and I will play together, right? That's what I couldn't tell you until you *signed*. That's why I was weird and stressed. Because this is the plan! Together we will rule the galaxy as manager and subordinate!"

He rolled his neck around. "Emma, would you be mad at me if I fired Max right now?"

"Yes. Sorry."

"*Merde*." He sighed. "Max, you're quite mad. Your plan has more plot holes than *Inception*. You're right that I would have tried to talk you out of this." He closed his eyes and shook his head, letting out a stream of invective in his mother tongue. Finally, he started to pour the wine again. "I will play for Chester and they will finish mid-table. A perfectly respectable season. You will *not* find a club willing to take a chance on you as a manager, and you will finish the season at Darlington as a player and *not* ruin your reputation. *Eh bien*. I understand that you have tried to create something magical today. A delicate and beautiful shoot of hope, and it falls to me to stamp on it, to extinguish its life. It is not your fault you will fail; it is the world's. I remain pleased to have met you. You remain privileged to be my agent." He nodded a few times. "Follow your course until the transfer window closes. Then when you are forced to remain here, in this nice market town, close to the joys and delights of Newcastle, remain with all your heart. Spare some time to talk to clubs in League Two. Get them to send scouts to watch the magnificent Henri Lyons. There. I have spoken."

He finished pouring and distributed the glasses.

"Let us drink," he said, "to the best and worst dual date I have ever been on."

We all took a swig.

Emma said, "Well, now that Max is normal again, to a certain value of normal, maybe we could try it again next week? Without all the contract talks and worries? Talk about Max's debut?"

"Love to," I said. "But can't."

"Why not?" said Henri.
"Next Sunday," I said. "I'm going to church."
"You can skip it," he laughed. "For Emma."
I smirked. "Can't. I'm giving the sermon."

16

DIGS

Football glossary: *Digs. Digs are cheap, shared accommodation owned or run by a football club for use by their junior players.*

At around six o'clock, Henri kicked us out. That is to say, he kicked me out, and then he kicked Emma out. I waited for him to do the same to Gemma, but he must have forgotten she was there.

With a grin, I shook hands with my new client, then took Emma to the train station.

I waited with her until her train came. "You know the way you're a strong, independent woman?" I said.

"I am?"

"I'd still rather you didn't come to the match on your own. Can you, sort of, get one of your football lads to come with you to the match?"

"More testosterone in the area to boost your competitive spirit?"

"I'm thinking of rowdy fans. Hooligans. I don't want to be worried about what's going on off the pitch. Please get some beefy dude to drive you so you don't have to get on the train with thousands of drunken nutjobs."

"I don't think many Darlington fans live in Newcastle, Max."

"Just—"

She put her hands on my chest and looked up at me. "Okay. I hear you. I'll find the strongest, tallest, most handsome knight in shining armour and spend the day with him. Okay?"

"Good," I said. "Good. But yeah. Second strongest is fine. I mean, doesn't even have to be a knight. Maybe a . . . what are they called? Squire."

"I already have the perfect man in mind," she said. And then she snuggled against me.

She was the absolute queen of mixed messages.

Her train pulled away, and as I watched it go, I realised something. This was the start of a ten-week chapter in my life called Max Best: Player.

I got back in my car and drove to my temporary new home—The Darlo Digs.

It was on a quiet-seeming side street. A detached house—one of those that seemed to have three floors but when you got inside there were actually five. The driveway full, I parked on the street.

I didn't have a key, so I knocked on the door. No answer. I knocked louder. Nothing. Looking through the bay windows of the front room, I saw four guys in there playing *FIFA* on console. With a brief spike of anger, I went back to the front door and was about to start pounding when I tried pushing—it opened.

I walked straight upstairs, cleaned out all their valuables from their rooms, went back to my car and drove off a rich man.

Okay, I didn't do that. In fact, I closed and locked the door behind me, and vowed not to leave any valuables in the digs. Not that I had many valuables. I only had one set of clothes—which I'd been forced to wear for three days—my only pair of football boots, shinpads, my phone, my laptop, my wallet. The rest of my stash was back in Manchester, behind a locked door. What to do about my house was a headache for another day.

The *FIFA* tournament, or whatever they were doing, was loud and punctuated by shouts and banter. The two lads currently playing were young—two of the scholarship players, as the guys on starter contracts who still did schoolwork were called. I wouldn't know if they were any good until I'd scouted an eighteens match. Maybe I'd try to be polite to them until I knew for sure. Didn't want to piss off any potential superstar clients.

Watching and bantering (in sentences of never more than four words), were two players who'd been in my trial match—my direct opponent, Chumpy, nineteen, and Glynn, eighteen, a crafty midfielder who would probably end up bouncing between the sixth and seventh tiers.

Chumpy spotted me first and raced over, hand extended. "Max! We been waiting for you. Good to see you. You never thanked me, though."

"What for?" I asked, cautiously.

"I made you look good in your trial," he laughed. The guy was totally different off the pitch. Totally different. Here, he was charming, in a rustic kind of way. Not to the point where I'd worry if Emma chose him as her footballing bodyguard, but he was certainly making a potentially difficult introduction go down easy. "Lads, fucking pause. Fuck sake. Max is here." There were brief introductions. There was Barkley, who I'd later find out was a sixteen-year-old half-Jamaican winger, and Benzo, a seventeen-year-old English right back. "You watch and learn, Bark," said Chumpy. "This guy's the new Ronaldo."

Bark *tsk*ed. "Child, please."

Benzo said, "You play *FIFA*, Max?"

"No. Gives me a headache. Don't play games much. I've got a PS3. Showing its age these days, I guess."

"Nah, this is only a PS4," said Benzo. "Five's been out for time, yo! Club got to be spending!"

"Are you dissatisfied with the amenities?" I said, like a hotel manager slash serial killer. That freaked him out a bit and he backtracked and said the PS4 was a good machine and the 5 was out of stock anyway.

"Supply chains are hard," I agreed, putting my hand on his shoulder. "Hey, where's my room? I'll dump my stuff then go get some dinner."

"I'll show you," said Glynn. "But you don't need to go out. We've got food here."

"Not in the mood for cooking, mate. It's been a long and weird week."

"Nah, mate. It's made. Just heat it up. There's a woman who comes to cook. Mrs. Ratliff. She's the landlady. Takes care of us. Does our laundry and that."

"She does your laundry?" I said, stupefied.

Glynn looked embarrassed, so Chumpy helped out. "It's not that we can't do it! I mean, some lads when they come don't really know how to use the machines and the temperatures and all that. The academy does sessions, like. Life skills and that. But it's also, we do training and meetings and sessions and the like. Scholarship lads get homework, even. Having someone like Mrs. Ratliff sort of helps us focus on improving as players, like."

I eyed the already-unpaused *FIFA* game. "Right." Then my eyes swept the area—the sink was full of dirty dishes and cups. The bin was full. There were sweet wrappers and crisp packets everywhere. Someone really liked Mars bars. Living with four boys was basically my worst nightmare, but I resolved to clamp my mouth shut. This was just temporary. It wasn't my job to get involved in their living arrangements.

My room was small but fine. I dumped my stuff there and tested the bed. Way too soft and I could feel the springs pressing into my back, but I guessed it'd serve its purpose. The walls, though, were far too thin to cope with the noise from the TV. The din or the shitty bed—I could deal with one, but not both. I took a last moment to look around and saw a Neymar poster. The most fouled player in world football. I gave him a little nod.

Down in the kitchen, I ate and chatted to Chumpy and Glynn, who were very agreeable. Chumpy gave me my house key. I pumped them for information. What time did they go to bed? What did they eat before training? What should I expect from a Monday morning session? Where do I park?

One nice convenience was that a sort of shuttle bus would pick us up from the digs and take us to training. The driver would take us home when we wanted, so long as he wasn't doing anything more important. The training ground wasn't far, so we could walk, but it wasn't very scenic.

Plain, simple food and plain, simple company is a good way to start an adventure. I told the lads I was going to have an early night and rest my ankle.

The scholarship lads grunted and carried on playing. I bent down into their field of vision, turned to look at the screen, then back at them. "I said I'm going to have an early night. And rest. Like a professional footballer."

They looked at each other, trying to parse what I was saying. "You telling us to go to bed?" said Bark.

"No, mate," I chuckled. "I'm not your mum. You do whatever you want. But I'm going to bed now. To rest. Yeah?"

Benzo scratched his temple. "You want us to stop playing?"

"No, mate," I chuckled again. "I can't see the screen from my room, can I?"

"Oh!" said Bark. "Turn it down, yeah? Oh. Can do."

I snatched the remote control before he could get it. "Let me," I said, and hit the mute button. "Ahh. Perfect. Now you can play all night and I can sleep. What a great solution!"

"Okay, Max," laughed Benzo. "We get you."

I turned to look at the screen again. "Hey, Bark. Are you the red team?"

"Yes, Max."

"Do you choose the formations in this, er, game, or does every team have a default?"

"You can change them. I'm doing three-four-one-two because I'm Portugal and my best player's Felix. So he's my CAM."

"*Tsch*," said Benzo. "That's why I've got a DM. Shut Felix down and they've got nothing. I keep whupping him on counters."

"Holy shit," I said. These brats were six years ahead of me in tactical knowledge! "Did you learn all that from the academy or from the game?"

Benzo shrugged. "Both. Game mostly, suppose."

I did a one-eighty on the whole "wasting their time playing *FIFA*" thing—they weren't simply killing time. They were also absorbing tactical thinking. Would that filter into their performance on the pitch? Allow them to learn new formations quickly? Understand why managers were asking them to do X, Y, and Z? I watched the match they were playing for about ten seconds. "I hope I don't have to stay here long, no offence, but maybe you can teach me a few things. You up for that?"

"You're too old to play," said Benzo, now that my air of authority had evaporated.

"What?"

"You've got those old person hands. Sending texts one finger at a time. Playing *FIFA* being like 'Yo which button is shoot?'"

The kids fell into each other, laughing. Disrespectful little shits! I would never dig into someone older than me like that. Except Jackie Reaper. And Mike Dean. And Ian Evans.

I went to bed and fired off some texts.

Sleep came before I got any replies.

Emma: Good luck!

Henri: By the way. They are called mannequins. Do not be a dummy. Do not say wire men.

Unknown number: HMRC Refund: You have an outstanding Tax refund of £277.32 from 2020 to 2021. Follow instructions to claim your retund at englandgovermet.com/IRS

Raffi: Been good. Training good. Vibe good. You in Darlinton no joke? Weird but good.

Ziggy: Darlingont? That makes no sense. Your turn to buy a round though!

Kisi: Yes, Mr. Best. All is well. Thank you for asking. Sometimes the training is too hard, but the girls are helping me through. James is well. He brings a notepad to the sessions and gives me feedback on the way home. I let him do this for you, Mr. Best. You owe me.

Kisi: No, really. You owe me. He is very boring.

Monday, November 14.

My first day as a professional footballer. Woke up bright and early, ankle already better. It was still bruised and sore to the touch, but it seemed perfectly flexible. No swelling. Ready for training. Ready to start learning the ropes. Get to know my team properly. Get to see what's involved in running a football club—from the inside.

A minivan beeped from outside. I grabbed my boots and slung them over my shoulder. I carried my shinpads by hand. The other guys had bulky kit bags.

A bleary-eyed Bark and Benzo got into the van first and sat at the back. Glynn got in the middle row, and I was about to follow when I realised that Chumpy was hesitating. I took in the situation and realised that he was hoping to get in the passenger seat. Presumably that was either more comfortable or came with higher status. Either way, I had this kind of pathetic impulse to stake my claim to it. "I'd better go in the front," I said. "Because of my injury."

"Oh, right," he said. He tried to think of some comeback, but I was already halfway round the front of the van.

I regretted it immediately—the driver, Pat, was incredibly chatty and after asking me who I was, what position I played, and where I was from, he proceeded to tell me about his life as a Darlington fan.

He remembered the date, score, and scorers of every match he'd ever been to, it seemed. It was as though someone turned Wikipedia into an audiobook but forgot to programme a pause button. These are the worst kinds of people because they get upset if you ask them to shut up.

Still, he was a good driver. Not trying to show off, not taking crazy risks, and the Darlington logo on the van meant other drivers let us turn onto roads and that sort of thing. So that was one positive. There wouldn't be many more that morning.

Chumpy and Glynn came with me into the dressing room. They left their kit bags and I left my boots and shinpads on a section of bench labelled *NEW PLAYER*, as instructed. Then it was off through a few corridors to a function room with a bar off to the side. There was a metal shutter there—the boundary between a bunch of professional footballers and many thousands of units of alcohol. It didn't seem ideal.

The first team ranged in age from my late-teenage housemates to battle-scarred thirty-three-year-olds. We had a reserve goalie who was thirty-seven, and a player-coach who was forty. An experienced group, but unlike Ian Evans, Dave Cutter didn't mind throwing a young player onto the pitch if he was doing well in training.

The main man strode through us all, resplendent in his club tracksuit. He and his two main assistants took a position at the front of the room, and the hubbub of chat died down.

"All right, lads. Good win at the weekend. We've got to build on that this week. Tuesday there's no league game so we've got a friendly against Whitby Town. You all know full well how friendly they are." Knowing chuckles from all quarters. "If you don't match their physicality and workrate, they'll tear you a new one. All right? It's not a league game but I expect you to put a shift in. We graft, we win our battles, we put them on the back foot, and we earn the right to fucking play the way we want to fucking play. All right? Saturday it's the FA Trophy against Alfreton at Blackwell. The office tells me it could be a big crowd, so it's an important game. It's a home game. We're better than them; we want to win. We have to win. But the priority this season is winning this league and getting out of this division. So we'll rotate where we can. Which brings us to our new addition. Max Best. You met him the other day. He's come in to give us an extra body. Max, we'll see how you go in training but I'd love to get you some minutes tomorrow night and if your fitness can handle it, start on Saturday. You good with that?"

I wasn't sure how people addressed him in these kinds of settings, so I guessed. "Yes, boss."

"Right. Any questions?"

One hand went up. It was the team's best centre back and captain. "Yeah. If he's here, does that mean the Frenchman will be back?"

"No. He's out. For good." That unleashed another hubbub of chat. "Right. Get changed. On pitch two in ten. Hop to it."

All the guys stood and filed out back towards the dressing room. All except for the goalies. They went past Cutter and through a different door. So the keepers didn't train with the rest of the squad? Weird.

One of said squad, a midfielder who was a rare example of Cutter overrating a player, came up to me and blocked my path. "So, Max, isn't it?"

"Yeah."

He didn't introduce himself, a fact that I didn't notice at the time because thanks to the curse, I already knew who he was. "I'm Darlo's union rep."

"Union?"

"For the PFA." The Professional Footballers Association. I'd heard mixed things about them. "Just want to check that you'll be joining."

"I'll have to read up on it," I said, and tried to sidestep him.

He blocked me again. "What? Are you against unions or something? Are you a fascist?"

I eyed him. He was acting very strangely. "You've convinced me," I said. "I'll join."

I moved again, and again he blocked me. "Thing is," he said, but I faked a step and moved past him on the other side.

It had finally clicked—he was trying to delay me from getting to the dressing room. Trying to make me late so that the captain could levy a fine on me. Cutter had warned me about all the little fines there were for everything. Presumably, this was how the captain established dominance over the dressing room. How he kept himself as top dog. I couldn't really give a shit about that, but the idea of being out of pocket within twenty minutes of starting my career was maddening.

I raced to the dressing room and there was a palpable mood of merriment. Driver Pat was also the kit man, and he was laying out fresh tops, shorts, and socks for all the guys. In the middle of the room were two large, portable bins, and after training we were supposed to chuck our dirty kit in there to get washed. I picked up the gear he'd left me and swapped it with another player. The level of merriment wobbled.

Something's up, I thought, *but it's not the kit.* While I was undressing, I scanned the room as the rest of the lads pulled on shirts or applied unguents to different parts of their bodies. All pretty normal. I folded up my jeans and placed them next to my hoodie. One guy was doing something weird to his boots—sort of using an Allen key on them like they were flat pack furniture. I glanced down. My boots were gone. My shinpads, too. The levels of excitement in the room trebled.

Instant, deafening fury. Then a snort through the nostril.

The plan, Max. Stick to the plan. Got to play ten league games. Got to. Games first, revenge second.

But fuck. They were my only boots and my only shinpads. They were a gift from my mother when I was about seventeen and still playing regularly. Before she'd started to get sick. Her happiness seeping into me. "Do you really like them?" she'd said, and she'd been so, so happy that she'd picked the right ones.

Someone had installed a massive, industrial pump somewhere in my chest and it was forcing gallons of angry hormones into my brain. I clenched my fists, then with a tremendous effort, unclenched them.

Games first, revenge second.

"Pat," I said, so that the whole room could hear. That was the point of this, wasn't it? I should be humiliated to entertain a room full of pricks? So then let's do it out loud.

He paused with some socks in his hands. "Did you say something, Max?"

"Yes, Pat. Did you see a pair of football boots here?"

"There? No, Max. There was nothing there when I came in."

He looked worried for a second, but then he looked around the room and sort of sagged a bit. "I'll let you get your own kit," he said to no one in particular, and left with a shake of the head.

That was the cue for the captain to walk over to me. He was fully ready to play—I was only in underpants. The fact that he was wearing boots and I wasn't seemed like a huge disadvantage—like he had a sword and shield and I was unarmed.

He held out a piece of A4 paper. A printout. At the top it said *Darlo Player Fines*. "So, Maxy boy. Looks like you'll need to find your boots. Looks like you'll be late for training. That's a fine." Laughter from all corners of the room. He smiled and tapped the paper.

I appraised him. He was a tall guy, strong, not very fast, pretty good in the air. Slightly above average technical skills for his position at this level. "Where are my boots?" I said, and that triggered another bout of sniggering.

"The fuck should I know?" he said. "They're *your* boots." More laughter. Some guys slapped each other's hands they were enjoying the show so much.

I looked through his eyeballs right into his tiny little soul. I took the paper in both hands and tore it in two. Still watching his appalled face, I squashed one half of the paper into a ball, then repeated it for the other half. Then I tucked them into my underpants and grabbed my newly-swollen junk. Merriment had turned to horror. There was no sniggering now. The guy's face briefly contorted, and that triggered a massive reaction in my own body. If he'd so much as twitched I would have gone for him. He saw that in me.

"Fucking nutjob," he said, backing away.

Once he'd gone, I stepped around the U-shaped space staring at my so-called teammates. When I got to Chumpy, he wouldn't meet my eye, so I got closer until he looked at me. That lasted less than half a second. "Shower," he mumbled.

I stood tall and went into the showers. At the very back, in the darkest corner, two of my very, very few possessions in this world were soaked. Maybe with water, maybe not. I thought about my poor mum. Her happy smile. One of the connections between us cut forever. The boots lying on their sides like they'd been mugged and left for dead. The laces reaching out for help that never came. The shinpads ruined; no longer able to protect me.

I left them there. I walked the few yards to the place where the dressing room met the showers. Some of the team were looking at me, waiting for my reaction. Hoping I'd say something they could laugh about later. *Did you hear what he said?* They'd snigger. *What a prick!*

So I said nothing. There's no point talking to a dead man, and they were all dead to me.

With no particular urgency, I pulled on my jeans, hoodie, and trainers and left.

17

TOP GEAR

I demanded the minivan keys from a very, very reluctant Pat.

"I'll drive you, lad. Where are you off ter?"

"Please hand over the keys, Pat."

"You're not insured!"

"The keys if you please." He dropped them into my palm. "My boots and shinpads are in the shower. Please leave them there."

"What?" He seemed dismayed, not by the news, but by my request.

"Leave them, Pat. Whoever cleans in there, let them know."

With that, I zipped out to the car park, looked up my destination, and hit the road.

A bell rang as I entered the shop. There was a youth hanging around tidying the shelves. Pretending to work, it looked like.

"Canneelpya?" he said.

I spent a few decades trying to understand what he said, then nodded. "Yes, you can help me. Can you get your manager, please?" It always sounds obnoxious when you ask for the manager, so I did my best to be friendly.

"I'm the manager, like. It's my shop."

"Oh," I said. "You're . . ." I checked my phone, "David Longstaff?"

"Aye! Everyone calls me Longstaff."

He was only a bit older than me, it seemed. Thin and friendly and a sort of blank face. But that was deceptive—he'd built a small business. He had something about him. "Awesome," I said, holding out a hand. "I'm Max. Just started playing for Darlington. Are you a fan?"

"Yeah! Course!" He looked worried. "I've not heard boot any noo playa!"

That's the end of me trying to faithfully recreate the northeast accent, by the way. From now on, I'll leave it to your imagination. Just elongate vowels wherever you want. "Literally just started. Not even started, really. I've had an equipment failure. I need new boots, and shinpads too, ideally. And the best thing is, I don't have any money. I've just moved from Manchester and I don't know when I'll be getting paid. That's why I wanted the manager—to beg for help!"

A lot of looks flashed across his face—doubt, interest, suspicion, calculation. It settled on helpful. "Right. Right. So you want to open a tab, sort of thing?"

"No," I said. "I want to open a tab and close it as soon as possible. I know times are tough. Um . . . why is all your stock squashed into half the space?" His racks had been pushed together so that the gap between aisles was virtually nil in some cases.

"Save on leccy," he said. "Electricity," he added. He looked up at the shop lights—about half were turned off.

"Oh, right. Of course."

"Price trebled a few weeks back. It's murder. Can't even have the open sign lit up. Had to cut the hours on me staff."

"Fuck," I said. Maybe this had been a mistake. "Look, er . . . I just need some boots. Forget the shinpads. Do you have, like, some ex-display models in storage or whatever?"

"What position do you play?" he said, moving over to his rack of boots.

"Right mid."

"So you're fast? Want something light?" He picked up a boot that seemed to be made of tissue paper.

"I get fouled a lot. Those look pretty insubstantial."

"They are, aye. Lot of players like that. Feel the ball better. Improve your touch."

"I wouldn't worry about that," I said, my eyes dancing around the shelves. At first it had seemed like a limited stock, but actually there was a lot of variety. "Shit. I don't even know what I want."

"Anti-clog?"

I looked at him. I had no idea what he was saying, but it seemed stupid to actually let him know that. What sort of professional wouldn't know the basic options? "Just give me the cheapest ones and I'll be back when I've got something in my account."

"Come on, now. Let's get you the right pair. If it's worth doing, it's worth doing right."

"The thing is, I haven't bought a pair in . . . years. I've been using the same ones since I was . . ." My throat briefly clogged up.

"Come on," he said. "I'll talk you through it."

So we spent five minutes going through the pros and cons of the various options, then found a boot that had a good balance of what I needed.

"Okay," I said, with my foot in one boot. "This feels good. Let's do this one."

"That's the most expensive pair," he laughed.

"Shit."

"What about those shinpads?"

"They can wait."

"In for a penny, in for a pound. Come on." He helped me choose a pair with ankle protection, but mentioned some kind of super-shinpad that he didn't carry in stock. "I'll order some for you when you get your money coming in. Now, then. I'll just take some details from you, if you don't mind. To set up the tab, like. What's your address?"

There followed a slightly ludicrous couple of minutes where I offered him my address in Manchester (which didn't impress him) or the digs (where I wouldn't be staying for long), which led to him apologising but having to ask for some proof that I was actually a Darlington player.

Which led to a total brain freeze. It's not like the club had issued me a special passport valid in County Durham. I wasn't on the club's website, and the guy who ran the club's Twitter account didn't know I existed. I didn't have my contract with me and I hadn't taken a photo of it—why would I? There were no photos or videos of me in a Darlington shirt.

I was standing there, staring up at one of the fluorescent ceiling lights, trying to come up with a clever way to prove I was who I said I was. Finally, I laughed and said, "Come outside and I'll take a good corner."

"That wouldn't prove you were a Darlo player," he said. "Just the opposite. We're shit at corners."

Just then, a postman came in. What kind of place had postmen delivering mail to the counter of a shop? Had I gone through a portal to 1955? "Morning, Longstaff. Who've you got from Darlo in here?"

Longstaff glanced at me, then turned back to his mate. "What do you mean?"

"Club van's parked on your spot."

I clicked my fingers. "Club van!" I said. I went and shook the postman's hand. He'd gotten me out of a jam. "Max Best," I said. "I'm picking up some gear. Come to the match on Saturday. I'll score a goal in your honour."

"Oh!" he said, and actually got a bit flustered.

"So," I said when I was back at the till. "That's sorted. I'll tell you what, though. I'll score you a goal, too, if you let me take a couple of those black hoodies. I've been wearing this one since I got here."

"When was that?"

"Feels like a lifetime," I said.

I strode out onto the training area and headed to pitch two. The first team squad were doing some running drills. I grabbed as many balls as I could carry (four) and dribbled another one over to the empty pitch one. I scattered them on the ground about thirty-five yards from goal. Just far out enough that most goalies wouldn't expect me to shoot.

To start with, I tried hitting the ball in a conventional way. My default method was pretty textbook, really. Very loose and natural. I didn't have any footage of me taking a free kick, but I imagined I looked something like David Beckham. Relax your posture, approach the ball, weight on the off foot, fast follow-through, lots of side spin, big curve, big dip. Hit the near post or the far post with the same action. Very difficult for a goalkeeper to read your intentions. Nice.

I aimed for the intersection of the crossbar and post and had pretty good accuracy.

While I gathered the balls, I thought about what else I wanted to try.

Some different techniques. More power. Some free-kick takers placed the ball on the grass very carefully so that the air nozzle was facing them, then they struck the ball on that exact spot. I'm not sure Ronaldo was the first, but he made it famous. The idea was that the ball would travel in a very weird and unpredictable manner. At first it moved exactly like a cannonball shot, but sometimes it would veer wildly just as a goalie was closing in on it. Sometimes the ball would dip at the last second in a way that defied physics. Normally when Ronaldo tried it, the ball ended up high in the stands, but still, when it worked, it was spectacular. Perfect for someone who needed to get reputation, fast.

I tried it a few times with no luck, but after the fifth try, I got a massive pang of headache.

Great! Exciting! Something had changed.

I retrieved the balls and was about to do another wave of shots when one of the coaches came over to me. "Max. What are you doing?"

"Training," I said.

"Training's over here," he said, pointing to pitch two.

"Huh," I said, "Must have missed that. Where are the goalies?"

That question interrupted his subroutine. "Uh, they're inside. In the gym doing goalkeeper things."

"Thanks," I said, and started that way. With a quick click of my fingers, I remembered my Longstaff Sports carrier bag and jogged to get it. All my possessions were in it.

"Leave that in the dressing room!" called the coach. He was actually annoyed by my stupidity, which meant he wasn't in on the plot. Or he was a good actor. Or he wanted me to leave more stuff in there to be destroyed. No point in taking a chance. I'd engage with the coaches if they were teaching me about football or telling me about the logistics of where I needed to be at a certain time. For everything else, they would get the same treatment as the first team.

I went inside and found the goalkeepers. The trialist had vanished—some trial—so there were the three I'd humiliated a few days before, plus the goalkeeping coach. I watched them for thirty seconds and what they were doing was as incomprehensible to me as Champion Manager. Something with elastic leashes, weights, and rhythmic dancing.

"Max," said Taff. He was the goalkeeping coach. I wasn't sure if I should treat him as part of the general coaching staff—the goalies seemed to always be off to the side doing their own thing. And now that everyone had turned to stare at me, I wasn't sure how welcome I was. These guys had more to dislike about me than the first team. Well, only one way to find out.

I pushed forward and shook hands with everyone, starting with the coach. "Taff! Smokes. Paul. Sky. You're all looking well. Thanks for your time last Friday. Highlight of my year, that."

"Was it now?" asked Taff. He checked his watch. "Training finished?"

"Not for me. I asked for three nutjobs to help me with a few drills I want to try and they sent me in here."

"Nutjobs?"

"I said, boss, I need to leather a football so hard at someone it could make their eyes pop out. And I want to do strange, weird experiments that push the art of the free kick to dizzying new heights. And I want to—"

"All right," said Taff. "You want to take more shots on us?"

Us. That was interesting. I hadn't taken a shot on him but he was so much a part of the group it came out in his language. "Five free kicks each. Five corners each. Five pens each. Then I want to brainstorm some scenarios."

"Brainstorm?" said Smokes. He was the first team goalie. Maybe the best in the division, but I hadn't seen every team. His rival, Paul, was much younger and had a much higher PA, but I guessed it would be a year or two before he overtook Smokes. Sky was the thirty-seven-year-old backup goalie. He had a good PA, but his peak was obviously far in his past. His profile said he hadn't played a single game last season. Was his an easy life? Train in the morning, have loads of free time, most of the benefits of being a footballer with none of the pressure of actually playing? Or was it a personal hellscape?

"Look," I said, "I have no experience. I don't know what I'm doing. I've got some ideas. I want to test them on you."

"Like what?" said Taff.

"Like . . . example. I'm running down the wing. I get to the edge of the penalty box. There's a striker running along with me. At what point do I square the ball to maximise his chance of scoring?"

"Early," said Paul.

"As late as possible," said Sky.

"Different every time," said Smokes.

"Whoa whoa whoa!" I said. "This is what I'm talking about. Everyone's got an opinion. I've got an opinion. But let's go test it."

"Why are you asking *us*?" said Taff.

I frowned at him. Was he joking? "My job is to terrify the other team. Be as dangerous as possible. Who knows danger better than a goalie? Same with penalties. Teach me where you don't want me to hit it. Corners. What do you hate?"

This animated the crew like nothing else I could have said. I'd unleashed a torrent of thoughts, theories, ideas. Taff held up his hands to shut it all down. "I've been coaching a long time," he said. "No one's ever asked the goalies to coach the forwards before."

"Well, that's dumb." I glanced up at a big digital clock on the wall. "Lads, I might play tomorrow night and I'm clueless. Are you going to help me or what?"

Taff brought out a huge bag of balls. Smokes and Sky carried a two-headed wire man—I mean, mannequin—while Paul and I lugged a three-headed one.

Once the goalies had positioned the defences, I started by whipping my basic Beckham free kicks at them. They fucking hated it.

"Okay," I said. "I think that's working pretty well. Can I try something I've been working on?"

I began firing Ronaldo cannonballs at them. At first, they squirted off my foot at strange, impossible angles. But then it clicked. My arms were all wrong. I had to commit to the style. From that moment, the gentle teasing that accompanied my first attempts was replaced by genuine terror.

"Guys," I said, waving everyone towards me. "Let me tell you if this sounds right to you. If I'm close to the goal I should do the Beckham technique. It's got more predictable whip and as long as I've got an angle on either post, the goalie's in trouble. Does that sound right?" Nods. Assent. "If I'm farther out, I'll do the Ronaldo one. It seems to mess with your head, that one."

"Say that again," said Smokes, and the others laughed. This was fun! This was collaboration! This was teamwork!

"Taff. Any thoughts?" I said.

He shook his head. He'd been subdued ever since I'd got to grips with the Ronaldo method. "Honestly, I'm shocked by how many the lads saved. You're like a ball launcher. But more accurate." He moved between Smokes and Paul, put his arms around them, and added, "I'm proud of 'em. What do you think, Sky? We doing a good job?"

"Looks like," he beamed.

"Oh," I said. "So what you're saying is I can stop going easy on them?"

Big laughs all round.

I clapped my hands together. "Quick penalty contest?"

Taff shook his head. "You won't be taking the pens tomorrow, Max. Postpone that." He checked his watch. "Lunch soon. One more quickie, as the bishop said to the bishop."

"Okay," I said, scratching the back of my neck. "Okay. I'll go right wing." I pointed. "One goalie. Obvs. Start on your line or thereabouts. The rest of us in a row. So from left to right, one striker running towards the far post. One defender trying to block the pass. Then me over here on the right." I scratched my neck again. "What I want to know is, when I'm running to the by-line, can I sort of trigger the goalie to try to intercept the pass I'm about to play? Because he won't get it, and then my dude has an open goal." Despite my obvious brilliance, there was still some scepticism. I guessed they were the types who learned by doing. "You'll see what I mean. Let's do it once then discuss it."

I took my place on the right and immediately saw a flaw in the plan. These were goalkeepers. They were slow. Paul was no sloth, but still. He was a goalie. If God wanted him to run fast, he wouldn't have made his legs so spindly. "Paul, Sky, push forward about ten yards."

"Ten?" said Sky, disbelieving.

"Fifteen if you want. Taff, got a whistle?"

He paused, then when I looked away from the ball to see what he was doing, he peeped. Trying to give his lads an advantage. It made no difference—I hit top gear in no time. Sky's 10-yard head start evaporated in about two seconds and I was once more feeling the joy of air resistance trying and failing to slow me down. I glanced to check where Paul was—some distance behind, but I could work with that. I cut towards Smokes's goal so that he'd be forced to come towards me. He twitched and I pulled the ball back, diagonally, right into Paul's path. Smokes reacted brilliantly, scampered across goal, and easily saved Paul's feeble shot.

I summoned the group. "Great demo. Perfect. Thanks. So you see what I'm saying? I know there's a point where Smokes will have to come and close me down. When he does, I can pass to Paul with no chance of recovery. Open goal. Yeah?"

"But if you wait too long," said Paul, "Smokes will be able to dive and intercept the pass."

"Exactly," I said. "It's all about timing. Normally, I'd have learned that by having a hundred such situations in matches at the academy and for the age groups. But I don't. So you guys need to teach me."

"I get what you're saying now, Max," said Taff. "Get back in position and I'll shout when I think's right. But you have to give yourself the option to shoot."

"Shoot?"

"If you're going to shoot, he'll come to narrow the angle. That's primal instinct for goalies. Look like you're going to pull the trigger, that'll trigger him. One thing, though."

"Yeah?"

"Just for today, can you slow yourself down? Go as fast as Sky."

"As fast as Sky?" I said. "I haven't run that slow since the last mile of the Great Northern Run. When I was in fancy dress. Wearing a snorkel and flippers." It must have been the last word that made Sky flip me the bird. In return, I gave him a breezy Maxy two-thumbs.

Peep!

I went again, this time with my brakes on. I kept slightly ahead of Sky, and it felt really sarcastic. But within seconds I was moving into the penalty box from the right-hand side. I glanced at Paul and faked a shot that Smokes knew was a fake. Still, he twitched, and his balance shifted towards me. A shout came from Taff. Instead of passing, I turned perpendicular to the goal line and gave my entire attention to a possible shot. I could sweep it low to the goalie's left, or smash it high towards the near post. Either way, I liked my odds. I went through the motion of smashing the ball, and Smokes jiggled to my right to close the angle.

I backheeled the ball square—in front of Sky, perfectly into the path of Paul. This time his feeble shot dribbled in. Open net.

The group meandered towards me. Sky had his hands behind his head. He was thirty-seven. Those two little sprints had exhausted him. *Never get old, Max!*

Taff shook his head. "I think your instinct for the timing is better than mine, Max. Just go with your gut, I'd say."

"Hmm. Well, look. If you ever see me make a bad decision or take a wrong choice or whatever. Something I can obviously, easily improve on . . . will you tell me?"

"Sure," said Taff. "Can do. Can do. Now, that was a fun little session, if you ask me. Lads, you like that?" They did. "Satisfied, Max?"

"It's not *completely* what I was looking for," I said, which sounds a lot more dickish now than when I said it. They all knew what I meant. "But yeah. I think that was helpful. You've basically got to make the goalie commit. I've noticed that when you guys decide to do something, no matter how daft, you go at it a hundred percent."

"It's the only way to be a goalie," said Taff.

"No matter how dumb," I said. "No matter how moronic. No matter how ill-advised."

"Right," said Taff. "Max can get all the balls himself, I reckon."

"Noo!" I said, with a chuckle. "I deserve that. But seriously, you get your lunch. I'll bring all the stuff back."

I walked off to the furthest ball, and when I turned around, two of the lads were carrying a mannequin away, and the other two were collecting balls. Whoa. It did something to me. I can't explain it. Just sort of broke through the dam I'd constructed between me and this squad. I turned away in case I started blubbing, but I swallowed the emotion. Let the feeling make my heart even harder to some, while still being the full me for others. It wasn't Max versus the universe. I had allies. Or at least, some teammates I wouldn't mind sitting next to on a long coach ride.

I fucking zoomed towards the next nearest ball, chipped it towards the bag, and slalomed to the next one. If there was a world record for collecting balls after a training session, I broke it. Smashed it. Then I sprinted to catch up to Taff, and took the bag out of his hand. Then I groaned, put the bag down, raced off to collect my plastic carrier bag, and rejoined him.

"Didn't they give you a hook?" he said, eyeing my bag.

"Never mind that," I said. "I've got questions, if you don't mind me picking your brain."

"Picking my brain?" he said, with a lopsided grin. A bit nervous, I think. "Not many people are interested in the contents of my brain, lad."

"Course they are. Listen. First question. Why do the goalies train separately? No, wait. First question. Should goalies punch crosses or try to catch them? No, hold up. What's more important—handling or jumping? Do keepers need stamina? Take two goalies. One's worth a million pounds. Another one's exactly the same, but he's as fast as me. How much is *he* worth?"

Taff laughed and slapped me on the back. "Not sure what's worse—being on the end of your free kicks or being on the end of your questions." He laughed again. "Let's put this gear away. We'll show you where. Then I'll answer a few. Are you staying for lunch?"

It seemed like an invitation to eat with him. "Absolutely."

"And by the way," he said. "I can carry a wee sack of balls."

"I know," I said. "But today, you don't have to."

18

WHITBY TOWN

I had a hearty lunch in the staff canteen—apparently it was the done thing to load up on carbs the day before a match. The goalies were great company but were puzzled that I had chosen not to take a shower after the session. They kept ribbing me about it until I announced that while I didn't mind the joke, we were wasting valuable time where they could be teaching me about football.

After lunch, I walked back to the digs, took a shower, and drove back to the training centre.

Once there, I went into the Darlington FC office. There were four little tables with computers and phones, but only one was occupied. The occupant was Darlington's equivalent of Inga (from Chester, you remember). She was called Margot and was absolutely ancient. At least fifty. She had a lively look in her eye, like she'd seen it all before but didn't mind seeing it again. One thing she hadn't seen before was a player asking detailed questions about the admin side of the club. I asked her to talk me through her job and show me some bits of work she did. The software used for most club business was ancient. She said it was an ICMS—an integrated customer management system.

"Integrated with what?" I wondered aloud as I used the keyboard to explore the MS-DOS-looking screens. "Zork? Pac-Man? The moon landing?"

She laughed and assured me that while it didn't have bells and whistles, the software was rock solid. She showed me a couple of neat features it had. I was entranced.

My being there was absolutely insane to Margot, but after half an hour she started to understand that I really was there to learn and it wasn't some prank. I finally completely won her over by offering to make tea for us both. She opened a drawer and let me have two of her milk chocolate Hobnobs. What a woman!

The reason Margot was employed full-time was that the football club and rugby club shared her. They also shared the stadium, an obvious fact that had somehow passed me by. She warned me that the pitch would be cut up sometimes, but that generally the ground staff were excellent. "Very well-respected in their field," she said, which seemed to be the setup to some joke, but she never delivered the punchline.

While there I called the FA and got them to link my player profile to my agent application. Easy! Done! I was a licensed agent. Time to smash a bottle of bubbly on the hull of the good ship Max.

I called Mike Dean from the office phone and put on a Darlington accent. Margot tried to look disapproving, but had to laugh at how inept I was.

"Is that Mike Deeeyun?" I said. "I'm calling on bee-alf of the Footy Socia-shun."

Big pause. "Max?"

"I can't believe you saw through that accent!" I said. Margot scoffed and turned to her work. I explained that I had my license and he could discuss a starting date with Raffi.

When our business was concluded, MD said, "So, how are you doing?"

With the tea and the Hobnobs it was easy to pretend. "Doing great. All shipshape and Bristol fashion. This week's been a banger. Making my home debut for Darlington on Saturday. If you want to come and watch, my best friend Margot will get you a ticket. Won't you, Margot?" She extended her hands—who is it? "Managing director of Chester." Thumbs-up. "Yeah. Call this number if you want to come. I've got to go. Very busy." I moved the phone back to its cradle. As I did, I heard some frantic questions.

"Max, wait. You're at Darlington? Debut? Player or manager? What's going on? Max!"

I sat around a while longer, trying to learn what went on inside a sixth-tier football club. It wasn't a hive of activity.

"Most of what I'm doing is for the rugby club, Max. The football side is done on match days, mostly," she said. "Ticket sales, media enquiries, vendors, police liaison. It's all hands on deck on a match day. You win that cup match on Saturday, get us through a few rounds. Once people smell a trip to Wembley, things will heat up in here, I can tell you."

I'd be long gone before the FA Trophy final, but she didn't need to know that. "This was interesting, Margot. Thank you very much. I might pop by again if that's all right. By the way, what did you think of Henri Lyons?"

"He was very handsome," she said, as though he'd died.

"And?"

She took her hands away from her keyboard and her head tilted forward. "Me, now, I liked him. He was always very polite, very friendly. A perfect gentleman, really. And we were very lucky to get him, mind. Player of his quality down here. People forget that. A lot of people turned after the newspaper article, but not me. It's a great shame. It's best he's gone so's we can all move on. But it's a great shame, it is. But that's football, isn't it? It's not rational and never will be."

"Do you watch the games, Margot?"

"All the home games, yes. I sit up on the balcony. Have you seen it?"

"Balcony? No."

"You know The Clubhouse? It's got a balcony on the right-hand side. You'll see it next time you're on the pitch. It's like at cricket matches where the batters who aren't batting sit and watch from up high and wait their turn. Best view in the house. The directors and VIP guests hang around inside having a few drinks. It's the closest we have to a proper executive box. And they let me in, too. Of course, it's mostly so they can get their expenses processed faster! Still a nice perk, though."

"If the balcony is where I think it is," I mused, "you'll have an incredible view of me scoring direct from a corner. I'll give you a cheeky wink just before I do it."

She rolled her eyes. "I think I'll get back to work now, Mr. Best."

I didn't know what else to do—most of the players seemed to have left and the place was getting a bit like the Marie Celeste. I didn't have walking-around money, so I went back to the digs to chill out. The PS4 had *Mortal Kombat* on it, so I worked out some of my stress by punching people to death. I genuinely think it helped calm me down for the rest of the day. Stopped me doing something I might regret.

When the scholarship kids turned up, they went and slumped right in front of the PlayStation. "Whoa whoa whoa," I said, running to block their view of the TV. "Come over here a minute, maties."

With extreme reluctance, they stomped over to the kitchen table that the housekeeper had cleaned while everyone was out. I sat at the head of the table and made them sit side by side. "I wanted to watch you train today but you weren't around. What's that all about?"

"We go to the college and study and train there."

"Oh. You'll have to tell me the times so I can scout you. Right. Check this out." I turned my laptop around and showed them what was on my browser. It was lots of YouTube tabs. "We're playing Whitby Town tomorrow night. If you don't mind helping me out for ten minutes, I'd like to watch some of these clips together and see if we can spot any weaknesses or anything. See what we can see about their left back in particular."

"Why scout," said Bark.

"Why scout?" I said. "Because I'm a professional. Because I want to play well."

"No, Max," he said. "Wyscout. W-Y-scout. It's a scouting tool. You get proper clips, not this shaky iPhone stuff." He pulled my laptop towards him, opened a new tab, and showed me the website.

"What!" I said, looking at some of the linked pages. "Agents, transfer zone, coaches, scouts. Oh! I saw Mike Dean using this once." It was instantly clear that I needed access to this, so I clicked on the pricing. It was three hundred pounds a year for the basic plan, which *seemed* reasonable. But it only came with seventy minutes a month of videos. Me being me, I'd burn through that in half an hour. "Bark! You little wizard!" I gave him a little hug that he pretended to resist. I looked at the website again. "You know what? I'll check this out later. Let's focus on what I've prepared. Are you up for it?"

Benzo frowned. "Why you gonna listen to us?"

"I'll take ideas from anyone."

"Let's wait for the other two, then."

"I'll take ideas from anyone in this room," I said. The lads looked at each other. "Do you want to help me rip this left back a new one, yes or no?"

They laughed. "Aight, Max. Let's do it."

"Okay, clip one."

They had an absolute blast. It was a bit like schoolwork, but about football and to help a mate. Some of the clips led to zero analysis but lots of banter. One poor piece of play led to Bark accusing Benzo of doing the exact same thing in training and Benzo trying to defend himself in extremely feeble fashion. He was obviously guilty as hell.

There weren't a lot of recent clips of Whitby, but the kids didn't leave the table when we'd exhausted the ones I'd found. They began tapping away on their phones, joining Whitby Facebook groups and looking for fan rants on TikTok. They got distracted a lot, but every now and then they'd find a data point. "Yeah, this guy's complaining they always play four-four-two." "This one says the left-sided CB is a red-card magnet." "They're pretty dirty."

When I thought things were winding down, Bark asked for my laptop. He went through the clips I'd found again.

"Max," he said, after a while.

"Sup?"

"Your left back here," he said, quiet, serious. "I think he likes to tuck in."

"Show me."

He showed me one clip, then another. Somehow he'd made the replay very slow. He touched my screen, which normally winds me up. Not this time. "See here? He's very narrow." Bark switched to another tab. "Here again."

The guy most likely to be my direct opponent—if I played—was standing slightly ahead of his centre backs. From what I'd learned, that was pretty optimal in relation to the offside trap. But most fullbacks left a space between themselves and the nearest centre back. This guy, though, seemed to like to get close to them.

"It's only two little moments," said Bark. I think he gave me a worried look, but I can't be sure because I was locked on to the tiny, pixelated man on my screen. *Why you so far across, bro?*

"Interesting," I said. "What would you do against this guy?"

"Stay wide," said Bark.

"Why?"

"Make him do what he doesn't want to do," he said.

I closed my eyes. Imagined wandering around the pitch, dragging the guy all over Whitby. I grinned, viciously. I opened my eyes. "It's too good to be true. No one would give me that much space. I'll whizz past him once and force him to stay back. Probably drag the midfielder back, too. Are you guys going to the match?"

"No. No away trips on school nights."

"Shame. Well, thanks for your help. It was fun."

The front door opened. Chumpy and Glynn came in, dumped their bags against the nearest wall, and said hi to the kids. They walked over to the dining table and Chumpy said, "Hi, Max."

My reply was a death stare for the ages. It was so intense that he did a sort of Mr. Bean-retracing-his-steps walk, picked up his bag, and escaped to his bedroom. Glynn copied him.

"What the fuck?" said Bark.

"What happened?" said Benzo.

"They chose war," I said. I closed my laptop and gave them each a friendly pat on the shoulder. "If you're still allowed to talk to me on Friday, let's do this again, yeah? We're playing . . ." I'd forgotten who we were playing. My big debut!

"Alfreton," said Bark.

"Oh, right," I said. "I've seen them. They play four-five-one. Defensive as fuck. Aim their set pieces central and they leave this slow player as the last man at corners. Osgood, his name is. I will fucking tear them a new one if they try that against me. So I suppose I won't need your help for that one."

"Can we do it anyway?" said Benzo. He seemed to have enjoyed the little scouting session.

"Yeah! They might have changed their default formation. I might have missed something. If I remember, I was off my head on painkillers for a lot of that time. If you want, we can have dinner on Friday and talk about it?" Just then, Chumpy walked past to get to the kettle. So he heard my next question. "So tomorrow night there's this match. What about Wednesday and Thursday? I want to go watch some footy. Where's the best place?"

"Middleton Rangers," said Chumpy, and the kids laughed.

I glared at the twat, then said to Bark, "Is that a real thing?"

He nodded, so I typed it into a search engine and scanned the Middleton Rangers website. "'*Inclusive football in Darlington for all ages and abilities.*' Absolutely fucking perfect." There was a team photo. "Look at this guy! He's a goalie with a metal hand or something. He looks fucking badass!"

"I think it's just black gloves, Max," said Benzo, leaning over.

"One way to find out. I'll give you twenty quid if the tall guy in the middle isn't a striker. And this guy here, he looks like he can only achieve an erection if he's had a yellow card in the last forty-eight hours. Look at his eyes! I love this. I'm excited. When do they play? Adult men, Wednesdays at seven. The airport? There's an airport here? I thought it was all shipyards over here."

"You're thinking of Sunderland. This is Teesside Airport, Max. It's not that far. But Middleton, Max, they're, you know . . ."

"What?"

"Disabled and that."

I scoffed. "It's still football, isn't it? You think I'd rather go clubbing and meet women and bring them back *here*? Dream on, mate. Now that's Wednesday sorted, what else have we got?" I clicked around. "Most of the age groups play on Wednesday, too. Ah! Pan-disability all ages, Thursday. Sponsored by a pie shop. This just gets better and better. Fuck. I want a pie now."

"Are you seriously going to watch disabled football on your nights off?"

"Yep. Want to come?"

They didn't.

Tuesday morning I drove to Eastbourne early and parked right in front of reception. If anyone wanted to vandalise my car, the receptionist would see it. I'd stowed my laptop and other valuables in the safest place I could think of—the landlady's house. She hadn't been very pleased to see me at that time of day, but I'd turned on the charm and she'd melted.

So I got changed, grabbed five balls from storage, and went out onto pitch two.

I did some dribbles as a light warm-up, then did a few Beckhams and then a few cannonballs. The latter was extremely addictive. The feeling as the ball left my foot was like nothing else. Imagine you could cast a fireball, punch through bricks, or bend bullets around corners—it was like that. Boom! The raw power of the shot, then the vicious, evil dip. Even though I was the one doing it, I felt the shock and awe every time. I could only guess what it looked like from the outside.

I had to force myself not to endlessly repeat the skill. This wasn't something to be practiced and refined. This was something best left raw. Untamed.

So I mixed it up by doing some slow dribbles, some little skills, some stretches. Eventually, the first team appeared. I got some dirty looks, a bit of evil eye. There was sniggering. The captain puffed out his chest when he saw me looking. Puffed himself up like a scared cat. Little groups of players formed. Groups of three or four. Chatting away. Helping each other stretch. They left me on the outside. Turned their backs to me until the session started.

Cutter got us doing shape work. That involved a lot of highly tedious standing and moving in the formation we'd use in the game. It was very much like a gun crew going through the motions of loading and firing a cannon, but without the gunpowder and certainly without the ammunition.

I wasn't in the first eleven for this one, so I mostly stood on the sideline and tried to absorb what Cutter wanted. But every now and then he'd take Webby out and put me in the right mid slot.

What Cutter wanted was for us to be very compact when we didn't have the ball. If Whitby attacked down our right, where I'd be playing, the entire team would squash over to that side.

If the ball went to the other side, I was supposed to race across into the middle of the pitch. Turn one small rectangle into a minefield.

Cutter used the verb *shuffle* a lot. Ditto *slide*. "Shuffle! Right right right! Okay, they've switched it! Slide back. Slide back!"

Then if our imaginary opponents got forward, we'd also squash *vertically*—the verbs were *sink* and *lock down*. The strikers had to sink—come back to help the midfield. The defence had to stick to a zone equivalent to a second six-yard box. The idea was to make sure there were always two or three defenders just in front of the goalkeeper. That was, apparently, where most goals were scored from. The "position of maximum opportunity," Cutter called it. It made sense that most goals were scored from such close distance. And it made sense to reinforce the message that there always needed to be defenders there.

But it was all very negative. Don't make *this* mistake. Don't be out of shape in *this* situation. Don't let them do *this*. Be aware when they do *that*.

The entire session was without gunpowder. We didn't practice attacks. We didn't talk about being creative. We talked about running, about doing the "hard yards" (meaning the boring work of shuffling, sliding, squashing, and sinking), and about being compact. Did I mention the word *compact* yet? I heard it at least three million times that morning, and if you think that's an exaggeration, you're right.

Still, it was a session with the team. I didn't speak to anyone, but I was there. I was in it.

Tiny, tiny, progress.

"Class dismissed," said Cutter. The first team started to disperse. I wandered over to him.

"Dave," I said, because although there were loads of people around, the conversation was just the two of us. "Are we all driving to Whitby separately?"

"No, Max. Meet back here at three. We'll have a last chat about the game and then get on the coach together. Leave at four, get there at half six, game's at half seven. Good?" I nodded. "Max," he said. "About yesterday. First day can be hard, I know that. But you can't wander off and do what you want. We run a tight ship here." *Tight ship*, I thought. I'd watched James Yalley's favourite film, *Master and Commander*. A *tight ship* meant public flogging, endless back-breaking labour, and above all, the centralisation of decision-making to a single point.

"I suppose it's good my contract is so flexible, then," I said.

"What do you mean?"

"I mean if I can't fit in, you can easily get rid of me."

I kept my face neutral, bordering on pleasant, but Cutter heard the opposite of what I'd actually said. He'd heard me say that if *I* didn't like it here, *I* could leave.

"Max," he said, but one of his lieutenants came with some question. I wandered off. I had some time to kill.

The coach ride to Whitby was very tedious. I should have been excited to play a real match, but it seemed like I would only get on the pitch for five or ten minutes (with a two-hour drive before and after).

Since this was a friendly, I wasn't being paid full whack. Because of employment laws I was at least getting minimum wage. That meant I had no incentive to score and assist, except to make sure I got in the team for Saturday.

And crazily, I hadn't done any ball work with my teammates. Not a single pass or a single conversation about what was expected from me from a creative point of view. It wasn't completely unheard of—a lot of new signings got thrown straight into a team.

But my lack of verve was also a function of the fact that most of my teammates were pricks and I not only hated being in an enclosed space with them, but also hated the idea of being on a pitch with them. In public, I'd have to pretend to like them.

Huh.

I looked out of the window where there was a low, early moon.

I'd have to pretend to like them.

Or would I?

We got to Whitby—some kind of fishing village—went into the away dressing room, started getting ready. Warm up on the pitch, back to the dressing room, blast some music, sweary pre-match hype session, and back onto the pitch to line up and shake hands with the opponents.

The match kicked off on time and on a pitch that was just turning from decent to muddy. There were about four hundred people in the stadium, which seemed like a decent turnout. Darlington was a pretty big draw. The stadium was tiny, of course, but looked more like a football venue than Darlington's. There were terraces in the middle of the pitch and not much at the corners or behind the goals. The sea felt very close and the air was salty.

My role was to sit patiently on the bench and wait my turn. Naturally, I picked up some XP and checked out the tactics of both teams. Whitby played a basic 4-4-2, of course. Cutter modified our 4-4-2 so that the fullbacks were pushing into midfield and one striker was "sinking" so that he was basically a CAM. It rang a bell, and I realised that this was the exact same tweak he'd used against Chester, the first time I'd laid eyes on Henri Lyons.

I shook my head. Although it was innovative, it remained a throwback way of playing. How had I got the impression Cutter was modern?

He'd charmed me, found that I liked when he talked about modern ideas, and played up the side of his personality that resonated with me. But barely a millimetre under the surface he was just as much of a dinosaur as Ian Evans. Incredible. I'd fallen for it hook, line, and sinker.

I took in a deep breath and let it out. I'd told myself I'd be bored to death playing for a defensive team, yet somehow I'd ended up in one. While I'd learned a lot and was learning quickly, I was still very callow. No point crying over spilt milk, but I'd have to be a lot more careful in future. A lot more switched on.

The coaches asked me to warm up a few times, but there was no chance of me getting on in the first half, so I didn't put much effort in. Halftime came and went. The halftime team talk was big on shape and workrate and winning battles, and light on tactics, flair, and creativity. I would have sold my soul to have Mr. Yalley pop in and talk about taps.

But this complaining borders on unfair. At halftime, Darlington were winning 2–0, and scored another soon after the break. Cutter's methods *worked*. In fact, I'd go so far as to say that superficially, our tactical ideas weren't so different. His modified 4-4-2 was not a million miles from the 2-6-2 I'd proposed to Ian Evans. If my ideas were sometimes clever, then credit where it's due—Cutter's were clever too. And extremely pragmatic.

I stewed at the back of the dugout, with no one on the seat next to me, for seventy minutes. But then he signalled it was my time to get on the pitch and my heart finally started beating. I noticed the floodlights and heard the fans. My match was about to start. My *career* was about to start.

I'd get twenty minutes to run around in the red-and-white kit. It was a blank shirt; there was no name or number on the back, and the stadium announcer actually said, "Sorry, I don't know who this is," when I walked onto the pitch. The Whitby fans soon began chanting "Who are ya? Who are ya?"

Which was pretty funny. I blew them a kiss.

Whitby were wearing an unusual blue kit with three stripes—black, red, and white. It reminded me of a team in Italy. That was the last interesting thing about them. I certainly had nothing to fear from their left back.

While I was strolling around, getting my bearings, feeling the pace of the game from the inside, the ball came to me. It was at shoulder height and wasn't coming very fast. So I got into position to control it on my chest. The plan was to let it drop and play a simple pass into the midfield.

Duff!

I was rolling around on the turf, arching my back, holding the base of my spine with both hands. It was a dull pain. No doubt I'd have a huge bruise there. I suppose I should be grateful I wasn't paralysed.

While the match went on around me—not even a free kick!—I tried to work out what had happened. I checked the match commentary and sure enough the answer was right there. My opposing left back was a nobody called Andrews.

It's a high, looping pass hit out towards the right.

Best is there, ready to collect.

He controls the ball beautifully.

But he's fouled!

Andrews came through the back of him, knee-first.

The referee lets the play go on.

Andrews is lucky not to be booked.

I stayed on the ground for a while. At the next stop in play, the referee finally blew his whistle to allow a physio to come and check me out. He gave me some magic spray and basically confirmed that I was not going to be in a wheelchair for the rest of my life.

Up on my feet, I bent with my hands on my knees and gradually eased myself into a fully upright position. I stared at Andrews. Obviously, my first impulse was to rip out his spine and use it as a whip against the rest of his team. My second impulse was to wonder what was wrong with my first impulse.

I began to potter around again. We had the majority of possession, but the ball wasn't coming over to the right. The other guys didn't want to pass to me. They hadn't in my trial, either, but that felt totally different. That had been based on sound footballing reasons. This now was pure spite.

Finally, a pass came. Colin, the right back, the guy who played behind me, the guy I was supposed to develop a fruitful working relationship with, chipped the ball towards me.

Alarm bells rang all over my body. I slid to the side—not exactly the way Cutter had intended—and Andrews attacked the spot where I'd just been, knee-first. Fucker trying to cripple me! And best of all, Colin had set me up for it.

I scoffed. So. They'd decided to escalate.

Oh, boy.

I went back to walking around. So far, I hadn't broken into a sprint, and I'd been on the pitch for five minutes. I'd been fouled once—nothing given—and touched the ball once. Some debut.

Not a problem. I only had to do enough to get picked for the cup match on Saturday.

A couple more minutes went by before the next pass came. This time it was the captain, hitting—you guessed it—a slow, chest-high chip that would give Andrews plenty of time to commit actual bodily harm on me.

"Maxy ball!" I screamed and spread myself wide like a Sumo wrestler. I literally heard Andrews's eyes bulge with delight. Nice, big, juicy target! He launched himself towards me. I sank, slid, and shuffled, and after Andrews dashed past like a tricked bull, I threw a foot up to stop the ball going out for a throw-in. Now, finally, I had control, and although I was deep in my own half there was no one in front of me. I was Johnny Winger—free to run.

So I ran.

The Whitby centre backs had an enormous head start on me and turned and ran back towards their goal—but it didn't matter. I caught up to them around the edge of the penalty area, eighteen yards from goal. I surged forward, like I'd practiced with our goalies. I shaped to shoot. Calculated. Bottom left, sixty percent chance to score. Top right, fifty percent but extra points for drama.

Out of the corner of my eye I saw our CA 50 striker making a lung-bursting run. The pass to him was a ninety-nine percent chance of a goal. One hundred percent, really, if the pass wasn't blocked.

I faked the goalie—he almost bought it. He shifted his balance, but then readjusted. I faked again. One of the defenders launched himself between me and the goal—I was out of time—I played the ball slightly backwards, nice and soft, no alarms, no surprises, right into the path of the striker. He had an open goal. Zero percent chance to miss.

He hit it so far over the bar I waited—unironically—to see if I could hear it splash in the sea.

He called out to me, but I turned away and walked back to my zone. Andrews was staring at me like he'd seen a ghost. I thought about warning him about his conduct. Perhaps something with homes and ambulances.

But I decided to remain impassive. I hadn't quite worked out what persona would suit my purposes best, and didn't want to get into mischief before Saturday.

While I watched the match unfold, I started to doubt myself. If the team weren't going to pass to me and if they were going to blast my assists into orbit, I was in trouble.

Whitby had worked out that Darlington weren't trying to attack down my side, so they shuffled over to the other side and made that space compact. I watched with a huge grin as Andrews went weirdly close to the nearest centre back. I had about twenty yards of pitch all to myself.

While the rest of the team shuffled left, I drifted farther right. Oceans of space, and smooth seas ahead. Get the ball and pass to me, you mangy dogs! I'm wide open! I'll murder them!

The ball, of course, never came. And Cutter was turning red from screaming at me to get into position. So I did.

I spent the rest of the match shuffling and sliding. Squashing and sinking and locking things down. My match rating dropped to 5 out of 10. Almost a shipwreck. When I trudged off the pitch, Cutter told me I'd done a good job.

I kept my thoughts to myself. I'd done it to book my passage into the cup team, but I wouldn't do it again. Swabbing the deck with all the other sailors wasn't going to get me noticed. No, come Saturday at 3 p.m., at the first opportunity, I'd climb the mainmast and raise my flag.

And if Cutter didn't like it . . . that's what mutinies are for.

19

JAM TOMORROW

Wednesday, November 16.

I was first onto the training pitch again, getting my day off to a good start by smacking free kicks at goal. Five right foot, collect the balls, have a think. Five left foot, collect, think. It was a good rhythm. I could have taken a whole bag of balls but then I would have only been shooting and not reflecting.

That morning I was reflecting on the curse. I'd been gathering bits of XP here and there, slowly paying down my debt. But where was the monthly perk? Well, the World Cup started in four days; I had to be patient.

Patience. That was my whole life, it seemed. Jam tomorrow, never jam today.

If I looked forward to the day I got my first real job as a manager, I saw that I still had almost the whole road left to travel. But if I turned around, I'd actually come a long way. I had contacts and contracts and was learning every day. Sometimes I was learning what *not* to do, but that was okay. You can't navigate unknown waters and expect to not scrape against the occasional reef.

I kept reminding myself that I only needed to play ten league games for Darlington. *Just suck it up, Max!*

Another thing—It felt like Captain Caveman and his minions had taken their best shot at me. If they pulled the same hospital pass stunt in a cup match in front of three thousand people, someone would notice. Then again, sports fans often took the wrong lessons from what they were watching. It was fifty-fifty if they'd blame me for not controlling the passes. Hmm.

Anyway, I had a bit more spring in my step, so when training started, I wasn't chatty, and I wasn't cheerful, but I wasn't morose either.

And—wonder of wonders—we worked with the ball! A little blob of jam with my breakfast! It was a morning full of the sorts of drills I'd seen the first team doing when I'd come for the first time. Run, pass, run pass shoot. Run, pass, run pass recover. Slalom past poles and sprint to a line faster than someone else. Slalom, sprint, recover, pass. It was easy, and the rest of the guys were forced to pass to me. Sometimes they'd try to show me up by hitting it six inches above ground instead of along the deck, but the curse had given me high technique.

"Max," called Cutter near the end of the sesh. "Want to show us your corners?" The goalies were in the gym again, and it made no sense to practice corners without them. But in the spirit of not being a miserable bastard my whole life, I gave him a Maxy two thumbs. "Which side do you prefer?"

"I'm top from both," I called back.

There was some sniggering.

But get this—over the course of the sesh I'd realised yet another of my countless mistakes. The Darlington first team was far from a unified bloc of cavemen. There were cliques, and there were cliques within cliques. Captain Caveman was the dominant figure, but he wasn't universally liked and wasn't universally respected. As an example of a potential fracture, the reserve centre backs never seemed to be close to him—in the sessions, in the changing rooms, or during meals. A couple of times it had seemed like they wanted to talk to me, but of course I pretended not to notice them. I could go on, but suffice to say that it occurred to me that I was shooting myself in the foot by treating everyone as enemies.

I needed to be more . . . political.

As for the corners, I waited for the guys to set up in the penalty area—four attackers versus five defenders, including Caveman—and sent in a bog-standard Max Best cross. No frills. No optional extras. A stripped-back model. Your basic curving thunderbolt aimed at the area between the six-yard line and the penalty spot. Too far for a goalie to come and punch, but close enough that, with the ball traveling at such velocity, any decent attacking header would result in a high chance of a goal.

Bosh! "My ball!" *Donk! Swish!* Back of the net!

"Fucking hell!" someone shouted.

Caveman had been outjumped and it was his man who'd scored. Still, he turned to give someone else a bollocking.

I tried not to be smug. Blank faced, I rolled another ball onto the little arc by the corner flag.

"Fore!" I shouted, to signal that I was about to take the next one.

I did it again.

I saw the excitement among the coaches. I could practically hear Cutter rubbing his hands with glee, even though he had his arms folded.

Well, I thought. *The old Max Best Special is still on the menu. No real need to keep practicing. Time for some anarchy.* I pottered away from the corner and waved Cutter over. He met me in between the attackers and defenders.

"Boss," I said. "Can I reposition the attackers?"

"Let's hear it."

I pointed to the edge of the penalty box. Eighteen yards from goal. I turned to the attackers. "Guys, start over there."

"And run in?" said one. It was virtually the first thing any of the first team had said to me since the incident.

"No," I said, turning away. "Just stay there."

Cutter shooed the attackers to where I had said, then took a few steps away. The defenders milled around, not sure what to do. There are two ways to defend corners—zonal marking or man-to-man. With no men to mark they spread out covering as many zones as possible.

I bent to rest a ball on the very very edge of the white line. I smoothed the grass in front of the ball so that no stray blade could interfere with my contact. I closed my eyes and savoured the moment. I imagined Caveman looking at the attackers with sweat forming on his top lip—what were they doing over there? What was the plan?

Laughing, I opened my eyes and took a few steps back, allowed my weight to centre, and zipped forward like a triple jumper. My leg hit through the line of the ball and I tweaked my foot at the last second to impart spin.

The ball flew like a wizard's wand, like an architect's charcoal, like an air-defence missile. Over Caveman's despairing leap, under the crossbar, and into the net.

I picked up the two balls that were still near me and followed the path of my shot. When I got a few yards in front of Caveman, I called out to Cutter. "Boss, if you want me to scout some taller centre backs, let me know."

There was sniggering again, but this time people were laughing *with* me. One–nil!

I rolled the balls towards the other corner arc and when I got there, placed one. I got ready to cross. "Guys!" I said, laughing at the attackers. Big smile. Big charisma. "No point standing out there, is there? Get in the box!" I flapped my arms to express good-natured disbelief. From this side, with my right foot, I could only take an out-swinging corner. "It's not like I can score from this side." I'm not sure why I was lying. It felt right to keep the true extent of my two-footedness under wraps for now. Maybe it was because Ian Evans had said I needed to learn a position, and if I was two-footed I'd get moved around filling whatever gaps existed in the team. This way, I might play right-midfield often enough to actually start doing it well.

A good morning, then. On the footballing side, I was now hyper-confident in my free kicks and corners. Even if I was abysmal in open play (the dynamic parts of a match), I was going to be an absolute menace at any set pieces I was allowed to take. And I'd taken the tiniest steps towards integrating into the team.

But the most satisfying part was landing my first little dig on Caveman. The satisfaction of hearing people laugh at him led to me offering myself a side quest.

Quest offered!
Destroy Captain Caveman, the prick.
Quest rewards: 0 XP, 0 gold, 0 reputation, 0 long-term benefit.
You have accepted this quest!
You are a bit of a cretin sometimes lol!

I grabbed a shower at the digs then went back to eat lunch with the goalies. They promised to let me humiliate them at penalties before Saturday. Then I hung out with Margot for a bit. Ten minutes of pestering her with questions. Ten minutes of skimming a very dry book on the history of Darlington Football Club. There wasn't enough action there and I got restless.

I asked where the scholarship kids went to school, so I drove there and wandered around, poking my head into classrooms until I saw them.

They were slouched, bored to death. And that made no sense because their teacher was a stone-cold fox. Short hair, slim, pert, tight pencil skirt. Jesus, she even had sexy secretary glasses. Maybe the kids had gotten used to it, but it was hard to imagine. I knocked and went in. Benzo and Bark sat up straight as though jolted by electricity.

"Hi," I said to the teacher. "I'm Max. I just started at Darlington and I came to check on the lads."

The teacher frowned. I expected her to say, "Well this is most improper. You must leave at once and next time go through the proper channels." Instead she looked me up and down and said, "I'm Miss Fox."

"Miss Fox?" I said, treating the room to a huge, incredulous smile.

"Miss Faulkes," she said, but the corners of her lips were twitching.

Wow. This was highly enjoyable. "Can I quickly ask the kids when they're playing footy?"

She nodded, gestured at them.

"Er . . . it'll be a couple of hours, Mr. Best," said Benzo.

"Well, shit." That meant hanging around the school for ages or going to the digs and then coming right back. I sighed. "What's this subject?"

"English," said Miss Fox.

"Wait, what?" I said. "I thought this was a football school or something."

"It's a normal school," she said, "with some special lessons." She looked out of the window. "And a crazily overspecced sports complex."

Bark piped up. "We do BTEC Sport. That's the main thing. We can do other A levels if we want. One kid is doing German because he thinks his pathway will take him to the Bundesliga. But almost everyone does English because of the media training module."

"Whoa whoa whoa," I said, turning to Miss Fox. "Stop the presses. Are you trying to trick them into learning English by making it relevant to their needs?"

She smiled. "Yes. Trying."

I rubbed my lips. "Huh."

"What?"

"Can I sit in?"

"You can't be serious."

"I've never had any media training. I played last night. I was absolutely abysmal. If some newspaper dude comes up to me, what am I supposed to say?"

She looked from me to the class. When she looked at me again she had a glint in her eye. "Who wants to interview Max?"

This was an amazing and useful time killer. The lesson went on for another hour and my enthusiasm slowly brought more of the kids into the mix. They delighted in taking different roles—the bland interviewer, the hipster podcaster, the gotcha journalist. They especially loved being vicious. "Max, our post-match poll named you the worst player on the pitch. How do you feel about that?" "Max, the fans booed when you were substituted. What do you say to the people who want you out of the club?" "Max, you're shit. Thoughts?"

Apparently, I was supposed to smile and nod and talk in cliches. Once the kids got the idea that I really actually wanted to hear all their thoughts and opinions, they repeated a lot of the things they'd learned in that course. So they had been paying attention! And Miss Fox got them to role play scenarios which were followed by a class-wide feedback session.

The bell rang and the kids collected their bags and started to dribble out.

"Well," said Miss Fox, smoothing down her skirt. "That wasn't the lesson I had planned but I'm actually very happy with it. They haven't been that engaged in a while."

"They like real scenarios, I think," I said. Spoken like a true expert!

I checked my phone. Still ages to get through until the football started. The last kid trudged off and I was alone with Miss Fox. I closed the door, looked at the floor, then up at her with a provocative little smile. "Any ideas what I can do for an hour?"

She looked at me. She looked away. She thought about it. Sadly, she decided to be sensible. "I'll bring you to the school library and you can watch videos of post-match interviews."

I nodded. That was a good idea. "Aren't the computers, like, locked or whatever?"

"I'll give you my number," she said.

She was teasing me. Otherwise she would have said she'd give me her password. I shook my head, laughed, and opened the door nice and wide.

As she walked past, I touched her on the elbow. Not aggressive—just enough to stop her. "My full debut is this Saturday. If I do a shit interview can you turn it into a lesson?"

"Of course. We did a whole week on Henri Lyons."

I let her go. Flirting was over. "That wasn't a shit interview."

She tilted her head. Considered me. "It didn't achieve his aims, did it? It backfired."

Hmm. That was actually a helpful framing. Most footballers being interviewed had the aim of not looking like an idiot. My aims were quite different. The media could help me get the reputation I needed. "I need to get good at this. Really good, really fast. What do you suggest?"

"Oh. I don't know . . . I mean, no offence but you play non-league football. What sort of media challenges are you expecting to face?"

I closed my eyes and tried to think of a way to explain what I wanted without telling her anything of substance. I realised I could be pretty truthful. "I get fouled a lot. Any tackle could be my last. I want to stay in football. Be a coach or a manager or something like that when my playing career is over. Do you know what I mean? So I'm thinking . . . what can I do *now* . . . for *then*? So that when there's a press release that . . . I don't know . . . Chester have appointed thirty-one-year-old Max Best as their manager, everyone nods and says yeah that makes sense, he'll do well there." She frowned. I'd gone from light and flirty to brooding and intense and the switch had been jarring. I shuffled back a few inches. "I'm making you uncomfortable."

"No, not at all. It's just . . . You don't talk like a footballer. You sound like a . . . like a politician."

"Ouch," I laughed.

She looked me up and down again. "The people who achieve unlikely goals that rely on the support or approval of others . . . People like Steve Jobs. Oprah. Zelensky. They all have one thing in common."

"Oh, I know this! Cold showers."

"They're storytellers."

I thought about what she'd said while watching videos in a deserted school library. People loved stories. Telling the story of why I liked football was what piqued Emma's interest in me. Teasing Henri Lyons that a cool story was happening was what made him come to watch me manage the Chester Knights. One time I hadn't told a story was with James Yalley, and look how that turned out.

Were football managers storytellers?

The most famous post-match interview is probably Kevin Keegan's in 1996. He was the manager of a thrilling Newcastle team who were competing with Man United for the title. United's manager, Alex Ferguson, had been winding Keegan up, putting pressure on him by suggesting other teams wanted Newcastle to win the league so they wouldn't play as hard against them as they did against United. Keegan snapped live on camera, jabbing his finger and saying, "I will *love* it if we beat them! Love it!" The interview is said to have killed Newcastle's title chances. It certainly killed the phrase *I will love it if . . .*

Ferguson had told an extremely basic story—Newcastle had it easy and United didn't. And that proved to be explosive.

Could I really use post-match interviews to position myself as a future football club manager? Given enough time, yes. But in a couple of months?

Stories weren't *that* powerful, were they?

Such thoughts were swept aside when the clock struck three. I paced out of the dim library into some harshly lit corridors and then out into the dim Darlington afternoon sun. How can the sun be grey?

It was bright enough to watch the training session and to scout the scholarship kids. The guy who wanted to move to Germany wasn't there, and a couple were out injured. But I saw twenty lads. Half were impressive physical specimens who had been noticed because they were fast and strong, but who, according to the curse, had no future in the game. No jam today, no jam tomorrow.

Tough break.

Even tougher was Benzo. I'd hoped he would be close in standard to the starting right back, the abysmal Colin. If he was, I'd work to get him in the team and then try to make him look good. I had multiple elaborate theories about how to do that. Sadly, Benzo was CA 6, PA 6, which meant he could improve no further. If the coaching staff were easily misled or over-indexed his winning personality, he might get a pro contract, and he could even play in a match or two. But he'd never be a starter. If I had the power to make him quit the game right there and then, I would have used it. As it was, there was no way to tell him. Would it hurt more to be cut at twenty than at seventeen? I could only speculate.

But there was no guesswork involved with Bark. He was a special talent.

CALABASH "BARK" BARKLEY		
Born 16.7.2006	(Age 16)	English/Jamaican
Acceleration 13		
	Handling 1	Stamina 5
	Heading 4	Strength 5
		Tackling 4
	Jumping 4	Teamwork 9
Bravery 5		Technique 7
	Pace 11	preferred foot R
	Passing 7	
Dribbling 9		
Finishing 9		
CA 11	PA 130	
Attacking Midfielder (Centre; Right)		

Definitely worth taking the time to come and scout him! PA 130 was *very* juicy; only a bit short of Raffi Brown. If I could insert myself as Bark's agent, I would. What was the best way to go about it? Charm his parents, probably. Tell them a story. At the very least, I'd make sure they didn't sign any long-term contracts. The most sensible first step would be to gauge what the Darlington coaches thought about him. That shouldn't be too hard.

That evening I went to Teesside Airport to watch Middleton Rangers. They played eleven-a-side on grass. I supposed I'd been expecting a sports hall or something, but it was a bit more like Sunday League. The pitches reminded me of Hough End in Manchester, but with four pitches instead of forty.

And I was a bit surprised that the players were . . . well, they weren't very disabled. There was a guy with a prosthetic arm, but the curse didn't give a shit about that and treated him like everyone else.

I watched the first half—for a CA 1 team they played some really, really nice football—got 45 XP—and at halftime wandered over to chat with their coach. After introductions and small talk, I got to the heart of the matter.

"Listen. I heard that you guys were a disabled team. Why would someone think that?"

"Oh," he said. "We've got loads of teams. We're actually a big club! If your mates have seen a disabled team in the area, it's probably us. They might have thought that's all we did. Oh, and we do walking football, too."

"What's that?"

"Over-fifties. You're not allowed to run, so it's good for when you've got no hips or knees. It's the football equivalent of that walking thing at the Olympics where you do ten miles then get disqualified for going too fast."

"Huh." Walking football. I'd have to check that out. It sounded absolutely terrible, but I wanted to know if the curse counted it or not. "Where can I see one of your disabled teams?"

"Tomorrow night. Same time."

Jam tomorrow! "Here?"

"Yep."

"Does that goalie there have a metal hand?"

"Er . . . no. It's a shiny glove. Why are you so interested in para football?"

"I'm about to start my coaching badges. Ideally, I'd have a team I could do little sessions with. Not looking to take over," I lied. "The course organisers will send people to watch me do some live coaching. If I can do a few sessions here and there beforehand, that'd be ideal."

"Okay but why para?"

The honest answer to that was that there was less interest in para football so it seemed like an easier way to get gigs. "Oh. I suppose it doesn't have to be." He wasn't sure what to make of me. I realised this was a good time to try some storytelling. I gave him a bit more of my energy. "It's more rewarding, though, isn't it? I've managed men, boys, women, and the Chester Knights. That's Chester FC's disabled outfit. The men and boys were pretty easy, truth be told. Eleven-a-side. That's kind of what I've been training for all my life. Do you know what I mean? The women's team was cool because it was seven-a-side and I had to come up with some mad tactics. But the disabled games were really hard. Really hard! I didn't have much time to work with them and I have like, zero experience with disabilities. I was really thrown in at the deep end. And I loved it! I know it won't be the same the next time, but if I could choose, that's where I'd start." I lost confidence. "Sorry for rambling!" I said, "Is it all right if I watch the rest of the match? You play some lovely football here."

"Yeah, sure," he said. He seemed a bit confused.

I really needed some media training.

Thursday morning's training was good. It was more shape work, but with a ball this time. We also did some rondos. You've seen those in the warm-ups before big games. At school we used to call it Piggy in the Middle. A few players form a square or circle and pass to each other. There are one or two people inside who chase the ball and if they touch it, the guy who made the mistake becomes the piggy.

My rondo included Captain Caveman and Colin, and at first they delighted in tormenting me. At least they thought that's what they were doing. But I'd quickly seen the folly of chasing the ball wherever it went, and I slowed down and got a bit more cerebral. As they taunted me—"He's given up!" "He's cracked." "Head's gone."—I was learning. Caveman had two moves: One, a quick, high-energy pass to his left. Two, bouncing the ball the exact way it came. Colin also had two main go-tos: One, pass to his captain. Two, a sand-wedge kinda hit that got him out of trouble but put the guy he was passing to firmly in the shit. I'd seen *that* before.

Once I'd cracked the case, I felt I could anticipate what the pricks would do in nine out of ten scenarios. The time for thinking was over, and the time to throw myself into the drill had arrived. The first time I intercepted a Caveman pass there was dead silence. He stepped forward into the middle as per the rules of the game, but I had a better idea. "You can stay out there, Captain. I quite like it where I am."

He shook his head and mumbled something, but the drill continued. Except that I made no effort to intercept the ball from anyone other than him. And the more I got the ball, the more frustrated he became. I was getting pretty excited—he was on the verge of a *volcanic* eruption. I was toying with the idea of saying things like, "ooh, nearly!" as I intercepted his passes. But a whistle blew, most of the tension evaporated, and we walked to pitch one for the next drill.

One of my fellow rondo-ers overtook me and gave me a friendly pat on the back.

It was happening.

I did the next drills with a massive, shit-eating grin plastered on my face.

A strange thing happened that evening. I finally got some jam. And then some more.

My bank app pinged to say that my salary from the call centre had come through. Not my redundancy money, just my normal wages. Most of it would go to rent and bills from my house in Manchester, but I had a bit of disposable income for the first time in a while. A hundred pounds. I wasn't sure how long it would have to last, and I'd probably need it for petrol. But I allowed myself to go to the nearest shops and have a potter around. Started to properly explore Darlington.

So at half five I was in a cafe drinking a builder's tea and reading their tabloid newspapers when I got a message.

Unknown number: Yo Max this is Bark. You should come back to the digs. Yeah, like right away maybe?

Bark: Yeah like right away.

Bark: Max jeez hurry up.

I hopped back in the car and was at the digs in two minutes. All kinds of scenarios were running through my mind, and they all involved Caveman and his crew. They'd trashed my room, they'd put my new boots in the dishwasher, they'd filled my pillow with anthrax.

It's just a prank, bro! Where's your sense of humour?

I stormed into the house, into the kitchen, fists clenched, face thunderous.

And what I saw was Benzo and Bark on one side of the dining table, just like when we'd done the Whitby scouting together. But sitting across from them, having a cup of tea and spreading jam onto a piece of toast, was the last person in the world I would have expected.

20

MANAGING EXPECTATIONS

Teenage boys, teenage men.

Dirt, decay, and debris.

Stale sweat, discarded sweaters, bags of socks both sweaty and discarded.

A woman comes to tidy, to clean, to rub, to bleach. King Canute goes to shore and instructs the tide to turn. Same result.

By the standards of the entire sweep of human civilisation, the digs is habitable. Compared to Henri Lyons's house—tasteful, respected, *clean*—the digs has the vibe of a museum recreation.

This is how the Victorians lived. 18 people shared this one room and self-respect hadn't been invented yet.

And there, somehow managing to not gag at the stench, looking perfectly at ease, was my dream woman. Dressed like a lawyer, but a sexy American one. Why was she here? I didn't care—my heart soared. Her lips twitched—I took this as a signal to be playful—and the scholarship boys turned in their seats to see what she was smiling at.

Frowning, I moved slowly but carefully towards the table, with my arms slightly raised and my palms facing down. Trying to project a calming, soothing vibe.

"Bark," I said, my voice setting him on edge. "Benzo . . . Who let this person in?"

"Er . . ." said Benzo. The boys were clearly smitten with this sexy blonde who had entered their lives, and why wouldn't they be? She was the perfect mix of attractive and approachable.

"That's my *stalker*," I murmured. In a slow, loud voice, I said, "Hello, *Emma*. Why are you here?" She was wearing a suit, but with a smart grey sweater instead of a shirt. She must have come straight from work. Big law firm in Newcastle.

Her face smoothed out as its expression changed. A crazy kind of look came into her eye. "To see *you*, Max. You know I always want to see *you*."

I shook my head. I looked at Bark. "Do you know she's got a tattoo? Of my face?"

Two thoughts entered his head. One was *Oh my God*. The other was *Yeah but where?* He swallowed.

"Do you want to see it?" said Emma. She started to lift her sweater.

"They're too young," I snapped. Her hand relaxed, and so did the young men. "Now, Emma," I said. "Push the knife away."

We all looked down at it. It was slick with strawberry jam, which looked very much like blood. "No," she said, gripping the handle. "I need it." She scraped the jam onto her toast. The hairs on my neck stood up; I can only imagine what the boys felt.

"Guys," I said, licking my dry lips. "Don't move." Benzo shifted. "Benzo, *really*. Don't move. She can throw that with deadly accuracy over twenty yards . . . She was raised in a circus."

"Oh," groaned Bark. He flopped forwards, arms on the table, head on his arms. He sat back up and laughed. "You had me going! Fucking hell, Max!"

I grinned and went over to Emma—she stood, knifeless—and we hugged. It was very sweet, very chaste. "Miss Weaver," I said.

"Mr. Best," she said.

The fun mood didn't survive long. That seemed to be a theme in Darlington. "I thought you didn't *like* pranks." This came from the kitchen, behind me and to the right. It was Glynn. By my reckoning, he was a Team Caveman wannabe.

"Max?" said Emma, reacting to the hostility.

Well, now. He didn't know it, but Glynn had sent me through one-on-one versus the keeper. A tremendous opportunity! My aims were many—beat the cavemen, get closer to Bark (if possible), and test my man-management skills. If I wanted to be a football manager, I couldn't rely on the curse. I needed to actually manage footballers. Off the pitch, anyway. And this was a low-stakes way to practice. Benzo, sadly, didn't have "it." Bark was at a good club and was on track to have a good career without me. And both of them would be disposed to take my side while Emma was around.

So then. Storytime.

My natural inclination had been to keep the whole hazing thing to myself, to keep it internal, but that wouldn't help me achieve my goals. I knew which story angle would work best, and while it was extremely distasteful for me, I had decided to go for it. The snag had been—when? When could I launch into it without my intentions being obvious? Well, Emma had solved that problem.

I coaxed her to sit down again. I sat close, held her little hand, and launched into my little tale. The real audience, of course, was Bark and Benzo.

"Emma. I told you my mum is sick. In the home. The things she remembers best are from when I was a teenager. When I was a total dick, in other words. She used to try to connect using football. 'Did you see the match? How did you play?' It annoyed me. I didn't *get it*. And now that I lose her a little bit every day, I look back on those times with . . . shame. One thing, though. One thing I wasn't a dick about. She must have asked my friends or something because I don't know how she knew, how she got it so perfect. She bought me these football boots for my seventeenth birthday; I was playing for a Sunday League team. We were bottom of the league but the boots were top. I felt like George Best in them. Well, Sunday League wasn't for me, but you know I kept those boots. Thought I'd keep them forever. Fast forward to Monday and I come to Darlington for my first day of training. First day as a professional. I haven't even told my mum about it. I want my photo in the newspaper so I can take it to her. 'Look, Mum! I scored a goal in the boots you bought me! Do you remember?'"

I'd started this story as a mathematical exercise in manipulation, but holy shit, I'd manipulated myself. I had a stream coming from my right eye and my throat was trying to close so that I couldn't cause myself further pain. I let go of Emma's hand so I could wipe my cheek. "The guys," I said, legit furious at the memory, "decide to prank the new boy. They don't like me because I'm taking their mate's place in the team, because I'm Henri's agent, or this is what they do to everyone because they're fucking cavemen. They tell me to leave my boots in the changing room . . ."

"Oh, no," said Emma, whose eyes were not dry. She glared in the direction of where Glynn had been—I sensed that he had fucked off during the story. Guilty as fuck.

"While one of them distracts me, the rest take the boots into the shower, run the water, and piss all over them. They think it's fucking hilarious. They think I'm supposed to just take it. But those boots are one of the only things I have left from my . . . from my . . . One of the only things that mean anything to me. I've done some shitty things in my life, God knows I have, but I've never done anything *unforgivable*."

There's a silence that finally ends with Benzo saying, "Holy shit."

And that's how simple it is. Word will spread. The guys in the first team who think I'm a crybaby because of my reaction to the prank will have a choice. Some will choose poorly. That's fine; it'll give me something to do when training gets boring. A man needs a hobby.

The scene ends with me getting a warm, moist hug from the northeast's greatest achievement, while Bark retreats to his room and calls his mother.

Five minutes later, the mood had normalised enough for me to quiz Emma on why she was there.

"To stalk you, of course. And to hang out. You're not that far anymore! I got Gemma to get the details from Henri."

"Are you really Henri's agent?" said Benzo.

Bark came back into the room. "Yeah," I said, looking at him. "And I'm always on the lookout for talented players."

Bark eyed me. "What about Benzo?"

"Like I said, I'm always on the lookout for talented players."

"Prick!" said Benzo, laughing.

"So," said Bark. "Where you taking your girl? Raby Hunt?" That was a restaurant in the area with two Michelin stars. The kind of place—I imagined—that pumped vegetables full of helium and served it as a dish called pea balloons. Or made a lovely cheesecake then had the waiter smash it with a hammer in front of you.

A chance to drop in another little nugget of the story. "Slap-up dinner? I spent all my money on new boots, didn't I?" He had a point though. What was I supposed to do with her? "Emma, I promised to take you to a football match."

"You did!"

"Okay," I said. "Let's go."

"Wait," said Bark. "Who's playing? There's no match tonight."

"Bark, mate. Middleton Rangers. I invited you to come. You're the one who *told* me about it."

"You're not . . . You're serious? You're going to take your girlfriend to watch . . . that?"

Emma and I looked at each other. Was I going to let the girlfriend tag stand? I grinned. "I spend most of my time watching football, Bark. My girlfriend has to be the type of person who knows that when she suggests going on a minibreak to Dublin, she knows I'll be checking to see if Shamrock Rovers are playing. And if she pops in to visit me when I'm in the arse end of nowhere, she's always ready to be swept away to Teesside Airport to watch a terrible match in the cold and the rain."

"It's not raining," said Emma. "And I brought a hat. So quit yapping and get in the car."

"Are we still invited?" said Benzo.

Now that was interesting. I wouldn't bring Emma back to the digs and I'd made a big deal of our first kiss being after I'd scored a goal. Our evening would be child-safe. "I'd like that."

"Do you mind?" he asked Emma, which is a question I should probably have asked.

"It'll be nice to have someone to talk to," she said. In response to his confused expression, she added, "Apparently, he gets carried away and starts coaching the teams."

"Managing," I said. "I'm not good at coaching."

"What's the difference?"

"I'll explain in the car. Bark, are you coming? Yeah? Great. Can you guys put on a Darlington training top or something? That might help me out. Thanks."

So the four of us headed out to the airport. I tried to tell Emma that for me, managing meant picking the team and choosing the tactics, and in real clubs, being involved in transfers. And coaching was about improving the players. But there was more and more overlap between the roles. She said she didn't really get the difference.

"I want to be a manager," I said. "And not a coach. That'll do for now."

"But . . ." she said, "didn't you tell me you wanted to get your coaching certificates?"

"Yes," I said. "I need those to become a manager."

"So it's the same thing."

"Guys," I said to the kids so I could focus on the road. "Help me out here."

Bark stepped up like a champ. "He needs to learn to coach so that when he's the manager he can make sure the coaches are doing the right things."

"The manager is like the head chef," said Benzo. "And the coaches are like the chefs. But this head chef doesn't make any food. He writes the menu."

"And flirts with the waitresses," said Emma. "Gordon Ramsay was a footballer," she added, and we were all relieved to get out of that conversation.

It was a cold evening and the lads were soon complaining. Emma looked, for the first time, regretful. Within seconds she was blowing into her hands.

But I was in heaven. Two dozen kids split into four teams, playing on a quarter of a full-sized pitch each. Wonderful! They'd come from all over the region. Plenty of cars, plenty of parents, but there was only one main coach guy, and only one assistant. Plenty of scope for me to insinuate myself into the sitch.

I made a beeline for the coach dude. The curse told me he was fifty-two. He had enormous bags under his eyes and that gruff northern way of being suspicious but friendly.

"Hi, I'm Max," I said. "I play for Darlington. I'm here with two scholarship lads and one lucky, lucky lady."

"Oh, hi. Hiya. I'm Trev. I think Nas warned me about you."

I laughed. "Warned? Yeah, that sounds about right. Nas is the coach of the men's team?"

"Yeah. He said you're doing your badges. Looking for guinea pigs."

"I wouldn't put it like that," I lied. "Thing is, I'm making my debut on Saturday." Benzo made a weird noise behind me. I ignored it. "So I'm close to achieving my dream of being a professional football player. And I want to give something back. Help these kids get where they want to get. But look, today I'm just here to watch. If you need a hand with anything, give us a shout. And these lads are whip smart, too. You need a UEFA B license just to play them at *FIFA*."

"Yeah?" He nodded at the lads. "They teach you that at Darlo? That's good to know. All right. Max, was it? Nice to meet you." He wandered off to get things ready.

Me, my bros, and my girlfriend, question mark, watched and made small talk with each other while the session began. Trev got the players warmed up, did a few drills, and then split them into four teams—A, B, C, and D. A played B, and that's the match we watched.

As the players started swarming around and crashing into each other, I gave my companions a quick primer in para football—told them all the stuff I'd learned in Chester. But while I was externally calm, inside I was bouncing. The curse was still struggling with the player profiles, but instead of switching from nothing to all question marks and back again, now it was switching from all question marks to actual numbers! For almost every attribute, a player would have one of three numbers—1, 10, or 20.

	TOMMY GORDON	
Born 24.12.2010	(Age 13)	English
Acceleration 1		
	Handling 1	Stamina 20
	Heading 1	Strength 20
		Tackling 20
	Jumping 1	Teamwork 10
Bravery 10		Technique 1
	Pace 1	preferred foot R
	Passing 1	
Dribbling 1		
Finishing 1		
CA ??	PA ??	
??		

Very mysterious!

My best guess was that the curse was trying to map the abilities of the disabled players onto the template of the professionals. And it was rating players as either shit, okay, or excellent for every attribute.

Which wasn't ideal but it was clearly trying hard to be less of a dick. Which—in my opinion—reflected very well on me and my personal growth.

The thought nearly made me kiss Emma right then and there.

The lack of CA and PA data didn't bother me, but I did wonder if it would appear one day. Maybe if I watched para football at a higher standard? So the curse would have points of comparison? Becoming an expert on this topic really wasn't one of my life goals, but maybe I'd one day get the chance to—

"Max," said Emma.

"What?"

"What are you grinning at?"

"I was thinking about kissing you."

Bark and Benzo moved away, probably cringing, but Emma was unmoved. Perhaps a slight lifting of the corner of her mouth. "No, really. Come on."

"I just love this. I know it makes no sense to anyone normal."

"But what are you doing? You're doing something."

She wanted to know what was going on inside my head. Huh. "Okay . . ." I said, carefully. "A day in the life of Max Best. So . . . I've come to a football match. Er . . . I've never verbalised this before. I start by scouting the players. That's the foundation, right? You need to know if a player is fast or technical or whatever. What can they do? What can't they do? Then you work out their best position and take a guess at how good they could be, one day. That step is for my little agency business. I'm not doing that now. There's no money in this." I gestured towards the pitch. "But I went to see the Darlington scholarship kids, and Bark is good. He'd be a great client."

"What about Benzo?"

The lads were in earshot. I hoped they were both listening, but I needed to be careful. "He's a defender," I said. "I don't have any defensive clients." That was true, but only by coincidence. "I might one day, but right now I think I'm better with attacking guys. I can help them more."

"What's Bark?"

"Right midfield. Same as me."

"Oh, perfect! Did you talk about signing him?"

"No. He should probably stay at Darlington until he finishes his scholarship. I'll check on him every few months, make sure he's progressing. He might be best staying here, trying to break into the first team."

"But you won't make money from that. Henri said he wouldn't pay you to keep him where he was."

"If I manage a client's career well and take them to a big club, I'll make more money from one week up there than five years down here. It's actually better for me to put the football first. Anyway, we shouldn't discuss it before I've talked to Bark. So I've scouted the players and the match has started, and now I'm thinking of tactics and formations and so on. When you play chess the pieces have to start in a fixed position. But if I was the manager of team A I could do whatever I wanted."

"What would you do, Max?" said Benzo. So they'd been listening. Perfect.

I jogged away and got one of the tiny magnetic tactics boards that Trev had with him. I was on my way back when I thought that a marker might be useful, so I grabbed one of those, too.

Back next to Emma, I used the magnets to show what the team was currently doing. "It probably looks quite chaotic to you, but they're doing two-two-two. The goalie, two defenders, two midfielders, two strikers." I moved all the magnets to the side of the board and pushed one back. "The goalkeeper. Imagine he's got the ball in his hands."

"She," said Bark.

I looked up. "Right. She. Now my question is, how do we get the ball from there to a position where we might score a goal?"

"Close to the other goalie," said Emma.

"Right. What's that called, Bark?" When did I become a fucking schoolteacher? Jesus.

"Position of maximum opportunity."

"Yep. What I did at Chester was this," I said, and laid out the magnets. "I had this girl here who could pass and told her to pass to this guy. Johnny Winger. Then he could run down this whole side of the pitch." I moved the magnets away again. "But we don't have a Johnny Winger comp here."

"Comp?" said Emma.

"Comparison," said Benzo. "Equivalent player."

I pointed to sets of players. "See here? I've got two defender types. Three passing types. One finisher. And one goalie," I added, as an afterthought. "When we say two-two-two that shows it's seven-a-side because there's always a goalie. On Saturday Darlington will play four-four-two. That adds up to ten, plus you've got the keeper."

"Right."

"So what I'm thinking now is something like this . . ."

I split the pitch into nine zones like I'd done in Chester. In the right-hand zones (zones three, six, and nine) I wrote a letter *P*.

"P for passer. Goalie gives the ball to this guy, who passes forward to this girl, who passes forward, and now we've got one of our best passers, with the ball, in a forward position, and we put our finisher in zone eight." I wrote *F* at the top of the board. "Easy. Boom."

"That's five players," said Emma. "Where do the others go?"

I shrugged. "Wherever. Defending is overrated. Isn't it Benzo? But fine. Let's defend. I'd probably put them in zones one and two." I wrote D in those boxes.

"Max!" complained Bark. "You've got nothing in the centre of midfield and you've given the other team the entire left flank."

"So?"

"So that's mad."

I laughed. "This would work. One hundred percent."

"At least move the guy from zone one to zone four."

"Why?" said Emma.

"He can still do his defensive work there. He can support the middle. And he might get on the end of some attacking moves. Like if the pass is too hard from the right, it often goes to the left."

"Bark!" I said. "I approve." I resketched the tactic.

"I actually understand this," said Emma, with a little smile. "It's like laying out a factory. But the other team has a manager, too, right? They can try to stop you."

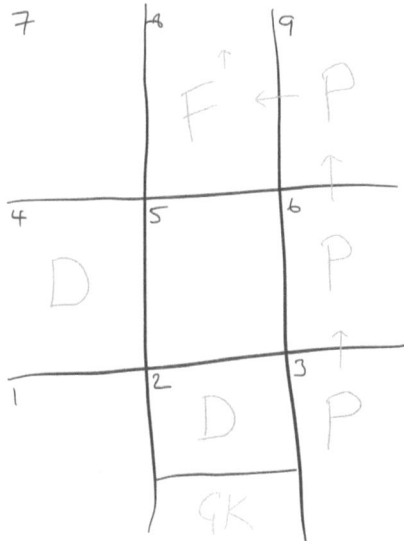

"Oh, sure," I said, cleaning the board. "It normally takes people a while to work out what I've done, and as you can see, even two minutes in these matches can produce a lot of goals. But yeah. Let's say I'm the manager of team B and my opponent is a Max Best-level genius."

"Yes, let's," said Emma. Teasing me.

"How do I beat myself? That's easy. One passer in zone three, somebody in zone nine. That's our attack."

"You never go down the middle?" said Emma.

"It's normally congested, there." I added a *D* in zones four and seven.

"Mate!" said Bark. "You're doing it upside down."

"No," I laughed. "These guys block the passing lanes."

"But there's someone behind! Unmarked."

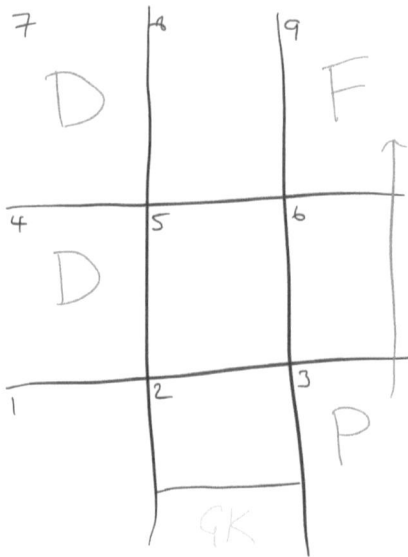

"It doesn't matter," I said. "The ball will never get to her. Ditto their striker. So we've got two attackers on the right, two defenders on the left. Shit, that might be enough. Five against seven. This is why I want to run a football club, Emma. So I can do these mad experiments without having to get permission from everyone."

"Hold on," said Emma. "I don't know football but can't the goalie kick the ball all the way to the other side?"

"Sure," I said. "It's called long-ball. But these kids don't do it because half of them can't see that far."

"What about when you guys play? You can do all this fancy chess planning but then oops!" She mimed kicking a ball. Definite CA 1 talent, there. "I just bypassed your entire plan."

"That's why every team has a caveman in defence," I said. "To head the ball away with his massive atavistic slab of a head." I looked around. We were watching para football for no XP and I was holding a tactics board the size of a Christmas card. I was basically playing imaginary chess against myself, out in the cold. The lads were engaged, but only just. Emma was interested but shivering. "All right. Guys. We don't need to stay all night. This is me. This is what I get up to. What do you think?"

"I can honestly say I've never seen anything like it," said Emma. She gave me that smile. The one I dreamed about. "So we can go? Thank God. Who wants dinner? My treat."

"What, really?" said Benzo.

"Yeah. Preferably somewhere with heated seats. My arse is numb. What do footballers eat?"

"I don't know," I said. "No one's told me." I closed my eyes. "I don't know why, but I'd love some pea soup."

"Footballers eat chicken," said Bark. "I know the perfect place."

We said thanks and bye to Trev, and went to Nando's, famous for its chicken-based meals and weird ordering system. We talked about anything and everything and got warm. After half an hour Emma turned the conversation to my debut. She told the boys she was coming— What should she expect? Had they seen me play? Would they be there? She was very excited, and Bark was happy to answer all her questions.

But Benzo started to look sick.

"Are you okay?" I said, leaning towards him.

"Yeah," he whispered. "You're dead nice. And Emma's . . ." He munched a chip, unhappily. "Max, listen. Your debut. I heard . . . Look. Look, maybe you'll get kicked in training tomorrow. And maybe you'll miss the match. I just think . . . Maybe she should check you're in the team before she leaves home. So she doesn't waste her time. You know."

I thought this through. Of course the cavemen would try something like that tomorrow. It could be their last chance. Once I got in the team it would be hard to get me out. Their best bet was to stop me from ever playing.

Meh. There were a hundred ways to deal with that. For now, I was happy. Emma didn't know it, but she was helping me get a new client. And Benzo's confession was proof that I had achieved at least one of my aims.

I pointed at him with a chicken drumstick. "Mate," I said, "That's not how this story goes." I smiled. "No one at training will get within a hundred miles of me. You can count on it."

21

A NEW LIGHT

Guys slapped each other as I walked through the changing room. *Get a load of this!*

Dudes got out of my way as I slammed open the doors to the outside world. *Oh my God, what happened to him?*

I walked across the pitch towards David Cutter, manager of Darlington Football Club.

I say walked, but what I really mean is hobbled. Actually, I mean wobbled. The crutches sank into the dewy turf, slowing me down.

He saw me and, once over the shock, dashed over.

"Max, what the fuck?"

"Boss," I croaked. "I'm on crutches."

"I can see that! Why? How?"

I looked down. Forlorn. "Pretending to be injured, boss."

"What—Oh, for fucks' sake."

"Apparently it's all pranks around here. I'm trying to integrate. I'm thinking that when you name the team tomorrow, I burst into the dressing room. Surprise! He was fit all along! They'll absolutely lose their minds. I can't wait to see their faces."

"Don't be daft, lad. We're a professional football team. You missed training Monday. You can't miss today an' all."

I eyed him. "Dave, this is just to make the best of a bad situation."

"What do you mean?"

"Er . . . it's private." A couple of players and coaches were coming to get the goss. Cutter shooed them away. "Boss, er . . . Thing is, with your permission, I'd like to go and see my mum. In the home, you know."

"The home?"

"The care home. In Manchester. I told you," I lied. The next bit was true. Sort of. "Anyway, the specialist said if it was possible, I should go and see her. I mean, if it's going to cost me my place tomorrow then I'll stay and train. But, you know. If I can be there, I'd like to be there. There's a park near the home. I can do however much running you want. But I'll still be close by, you know? With her. Just in case."

"Oh." He seemed to replay the entire conversation in his head. His posture changed, and he put his hand on my shoulder. "Listen. If you need time off . . ."

I shook my head. "She always wanted me to become a footballer. Tomorrow I'll play so well I'll be in the papers. And I'll bring them to show her. That's her generation—newspaper clippings."

Cutter took his hand away and smiled. "My ma kept my cuttings in photo albums."

I sighed. "I don't have any. This is my first chance. It might be my last. I want my time at Darlington to be a success. I want my mum to be proud of me. Missing training isn't in my interest, but some things are more important."

He pursed his lips. "You better believe it. Took me far too long to realise that." He looked away at some tree or something. "Fuck it. Your natural fitness is off the scale. Go see your ma." He checked his watch. "Kickoff's at three tomorrow. We hand in the team sheets at two. If you want to do a dramatic entrance, two p.m." He surveyed my crutches with a sparkle in his eye. "This is my sort of caper. At the end, everyone's laughing. Go on, lad. Waddle away."

I drove back to the clinic that had lent me the crutches and dropped them off. Cost: one cheeky smile for a bored receptionist.

Then it was two hours to Manchester. Spending some time with Mum, Anna, and Solly. It was actually fun until I discovered that Mum's bedside table lamp needed a new bulb. I asked how long it had been out and she wouldn't tell me. Trying to protect the nurses. It wasn't the nurses that I blamed. It was me. I had this fantastic talent and couldn't even provide basic things for my own mother. And she'd rather sit in the darkness than tell me, because she knew I couldn't do anything about it.

I bought a new bulb, changed it, and went to work my anger off with some sprints around the endless, empty pitches at Hough End.

Back at my house, I took a long shower and packed all my clothes and possessions. I left them in the entrance corridor.

I lay on my bed for a while and looked at the ceiling. I decided to stay home the whole evening, other than a quick pop to get some food. The plan was to completely, utterly rest so that I was daisy-fresh for the match tomorrow. There was a lot riding on it.

The boredom, though, was crushing. So I went to Platt Lane and watched some garbage footy. I pumped 90 XP into my veins, grabbed my last "free" kebab from Emre, and demanded his phone number.

"I won't be back here," I explained. "But I'm going to clear my tab. Maybe I'll get your bank details or something."

"Nah," he said, which sounded very Mancunian. "We say in Turkey: You always meet twice. You'll be back. Pay me then."

"You always meet twice. Could be the name of a Turkish James Bond movie."

"The Spy Who Loved Meat," he said, attacking his giant kebab skewer with his carving knife.

"The Ottoman with the Golden Gun," I said. "Die Another Salt Bae."

He pointed the blade at me. "I told you to stop talking about him! He doesn't know meat! He's a hack!"

"Emre," I said, pushing my luck. "It's going to be ages before I see you again. Are you going to let Turkey's most famous chef come between us?"

He took a minute to calm down, but then came out of his little booth thing and gave me a hug. "Take care, Max."

"Nasilsin, bro."

He shook his head and for a moment I thought he might grab the blade again. But he smiled, launched himself back into the hug, and mumbled, "Güle güle."

"Right back at you."

XP balance: 1,565

Debt repaid: 174/3,000

Saturday, November 19.

I stuffed my car. I still had a few bits of furniture in the house, but it would probably be cheaper to buy new pieces than move what I had.

I threw the crutches Jackie had found for me onto the passenger seat and locked my front door. I'd probably be back one last time, but this felt like an ending.

Of course, if I didn't play well, if I had some kind of Maxy meltdown, then I'd be back. Back with my tail between my legs. Which is why I hadn't called my landlord yet.

Some impulse made me hesitate before starting my car. I walked round the corner to the little park where this whole adventure had started. I walked to the spot where I'd met Old Nick. Then to the place I'd fallen over the first time I'd seen the player profiles.

It was a park. Just that. Some trees, some paths. A couple of plaques set into slightly raised concrete memorials. One for a shooting, one for a stabbing. The names of those killed were well known in the area. Why had I been drawn there?

Someone had placed a flower in a little vase, but it had blown away. I put it back.

It was a very stop-start drive to Darlington, which gave me a little more time to think. I put the radio on just in time to hear the start of a very smooth song with a playful karaoke hook. My stereo said it was "New Light" by John Mayer. I wasn't familiar with his work, but there was one bit that went "Woooh," so I paid extra attention.

I let the song finish then turned off the radio. It was a song about a guy hoping to change a woman's opinion of him. Give me a chance and you'll see me in a new light.

It resonated.

But why? Almost nobody on the planet knew who I was. I certainly had zero reputation in the world of football. That wasn't helpful in terms of achieving my goals, but it also meant I had no baggage. No previous. When I stepped onto that pitch I would be reborn. Load up a new RPG and choose your character. In a video game you had the same missions whether you were a warrior, a mage, or a monk. I was starting the game hoping to get a certain quest line—help the townsfolk and become the new mayor!—and was reverse engineering my character based on that.

Not see me in a *new* light, then, but see me in the *right* light.

How could I play football like someone on the fast track to management while generating hype?

How could I ensure I was picked for every match?

I mentally sketched out a few possibilities.

Option one. Some kind of superstar diva. The curse had given me physical gifts that took me way past what the average sixth-tier player could cope with. I was much faster, had better technique, better finishing. I could flap my arms around like a goose every time my teammates didn't pass to me—really make sure the crowd saw that I was a cut above. It didn't seem very mature, though. Not very managerial.

Option two. Some kind of team-first fundamentalist. Lots of recovery sprints, helping my fullback, short passes to bring my comrades into the match, winning headers, thundering into tackles. Yeah, I could be the kind of inspirational player that got management jobs easily. And Cutter would love it. On the other hand, most of that would be indistinguishable from what any other player on the pitch was doing, and all the tracking and shape work would be invisible to the fans.

The fans. It was all about the fans, wasn't it? I had to make a connection with them. Once they were on my side, they'd howl when the cavemen didn't pass. They'd rage at the strikers who didn't turn my passes into goals. They'd chant my name when I wasn't named in the starting eleven.

Yep. Fans first. Had to be.

So option three. A tricky winger. Fans love wingers. Run fast, do skills, beat defenders, hit crosses. Don't bother with all that defensive stuff. But if I didn't do my defensive work, Cutter wouldn't pick me, no matter how popular I was. And the winger-to-manager career path was not a common one. Wingers kept their brains in their feet and never lived up to their talent.

I tapped the steering wheel.

It seemed like I could play mostly in the confines of Cutter's system and occasionally break out to enthral the fans. Or I could be an entertainer first and foremost and risk being dropped.

Tricky.

I didn't need to settle on a character right away. It wasn't like wrestling where you needed to pick a name and an outfit before you even got in the ring. I didn't even have an outfit yet. Pat the kit guy had said the kit-printing machine was broken and he needed a certain spare part. He'd hinted that I'd be playing in a blank kit again.

At one minute to two, I swung myself into the dressing room. The hubbub decreased in volume briefly, but then came back slightly louder. I tried to look blank and found it pretty easy. Most of the guys were fully ready to play, except a few with mad superstitions—they would put one sock on now and the other just before the match, things like that. Absolutely bonkers. I noticed that Webby was fully ready to play—he was the first-choice right mid. I wondered if Cutter had double-pranked me and I wasn't going to play after all. A light sheen of sweat formed on the back of my neck. I needed this!

Cutter stood where we could all see him. "Lads. Big cup tie. Big crowd out there. Do you hear them?" We all looked towards the door to the corridor that led to the pitch. What we mostly heard was crazy-loud pop music being blasted out, drowning the atmosphere the fans were trying to create. "So. We're starting pretty strong, get a few goals to the good so we can give more lads a chance off the bench. Right? Solid start! They're physical, this lot, so win your battles! Get up their arses! Then fucking play! Right, we're doing our squashed four-four-two. Here's the team. In goal, Larkin." That was Paul, the talented backup goalie. An immediate sign that Cutter was resting some of his big guns for this match. Perfect. But when he ran through the back four, Captain Caveman and Colin were both in the team. The only change in defence was that Chumpy got a start at left back. Fuck. The defence was more caveman than ever! "Midfield: Tim, Doop, Glynn . . ." Glynn! That weasel-faced fuck. He'd be the midfielder closest to me. I'd be *surrounded* by cavemen! I briefly hoped I wouldn't be named in the team, after all. "Strikers: Blondie, Junior." There was a bit of restless movement—Cutter wasn't the type to forget to name a player. He grinned. "Oh. Right mid, Max."

Pat, the driver and kit man, stepped forward with my shirt on a hangar. I glimpsed the back and he'd printed something on there after all. He'd pranked me! He put it on the hook behind me, even though I was standing in his way. But it made sense. It was something of a rite of passage. Seeing your name on the shirt for the first time. Proof that you'd made it. All your hard work had led to this moment. Well, I hadn't worked hard in the slightest but seeing the shirt there still hit me in the feels.

BEST 77.

Yes, mate.

While I stared at the shirt, I was aware that something had changed in the dressing room. Cutter had played his part in the prank beautifully, but the punchline had played to zero reception. From his point of view there should have been an explosion of laughs, banter, handshakes. He looked puzzled, but shook it off and launched into his pre-match motivational speech.

I put the crutches down, pulled off my hoodie and t-shirt, and held the Darlington top up in front of me.

The back was all white, except for my name and number. The front had chunky horizontal black and white stripes, with the sponsor and half the club badge in red. Good football kit!

The badge featured a Quaker hat and an old steam train. Big parts of the city's history. The football club was 135 years old and no one had ever worn shirt number 77. Whatever happened today, I would be a small part of that history.

I didn't listen to the motivational speech; I didn't need it.

The warm-up was the last chance for a caveman to kick me, so I went over and helped Taff get Paul ready. I hit soft shots at him, then some slow, lobbed crosses for him to catch. Trying to make him feel good before kickoff.

Then with the last obstacle safely navigated, we went back inside for the last hype session, and back out. Ready to play.

The stadium announcer read out the teams, leaving pauses for the crowd to react.

"Number nine, Owen Thorpe." Big cheer from the home fans!

"Number thirty-four, Junior Howland." Warm applause for the young striker.

"Er . . . number seventy-seven . . . Max Bent." Half-hearted cheer.

The match kicked off and I spent my usual few minutes wandering around my zone, checking out the sitch.

The sitch was that Alfreton were playing a weakened team, as well. I don't know what their fans call them, but let's go with Alfy. They were in a 4-5-1 formation. The goalie had CA 35. The back four averaged 33. The midfield was 33, too, and their striker was CA 43. So their team average was about 34.

Paul had CA 39. Chumpy dragged the average of our defence down to 43. Our midfield, excluding me, obviously, was 35. Pretty weak because Tim (The Invisible Man) was really a nonentity and Glynn, while he had some positive *footballing* attributes, wasn't getting regular game time. The strikers were decent. Blondie had CA 50, and the other, Junior, was a fairly promising youngster. Although he only had CA 37, his PA meant he'd probably end up at a decent level.

So Alfy averaged 34, Darlington 40.

My direct opponent was way below average, even for this level. I wondered why the Alfy manager had rotated his team so much. Alfreton had an outside chance of getting to the playoffs, so the league was obviously their priority. But if they lost, say, their next four league games their season would effectively be over. Have a go at the cup, man! Maybe he thought Darlington were just too strong.

My first involvement was when Alfy's goalie launched a booming goal kick towards my side of the pitch. My opponent had 10 in jumping, but I leapt much higher and nodded the ball sideways to Glynn, the prick.

Glynn, the prick, turned away and scurried off like a crab to the other side of the pitch.

The pitch was a bit sticky. A bit bobbly. Most of the guys were having trouble controlling and passing the ball, and even I had problems in the warm-up. You could have perfect technique but if the ball bounced up before you struck it, you were going to look shit. Glynn passed and it bobbled right over the foot of Tim. Out for a throw-in.

The fans were in good voice. A cup run would have been a nice distraction, but it wasn't the be-all-and-end-all of Darlington's season. Great if we win, not so bad if we lose. Also, there didn't seem to be any particular rivalry between the clubs, so losing wouldn't come with gifs and memes and banter.

We got a throw-in on my side of the pitch. It was Colin's job to take them. He almost always threw it backwards to Captain Caveman's mate, who I'd started to call Shrek. But the one time I wasn't paying close enough attention, he threw it to *me*, knowing that I had no chance to do anything with it, surrounded as I was. Damn! It *looked* like he was trying to link with me, without actually doing it. Maddening. From that moment, I made sure I was farther away when we got throw-ins.

I spent the first five minutes shuffling and sliding like a good boy. Cutter said he wanted to keep things tight at the start—don't let Alfy have a sniff. Don't give them any encouragement! So I did the hard yards. Actually, hard yards sort of implies a lot of virtuous running. I mostly just walked from spot to spot. A couple of times Alfy got too close to me, and I nicked the ball off someone's feet and played a one-touch pass.

So after five minutes I had a match rating of 7. I was a good and diligent boy!

After a bombastic start from Alfy, we got a stranglehold on the game and started to push them back. When we had the ball, I was allowed to take up a position on the right wing. Very attacking. Ready to drop some hand grenades!

But seven minutes in, I hadn't received a single intentional pass from a teammate.

So. It was going to be like that.

I spent another few minutes analysing the tactics and the strengths and weaknesses of the Alfy guys. The left back had a habit of taking a heavy touch when the ball came to him and then turning to the touchline (my right) and whacking the ball down the line. It was his get-out-of-jail-free card. I tucked the knowledge away. For now, I was content to let him do that and put pressure on Colin, the prick. My dream was for Alfy to get a corner, because they had their slow midfielder, Osgood, playing. He was the one vulnerable to fast counter-attacks. And, mate, having spent zero calories in the match so far, I felt fast.

Ten minutes in and I hadn't had a meaningful touch of the ball. Time to step up!

I waited until the ball was passed to the left back, then sprinted at him, aiming my run for his left. He turned towards the right side of the pitch, as I knew he would, and I nicked the ball off him, dabbed it ten yards down the line and chased it. The guy, surprised, tried to grab my shirt to stop me. *Mate, I'm strength 20.* I collected the ball, ran on, ran on, then cut diagonally into the penalty area. Junior was trying to get to the far post, but the highest percentage chance was our number 9, Blondie. He'd sent my last assist into the sea at Whitby. Surely today he wouldn't dare do that shit? There were a few defenders near him, so to make it easier I chipped the ball up to his head. He only had to redirect it towards the left of the goal.

He met it and booped it almost vertically. It stayed up in the air so long that the goalie had time to get close, jump, and catch the ball.

I stood there, honestly kind of stunned, simply staring at Blondie. It seemed definitive proof that he was a closet caveman. We were attacking the Tin Shed, the noisiest set of fans, and they shouted their encouragement at me. I started walking back to our half of the pitch.

Big demonstrations of my unhappiness wouldn't go down well. This was supposed to be a team game, after all.

But Blondie had given me the first hint of an idea about how to play this match . . .

We got a throw-in. As I said, it was Colin's job to take them, and because he always threw the ball backwards to his mates, Alfy tended to switch off in these situations. A bit of a mental breather.

I picked the ball up and held it, ready to give to Colin. Normally, then, I'd sprint down the line so he couldn't try to involve me in a situation that could only be bad for me. But this time I had other plans.

"*What* did he say?" I said, nodding towards Shrek. The first thing I'd said to Colin since my trial the previous Friday.

Colin turned to look at his buddy. While he was looking away, I threw the ball at his back, which made it live, then I dashed to gather it and started dribbling. I burst past two Alfy players before they even knew what was happening, and powered towards the byline. I glanced up to see where the strikers were. Junior, annoyingly, was in a glorious position. But that didn't fit the story I was writing. I lashed the ball shin-height at Blondie. It bounced off his leg at a mad angle.

The Tin Shed lost their minds. From their point of view I'd served him a goal on a plate again, and he'd made a mess again.

I let myself end up just in front of the fans. I stared at one guy. He must have been twenty-five. Some boring job and this was his weekly release from it. I glanced in the direction of Blondie then stared at the fan again. I did the tiniest little shrug—hopefully it wouldn't show on camera. It worked on this guy, though. I think. He got a manic look in his eye and yelled, "Come on! Come on!"

I walked back to our half of the pitch again and checked the match ratings. I was on 8. Colin and Glynn 6. Blondie was on 5. I smiled. This was tremendous. One more miss from Blondie . . .

Although some guys weren't playing well, we were still the better team. And so it came to pass that we finally got a corner. Cutter had been very, very clear that I was on corners and free kicks. Even the cavemen knew better than to defy him when it came to set pieces.

The timing was annoying. If we scored, my narrative would be stillborn. There wasn't really a way to take a corner in such a way that would make me look good but would lead to a lower-than-average-quality chance for a teammate. As I strolled to the far corner, something caught my eye up on The Clubhouse. The balcony where Margot, presumably, was sitting. I thought I'd seen someone I recognised, but apparently not. Someone had draped a couple of banners there. One had some text and a big Darlington FC badge. The one I was wearing over my heart. Emma once accused me of being romantic, and I suppose when it comes to the traditions of the game, I am. Taking a shit corner on purpose seemed . . . disrespectful . . . in a way that giving a prick a difficult pass wasn't. Maybe it was because from the corner I would be aiming at an *area*, and any of five or six different people could score.

I prepared to whip in a Max Best Special. I put both hands up because I was a professional football player now and that's what we did. I stepped back and ran on the spot briefly.

Then . . .

The cross was delicious. Mm mm mmm! Spicy and flavourful; I leaned back and savoured it.

Someone headed it straight onto a defender—unlucky!—and the ball bobbled around the penalty area. A Darlington guy swished his boot at it and missed. An Alfy bro tried to clear and only nudged the ball a yard sideways.

Straight to the feet of Blondie! One of the best strikers in the division!

Best takes the corner.
A perfect delivery! Onto the head of the captain!
It's blocked. There's a desperate scramble.
The ball breaks to Blondie.
An amazing chance to put his side ahead.
But he puts it wide!
The fans can't believe it.
And neither can he.

I let out a single laugh. This was incredible. He had a fucking open net! Why had he tried to hit it so hard?

I knew why—because he'd missed the previous chances. The narrative in his own head, working against him. Footballers weren't supposed to think like that. Sports people were supposed to forget what's happened before and focus on their process. Not this guy, though.

Lol.

For the first time I didn't walk back to my zone. I jogged. Practically skipped!

And I was bouncing on my heels as the goalie kicked off. I needed to get the ball. He thumped it into the centre of the pitch. I left my zone and raced towards where the ball was likely to go next—it was a piece of piss to intercept a weak pass, and now I was dribbling towards the left of the pitch. I eased past a player, then touched the ball towards Tim and sprinted down the line. All the fucker had to do was pass it anywhere! Anywhere in the northern hemisphere!

But when I realised the ball wasn't coming, I turned back and saw that Alfy had a throw-in. What the fuck had Tim *done*?

I put my head in my hands, absolutely stupefied, and it wasn't even an act. I genuinely couldn't believe it.

I trudged back towards my side of the pitch, but some noise from the crowd was getting through to me. They were roaring me on, and they were getting on the backs of my so-called comrades. My narrative was working.

The story of this match was one man (Max Bent, apparently) trying to drag his team single-handed across the finish line. Let down at every turn by his inept teammates. I rubbed my temples. It was a way of conveying my annoyance that didn't come with football-related baggage. I certainly knew better than to flap my arms!

Tim's match rating dropped to 5. Most of our midfielders and forwards were officially having stinkers, so even though we were better, Alfy got a foothold in the game. Our defence was pretty solid, so I wasn't worried about conceding so many goals that we'd actually lose. I was delighted, though, when Chumpy gave away a corner.

I walked to the edge of the penalty area—I hadn't actually been given a specific role by Cutter. Caveman spoke to me for the first time since Monday. "Best! Get back here! Mark fourteen. Best! Fourteen is your man!"

I ignored the shit out of him—as I'd seen when I scouted Alfreton all those weeks ago, they left this guy Osgood back as their cover. It had cost them one goal already this season, and if the ball bounced right, it'd cost them another.

The alternative was that Alfy would score and Caveman would tell Cutter that I'd disobeyed him. It wasn't much of a dilemma—I had to feed my narrative.

The corner came in, and Caveman was first to the ball. He headed it away and to the left. Glynn was fastest to respond. I pointed to where I wanted the ball. "Glynn! Line!"

If he passed, I'd have an almost clear path to goal. Of course, the twat crabbed even further to the left.

I lost my shit. Absolutely lost it. I was already running at half-speed, and I changed direction without losing a joule of momentum. With a little extra burst I caught up to him, and shoulder-barged him. He. Went. Flying.

I sensed the referee bring his whistle to his lips, but there wasn't really any reason to stop a player fouling his teammate. He let play go on. The delay had brought a bunch of Alfy guys level with me, and I was way over on the left side of the pitch, not that far from my own penalty box. So I straightened and increased my speed. Eighty percent. Osgood came over and I knew he had decided to try to foul me. He'd probably only get a yellow card because I was so far from goal. So I kicked the ball forward thirty yards and accelerated. I sensed the crowd around me straining for a better view. Everyone on the Darlington dugout took three steps forward to see what I'd do next.

I wasn't the only guy who had lost his mind. The Alfy keeper had reacted to my ball down the line by racing out of his goal to try to get there first. His problem was that I was much, much faster than he'd anticipated.

Now if *he* fouled me, that would be a definite red card. What was better for me? Obviously to go past him and score. It'd be the thrilling climax to the little story I'd been writing. But for the team it was definitely best if the other lot were down to ten men so early in the game. It would make the rest of the ninety minutes a cakewalk, and our best players would be able to get a rest. If I were Cutter, I'd have wanted the red card. So I slowed down enough that the guy would smash into me. When he was close enough, I knocked the ball a little farther away.

"Oh, shit," he said. He wasn't the first-choice keeper. This was his first start of the season. Getting sent off was not good for his career. So he threw himself to the side to try to avoid me. He actually clipped me, but I decided to take pity on him and battled to keep upright.

Again, the ref brought his whistle to his mouth, and again he decided to let play continue.

So now I was bearing down on an empty goal from the left-hand side of the pitch. I angled my run towards the near post. The thousand people in the Tin Shed were going bonkers, screaming at me to shoot. It was an open goal! What was I waiting for?

But all the delays had allowed two of Alfy's faster players to scream back, and they were on an intercept course, both running with all their might towards the post that I was heading for.

I was ten yards away and they were twelve.

I was eight and they were nine.

The Tin Shed were bouncing up and down like a mosh pit at the last leg of a horse race. Why was I slowing down? Why wouldn't I shoot? Some of them would have shot *me* if they could.

Six yards from goal and I finally—finally!—cocked my right leg. The two Alfy guys hurled themselves forward, legs first, trying desperately to block my shot. The farthest one even raised his leg in case I tried a chip, a wall between me and glory.

But it was a wall that was very quickly sliding away. A wall on wheels.

With my foot on the ball and a quizzical look on my face, I watched them go by. Then I rolled the ball into the empty net. The Tin Shed went even more bonkers. I looked at them and gave a little shrug. *What were you worried about?*

While the fans cheered and hugged, the celebrations of the players were pretty muted considering it was a cup tie. Junior and a few nearby guys came to embrace me, but only because not doing so would have raised more questions than it was worth. The cavemen mostly huddled around Glynn, who was sitting up on the grass, looking a bit groggy.

None of his attributes had turned red, so I wasn't worried about it.

So it was time for the next stage of Project: Project, in which I tried to project an air of maturity and tactical awareness. I went over to Cutter and pointed to spaces around the pitch, almost at random, while I asked him if I was allowed to push forward a bit more. The idea was that, seen on a TV camera, it would look like we were discussing tactics. As an afterthought, I covered my mouth in case of lip-readers.

A slightly bemused Cutter congratulated me on my goal but asked me to keep the shape until halftime.

As I made my way back to my side of the pitch, I made eye contact with Glynn. He looked sullen, but wary. Now that I'd bitten back, he was seeing me in a new light.

"Glynn, mate," I said. "You want to play in my midfield? Pass or get off the pot."

Caveman heard and shouted back. "It's not your midfield!"

I waved at the fans to cheer louder. They responded. My heart beat harder. I turned back to Caveman and pointed around the stadium. "It is now."

22
NO BACKSIES

Alfy took the kickoff and had a little go at us. Trying to get a quick equaliser. I shuffled and slid and kept the shape. I even sprinted to help Colin, the prick, out of a jam.

All the while, I thought about my ideal next steps. The absolute dream would probably be for me to score the second goal, really whip up the fans, and then . . . Then what? There would come a point where me shooting all the time would stop being inspirational and start being obnoxious.

I looked around at my teammates. The only guy who liked me was Paul, and he was a goalkeeper. We wouldn't interact too much. Ahead of me, Blondie was on my shit list. Either he was missing on purpose or he was just playing like crap. My instinct was that he'd missed deliberately in Whitby and the first header here, and everything after was incompetence.

Behind me, the defence was pure caveman, and in midfield there was only Tim (useless) and Doop (not much better). I could try to get Cutter to bring on a substitute, but that was a minefield. A nobody asking for certain players to come on would backfire; it wasn't my place to comment on our lineup.

That left Junior, a young striker trying to make a name for himself. I focused my attention on him for a while. Watched how he ran, where he liked to move, how he controlled the ball and interacted with the guys around him. The curse told me he had high PA—80—but I'd like to think his talent would have been obvious to me even before I met Old Nick. Junior moved like a player at a much higher level.

We kept our shape and began pushing Alfy back into their own half. In these phases I was stationed up the pitch, hugging the right touchline, close to the offside line. I imagined what I'd do if I played in a team that *wanted* me there. The most obvious thing would be to get the ball to feet and whip in a series of David Beckham-style crosses. Beckham didn't even bother with dribbling past his opponent—he could bend the ball around an obstacle and make it land wherever he wanted. They made a film about this talent. I think it was called *Snowpiercer*. Okay, fine: *Bend It Like Beckham*. The downside to that plan would be that Junior didn't have the technical qualities of the guys Beckham was passing to; Junior would find it hard to turn such crosses into chances.

So maybe the best thing would be—

All activity in my brain ceased. Glynn had crabbed his way over to the right and passed to me. I controlled the ball and looked at it like it was a ticking bomb. I glanced up and saw that Junior had made a run to the far post. I returned the ball to Glynn and he crabbed his way back over to the left.

Well, well, well.

The game continued. It was a scrappy affair. Each team would string two passes together, but not three. Glynn passed to me again, and I one-touched it right back to him.

Colin chipped the ball down the line, a pass indistinguishable from a deliberate attempt to get me injured. I cushioned it right back towards him—the defender came close but didn't foul me. In a properly functioning team, my teammate would give me a signal, next time, and play it above my head for me to run onto, knowing I was much faster than the defender.

But I didn't play for such a team. I played in a team where Caveman was captain.

Talking of whom . . . He got the ball, did a three-point turn like someone using your driveway to turn their car around, and did his trademark soft, slow, chest-high chip towards me. A handwritten invitation for the defender to launch himself into my back, knee-first!

I stepped away and turned round. The left back was confused by this and hesitated—it helped that he'd seen me run at the speed of sound earlier. As the ball went out of play past me, around nipple height, I shaded my eyes with my hand, almost like doing a military salute, and peered up into the stand, looking at the metalwork up there. The ball hadn't gone that high, but that's the thing about gaslighting— the facts don't matter. After a bit of fake searching, I raised my arms vertically above my shoulders, then flattened my hands. It's the same signal used in at least two sports, and this was a rugby ground. But for some reason I shouted, "Touchdown!"

A few in the crowd were amused. A few were angry at me for not trying to get the ball. I grinned at the latter.

Then I plastered a huge, charming smile on my face and turned back to Captain. I gave him a little thumbs-up and a big clap. That's football code for "Ooh nearly, thanks for trying."

Then I shuffled and sank and did some hard yards, and for the first time, loved every second of it.

You can imagine that I was having a lovely old time. I was sailing my little plague ship all around, chucking barrels of poison at people whenever I wanted. But I had a magic mainmast that made anyone on dry land see me as a glimmering hero.

It was perfect. Dreamlike.

And that's the problem. Dreams end.

Now that Glynn had started to pass to me—in moderation—the midfield was feeling more of a unit. Glynn hit me a nice, fast pass that I controlled in a way that gave my body a bit of kinetic energy—an invitation to myself to go on a dribble. It didn't feel right, though, so I shaped to pass to Glynn. Since that's what I'd been doing a lot recently, Alfy's midfielders moved to intercept. So I played a longer pass, sideways, across the crowded pitch, which can be risky. But the pass found its target, Doop, and he played a 1–2 with Tim. Doop was pushing towards the penalty box when he was fouled. As always, I scanned his player profile to see if anything was red. All clear. But something about the challenge infuriated Doop, and he was up on his feet pushing his opponent. That triggered a melee. First the hotheads ran in to vent their testosterone, then the peacemakers piled on to make things worse.

Now, football melees are often described in phrases that use the word *handbags*. Commentators say, "Oh, we've got a bit of handbags here." Think of a group of older women getting rowdy and swinging their handbags at each other. (I wonder if this has travelled to America but with the word *purse?*) Now personally I wouldn't like to be hit by a thirty-litre handbag full of phones, metal canisters, and tiny blades, so I don't know where the phrase comes from. I suppose it's better than a cricket bat or a .44 Remington. In these melees, football players almost never punch, or kick, or do anything other than bounce into each other like baby rams, so it's really a pointless endeavour.

I wandered over in the direction of the melee, but only because I was going to take the free kick. I stayed ten yards away and took the opportunity to look around the stadium. Until that moment, I'd been almost wholly consumed by the game, by achieving my goals. Emma and her date were probably in the stand where I'd pretended Caveman's pass had been absurdly high. That was on the far side from me, now. Who else had I invited? Well, almost everyone I knew. I doubted anyone would actually come. But maybe, just maybe, Mike Dean would be here. I guessed he'd be up on the balcony. So I walked a bit closer. I glanced back at the contretemps; it seemed to be disbanding, but there was still time to have a look around.

The balcony, then. It was packed. People were two or three deep along the whole length. It made sense, I suppose—those guys had a great view and could pop inside for a beer. I started on the right-hand side because I had the idea that Margot would be there. That was absurd—*I* was the one who had imagined her being there to watch me score direct from a corner. Anyway, I didn't see her, and I didn't see Mike Dean.

At the closest point to where I was, there stood an extremely handsome old man. I was briefly impressed by his clothes—it was all soft fabrics, a hint of a tweed jacket underneath a really superb coat, and what looked like two scarves. I smiled. It was like seeing a future version of Henri Lyons. I scanned the rest of the balcony, saw no-one I recognised, then turned to pick up the ball. I placed it with the nozzle facing me. Then I hesitated. Maybe it'd be a good time to let someone else score? A cross to the far post, then? Financially, it was the same if I scored or assisted. Nah. I should score again. Two goals on debut and the rest of the match trying to create chances for Junior. That was the story.

The goalie was shouting at his players to form a two-man wall. I was so far out that there was almost no chance of a direct shot. I tried not to smirk. This would be the last time anyone underestimated me.

Cannonball, then.

The exact moment I made my final choice was the exact moment I felt a wave of hostility assault me. It felt like the blast of air you get when you open a sauna door. I turned, bewildered, but knew exactly where to look.

The distinguished older man, the guy wearing clothes that cost more than the stadium, the silver fox with those prominent shoulder muscles you only get from chucking weights around a gym for an hour a day, was glaring at me. Calling it the evil eye would be way too on the nose.

It was Old Nick.

I hadn't recognised him at first because when I'd met him he was pretending—yes, pretending, I'm sure of it—to be a thin, old, doddering fool. This was more like the real Nick. Strong, powerful, serious. His hair was all silver now. His haircut was as modern as any Premier League footballer's, but it suited him to perfection. His beard could have been sculpted by Guillaume Geefs.

And he was furious.

I knew. I knew what had happened as lucidly as if he'd sent me a readme.txt file explaining our entire interaction, step by step in words of no more than two syllables. When he'd given me the curse he hadn't intended for me to be a player. He just hadn't. He'd given me the management skills. Seeing me dominate this match as a player was shocking to him. So shocking he'd emerged from the shadows to . . .

To . . .

To . . . what?

To make me stop.

His head tilted forward—almost a nod.

Someone bumped me. With extreme reluctance, I broke eye contact with Nick. "What?" I snapped.

It was the referee. "It's a bit early in the game to be timewasting." A tiny joke to get me to hurry up and take the free kick. But he saw something in my expression. "Er . . . Are you all right?"

"Ref," I said. "Look up on the balcony. Do you see a tall man with silver hair? Looks like he just stepped out of a fashion magazine."

"Best," he said, shaking his head.

"Please," I whispered.

He sighed and looked. "Oh!" he said, a bit shocked. "Yeah he's there. You weren't joking about the hair. Is this . . . er . . . Is he your . . .? Do you want me to get a policeman or something? I'll be discreet."

"No, thanks," I said. "I got this." I touched the sides of the ball. The ref jogged off into his position.

I took a few steps back, then a few more. I sank into my body, then, face distorted with fury, smashed the ball towards goal. It was halfway there almost as soon as I finished my follow-through—so far above the goal that the keeper didn't even take a step towards the ball. At that point, with the ball flying a full two yards above the crossbar, I turned towards Nick and locked eyes with him. The moment the ball began its wicked dip, his eyes flickered towards it. I wanted to roar, to scream, to yell defiance. And I did. Silently.

The silence lasted no more than half a second. The Tin Shed did my roaring for me as the ball smacked into the net.

I stared at Nick until we were both enveloped—him by rampant Darlington fans—cheering, jumping, spilling their beers, but never actually seeming to touch him—me by teammates. Junior, Tim, Doop. Even Glynn. Most of the subs and coaches had run on to the pitch, too.

I let it wash over me, and when they finally fucked off, I checked the balcony. He'd gone, leaving only ripples of menace in his wake. I made a beeline for Junior. I grabbed him by a fistful of shirt. "Junior, mate. I need someone to score from my passes."

He tried to free himself, but I was too strong. "I've been making runs!"

"Keep making 'em," I grunted. In trying to release my grip I accidentally pushed him away. Then I paced towards the centre circle. Alfy kicked off and I stormed towards the ball. They passed it and I changed direction, sprinting at full speed. Another pass, another sprint. Another pass, another sprint. I was zooming around like a man possessed. An unfortunate turn of phrase, perhaps, but vivid.

I ran, ran, ran, and all the while the fans went nuts. Normally, a player who lost his head like I had would make three sprints then get tired. Four, maybe. I was on eight, nine, and Alfy were buckling. Every time I turned I got a little closer to the ball. Finally, a guy played a pass back to the goalie and when he saw me bearing down on him he tried to kick the ball long, first time. The ball bobbled up just before he made contact and he sliced it over to the right-hand side of the pitch. The zone where I should have been anyway. I sprinted and collected it. Blondie was unmarked at the near post. Junior was making his usual far-post attack but with two defenders near him. I curled it high enough to evade the backtracking goalie and hard enough so that Junior wouldn't have to add any extra energy to score.

Bop. Boof. Swish. Come on!

Three—nil!

I collapsed to the ground, breathing hard, sweating freely. At some point in my manic sprinting, my legs had turned to jelly. I put my hands under my head and spent a couple of seconds enjoying the absolute delirium coming from the stadium.

Junior had been celebrating over on the far side, near where he'd scored, but now he was standing over me. He pulled me up and hugged me. "Thought you was being a one-man team."

I held out my hand and we did a manly, grasping handshake. "We're a two-man team, now."

"Guy, you're fucking crazy," he said. But he was smiling.

I didn't do anything crazy for the rest of the half. I had what Cutter had called natural fitness, but I was nowhere near the Premier League norm of firing off a hundred sprints a game. I needed to conserve energy and explode at the right moments.

Twice I got a pass from Glynn that I instantly sent forwards to Junior. His movement was great, but the first time he lost control of the ball and a defender knocked it away. The second time he gathered the ball but hit a weak shot. He was delighted, though, to be playing with someone who could find his runs. And part of me was delighted that he was missing. If I scored and assisted too many times it would cost the club too much money. There was a chance Cutter would get told not to pick me in every game!

One more assist would be fine. I planned to get through to halftime, dose myself with those energy sachets, do ten or twenty minutes of the second half, then suggest to Cutter that he sub me.

At halftime, in the dressing room, I rushed to my kit bag. I grabbed my phone and typed *Champion Manager*. The results were gibberish. I clicked *images* and they were as insane and baffling as always. I went back to the first results and clicked on one. I got a pang of headache. I nodded a few times and slipped my phone back into my bag.

I was deep in thought when Cutter announced his plans. "Max, well played! That free kick, holy shit. Let's save your legs for the next match, though, yeah? So, second half, Webby you're on . . ."

"Whoa whoa whoa," I said, standing up from the U-shaped bench all the players were on.

"Max," he said, annoyed. "I've made up my mind. The priority is the league."

I showed him my palms. "I don't mean that. I mean, can I go?"

"What?"

"Can I go? To Manchester. To the care home."

He relaxed, microscopically. "Oh. Normally, I'd say no. You saw what happened with Ronaldo." Ronaldo, when he realised he wouldn't be getting onto the pitch, had left a Man United match early and caused a big media storm. It's disrespectful. Shows you aren't a team player.

This, though. I'd already played and done my part for the team. Preventing me from leaving early served no purpose other than to show who was in charge. My head dropped a fraction and I went back to my part of the bench.

"Maaxxx," he said. "You're going to be man of the match! You have to do media." Yeah, that was something. If I stayed, I'd get 90 more XP for watching the second half (I'd only got 45 for playing), and I'd get to tell my story to whichever journalist had the misfortune of reporting on Darlington's games.

"Don't worry," I said. "I'll be man of the match next time, too."

"Jesus prick," said someone. Almost certainly Caveman.

"Are you going to keep sulking unless I say you can go?" said Cutter.

"I'm not sulking," I said, and everyone burst out laughing. That brought a proper smile to my face. I shook my head. "All right, I won't mention it again."

"Great. I'll finish my halftime team talk now, will I?" I gave him a thumbs-up. "Oh, thank you very much, Best."

He went through the changes he was making and told the guys what he expected from the second half. It was interesting because from what I'd seen on documentaries the halftime talks were very sweary, very much about getting up people's arses. This one was calm, rational. Trying to get the players to save energy by letting the system do the work for them.

"All right, get back out there and get up their arses!" Ah, there it was!

The lads filed out, *clomp clomp clomp*, and I stayed back. I'd have an early shower, at least.

"Best!" snapped Cutter as I was taking my shorts off. "Are you planning to sneak off?"

I looked around the almost-empty changing room. There was Pat and a coach. No cavemen. "No, I just wanted a shower."

Cutter came closer and folded his arms. "Best. Have a shower. Get a massage if you want. Get dressed. Then go see your ma."

"Oh," I said. I looked towards where he'd given his team talk from. "You wanted to stamp your authority but don't actually mind me going."

"No, Max. I don't want the lads distracted for the second half. We don't invite extra drama." He slapped me on the upper arm. "Well played. Bright and early for training Monday morning, yeah?"

"Absolutely." Cutter left. "Pat!" The driver-turned-kit-man looked at me, surprised. "Pat. Can I borrow your cap?"

Disguised as a sixty-five-year-old man, I wandered around The Clubhouse looking for Nick. Then I paced my way all around the ground until I got to the terrace where Emma was most likely to be. I saw her blonde hair peeking out from under a stylish grey hat. There was an older guy next to her. He was very good-looking. Some kind of sugar daddy? Emma didn't seem the type. But maybe this guy had helped pay her way through law school and while she didn't see him *that* way, it was possible that, eventually, she would. I paused. Maybe I should let that scenario play out?

Well, it would have been rude to leave without telling her. So I snuck up the steps and sort of loomed next to her with my finger on my lips. She looked at me and nearly blurted out my name. Just in time, she saw my shush gesture. I bent down and whispered. "Emma. I'm not playing the second half."

"I know," she whispered back. "They said. They got your name right this time!"

I grinned. It faded. "I have to go to Manchester," I said.

"Oh," she said, disappointment writ large. She gave me a look not dissimilar to the one Old Nick had given me. "You promised me a K-I-S-S."

"I'm in a state," I said. "You wouldn't enjoy it."

"I fucking would," she said. I took a moment to admire her. Beautiful, smart, soft, fierce. Her lips twitched. "What?" she said.

"I have to go." She did an angry little shake of her head. This wasn't the first time I'd ruined a date. "I'll make it up to you."

She went through some kind of internal process, then spoke in a flat voice. "Did you talk to Henri?"

"When? No."

"Talk to him first."

"Er . . ."

"He's down there somewhere." She pointed. I nodded and got up to go. "Max," she said. It was clear she wanted to say something important, but changed her mind. "Nice hat."

"Nice knight in shining armour," I said, nodding to her companion.

"The best," she said, hugging his arm.

What?

I spotted Henri. He was in amongst a bunch of Darlington fans, leaning against one of the railings. They were blocking the view of people in the terrace behind, but it seemed to be the done thing. Weird. I forced my way through until I was next to him.

"The rain in Spain," I said, looking at the pitch and not at him, "stays mainly in the plain."

He glanced at me and took in my preposterous old-man cap. "My eyes despise this guy's disguise. Why are you here?"

"I'm sneaking off. Got to go to the care home."

"Is everything all right? I'll come with you."

"Everything's fine. I just . . . have to go."

"*Bien entendu.*"

"Emma said you wanted to talk."

"Not to talk, no. I have a gift for you. I was going to surprise you after the match." He reached into his pocket and pulled out his keyring. He removed one key. "You know the address," he said, handing it over. "And the code is the number of women I have slept with." He grinned at my blank face. "One two three four."

I stared at the key. "I can't afford the rent on a place like that," I said.

"You can," he said. "It's free. I always wanted to be a patron of the arts. A modern-day Medici. And now I am. You are an artist, *mon ami.* Plus it's only a couple of months until you flounce out of the northeast forever."

"But—"

"Just take the key and go! We can discuss it some other time." He gave me a strange look. "Or perhaps you would prefer to stay in the digs?"

Over at left back, Chumpy was running around like a puppy dog, wagging his tail with delight because he got to play alongside his master. His CA had improved by one point. If I moved into Henri's place, I'd never have to talk to Chumpy again.

"No backsies," I said to Henri.

"What does that mean?"

"You can't change your mind. Can't take it back."

"Ah! I've heard the phrase. No backsies, no. If you decide to stay beyond . . ." He looked around. "Beyond you-know-when, then we'll have to talk."

I nodded and slipped the key into my pocket. "Am I allowed to have orgies?"

"I would be disappointed if you didn't. It is your home now. There is only one rule. There is a door. You will know it when you see it. You must not open that door. Also, no smoking. Now go."

I drove to Manchester, faster than I'd normally go. At times my speed was reckless and I'd force myself to calm down, but then I'd see I was way above the limit again.

With a tremendous effort, I got a grip, and pushed my mission to the back of my mind. When I got into Manchester, I hit a red traffic light. While I was waiting for it to change, the thought bubbled up again.

This whole curse thing had something to do with Champion Manager. That so-called game was the locked chest that held all the answers. And I couldn't open it on my own.

I needed help, and there was only one person in the world I could trust.

23

WHOEVER HAS WILL BE GIVEN MORE

I knocked on the door of a shitty terraced house in north Manchester. If you don't know what a terraced house is, don't think of charming Italian vineyards or majestic football stands—it's not that kind of terrace. I think in some countries they're called row houses. You might remember that I used to live in one. That was in the old days, though. Now, I'd moved up, skipping the semi-detached phase of the property ladder, going all the way to detached. Next stop, the moon!

"Max! Long time no see."

"Chris," I said, stepping into the house. It was getting cold. I pulled the door closed behind me.

"Will I put the kettle on?"

"No, thanks. I need to grab a box and bring it to the home."

"Your mum? How is she?"

I mentally gritted my teeth. Chris was my cousin or second cousin or some shit, and thus was one of my closest living relatives. He was a good guy, a charming guy, a talented guy, a guy who had decided to live on the dole (i.e., get unemployment benefits) and smoke weed pretty much constantly. When I was a kid I was in awe of his artistic abilities. He drew incredible little comic strips that made me crack up laughing. Once I'd read them, he'd take them back off me and keep shading and shading until—in my opinion—he ruined them. He never grew out of this self-destructiveness and seeing him waste his life infuriated me to the point I actively avoided him. "She's . . ." I bit back a vicious remark. Needless. *Come on, Max.* "She's actually doing better. She'd love you to pop in."

"Yeah! Sure, I'll be there," he lied, the twat.

I sighed. Incredible self-control. Without asking, I jogged up his stairs, let myself up into his attic and found a certain cardboard box. All the contents were still inside, which was a relief. Chris wasn't such a fiend he'd sell the family silver for one more hit, but you never knew who he might befriend. Anyway, seeing all my mum's stuff taken care of (or at least not despoiled) made me sentimental, and made me vow to be a fraction nicer to Chris in the eight seconds before I left his house.

I slid down the ladder and folded it back up against the ceiling.

"Christ, Max," he said. "What happened to you?"

"What do you mean?"

"You're fit. You look strong. You're . . . are you *taller*? You on steroids or something?"

"Something a lot more powerful," I said, going down the stairs. "Chris, go and see my mum. I'll be busy for a while. In Durham."

"The city?"

"The county. Just check in on her. Please."

He scratched the back of his head. "All right. I'll . . . yeah. Sure."

"One more thing." I got close to him. Uncomfortably close. "Don't talk to anyone about me." He looked alarmed. "And don't believe anything you read."

Chris licked his lips. "Uh . . . right. Hey, Max. What's in the box?"

My humorous reply was and is a spoiler for a great movie, so I won't repeat it.

"Max! Visiting times are over."

"Stacey, are you seriously going to stop me going in?"

"No, but . . ." She softened. I was always nice to the nurses. Not *that* nice. Get your mind out of the gutter.

"What time do you finish?"

"Nine."

I pulled a face, and rubbed my lips while calculating. "Is there any leftover food? I am *famished*. I forgot to eat. It just hit me."

"Your mum never finishes her spag bol. There's probably half a plate in her room."

I laughed at the absurdity of it all. I was a big-shot football star now. Why was I eating cold leftovers? "I'll take a look. Is there a microwave I can use?"

"I'll do it for you."

I adjusted the box in my grip. "I'm going now," I said, dramatically. "I may be some time."

She laughed.

As soon as she was safely behind me, my cheeky smile vanished.

"Max, is that you?"

"Yes, Anna. How are you doing?"

"Well. But I'm confused. What time is it? What's in the box?"

"Some old stuff. No, you stay in bed for now. I need to set it up."

With great difficulty, she pushed herself to the edge of the medical bed, then caught her breath. "Stop at once. I am detecting residual spiritual emanations from the box. I wish to examine it."

I smiled. "Anna, I promise you, there are no emanations from this box."

"Tisch. I can feel it from here. Just let me . . . steel myself."

I left the box and went over to her. I bent to peer into her eyes, as though that was some kind of medical test. She didn't seem to mind. How many tests a week was she subjected to? "You're not in peak condition."

She scoffed. "Peak condition was fifty years ago, young man." She coughed a couple of times. Not like in the movies where they cough and you know they're going to die soon. Her amusement turned to wonder. "You didn't come to talk to your mother."

"No."

"And you don't need Solly."

"No. Where *is* the little prick?"

"He isn't . . . that. He's in with Jessica Avery. She needs him. So . . ." She closed her eyes. I thought she was asleep, but she was just thinking. "I can't for the life of me imagine why you're here." She opened her eyes. "You're different. Your aura has changed."

"In what way?"

"More light. But more dark, too. Fascinating boy." She lowered her head as though preparing for the ordeal of standing up.

"Anna," I murmured. "Will you let me carry you?"

"Of course not! Foolish child. I am not so infirm. Not yet."

"Right," I said. "But you *are*. And I need you."

That made her pause. She reappraised me. "Oh?"

"I need you. I can't let you waste energy on bravado."

She chuckled. "Me? Bravado?"

"Yes, you. Now stay there."

I went back to the area where I'd placed the box and moved some items around. Pulled a table slightly away from the wall. Took a photo of her ornaments and photos and shit so that I'd be able to put them back where they'd been. I shoved them all away. Moved some chairs. I paced around, looking at the area from all angles. I narrowed my eyes at the windows; I closed them all, peeked out into the grounds, and shut the curtains. Finally, I closed my eyes and thought things through. "Will you be warm enough over here for a while?"

"A while?"

"An hour?"

"Yes. But you may bring my cardy."

"Cardy?"

"I thought that was Manchester-speak for cardigan."

I nodded and got the garment. I spotted some slippers with suspicious bite marks. "Are they for you or the dog?"

"Both."

"We're nearly ready. How about a hot drink?"

She spoke, then looked away quickly. Ashamed to confess weakness. "Later. If you need my energy, I suggest you don't waste time."

I went to the bed and thought about how to pick her up. I shifted to the right of her so I could put my left hand under her left thigh and my right behind her back. Before doing it, I eyed her. She gave me the go-ahead. I picked her up—it was like lifting a sack of doughnut holes—and she put her arms around my neck for stability. We walked across the room.

"Max," she whispered. "Wait." I waited. "Go to the mirror."

I went to the floor-to-not-ceiling mirror. We looked like a romantic vision from a black-and-white movie. A cavalryman, tall and strong, carrying off some woman in a flowing dressing gown. I wondered what face she was seeing instead of mine. "Would you like me to look away?" I was offering to make it easier to remember whichever dashing young Pole had swept her away from whatever ballroom they'd courted in.

"You're not so bad-looking. For an English."

Just as I suspected! She was so deep in her memory she was thinking in Polish. I wondered how often that happened, these days.

"We continue," she whispered. I took her to the chair and set her down. It was insane to do things in this order, but such was my life. She took a moment to revivify herself. I went over to the phone by her bed and called reception. I asked Stacey to bring us some drinks. It wasn't really her job, but Anna was popular.

I'd set up a second chair with its back to the wall, facing Anna. She was touching the box with both hands. "What do you sense?"

"Positive energy. Optimism. Love."

"Tell me when I can open it."

"You may."

I sprang to my feet and began emptying the contents.

It was my old computer. My one-time pride and joy. I nearly burst into tears when I saw it again. AMD processor; Radeon graphics card; Windows 7. For about twenty seconds, I looked at the back of the machine, stupefied by the weird, random holes and slots. Would I be able to reassemble this? I felt like someone in *Star Trek* encountering a dead civilisation and needing to work out how to use their tech in order to send an SOS. But then I clipped the monitor into its slot, and everything else came flooding back. I assembled it and turned it on. The boot-up sequence was as nostalgic as an old school photo.

I plugged the mouse in and put Anna's hand on it. "Do you know how to use a computer?" I said.

She inhaled. "Max Best. Have you ever heard of ICQ?"

"No."

"Then do not be a moron. I was using the internet before you were born. What are we doing here?"

I glanced at the screen. Windows was still thinking about loading. I sat and leant forward. "Anna, do you believe in God?"

"Yes."

"So you believe in the devil?"

"One doesn't follow the other."

"Do you or not?"

She gave me a curious look. "I do not. Evil doesn't need an avatar." She tilted her head. "Do you believe in the devil?"

"Yes."

"Do you believe in God?"

"No."

She laughed. "Your position is less rational than mine."

"I have evidence," I said.

"We all have evidence of the existence of evil."

"I don't mean that. I mean—" Stacey came in with some herbal teas. She stared at the computer and the fact that Anna was out of bed. She raised her eyebrows but left without a word. "Anna, here's the thing. I met a guy. And since then, everything's been bonkers. Okay, wait. The desktop is up. See the cursor? Tell me when it stops spinning. So this guy. He took away one of my memories. I think. Of a computer game about football. I *think*. And he used it to . . . hmm." For the millionth time, I replayed what I remembered of my conversation with Nick in the park. "He used it to make my wish come true. It's one of those cursed wishes." I shuddered. I hadn't said the word curse out loud since it had happened. I looked at my wrist—it was covered in goosebumps. "And now he's mad that I'm . . . I don't know. Overpowered."

She took her hand off the mouse and leaned back. "Why are you telling me this? Why *me*?"

I indicated her books on astrology, her tarot cards, her crystals. "I need someone I can trust completely. Someone who understands esoteric things." My eyebrows shot up when I realised one of the reasons I hadn't admitted to myself. "Yeah, and I need someone who won't laugh at me. I know this is insane."

"You don't seem particularly insane. You seem afraid. But calm. The icon is no longer spinning."

I glanced at the monitor. There was one part of the screen that I couldn't see. It was blurred and unwelcoming. I pointed to it. "There's something here. Something about football."

"There's a picture of a football."

That was easy. "Can you double-click it, please?"

"This seems like something you could do, Max," she said, as the mouse made a familiar *keek keek* noise.

"I can't," I said. "That's the point. He's removed and protected the memory so completely that when I try to get close to it, I get a headache. I'm supposed to sort of learn it all again, step by step. It's the price of my powers. Got to put the time in."

She gave me a sharp look. "Perhaps you should follow the rules."

"If you start getting a headache, we'll stop right away." Her face told me that was *not* what she was worried about. I continued. "This isn't breaking the rules. You might consider this . . . checking what the rules are."

Anna looked dubious. "What now?"

I looked at the screen and was overwhelmed by a tide of nausea. "I'm sorry, Anna, but I'm going to have to ask you to describe what you can see."

"You can't . . . you can't *see* it?"

"No. It's distorted and crazy. It makes me sick."

"I'll describe what I see but I would like you to tell me the whole story from start to finish."

"Maybe," I said. It would be nice to tell someone, that was for sure. "But let's solve the mystery first. If you have spare energy, then we'll see. Otherwise, some other time."

She inhaled in a way that suggested she didn't really believe me. "There are many boxes that I could click. What are we looking for?"

I narrowed my eyes. "I think it's a game. I'm the manager of a team. Is there one that says 'go to team' or something?"

"Start new game," she said. "Restore saved game. Network play."

"That's it!" I said, a film of sweat pushing itself out of my skull and onto my forehead. "Restore game. Choose that."

I heard the hard drive go clicky click. Had it always been that irregular? A bead of sweat dribbled down my spine. What if the drive died right now? What would I do then? Anna peered at the monitor. "It's a list of filenames. Manchester United two. Manchester United one. Queen's Park. Carlisle United."

"Yes!" I said, trying to smooth a vein that was throbbing on my temple. "Mum said I was always Carlisle. Being Man U was too easy. Choose the Carlisle one."

I heard the click of the mouse and the click of the drive. "Good. New screen. At the top it says 'Max Best News.' Ah . . . It seems to be a message. Like Twitter. *'The five goals scored by Tonton Zola Moukoko in the Worthington Cup is a new record.'*"

Worthington Cup! That was one of the many past names for the League Cup. It was currently called the Carabao Cup. That phrase would allow me to carbon date this data to within a few years. My pulse accelerated. Forbidden knowledge was a few well-chosen words away! "Amazing!" I murmured. "What else?"

She looked up, a little flash of annoyance. "There's a lot on the screen, Max. I don't know what you need to know."

"That's okay. I know this will be frustrating. Maybe just say things at random."

She cleared her throat and picked up her tea. It was still too hot. "On the side there are boxes like Continue Game, Max Best, Competitions."

"Choose Max Best."

"You would say that . . . Oh. There's a *lot* of new things here." She closed her eyes and grimaced. "I'm fine. I'm fine. Did you say this was a game? It seems to be a databank. I once had to learn SQL. Okay. Breathe, Anna. This is a list of names. After every name is something. A code."

"Give me an example."

"Smith, GK."

"That means goalkeeper."

"Of course. I get it now. What is . . . AM RC?"

"Attacking midfielder right or centre. Don't get stressed trying to understand everything. Can you please click on the AM RC guy?" Close, now! My heart was struggling. Trying to play Beethoven. Dum dum DUM dum!

"Done. New screen. It seems to be the databank entry for that footballer."

"Does it say things like acceleration, heading, dribbling . . . and a number?"

"Yes, exactly."

Dum dumdum dum dumdum dum. I was starting to feel lightheaded. Lack of food or the thrill of discovery? Fear? I saw Old Nick up on the balcony, flames either side of him. The smell of brimstone. How would I know what brimstone smelled like? I let the moment pass through me. "Can you go back to the previous screen?"

"Oh. How? Never mind. Yes. Done."

"Does it say Max Best as one of the players?"

"No."

"Huh." I rubbed my lips. Without being able to see the screen, this was incredibly difficult. A brute force attack would do, but I couldn't push Anna too far. I had to be scientific. What would a scientist do?

"Found it," she said.

"What?"

"There's a button that says Find. I clicked on it and typed Max Best. There was one entry. It says Max Best, Barcelona. Should I click on it?"

Max Best, Barcelona? What? "Er . . . yes, please."

"Okay. Now what?"

"Er . . . You can see the acceleration and everything else?"

"No. Only some of the things. With the other one I could see a lot more."

"Tell me some you can see."

"Acceleration. Bravery. Dribbling."

"Finishing?"

"No."

"Teamwork?"

"No."

"Jumping?"

"Yes."

I flexed my fingers. They felt like all the blood had been pushed out, like I'd slept on them. When I flexed, I felt the blood rushing around. Horrible.

"Max? What does this mean?"

"It's fine. It makes sense."

"It does?"

"Yes. The things you can see there are the things I could see the day I got cursed. I've added to my knowledge since then, but what you can see is how it was on day one."

"Why is some of it missing? The other player had more data fields."

"Because . . ." I said. Why was it? I understood why the curse blocked some entries for modern-day me—it wanted me to grind to unlock new skills. But in the game I played years ago? "It's the fog of war," I said. "The first player you looked at is in my team. I see him every day so I know everything about him. But this Max Best person, he's gone to Barcelona. I knew about him at one point, but I lost track of him over time. I suppose if we play Barcelona I'll re-learn everything about him."

This was fascinating—to me at least—but I was burning through Anna's precious energy. I needed to get to the point. She was engaged, though. "Would it help if I went back to the first player and told you the missing fields? One was aggression."

Oh! "That's good to know. But I don't want to push my luck. Like you say, I should follow the rules. Mostly. So . . . this screen you're looking at. Max Best, the player. Let me guess. For all his attributes, the number afterwards is twenty."

"That's right."

"Like, all of them?"

"Yes."

I laughed. A kind of disbelieving exclamation. I was such a *prick*. "Is there a place where it says PA and CA?"

"PA and CA?" Her eyes darted around all over the place, but never locked on. "No. At least, not that I can see." She was starting to struggle.

"Nearly done, I promise. The codes for the position. Like AM RC. Can you see that?"

"Yes. GK; SW; D LRC; DM LRC; M LRC; AM LRC, F LRC, ST."

I laughed some more. By now I was equal parts fearful and giddy.

"It's so fascinating. Thank you, Anna." I squeezed and rubbed my eyebrows between my middle finger and thumb. This was what I'd driven three hours for. This was what I'd abandoned Emma for. What else could the computer tell me? A lot, probably. But how much did I want to tax Anna? And was I potentially putting her at risk by including her in this little escapade? "Just one last thing. Can you do the findy thing and type . . . Haaland." I spelled it for her.

"One result. Alf-Inge Haaland."

I clapped my hands together. I'd thought to find Erling Haaland, the striker who was terrorising the Premier League. I wondered if his attributes on the file matched what I'd seen on the pitch. "That's his father. Amazing." I grinned for a while. "Can you exit the . . . the programme?"

"Ah . . ." She clicked a few times, then her head sank. The fact she was too tired to even say "done" was concerning. I picked her up and put her in bed. Tucked her in. Went to open the curtains. I turned the PC off and packed it away. I left the box by the door, then restored all her ornaments to the way they were.

I sat by Anna's bed. Her skin suddenly seemed thin, like a butterfly's wing. I took her hand and held it. After a while, she let out a slow sigh. Had she died? Had I fucking killed her? I must have expressed panic through the muscles in my fingers because her eyes opened and an amused smile crossed her lips. "No chance I'm crossing over until you explain what that little charade was about."

"Great," I said. "So if I don't tell you, you'll live forever."

"Max," she said.

"Can I eat cold spaghetti while I tell you?"

"Uhh," she said, which seemed more like a yes than anything. So I snuck into Mum's room next door and used my phone's flashlight to look for leftover scran.

Anna was halfway asleep when I came back with the plate. I guessed that she would enjoy me telling her about Nick. Bedtime stories for people who believe in crystals and angels. As for me, maybe it'd be cathartic. Maybe it'd help get my thoughts in order.

I wolfed down the food; it calmed me marvellously.

After sipping her tea, Anna indicated that I should begin.

"Right. The adventures of Max Best. See, I was thinking maybe I'd met the devil. But there's no chance. The guy I met was looking for action on the side streets of Manchester. If I was the devil I'd be at Davos and have a helipad in Washington and a yacht in Monaco. Moss Side, Manchester? Forget it. So, I met a demon, maybe." I let out a single laugh. "I don't believe any of this stuff. Listen to me talk like I'm an expert in demonology. The seven layers of hell."

"Nine," she whispered.

"Really? That many? Huh. So. This guy. Tries to get me to sell my soul or some shit. I'm not that keen. He starts talking about wishes. I'm salivating about Hobnobs and I think he's a Polish plumber or something so I humour him."

"The devil isn't Polish," she said.

"Can you please? Thanks. So this Polish guy tricks me into making a wish. Fine. He *grants* my wish. Fine. Insane, but fine. I get on with my life. But now he's acting like I've broken the deal or whatever. But there *wasn't* a deal. In this kind of story, you get something you think you want and later find out you don't want it. Right? That's how it goes. So what's he mad about? Here's the kick—he's mad because he's accidentally turned me into a top footballer."

"Pardon me?"

"I know. And I know what his plan was. He wanted me to have the *ability* to be a top manager, but be unable to ever get a job. Like one of those Greek dudes who knows the future but no one believes him. A lifetime of torment, yeah? That's Nick's plan, right? But see, he doesn't know the first thing about football. But he knows that *I* do. The first thing, at least. Right? So he peeks inside my little head and finds this treasure trove of info. Players, tactics, formations. It's all there, stored in a set of memories called Champion Manager. That's the programme you were just helping me with. Apparently, despite appearances it *is* a game and I used to play it endlessly. So Nick's laughing. All he has to do is turn my memories of the computer game into a . . . into an *interface*. And delete the memories and stop me recreating them. He's basically taken the game and turned it into real life. Amazing. Efficient. Or maybe . . . lazy? And he's made one big mistake. I seem to have been playing an old version of the game. Ancient. In using the game as his interface, he's also used the players from the database and made their stats come true. All those players are probably retired now. There might be a few still knocking around, but they're all old so no one will notice if they are suddenly ten percent faster or slower. But guess what? I was an insufferable little shit as a teenager—no surprise there—and I found a way to edit the database. My mum said, 'He put himself in the game.' I thought she was having an episode, but no. That was a vivid memory of something that happened. But I didn't just put myself in the game. I made myself into a superstar! Beyond superstar, really. The first time I played football since meeting Nick, I got this crazy sense of . . . disconnection. Nothing was right. I was existing on two planes. When it finally resolved, I was me, but I was also Max Best."

"Uuh?"

"From the game. The guy you saw from Barcelona. Knowing me, I probably made myself start in the team I was managing. Carlisle. But then another team scouted me and bought me. So Max Best the manager was unable to keep Max Best the player. Rebelling against authority, as per usual, even when that authority is me. Yeah, when I played for Ziggy's team, the curse got confused and decided to merge the files. But that's wild. That means when I was at FC United, Jackie thought the *old* Max Best had potential. Maybe I *was* good!"

"Uuuh." She didn't understand.

"Don't worry. The upshot is I'm . . . really good at football now. I don't know what my CA and PA are. I don't know if I knew about those things back then. It could be that I've got twenty in all my attributes but I'm still CA one. That would explain a lot. The curse doesn't help me to know where to stand and how to deal with problems in a match. I'll still have to learn loads. But I'm probably already good enough to become a star." I clicked my fingers. "That's it! That's what Nick is worried about. If I get world famous or whatever, the other demons will realise someone made a mistake. Nick will get *done*." That thought delighted and terrified me. "So . . . he's probably going to try to stop me . . . But I need to get a *bit* famous to become a manager. What does he think? I'm not going to use this talent because *he* took a shortcut? He's clueless. I made two thousand pounds today." Visions of Jacuzzis and supermodels and fast cars. "On the other hand . . . if he can change the world to fit how the game worked . . . what else can he do?"

"Boil you and eat you and repeat every day for the rest of eternity."

"Yeah," I said. "But two thousand pounds. That's a lot of avocado on toast."

"Max."

"I could use this talent to make a ton of money. Take proper care of my mum. And you."

"You're not my family. You don't owe me anything."

"I'm a footballer now. I don't have family. I have teams. And you're on my team. I'm going to hire some guy to come here dressed as a hussar and read Adam Mickiewicz to you in the original Polish."

She laughed and turned away. A moment later, she turned back to face me. "I don't understand why Solly disapproved of you. A rare mistake. But you must not use this power if it means angering this demon. I speak for myself and for your mother. We do not want your help if that is the cost."

"Okay," I said. "I hear you. I promise I will not use my powers ever again. Starting . . . now."

She shook her head. A little bit amused, a little bit angry. "Solly is always proven right. Just . . . please don't do anything rash. Please."

I didn't sleep. One, because my house—the terraced one I was supposed to have evolved away from—was sub-zero. I'd left the heating on a bare minimum so the pipes wouldn't freeze and got home too late for the place to really warm up. Two, because the thrill of discovery had ebbed away by the time my head hit the pillow. Now all I could think of was some fragment of demon lore from a book or movie—they got you in your dreams, didn't they? The thought stressed me out.

To make matters worse, I had packed almost everything I owned and brought it to Darlington. I still had my bed and bedding, but no phone chargers. So I couldn't even play a tower defence game to pass the time. I turned my phone off so I'd have enough battery to get through most of tomorrow, then stared at the ceiling.

Sunday, November 20.

The day the World Cup would start. The first-ever winter World Cup, the first in the Middle East, the last chance for Messi to fulfil the prophecy and lift the trophy.

I stayed in bed for as long as possible, but when I turned my phone back on it was still only 4 a.m. Absolute nightmare. If the monthly perk had appeared I would have had something to think about, but it was conspicuous by its absence.

This was crazy-making. Not half a day ago, I'd made two grand in forty-five minutes' work, yet here I was still freezing to death, still lacking the ready cash to go and treat myself to an early breakfast. Where could I go that was warm? On a Sunday morning? Maybe there was an obvious place, but I was too cold to think rationally.

There followed hour after hour of torture-by-cold, which put me in a pissed-off, acerbic, defiant kind of mood. Pretty much the perfect vibe for the next item in my diary.

It was close to 11 a.m. when I moved the chair a little closer and opened the door another crack. No one could see me, I was sure. I opened it another half an inch to let as much sound in as poss. A deep, resonant voice rang out.

"Not so long ago, we had an unexpected visitor. Many of you remember his . . . dramatic entrance." The voice chuckled. "Mr. Best returned and I was foolish enough to ask if he enjoyed my sermon. He told me off. 'Your sermons are too long,' he said. 'I could do it in five minutes.'" Lots of chuckles from the congregation. "I said I would like to hear a sermon of *his*. Imagine my surprise when he invited himself to do just that! Today, we have competing speakers, ladies and gentlemen! One of five minutes, one of fifty. Afterwards, you may tell me which one you preferred. As long as it's mine." A little bit of hubbub. Nothing like this had ever happened before. "I must say, I am burning with curiosity. Please help me to welcome . . . Mr. Best."

Warm applause. I rose, went through the door and up to the pulpit. Lots of intrigued faces were checking me out. There was a section of the pews that I studiously ignored.

"Thank you, pastor," I said. I tapped on my phone until a five-minute timer appeared. I showed the screen to the congregation, and that got a laugh. I invited the pastor to touch the screen to start the timer, and that got another one.

I looked around at south Manchester's Ghanaian community. I wasn't sure if they were good Christians or if it was more that they had to show up to church to fit in. I cleared my throat. "I'm very grateful to Pastor Yaw, but I shouldn't be here. I don't believe what you believe. I would happily lie and cheat to get what I want from you. There is one way we are alike, and that's the way we all want to make our lives better. I think we make a better world by doing what we're good at, and trying to get better at that thing. And if you're exceptional at something that can make the world a better place, it is infuriating to think you would refuse to use that skill. But hold up! This isn't about my opinions. I already said you shouldn't listen to me. So check this out." I lifted the copy of the Bible that was on the pulpit. "I'm going to read from this. Just read with no annotations. Well, that was my plan. The problem is I find some of the language incomprehensible, so I'm going to modernise it. Will I get smited?" I said, addressing Yaw directly.

"There will be no smiting today," said Yaw. "I will cut your mic if you are in danger."

"Top. So it's Matthew twenty-five, verse fourteen," I said.

"Ah!" said Yaw, beaming. "Of course." He looked around to see how many of his flock knew where this was going. He folded his arms, which was an expression of him trying to contain his excitement.

"Once upon a time," I said.

Yaw unfolded himself. "Max, no. Bible stories do not start with *Once upon a time*. No. Please."

I squashed my lips together in fake annoyance. "The story begins . . ." I suggested. That got a nod. "With a rich and famous football manager. Actually he was a player-manager and he liked to take all the free kicks and penalties himself. But that's by the by. One day, he got a job offer to go to the far side of the world and commentate on the World Cup. He didn't want to leave his club, but it was silly money so he said, 'Yeah aight.'"

"Max."

"Now, the manager had three talented players. And he said, guys, when I'm away making paper, I need you to step up. We're going to

West Brom on Saturday and we need three points. Then it's Stoke and you know how physical they are."

"Max." Yaw had his nose in his fingers, but he was enjoying my performance. What I was saying was actually pretty faithful to the original parable. In my opinion.

"So Max goes off to the World Cup, and yeah he's a big star because he's kinda dreamy and intense and whatnot. And he has a nice time and gets back to his club and he calls in his players, one by one. And he says, 'Henri, I've been away. What have you been up to?' And Henri says, 'Oh! I scored five goals and got a defender sent off.' And the manager says, 'Well done, you good and faithful servant to the club! Here's your goal bonuses and by the way, you're my new assistant manager.' And he gets the next player. And he says, 'Raffi, what have you been up to?' And the guy says, 'Gaffer! You asked me to dominate the midfield and I did. Look at my tackle and interception stats!' And the manager says, 'I knew I could count on you. You're class. Here's twenty thousand pounds, tax-free.' And the third player comes in. Max says, 'Hey! These other guys have been dominating. What about you?' And the guy says, 'Oh I didn't want to play bad so I said I had a groin strain and got back into Fortnite in a big way.' And the manager says, 'Bro! I'm fining you two week's wages and giving it to the first guy.'" At this point, I read from the actual Bible to make sure the point was unmistakable. "For whoever *has* will be given *more*, and they will have an abundance. Whoever does not have, even what they *have* will be taken from them."

I left a bit of a space there. I'd tried to improve the pacing of the Bible story by cutting out a really weird part, but my version had a beat missing, and there was a general air of confusion. I didn't mind. There was only one person who needed to completely understand what I was saying, and I had no doubt that he knew this verse better than me.

"This story is often called the Parable of the Talents. Talent being an old word for a gold coin. But it's not about money, is it? It *is* about talent. It's an instruction from God to use the talent he's given you. When you do that, money comes. And so does happiness and fulfilment. That's it. Boom. Can I do a mic drop?"

"No, Mr. Best."

"Okay." I showed everyone my clock. Loads of time left. "Follow that!"

"This is not a rap battle, Mr. Best." Yaw shook his head at me. "I know which Bible verse will form the basis of next week's sermon. Perhaps in a not-so-modern form."

"Did I get it wrong? The style was flippant but I actually did a lot of research."

"You found in the parable what you wanted to find."

I hesitated, then grinned. "Yeah. I seem to have quite the *talent* for that. Maybe I should use it more." I gave a jaunty little wave like I'd said something hilarious, then left through the nearest door.

I walked to my car and leaned against it. Waiting for the second most talented footballer I knew.

24

TIMING

So much of football is about timing.

Egypt are due to play in the first World Cup, but miss their connecting ship to Uruguay. If only they'd arrived, they might have won, and people might have taken African football more seriously in the subsequent hundred years.

Lucas Digne signs for Everton. He loves it and the fans love him. Things go smoothly until he falls out with his manager. After a very public spat, Digne demands a transfer. He moves to Aston Villa. The manager he hates is sacked three days later. If he had only waited . . .

Euro '96, the semi-final, extra time. England versus Germany. Paul Gascoigne slides towards a cross. He's inches from goal—any contact will do. If he had only started his move nought point nought nought seconds earlier . . .

The church building was grim. It had the aesthetic of a prison, and not one of those cool ones where supervillains are kept in transparent boxes. No, a boring prison. A box with iron bars surrounded by iron railings. Vandal paint on the roof.

So why did being there bring me such calm? The answer's obvious: because I felt safe.

Not that being in a church would save me from a demon and his trident, but at least I'd die surrounded by warm, friendly people. Maybe as I lay dying they'd sing *Jerusalem*. Or is that too colonial? I'd once asked Ziggy what his favourite football chant was. I wondered if James Yalley had a favourite hymn. Dumb question. I *knew* he did.

While I was letting my mind drift around, latching onto and releasing ideas, I spotted movement near the church's entrance. James had poked his head out, seen me, and retreated.

I laughed. How can you be so serious, so studious, strive to have maximum dignity at all times, and yet be so goofy?

He came back. I knew he would. His jaw looked clenched. For him, this was round two of our epic battle. The tedious moment in a video game where you have to beat the guy you already beat.

He was wearing his big mustard suit. My heart broke a little bit. The kid was as poor as me, but he had something I didn't. He knew how to be content with what he had.

"Mr. Best," he said. "That was quite a performance. A masterclass."

"Good to see you, James. What's your favourite hymn?"

"Oh." This disarmed him. It disarmed him so much he grew suspicious. "Why do you ask?"

"I was thinking if I got stabbed to death, what song would I want you guys to sing? You know, as the last thing I ever heard."

"If you were stabbed during the service we would scream and panic and run around. There would be no hymns."

"Great. Forget about stabbings. What's your favourite hymn?"

"*O Holy Night*. The David Phelps version." I tapped this into my notepad. I had eight percent battery left. I hate when it says eight percent. It's never seven or nine. Check your phone. If it says eight percent it's just guessing. It could last another minute or another hour. James scanned the car park. Maybe he was looking for the people who had made me think of knife attacks. "Are you going to listen to it now?"

"No. What are you doing out here, James? You're missing the second-best sermon of the week."

He glanced back at the entrance. Wishing he could go back? I couldn't read his expression. "You want to talk. Don't you?"

"No. It's quite vain to assume my sermon was about you. Isn't that one of the sins? Vanity?"

"Oh, Mr. Best. Why are you like this?"

I laughed. "I don't know. What time is it?" He looked at his pound-shop digital watch and told me. Still loads of time before the first World Cup match. Kickoff would be 4 p.m. in the UK. I could have this chat then drive to Darlington. Easy. "James. You know I think you'd be an amazing football player. That's why I asked your pastor to let me do a quick bit before his sermon. But I asked him weeks ago. Feels like weeks ago, anyway. I was all pumped for it. This'll be the final push that James needs! I was actually going to do it all blood and thunder. Fire-and-brimstone preacher, I think you call it? Get really mad about your wasted talent. I was genuinely going to shout: *'Can I get an amen?'* Do you do that here?"

"Only by accident."

"Yeah, well as you heard, I didn't do that. I didn't have it in me. I just don't know how I feel about it all now." I rubbed my nose. "So how was it? Did it persuade you?"

"No."

That was the strange thing about talking to James. I found it really relaxing. He was so implacable. I had to try, but I didn't mind failing. "Okay."

He shuffled his feet around and glanced at me. "Aren't you going to tell me how amazing it is to be a football player? How there's nothing like it?"

"What?" I laughed. "I wasn't planning to do that, no. I used to think about taking you to a stadium, showing you around the facilities and the secret chambers and all that, and then we'd go into the dressing room and there'd be a kit with YALLEY written on the back."

The lack of sleep must have been messing with my head, because I could have sworn I saw a wistful, dreamy look come into his eye. "Why didn't you?"

"Because I'm stupid," I laughed.

"But you could still do that," he said.

"James, there's this dude. He's trying to get me to live my life the way he deems fit. And I find that super annoying. I think I'd prefer to do whatever I want, to be honest. Anyway, I was up all night wondering if I'm doing the same with you. I know it's not exactly equivalent, but I decided to drop it. Respect your wishes."

"You still did the presentation. I won't call it a sermon."

"Yeah, well. I put a lot of work into that three minutes!" I thought about telling him I'd lost my job because of all the Christian chats I'd had on company time, but it seemed overly manipulative. "I got suggestions of Bible passages and I spent hours on aggressively tedious and weird websites trying to understand them. In a way, I'm glad the sermon didn't sway you. Everything you said last time is still true."

"Well . . ." said James. "I think it might have worked, the fact of you making one final effort like that, had the situation been different.

And if you had chosen a different parable. That one does not mean what you think it means."

"Yeah it does."

"But—"

"I'm fine not knowing, James. Thanks."

He looked frustrated. "I have to tell you something, Mr. Best. From the Bible. Please."

I was really all done with that book, preferably forever, but it didn't cost me much to listen. "Fine."

"You should have chosen the story of Zacchaeus. He was a tax collector, and they were despised because they worked for the Romans. And because people at the time did not like paying tax. And people were astonished when Jesus asked to share a meal with this tax collector. Jesus did not spend time with the great and the good. He gave what he had to those at the bottom of society. Labourers, dockworkers, normal people. His philosophy was that healthy people do not need trauma surgeons—injured people do. Do you see?"

"Not in the slightest."

He swallowed some more frustration and nodded. "When we talked, I was prepared to defend all my points. But you agreed with me about most of them. That was very unexpected. I had the strangest feeling that although I was right superficially, I was wrong on a different level."

"Because I didn't argue about every little thing?"

"Yes. Is it strange?"

"I don't know. It makes me feel better about that day. I thought I'd done everything wrong."

"No, Mr. Best. You made me reconsider. I spoke to Pastor Yaw about all this. He agreed with me that football is problematic and troubled and full of problematic and troubled people. And he said, 'Would Jesus, then, spend his Sunday mornings in church with people who already believe in him, or would he perhaps go to a football match?' I told him there aren't many matches on a Sunday morning and he suggested I might try to be less pedantic." He grinned sheepishly.

I was listening to all this in an interested but detached way. If Jesus came back, it wouldn't affect me in the slightest if he chose to go to watch Exeter City versus Port Vale.

"Pastor Yaw suggested," continued James, "that if God has given me the talent you think I have, is it not so that I may pass through doors into rooms that the average person cannot even approach? A football club is full of people who need Jesus. Who is going to be salt and light to them? Who will be their example?"

My skin started to buzz. I was finally starting to understand that I'd misread this situation. He hadn't steeled himself to defeat me again, but to join me! This was a massive moment in my life. The winning lottery ticket had blown all around town and come to rest wedged under the windscreen wiper of my car! I only had to cash it in!

I stared at the young man, soon to be the perfect specimen of a defensive midfielder. With a kind of fascinated horror, I imagined him inside a football club. Giving Bibles to the entire first team squad as Christmas presents. Having the captaincy removed because he tried to organise a team bonding session not in a nightclub, but in the ruins of an abbey. I imagined him openly forgiving Caveman for pissing in his football boots. What a response that would be! I wish I'd thought of it!

Why was this happening? What could I learn from this?

"Do I have this right?" I said. "*Before*, you didn't want to be a footballer because football is wicked and sinful. And now . . . you want to be a footballer *because* it's wicked and sinful?"

"If I have the talent, yes."

"Unreal," I said. Then I paused, trying to work through the timeline. "You didn't just decide this *now*."

"No. I made my mind up some time ago. But Pastor Yaw asked me to wait to tell you."

"Until after I'd pranced around the stage shouting '*Hallelujah*'?"

"Until after you had studied the Word of God."

"He thinks me reading about Jesus smashing up a casino and cooking loads of fish sandwiches is going to convert me?"

"It might."

I laughed. "That's optimistic."

Once again I got mentally stuck on the timing. If James had told me his decision the day he had made it, I might not have joined in the trial at Chester. I almost certainly wouldn't have become a player. I wouldn't have riled up Old Nick. It was, if I was being suspicious, as though I'd been manoeuvred into conflict with him. If there were demons, were there angels? I chewed on my thumbnail and looked away. I was making things needlessly complicated. The timing—and what it meant—was a coincidence.

James wrung his hands. "Mr. Best, I would like to thank you."

"For what?"

"For trying to respect my wishes. It would have been easy to use your playing career as a selling point."

"My playing career? Did Kisi find some match report that mentioned me?"

"She did not need to, Mr. Best. We were there."

"What?"

"We were at the match yesterday. All of us."

"Oh." I didn't know how to feel about that. I must have included Kisi in my text blast. And she'd insisted on going and for some reason, the whole family had decided to make it a day out. I smiled. It made me feel a bit better about showing off. At least they'd have had something to talk about on the long drive home. "Did you enjoy it?"

"The first half, yes. I have to say, Mr. Best, that when it comes to your personal performance . . ." He sighed. "Such tactical indiscipline." He waited for me to react, then burst out laughing. "I am sorry. That was a joke. I am trying to do more jokes. You were incredible. What more can I say? Kisi burst into tears when they announced your substitution." He smiled nostalgically. "And I was, to be truthful, almost as disappointed. I trust Pastor Yaw when it comes to Bible scholarship. I trust my father when it comes to aeronautics. I trust you when it comes to football. If you say I have the talent to go far, then I believe you. Strange as it may be. I am ready to put my career in your hands."

Huh! I thought about explaining that my playing skills were quite separate from my scouting skills, but that would have been a very James way of communicating. In the end, he was right to trust me. Probably. "James, wow. Your career in my hands? This is really unexpected. Wow. I thought this was over. Maybe I shouldn't . . . No, this was his idea. He can't be mad about this."

"Who?"

"Oh, nothing. Just thinking out loud. I'll have to find you somewhere to train. Get you started."

"Is your club not an option?"

"No. Nor is Chester. That youth system is a mess. FC United maybe. But that means talking to . . . Or I suppose I could get Ziggy to do it. No, it doesn't feel right. I'll have to think about it." My head started fizzing with options and possibilities. I grinned. I was reenergised. "James Yalley! Youngster! My new DM client! I'm building quite a team! All right!" I held my hand out for him to shake.

And of course, when we shook hands, the monthly perk dropped. And it was a corker.

25

COPA MUNDIAL

I read through the perk—twice—then looked at James. "Would you like to help me with a project?"

"Oh. Yes. Probably. What is it?"

"Two things. One. You're a big movie buff and you like Bible stuff. I've often thought of writing a screenplay. Maybe one where there's a guy who's made enemies with a demon. Maybe you could find out what the Bible says about killing demons. Silver bullets, holy water, garlic, whatever."

"Well—"

"And the most important. Watch Qatar versus Ecuador with me later today. It starts at four p.m."

"Oh. Is this part of my training? You will teach me about football?"

"No. It's . . . my training. This is for me. You can say no quite freely."

"But I would like to watch football with you."

"Great. Go back to church. I need to go somewhere warm and get a tea. Slice of toast."

James reached into his pocket and handed over his house key. "We have tea. And bread. The house is warm."

I hesitated. "You should check with your mum."

"There is no chance she will refuse. She might even be upset if I check with her. She might think I was not sufficiently forceful with my hospitality."

"I feel like I should ask if you're sure three times or something, but fuck it. I need a tea. Thanks. See you in a bit. Don't forget to boo when your pastor finishes."

I drove to their house, let myself in, made a tea, and pottered around while drinking it. On the side table where the red-eyed photo of young James was, there were two copies of our contract. Both signed. I was briefly emotional. The family believed in me so much! I had to repay their faith.

I sat on the sofa, but then my brain finally processed something it had seen a few moments earlier. I stood again and wandered over to the coffee table in front of the TV. There was a printout—an unformatted printout of some website. It had the word *Darlington* on it—that's what caught my eye. The publication was the *Northern Echo*.

DARLINGTON 4 ALFRETON 1: MYSTERY WINGER THRILLS IN CUP

A sensational 45-minute performance by previously unknown winger Max Best secured Quakers progress to the third round of the FA Trophy. The 22-year-old debutant, who was not only playing his first match for Darlington but for anyone, scored with an 80-yard solo dribble, a 35-yard free kick, assisted, and caused havoc every time he surged forward.

Quakers manager David Cutter said, "The lad's done well. He takes free kicks like that in training, but you sometimes never see players do it in a match. We're made up for the boy. He's put us in the next round and given the club a boost and no mistake. But we're fuming about their goal. It was miles offside and I've said that to the ref."

There followed a surprisingly biased match report that at least got the basic facts right. It was interesting to find out what happened in the second half. I had heard the score on *talkSPORT* but didn't know more than that. And didn't care much, either.

I went to make another cup of tea. Mystery winger! That was fun. Good for my reputation and storytelling project. Not so good in terms of pissing off demons or whatever. But I didn't need to worry about that until our next game, which would be on Saturday.

I sat back down on the sofa and sighed. I reopened the message that introduced the new perk. It was bonkers.

Quadrennial Assigned TINO Accumulator/Reducer
VERSION COPA MUNDIAL

Cost to enter: Free. However, your existing balance of XP (1,606) has been converted into TINOs.

Effects: Chance to win/lose/retain TINOs by answering World Cup-themed questions and completing tasks.

Stipulation: To participate, you must watch every match in the Qatar 2022 World Cup. Failure to heed this rule will result in irrevocable XP loss.

Bonus! At 3:59 p.m. you will have a chance to greatly increase your starting pool of TINOs.

The sofa was really quite cosy, so I took my shoes off and stretched out.

I'd waited for ages for this perk, and it turned out to be not just bizarre and aggravating, but actively destructive. It had literally stolen my XP! The curse shop was still open, but I had no cash. It felt really strange. Being broke in real life was one thing, but losing my XP left me feeling like I'd been mugged.

Only a bit, though, because if stealing 1,600 XP from me was the full extent of Old Nick's revenge, I'd probably take that. It was a couple of Premier League matches, and I was going to have some disposable income very soon. And obviously there was no way that this tiny sacrifice would satisfy him. Sixteen hundred XP to placate a guy who wore two scarves? No chance.

Which led me to wonder if this stolen XP thing was perhaps *not* a punishment. I had 1,606 TINOs, whatever they were. I knew this because I had a new tab on my interface called MUNDIAL. It was pretty sparse for now—just a record of my holdings. And maybe after the World Cup I'd be able to convert the TINOs back into XP.

So yeah. Crazy. I supposed I'd find out soon enough what it all meant. For now, it was clear that I had to try to watch every match. There was no way to watch absolutely every one—for a start, the final group games were played simultaneously! So I'd miss eight of the sixty-four games at least. And non-league football wasn't taking a break for the World Cup, so I'd probably have to play for Darlington during some of the fixtures. Maybe I could avoid the result and watch on catch-up?

I had a bit of a think of what it all meant.

And then I was shaken awake by James Yalley.

They had let me sleep, cooked their Sunday feast in near silence, and taken their meals into the master bedroom so they wouldn't disturb me.

Mr. Yalley had wanted to rouse me because my neck was in a bad position, but Kisi had flipped out and insisted I be allowed to rest. James had agreed with both of them, but eventually decided I wouldn't want to miss the match. He'd woken me with ten minutes to spare!

Groggy, feeling weird, and in a slight panic, I grabbed James, staged a photo of him signing his contract, then virtually dragged him towards the nearest pub.

"I'll explain in a bit," I said. "But the next few minutes are key. Just go along with me, okay?"

He was following like a toddler, drifting behind then rushing to catch up. "Okay, but Mr. Best, we could have watched the match at home. It's on BBC1, not on Sky."

"Oh," I said. "Good point. Well, you wanted to meet some degenerates. You're welcome."

"Why are we rushing? Are you so excited by the World Cup you wouldn't want to miss a single second?"

That was a good question. Was I excited? "I'm not into it right at this very moment in time. I've been too busy. Too much going on. But I'm *ready* to be into it. Do you know what I mean? Once it starts, once England play, I'll probably be excited, yeah."

"Oh." His tone put me on alert. *He* wasn't excited. I didn't think I could say anything that would make him go home and rip up the contract, but why take the risk?

"You're dubious."

"Mr. Best. Please tell me what you really think about it."

"About it being in Qatar? That's what you mean, right?" I grabbed his wrist and checked the time. We had ages and the pub was in sight. This would be a good use of my time. "It's obviously problematic. There was corruption right from the off and everyone knows it. So that's kind of hilarious if they were trying to promote a positive image. Then there's the fact that football isn't normally played in a desert. So they had to move it to the winter, and that has messed up the football season. FIFA and UEFA really seem to be trying to destroy the sport. They'll do literally anything for a sneaky dollar. They're abysmal."

"Why do I feel like there's a 'but' coming?"

I laughed. "Yeah! I was planning a *but* ages ago but I kept remembering more godawful shit. Here we go: but. But the World Cup is the pinnacle of the sport. It's top. Yeah, the Champions League is the most elite in terms of actual matches, actual quality, but nothing beats the colour and sound and surprise of the World Cup. I told my . . . uh, I told this girl that surprise was important in sport, and you don't get much surprise in the Champions League.

"In the Champions League, we know all the teams and managers and players. But the World Cup! There's always some rando who turns up and is amazing. Roger Milla. Goycochea. Man City, the pricks, have two great players in every position, but national teams are more flawed. It's kind of random who is born in a certain geographical location at a certain point in time. There's probably a country with three amazing strikers but no goalies. There's definitely a team with two elite left backs and nothing else. That's Scotland, and that's why they didn't make it to the finals. And unlike the Premier League and Champions League, which are annual, the World Cup is every four years, so like the Olympics great players might only get one chance to take part. The rarity makes it special. I'm twenty-two. If I turn out to be the GOAT, I'll still only have two World Cups in me. And chances are I'll be injured for one.

"That's the stakes for the players. For the rest of us, the whole thing is great fun. Shakespeare on Ice. And listen. The World Cup should never be in the winter, that's obvious. But once in a thousand years, it's interesting! Take the English players. They normally play nine months with more games at a higher intensity than in any other country and then they get two weeks off and fly to the World Cup shattered and lose to Iceland because their legs are gone.

"But this time anyone who isn't injured is in peak condition. Peak condition! There's never been a World Cup where everyone's at absolutely full fitness. The quality should be really high."

I looked at James. He was deep in thought, looking at the ground in front of his feet. I got the feeling he wasn't very happy with what I'd said. I mentally sighed. He'd probably read about all the bad news coming out of Qatar. I had tried to skip it as much as poss. It was depressing.

I realised I'd been waving my hands around in an excited way, so I tried to match James's subdued energy. "Well, we're here now. Let's find a good spot."

The pub was an absolute hellhole, but it had nice, big screens. It was only a quarter full, but people were starting to file in, wanting to watch the match in public. Shared experience. Covid lockdowns had made people crazy for contact. I understood it.

We got a good table with a view of multiple screens. A guy was going round taking orders. With my hundred-million-pound midfielder next to me, I decided I could risk a splurge, and ordered two big cokes and some cheesy chips. I also asked why the sound was off on the telly.

"Gary Lineker is telling us why the World Cup shouldn't be in Qatar," he said. "Woke snowflake tripe. Stick to the football. We'll put the sound on when the actual match starts."

"Cool," I said, and he fucked off.

"Mr. Best," said James. "Do you share his views? That caring about human rights is woke snowflake tripe?"

I shrugged. "James, maybe on balance the tournament shouldn't be there, but it is. What do you want me to do about it?"

He shook his head. "Nothing, I suppose. Although . . ."

"What?"

"I suppose I would like you to say something to that man."

"He wouldn't listen. What's the point?"

He did that unhappy face again, and rubbed a knuckle. "If I am to be a professional, I should watch the matches. And learn."

"Good," I said, and something about the way it came out kind of sickened me. "Look, James. Nobody gives a shit what we think. But when I'm a top manager and you're the best midfielder in the league, people will listen. That's what I'm working towards. Until then, I'm not going to beat myself up about it. No one listened to Jesus until he started going to parties making wine appear out of thin air. Then people really started to take notice."

He nodded a few times. "Not accurate but yes. I take the point."

I kept an eye on him for a while. I felt—as usual with him—that I'd done a bad job with that conversation. "James, I'm going to need your help. You ready?"

It was 3:58 and some number of seconds. I bit my nails. The next time the clock changed, something big would happen. I could feel it.

Time pushed forward one digit with a huge *GONG* that only I could hear.

TINO Accelerator Round Begins!

Task: Choose one box.

The number corresponding to the text in your chosen box will be added to your store of TINOs.

Once all boxes are revealed, you will have fifteen seconds to make your choice. If you do not choose, a box will be chosen randomly. The box with the highest number will not be included in the randomisation process.

GET READY

This was going to look absolutely insane to James. I had a sudden inspiration and grabbed my earphone case. I opened it, shoved one bud into my right ear, and tapped on my phone. The shitty earphones I had didn't even work if you only had one in, but James didn't know that.

"James, I might ask you some questions. Get ready. Oh, shit."

It was happening.

There were five squares on the screen. Each had a padlock-style five-digit number inside, but every digit was spinning round. The intention was clear—the number would be revealed at the end of the mini game. The numbers faded away, still spinning.

The first box turned red and text in a white font appeared. This particular palette seemed incredibly familiar and comforting to me, but I couldn't think why. The text said:

Number of billions of dollars spent by Qatar in preparation for the World Cup.

I turned that into a question for James.

"Oh," he said. "Lots, I would think. They had to build eight stadiums. Perhaps eight or nine billion?"

They had to build eight stadiums? They didn't have any before? What?

The next square filled up—it had the same red-and-white colour scheme so there were no clues there.

Qatar's FIFA world ranking when they were named as hosts of the 2022 World Cup.

"Oh!" said James again. "These questions are hard. What is this for?"

Do you fucking know or not, I nearly hissed. "Guess."

"Not in the top twenty. Perhaps forty? I do not know."

So if James was right, choosing box one would get me 9 TINOs and box two would get me 40. Barely seemed worth the stress of playing this mini-game, and believe me, it was stressful. And it only got worse.

The next square:

Number of workers who have died building World Cup-related infrastructure.

Holy fuck, that was dark. I didn't have time to think it through.

"James, how many workers died building these stadiums and stuff?"

He frowned and whipped out his elderly smartphone. He tapped away with a maddening lack of urgency.

The next square filled in.

Number of FIFA Executive Committee members who were arrested in 2015

multiplied by

Maximum penalty for same-sex relationships in Qatar, as measured in years in prison

multiplied by

Amount of carbon set to be emitted during the World Cup, as measured in millions of tonnes.

Oh my God. I broke out into a cold sweat as realisation set in.

This was Old Nick's doing, I was sure. He'd written all this stuff to make me feel like shit. Presumably, if I'd told James I was *against* Qatar hosting the tournament, all these options would be *positive* things. Number of jobs created, number of solar panels installed, whatever. Nick just wanted to provoke me. To stop me enjoying the best tournament in the world!

The last box:

Number of litres of water needed per day to maintain one grass pitch in one stadium in Qatar, a desert country.

"I don't fucking care!" I said. James looked startled and appalled, but I got my act together and gave him a placating arm-touch and pointed to my earbud. "Soz," I mouthed.

This was beyond frustrating. I just wanted my XP so I could buy perks. I rubbed my face like a maniac, until I noticed that the fifteen second timer had started.

I froze. There was too much information provoking too many feelings, and too little time.

"The official line from the Supreme Committee," said James, looking at some website, "is that there have been thirty-seven deaths at World Cup stadiums, three of which were work-related."

That snapped me out of it. "Thirty-seven died but only three were because they were toiling in the fucking desert sun building eight stadiums from scratch? Is that a joke?"

He didn't react well to me haranguing him. He spoke like a schoolboy addressing a fierce teacher. "Was that the wrong answer?"

I didn't reply. The brazen lie had me fuming. I turned the heat into steam to get the cogs in my brain whirring.

Options one and two, the billions spent on infrastructure and the world rankings seemed like they'd be relatively low numbers, so even getting them right wouldn't make all that much of a difference to how many TINOs I had. I wasn't going to touch the multiplication one in case any of the three numbers were zero. Seemed like it might be a trick question. The water one—who knew?

So I slammed the worker deaths option, and with the shittest animation yet, the five red backgrounds melted away to reveal the padlock combination behind. Two hundred billion spent. World ranking 112. 6,522 migrant deaths. The multiplication added up to 560, but I'm not reckless enough to show the workings. And each pitch needed ten thousand litres of water a day.

I'd chosen the second-best option, then!

Great news.

I relaxed. Hopefully that would be the end of the unwanted social commentary and I could focus on the football.

On the TV screens, the referee was getting ready to blow his whistle to start the tournament. In my vision, I had cursemail. I opened it.

DIVIDE AND CONQUER

Your TINOs will now be evenly split across all World Cup matches.

You have accumulated 8,128 TINOs.

You will have 127 TINOs to stake on each of the 64 matches.

Your current TINO balance: 0.

Stake? Did it mean gambling? Balance zero? What?

I didn't need to wait long to find out. Almost as soon as Qatar versus Ecuador started, I got two notifications.

QAT-ECU QUESTION 1

Stake: 12.7 TINOs

Which Qatar player in the starting 11 has the highest acceleration?

Time limit: end of first half

QAT-ECU QUESTION 2

Stake: 12.7 TINOs

Which Ecuador player in the starting 11 has the highest stamina?

Time limit: end of match

Ah! Finally! Some football stuff!

I let some air into my lungs and took a few seconds to calm down. That half a minute had been incredibly intense. I gave James a bump on the arm and a thumbs-up. I popped the earbud out, fussed my slightly clammy hair, and thought about how to explain what the fuck was going on.

26

HOLY MOSES

While I was touching a two fingers to my neck to see how fast my pulse was going, a couple of young women approached our table. White, thin, fake tan, high-waisted jeans, big hoopy earrings. One's neck was bare, the other wore two different necklaces. Now that I was spending most of my time with tall, powerful footballers, these women seemed hilariously tiny. They made up for it with oversized personalities, though.

"Can we sit 'ere?" said one. James and I were on one side of a table for four. "We wanna watch the match and not get bovvered."

"Oh," I said. "And you think we won't bother you."

"Nah," said the other one. "You won't."

I would have invited them to sit down, but they already had.

I gave them a double-barrelled blast of attention, then got on with my life. "James," I said. "We need to watch carefully to find the fastest Qatar player. And the guy from Ecuador with the highest stamina."

He didn't respond. I realised he was staring at the women with wide eyes. The horny little scamp! He felt me smirking at him and sorted his face out. "Fastest. Highest stamina. Yes."

"What are you doing?" said the first woman, eyeing my earbud.

Good question! My answer would be for James's benefit too.

"I'm doing a kind of analysis of the match, like for the TV coverage. Have you seen those little graphics that come up to show who ran the fastest or who did the hardest shot? That kind of thing."

"Oh. Like an expert."

"Yes," I said, flicking my gaze away from the screen just long enough to be polite.

"Is the money good?" They'd brought drinks with them from the bar, and this one was stirring her straw in a very suggestive manner. James looked away. Then back.

"It can be. I'm just starting. You could say I'm being paid in experience."

Just then, something insane happened. The camera picked out a stupendously disagreeable face in the crowd and the curse started spamming my vision with buttons. Each one demanded that I "SHOUT 'TINO.'"

What? Why? It was absurd. But I wanted my XP back. Just in time, I obeyed. "TINO!" I said, for some reason pointing at the screen.

The second woman laughed. "What the hell was that?"

"That was the boss of FIFA," said James, who then tried to pull his neck into his jacket, like a turtle.

I mentally slapped myself. Of fucking course. *Infantino*. The president of FIFA. When I'd said his name, all the buttons had popped and a green number 1 appeared, then faded away. I went into my MUNDIAL tab and found I'd been awarded one TINO. Huh.

"Yes but why—"

"Wait wait wait!" I said, pointing at the screen, spider senses tingling. Two minutes in and Ecuador had a free kick in a good position. The pitch, apparently drenched with ten thousand litres a day, was a frankly gorgeous shade of green that made the all-yellow Ecuador kit look dream-like. Qatar's maroon kit was a phenomenal counterpoint.

The Ecuador player chipped the ball, the Qatar goalie came and tripped over himself, and Ecuador scored. Easy! Two minutes and the Qataris were being humiliated in their own tournament! But the goal was disallowed for offside. That was shocking to me—in all the replays the Qatari defenders were virtually on the goal line. How could it be offside? The TV guys started to show replays, and finally they gave an angle that proved that the call was, in fact, correct. "Wow. Impressive from the linesman."

"Mr. Best," said James. "They are using artificial intelligence to help with the offside decisions."

"Huh. Cool. I guess?"

That's when questions three and four dropped.

QAT-ECU QUESTION 3

Stake: 12.7 TINOs

Which Ecuador player in the starting 11 has the highest transfer value?

Time limit: end of match
QAT-ECU QUESTION 4
Stake: 12.7 TINOs
Which formation are Qatar using when out of possession?
Time limit: next 50 seconds

Whoa! The last one had a tight limit. I repeated the question to James.

"The same one they use when in possession, surely? The graphic said five-three-two."

"Not necessarily," I said. This was something I'd been coming to realise. What looked like teams splintering and buckling under the weight of an opposition attack was, in fact, often intentional. For example, Darlington were 4-4-2 with the ball and sometimes 4-5-1 without it. "Quick time limit on this one. Forget the other questions."

We stared at the screen—even the women—in rapt silence. It was a strange way to watch a match. I started to get the feeling that I was taking an exam. Midterms.

"Mr. Best," said James, cautiously. "It looks like five-three-two to me."

"I agree. Let me try it." I pushed my earbud further into my ear and said "Five-three-two." Although, of course, actually answering the question was done via the interface.

You have chosen: 5-3-2
Your answer status: CORRECT

"Yes!" I said, punching the air. "James, mate. Yes. Come on! Whoo!" James was almost the perfect companion for this. If I was being arrogant, and nobody has ever tried to stop me being just that, I would say that I was mentally quicker than him. But he was more methodical, more thorough. In school, he probably didn't have moments of brilliance that got teachers buzzing like I did, but he was pretty much a straight-B student while my grades were a surrealist scatter graph. On a football pitch, he'd virtually never be out of position, would rarely let the team down, but might not create much, either. He was a born defensive midfielder, while I was a born winger, wild and instinctive. I clamped onto his shoulder and shook him. He grinned happily while I chanted: "James! James! James!"

I checked my screens. I now had 13.7 TINOs. I bit my nails while I calculated. If this mini game allowed me to win up to 127 TINOs per match, and if it played fair and converted my TINOs back into XP at the end, one to one, with a sixty percent answer rate I could end up with something like 5,000 XP.

Which was obviously fantastic, and motivational in its own right.

But something else was happening, too. The questions so far had been pitched near the limit of what I could answer. Guessing a guy's stamina just by looking seemed really hard, like maybe just a bit beyond what I could realistically do without the curse. But the acceleration one and the formation one seemed doable. Very doable. And the other one . . .

"Now, James. This one might be fun. From those players on the pitch, who has the highest transfer value?"

He frowned. "That's impossible to know."

"No!" I chuckled. "This is one I'm confident about. We can work it out. This is as close to science as football gets. It's pure economics."

"What makes one player more valuable than another?" asked one of the women.

I couldn't keep thinking of them as "the women." "What are your names?" I said, half-expecting them to say Emma and Gemma.

"Stacey. Chloe."

"It's a great question, Stacey. The main thing is skill level. If I had to summarise that into one phrase, I'd call it 'current ability.'"

"His FIFA rating," said Chloe.

I stared at her. That phrase seemed familiar. I looked around my mind to find it, but there was nothing there. Deleted by the curse, maybe, along with the Champion Manager stuff. "Yeah. Something like that. Are they out of two hundred?"

"I don't know. My brother never shuts up about it. I could text him."

"Nah. Let's say it's out of two hundred. So there's James, here, and me, and Chloe, and Stacey. We've all got FIFA one fifty or however you say it. Which one of us has the highest market value?"

"You," said James.

"Why?"

"You're a winger. You score goals and assist."

"Yeah yeah yeah I'm amazing," I said, waving the evidence into admission. "Goals are valuable, sure. But the main thing is I'm a man. Sorry, ladies, but the market isn't there for women yet."

"It is growing, though," said James.

"It is, mate, it is. I'm keeping a very close eye on it, let me tell you."

"I bet you are," said Chloe, trying to challenge me with strong eye contact. I gave her a steady stare back until she blushed and looked away. Tsk. Too easy.

"I'm twenty-two and James is sixteen," I said, eyes back on the TV.

"I am seventeen," said James.

"What?"

"My birthday was in October."

I checked his player profile. He was right, not that I was seriously expecting him to not remember his own birthday. "Shit. If you hadn't shot me down I would have got you something."

"That is all right."

"Basically, at twenty-two I'm coming into my peak. Imagine I'm a car. My engine is good, there's no wear and tear. If you buy me today you're going to get five or six years of awesome service from me. Or, you might sell me to a bigger club in a couple of years and make a big profit. Someone who's seventeen, if they're already great, that's worth more money because you get ten years of service *and* resale value. But if it's a seventeen-year-old with *potential*, he might never reach that potential so buying him is a risk. When I look at Ecuador, their best player is Enner Valencia. He's really top. But he's thirty-three. If you buy him today you might only get a year out of him. He's had the engine replaced, his axle is worn down, the tyres are frayed, and someone's stolen his hubcaps. If you're paying a lot of money for him, you're doing something wrong."

"Skill. Age. Gender," said James. "Is there anything else?"

"Yeah. The Premier League has the most money these days. Premier League teams have to include a certain number of English players in their squads, so there's a bit of a premium paid for English players. Marketability is another factor. James, you're cute in your own goofy way, but my fee would be higher because I'm *unbelievably* attractive and I'm into disabled football and I'm good with kids. I'm fucking *dreamy*. And I've got my own branding, already. Max Best seventy-seven. A club that buys me can sell more replica kits. What else? Yeah just the fact that the Premier League is hard. Some really good foreign players can't fit in. Can't hack it. No shade on them, it's just how it is. So someone who has already played in the Premier League should command a higher price than someone who hasn't. Oh, and of course, the position on the pitch. There are loads of centre backs and centre midfielders. There are fewer left-sided players. There aren't many elite DMs, which is why I'm excited about your future, James. Ladies, this guy's a hundred-million-pound player. No joke. And strikers who score loads of goals, of course *they* are the rarest thing of all." I turned back to the screen. "But like I said, the best striker in this match is old."

There was a brief break in the conversation. A lull. Stacey and Chloe were giving me a look that I can't describe. Sceptical hope? Is that a thing?

"Moisés Caicedo," said James.

"Explain."

"He is twenty-one. He plays for Brighton in the Premier League. He is a midfielder or defensive midfielder. I am no expert but he looks to be a cut above the others."

"Amazing," I said. I'd seen the player in question, but I would have sworn he was a thirty-year-old veteran. If he was playing like *that* at twenty-one, he was clearly destined for bigger things. It seemed clear that this was the answer. No one else came close.

"Why don't you check his FIFA rating before you decide?" said Chloe.

"Hmm," I said, and brought my phone closer.

The curse hijacked my vision.

THE REFEREE IS REACHING INTO HIS POCKET.

It would *know* if I cheated. The punishment, I was sure, would be disproportionate. What card would come out of the pocket? Straight red? "No, thanks," I said. "I have to do it just by watching."

"They won't know," said Chloe.

"I'll know. It's not just about the answer. It's about how I get there. James, I think you've nailed it. I didn't notice he played for Brighton."

"It was shown just before the match when you were distracted."

This mini game was starting to feel like a two-man job. It was strange that the curse allowed me to get help. Maybe it wanted me to have these kinds of discussions. "Moses Caicedo," I said. "I'm going in."

"Moisés. Not Moses."

You have chosen: Moisés Caicedo
Your answer status: CORRECT

"Yes!" I loved this mini game! It was like my own personal pub quiz. "I'm on a roll. Let's do the player with the highest stamina. Who do you think?"

"From Ecuador? It makes sense to choose a Premier League player. I hear it is the most intense league in the world. Caicedo has to run around a lot. Estupiñán, the left back, also plays for Brighton."

"I'm going to double up on Caicedo. He looks pretty fit to me."

You have chosen: Moisés Caicedo
Your answer status: INCORRECT

"Well, shit," I said. There were only three people there, but it felt like the eyes of the world were on me. Watching me fail. I supposed if I wanted to be a football manager I'd have to get used to this feeling.

"What was the right answer?" said Chloe. Or Stacey. I wasn't really paying attention.

"I don't know," I said. "They didn't tell me. Maybe they'll reuse the question in the next match." I sighed. That had smacked my accuracy from 100% to 66%, but my TINO balance didn't go down. I was allowed to make mistakes.

I went internal, and the women sensed that. I watched the match while the women talked to each other and—increasingly—James. I was aware that they were asking him about his football career, and he said he hadn't really started yet but Mr. Best had been pursuing him for weeks.

"I wonder what *that* feels like," said Chloe, and there was some sniggering. "*He's* a player, though, right?"

"Yes," said James. "And he is a footballer, too." I shook my head. His jokes were getting worse. How was that possible?

"Found him," said Stacey. "I typed Max Best seventy-seven. There's one video."

"One?" said Chloe, dubiously. My sex appeal had just fallen ninety-seven percent!

While I tried to focus on the World Cup, the women started making little gasping noises as they watched some TikTok. I checked James. He was back to being wide-eyed. I tried to remember what it was like being seventeen. All I could remember was being kind of desperate the whole time. The noise from the video was annoying—the women kept repeating the same part again and again. "Let me see that," I said, holding out my hand.

Instead of passing the phone over, Stacey came right next to me and held it in front of us, more or less as though she wanted to take a selfie. Chloe, not to be outdone, came and pushed into me from the other side. It was all a bit obvious, a bit cheap, but strangely, I didn't mind.

I reached out and gently prised the phone from Stacey's hand. While the women squashed into me, I homed in on the screen and watched myself barge Glynn off the ball and burst past Osgood, the Alfreton player. The noise from the people around the cameraman was thrilling—I got goosebumps. Then when I accelerated past the goalie, the excitement increased in pitch and volume. While I dallied in front of the open goal, one guy shouted, "What's he *doing*?" The same guy then made an orgasmic *ooaaaaaoowwww!* noise as my feint took the two defenders out of the game, and then as I scored the camera and mic were swallowed by fans. One shitty transition later, I was blasting the free kick into the goal. The camera guy must have been standing near Old Nick, because I turned to glare almost down the lens. It was pretty fucking weird-looking, especially because either side of me in the present day, the women sank into me like my defiance was the hottest thing they'd seen in their brief lives. The video continued with a rapid-fire selection of me trying to assist Blondie and Junior, and some of my one-touch passes. It was only seeing it on camera that made me realise how balanced and composed I looked compared to all the other players. I was different gravy.

I stopped the video and checked the title.

MAX BEST DARLO PLAYER OF SEASON AFTER 45 MINS LOL

"Do you want me to send it to you?" asked Stacey. Trying to get my phone number.

"I don't need to see it again," I said, with a PG-13 smile. "I did it."

I returned her phone, gently pushed them both away from me, and gave James another glance. I was worried all this female attention would be off-putting for him. If he became a star player, he'd have to deal with it, too. Would that make him change his mind about his new career, maybe?

The look on his face said: no, please.

With help from James and the two randos, I answered more questions. The last one in the first half popped up when Ecuador got a penalty. Enner Valencia got ready to take it, and a button appeared:

Will he score yes/no?

Everyone on the table was confident. I hit yes, and we all high-fived each other when the ball rolled in. James was sweating with pleasure.

The first four questions in the second half were about attributes, formations, and things you could try to work out based on the information given by the broadcast. Having a helper was definitely a bonus, but I'd probably want to watch most of the games alone so I could focus on them absolutely to the exclusion of everything else.

Near the end I finally answered question 1. We thought that Qatar's fastest player was either Ahmed Alaaeldin or Akram Afif. I chose Afif because it was FIFA backwards, and that turned out to be right.

By far the most interesting question was the very last one. It was basically a mini essay. I filled it in by thought-to-type, which took about four seconds, and then fiddled around adding and removing commas and semicolons for what seemed like four hours.

Rate the Qatar manager's performance, then justify your opinion.

I gave him a nine, and wrote that he didn't have a lot of quality to call on, that his normally reliable goalkeeper had performed like shit, and that his team had actually created two golden opportunities that could have got a very impressive draw.

The curse liked my analysis and awarded me the TINOs. Great, but I'd have loved some feedback.

At the end of the match, I had got six out of ten right and earned 76.2 TINOs, with a bonus of 1 for shouting TINO.

XP balance: 0

Debt repaid: 178/3000

TINOs: 77.2

James walked with me back to the church, where one of the volunteers was waiting to unlock the gate for me. Apparently, James and the Yalleys had organised some kind of CIA mission with SMS relays and walkie talkies and whatnot to ensure that I'd be able to pick up my car whenever I wanted. Too good for this world.

"Did you have a nice time?" I asked.

"Yes, Mr. Best," said James. He seemed to want to say something. I only needed to give him the right prompt.

"Is there something you want to tell me?"

He looked away. "Only that I am very motivated to become a player. To learn. I will watch all the World Cup matches and study them. If you would like to send me questions to think about, I would greatly enjoy it."

"You'll hold your nose, will you?"

"I do not know," he said. "I get the feeling I was overly critical of Qatar. Perhaps I should study the issues more."

"Or," I said, slapping his upper arm. "Study them less. Or not at all. Because no one gives a shit."

"Mr. Best," he said.

"Just learn your trade. When you've got a few mil in the bank, you can get religion." I smiled. "So to speak."

He smiled back at me. I was wrong to suggest he was less marketable than me. That smile could open a lot of hearts. "Yes, Mr. Best."

I gave him a final handshake and drove back to Darlington.

I went to the digs first, and loaded my car with my stuff. Everyone was out, so I sat and ate some of the food that the landlady had prepared. I drove to Henri's house and brought all my boxes in. After sitting on his comfy chair for about six minutes, I plugged my phone in and then wandered around the house looking for the room that I wasn't supposed to enter. Finally, I laughed. He'd been joking. I mean, I *knew* it was a joke, but with Henri you never *really* knew. It was perfectly possible he had converted one room into a sex dungeon or whatever.

Since I'd bagged a hundred-million-pound client, I treated myself to a large glass of wine and took it back to the comfy armchair. I sent texts out to Henri, Ziggy, Raffi, and Kisi. I thought about what to say to Emma, and agonised over the wording for so long I got sick of the process. So I tried to write a kind-of honest summary and if I chose the wrong phrasing, so be it.

Everything turned out great at the care home and the Christians loved my sermon. Signed a client! The biggest fish! Making progress. Hope your knight took good care of you.

Social interaction done, I listened to the hymn James had recommended. It started pretty boring, pretty generic. The guy had a good voice, sure, but so did loads of people. But after three minutes I touched my face to check the guy wasn't literally melting the skin off my skull. He had Rolls Royce jet engines for lungs. It was fucking awesome. I played it three times and realised the singer was telling a story with his performance. You had to see the majesty of the end to appreciate the subtlety of the beginning. Ten-out-of-ten choice, Jamesy boy.

By then, I'd received a few replies.

Raffi: *thumbs-up emoji*

Henri: Yes, eat anything in the fridge. But there's one thing in the freezer you shouldn't touch. You'll know it when you see it.

Ziggy: I can't believe I had to sit in the stands watching FC United draw 0-0 and miss your debut. I watched the video though. Holy shit. I can't believe you're my agent.

Kisi: I know he isn't boring, Max. I was joking. Come on. Did he tell you we went to the match? It's sooo far away lol. James cried when you were subbed off. Don't tell him I said that. Do you really think he can make it as a pro? He's so . . . nice. Meghan is nice, but, you know. Different nice. Bad nice. Max nice. I don't see it from James. God, I'm stressed now. Please tell me he'll make it.

And the big one:

Emma: I'm glad to hear that. My knight doesn't want me to see you again. But he wouldn't mind if you signed for Newcastle United.

Well. I didn't know how to reply to that. So I didn't.

So, finally, a little time to plan. A little time to myself. I checked the World Cup schedule.

The games were going to come thick and fast, sometimes four a day. I'd train at Darlington in the morning and then watch TV all day. A new, weird kind of grind. Twenty-nine days of virtually nonstop football with pop quizzes the whole time. Would I get sick of it? Would I be able to hone my skills? Would it pay off, or would Nick turn my thousands of TINOs into, like, 6 XP?

There was only one way to find out.

27

MONKEY ISLAND

Henri's bed was so incredibly comfortable and I was so terribly fatigued that I overslept. I jumped out of bed and zoomed to training. To save three seconds, I even left my kit bag on the dressing room bench for the first time since Captain Caveman's Wet Welcome.

Fortunately, Henri's house was so close and the roads were so clear that I entered the meeting room for the weekly planning just before 9 a.m. Made it! Even though I was on time, Cutter gave me a murderous look.

"Glad you could make it, Best," he said.

Apart from the mild anxiety I always get when in a rush, I felt great. Refreshed, healthy, powerful. Maybe I should have been a bit conciliatory or whatever, but I hadn't done anything wrong. I set my demeanour to "Max is in a good mood and wants to share his joy."

"Had the best night's sleep I can remember," I told him.

"Aye, grand," he said, his eyes sweeping around the first team squad. "But if you're not twenty minutes early, you're late." I laughed because what he said was so moronic it had to be a joke, but he seemed to be serious, which was borne out by the fact that he barely spoke to me the rest of the week. I wish I was exaggerating.

It didn't bother me . . . at first. I wasn't at Darlington to get his approval, and all this mad kindergarten shit would simply make it easier to leave.

Later, when I reflected on this incident, I decided Cutter was trying to make sure my amazing debut didn't go to my head, and to tell the team that he would take a stance even against its star player. Those desires made sense on an abstract level, but I could imagine the ploy backfiring on a lot of people. One of the side benefits of being a player was watching up close how this experienced, highly regarded manager acted, what he communicated and when, and how often and in which manner he interacted with players.

So far, I wasn't all that impressed.

We went to the training pitch—my boots were untouched—and had a good session with lots of passing drills. I used the team shower for the first time, then went home and made some phone calls.

First, I called my landlord and told him I wanted out of my contract as soon as poss. He was delighted. Although I was a model tenant, rents had rocketed and with me out he could get a few hundred quid a month extra. He said he might buy my bed from me, or store it for a while. So, part grasping capitalist, part good guy. We contain multitudes, as James would probably say if there weren't any women around.

So that was that. I was basically homeless.

Then I did some web searches that led me to Altrincham FC's website. Alty were a fifth-tier team, the league above Darlington, along with Wrexham and Oldham. They had a lot on their site about inclusivity and diversity and took the time to take and post large colour photos of their academy players. Just a good vibe, good first impression. They seemed to care about their youth system, and James lived within walking distance.

I left a voicemail.

"Hi, this is Max Best. I represent a few players in Manchester. One's sixteen, no, just turned seventeen. Defensive midfielder, lovely kid, very talented, bit raw, lives really close to you. I was wondering if he could go and train with you for a while until I can find him a club. I'd come in person to beg you but I've just started playing for Darlington and the drive back home is starting to do my head in!" Also, it was putting a big dent in my bank balance. "Anyway, thanks for listening. This is Max Best," and then I gave my phone number.

It seemed the right tone. Not too pushy, bit of self-deprecating humour. Yeah, happy with that.

Those were the most pressing things on my to-do list, so I pottered around the house, thinking of what else I needed to get ahead of. Most of my next steps would involve money—paying off my debts, for example. Buying a second pair of football boots! But since I had no spare money, I would stay home and focus on the three World Cup matches. I couldn't find a notepad, so I emptied Henri's printer and found loads of pens and highlighters. The number of highlighters I found was surprising. I didn't associate Henri with bright yellow lines. Don't ask me why.

One thing I wanted to do between matches was to take the pulse of the Darlington fans. There was this thing called Darlo Fans Radio where you could listen to matches online, which was a really awesome feature. But they didn't save the recordings, as far as I could tell. You could only listen live. Which meant I'd never hear it . . . Maybe it was for the best, but it did seem like if a particular player was extremely unpopular with the fans that would be a way for me to find out. And exploit it.

I was all ready for the first game of the day, England versus Iran, when my phone rang. It was someone from Altrincham's academy. Basically, he asked me to confirm who I was and quizzed me about my debut. He got more and more excited—turns out he'd looked me up and found the Player of the Season video, then checked me on Wyscout. He went on and on about how amazing my goals were, to the point that I had to laugh and tell him I had a contract and wasn't available to play for Alty. He was a bit reluctant to change the subject, but agreed to let James train with his lads for a few weeks. A few weeks! That was way better than I'd expected.

"And maybe one day you can come and do a free kick clinic with us," he said.

"Sure," I said. "That might be good anyway. For my coaching badges."

"Unless that one was a fluke," he said.

"A fluke? That free kick? Just be thankful we're not in the same division, mate, or you'd get to see one up close."

"All right, Max. Give me this kid's details and I'll sort things out with him. I'll take care of him, don't you worry. What's his name again?"

"Youngster." James Yalley was bad branding. Youngster was cool. Intriguing. Could be a rapper.

I hung up the phone and had a big old think. I'd only had forty-five minutes of being a footballer and it was already opening doors.

As if I wasn't busy enough, Mike Dean called. He joked that he'd tried me at the reception of Darlington Rugby Club. At least I think he was joking. He was calling to get me to sign some document sometime in November so Raffi could start being put in match day squads from December 1.

"Already?"

"Ian loves him. Everyone does."

"He's not quite ready."

"Isn't it exhausting trying to micromanage every football decision everywhere in the country?"

"No. It's my duty. Listen, I'll drive to Chester if I have to, but as a favour, can we meet somewhere a bit closer?"

We bickered for a bit, but MD had a great idea. "Let's run this up the flagpole, Max. This Saturday, you lot are playing in Hereford. And we're away at Scarborough. We can meet in Manchester!"

"Cutter is mad at me, or pretending to be. If I go ask him to drop me off in Manchester he'll go full hairdryer on me."

"I'll get Ian to call him. Don't worry about it." I paused to nibble my lip for a while. MD stepped into the void. "Max, it'll be fine."

"I'm not worried about that. It just means I'll miss another World Cup game."

"Which one?"

"Argentina v Mexico. If Argentina lose, they're out. No World Cup for Messi. It's one of the most important games in the group stage."

MD made a *hmm* kind of noise. "I don't want to miss that one either. Tell you what, let's meet somewhere. We'll sign this paperwork. Then we'll all watch the match. Make an evening of it."

"You, me, and Charlie's Angels?"

"Me, you, Raffi, and whoever else is interested. It'll be nice to spend some time with you when you're not being weird."

"Ah. Yeah. Riiiiight. I mean, I can think of one weird thing I might do. Nah, never mind. You probably won't even notice."

Training, landlord, James, MD. Busy morning!

Day two of the World Cup came with three interesting matches and a variety of trivia questions. They followed the same pattern as the first day. Five questions in the first half, five in the second. Some that I had the whole match to think about, some that I had to answer quickly. And an essay at the end.

I had to shout "TINO" every time the FIFA boss appeared on screen, which was, bizarrely, a lot. Spoiler alert—he was on screen during every single match of the World Cup. Every. Single. Match. Yes, even though some matches were played simultaneously! The dude waited till he was on screen in one, then hopped out and zoomed to the other stadium.

World. Class. Prick.

But I'm getting ahead of myself.

I did okay on the highest attribute questions. Some of it was pretty guessy. Spotting the difference between a pace 16 guy and a pace 17 guy was virtually impossible. Even though I lost TINOs every time I got one wrong, it was interesting to be reminded of what it felt like to watch football as an uncursed person.

I did fantastic on the highest transfer value questions.

Questions about formations were quite hard, but with Henri's TV I could pause the feed and rewind and go forward frame by frame and all that stuff. There was a risk of losing time for the rapid-fire questions, but the curse didn't seem to mind me overanalysing certain passages of play. And I did quite well on the final questions, which were all essays about how a certain manager did.

I got twenty-one out of thirty questions right, plus picked up three bonuses for shouting "TINO."

That gave me 269.7 more TINOs, bringing my total to 346.9.

They say a top-level chess match is as tiring as boxing, and I can imagine that's true. Concentrating so much was hard, but at the end of the day I felt pretty good. I slept well.

The next few days were more of the same, but with four games per day. Every match was bursting with self-contained dramas, plots, subplots, twists, turns, the whole Shakespeare. Getting sucked into the narratives made the matches more interesting to watch, but also more tiring. And, I noticed, led me to draw bad conclusions.

If the commentator said that a player had just returned from a long injury, I immediately discounted the possibility that they were the fastest or had the best jumping. Which was dumb. I turned the sound off, and that helped in terms of my answer accuracy, but made the whole thing feel more like an exam. An endless exam.

My motivation dipped. Trying to concentrate on every player's pace or heading was burning me out, so with the attribute questions I switched to best-guess mode. I always put a lot of effort into anything about player values and formations, because those didn't really feel like work. Trying to get to those answers was fun.

But my overall response rate was dropping, so from twelve games, I scored 63 out of 120. Not that impressive, really. But by Friday I had added another 812.1 TINOs.

TINOs: 1,159

Friday, November 25.

Training on Friday morning was the best one yet. It was all about duels! That Liverpudlian coach I used to know would have loved it.

There were duels of all kinds. Headers, sprints, tackles, and one-v.-one dribbles. One of Cutter's assistants must have known what was up because I was pitted against a caveman in every drill. So you better believe I was motivated. I ran hard, jumped high, and thundered into tackles.

Strangely, the part I was shit at was dribbling one v one. In a real game, I had the freedom to feint, pass, or shoot. But in these drills, the cavemen knew I *had* to dribble past them. I had the physical skills to do it, but not the experience.

I bombed. There was no backchat because I'd been beating Captain Caveman at headers and out-tackling other members of the caveman crew like Chumpy and Colin. I wished there had been some banter; it would have relieved the stress I was starting to feel.

So far, the Darlington coaches had been absolutely useless to me. But now, one of them took me aside and hosed me with two minutes of liquid footballing education.

"Max. You've got the ability to put these guys on toast. What's up?"

"I never dribble straight towards people." He opened his mouth to speak, but I got there first. "I'm not complaining about the drill! I'm just saying I don't play like this. So I don't know what to do here."

"I heard you talking to Junior about movies. I'm guessing you're a big movie guy. That right?"

"Yeah, I suppose. Less so recently."

"Have you seen *Leon: The Professional*? It's about an assassin who spends way too much time with a teenage girl."

"Er . . . no. My search history is problematic enough."

"It's good. The assassin teaches the kid how to kill. Level one is long distance. Sniper rifles and the sort. Level two is a pistol. Level three is a dagger. The better you are, the closer you get to your target."

That didn't necessarily make sense to me, but I hadn't seen the movie. "Okay."

"You're level one."

"Does he say level one in the movie? Is it CinemRPG?"

"No. I've adapted it. Level one is your corners and free kicks. Your long dribbles. I tell you what, if that's all you ever do in your career, you'll have a good career. Level two. That's your passing and making connections with other players. That's missing in your game."

"Yeah, well," I said, glaring at the cavemen. *You should see me play with Raffi and Henri.*

"I'm not too worried about that, though. I see you trying. You've nearly got something going on with Junior. Keep at it. But level three. That's your close combat. Your duels. Close-up magic. Sleight of hand. If you're in a tight spot, how do you get out? Can you win us a free kick when we're under pressure? See Harry Kane? Watch him—he's very sneaky. He'll back into a defender until the defender fouls him. Gets hundreds of free kicks doing it. Team goes from defence to attack like that." He snapped his fingers. "All those details, Max. If you want to get to the very top, that's what it's going to take. First things first, though. You're playing right mid. Three main skills there. Get the ball, dribble past your man, put in a cross. You're top at the first and last. The middle . . ." He pulled a sour face.

"Yeah, I get it," I said. "I agree with everything you've said. But I've not been in an academy or anything. I played five-a-side. One of my best moves was bouncing the ball against the wall! I was hoping the training here would be more . . . what you said. Obviously, the other players don't need it as much as I do, so I get it. Maybe when I get paid I'll hire a private coach or something."

He frowned and had a little think. "You could do that, sure. If you're on Henri Lyons wages. Have you ever heard of *Monkey Island*?"

"Gibraltar?"

"No. It's an old computer game. You had to learn sword-fighting."

"Cool."

"No it wasn't cool. Well, it was, but not the way you're thinking. There was no action. It was all about insults and comebacks. You had to learn the insult from one fighter and then go and use it on another. Then you'd learn the comeback and the next insult until you'd mastered it all."

"I love talking about computer games I'll never play."

He laughed. "You're such a prick. I'm trying to help."

"Bad joke. I'm listening. Really."

"Let's put you on defence. Let someone use a trick on you. Watch what they do, learn it, then use it on someone. Just like in *Monkey Island*. Yeah?"

"Thanks," I said.

So that's what we tried. One of the attackers tried to get past me, and I blocked it. Another one came at me, and I came away with the ball. And that's where the coach's scheme failed. I'd been watching these guys—Junior, Glynn, Tim, Doop—in training and in matches, and I knew their styles. It wasn't like I knew every single move they could ever possibly try, but they came at me with their best stuff and I defended it all easily.

Still, the idea was great. If anyone ever beat me in a match, I'd learn that skill and add it to my repertoire.

After training, I popped into the Longstaff sports shop. I wanted to go back when I had cash in my pocket, but Longstaff was delighted to see me anyway. I explained I hadn't been paid yet, etc., etc., and he said he didn't give two shits and would happily go bankrupt if I quote *did that again* end quote.

"Thing is," I said, "you're one of the coolest guys I've met here. And I need help watching the World Cup."

"You need help . . . watching the World Cup?"

"I do it different than most guys."

"I bet."

He said he had plans for the England versus USA match but he'd love to watch the third game of the day, Netherlands versus Ecuador, with me. I had to watch the two earlier ones on my own, then drove back to the shop—his flat was upstairs.

Longstaff was hospitable, but somewhat intimidated at first. Presumably this was a function of my otherworldly attractiveness multiplied by my astonishing debut performance multiplied by the weirdness of the questions I was asking him. Who's faster: Gakpo or Dumfries? Who would you rather see at Darlington: de Jong or van Dijk? I used self-deprecating humour to make him feel relaxed, and only a few times did I go internal.

At halftime he asked me what it was like at Darlington FC, and I told him some things. It didn't seem right to slag off the other players, so I didn't get very gossipy. I did let the handbrake off for a vivid retelling of the post-training penalty-taking practice I'd arranged with the goalies. I'd organised it as a competition, so it was in Paul's interest to tell me where to shoot to score past Smokes, and vice versa.

"So you were learning their weaknesses from the people who know them best?" he said, ecstatic.

"Yeah. But after a while the goalie coach, Taff, got annoyed. He said, *'If you can hit it wherever you want, just hit the top-left or top-right corner. No one can save that.'* So I tried that for a bit and then he ended the sesh because the sound of me pinging balls into the net was demoralising the lads. Kind of a reverse Pavlov's dog."

Longstaff got annoyed. "You're pulling my leg," he said.

I smirked. "Am I?"

Watching the match with a friend was mentally soothing. It broke up the monotony of the day and made me feel less like a prisoner of the tournament. I decided to try to watch one game a day with someone, or in public, for the mental health benefits.

But there was more. I got seven out of ten right for the Longstaff match, compared to four out of ten for the dreadful England versus USA, which I watched on my own. And I'd done better than average in the match I watched with James.

Interesting.

I ended the day lying fully clothed on the top of Henri's bed, staring at the ceiling. I wanted to be a manager. That meant taking final responsibility for picking the team, making substitutions, all that guff. And sure, I thought I'd be good at it. But if this mini game was teaching me anything, it was that discussing my ideas with someone else led to better outcomes.

Very, very interesting.

Darlington's next league game was on Saturday, deep in the middle of England in a little-known village called Hereford. Wikipedia said it had a cathedral, a river, and its chief export is cider. As soon as I read that, I could smell the cows.

I'm joking. It's a beautiful part of the country.

But what was most interesting about my research was that Hereford FC was yet another fucking phoenix club—one set up by fans to replace the original after the original had been bankrupted by mismanagement or fraud. How many shitty owners had destroyed hundred-year-old teams? Almost every team in the National League had either been wiped out by a former owner, or come very very close. It was shocking; these clubs were the backbone of the local community.

Getting ready at the ground and our long drive from the northeast meant I missed two World Cup matches. The curse deducted 127 TI-NOs from my balance for each. Quite harsh, but there was one silver lining—Hereford's Edgar Street was my favourite stadium so far. The stands enveloped the pitch—no gaps—and that made such a difference. It all seemed proper. Meant. I loved it.

So when Cutter announced the team, and that Webby would be playing right mid, I was pissed. But only briefly, because there was a very definite atmosphere. A mood that came to life in the dressing room, and then spread to the dugout and the pitch. Uncertainty. Doubt. *No Max? Why not?*

And during the match, when we got a corner or free kick, or Webby did something shit, there was this weird kind of moment where everyone, including the cavemen, turned to look where I was sitting. *Best would have scored that. Best would have made that pass.* In other circumstances, I would have loved it. But all I could think was that I was missing France versus Denmark for this.

That's not quite true. I was also thinking through the implications of the fact that I was earning XP for watching this game. Two per minute. By halftime my XP balance was 81, and I had a choice. Buy something—anything—ASAP so that it couldn't be converted into TINOs, or let it accumulate. I mean, once I'd gotten over the resentment of having my XP stolen, I had to admit that the World Cup mini game seemed to be not only fair but actually beneficial. Even if I lost XP overall, I felt my understanding of football was deepening, and that was worth paying for.

I quickly checked the perk shop—the cheapest one currently available was Match Stats 2 for 300 XP. I wouldn't get enough from this match, and any grinding I did (e.g., watching Middleton Rangers) would stop me doing the World Cup mini game. Once the group stages of the World Cup were over, there would be fewer matches per day, and even some days with no football! So I could try to grind for XP then. The thought . . . exhausted me.

While I was considering all this, Hereford scored. Darlington were looking shaky. Webby was steaming around like a madman, trying to justify his place in the team, but nothing was working for him. His match rating was 6 out of 10, which I felt was generous but to be fair, he *was* doing his defensive work. It was just his passing, crossing, dribbling, and shooting that was abysmal.

At halftime, though, Cutter didn't bring me on. I started to worry. I needed to play every league game so that I'd have ten appearances by the time I left. Even if I came on for the last five minutes, that would do. And of course, five hundred quid was on the line.

Over the next twenty-five minutes, I started to resent Cutter for his management style in a way I hadn't before. I hadn't been late for the team meeting. I'd stayed late to practice penalties. I hadn't bought a Ferrari or started a fashion label or given a bizarre newspaper interview. I'd done absolutely nothing to warrant this treatment. There he stood, the big boss, infallible as the Pope, jaw working over some poor, innocent piece of gum. My resentment simmered, getting dangerously close to contempt.

Desperate for an equaliser, Cutter summoned me on the seventieth minute and told me to warm up. I pottered up and down the touchline a few times. There was a break in play but I didn't go on. I jogged around some more. Another break, still I didn't go on. I think Cutter was hoping that seeing me on the touchline would motivate Webby to finally do something, and if there had been a goal in those minutes, Cutter would have been very pleased with himself.

Reluctantly, he signalled for Webby to come off. As Webby trudged towards the side of the pitch, several plotlines decided to intersect and climax. Me versus the cavemen. My loneliness. My resentment at my recent treatment.

"Junior was sharp in training," I told Cutter. "He makes the kind of runs I can pick out. If you want a goal, Junior's your man."

Time stood still.

My tone was superficially friendly, solicitous even. Just trying to help! But Cutter knew what I was doing—telling him how to do his job. Neil at FC United had hated me doing it. Ian Evans had hated me doing it. And now Cutter hated me doing it. His eyes narrowed and he stopped chewing—there was still time to cancel the substitution.

Had I just talked myself out of my five-hundred-pound appearance fee and my league winner's medal?

28

ALL-OUT ATTACK

"Well played, Webby, lad," Cutter called out, and gave the guy a pat on the back as he left the pitch.

That was my answer, then. Cutter needed me more than I needed him.

I strolled over to the far side of the pitch and waited for someone to pass to me.

Hereford were well up for the game. There were a lot of 7s in their match ratings, and a couple of 8s. Darlington had a lot of 7s and a couple of 6s. The left back smashed into me the first chance he got. Trying to bully me out of the game. Bottom-feeder mentality. I ignored him; I was seeing the bigger picture.

If I went on a rampage now, we could turn things around, win, and take home three points. If I waited, we might get a draw (one point) or end up losing (no points).

It might seem obvious that the best move was to win the match. Me playing ten games would only lead to a medal if Darlington actually won the league. If they were going to finish fifth, for example, then it didn't matter how many games I played. So getting at least a draw from this match was pretty important.

But I couldn't mope around Darlington on my own for two months. I mean, I could, but I didn't want to. I wanted to use the word teammate without mentally rolling my eyes. I wanted someone to score from my passes and I wanted someone to talk to on the long coach rides home. And the man I had chosen for that task was Junior. He was on the bench. Could I play in a way that would make Cutter send him onto the pitch?

Or should I just score a couple of quick goals and follow my January 31 masterplan?

Watching so many World Cup matches alone had started to remind me of life during lockdown, and the need for human contact outweighed my other considerations. So for the next ten minutes, I got into defensive shape, I played sideways one-touch passes, and I learned about the opposing players. The left back was delighted—he felt like he'd kicked me out of the game. The more I played my role exactly as Cutter had designed it, the more animated he got on the touchline. *Go, Max! Attack!* I didn't go. I didn't attack.

When we got corners and free kicks, I played them short to a teammate. Not my fault if that guy did bugger all with the chance.

With ten minutes to go and the team still losing, Cutter cracked. Junior came on, but to my dismay, he didn't replace Blondie. Blondie remained on the pitch, and as the senior striker, he would take all the best positions. Junior would have to play around him.

Hmm. That increased the degree of difficulty, but I was suddenly energised. There was an outside chance I could have my cake and eat it.

Nine minutes to go and I got the ball in an awkward position. I played it square to our nearest CM and ran down the line—my first serious sprint of the day. The ball came back, but slightly too far towards the touchline. I had to adjust to get it and lost all momentum.

I turned back, saw Blondie make a good run to the near post. I could easily have clipped the ball with my left foot, and Blondie knew that. I played the ball safely backwards. Blondie shook his head but got back into position. There wasn't time for histrionics.

Seven minutes to go and we got a corner. Blondie was jostling with an opponent at the near post, and Junior was in a mass of guys over by the far post. I swung it a bit higher and a bit longer towards Junior. A low percentage kind of play, but it led to another corner. I raced across to the other side of the pitch to take it. Again, Blondie was at the near post, but this time, Junior joined him there. I waved at him to go away, then hit it to the back post. It came to nothing, but Blondie was scowling at me.

I jogged past Junior and told him to stay away from Blondie at dead balls. "To give me more options," I said.

He said, "Aight."

Six minutes to go, we got another corner. Blondie was at the far post, but even from distance I could see he had a strange, calculating look in his eye. I repressed a grin and fired the cross . . . to the far post.

Blondie had charged towards the front. Nothing came of the chance, and I trudged back to my slot shaking my head. It had been funny at the time, but my teammates and I were using game theory against each other. We couldn't go on like this.

Four minutes to go. In my right-mid slot I got a pass and threatened to launch a high, hopeful ball into the box. Really, the left back should have just let me do that. The chances of it leading to anything were very low, but footballers try to block crosses. It's in their DNA. Naturally, I knocked the ball round the defender and chased after it. I got to the by-line and was about to smash the ball square when I saw, out of the corner of my eye, that Blondie was sliding in to convert my cross.

Nah.

I stopped the ball dead, then chipped it diagonally back to where Junior was racing forward. He got to the ball first, but his shot was wild. Maybe in the first minute of the game he'd have been calmer, but the pressure of the match situation was telling.

Hmm. I decided I might have to try to do this on my own. Meanwhile, the left back was trying to kick me every time I got anywhere near him. When the ref wasn't looking, he'd grab my shirt, pull at my arm, stand on my toes. Well, there was an easy solution to that. I man-marked the referee.

"Max!" called someone from the bench. It sounded like the plaintive cry of a lost whale cub. "Maaxxx!"

But the next time I got the ball, I was in the dead centre of the pitch, thirty-five yards out. Ideally the other team would have known about my dangerous long shots and stood between me and goal, giving me an easy way to dribble to the right. But these idiots kept launching themselves into tackles! Which made things simultaneously much harder and much easier.

Best shapes to shoot. Venable slides in.

Best knocks the ball sideways and pushes forward.

West makes a challenge. Best is forced further wide.

Best plays a pass between two defenders—but there's no one from Darlington there!

Best chases his own pass.

Suddenly, he's through! He's one-on-one with the keeper! He's got Blondie haring up beside him.

Best chips the ball above Blondie's outstretched leg. A poor pass. The ball lands in the path of a defender.

But Howland slides in and tackles the ball into the net!

GOOOOOAAAAAALLLLLL!

Darlington are level!

So late in the game!

I laughed as Junior dashed into the net and retrieved the ball. Passing to the defender wasn't *exactly* what I'd intended. The ball had bobbled up off the shitty pitch and made me look awful.

There was activity from the Hereford bench. It seemed familiar; I checked the match commentary.

Hereford have adopted a more defensive stance.

They look like they will be happy to survive with a point.

I ran around the pitch yelling at everyone. Yeah, even the cavemen. "They're turtling. Full attack! All out! Come on!" Not many of them seemed motivated by my words, but they all paid attention. And it didn't take long to confirm that Hereford had dropped back. They were basically playing 5-5-0. Two long banks of defenders. Making it hard for us to get through. Which, yeah, against a normal team might have worked. But you don't give Max Best time and space to get crosses in. I was camped on the right touchline, whipping in crosses with pinpoint accuracy.

Now that Junior had scored and increased his reputation, I didn't care who got the winning goal. I wanted that win now, even if it meant picking out Blondie. The more crosses I sent into dangerous areas, the more our players pushed up the pitch, until even Caveman himself went up as an auxiliary striker. And that was the combination that did it.

Best gets another chance to cross. He whips it towards the penalty spot. Caveman rises highest.

A thumping header!

Oh! It's a tremendous save from the goalkeeper! Fantastic agility.

The ball rebounds to Junior. He shapes to shoot . . .

But passes to Blondie. The keeper is stranded. Blondie has to score!

GOOOOOAAAAAALLLLLL!

As most of the players raced to the away section, where fifty to a hundred Darlington fans were going tonto, I walked back to talk to Cutter. On the way, I realised that although I'd made both goals, I almost certainly wouldn't be credited with an assist for either. No bonus! I'd told myself I didn't want to cost the club too much money too soon, but after another penniless week, I wasn't quite so resolute. Ah, well.

I waited for Cutter and the coaching staff to stop hugging. My inspirational manager glared at me. "What do you want, Best?"

"Is there anything we can do to make sure they don't score in the last seconds?"

"Yeah. Keep your shape."

"I could pressure them from the kickoff like I did the other day."

"Keep your shape."

"Yes, boss," I said.

As ever, this was just theatre to make it look to observers like I was manager material. That said, it was an interesting enough question to ask. I think if I was the manager I'd want me to stick to my role, but as a player in that situation, I felt like a bit of headless chickening could have paid off.

Anyway, the match lasted about a minute more, and that was that. Job done.

Junior, high on being the catalyst for our win, was very chatty. He talked my ear off all through the showers and onto the coach. I sat by a window, and he sat next to me.

Starved of human contact as I was, I loved every second of it, and was looking forward to the drive back. That's when things got spicy.

Most of the cavemen got on and went to the back, which was their spot. Because they were man-children. Cutter and the coaches were still either in the stadium or stowing the gear underneath the coach. So when Blondie got on, there were only players around.

He glared at me as he stood in the aisle, trying to loom over me. He said, nice and loud, "Why don't you fucking pass the fucking ball, Best?"

I blinked. What was he doing? I accidentally let out a squashed, repressed sort of laugh. I don't know what the proper name for it is. You know the sort—it starts in your throat and tries to escape through your cheeks.

He didn't like that. "The fuck is funny?"

I got to my feet and eased past Junior. Blondie probably should have tried to stop me getting into the aisle, because once I was there I stretched out and made sure everyone was watching. I'm not sure how much personal responsibility I should take for what happened next. I'd probably given myself aggression 20 in Champion Manager. So if you think about it, this outburst and almost all the others, are Nick's fault. Yeah. Nick's fault.

"Are you seriously asking why I don't pass to you?" I beamed at him. The question was absolutely delightful to me. I turned my head left and right to bathe the rest of the squad in my radiance. "What an interesting question! Here's four answers, buddy." On my right hand, I stretched out my index finger to indicate my first point. "You pissed in my football boots. The last gift I ever got from my mother, and the last I ever *will* get." I stretched my middle finger. "To keep me out of the team, you blasted my assist at Whitby into the North Sea. And you know I hate pollution." On my left hand, I stretched my index finger. "You and the rest of the cavemen plotted to cripple me in training so I'd miss my debut." I stretched my middle finger. "You deliberately missed an open goal against Alfy. There's four reasons."

Now, visual learners will have a clear mental image of what my hands looked like at this point. A V-sign on my right, a V-sign on my left. I waved my hands around in front of his face. You know, to emphasise the four incidents. It was entirely accidental that I'd formed a gesture considered rude in my culture.

He slapped my hands away. "I didn't piss in your boots!" he yelled, and for some reason I found it funny.

"Gotcha," I said. "So it's Whitby, cripple Max, Alfreton." Now I was showing him a V-sign on my left hand and just the middle finger on my right. A very transatlantic way of expressing oneself.

He turned and punched the side of a headrest. It looked soft, but the padding didn't go very deep. It hurt. It hurt him so much he did it again, twice.

"All right, Blondie? We all clear now? I came to this club with good intentions. Win this league and have a blast doing it. But you chose to be a dick. I'm a fucking assist machine. You could have had ten goals in these three games. But you chose to be a dick. I'd fucking set you up for a hat trick in every game. But you chose to be a dick. If I met a demon who offered me a choice—pass to you or let Putin conquer the world, I wouldn't hesitate. I'd start learning Russian. Aight? That's why I don't pass to you. Because you're a dick. Now go fuck yourself."

"Max?"

Ooh. Not good. Cutter had come onboard mid-rant. I turned and smiled at him. "Good win today, boss!"

"Shut the fuck up. What's this? We've won and you're at each other's throats? Are you tugging my todger?"

"No, boss. We're top friends. It's just banter."

"Banter? It didn't sound like banter. I could hear it from inside the stadium."

That wasn't true, but I didn't have time to think through his motives and the various dialogue trees that could spring from this moment. I had to act on instinct. "We're just letting off steam. Blondie was pissed I messed up my pass near the end there. The one Junior turned into a goal. And I got a bit defensive. But he's right. It was a shit pass."

Cutter got close to me, very close and very aggressive. It was a hundred times more intimidating than Blondie's weaksauce attempt. I wondered how many times in his life he'd headbutted someone. More than five, less than ten. "I've got half a mind to take you to Manchester and leave you there . . . permanently."

I returned his eye contact. I think I was supposed to look away. Let him win, you know? But nah.

Eventually, he eased up, shrugged boxer-style, and went to the front.

I squeezed past Junior and retook my seat. He was looking pale.

"Still want to sit next to me?" I said, with a cheeky grin. But underneath the grin was a desperation I didn't know was in me. *Are we still friends?* Pathetic.

He gave me a weird look, then bent to grab his bag from under the seat.

My heart broke. I was so toxic that in trying to make a friend, I'd pushed him as far away as possible.

He zipped the bag back up and with a jolt I realised he was handing me something. An iPad.

"What?"

"Hold that a sec."

He bent, fiddled in a side pocket and came back up with a dongle thing. He took the tablet back and plugged the dongle in.

"So we can watch France v Denmark," he said. Then he looked worried. "If that's all right? I can put my headphones on if you don't want."

"Junior," I said, feeling the kinds of emotions I'd only ever felt when a crush had texted me back. "France v Denmark? I'd fucking love that."

29

POKING THE BEAR

The coach pulled over. The rest of the first team craned their necks in baffled amazement as I stepped off and got cosy at a random bus stop on Princess Parkway. I felt a bit odd wearing my Darlington hoodie and clutching my Darlington kit bag not all that far from my house in Moss Side. From the back seats, the cavemen gave me dead, flat looks. I blanked them; I'd already poked that bear enough for one week.

I checked the MUNDIAL tab and my accounts.

XP balance: 144
Debt repaid: 194/3,000
TINOs: 1,227.5

In the last couple of days I'd watched five World Cup matches and added fewer than one hundred TINOs! The 127-TINO penalty for missing games was really crushing. And the path to 300 XP was covered in treacle—I couldn't go to watch some amateur game if it meant missing a match from Qatar.

Still, the group stage of the tournament would finish the following Friday, and then there would be a maximum of two matches per day. That would free up my time considerably.

It wasn't long before Raffi picked me up and drove me to his place.

The plan had changed several times. The first idea was to go to a curry house. That fell through, so next came Chinese, then a sports bar, then somewhere fancy. Finally, Shona offered to host us and that suited everyone. She said that since Max Best was visiting, she would leave Jamaica's favourite dish off the menu, as there would be enough jerk.

See what I have to deal with?

I gave her a hug anyway, and told her the house smelled incredible. "Have you been cooking all day?"

"She always goes overboard," said Raffi. "She's missed this."

Shona stirred a pot of something. "We followed the rules in the pandemic—no parties—and we haven't had guests since I had Serina."

"Is she here? Why aren't we whispering?" I glanced around the kitchen. There was a pile of cardboard boxes in one corner. They were getting ready to move.

"She's with Raffi's mum. His dad is here for the first half, then we'll swap."

"Swap the mum for the dad?"

"Ha ha. No."

"Who else is here?" I said, pottering into the living room. I stopped dead. There was Henri and Gemma. An older, meaner version of Raffi. Mike Dean. Dramatic pause . . . and Ian Evans.

Obviously, what I did next was smile and go round the room shaking everyone's hand. And then spent the next two hours being charming and witty. Ah, wait, no. That's what I *should* have done. Instead, I poked the bear.

"Bonjour, Max," said Henri. He shook my hand.

Gemma did a European double cheek-kiss thing. "Hi, Max."

"Er . . . Are we in Paris?"

"Henri's civilising me," she said.

"Gemma. This is Manchester. It's the height of civilisation."

"Sure, Max. Anyway, when I asked him to teach me French kissing, that wasn't what I had in mind."

I liked this new, relaxed Gemma! There wasn't time to dwell on it, though. "You must be Raffi's dad."

"I'm Moss," he said.

I clicked my fingers. Remembered a nugget of info from the dawn of time. "You're a Chelsea fan."

Raffi came in and handed me a cold bottle of something. He was beaming—delighted that I'd remembered. His dad put his arm around him and both clinked their bottles against mine. Moss half-closed his eyes. "Chelsea had a Black winger that I used to like watching when I was working down in London. He took all kinds of abuse and kept going. I looked up to him. Very much."

"Paul Canoville," said Ian Evans from the corner of the room. It wasn't the chair with the best view of the TV—he was too good-mannered to take that from Raffi, who of course would give it up for his dad. But Evans had a view of all the comings and goings.

"That's right," said Moss, impressed.

"I played against him," said Evans.

"You did?"

"What position were you, Mr. Evans?" said Gemma.

"Centre back. Like all good managers." That was a little dig at me, by the way. In case you missed it. The following people didn't miss it: Henri. Mike. Raffi.

I smiled at the soon-to-be-humiliated-by-me pensioner. Raised my bottle with a little nod. That was a combined hello to Evans and MD. "Alex Ferguson was a striker. Guardiola midfield. Cruyff . . . Cruyff played a lot like me, from the tapes I've seen."

Comparing myself to one of the best players and most important tactical innovators the game has ever known went down well with everyone . . . with one exception. Evans had a tiny surge of anger that expressed itself through the vibration of his hair.

MD noticed and looked slightly panicked. "Er . . . should we get the papers signed before . . . ?" *Before violence breaks out.* "Before we get sauce on our fingers."

"Great idea!" shouted Shona from the kitchen.

We signed the papers, staged some photos, and Raffi and Shona celebrated. There were no more hurdles—in a few days he'd be a real, actual professional footballer. The couple hugged Moss, which was correct and totally normal, but still, I had a tiny stab of jealousy. I was the guy who had made this happen! Max first, then dad. Jesus.

We took our positions in front of the TV. I could write a thousand-word essay on who sat where and why, but suffice to say that Moss was in the best spot, Henri the worst, and I was on the floor, cross-legged as close to the TV as Shona would let me get. Argentina versus Mexico. Let's do this! I grabbed the remote and turned the sound off, which led to a chorus of complaints. I snapped back telling them I had to concentrate for my coaching badges and that we'd discussed all this. They pushed back. I was winning until Moss said he hadn't agreed to any such thing and he wasn't going to watch the noisiest World Cup match in total silence. Shona held her hand out and I was forced to give up the remote. That was almost as annoying as being pushed down the hug queue.

I sulked for a minute, then got my post-it notes and marker pens out of my bag. That reminded me.

"Henri, why are there so many highlighters in your house?"

The slight delay until he replied made me snap my neck round to check out his face. Those few seconds were enough for him to go blank. Hmm. "I have a completely normal number of highlighters, Max. You really are excessively strange sometimes. Why don't you tell us what your project is and let us help you?"

I decided to let the highlighter thing go. He was lying, and it was extremely obvious to me. Gemma was giving him a slightly curious look, too—she didn't believe him but was puzzled about why he'd be sensitive about stationery. What possible reason could there be? "Actually, Henri, you *can* help me. Over the course of the match, I'll be getting nine questions and writing them on these post-it notes. I'll have until the end of the match to answer most of them, but some I have to answer fast. Like if there's a penalty I might have to say if Messi will score or not."

"Messi's bad at penalties," said Mike Dean, which was disappointing. Messi was average at penalties, and people lost their minds about it because it was the only aspect of kicking a ball where he wasn't superhuman. MD had clearly been listening to the same radio shows as me, but unlike me, fallen into some narrative traps.

"Nine questions?" said Gemma. "That's an odd number."

"Nine *is* an odd number, Gemma. Well done." She gave me the middle finger. I smiled at her. "There *is* a tenth question but it's an essay about my overall impression of one of the managers."

"Managers?" said MD. "Why managers? What kind of coaching course are you doing?"

I smiled. "One that will help me to become a manager. You know that's why I'm playing for Darlington, Mike. So that when a struggling manager"—I accidentally raised my eyebrows in the direction of Ian Evans—"gets *sacked*, the fans will be excited when they find out I've applied for the job. Max Best, superstar, wants to manage my team? Yes, please! He'll save us from relegation and guess what? He's a tactical genius! He knows two formations!" I laughed a bit too hard and checked what I was drinking. Red Stripe. Jamaican beer. I eyed Raffi while I pointed to the bottle.

"Celebrating," he said, with a shrug.

"So what are the questions?" said Gemma. She didn't know football but she understood something was not right between me and Evans, and was playing peacekeeper.

"I normally get two at kick-off then three more in the first half. I'm pretty sure the goal is to keep me concentrating for the longest possible time."

"Absurd," said Henri.

"How's training?" I asked him.

He shrugged. "Acceptable. But it's a long time until I can play in the first team. And the defenders aren't competing with me in training. I'm losing my edge."

"What? Why aren't they?"

"I think it's because they are afraid of what will happen to them if they hurt me. They think they will get into trouble with . . . the manager."

Wow, there was a *lot* of subtext in this conversation. By "the manager," everyone thought he meant Evans, but of course he meant me. I'd lost my rag when Ryder, an imposing centre back, had fouled Henri in my trial match. I chose my reply carefully. "They'll probably start kicking you on January first, once your move is all officially official."

"Let's hope so," sighed Henri. We had never discussed why he liked to get into scraps. That didn't resonate with me at all, and didn't fit his whole football-as-creation vibe.

I turned away and checked the TV. The anthems were winding down and the match would start soon. Moss and Evans were talking about old footballers. MD came out of the kitchen with a plate laden with meat and sauce and rice. He eased into place on the floor next to me. "Go grab some food," he said.

"Can't. Got to watch. I'll wait till halftime."

"Are you serious?"

"Mike," I said.

"This job isn't worth it," he said, getting up again. "Take this." He handed me his plate, and went to get another one. Once he'd cloned his last order, he came back and sat next to me. We made small talk, but I hushed him when kickoff was about to happen and stuck an earphone in. I shoved some rice into my mouth, popped the lid off a marker pen, and waited for the first two questions to appear.

I scrawled on two post-its, then took the earbud out. I crawled forward and stuck the notes onto the TV, on the left-hand side at the very top. By the end of the match I would have created a whole yellow-brick road.

"What's that say?" said Moss. He didn't have good eyesight, it seemed. One of those older guys too proud to wear glasses in public.

"ARG Jump. Which Argentina player has the best jumping skill? MEX Fin. Which Mexico player has the best finishing?"

"Doubly absurd!" said Henri. "Absurdity ad infinitum! There's no way to objectively know that."

"This is me crossing you out of my list of helpers," I said, miming with the marker pen. I shuffled back to my spot on the floor and ate.

"The answer to every question about Argentina is Messi," said Raffi.

"Normally," I said. "But jumping? No chance. Lisandro Martinez is way better at that."

"He's a flea," said Moss. He meant he was short.

"Yeah. And fleas can jump."

"So is that the right answer?" said Gemma.

"I don't know. But I've seen Martinez in the flesh so that's helpful. I'll answer that one near the end of the match. Gives me more time to see if there's someone else."

"But Max," said Henri. "What does it mean, best jumping? Martinez jumps well for a man of his height, but he doesn't jump higher than Otamendi or the goalkeeper."

"I think it's relative to his size," I said. "So a flea has better jumping than an elephant, even if the elephant gets higher."

"Elephants can't jump," said Gemma.

"There you go then."

"You're guessing," said Evans, ridicule in his voice, and the mood shifted again.

"It's called an *educated* guess."

"Mexico won't get a shot the whole game," said Raffi. "How you gonna know how they finish?"

I nodded. "Could be hard. I'll have to use other information."

"Like what?" said Gemma. "Wikipedia?"

"No. I'm not allowed to look things up. The Mexicans might not shoot, but they will try long passes and make clearances. I'll see them striking the ball under pressure. That plus their technique plus their coldness should give me a rough idea of, say, the top three finishers. Then I'll take my best shot, so to speak, from that shortlist."

"Guesswork."

"I'm getting about forty percent of those kinds of questions right. If I was purely guessing, it'd be about fifteen percent. It's hard, but possible."

That led to a lull in conversation, and when people started talking again, they cut me out. All except Mike Dean, who had foolishly placed himself right next to me. "How's life as a player?"

"Pretty boring," I said. "Most of the training is very defensive. Lots of repetition. Shape work, they call it. As a kid, I always thought being a professional meant playing games every day like we did in school. We barely do that, and when we do, it's with empty nets because the goalies train separately."

"I noticed on the videos," said MD, with care, "that you don't celebrate goals."

I frowned. "Sure I do."

"You don't. You walk back to your half, or you go to talk to the manager."

"I'm discussing tactics with him," I said. "You know, because I think in terms of tactics."

"I see," he said. "You think it'll help you get a management job." I closed one eye and fired a finger gun at him. He shook his head. "I'd be careful with that. You risk looking ridiculous. Either people will think you've got ideas above your station or even worse, that you're always asking for reminders of what you're supposed to be doing. Which would explain why you're always out of position."

I felt my eyes narrowing as an automatic defensive response. Like in a bank where shutters fly down to protect the money from the robbers. *He's only trying to help*, I told myself. "Okay, I'll bear that in mind. Thanks."

"I had a friend at your match today. Hereford fan. I asked him to keep an eye on you and tell me what he thought. He said you got kicked to bits and didn't react. Not even once. I said he must have been watching the wrong player."

"Why?"

"Because you fly off the handle at every little thing!"

"Oh," I said. I had a little think. "Well, maybe. If it's you blocking my path, that's infuriating. You should listen to me. And those old guys. Holy shit. It's incredibly frustrating to have a talent I can't use. TINO! But this guy who was kicking me today, he's shit. I mean, he was probably by far the best player in his school and all that. You put him in those credit card games at Chester's training ground and he'll dominate. But he's basically a carpet fitter who's got lucky with a full-time contract. I don't mean shit shit. I mean for-this-level shit. He should be part-time."

"You don't have to explain that to me. I know what you mean."

"Yeah. It's just context. I'm miles better than him. Miles faster. Great technique. How's he supposed to stop me? He can kick me or try to make me self-destruct."

"So you can rise above it?"

"No. No, it's like I don't even see him as a person. He's basically a mannequin on wheels."

"Jesus Christ."

I shrugged. "I'm just saying that when I play at this level, it isn't emotional, it's mathematical. So far. Off the pitch I mostly think about my shitty teammates and how they're going to try to make my life miserable next. And I spend most of my time on the pitch working out how many goals I can create without costing the club so much money they have to leave me out of the next game."

"What?"

"I'm pay-as-you-play, with a big goal and assist bonus. Flexible contract so's I can take that manager job whenever it comes up. Keep that under your hat, please. I don't want Darlington to know that's my intention. Anyway, yeah, how can I help the team win without bankrupting them? Check this out: I've had an idea for a new free kick. I'm going to hit it straight at the keeper so that he'll definitely block it, but it will dip viciously just before it gets to him. It should bounce right off him. And it's fifty-fifty if it lands in front of a defender or one of our strikers. I'll let you know if I can get it working in training. Then you can check it out on Wyscout next week."

"If you cause the goal, you get the assist, no?"

"No. That's a saved shot and a rebound. No assist. According to my contract, anyway."

MD moved closer and got quieter. "Why didn't you do this superstar act at your trial? Why did we do all that hide-and-seek stuff?"

I matched his volume and tone. "Because I didn't know. I told you. I hadn't played for years." I leaned back. I couldn't leave it at that. My meteoric rise in ability needed to be explained. "I think it's because I'm playing with better players. In Sunday League they used to just pump the ball forward as far as they could. No one ever played a short, clever pass. And the pitches were like turnip fields. How could a player like me do anything?"

"You could have taken the free kicks."

"When I was sixteen or seventeen? Ahead of some senior player who thought he was God's Gift to dead balls? Nah." I finished my exotic beer. "Anyway. At least we tried, you and me. I wish it had worked at Chester, but it didn't. I've moved on. I've got my eye on Telford United."

"Telford? They're bottom of the league. Ten points from the nearest team, fifteen points from safety. They're going down, Max."

"Not with me in charge," I said, stating it as the undeniable historical fact that it was. MD wanted to reply, but I raised a finger to forestall him, put my earphone in and scribbled out two more post-its. I slapped the first one on the TV. "Which Mexican player is out of position most often? That's a new question type. Can't say I've noticed or would know what to look for." Next one. "Which Argentina player has the highest transfer value?"

"Messi," said at least four people.

"No," I said. "He's thirty-five."

"And his contract is incredible," said MD. "If you've got fifty million to spend on Messi, that's just his wages. You've got nothing left for a transfer fee." I felt a pang of regret. Squadbuilding with MD would have been fun.

"Alvarez," suggested Raffi. He was a striker Man City had bought. I'd seen him when I went to watch them that one time, and he was slightly overrated.

"Maybe," I said. "Maybe if he has a great World Cup, but I doubt it. Lisandro Martinez moved to United at the same time and he was much more expensive."

"Martinez is too small to play centre back," said Evans, which was incredibly stupid because the guy was literally playing centre back for

Argentina in the World Cup! He had a better answer. "Enzo Fernandez," he said, referring to a young player who had impressed in the first match.

"He seems top," I agreed. "And he's young and all that. But it's starting eleven only, for this question."

"Mac Allister," said Evans.

"Are Scotland playing?" said Gemma. I'm not sure if that one was a joke or not.

I wasn't sure if Evans was trying to help me or just prove he knew more about football than me. I gave him the benefit of the doubt and turned towards him to show I was interested. "Mac Allister is a solid midfielder and he's at a Premier League club, but I think Lisandro Martinez would cost more. This kind of hyper-modern defender that can progress the ball up the pitch, that's the future. That's why I was so excited about Future from your under-twelves. He's the kind of player every big team will need ten years from now."

He stared at me like I was offering to pickle his hair in formaldehyde for future generations to study. He had no idea who Future was! Maybe the most talented kid in the entire youth system and the manager didn't know about him. Wilful ignorance. He bypassed the whole Future topic. "You need someone in midfield to receive the ball *from* the defender. One isn't good without the other."

"True," I said. "But there are plenty of players like Mac Allister. There aren't many like Martinez. You can say United paid a premium for him, but that's the point. If you need that type of player for your system, he's one of the only ones."

Evans shook his head, said "He's too small," and returned to watching the match. There was something about the way he dismissed my reasoning and kept repeating an obvious untruth that wound me up.

I glowered at MD, who pretended to be very interested in the match even though nothing was happening.

Halftime should have been the point where normalcy resumed and my feud with Evans took a back seat. If you'd asked us, I'm sure we'd both have agreed that everyone having a nice time was more desirable than continuing our fruitless bickering.

We were all in the kitchen, enjoying being on our feet, having some snacks, when all hope of normalcy died.

The trigger was when Moss started getting ready to go. He put his big coat on and had one last joke with Evans. They had really hit it off. Two old, fierce men completely convinced they knew what was wrong with the world and how to fix it. There was mutual respect there.

Raffi picked up his car keys. The plan was for Raffi to drive his dad home and pick up Serina.

Moss said, "Ian, maybe by the time she's growed up you'll have a girl's team there at Chester."

"Aye, the way things are going, I'm sure they will." *They? They? It's your team, you prick!* "They'll *try* anyway. Max Best will probably tear it down."

All eyes turned to me. "What?"

"Oh, didn't you hear? Half the team left."

"Half what team?"

"The youth team, Best. The one you broke."

"Is that right?" I said, popping a crisp into my mouth, not showing how fucking aggravating his words were. I turned to MD. "Benny?"

He nodded. "And four others. The one you called Future."

"Where did they go? Where's the nearest academy?"

"There isn't one. They've gone to Broughton."

Broughton! The team we'd played against during the whole Benny incident. A slow smile spread over my face.

"Max," said Henri. A warning. I'd heard that from him before, and like before, I ignored it.

Raffi and Moss were both standing, half-turned, ready to leave. But they stayed to watch. It was crazy. Everyone in the room just stood and watched as I got my phone out, tapped a few times, and tried to stop smiling long enough to talk.

"Nice One!" I said. "It's Maxy Two Thumbs. How you doing?"

I let my eyes sweep the room, enjoying the looks on everyone's faces.

"Great. We're watching it, too. Bit drab so far, isn't it? Listen, I won't keep you long. I just this second heard that Benny left Chester." I let Nice One quickly tell me what I already knew. "From bad to worse, you say?" He spoke some more. "Yeah, probably the best move. If some rando from Manchester cares more about their careers than their own manager, that's a bad sign."

Henri stepped forward to make me stop, but I pointed at him and looked so furious that even he backed down.

I smoothed out my face and continued. "Thing is, I told Benny I'd try to sort things out there and I didn't get the chance to do that, sad to say. I want to make it up to the kids. Help them out somehow. They always play on Sundays, right? I don't suppose you've got the next fixtures, have you? Oh, on the fridge! Yeah, I'm at Raffi's house now. The fridge seems to be where they organise things, too. Is that a parent thing?"

Nice One told me the upcoming fixtures. When I heard what I wanted to hear, I punched the air. Who says I don't celebrate? "They're playing Chester on the eighteenth of December? Oh, that's fun. That's my one Sunday off. Listen, how about . . . Do you think the kids would like it if I went and managed that match? Yeah? You'll talk to that manager guy? What's that? Four-four-two diamond?" I laughed. "Maybe. I've got some new moves, Nice One. They're going to love it. Henri as assistant? Er . . . I don't think so. He's a Chester player now. He might think it's disloyal or whatever. He might come and watch, though . . ."

I was grinning like a crazy person, now. This was better than beating Hereford—it wasn't even close. I was going to get another chance to manage a game, and I was going to humiliate Chester, Spectrum, Tyson and the rest.

I ended the call, placed my phone down on the kitchen counter, and showed my two thumbs to Ian Evans.

"Dad, let's go," said Raffi. They shuffled towards the front door.

Henri grabbed me by the arm, quite hard. "Max," he said, pleasantly. "I need to gather some clothes from my house. Then I will take Gemma home. Would you like to join us in the car?"

Not really, no. I wanted to stay and find more ways to throw haymakers at Ian Evans.

Shona said, "I'll put some food in a Tupperware for you, Max." She was pushing me out. Seconds later, Henri was by the front door holding my kit bag and Shona was pressing a container full of home cooking into my hand. She looked up at me before taking her hands away. With a tiny, sad shake of her head, she simply said, "Jerk."

30

YELLOW CARDS

I paused as Henri opened a car door for me. "Enchanté," I said.

"I'm opening the door *for Gemma*. You get in the front."

"Why?"

"Because you're a professional footballer and we're going to be driving for two hours."

I didn't really understand what he was talking about. "What?"

"Being scrunched up in cars is bad for your hamstrings. The passenger seat has been *calibrated*. Now get in and don't press any buttons."

Gemma pulled me out of the way. "It's okay, Max. I don't mind."

I walked round to the other side, then scratched my head. "This isn't a Lotus Seven."

"That's right, Max," said Gemma, mimicking the way I mocked her. "Well done!"

I got in the passenger seat of this ugly silver Volvo and placed the Tupperware down between my feet. I settled into the seat, then sighed. "Made a mess of that party, didn't I?"

"No, Max," said Henri, buckling his seatbelt. "You were provoked. You had no choice."

"Do you really think so?" I said, but my burst of happiness flew away as soon as it grew wings. "Oh. You're taking the piss."

"Yes. I am taking the piss. I am disappointed in you. You were immature. Shona worked hard to host us. That is *my* career you are playing with. And Raffi's. He just signed a three-year deal!"

"Evans isn't more annoyed with me now than when he signed the deals."

"Everyone has a limit, Max."

"He'll be gone soon."

"He's connected. He knows everyone in the game. Be careful. Be very careful. Consider this a yellow card from me. Pray Raffi is as tolerant. There. I have spoken." We drove off, then almost immediately pulled to the side of the road again. Henri checked me out. "Watching these games is important to you, yes?"

I was feeling that sort of numb buzz you get when you realise you've made a big mistake. Yes, I felt justified. Yes, the situation was patently unfair. But Henri was right. Of course he was right. I'd gone too far. A lot of risk for almost no reward. Self-sabotage to the max—literally. I'd put myself in a position where I'd endangered a huge chunk of my guaranteed income. Lost in a mist of self-pity, it took me a second to realise he was talking about the World Cup. "Yes."

"Then go ahead. Watch on your phone. When the match is over, we'll still have more than an hour to complain about your behaviour."

Poverty kicked in. "I don't have that kind of data plan."

"Here," said Gemma. She gave me her phone. I say phone, but it was practically a tablet.

"You sure?"

"Sure I'm sure."

I wasn't going to argue. I went to a website that had links to lots of exceedingly legal ways to stream live matches. As soon as the feed came on, I saw that I'd only missed two minutes, and questions six and seven popped up in my vision. "Oh! Amazing. You're a lifesaver."

"You can leave the sound on," said Henri.

"I prefer it with the sound off," I said. "I can concentrate more. Also, I need to listen out for the questions." Saying this, I popped the earphone in.

"This is what you do, is it? With your free time? Watch matches and answer strange questions?"

"Yes," I said.

"And what do you hope to get from it?"

"Opportunity."

"But you are a football player. You are playing well, scoring goals. Building your reputation. That's opportunity enough, no? Your January thirty-first plan remains insane, but it's growing on me. There's a long way to go but . . . if a club is desperate enough . . . why not give you a chance?" He sighed. "However. This *extra* work you are doing, this online course, it is not healthy. You look exhausted. You need to take better care of yourself."

"Max," said Gemma. "Why did you do that?"

"Do what?"

"Put yourself forward to manage a children's match against Chester? It's going to annoy the management, and you've got two clients there. I don't get it."

"It is not gettable," said Henri. "It is diabolical."

His word choice made me wince. "Why would it annoy them? It's coincidence that the match is against Chester."

"Come on. I'm not *that* stupid. You knew it was a mistake when you were doing it. I want to know."

I shrugged. On the phone's screen, Argentina were struggling to create chances against Mexico. I'd probably struggle to explain my motivations. "Okay, fine. To annoy them."

"To annoy Ian Evans," said Henri.

"No. Both of them. I like MD, but he doesn't give a shit about the youth system and he should have defended me against what Evans was saying. I didn't break that team. It was already broken. Fuck sake, Henri. You were there. Tell me you agree with me."

"I don't completely agree with you, Max."

I fumed for a bit. "Gemma, it's like this. You smother your teeth with . . . I don't know . . . what's that fizzy sweet that tingles your mouth? Then you forget to brush your teeth for four years, then one day Max Best comes along and offers you a KitKat. You take a bite and five of your teeth fall out. Who do you blame? Max or the KitKat?"

"The KitKat."

I laughed. "Come on. It's *your* fault! You didn't brush your teeth. You did it to yourself."

Henri nodded once. "Your analogy has some merit, Max. But to make it more realistic, once the teeth fall out, Max Best breaks the KitKat into four pieces and uses them to make rude gestures at the person who trusted him."

Amazing. Had he somehow heard about what I'd done on the team bus? No. Surely it was just coincidence. I smiled, very slightly. "You missed the bit in the middle where I *told* them not to eat the KitKat and said I had a special toothpaste that would heal their teeth and make them grow bigger and sharper than ever. And instead of using my toothpaste, which only costs three hundred and fifty pounds a week, they keep yelling 'What have you done to my teeth?'"

Henri shook his head, but he was smiling now. "You're certifiable."

"Guys, listen. I feel bad for Shona. That was shit of me. I need to get a grip. I really do. I promise I'll work on it. But that's me. Me the person, me the agent. But the kids! The youth team! I have to be honest with you now. I'm annoyed. At everyone. Everyone except Gemma. Yes, Henri, I'm annoyed with you. I don't expect you to take my side in front of Ian. We can't both have a bad relationship with him. But I do expect it here in the car. I admit I struggle to keep my temper in check and I have to be more diplomatic, but this thing with the under-fourteens presses *all* my buttons."

I put the phone on my lap so I could count on my fingers.

"One. Wasted talent. These kids are good! One's *really* good. Two. Toxic workplaces. Imagine being that age, excited to get a chance to train and play five times a week, and then you find out what it's really like. Fucking winds me up. By the way, you could have told me Darlington was wall-to-wall pricks. Three. Indifferent, incompetent, and distant management. Am I describing my bosses at the call centre, or am I describing a man who doesn't even know the name of the brightest prospect in his own youth system? Infuriating. Four. Lies and cowardice. Spectrum and the guys who told Evans none of this was their fault. And above all, five. Bad football. Imagine how much shit the average kid would put up with to play for their local team, then realise that *half of one whole team* has walked out. That's how shit it is to be on the same team as Tyson and Henk. But yeah. That's my fault. It's all *my* fault."

I took a moment to calm down, and remembered the Argentina match. But no sooner had I picked the phone up than I put it down again.

"That Benny kid means a lot to me. It's weird, but he does. He's not the most talented, but he wants to be a professional like his dad and he can certainly get that far in the game. He's a top lad. I *will* bring him to his mountaintop. I will. He's well out of that Chester team. He's in a good place, now. It's not going to be the best training and the best facilities, but he's not breathing poison every day. Know what I mean? I can't be there to watch over him, but I can check on him every now and then. Make sure he's on the right path. And while I'm doing it, I can stick it to Ian Evans and his fucking lackeys. Why did I do it, Gemma? For me. For pride. For stubbornness. Ninety percent for me. And ten percent for the kids. And I promise you one thing, that's ten percent more than they'll ever get from Ian Evans."

I faced the front. I was spent.

"Fighting Ian Evans is a mistake," said Henri.

"No, Henri. My mistake was starting to care about some random under-fourteens. But I do."

"You can't care more about the under-fourteens than your actual, paying clients. And if you do, you need to rethink that."

I bit back a response. He was right.

"Max," said Gemma.

Her tone made me turn back again. There was something tender about it. "Yes?"

"You're fighting Ian. You're fighting your teammates. You're fighting for these kids."

"Yes." I expected her to tell me to try being less aggressive.

"Why don't you fight for Emma?"

I looked away. "Because," I said. But I had no clue how to go on. I felt completely drained.

I faced the front again and picked up the phone.

"Messi just scored," I said. I answered all my open MUNDIAL questions the best I could, closed the browser, and gave Gemma her phone back. I was done for the day.

We pulled into Henri's driveway. I got out and said, "Huh."

"What?" said Henri, opening the back door for Gemma.

"I feel great. Not stiff at all. You'll have to teach me how to adjust the car seats."

"Not until you're done trying to destroy my employer."

He used his own key to let himself in, and, too late, I remembered the state I'd left the house in. I raced up behind the lovebirds, but what was I supposed to do? Rugby-tackle them?

"Fucking hell, Max," said Henri.

"Oh my . . ." said Gemma.

I rushed to the island unit in the kitchen and tried to swipe the nearest post-it note. Henri grabbed my wrist.

"I'll make sure it's clean," I said.

"Max," he said. "I do not care about the countertop." He released me and let his hand float over the rows and columns of post-it notes that I'd arranged on the island—pink, yellow, green. There were post-its *everywhere*, arranged in neat horizontal or vertical lines. The kitchen island looked like a spreadsheet with many columns of ten colourful little squares. My intention was to see if there were any hidden patterns in the questions, any deeper meaning I could get out of the MUNDIAL mini game. Of course, it made me look like a serial killer.

"What is . . . this?" said Henri, pointing to one note.

I peered at it. "England player with the best heading. Harry Kane."

"And this one?"

"What formation did Japan switch to against Germany? It was when that sub came on and changed the game."

"This?"

"That was a weird one. From that day's matches, who was the best goalkeeper? Very, very tough. I didn't get it."

Henri was lost for words. My mania wasn't a mania. It was way beyond that. He did one very slow blink, then wandered off to collect what he had come to collect.

Gemma was standing by the fridge, looking around the room, spotting more little columns of post-its here and there. Duplicates so I could seek inspiration in different parts of the room. She was rubbing one arm like she was afraid of me. "What is this?"

I sighed. I placed my palms on the island and leaned on them. "This is a colossal waste of time. Or a huge shortcut. I won't know till it's over."

"Oh."

"I don't want to feel sorry for myself. I chose this. But . . . you know." I waved my hand around the room. "Not exactly knight-in-shining-armour material right now."

"No."

Henri returned. He had a load of clothes and something in a little zipped-up case. Headphones, maybe. He went through into his office and came back with two envelopes. "Max. I thought this could wait but . . . despite your behaviour, a gift. World Cup final tickets."

The envelopes were glossy and expensive, but I could still see the glowing, Willy Wonka golden tickets shining from within. I felt dizzy for a second. "Are you serious? They're like gold dust."

"I have contacts. Now listen. Do you want them?"

Huh. Some tiny moment of hesitation. On the one hand, the World Cup final! On the other hand, Old Nick's little burst of anti-Qatar propaganda made me pause. For almost a tenth of a second. "Yes, absolutely."

"Great. The final is December eighteenth."

"Cool," I said, hand outstretched.

He waited. Stared at me. I was supposed to think something, but I was tired to my bones. He crossed the T. "That's the day Broughton are playing Chester."

"Oh." Now, *this* was a dilemma. Go to the World Cup final, in person, or manage a bunch of—sorry to say—fairly terrible players whose careers—let's be honest—wouldn't ever amount to much. I brought my hand back, and rapped a knuckle on the countertop, one beat for every second of calculation. Three beats. "Yeah, okay. I'll pass. Thanks."

"You'd put Benny ahead of the World Cup final? Seriously?"

"Yes, Henri," I said, getting hot. He was getting on my tits. If I had a spare house to live in, I might have really let loose. "Seriously."

"You said this rematch with Ian Evans was ninety percent for you, ten percent for the kids. What is it really?"

"Just that."

He slapped the tickets on his other hand. "No! No, Max! You do not miss the final, the World Cup final, for some meaningless kickabout. Be serious."

"Fine. It's twenty percent for the kids. Jesus. Who cares?"

"I care." He looked stern. "I put it to you, Max Best, that it is ninety percent for the kids. Ninety!"

"Come on," I said.

He tossed the tickets onto the counter and placed his hands on my shoulders, as though my first kiss in Darlington would be with him. "Look at me, Max. Tell me the truth. Is this big fight, this title bout, for *you*? Or for *Benny*?"

He was so close I had little choice but to return his gaze, but before I spoke I looked down and away. "Benny *is* me."

"Explain."

"No."

He did something strange then. He released me, slipped the envelopes into his jacket, then walked away and sat on the bottom stair. He jiggled a nail in between two teeth, the way I did, as he stared into nothingness. "*Eh bien* . . ." He finished his deliberation and came round the island and looked me up and down. Then he walked around in a little circle. "The children are in your heart. You continue to surprise me. Sometimes I do not like it, but it must be the way that it is. You will manage Broughton against the club that pays two of your three clients. I will talk to Ian Evans. I will do my best to smooth things over and make sure no harm comes to Raffi. I will smooth things over with Shona and help her understand what happened tonight. I cannot support your revenge fantasy, but I will support your efforts to help the children. I will teach Benny how to be a fearsome striker like his idol, Henri Lyons." He stopped walking. "We *will* play a formation with strikers, yes?"

We! He said we! "Strikers? Yes," I said. "Three."

"Ah!" he said, smiling. "You've been trying new formations. Of course you have."

Not yet, but I would make practicing 4-3-3 a priority. "Your phone was here the whole time. How did you know when the final was?"

"I'm French, Max. When you support a national team as dominant in international competition as France, you learn the dates of the finals."

"Ha ha," I said. "Let me see the tickets, though. I've never seen a World Cup ticket."

"Ah," he said, and immediately everything about him became shifty and slippery. "It's late, we have to go."

The whole scene suddenly clicked. There were no tickets. He was just testing how serious I was. I put my hands to my head. "Oh my fucking God! You absolute prick! What if I'd said I wanted the tickets?"

"I didn't think that far."

"Why is it that when I do plans everyone thinks I'm manic and childish but when you do it, it's cute and whimsical?"

"Because *my* plans don't drag dozens of other people into them, Max." He stepped close again and gave me a hug. When we separated, he pointed to the post-its. "Please do less of this."

Gemma followed him towards the front door, took one last look around the room, and said, "I don't understand any of this, but don't let anyone stop you. You do you." Then she gave me a double kiss goodbye, and I was once more alone with my block of post-its and my marker pen.

You do you. She was talking about watching all the World Cup matches, but it was all the encouragement I needed to forge ahead with what Henri called my revenge fantasy. I took a piece of A4 paper and drew a timeline from then until December 18. I plotted out all the things I could do to make sure Broughton won that game—chuckling as I thought of ways to annoy Spectrum and get under his skin—and arranged them into some sort of sequence. A few things, for example managing a Middleton Rangers game, would mean missing World Cup matches, but I had a plan for that. By the end, looking at my scheme, I was pretty convinced we'd beat Chester.

I pottered around, picking up Henri's books and putting them down again. One was called *Maxy-Dick*, which shocked me into a double take. Of course, it was *Moby-Dick*, about a dude who destroys himself fighting something he should have left alone. A stiff, solid rectangle of card was wedged in, halfway through, used as a bookmark. It wasn't yellow—it was orange—but close enough.

"Fine," I said, out loud. "I get it. Jesus."

I went back to the timeline. I'd been focused on winning the match and crushing Evans and Spectrum and all that bad stuff. But now I brainstormed how else I could make use of that day. Things that would be beneficial to Benny and the other rebels beyond the thrill of victory. I worked on that for a while, took a last look at my creation, nodded, and stuck it to the fridge.

I got into bed, but after a restless half hour, went back downstairs and plucked all the post-its from the kitchen island. I placed my laptop there instead and went to YouTube. I typed *anger management*.

When I eventually went back to bed, I slept like a lamb.

31

HERE ENDETH THE LESSON

Sunday felt like climbing out of a hole. First, I got a lunchtime text from Emma. Just a light kind of checking-in message. I responded in kind. I guessed that Gemma had told Emma what she'd seen, and that while I was bonkers, I wasn't bonking women left, right, and centre. So Emma was trying to stay friends or whatever and was no longer mad at me. I didn't really need an outrageously sexy blonde friend, but it was better than nothing.

Then I got invited to watch World Cup matches with Longstaff and Junior. I did one each with them, and two on my own. Perfect!

With Longstaff, I asked him what it was like supporting a small team, how it had affected him when the previous owner had built an enormous white elephant stadium that led to the bankruptcy of the original Darlington FC, and what it meant to be a phoenix club.

One interesting thing was the frequency with which he mentioned the pandemic. By far the hardest part of the lockdowns, he said, was not being able to go to the football. Absence makes the heart grow fonder, even when it's sixth-tier Darlington playing a dogged 4-4-2. It might have been the hundredth time someone told me what their local team meant to them, but I think I was finally starting to get it. Like, really get it.

With Junior, I focused on his experiences as a player. What it was like in youth teams, his ups and downs, being out of contract for long stretches and struggling to get noticed. I asked him about other clubs, other managers, what he really thought of Cutter and the cavemen, how he trained, how he ate. Like Longstaff, it wasn't hard to get him to talk and I loved every second of it. Even when he praised Captain Caveman and his bully boys for being good defenders. *Tsch.*

As I was leaving his flat, he begged me to keep my head down. Don't rock the boat for a while.

"I don't rock boats," I said. "I just point out when they're rocking."

"Well, give it a rest for a spell. Don't put a target on your back. With the gaffer or the squad."

"Absolutely."

I wasn't just learning loads about life in the lower leagues, I was also racking up TINOs. My stash was starting to look impressive. If I kept grinding, I'd soon have more TINOs than I had XP at the start of the World Cup, with half the tournament still to come.

The only problem was that they surely wouldn't be converted back to XP until after the World Cup final, so I wouldn't be able to buy new skills and perks to help me in the Broughton match.

Monday, November 28.

I got to the training ground at 7:30, ninety minutes early. In-before-Cutter early. Sarcastically early? You decide.

I set up a net on my own and smashed Beckhams and cannonballs into it, right foot and left. Then five penalties on each foot. Then a light jog around the pitches. Then, because I was bored, some kickups. I got to fifty without the slightest concern, and that's when I stopped. I tried doing some skills against mannequins but it wasn't much fun.

At 8:40, when one of the coaches started putting the chairs out into rows, I was in the meeting room. As soon as he put the fifth one down, I said thanks and sat on it. He sighed and shook his head and finished his work. My spot was right in the middle, right in front of Cutter. Sarcastically eager? You decide.

The rest of the team filed in. Junior sat behind me and leaned forward. "Is this your idea of keeping a low profile?"

I smiled back at him. "I'm the reserve right midfielder for a team in the sixth tier. How low can my profile get?"

"You know what I mean."

The meeting started as something of a bollocking for the team's poor performance on Saturday, a promise that training would be extra hard, and a bit of a heads-up about what to expect from the Kettering game on Friday.

I shot to my feet, then sat down again. "Friday?"

"Yes, Best. Friday night. Under the floodlights. Is that okay with you? Does it fit your schedule?"

"Yep," I said. "Does that mean I can make plans for Saturday afternoon?"

His first instinct was to get mad at me, but his second was patience. Maybe one of the coaches had reminded him that I had almost zero experience. "Yes."

"Oh, top."

Cutter wanted to move on, but curiosity got the better of him. "What will you do?"

"Oh, I'll see if any of my mates are playing and go and watch them."

"Mates or clients?"

"My clients are all mates."

He pushed his bottom lip out and turned his head—conceding the point. He'd seen me and Henri together. "What if no one's playing?"

This was ludicrous. The whole first-team squad was watching him chat to me about my plans for the weekend. A cheeky grin slid over my mouth and I half-turned so the others could see it. "I might go to the zoo. Do you want to come, boss?"

Cutter grinned back. For once I'd pitched my cheekiness just right. "No fear. There's enough animals round this place. Primates everywhere."

"Snakes, too," said Captain Caveman, which drew snickers from his goons.

"I've spotted a couple of endangered species," I said, stretching out to cover more space.

"Donkeys!" said Glynn, because that's what people call footballers with poor technique. Funny but not quite pitched right. Or maybe it was the perfect pitch, since it ended the banter.

"Lovely stuff," said Cutter, ending that little escapade. "That's it. Pitch two."

Training was okay, with one interesting discovery and one minor incident. The discovery was that as Junior started the session, his CA increased by one. Then at the end, it increased by another point, to bring him to 40. I hadn't seen a two-point increase in one session since I'd been at Darlington. I wondered if I'd helped him build his confidence to the point where his natural talent could really flourish. It might have simply been that he was getting more game time.

The second incident was after we'd done all the boring sprints and shape work and blah blah blah. We got some small-sided games going on. Five-a-side in a quarter of the pitch. Really congested. We didn't have a full-sized goal to aim at, though, nor even the smaller one. No, we had the absolute tiniest goals available—as big as the ones you'd buy for a toddler. There were two for each team to aim at, set back from the playing area on diagonals. To score, you simply needed to pass the ball into either of the mini goals.

It's not *that* important that you can visualise the drill, but maybe imagine a late-night talk show—the playing area is the main stage, and the goals for team A were angled away from it like camera one and camera two. And of course, there was the same setup on the other side, so that our attacks could turn into defensive situations in a microsecond.

I guess the intention was to simulate a match situation where you'd compete in a small area then try to get some space to play a forward pass to a winger, while stopping the other team from doing that.

I was on a team that included Captain Caveman and Colin, and we were doing exceptionally well. We had a pretty ideal mix of skills for this game. Our opponents found it hard to get past us, and then on transitions I'd open the other team up with a clever through ball or a little burst of speed. When one team scored two goals, the losing team went off and a fresh team came on. We were totally dominant, though, and had entrenched ourselves as permanent residents. I loved it—it felt like my teammates and I were, at last, in sync.

The incident came when one of the other teams finally scored. Caveman lashed out at me. "That was your man, Best!"

"Nope. I was here for the counter."

Since the prick had never said more than eight words to me in one go, I thought that was the end of it. But my attack on Blondie had changed something. He came back at me. "You can't weasel your way out of this one. That was your man. If he scores, that's on you."

"No," I said, genuinely quite calmly, though despite watching over three anger management videos I was ready to lash out when the moment inevitably came. "The goal is to progress the ball, so you need me to stay in an attacking position."

"Gloryhunting."

"No, *Captain*. That's my *job*. If we play with five defenders, they'll come with five attackers and we'll get dicked. I've got to be ready for the transitions. If I'm attacking, they'll keep two defenders back as cover."

"Best," said his lackey, Colin. "Maybe so. But *that time*, you should have tracked the man."

"I've been doing it the same way this whole game and we've crushed it. You didn't complain when we were scoring with every break. It's risk reward, isn't it? They get a five percent chance to score, we get a ten percent chance. You take those odds."

"Football's about giving the other team nothing," said Caveman. "Clean sheet, every match. That's the aim."

"Not my aim," I said. "If you're not attacking, you're just waiting to lose."

"Attack wins you games, defence wins you titles. You know who said that? Alex Ferguson. Remember him? Managed *your* club. Best manager of all time. Think he might know a thing or two more than Max fucking Best."

I wanted to tell Caveman that the logical conclusion of his viewpoint was playing with eleven goalkeepers, but Cutter stepped forward. "We need to find the balance. That's what this drill is about." He blew his whistle to restart the game.

Demotivated, I walked around for a while, half-heartedly contributing. Henri's yellow card warning popped up in the centre of my mind. Well, the only person I could hurt this time was me. I went to one of the mini goals and lay down in front of it.

Cutter stopped the game. "Fucking hell, Max! What the fuck are you doing?"

"Defending the goal with my life, boss."

He fumed at me, and I saw his internal rage-o-meter filling rapidly. It shot past *Conceding a sloppy goal in the first minute of a local derby* and was rapidly closing in on *Little Manc twat ruining my training sessions with his unprofessional antics*. But a noise made him turn—his assistants were laughing. I got a piece of luck, just then, as one of the cavemen on the other team decided I was a nice juicy target—he hit a hard shot right at me. I adjusted and volleyed the ball away, in the direction of the opposite mini goal. It didn't go in—I wasn't *that* good—but just for a second, everyone thought it might.

Cutter blew his whistle and gestured at me. "Get off the pitch. Red card. Lads, you're down a man. Five against four. What are you going to do about it?"

Caveman tried to murder me with laser vision he didn't have. I helped my team by springing to my feet, flicking a ball into the air and doing jaunty three-metre-high kick-ups. Cutter whistled again. "Best! You're done. Go and wait in my office."

I did as he said and hung around for half an hour. I started out defiant, but I got more and more depressed as the minutes ticked by. It wasn't just that I couldn't fit in with the cavemen socially. I couldn't even get through to them about *football*. It was the same thing with Ian Evans. He had his ideas and they were fixed, even in the weight of overwhelming evidence to the contrary. I needed to be able to talk to these people if I was going to survive in the world of football. So far, I couldn't, and my failures were making me act out.

Cutter turned up and yelled at me for a while. Really let rip. When he was done, he told me to get out and buck up my ideas. I didn't move.

"Best? I told you to go home."

"Boss. I need help."

"What?" I don't think any player had ever said that to him before, unless it was about moving house or something basic.

"I don't know how to communicate with people like Captain and Colin. I try, I take deep breaths, I count to ten, and it all goes wrong anyway. How do you talk to people you don't like?"

"If I knew that, I'd be in the Premier League."

He wasn't going to help. I nodded, and stood up to leave.

"Best," he said. "Are you really asking?"

"Yes," I said, though the S didn't really come out. Got stuck in my throat somewhere.

Cutter stood up from his spot behind the desk and came to the chair next to me. Down to my level. "Max. You're wild and flighty and some of the lads love it and some hate it. But none of them trust you. I don't trust you. You're out of position when I want you in, and in when I want you out. Do you see what I'm saying? It's not that you can't communicate. It's that you can't get people to trust you." He looked out of the window. "You've made a big effort with Junior. Everyone can see that. That's good. But me? I wonder why you're doing it. And then I wonder why I wonder that. Do you get me?"

"Okay but I don't want to be best friends with everyone. I just need them to listen when it's about tactics or what the other team are doing or whatever. I spotted Hereford had gone defensive and told everyone, but the guys didn't react until they'd seen it for themselves."

He sighed. He didn't have time for my weird garbage. "When I broke into the first team, I was a skinny oddball. I scored an own goal in my second game. The guys didn't trust me. You know how I earned that trust?" He stood. "One day at a time. Now fuck off, I need to make some calls."

I headed for the door. When my hand was on the handle, he called out.

"It's good you're trying, Max. I like that. You're starting on Friday unless you pull another stunt like today."

"Yes, boss. Thanks. I'll behave."

After training on Wednesday—in which I was a MODEL CITIZEN—to test a theory I watched part of the second World Cup match and then drove to the school.

I watched a few seconds of Miss Fox's English lesson—she was dressed to kill, again, holy shit—then let myself in without knocking. The lads all sat up. "Guys," I said. "I don't get why you're always slouching. If I was in one of Miss Fox's lessons, I'd be erect the whole time."

The boys loved it. Miss Fox less so. "Max Best seventy-seven. Nice debut. But scoring a lucky free kick doesn't mean you get to interrupt my lessons whenever you want."

"Noted," I said. I pointed to her desk and said, "May I?" Without really waiting for a reply, I settled onto the front edge, facing the class. She had to move to the side to be seen. "Miss F . . . Faulkes. I need help. If that's all right?"

She sighed. "If it's going to get you out of here faster. Tell me what it is."

I looked around. It was all the academy lads, including Benzo and Bark, who I hadn't seen since I left the digs. "Guys, I want to be a football manager. I need to present an image of someone who could manage a team. Which is hard because I keep flying off the handle all the time. But that's not my fault—society's to blame. So two questions, I think. One. During matches I've been going over to the manager to discuss tactics with him. Has anyone seen that?" Several hands went up. I pointed at one. "What did you make of it?"

"Looked like you was scheming what to do next," he said. "Like you was assistant manager or sumfink."

"Oh, I got the opposite," said another kid. "I thought you was saying you didn't know what to do."

"Right," I said. That was the end of that little bit of pantomime, then. "Thanks. All right, question two. The media have been calling me a mystery winger and stuff. Which is pretty cool. I like it. Being mysterious seems fun. Like I've got superpowers. Or a curse. That's not going to help me get a job, though. My plan is to score, like, ten goals in the next match and then do an interview where I show how much I know about football."

"Short interview, then," said Benzo, to much laughter.

"No, Benzo, it would be very long." A dozen innuendos sprang to mind, but I glanced at Miss Fox and she already looked bored by them, even though I'd kept them in my pants. "The problem is if I talk about formations and stuff, they won't print it."

"Print?" laughed one kid. "Print is from the 1900s. If you want to control the narrative, that's what socials are for."

I knew it. "Social media? Ugh."

"Another thing, Max," said Bark. "You need to match the message to the medium. If you want to show off your tactics, you need to go on a deep-dive YouTube channel, or do a podcast. The newspaper's just gonna take half one sentence as their pull quote. TV's the same. If it was me, I'd start with short tactics videos on TikTok and have longer ones on YouTube. Reaction comments on Twitter, lifestyle things on Insta. When you've got some content there, get invited on a podcast and talk them through a match. They'll link to your socials and you'll grow a following."

"Yeah!" said Benzo. "It's looking like it'll be England v France in the quarters. You and Henri Lyons could do a predictions video! That'd be lit!"

That got a big buzz in the room. Benzo had definitely hit the nail on the head there.

"Mr. Best," said a kid I'd never seen. Sometimes the scholarship kids were at the Eastbourne training complex, so he must have seen me then. "Your skills are amazing. You could crush it with kick-up challenges or free kick tutorials."

Oooh, no thanks. "Like a performing monkey?"

He flushed, but stood his ground. "No. Yeah, but. But no. I mean, you can talk tactics for an hour but that won't get eyeballs. That's just nerds that watch that. I'm saying, come to watch you score from a corner, stay for the tips on how to beat a press."

I nodded and gave the kid a thumbs-up. I still didn't like what he was saying, but I liked that he'd said it. His blush deepened; he seemed really pleased.

I bit a nail.

Miss Fox chimed in. "Excellent, boys. Good ideas. But we've missed two of our Ws. *Who* is Max's target audience and *where* do they live online?"

"Old white men," said a young white man. "CEOs. Managing Directors. Rich guys who own teams. They're in anti-vax Facebook groups."

"And LinkedIn," said another. The name was met with howls of derision.

"Jesus, guys," I said. "I'm not going on LinkedIn! No one's *that* desperate. Oh, wait. The one director I know listens to *talkSPORT*."

Miss Fox said, "You need to build your profile before you get invited to contribute there, Max."

"So that means Insting and Twitting and Tikting and all that?"

She shrugged. "If you want to use the media, yes. That's the standard pathway. I'd suggest ninety percent entertainment, ten percent showing that you're not just a pretty face."

I sighed and stared out of the window. There were football pitches visible in the distance. Calling to me.

"Guys, Miss Fox, thanks for your help. Ten out of ten lesson." As I got to the door, I paused, turned, and asked Miss Fox, "How many goals do I need to score this Friday to interrupt next week?"

Amusement flickered on her lips. "Two."

"Only two?" I said. "So you don't mind our little chats. Good to know." And I eased out of the room while the boys made the noise that boys make when they've seen some next-level flirting.

That interruption proved productive in two ways. One, the ideas about using social media and all that. It seemed exhausting and bad for my mental health, but I was doing a lot of things that were bad for my mental health, so what difference would one more make?

The other thing was that since I'd watched the first five minutes of the World Cup match and answered the first two questions before leaving the house, I wasn't penalised for missing the whole match. I didn't get the chance to answer the other eight questions, but I didn't get the 127 TINOs stripped away. So I could, for example, watch a few minutes of the Wednesday evening match, then zip out to watch Middleton Rangers and get some actual XP.

I didn't—I wanted one more incredible Darlington performance in the bank before insinuating myself into the Middleton setup.

But it was good to know.

Thursday morning was shockingly important, and it all started out so innocently. So bland. So average.

Drills. Shape work. Nothing too serious the day before a match, but it wasn't my finest hour in terms of effort and intensity. The coaches knew I was half-arsing things, but they couldn't really complain if I was "only" finishing third in races or "only" making ninety-five percent of my passes.

The truth was, with it being December 1, I was hoping I'd finally get paid my redundancy money. Margot said the Darlington payouts were on the fifteenth of the month, so if I didn't get my call centre cash, I didn't know what I'd do. I couldn't live for two weeks with zero spending money.

So yeah, distracted. Which is why it took me a while to notice we had two new guys training with us. I was pretty confused because they were both nineteen—too old to have been sent up from Darlington's youth system—and because they were both shit.

There was some rando mincing around the touchline, chatting away to Cutter, who seemed to think this guy was the bee's knees.

I got on with the sesh, then had my shower and lunch and what-not. As I was getting to my car, Cutter was returning from somewhere with this dude. Probably gone off to get lunch together somewhere a bit more upmarket than the canteen.

"Max, come here," he said. "Brad wants to meet you."

This guy Brad was on the short side and stocky without having an ounce of fat on him. He had short, fluffy hair, a fake perma-tan, fake perma-smile, and a big, chunky watch. Patterned shirt, striped suit, and a Bluetooth handsfree earpiece.

I fist-bumped the guy. One annoying thing about being a footballer was the sheer volume of handshakes involved. It was never-ending. I tried to bump where poss. "Hi, Brad. I'm Max."

"I bet you are," he said, in a camp way.

Cutter thought that was delightful. When he was done chuckling, he said, "What did you think of the trialists, Best?"

"That was just a trial? Thank fuck. I thought you'd signed them."

The mood dipped a fraction, which I only realised retrospectively. "Why? What's wrong with them?"

Finally a chance to talk football with my manager! "Carmine combines being slow with having bad stamina. He can play a pass, but where's he going to get the time? A retirees league, maybe. In Italy. Thornton has the worst technique I've seen in Darlington, and I've been watching Caveman and Shrek for weeks."

Cutter's face had solidified, the muscles going taut, pulling his lips up into a snarl. "You're just saying that because he plays right midfield."

I was astonished. "Which one?"

"Carmine."

I laughed. "Carmine? Right mid? He's a defender. Right back, maybe. Midfield? Forget it."

"Now listen here," said Cutter, but the Brad guy soothed him with that soft, sibilant voice.

"David, it's okay. You asked him! And by the way, not bad. He *has* spent most of his career at right back. His last coach moved him upfield to great effect."

Cutter's anger turned to confusion. How had I seen all that in one distracted training session?

I looked up at the sky and shook my head. "I've put my foot in things again, haven't I? You're their agent."

"I am. Bradley Rymarquis, at your service." He pronounced the last syllable of his name "kvis." He put his finger to his cheek and tilted his head. "You've made quite the start to your career, Max Best. *Very exciting.* Do you have representation?"

I was about to open my mouth to say I didn't need an agent, but it struck me as pretty stupid. Why not string this guy along for a while and find out what he did? Playing for Darlington was a way to see how a real manager acted. Why not see what a real agent got up to?

"No," I said. "I don't. Yet. Do you want to help me with my career?"

"I think I do, my dear boy. I think I do."

"Fine. Promise not to put either of those two in the same team as me and we can talk."

I couldn't have known it at the time, but I'd just made one of the biggest mistakes of my life.

32

KETTERING TOWN

Friday, December 2.

On Friday morning we did a light training session, just loosening up and going through the match plans one last time.

I ate in the canteen and really had a lot of questions about it. The food was the same as the day before, even though we had a match scheduled for that night. I didn't know much about being a professional, but I knew I wasn't supposed to eat the same food the day before and the day of. I didn't expect a small club to have its own nutritionist, but there didn't seem to be any help for the players in terms of what to eat and when. But look, I kept my mouth shut. The boat was rocking and I simply smiled.

Around 1pm I got a rare notification from my bank app. I logged in and found the call centre had sent my redundancy money. Two thousand pounds! The relief was inordinate. I went to my laptop and paid my rent and my last bills from Moss Side. I pulled the screen flat and exhaled. I had some walking around money! I could buy all sorts of things!

I thought about Henri's yellow card and opened the laptop again. I sent Shona the money she'd lent me. In the notes field, I wrote "Thanks."

Next I texted Emma, saying I had that Saturday free and if she wanted to explore Darlington with me, I'd like that. She replied right away saying yes and what time. Huh. I said I didn't really know what I'd feel like the morning after playing a night match, but maybe we could pencil in 10 a.m. so we'd be done by the first World Cup match at 4. That would be the first of the Round of 16 matches. Finally, a relaxation in my workload. How better to spend some of that free time than with a platonic friend?

I chilled until the evening, dipping into the final four World Cup group matches but without making myself crazy trying to answer the harder questions, then drove to the stadium. Our match was against Kettering, who were near the bottom of the league. Piece of piss. My intention was to set Junior up for a couple of goals, and if he wasn't playing, maybe help myself to a hat trick.

Cutter got us together and told us the team—I was in, as he'd promised, and so was Junior. Blondie was out. I nearly punched the air, but had juuust enough restraint.

The only cheeky thing I did—and it's astonishing really that this could be considered cheeky—was to ask who was on free kicks, corners, and penalties.

Cutter eyed me, but decided it was a fair question. "You're on set pieces. First choice for pens is Gray. Then Blondie if he's on. After that, it's captain's choice."

I nodded. Putting our lumbering second striker on pens ahead of me was wrong on all sorts of levels, but at least I knew.

An evening match is different from a daytime one. The fans have had more time to drink, for one thing. But there's also the floodlights, the colder air, the way rain seeps into your bones, the way the edges of the pitch build up a dewy mist.

We kicked off, and the opening was pretty sedate. Kettering's average CA was about 30. The worst team I'd seen in this division so far. Our average was fractionally lower than our usual 50 because Junior was playing instead of Blondie, but we were in total control. I was doing my usual thing of scoping out the opposition, learning about my direct opponents, looking for the goalkeeper's trigger movements, all that jazz.

I found it almost funny when Kettering scored in the first few minutes. Caveman was put under pressure and he passed it back to Smokes. He took a heavy touch and the striker nearly got it. But Smokes's clearance was weak, and Kettering had enough about them to take advantage. No big deal. I would tease Smokes about his mistake during the next week, because we were so dominant it wouldn't actually matter.

Even a man short, the game was too easy. It was a foregone conclusion that we'd win, so much so that I was trying to estimate the attendance and looking at the crowd to see if I recognised anyone.

I was reading some of the names of the local sponsors and wondering what services they provided when I saw a commotion on the far side of the pitch. My first instinct was that the ref had shown a red card to a Kettering player. I checked the match commentary.

That's a foul by Tim. He came in late.
And the referee shows him a red card!
It seems a harsh decision.
Darlington will play 85 minutes with 10 men!

I stuck my bottom lip out. We were down a man, but Tim was so technically insecure that it could actually be a bonus playing without him. The ball would come down the right a lot more, that was for sure.

So I continued strolling around, waiting for my chance to strike.

What happened next was the dumbest of dumb luck. A long ball from Kettering's keeper was contested in midfield, but neither player made contact with it. The ball bounced up towards our defensive line, and Caveman rose to head it away. In a one-in-a-million twist, his powerful header crashed into the head of Kettering's second striker and flew back towards our goal. Their first striker reacted quickest, dashed to the ball, and took it round Smokes, ready to roll it into the empty net. Smokes had one of those goalkeeper moments and flung out a hand—he tripped the attacker to the ground.

My skin tingled. Red card, penalty. Unless the referee would bail us out somehow?

Nope. The guy pranced forward, pointed to the spot like he was doing some fucking performance art, then took out the red card and stalked towards Smokes with it partly hidden. Fucking attention-seeking prick!

Smokes, normally such a bubbly character, tottered towards the dressing room like he was walking the plank. No wonder—like Tim, he was finishing with a match rating of 4, with a three-match ban to follow.

There was a slight delay while Gray—our least mobile player—was subbed off so that Paul Larkin could go in goal.

Kettering scored the pen and as they celebrated I looked around in shock. We were all shocked. We'd have to play eighty more minutes with nine men, and somehow claw our way back from 2–0 down. I looked over to Cutter hoping he'd seen a situation like this before and would know how to reshuffle us. And that's when I saw he was bright red, spitting venom at the referee. The telling-off he'd given me in the office was nothing compared to this. The referee inched his way towards Cutter, seeming to dare him to continue with his tirade. Cutter obliged. The ref, delighted, gave him the red card, too.

Down to nine and without a manager.

What the . . .

The match kicked off again. Junior passed it to me and I just kind of frowned at the ball. What was I supposed to do with it? Kettering players were storming towards me like an orc horde, so I did something I hadn't done much of since I'd realised how good I was. I fucking booted it as far away as humanly possible. But that only delayed Kettering's next attack by a few seconds. They moved the ball, uncontested, to the wing, and played a cross in. Their taller striker got a head on it, but put it over the bar. A lucky break.

Caveman screamed at us to wake the fuck up.

For the rest of the half, we shuffled and sank and kept our shape. I put a shift in, same as everyone else. Stuck to the task. We'd get in and Cutter would be in the dressing room and would reorganise us. And we'd come out for the second half and turn this fucking disaster around.

Clomp clomp clomp bang crash. The sound of nine footballers plus subs and coaches going back into the dressing room. I took my place on the edge of the U-shaped bench and squeezed some marathon paste into my mouth. Two coaches were having a whispered conversation by the magnetic team board. Because of the shape of the space, I was farthest from the coaches so I couldn't hear what was going on.

I turned to Junior. "Will Cutter be in?"

"He's not allowed."

"No one will know."

"Ref will check. Or a lino. Or anyone. If he's seen in here, it's bad news. He won't risk it."

I vaguely remembered some story of José Mourinho being smuggled into the halftime team talk in a laundry hamper, so there *were* some managers who'd risk it, but I didn't know the sanctions for being caught.

"All right lads," said the oldest of the coaches. I'll call him Titan. "All right, listen up." He was trying to be confident, but having all the responsibility thrust on him was not his bag. He liked being second or third in charge. He liked coaching. "Bad half. Bad news. Referee's done us up like a kipper." Lots of agreement. "So second half, put a shift in, keep tight to your man, keep things tight. If we keep it tight, we might get away with a two–nil. So keep things tight for the first five. Right, keep your chins up. No one's going to blame you for what the ref done."

This plan was garbage. I looked around the dressing room waiting for someone to speak up, but no one even seemed to be thinking about raising a dissenting voice. My heart sank. If I kept my mouth shut, we could all just go about our business. Live long, happy lives. So why not do just that? Just zip it. Keep schtum.

But if Darlington didn't win this, they'd be three points behind King's Lynn. It'd be so so so much harder to win this league. I couldn't say *nothing*. But I tried to keep emotion out of it.

I pointed at the whiteboard. It had a football pitch background and two sets of magnets to represent the teams. We were blue. "What formation will we play?"

Titan pushed the blues around until they were in a 4-4-0. "Two banks of four. Make it hard to play through us. Keep things tight."

I leaned forward and rubbed my face. "We're two–nil down. How are we going to score?"

Predictably, he didn't like being challenged. "We'll keep things *tight* and see what happens."

"You can score a free kick, Best," said the coach who had told me about *Monkey Island*.

"Not from eighty yards out."

"Oh, what is your fucking problem?" Caveman, full of pent-up spite.

Weirdly, it didn't provoke me. At that moment, he wasn't really mad at *me*, and I suppose I had *just* enough maturity to know that. "My problem is that I can't do *that*."

"Do what? Score a free kick?"

"I can't play to lose." I pulled my jersey off, which of course made the tension ratchet up about a million times. In fact, I just wanted to use it as a prop, but to the rest of the guys it looked like I was throwing a tantrum.

Titan lost his shit. He stepped towards me. "Are you refusing to play?"

There was a little moment where I tried to understand why he'd said that. I couldn't put two and two together fast enough. My mouth took over. "Play?" I stood and walked towards to the whiteboard. All eyes were on me. I put my hands on Titan's arms and gently moved him a few inches so I could get past. "I don't mean any disrespect to you coaches. I really don't. You're not responsible for this mess. But to me," I tapped the board, "this isn't *playing*. This is lying down in front of the goal. This is what I did in training and got a bollocking for."

There was a bit of an uproar. I waited for it to settle down. What had Cutter said? They didn't trust me. Well, I couldn't exactly build trust in sixty seconds. But I could be honest. I started by staring at Caveman.

"Most of you hate my fucking guts. Fair dos, I probably deserve it. Here's a little secret. Darlington can cancel my contract at any time. No penalties, no problem. You get onto your journo friends and your WhatsApp groups and say Max Best refused to play the second half. I'll be toast. I'll be out of the club by midnight. But just wait a fucking second." I paced back to my spot and gathered my jersey. I held it up so that the badge was facing them. "Those fans out there built this club brick by brick and some madman took it from them. So they did it again. Phoenix club. Darlington 1883 they were called, until they got the name back. There's fifteen hundred people who built this club, who bought tickets to this tonight, out there watching us play. Play. Not hope to get away with a narrow loss." I unclenched my balled-up hands. Looked at the badge. "You're all professionals. You do what you're told. I'm an amateur. I'm so stupid I always think there's a chance to win." I draped the top over my shoulder.

Caveman tried to help me understand the situation. "We don't have a chance to win! We've not got a manager and we're down to nine men!"

"So? We're top of the league, they're almost bottom. The worst player on our team is better than the best player on theirs. Our *reserves* would beat them six times out of ten. We're going for the title. We're the better team. We're at home. There's fifteen hundred of our fans out there. It's our fucking *duty* to *try* to win!" I paused and shook my head. Waited until I was as calm as I could get. I looked around at them. "If I'm the only one who feels like this, I'll shut up."

"Great, shut up, then," said Titan.

The other coach shook his head. "No. I want to hear him out."

I looked at Titan until he gave me a little nod. I spread my arms wide. "No big speech. I just want to have a go," I said. Simple as that.

Shrek, Caveman's brother-in-armpits, fumed. "And what if we go nuts looking for goals and lose six–nil?"

"We won't lose this league on goal difference, mate. We'll lose it by three points. These three points from today. It's already as bad as it can get. Seriously."

Junior spoke up. "Have you got a plan?" He looked around. "Guys, he does tactics. He knows football."

A little sigh built up inside me, but I squashed it down. "It's not my place to suggest plans," I said. I pointed to Titan. "Titan's in charge." I took the right mid magnet and pushed it off to the side. "Max Best has done a runner, the prick. What now? Bearing in mind we need three goals."

"Two," said Titan.

"Point's no good," I said. "King's Lynn are winning. We *have* to win. We need three goals. How do you get them without magic free kicks?"

Titan put his hands on his head and turned around, facing the corner. He wasn't paid enough to deal with pricks like me.

Monkey Island dude checked his watch. Time was running out fast. He decided he could yell at me later. He moved the magnets around. "Bring Blondie on. Play two strikers. Tight at the back, but try and cause a nuisance up front."

"Great," I said. "Team vote. Option one, surrender. Option two, have a go. Everyone votes. Ready? Option one?" Nobody moved. "Option two?" A few hands went up. "Everyone votes! Blondie. Glynn. Doop. Everyone. Option one? Nobody. Option two? That's pretty conclusive."

"You didn't vote," said Caveman, who also hadn't joined in.

"I'm in the car park trying to get my shitty Subaru to start."

He shook his head, exasperated but very very mildly amused. "Vote."

"Yeah," I said, looking at the whiteboard. "I vote for option three."

"Fuck sake. I knew you were up to something. Jesus Christ. Fuck! Fine. What is it?"

"Do you want to know? Or do you just want to laugh at it on the back of the team bus?"

"Both."

I inhaled. "Fine. Good enough." I moved the Blondie magnet off the pitch and brought the Max Best one back on. It was dumb because they all looked identical, but it made the point. I pulled my jersey back on, too. Then I shuffled the magnets around.

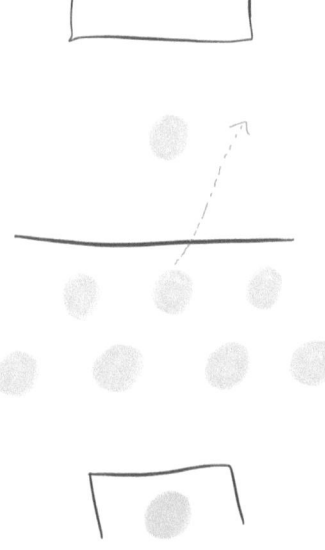

"Four-three-oh-one. Back four. Three defensive midfielders."

"What the fuck? I thought you wanted to attack?"

"Transitions *are* attacks." I heard a bell. It was just someone's phone, but I thought it was the one-minute warning. I spoke faster. "Here's how the half is going to go. They're going to have most of the ball. That's all right coz they're *shit*. They're going to get out wide and cross. Fullbacks, do your normal job. Try to stop them getting quality deliveries in. Centre backs, head it away. Three DMs here, get those second balls." This meant being first to the rebounds, deflections, defensive headers, whatnot. "This handsome character here in the middle of the three is . . . you guessed it . . . Max Best."

"You're going to play defensive midfield?" said Junior, showing a woeful lack of faith in my ability to hack Champion Manager.

"Bad news, mate. I might be the best DM in the world. True story. If I get the knock-downs, I'm going to drive forward five or ten yards." I moved the magnet up a little. "If it's one of the others, you pass to me. Right. Here comes the hard part." I wiggled the striker magnet around. "Junior, you know you're my favourite. But sorry to say, I need Blondie for this."

"Jesus," said Blondie, straightening from a slouch. "Are you going to fucking pass to me, then?"

"No, you're going to pass to me." I slid the Max Best magnet forward. "As I drive forward I'll play the ball to you."

"Oh, hashtag plot twist!" he said, the prick.

"This is the only really hard bit, I think. You need to give me time to get forward. Hold the ball up. Hold it, hold it," I moved my magnet until I was near the halfway line. "And go! Send me. Pass through, or over the top. I know it'll be hard to get good quality on it, but anywhere between the defence and the goalie and I'll get there first."

I stopped talking.

Caveman put his arms out. "And then?"

I smiled. "Then I score." I scoffed. "What else?"

"This is bonkers."

I stepped away from the whiteboard and looked at it. "Why?"

"Because," he said, but ran out of mental Scrabble tiles.

"Huh," said Monkey Island, moving closer to the board. "It's interesting, Max. Way more sophisticated than my idea. But they'll put a stop to it soon enough."

"Yeah," I said, going back to the magnets. "So when they adjust, we increase the pressure. If it stops working with just me and Blondie, one of the DMs joins us. Three in the move. I pass to Blondie and sprint, he lays it off to the DM who plays it over the top for me to chase. When they try to stop that, we get a fullback involved. At that point, it's four in attack. But we'll always have four in defence. That's plenty for most counters."

"Most," said Caveman.

"Yeah, man! Most! Most of our attacks will be more dangerous than most of theirs. It's just percentages. Odds. The odds will be in our favour. And by the way, as soon as we get some momentum, our fans will go nuts and their manager will sound the retreat. All these guys do."

Caveman wasn't sold. "You make it sound easy."

I blinked at him. "Well, that's bad communication from me. Let me correct that. This isn't easy. It's simple, but it's not easy. This will be the worst forty-five minutes of the season. Every one of you will have to put a hundred and twenty percent effort in. You'll suffer. You'll have to run more, win more headers, concentrate more. You'll need to make sure the passes to me and Blondie are crisp and clean or that whole attack cycle will be lost, and every time we go, it'll get slightly harder and slightly harder until by the end we're all running on fumes.

You'll have to rotate who supports the attacks. You'll have to save energy every way you know how, and more. Don't celebrate our goals. Don't come up for corners."

"Don't go for corners?"

"No. I need two in the box, that's all."

Paul, the goalie who had come on to replace Smokes, smiled. "You're going to shoot."

"I'm going to shoot from every corner we get. That reminds me, don't harass the keeper. Don't give this ref any excuse to disallow the goal. Got that?"

Lots of nods, including from Blondie. That's when I realised that we'd gone from discussing the plan to working on its implementation. I needed to take things back a step. Get consent. Make sure everyone was on board.

Caveman forestalled me. He walked up to the board and jabbed it with his index finger. "You want us to do a hundred and twenty percent, Best. But what about you? Seems to me you'll be doing the work of two men."

"Nah, mate. I'll be doing the work of three."

"You're so full of yourself!" It burst out of him. "How does this guy walk with balls that big? Fuck me." The bell rang. Time to get back out for the second half. "Right lads. Big shift coming up. Blondie, you warmed up?"

"Wait! We need to vote!" I said.

"We're not a fucking democracy, Best. It's like you said: we're professionals. We do what we're told. So we're doing Titan's plan."

I sucked in some air, but let it out again. Fine. Whatever.

But while I tried to stay calm, I felt the mist that was coming in the sides of the stadium wrap around me. Wrap around my eyeballs. All I could see was a tiny, plate-sized piece of the dressing room. A bit of wood and some damp corner of a towel.

I knew that at the end of the day, I'd feel good that I'd tried. Yeah, I needed to stop pissing off the world and its dog. But I couldn't just sit by and let shit happen. I wouldn't.

Still, being ignored hurt.

It really fucking hurt.

While these dark tendrils of thought swirled around, I heard a strange squelching noise. Caveman was writing on the top of the board: *TITANS PLAN*. When he finished, he dropped the marker into the tray and looked at the coach. "We're doing your plan, yeah?"

Titan nodded. "Yeah," he said, but it came out in a crack. He tried again. "Yeah, good lads. Four-three-one. Have a go. Yeah."

Caveman eyed everyone else. "Titan's plan. Anyone got a problem with that?" Nobody did. "Best?"

He was asking if I was cool letting the coach take the credit for my idea. He was actually trying to save me from the consequences of my actions. Or just trying to maintain dressing room harmony in a tough situation. Was it possible that *nobody* in the room would tell Cutter what had happened?

"Best?" he repeated.

I wanted to call out, "Three cheers for Coach Titan!" But I resisted the impulse. Talking was no longer part of the plan. The plan needed all my energy. Talking was wasted effort. I thumped the badge on my chest, which now that I think about it, cost way more calories.

Caveman yelled, "COME ON!" He turned and led the team back out.

Slightly dazed, I followed.

Junior, hoodie in hand, put his arm round my shoulder. He simply said, "Give 'em hell, Max."

33

GO FOR THE CORNER

We got into position for the second half. The crowd had visibly diminished. I hoped they were inside somewhere, buying beers, and hadn't fucked off home.

"Best!" Caveman was yelling at me.

I spread my arms. *What?*

"That's not the plan!"

Instead of being in the central DM slot, I was loitering out on the right wing. I was running one of my famous scams. Kettering's manager was a few yards away from me. Based on a cursory examination of the pitch, he'd assume we were doing something like 4-4-0. Maybe a little deception would help us out, maybe it wouldn't. But I hadn't communicated this to my team. There hadn't been time. I gave Caveman a double thumbs-up. *Trust me.* He didn't trust me.

Kettering kicked off and I slowly made my way to DM. To the outside world, it would look like typical Max Best tactical indiscipline. Another cross to bear.

The match went pretty much as predicted, with Kettering having most of the ball and most of our possessions ending quickly. No big deal. We had to be patient.

With seven people in defensive positions, we were solid as fuck, and Kettering defaulted to getting out wide and hitting crosses in. The kind of soft, slow deliveries you get at this level were meat and drink to Caveman and Shrek, and they dealt with most of the crosses with ease. Of course, one or two led to chances at goal, but that was always going to happen. All we could do was graft and make the chances as low percentage as poss.

We spent four or five minutes doing just that, when suddenly the ball was rolled into my path when I had forward momentum. I pushed forward and played it to Blondie. His marker tried to wrestle him, but Blondie was stronger and just as I crossed the halfway line, the ball was played towards me. A perfect pass! I couldn't believe it. I'd been drifting to the right, assuming any pass that came would be sliced. And even better—the goalie was rushing out to try to clear the ball. He had no idea how fast I was!

It was almost a dilemma. I could try to get the goalie to foul me before I shot. We wouldn't score, but Kettering would go down to ten men. And then we'd surely crush them. But a goal this early in the half would energise our fans. If things went tits-up from here, at least they'd have this one little moment of magic to talk about.

So I clipped the ball left-footed in a pleasing arc above and around the keeper.

It bounced exactly on the goal line, dead centre. 2–1.

The home fans cheered. It was some way short of a roar. Today, they didn't trust us.

I turned and walked back to halfway. The rest of the team stayed put. Saving energy. Yes! This was going to happen! I checked the tactics and match ratings. All good. While I was internal, Blondie got in my path and lifted his palms. We did a massive, bone-cracking high-ten.

"Nice pass," I said.

"Someone's got to teach you how," he said.

I remembered I was pretending to be playing right mid, and went over there. I stayed for a while, not just to sell the illusion, but because all the grinding in the first half and that big sprint had taken it out of me. I was about fifty times fitter than I should have been—I had the cheat code from the curse—but I was still human. I'd only had a short stint as a professional, and not that long ago I'd taken part in the trial at Chester and been absolutely destroyed by about twenty minutes of hard work. I *had* to conserve energy.

I took a thirty-second break, then drifted back into the middle. Back into the grinder.

So I was close at hand to see the mistake. A cross came in and Caveman jumped with the striker. He didn't get the ball, but neither did the other guy, which I suppose is good defending. But Shrek had just switched off for a second. The ball hit his chest, and he should have booted it away with all his might. Instead, in one of those inexplicable moments that you think about for years, he tried to spin and move the ball towards the other side of the pitch. Of course, being a giant green ogre, he lacked the agility, and the ball squirted off one foot and into the path of a Kettering dude.

3–1.

The home fans fell silent, and the stadium echoed with the whoops of eleven jubilant men from wherever the fuck Kettering is.

Shrek slumped to the ground. Paul was on his arse with his legs pointing straight out. Caveman was on his haunches, rubbing his head after that challenge.

I walked over to Shrek and held my hand out.

He shook his head. *Leave me alone.*

I bent down and grabbed his wrist, then leaned back until he lifted himself to his feet. I wandered around making eye contact with the rest. The goal had knocked some of the stuffing out of them. Well, that was natural. But they hadn't quit yet. Maybe I could inject a little dose of belief back into their veins.

I strode forward and took a position on the rim of the centre circle, towards the right, but nowhere near the right touchline. I wanted opposition players to come at me, but I wanted space, too. The ref whistled for the kickoff, and Blondie passed to me. I put my right foot behind my left and flicked the pass into the air, knee-height. From this position I did a few TikTok-style kick-ups. When the nearest opponent sprinted at me, I shifted my weight, looped my right leg over the ball, did one more kick-up, then blooped the ball over his head. I ran around him, control-pushed the ball a few yards ahead, and as I ran, pulled off a few stepovers, left and right. The Kettering guys were backtracking, wary, but finally two of them came at me. I did a no-look backheel pass to Blondie that was so obnoxious it even irritated *me*. I kept going. He hit the return pass first time, which was great, but this time he did slice it. Or since he was left-footed, I should probably say he hooked it. I went over to the right to gather the ball, shielding it from the fullback, and then stayed in place while he booted me up the arse. It was about the sixth time in that sequence where one of them had tried to foul me, and each failed attempt had been winding the home fans up a little more. I hoped it would have the same effect on my teammates.

I rolled around for a bit, pretending to be dying.

To my everlasting relief, the foul triggered a melee. Mega handbags! My guys burning their precious energy. The atmosphere had turned febrile. I clambered to my feet. Someone in one of the stands was banging a drum or slapping some sonorous piece of metal. Jungle fever. I felt my mania rising and fought to control it. I needed ice in my veins more than fire in my belly. The free kick was too far out and too far wide to do anything with. Deeply frustrating. So I passed it backwards and we had a short period of playing neat, simple passes to each other. A bit of a breather.

We wouldn't get many more.

With twenty-five minutes to go, Doop astonished the world by going on a little dribble on the left-hand side of the pitch. He played it to Blondie, who struck a highly optimistic shot from forty yards out. I couldn't tell you if it was on target, I'm guessing not, but it hit a nearby defender and we got a corner out of it.

"Max," called Caveman. He pointed towards the goal. *Should I go?* I shook my head. Stick to the plan. There was still loads of time in this game.

Blondie and Doop tried to make a nuisance of themselves in the penalty box, while every single Kettering player took up a defensive position. It was a weird sight—five of our guys taking a breather in the centre circle, then twenty yards of empty space, then a jam-packed box.

I positioned the ball where I wanted it, closed my eyes, centred myself, and opened them. Blondie was standing in front of the goalie, bouncing up and down. Being a dick. I put my hands on my hips. What had I *said*? I waited for him to get the message. Doop pulled him away from the goalie and with a last annoyed shake of the head, I looked down at the ball.

I hit it clean as clean can be, and got a little buzz of anticipation—the swerve on the thing was ideal, and it was dipping. Guaranteed goal, unless the goalie had brought stilts.

So I couldn't believe it when the ball crashed against the underside of the bar, bounced down the wrong side of the goal line, right to the foot of the defender who was at the back post. But the ball had so much spin that it squirted out from under his foot and went sideways, towards the crowded middle of the goal. Three players slid towards it, each trying to tackle the ball in a different direction. Blondie got a good chunk of it, but so did a defender. The ball popped out, bounced once, feebly, and was smashed into the goal by Doop.

Three–two, and now the fans really went nuts! We were playing towards the end where there wasn't a proper terrace, so the fans could mill around as they pleased. They zoomed from their spots to the place where Doop celebrated wildly—he didn't score many goals. I walked over to where he and Blondie were showing their biceps and waving at the crowd and all that. "Doop," I said. "Mate. My battery's on eight percent."

He gave me a look like a naughty schoolboy. "Aight." He turned, gave the crowd one last *Come on!* gesture, then we walked back to work.

Kettering's manager had seen enough. He ordered his team to defend. Men behind ball. Try to shut the game down. Sew up a famous win against one of the top teams in the division at all costs.

I signalled to Caveman and the rest. Four fingers. Four attackers. As all-out as my plan allowed. Caveman took over the organisation. He told Doop to stay back while the other DM and Colin from right back joined me. On the tactics screen, three of us had dotted lines emanating from our icons going up to the halfway line.

And the next phase of the match was pretty comfortable. We spent the next ten minutes in their half, like a little holiday. If they'd kept attacking us, we'd have been dead on our legs. As it was, only half our team needed to put any effort in, and Caveman was good at rotating the runners. After another five minutes, he called for subs. Glynn came on. Fresh legs, and a breath of fresh air. He and I passed to each other, brought in the third man, and tried to send chips over the massed defences for Blondie to run onto.

With quarter of an hour to go, all our probing paid off. A series of passes almost exactly like in our Monday training drill led to me having a bit of time and space thirty-five yards from goal. I didn't think about it—I fucking wellied it. Cannonball-style. The ball exploded off my boot—the keeper's eyes widened—then after ten yards there was a kind of second explosion, and it veered away to the right. The keeper threw out a hand, and very nearly deflected the shot wide. Close, but as a blind man says in a Ford showroom, no see car.

Three–three. I turned to walk back to our half, but this time there was no stopping the lads from celebrating. For the first time in my career, the whole team enveloped me. No holdouts.

When they were done, I took a step and called out, flopping to the turf in agony. Blondie came and gripped my boot and lifted my right leg up. Pushed it. Said, in a singsong voice, "Cramp, cramp, go away, come back another day."

I laughed, almost hysterically. I hadn't expected that! "What the fuck."

"Shut up, Best. It works."

Sure enough, when he pulled me to my feet, my calf felt invigorated. I had maybe two more long sprints in me. I switched roles with Glynn for a while. He got the job of marauding upfield while I stood just in front of Caveman, recovering, watching for counters. Kettering's manager was happy to stay defensive—a point against the mighty Darlo was good enough. He'd take it.

Glynn, Blondie, and our left back combined to win a corner.

Caveman and I looked at each other. "What do you want to do?" I said.

"There's only one thing left to do," he said. "Win the whole fucking thing."

We walked forward together. He ordered Glynn and Doop to stay back, while the rest of the team piled into the penalty area. It was now a target-rich environment. I placed the ball, took a breath, and hit it head-height towards Caveman. The goalie, burned by my recent shot, stayed on his line. So it was a mystery to me why I didn't see the ball power into the net. I didn't even see Caveman. I was mentally scratching my head when the ref blew his whistle and was surrounded by Kettering players.

I checked the commentary.

Best sends in the corner.

Caveman misses the header—he seemed to be pushed!

The referee blows his whistle . . .

He's given the penalty!

The Kettering players are furious!

Two yellow cards were shown. I walked away and checked the match ratings. I was on 9. Glynn was having a stormer: 8. Blondie was also on 9. His holdup play and movement were just as important as my dribbles and skills.

And now he'd get on the scoresheet, too.

"Best," called Caveman. "Take the pen."

"Blondie's on pens," I said. Cutter had told us the order. Blondie was second. Captain's choice was third.

"Fuck sake, Best. Get on with it. He's missed three of his last five."

Dilemma. If I took the pen, we'd win, but that would basically be me disobeying Cutter in the most direct way ever. But if Blondie took it and missed, all the team's hard work would be for nothing. How to balance everything?

I shook my head. I was fatigued and would make bad decisions. "Cutter said Blondie's on pens. Blondie," I called out. "Go for the corner."

Blondie had the ball in his hands—he knew the pecking order—and the Kettering players were milling around him, bumping into him, trying to put him off. The fans behind the goal were going feral—if the ref didn't get a grip on the shithousery soon, there could be carnage. A couple more yellow cards came out, and the Kettering mob finally retreated. Now the whole match came down to Blondie and the keeper.

He stepped up and hit a tame shot towards the bottom-right of the goal. Awful. But the goalie was too excited by the shitness of the pen, and the ball deflected off his wrist, down, and trickled into the goal. Dogshit, but we were winning 4-3!

The other manager took the handbrake off, and a look at the tactics screen showed them in a hugely attacking formation. It was something like 3-1-3-3. It was so far beyond all the 4-4-2s I'd experienced, I closed and opened the page several times to see if it was just a glitch.

"Guys," I shouted. "They're coming. Men behind ball!"

So the tone changed again. Back to the grind. At first, it was easier, physically, for me. I didn't have to do any of those punishing long sprints. All I had to do was shuffle around, get between some guy and the goal. Stop him from shooting. Let him turn and pass the ball back or sideways. Didn't take much energy. It was only when they started taking me on with dribbles that I got into trouble. If I didn't stab the ball away first time, I was toast. They started to target me. I'd turned into the weak link. I looked to the dugout and made the football gesture for *sub me off, boss*—two hands circling each other like a rolling wheel.

Blondie grabbed me and pushed me up the pitch. "No subs, Best."

"What?"

"We used all our subs. Get up top. I'll do this."

We used all our subs? When? Shit. I was more tired than I thought—I'd never missed a substitution before. Sure enough, Chumpy had come on at left back. I went to the halfway line and stood, basically helpless, watching our striker try to play DM. He was awful, but admittedly an improvement on my last few minutes.

The pressure mounted. Kettering got closer and closer. Paul Larkin saved a shot and immediately ran forward and got ready to launch the ball. What was he *doing*? But I suddenly realised that there was only one defender near me. I had the chance to wrap up the game!

I forced my legs to pump, chased after Paul's dropkicked punt, and was on track to get there. I'd be one-on-one with the keeper! It seemed too good to be true. But as I tracked the ball, it held up a fraction. Some tiny gust of wind. Argh! I had to slow and turn, and gathered the ball. That delay was enough for the defender to get in front of me. The clock said eighty-eight minutes had been played. Cutter would want me to take the ball into the corner of the pitch and try to keep it there for as long as possible. Me? I wanted to beat this defender and score. At 5–3, we'd be home and hosed. I started my dribble, and very nearly got space for the shot. The defender didn't slide in to block it like these clowns normally did, so I was forced a little wider. Since I was heading that direction anyway, I took the ball towards the corner flag and put my body between the ball and the defender. Ideally, he'd foul me and we could spend thirty seconds organising our team. But this guy was too wily for that. He simply waited until a teammate arrived, and between them they easily took the ball off me and launched an attack.

They moved the ball across the pitch, got an overload on the right, crossed, and a striker went up for a header. Paul Larkin insists the ball came off the guy's shoulder, which just about sums up our day. The header had been aimed at Paul's left. The goal was scored to his right. Four–all. Every single one of us slumped to the ground.

I don't remember much of the rest. We survived the last couple of minutes. I dragged myself off the pitch and into the showers because I knew if I stopped moving I wouldn't be able to walk again. Maybe someone offered me a massage. Maybe someone tried to talk to me. I don't know.

I do know that I couldn't drive, so Pat drove me home in the team's minivan, and he held the front door open while Junior lugged me inside.

I fell on the bed, face first. I didn't know what the consequences of my halftime intervention would be, but I knew that a draw at home to Kettering was a disaster. The fate of the league was no longer in our hands.

Footballers often talk about not being able to sleep after matches because of the adrenaline, but I didn't have that. Nor did I feel especially happy or sad or anything much at all. Mostly, the thought that kept coming to mind was a three-second phase of play. That moment where I could have attacked the goal but chose to do the so-called right thing and played safe.

Taking the ball into the corner?

I supposed I'd do it again if I was ordered to. But as a manager I would never, ever tell my players to do it.

If you weren't attacking, you were just waiting to lose.

34

THE MAX BEST MANIFESTO

By Saturday morning I had turned into a human brick. A few times, I woke up and wanted a sausage butty or to pee but simply couldn't move. My legs were eight times their normal weight. Henri's bedroom had different gravity. I assumed I would spend the rest of my life there, crushed under the pressure of my own fatigue. I couldn't even move my arms to put a podcast on, so I let myself curve in and out of sleep, before finally going deep, deep under.

A hand brushed my arm.

That was nice, this dream I was having.

A hand brushed my arm.

"Uh," I said.

"Max," someone whispered.

"Uh?" I was asking the person to prise one of my eyes open. They were locked up tight with weariness and that special night glue that eyeballs smother themselves with.

"It's Emma."

That did the trick. The shock let me get both eyes open a quarter. One eye half open would have been better, but I couldn't pick and choose. Sure enough, there was a mass of blonde hair and what looked like a leather jacket with too many zips.

"Uh uh uh?"

"It's our date, remember? A romantic tour of . . . let me check . . . *Darlington*? Starting twenty minutes ago."

"Uh uck."

"Ssh," she said, rubbing my arm. "It's okay. I know you had a big night."

"Ow in?"

"The key was still in the front door. Real horror movie scenario. Popped in to check how much blood there was."

"Orry."

"You're in the news. Want me to read it?"

"O-ay."

She adjusted on the bed. I guessed she took her jacket off, too, because I felt an extra pressure on my feet. Not ideal, tbh, but I wasn't going to complain. Also, I literally couldn't. She showed me her phone, which from my point of view meant she shone a fucking lighthouse lamp right into my weak, feeble, gluey retinas.

She double-cleared her throat. "'Darlington four Kettering four. Nine-man Quakers thrill Blackwell Meadows.' Is that the name of the stadium?"

"Eh."

"At first I thought it might be a local DJ or something. Okay, here it is. 'Darlington's title hopes were dented last night as they were held to a draw by lowly Kettering Town.' *Lowly*," she added. "That's mean. 'The match started with disaster followed by calamity, as Quakers conceded two goals and were shown three red cards inside the first fifteen minutes, including one for their manager David Cutter. Quakers spent the rest of the half . . .' Shouldn't it say *The* Quakers?"

I didn't reply; the answer would have needed more than a grunt.

"Quakers spent the rest of the half defending, and many fans left at halftime, fearing even greater humiliation was to come."

I heard Emma smiling and struggling to tame that smile. "They missed a second half full of passion and rapier-thrust counterattacks the likes of which this old stadium has surely never seen. Inspired by a bombastic, otherworldly performance from mystery winger Max Best, Quakers dragged themselves back into contention, and even held a brief lead near the end. Dreams of an improbable nine-man victory were dashed as the players' legs finally gave way. Those of the 1,441 who had stayed for the second half stayed longer to applaud their team from the pitch. An unforgettable night."

Emma paused. "Then there's some more details of the red cards and the goals. But you know all that. Then there's the interview with you."

"Uh?"

"Don't you remember? Well, they wrote it all down. So. Will I try to do a Manc accent? *Eee, our kid, nice one top one sorted.* Needs work? Yeah. Okay, they've done it in question-and-answer form. 'Echo.' This is in bold. 'Well played, Max. You're player of the match again. Tell us about the referee.' Then obviously it's what you said. Not in bold. 'If you're looking for a quote complaining about the referee, ask someone else. You won't get one from me. Echo. But did you think the red cards were justified? Max Best. If you print some angry tirade against the referee, you're giving yobs who read it permission to abuse refs in their Sunday League games. Leave me out of it.'"

Emma was shaking her head. "You get so indignant. 'Echo. What was said at halftime? Max Best. Our coaches reorganised the team, gave us a new structure to play from. A solid base with scope for counters. We wanted to give the fans something to shout about. Echo. Was it hard without your manager? Max Best. You want your manager there, but he prepares us for different game states. We literally had a session this Monday teaching us how to balance attack and defence. It was the perfect preparation for a game like tonight. Echo. Are you upset that your title charge has been derailed by one bad refereeing performance?' Then for your reply it just has an ellipsis."

She looked at me. "God, I can just imagine your face. 'Echo. Max, you've come out of nowhere and you're becoming a fan favourite. Can you tell us what your last club was? Where have you trained? Max Best. I want to thank everyone at Darlington for the chance to play here. The manager and the other players. People in town have been very friendly. We want to bring that league title here. We didn't win tonight, which is gutting, but I hope we showed that we're here to play and we're here to entertain and we'll always try to represent the badge in a way that the town can be proud of.'"

Emma blew some air out. "Well."

Well, indeed. It sounded okay to me, but I didn't think I'd really positioned myself as a manager type. I hadn't furthered my narrative. The scholarship lads were right—I needed to use social media. That didn't help my feelings of fatigue.

Emma went over to the curtains and opened them. Harsh, cruel light streamed in and assaulted me. It was a barbaric thing to do.

"What do footballers drink in the morning, Max? Green smoothie for recovery? Kale juice? Does Henri have a mixer?"

I summoned all my energy, shaped it into a small ball and pushed it into my throat. "Tea."

"Tea? Right. You wait there. I'll mek yous a mug. Then hows about a little massage to get you going?"

For the first time that morning, my eyes opened fully. You'll have to guess what facial expression I was doing because I don't know myself, but I saw Emma smirk. "I'll take that as a yes."

One very superficial but helpful calf rub later, I told her to shoo while I got dressed. A minute later I sent her a text and she came running back upstairs. "What? You okay?"

I grinned. This was not sexy. "I can't do the socks." I just couldn't bend!

She tried to hide a grin. Tried to get into nurse mode. "Right, then. I see you're planning to wear tracksuit bottoms and a plain black hoodie on our second date."

I tried to shrug, but lifting my arms hurt. Why did *everything* hurt? And what was I supposed to say about the whole *date* thing? I mean, if she wanted to cheat on her dude, I wouldn't stop her. But it would have to be some day when I was more limber. "This is what I wear most of the time now. I'm not really into drips and trims."

She was bending down. "What language was that? You been learning French?"

"Drips is what footballers call clothes, apparently. Trims is haircuts. Drips and trims is seventy percent of the banter."

"Oh, great. You're making friends."

I scoffed. "No. Far from it. I'm just nearby when some chat happens. I always wondered what players talk about all day. I assumed it would be all, 'If you could go back and watch any team from history, who would it be?' You know, 'What's your favourite chant?' kinda stuff. But no. I really wish I still had that mystery. Oh, what the fuck?"

She was putting white socks on me. White! That was criminal. "I'm just completing the look." She thought she was being delightful, but then she looked at me and said, "What?"

I adjusted my weight on the edge of the bed. I'd been in one position for too long. I thought about how to say this. "Emma. You're very stylish. You've got more zips on that tiny jacket than I've got in my whole wardrobe. If fashion and style are important to you . . ." I wasn't sure how to finish. I could hardly say this relationship wouldn't work, because we didn't have one. "Just. I've got enough on my plate. If I've got spare money I'm going to spend it on a personal trainer or going to watch matches I can't get into for free and things like that. Do you know what I mean? I genuinely don't care what I look like."

"Okay," she said. She fidgeted with the socks some more, but I realised she was putting them more *on* instead of taking them off. "So you won't mind wearing white socks with black everything else."

"I don't care what I look like *past a certain basic level*."

"Uh-uh, that's not what you said. Now come on. Get on your feet. This is the worst date I've ever been on. You need to raise your game."

It took about eight minutes to get down the stairs, but then we left the house and began our walk. Moving helped. My vague goal was to finally get to the centre and see the market and the Yards—Darlington's cute little side streets with random shops dotted around. I was willing to be distracted if anything better came up.

While we ambled, Emma asked me questions. "Why is *Moby-Dick* on the counter? Are you reading it?"

"No. It's just a reminder. Trying to be less antagonistic."

"That's good."

"I guess. It's just, when it comes to football, I've become really bolshy."

She laughed. "Bolshy? Is that Mancunian?"

"I dunno. You've never heard it?"

"No. What's it mean?"

"Just . . . argumentative. Difficult. Even when I try to tamp it down, it just . . . you know." I mimed an explosion. "Waah! When I was in my last job, I had a hundred ideas for how to run things better, but I kept my mouth shut, clocked off, and once I was out of the door I was out of the door. Do you know what I mean? But there's something about football that makes it stick with me. Gemma probably told you about my little disagreement with the guy at Chester."

"Yeah. But we don't understand it."

"Which part?"

"Most of it, really. It's some teenage boys playing football. How important can it be?"

I grinned. "Yeah. Good point. Fair. It's just that a club like Chester really should be trying to make sure the youth programme produces players for the first team. For a *thousand* reasons, really, but I'll give you an example. There's this team, Plymouth Argyle. They're in the third tier."

"League One."

"Holy shit! That was hot. So Plymouth have a young goalkeeper. I've only seen short clips of the guy, but there's a big buzz about him. Everyone agrees he's already Premier League quality."

"So why's he in League One?"

"That's the point! That's it! He came up through the youth teams. So he's probably on a hundred quid a week, he'll stay at the club as long as he can because he loves it, and they can pay him less than an outsider. And if he's as good as they say—which he probably is because he's their man of the match every week and they're top of the league—they'll get millions when they sell him. Millions! Almost all profit. I could find five players like that every year if someone would fucking let me!" I stopped to rub my temples. "Yeah it gets me worked up. That's what *Moby-Dick* is for. I need to stop caring."

"No," she said.

"No, I do. I can start caring when I've got a job where I can do something about it."

We ended up in the Yards, popping into the funny little shops. Round every corner was something completely random, so it was AAA date fodder. Funky hairdressers, tattoo places, bakeries, tea houses, all brightly painted, all trying to be social media friendly. With so many talking points, we had smooth, easy conversations even though I'd banned one topic. I had asked Emma not to bring football up—I didn't want to say something indiscreet that might be overheard in those ancient alleyways.

After the Yards, we checked out the big indoor market. It was the kind of thing you'd always want in your neighbourhood. A charming food court, plus all kinds of shops. Mostly friendly stallholders, with a few grumpytits thrown in for variety. Emma was impressed by the selection of cheeses and meats and the prices. "I could cook for us tonight," she said, examining an onion while a stall assistant tried to get an eyeful of her without anyone noticing. Fail!

I thought about her offer. There were pros and cons. Pros included spending the evening with my dream woman. Cons kind of stopped existing when I'd put the pro into concrete words. There was only one thing, really. "You know I'm doing this online course? I have to watch the matches. Answer questions. I can stick to the easy ones and skip the headscratchers, but I'll still be a bit distracted. As evenings go, it's on the other extreme from clubbing."

"We'll eat. You'll do your thing. I'll read *Moby-Dick*." She could see that I was undecided. "Max! I'm not going to harass you during the match. I promise. Hey, look at this turnip."

"I'd like to be harassed. But not tonight. And it's not just that. I'll feel guilty."

"Max?" New voice. Vaguely familiar. I turned and saw Glynn standing next to a woman. She was quite stocky with long, frizzy hair. The kind of face that breaks into a smile a lot.

"Oh. Hi," I said. A bit wary. I hadn't bumped into anyone from the club in the real world. But then again, I'd been at home almost non-stop. I looked around to see if anyone else was there, as though Glynn would only go shopping with Caveman or Chumpy.

"We saw you from over there. Soph wanted to meet you."

"Hi, Soph," I said, offering a fist bump. "Er . . . this is Emma."

They said hi, then there was an awkward pause because I didn't know what they wanted and yet everyone was waiting for me to take the lead. Glynn seemed nervous. His girlfriend had wanted to meet me and he'd been too ashamed to admit we were enemies. Him deciding to lose face with *me* instead of *her* was the most relatable thing he'd ever done. I noticed his eyes lock onto the number of zips on Emma's jacket. He got this look I can only describe as *aroused confusion*. A new contender for the most relatable thing . . . He finally got a grip. "Er . . . Soph was at the match last night. Watching me. Watching us."

"Oh, sorry," I said, joking.

"No!" she said, suddenly animated. "It was incredible. You were amazing. I've never seen anything like it. You were stunning. Absolutely stunning. Oh, I'm gushing. Sorry, Emma." Why was she saying sorry to *Emma*?

"No, keep going," said Emma. "He loves it. Made me read the newspaper to him this morning. 'Skip the parts that aren't about me,' he said." Soph was nodding slowly, drinking in every word. Emma realised she'd made a mistake. "Soph, I'm joking. He's not like that." Nervous release of tension from the weirdo.

I couldn't get a read on Soph's personality and now I wanted this whole thing to be over. "Well, Glynn was good, too. That was the best I've ever seen him play. When he came on, I was ecstatic I had another technical player on the pitch. It just relieved the pressure. Spread the load a bit, you know? We'd have lost six–three if he hadn't come on when he did."

"Oh!" said Soph. It took her a while, but my words finally seemed to land somewhere useful. "I'll keep him then!" Big, weird laugh while she grabbed him.

I smiled with about two percent of the energy she was giving off. "Do you mind if we wander away? I kind of used all my energy last night. Quiet night in. Emma's cooking."

"We should all go for a drink sometime!" said Soph. The words tumbled out, getting in each other's way.

"Sure," I said, glancing at Glynn, who was pretending to study a box of leeks. "I'm doing a World Cup project, then I'm starting my coaching badges. But maybe in, like, February?"

They fucked off and all that.

"That was mean," said Emma.

"What?"

"February. You'll have left by then."

"Shh," I said, looking around.

"Right, sorry. Sorry. Damn. But you have to be nicer to your fans."

"My what?"

"Didn't you see her face? We should google 'Max Best fan club' when we get home. We just met the founder."

"You're not worried? About the competition?"

"Max. I'm Premier League. You're in the National League North." She slapped my cheek a few times, then bought some vegetables from a beet-faced stallholder. Emma had fans of her own.

We bought more stuff, including a bottle of organic red wine. Emma expressed surprise that I'd have a drink, now that I was a big-shot player. I assured her two glasses was my limit, and anyway, no one had ever told me what to eat. I said that even though everyone hates induction days, especially me, I really should have had one. And that was my cue to start talking about my theories on a better way to run a non-league football club. I think all this stuff had been building up inside me since I'd started seeing clubs from the inside. And Emma uncorked me like a Pulltap.

Everything that had been happening recently poured out of me. Fermented. Ready to drink.

"There was a time I thought the guy at Chester was going to offer me a director of football job. He wasn't—I'm much too young and inexperienced. But ever since, I've been thinking about it. Writing a kind of manifesto. What if I was offered the job now? What's important? Where do you start?

"The start is, you've got to win games. That's the main thing. The mood in the dressing room depends almost entirely on the last game. The mood in the town, you can feel it if the team's done well. On the streets there's like, five percent more people who are smiling after a win. Winning's infectious. And if you don't win, you get fired. But why not win with style? Attack. Play attractive football. Try something new."

"And people don't?"

"Almost never. The other manager did something last night, something wild. I'm not sure if I imagined it because my brain was burning itself for fuel."

"What did he do?"

"Spread his players and pushed them forward. Threw caution to the wind. All-out attack. I've watched as much football as anyone in the last few months and I haven't seen a manager do anything like it."

"Why not, though?"

"Fear of humiliation. You're trying to be clever and there's people watching and it all blows up in your face. But you've got to try. You've got to play fearless football."

"Fearless football. I like that. What does it look like?"

"I'm still working on it, but some things seem burned into my DNA. No timewasting. No running into corners. Always have a plan to win. Always attack if you're the better team. Things like that. So that's tactics and stuff. My online course has been helping me with that kind of thing.

"Training. I think most of the training I've seen has been good, actually. Players improve. I'd want to change the focus to be more about technique, but you could persuade me not to. Half the pitches at this level are like turnip fields. Some slope like you wouldn't believe.

Or does that mean technique is even more important? Yeah, anyway, training's not the main issue.

"Squadbuilding. That's where you look at your team and try to get better players. Can you do that and keep the same wage bill? Do you spend your cash on your defence—they say defence wins titles—or your strikers? Goals win games. Youth versus experience. A genius who is always injured. Worth it? Maybe. It's a fun challenge. I'd be good at that. Really good. Plus just for funsies I'd bring in a handful of stars that we'd train up and sell for millions. Easy. *Ka-ching!*

"Youth team. Important. Serious. Manager's got to be informed, got to be interested, and there has to be a pathway from the bottom to the top. If there isn't, manager's fired. Develop young players or you're fired. People say, 'Oh but young players make mistakes, cost you games.' Like old guys never do anything wrong. It's pathetic. That's part of the fearless thing. Arsenal are winning the Premier League and they've got the youngest squad. Don't tell me it can't work.

"Culture. Enough caveman shit. It's moronic that someone like me should find it hard to integrate. If I can't fit in, neither can ninety percent of the population. And we're back to wasted talent. It's got to be more collaborative. More diverse. More grown-up. And I know *that's* ironic coming from me."

"Why is it?"

"It just is."

I went internal. Processed everything I'd just said. It felt right. Really right. It burned within me. I was going to get my hands on one of these shitty football clubs and turn it into a shining beacon. Number goes up. Money goes up. Attendance goes up. Talent flourishes. Stars are lifted to their next step. Memories linger. Everyone's happy to come to work. A virtuous cycle of achievement and improvement that will last long after I'm gone.

"Max?"

Eyes blazing, I looked down at Emma. She looked up at me. Lips parted. The stars aligned, everything was perfect. Be fearless. Still, I hesitated. Suddenly it *did* matter that she was seeing someone else. Trust is the basis for everything. "I don't know what your situation is."

"My situation is that you *owe* me a *kiss*."

I carefully placed the shopping bags on the path—we were in a park, suddenly, and every tree was a cherry blossom in bloom—and took one zip in each hand. I pulled her towards me, and as we kissed, seven flying cupids played "Zadok the Priest" on their little trumpets.

Eventually, after my mental stock of romantic clichés had been exhausted and a bulldog started giving my meat-filled carrier bag admiring glances, we walked on.

"This fearless football of yours," she said. "Is that why you organised the match in Chester? So you could practice?"

"It's one benefit," I said. "It's the only manager gig on my horizon. I keep having tactical ideas, I keep trying to innovate, but it's not meaningful if it's just in my head. Do you know what I mean? It's going to be ages and ages until I get a place to try out my theories."

Ha.

How wrong I was.

35

DO BETTER

We still had a bit of time before Holland versus USA, and I had a moment of inspiration. We put the shopping in the fridge, then got in my car. I checked I was fit to drive—I was, but it was borderline. So Emma drove my Subaru to a stationery shop that Henri seemed to frequent, based on the little paper bags in his office and bookmarks in his chill area.

In an ideal world they'd have sold large, football-themed whiteboard slash flipcharts. I'd need to order that kind of thing online, an assistant told me, but she showed me a plain A3 magnetic whiteboard with lots of little magnets. That'd work as a basic way of mapping out formations. I took it.

I wanted to ask the assistant how often Henri used to go there, but something made me hesitate. It didn't seem right to do it in front of Emma. Why? No clue. I let it go.

XP balance: 226

Debt repaid: 202/3,000

TINOs: 2,829

Matches remaining: 16

Forty-eight matches into the tournament and it had been a hell of a slog. But I was optimistic of getting to 3,200 TINOs very soon. That would see me double the amount of XP I'd started with, and everything after that would be pure gravy.

With kickoff fast approaching, I took my laptop to the sofa, turned the TV on, and let Emma settle in beside me. Her being around meant doing the whole earphone scam and trying to concentrate enough on my surroundings to not do something inexplicable. But it didn't matter. I felt so calm, so relaxed, so at peace with the universe that I was thinking of doing the first half and binning the second to be fully present with her.

Fat chance.

Ten minutes before kickoff, my vision was hijacked by two giant, flashing words.

GET READY

"Oh my God," I said.

"What?" said Emma.

"Something's changed."

"What?"

"Er . . . I think we're not doing the same thing. Oh, fuck. What do I do? Er . . . Right." I stood up and held my hands out. She extended hers. I helped her up, then put my hands around her waist and moved her. "You're too sexy. I need blood rushing to my brain instead of . . . other areas. You can sit here," I indicated the armchair to the side of the sofa. "Or there." The cosy reading space.

She gave me that amused lip curl. "Do you want me to leave?"

"No," I said. "Fuck no. But I need total focus. Until I know what's going on."

She sat on the armchair and crossed her legs. Her jeans pulled up a bit, revealing her ankles. Victorian men used to obsess over women's ankles, as it was often the only body part they would get a glimpse of. Dudes tried to estimate what the rest of the body would look like, based on that one element. Emma had perfect ankles. I found my eyes wandering up her legs. Goddammit. Stupidly, I allowed eye contact to happen. If she'd given me the slightest provocation, I might have launched myself at her. Luckily, she didn't. She simply waited for my next outburst.

I mentally took a cold shower. I scratched my chin. "The post-its," I said. I grabbed my store of notes—three inches of the things haphazardly stuck together—and put them on the coffee table. "What else?" I wibbled my bottom lip.

"What do you think is going to happen?"

"The next level," I said. "I've done all the scouting and been spotting formation changes. The course has . . . what's it done? It's made me think about tactics and players and I've assessed the managers. So now . . . The obvious next step is . . ." I bit a nail. "I don't really know. But something a level higher. Do you know what I mean?"

"Not in the slightest. But this is fun. You're really stressed. 'Mystery winger flounders.' Are you always this nervous at exams?"

"I never get nervous at exams. It's a genuine superpower. This isn't like that." I calmed down a bit. "I'm probably overreacting. It's probably going to be more of the same but even harder. TINO!"

"What?"

I didn't reply. I found myself on the floor, for some reason, between the sofa and the coffee table. Staring at the TV, wobbling back and forth. The Dutch and American players had warmed up, done the anthems, and the match would start very soon. "The US are playing four-three-three," I said, trying to distract myself. "That's interesting."

"Why?"

Talking would help pass the time until kickoff. My heart was *pounding*. "Where's that magnetic board?"

"Here," she said, dashing to get it. She knelt to the right of the coffee table.

"Turn it so it's oriented like a football pitch. Put one magnet for the goalie. Can you do a back four?" I stripped my eyes from the screen and checked her work. I adjusted the magnets, but she'd got them basically right. "Now three in the midfield, and three at the top." Eyes back to the screen.

"Like this?"

She'd got it close, but in her version, the magnets were spread wide so that there were players covering the whole width of the pitch. "Ah! Interesting. You've made a Rorschach test." I adjusted them so that they were more central.

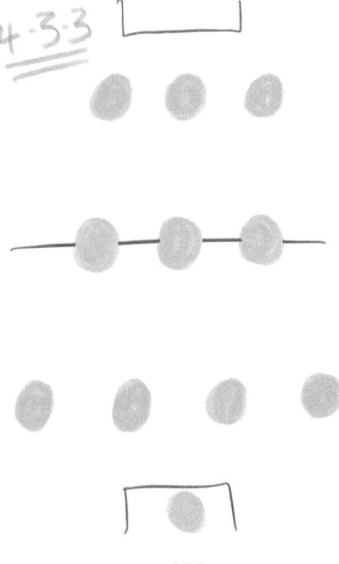

"So you can see the way they're doing it is quite narrow. The midfielders and attackers are all central. No width. So you get a lot of control in the middle, and give up the sides of the pitch. Oh, shit. Fuck. Hang on. Sorry."

Another hijack. Tiny trumpet sounds—real, this time. Real in my head, anyway.

NETHERLANDS VERSUS USA
Your team: Netherlands
Your mission: Do better

That stayed up for a few seconds. My mouth dropped open. Then:

MONTE CARLO SIMULATION BEGINS IN 10
9
8

"Whaaaa. What's a Monte Carlo simulation? Can you find out, please? Oh, Christ! Oh, Jesus fucking Christ!"

When the countdown hit seven, just before the action on the TV got underway, I suddenly had access to a Match Overview. At the top, it said, as you can guess, *Netherlands vs USA*.

The match commentary flashed up, orange and white:

The referee has finished counting the players. He looks at his linesmen. He brings his whistle to his mouth, checks his watch . . .

I froze. I was absolutely stunned by what was happening.

3
2
1

. . . and the match begins! Netherlands are playing from left to right. They try a long ball down the left of the pitch. But it comes to nothing.

"The fuck?"

I had the wherewithal to check the action on the TV. That wasn't what happened at kickoff!

I dipped into the tactics screens. The virtual Netherlands were set up the same as in the real match, and both USAs were doing 4-3-3. The match ratings screen showed everyone on 6 out of 10, the number players always started on. There was something different about the font that was being used. The player names looked . . . how can I put it? Clickable? I chose a player and his whole player profile popped up. More on that later.

"Got it," said Emma, gripping her phone two-handed. "Do you want me to tell you now?"

What the hell was she talking about? It was an epic struggle, but I eventually remembered I'd asked her to tell me what a Monte Carlo sim was. "No," I said. I closed my eyes. It was suddenly deeply frustrating that she was there. I rubbed my temples. "No, thanks," I said.

Back in the interface, I raced through the USA's tactics. They'd set Christian Pulisic as their playmaker. They were on hard tackling. The team's passing mentality was mixed, but some had been given personalised instructions. They were playing the offside trap, like every other professional team ever. I switched my attention to the TV, hoping to see confirmation of all that. The sample size was too small. I needed to watch ten, fifteen minutes to see such things.

Then I went to the Dutch tactics. It was a weird formation—3-4-1-2. Three centre backs, four across midfield, a central attacking midfielder, and two strikers. Quite unusual. There was something about it that I instinctively didn't like, but the Dutch manager was Louis van Gaal, a very, very experienced dude. A legend, to be honest. He knew a lot more than me, that was for sure.

I think I stared gormlessly into space for about two minutes.

There were no best jumping/fastest player type questions. No questions of any sort. There was just this interface. It all felt incredibly familiar, and not just because I'd been using these screens since I'd met Old Nick.

So. This was a challenge of some sort. Not trivia. Not player analysis. What, then?

What had it said? Do better? Better than what?

Right on cue, the camera cut to Louis van Gaal.

"What!" I spluttered.

"What?" said Emma, quietly. Worried.

I turned to her and beamed. One of those big smiles of disbelief. "I have to manage this match better than the real manager!"

"But—" she started, then closed her mouth and looked down.

I was back in the screens. So did that mean . . .? In the tactics area, I took the CAM and moved him back into midfield. He clicked into place. No restrictions! We were now playing 3-5-2. I looked at the TV and didn't notice a change. Of course, you wouldn't necessarily see a change that small. So I swapped the left- and right-sided midfielders, then stared at the TV screen for forty-five seconds.

"So I'm not controlling the actual match," I said, out loud, like a prize chump.

Emma boggled at me. I patted her hand. I swapped the players back to their original positions, including the CAM.

I had a decision to make here. I knew already that this was going to be intense. Concentration would be key. My instinct was to send Emma home, or upstairs, or whatever, so I could focus to the max. But what had I told myself recently? Having someone to talk to led to better outcomes? I had wanted the chance to put my principles into practice. Well, here was that chance.

"Emma. How would you like to be my assistant manager?"

"What's the pay?"

"You get paid in kind."

Her expression showed she didn't know that phrase, but she said, "Okay then. What do I do?"

"See these post-its? Can you go through and find all the ones that say *Ned* on the top?"

"Ned? Like Ned Flanders?"

"No. Ned like Ned Stark. And all the USA ones, too."

She started sorting the notes. "I see the assistant gets all the fun jobs. So what's the plan, Mr. Best?"

I thought about that. It seemed obvious I shouldn't make any big changes just yet. I didn't know why van Gaal had chosen this weird formation, and I didn't know why it rubbed me up the wrong way. I needed to let it play out for a while.

Also, to be honest, I suddenly had doubts.

I didn't think I was being arrogant when I said I'd do well as a manager in the sixth tier. Most opposing managers were predictable, most played 4-4-2, most were defensive as hell. Merely switching tactics a couple of times a game would frame me as the outstanding tactical thinker in the division!

But this was the World Cup! And van Gaal had been the manager of Ajax, Barcelona, Manchester United, and most impressively had turned a small Dutch team into league winners. Asking me to do better than him was genuinely preposterous. I felt I was learning fast, but even with the curse, even with constant grinding, it'd be ten years before I could challenge managers like him.

And that's when doubt turned to fear.

Because let me tell you, I'd only been playing this virtual game for a few minutes, but I was into it. I was deeply addicted already. The full player profiles, a complete overview of the match situation, the complete power to change things—this was everything I'd ever dreamed of.

"The cheeky fuck!"

Emma blinked at me, but didn't respond.

It had suddenly hit me. This is what I'd told Old Nick I wanted. To see football the way top managers saw it. Well, now I was seeing it like Louis van Gaal!

It was a cosmic joke. All the grinding, experiences, training, had led me to this—playing a virtual match. *In my head.*

Anger rose up in me, but didn't get very far. *No. Deep breaths, Max. Control your anger before it controls you.*

This was *not* a cosmic joke. This was the MUNDIAL mini game, nothing more. Out in the real world, I still saw player profiles. When I was a manager, I could do all the formation and individual instruction tweaks. So what was happening now was both an evaluation of what I'd been covering in the MUNDIAL "course," and a taste of things to come if I kept grinding. In short, this was a *good* thing.

I relaxed enough to realise it was not sensible to sit on the floor for ninety minutes. I pushed myself up onto the sofa.

So.

The fear.

My fear was simple—what if I lost this game? What if I won, but van Gaal won bigger?

Would I simply lose some TINOs, or would I be out of the World Cup?

I shook my head. Managing one game out of the remaining sixteen wasn't an option. I *needed* this. I'd *earned* this.

A quick aside on the player profiles. I *know* that in the final sixteen matches (the knockout stages) I saw the complete profiles for every player, including information I didn't have access to in the real world. For example, I could see a player's aggression, creativity, and influence. But when the match was over, the curse blurred those memories. So while I may have switched the captaincy mid-game to someone with higher influence, or moved a highly creative player somewhere he could do more damage, I can't remember any of that stuff. What I can say is that around ninety-five of my decisions were based on factors I already knew and was comfortable with—formations, player positions, pace, passing, heading—all the basics.

Excitement and fear simmered inside me, so I didn't change anything for the first ten minutes. Either van Gaal's 3-4-1-2 was too complicated for me to understand, or I was just too stunned by this whole turn of events to grasp it; I'd been expecting ten weird questions, as per.

Another reason I didn't change anything was the complexity of watching my match (via the text commentary, match ratings, and some other information that got memory-wiped) while watching the real match on the TV. I was hoping for clues, there. Now that I knew the endpoint of the MUNDIAL training, I knew what I was supposed to have been looking for—players and strategies that could make a difference.

Emma was laying out the post-its. They reminded me that in the group stages, I'd made special note of the Dutch right back Denzel Dumfries—he was incredible. Cody Gakpo seemed to be their main threat. I had mixed feelings about Memphis Depay, because although he was highly rated in the world of football, he'd been at Man United for a while and had a terrible time there that soured my view of him. Even with his real player profile telling me exactly how good he was, I couldn't shift the feeling that he was overrated.

On the USA side, everything revolved around Christian Pulisic. He was the one the others looked to. If he didn't play well, neither would the team. His teammates were no mugs, though. The U.S. had more players than ever playing in major European teams, and as a group they were extremely physical—fast, willing, great stamina. If I can oversimplify for a moment, they were athletes who'd been taught to play, while the Dutch were players trained to be athletes.

Disaster struck on the tenth minute, just as I had fallen into a mental rut.

The real Dutch team had the ball deep in their half. The Americans were pressing. With a series of unbelievably slick passes on the left of midfield, the Dutch moved the ball forward, back, central, then out to the right where Dumfries was having a 10 out of 10 match. He whizzed ahead, rolled it sideways, and Depay passed the ball into the net. Easy as pie, and beautiful.

"Oh, shit," I said.

"Do you want the US to win?"

"No. I mean, I don't care. That goal makes my job harder. I have to do better than the Dutch manager."

"Do better? In what sense?" She leaned forward to peek at my laptop.

I grabbed it away from her and opened several browsers and apps and resized them so that five resized tabs filled the screen. One tab had some random formation graphics. One was a text box where I could type gibberish. One was full of flashing, swirling green letters like in *The Matrix*. Basically, I tried to make it seem like there was some kind of interface there. It was all a bit rude, but better than the alternative. I tried to make up for it with a friendly tone. "Yeah, basically, in this simulation I'm Holland. I've got to do better than the real guy. Oh, maybe now's a good time. What's Monte Carlo?"

She picked up her phone and swiped a few times. "A Monte Carlo simulation is a model used to predict the probability of a variety of outcomes when the potential for random variables is present. Monte Carlo simulations help to explain the impact of risk and uncertainty in prediction and forecasting models."

I groaned. Typically baffling curse shit. "Not your fault but that's not helpful," I said. "Can I read it?" She handed it over. I skimmed the page. It was gibberish to the same degree as when I tried to look at Champion Manager images. "Holy Christ." I handed the phone back. "Never mind." I rubbed the back of my head and then let out a huge groan.

"Can I help?"

I exhaled. "Well," I said. "Er . . . The Dutch are using this system." I showed her with the magnets. "And I don't get it. It feels rubbish to me. It's crazy. He's got three defenders and the USA have three strikers. So that seems extremely aggressive. Very bold. But when you look at the TV, it's very dour. Seems defensive. It's a contradiction. I don't get it at all. I feel stupid. And that goal looked planned to me. Like that specific set of passes was the point of the formation. But how? I'm a bit out of my league here. It's like you said, I'm National League North."

She clambered up and sat next to me. Gave me a bit of a hug and a squeeze. "That was just me being playful. I know you're top class. Why would I choose you if you weren't?"

Tiny smile. "Wait a second. I chose you. I'm the protagonist."

"Sure. Now, this . . ." She looked at the magnets and counted. "This three-five-two formation the Dutch are using . . ." She didn't get it exactly right, but it was close enough to double the size of my smile. "It's messing with your tiny mind, right?"

Fair statement. "Yep."

"But you don't have to use it. You can change it?"

I went to the formation selector and saw every formation you could ever think of. "Yep."

"What would you do if you hadn't seen *this*?"

"Oh. If I had to choose the formation from scratch?" I hadn't thought about it. I'd been trying to tweak van Gaal's system. "Er . . . Against four-three-three? I haven't used that one myself yet. That's my next one. I think when I use the formations I get a deeper understanding of them. Does that make sense? Like with chess you can learn some of the openings and strategies but until you've used them wrong and seen some dude take your queen, you don't really feel it in your bones. But let's see. I mean, just visually, you'd say it has to be weak down the wings."

"So attack the wings."

"Absolutely."

"Great. What are wings?"

I laughed, but she wasn't joking. "Wow, yeah. So much jargon. Sorry. Please always ask. The wings are the sides. Like a bird's wings."

"Oh. That's clear. Sometimes the jargon sounds like it is. Sometimes it doesn't."

"Yeah. So let me think. Four-two-four. That's a formation with lots of emphasis on wingers. But look at the TV—do you see there's always loads of Americans in the box?"

"Which box?"

"Either box. Er . . . the box where the goalkeeper lives. There are two, right? The one you're attacking and the one you're defending. The Americans are running between the boxes like their lives fucking *depend* on it. It's exhausting to watch. Last night I did a fraction of what they're doing and it wrecked me. So we do need some numbers back. Some defensive bodies."

"You promised me fearless football," she said, in a mock whine. Like I'd promised to buy her a pony.

I put my arm around her and pulled her into me. "Yeah. Fearless. Not stupid. You know what, I want a DM." I tried to slide back down onto the floor, but she stopped me.

"Max," she said. "Was I helpful?"

"Yes!" I said. I felt energised. Ready to attack the task. Have a go.

"Payment in kind," she said.

"Oh, you know what it means?"

"I looked it up." She closed her eyes and tilted her head. When she sensed I wasn't leaning in, she pursed her lips and pointed to them.

"Don't make me laugh," I said. "I can't kiss when I'm laughing."

"Good point," she said, and poked me in the ribs. Annoying, but it worked.

One kiss later, I was back on the floor, shuffling the magnets around. The Dutch team was super weird. It had two guys who could play left back and two who could play right back. I wasn't that familiar with three of the team, but I had their profiles. I also had subs. There was nothing to stop me making an early substitution, right? To get things the way I wanted. I decided to use the players van Gaal had chosen. It wasn't exactly fearless football, but if things went tits-up playing the Max Best way, I could always switch back to the van Gaal way and hope to understand it better in the second half.

I started with the defence. Flat back four. I was comfortable with it. Then a DM to secure things. I mentally yelled at myself to *keep things tight!* Emma caught me smiling and raised her eyebrows at me. I blushed. Caught red-handed being an absolute weirdo.

Then two central midfielders so we weren't overrun. What else? One striker—Gakpo. And then the thing that the entire theory was based around—making Dumfries the heart of the team. Not a playmaker, because he was over on the right. The platonic playmaker played centrally. I actually left Dumfries where van Gaal had him, but gave him a big arrow all the way to the goal line—he would attack.

That left me with Depay. Looking at the formation, there was a big weakness on our left. I needed to put him over there, somewhere. But I wanted my attackers to attack! I wasn't going to do what Ian Evans had done when he used Aff to mark me. So I placed Depay as a left-sided forward. He'd give the Americans something to think about. They'd have to limit their attacks down that side or Depay would crush them on the break.

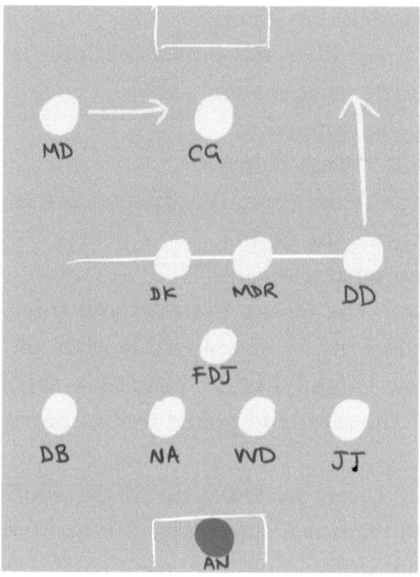

I took a long, hard look at my work. I didn't like it. It wasn't symmetrical. It felt stitched together like a real Frankenstein's monster of a tactic. But that was okay. I'd seen a lot of similar things in the World Cup. One thing the MUNDIAL training had made me realise was the extent to which good managers tried to shoehorn their good players into good positions. The rest of the team often looked as lumpy and misshapen as a comedy turnip. National teams weren't like club sides where you could buy and sell players to fit your favourite formations. You had to work with what the population had produced.

"Well," I said, with a sigh. "Until I make subs, this is the best I can do."

"You're not convinced?"

"No."

"Do it! What have you got to lose?"

I grinned at her. "Fine. Weapons hot! Go for launch!" I mentally made all the changes, said "Boom!" while miming an explosion, and started biting my thumb nail. Emma frowned. "Oh," I said, and then went through the whole rigmarole of mumbling into my earphone and typing on the textpad window and all that shit. After a while, I said, "Done!" Emma smiled, and went over to the cosy chair. Giving me a break. Five stars, girlfriend material.

Five minutes later, after my virtual Dutch boys had created three good chances, the in-curse American manager reacted to my tweaks. Went a bit more defensive. Amazing! I took it as validation of my ideas. I couldn't go *more* attacking because the American team had a lot of threat, so the next five mins were a bit of a stalemate. But they were a stalemate on my terms. The Dutch had the ball in the American half pretty much nonstop. Now we just needed a moment of magic to pick the lock, to carve out that one magical goal that would force the US to attack. At which point we'd murder them on counters.

I left my tactics unchanged. This was going well. I stood and moved around the room a little bit. Stretched my back. Touched my toes. I sounded like a bowl of Rice Krispies; every time I flexed a muscle there were dozens of tiny cracks and pops.

Emma looked up from her phone. "I think I understand Monte Carlo simulations now."

"Oh, top," I said. "Let me have it."

"It's basically, you get a computer, and you run a simulation. Like for example, a football match. And the first result is zero–zero."

"Nil–nil."

"But anything can happen in one game, right? So they do it again. And again. A million times. And then you get sort of averages. Useful data, maybe. After a million simulations, you can categorically say the most likely result is two–zero. Two–nil. Does that make sense? Is that what you're doing?"

I nodded. I thought I knew the concept but with a different name. "Yeah. Some kind of computer modelling. Probability thingies. That's definitely it. When I make a change to my team, the course organisers are using a computer to simulate what the likely outcome is. Yeah."

"But all this stuff I'm reading, it's all economics. Models about interest rates and that sort of thing. How would you do it with football?"

"You mean, which program would you use to model the results?"

"Exactly."

I shook my head and pushed my lips flat. "Champion Manager."

"What's that?"

"It's a game."

She tapped away and came and showed me her screen. Obviously, it was full of pictures of horrific space alien demons coming to slurp up my innards and use my bones as toothpicks. "Is this it?"

"Yes," I said, with a slight shudder.

"This is a game?" she said.

I scoffed. "I know, right?" But then I paused. Sudden clarity. I was literally playing that game right as I said it. And it was unbelievably good! I started to feel like I kind of remembered it. Not the specifics, but the generality. "Actually," I said, speaking from past and present experience, "I know it doesn't look like much from the outside, but when you're in it, it takes you over."

"No kidding," she said, scrolling. "There's a book called *Champion Manager Ruined My Life*."

That was a heart-stopping moment. I froze. Terror sweat burst out of me onto my neck. "Could you, ah, read the synopsis?"

She gave me a curious look. Caught something in my tone. She had a bit of a read while I waited, fearfully. Eventually, she said, "Seems to be a collection of anecdotes about this so-called game. Stories about boys spending all their time up in their rooms pretending to be managers of football teams. Taking it way too seriously. Is that right? So it's like you, but in the least sexy way." She let out a gentle little laugh.

I had stopped tensing—the book wasn't about someone who had been cursed. But it opened a new set of problems. I could ignore what she'd said, or I could try being honest. "Oh, Emma," I said. "It's probably fair to tell you now—I was one of those boys."

She looked at me with amazement. "No way!"

"Yeah. I don't remember much of it," I said, carefully, "but I know the game gives you a sense of control you can't get anywhere else in your life. A sense of purpose."

"Purpose!"

"Yeah. Getting Chester promoted. Keeping Carlisle in the first division. Trying to build a small Scottish team into a third powerhouse."

Where had all that come from? I listened to the words coming out of my mouth with deep interest and increasing emotion. "Everyone used to tell me to go out and get a girlfriend. That I was wasting my life. But I think . . . I think that was the only part of my life I *didn't* waste. It was an escape into a world where I could make things better. Where I wasn't angry and frustrated all the time. It was very important to me to have something like that." Some tiny shift in the clouds let a single beam of light in, illuminated one very specific memory. "Oh God, I remember it now. That feeling! My biggest fear. My biggest fear of all time was that a girl like you would laugh at me because I loved it so much."

She dropped her phone onto the sofa and came over. Put her arms around me, and pressed her cheek against my chest. "I'm sorry, Max. I'm not laughing at you and I'm not laughing at the game. I don't know what it is. It's simply that it doesn't look like anything."

"I know. You're allowed to laugh at me. And the game. But it's fair that you know. I'm not the quarterback, best-kid-in-school type. I'm the weird loner kid. I don't want to start anything under false pretences."

"You didn't."

"What?"

"In that restaurant in—what was it called?—Tisbury? With Ziggy and Gems. Where we met. I didn't know you were a player or a manager. I just thought you were a cool guy with an interesting way of thinking. I knew you had ambition. I knew you weren't intimidated by us. You were passionate and weren't afraid to show it or explain it. And then you didn't chase me. Almost at all. Do you know how often that happens to me? I had to find some excuse to call you, and then you hung up on me."

I tried to recall the incident. "A guy broke his leg."

"I know. You told me. About a week later." She smiled at the memory.

"You seem to like that I forget to call you."

"I like that I'm not the centre of your world. Right. So you see, I wouldn't have guessed you played weird games in darkened rooms, but I knew who I was pursuing. The, ah, athletic ability stuff is just a bonus." Lip smirk.

I cleared my throat. "I hope you aren't trying to get me hot right now."

"Why would you say that?" she said, making me hot. She detached from me. "Why don't you sit down and I'll make us both a cup of tea?"

For various reasons, including the restoration of proper blood flow to stiffened areas, I did some slow squats in front of the sofa. It had a calming effect. I checked what had happened in the last few minutes. My virtual opponent hadn't made any more changes, and the game was still 0–0. The real one was still 1–0. I sighed. I wasn't 'doing better', but there was no need to panic. There was a long way left to go.

Emma was behind me, filling the kettle. The sound of the water masked what she said.

"What?"

She finished pouring. "I was asking about this simulated match you're playing. If you're controlling Holland, does that mean there's *another* person somewhere in the world who's controlling the USA?"

That would mean another person in the world had met Old Nick and ended up as a football manager. I scoffed. Two people with the same curse. What were the odds? Hmm. I picked up Emma's phone and brought it over to her. "Emma, can you find out how popular Champion Manager is?" She had a look on her face that meant, oh no, you don't hand off small admin tasks to *me*. I am not your personal assistant. "Please," I said.

She shook off her first reaction and tapped away. "Champion Manager 2022 has sold one million copies."

I closed my eyes. Had a very tiny dizzy spell. It was not completely crazy that someone else would have the same exact wish as me. I stumbled back to the sofa and watched. Halftime was imminent.

I twisted my neck left and right, then paused. My opponent had changed his formation. Having weathered the storm of my attacking moves, he took a tentative step back towards his initial 4-3-3. It felt exceedingly . . . human. "Oh my God," I said.

"What?" called Emma. She came forward to look at the TV, thinking I'd reacted to something in the match. Holland had a harmless throw-in. They took it, played a couple of passes, and then that man Dumfries was pushing to the right touchline. He pulled the ball back across goal and Holland scored again! Virtually identical in its essence to the first goal!

Van Gaal was smashing me. Teaching me a lesson in football management.

"Oh my God!" I said again.

36
SIDE TO SIDE

I flopped against the cushion and felt something cold and wet press against me. For a second, I worried I'd spilled something on Henri's nice sofa, but it was just my sweat spreading around my lower back. "Quick shower," I said, and tried to bound up the stairs. I was still pretty rigid from the previous night's exertions, though, so it took me a while to get to the en suite.

The good thing about showers is that you can't bring your phone or laptop in there, so you get a break from whatever you're working on. It's a brief moment where your brain activity flatlines in the healthiest possible way—other, deeper processes can begin. But the MUNDIAL interface was *in* my head, and my head is pretty watertight considering how many holes are in it, so I could only get a break from the interface by consciously pushing it away. That was hard—I kept checking who my substitutes were and dipping into their player profiles. It wasn't a squad with an abundance of dynamism. I was uninspired and knew I needed a clean break.

I got dressed—switching to a less ugly sock colour—went downstairs, and grabbed Emma. "Quick outside time!"

"Where are we going?"

"Choose a direction. We'll do a ten-minute loop. No football."

That's what we did. We looked at gardens. We wrote backstories for the people who lived in certain places. The guy with the garden gnomes? Definite bigamist—each gnome represented one wife or child and each flower bed represented one of his families. The ornaments helped him remember everyone's names. Helped him keep his stories straight. The one house with the bricked-up attic window? An old woman growing weed on a semi-industrial scale that she sold at cost in local care homes.

That led to a whimsical chat about our dream houses. I told Emma that I'd like to live in a kind of grass-roofed hobbit hole with most of the living space underground. She accused me of joking, and said she knew I'd want something modern. I said I could imagine a lot of dream houses, but they'd all include a table tennis and snooker room, vintage arcade machines, a cinema, and, of course, secret passages and escape routes. She wanted a courtyard surrounded by a U-shaped bungalow, because she hated those big country houses where you had to walk from side to side all day.

Of course, I stopped dead. "Oh, shit."

"What?"

"That's it. Van Gaal. He's making the Americans go side to side all the time. And that's how the goals come. Drag them all over to the left, then burst over to the right. The Americans rush over to cover, but they're spread out. Diffuse. Unstructured. The Dutch guy has an easy pass, the goal-scorer an easy finish. If you only attack down the right, the defenders are well set. You've got to move them around before you strike. Well, shit." The thrill of discovery had given way to the realisation that there were tools I didn't have in my utility belt.

I looked up at the evening sky. The moon was out. A few stars were early to the party. I went into the tactics screens and checked the options and the sub-options, looking for ones that would let me micromanage our possessions—keep the ball left until the opposition lines are sufficiently disrupted, then move it to the other flank and go wee wee wee all the way home. Nothing like that had ever been there before, and sure enough, it still wasn't.

"Max," said Emma, rubbing my bicep. "What's wrong?"

"What do you mean?"

"Your mood just changed."

"Oh," I said. I didn't realise I was so obvious. I sighed. "So . . . I've been thinking I'd be a good manager."

"You will!"

I smiled at her misplaced faith in me. "Yeah, in the lower leagues. I'll bring in better players, have better tactics. It'll be great. I'll save Telford from relegation, and next year probably win the league! Why not? But this World Cup thing . . . What the Dutch guy is doing, it's way beyond me. It's beyond what I can do now and what I can ever imagine doing." I tried to picture myself explaining to players what I wanted and then coaching them in the patterns till they got it. And then repeating it endlessly until they mastered it. Maybe I'd for-real learn how to do that kind of thing when I did my coaching badges, but I just couldn't see myself in that role. Not only was I inept at dealing with footballers, but it seemed incredibly boring. That kind of work didn't float my boat in the slightest.

So if learning how to be top *coach* was one of the steps of being a top *manager*, then I wasn't going to arrive. It was the first time since meeting Old Nick that I thought there was a genuine limit to what I could achieve. I felt like I'd just discovered that I had CA and PA as a manager, and that my PA wasn't maxed. It was, truth be told, a bit of a punch in the gut.

We plodded along, a bit slower now. Emma was content for us to walk in silence, or she was giving me some space.

If I was right, how bad was it?

Let's say my curse-enhanced level was as a League One manager. Third tier. If so, I could bring Telford to three promotions and keep them in that league for a couple of seasons. That would be seriously impressive to a lot of decision-makers. So five years from now, I'd hit my ceiling. But my reputation would surely be high enough by then for some Championship club to give me a million-pound, three-year contract. They'd fire me after six months. And then what? I'd spend a year or two on the beach with Emma.

"Emma. Jamaica or Ibiza?"

"Jamaica."

Couple of years recharging in the Caribbean. Maybe I'd give walking tours of Tortuga dressed as a pirate. "Yarr," I said.

"What?"

"Just planning our pre-retirement. Where can we buy a nice house for five hundred K?"

"Newcastle." She squeezed my arm and smiled. "Why did *that* cheer you up?"

"Newcastle! It's so far! You might as well have said, I don't know, Wyoming."

"Max," she said, with a mood change of her own.

"Oui?"

"Your football problem seems to be something you can't discuss with your assistant manager."

"Yeah. Soz."

"That's okay. But you know hundreds of football people. Why don't you ask one?"

"Most of them hate me."

"They don't hate you. I bet there's six, tops, who actually hate you." There was a bit of a silence. Then: "Are you one of those boys who won't ask for directions even when you're lost?"

I did a kind of tut-sigh combo, mostly because she had nailed it, and because she'd used the word *boy*. Top class manipulation. I added it to my mental toolkit, grabbed my phone, thought about all the people I'd met in the last few months, and filtered out everyone who wouldn't understand what the eff I was talking about. That process left exactly one person. I sighed, and dialled.

"Max Best, as I live and breathe."

"Hi. Have you got a minute?"

"For you, Max, no. But go on. I'm curious."

I pointed to a low wall and went to sit on it. Emma copied me. "Have you been watching the Holland game?"

"Yeah. It's halftime."

"I know it's halftime, Jackie. That's why I'm calling. The Dutch are playing three-four-one-two. The U.S. are four-three-three. I've been trying to understand why the Dutch are doing that. It's a weird system. What do you make of it?"

"You know I hate to interrupt your flights of fancy, Max, but we both know you've cracked the case. Let's get to the part where you need me."

I grinned. "Yeah. Kay. So I think if I took some mushrooms or got locked in a sauna, I could come up with a plan like the Dutch are trying. But it's one thing having the plan. Let's say I'm the manager of, I don't know, Chelsea. And we're playing West Ham on Saturday. I come up with this kind of plan and on Monday morning I explain it to my coaches. Do they . . . Can they, sort of, make it happen?"

Jackie made some crunching noises. It sounded like he was nibbling on a carrot. "Maybe you'd better tell me what the Dutch are doing. I've been pretty bored by the game, to be totally truthful. Haven't noticed anything worth breaking a vow of silence over."

I quickly ran through the setup and my findings, then finished by excitedly saying, "I've never seen anyone attack *horizontally*! It's like in

Wrath of Khan where Spock tells Kirk to think three-D. It's fucking top, Jackie! I'm delirious! Well, I want to be delirious but that magnificent bastard *Louis* has just revealed my limitations. I can't do it. I can set up the team, but I can't coach this. I can think it, but I can't implement it."

More nibbling. "What's your question?"

"How do I do it if I can't do it?"

"You get someone to do it for you. Your example. You're the Chelsea manager. God help us all if you end up there, by the way. You've got an assistant and five first team coaches. You come in on Monday, tell them the plan, they work out how to implement it. These Dutch lads, they're elite players. They soak up all this tactical stuff from an early age. You tell them your plan is to pass it sideways, they're going to find it pretty rudimentary. No offence, lad."

"None taken. But watch those goals again. It's quite specific."

"You think it's a training ground move? Well, maybe it is, la. I'll watch out for the replays. But don't worry your little head about this kind of thing. By the time you're dealing with players who can do this, you'll know how to get them to do it. All right?"

"Yes. Thanks. One more thing. Are you available next Sunday to do some coaching?"

"No."

"Hundred quid."

"No."

"Livia will be there."

Pause. *Big* pause. No munching this time! "No. The session's in Chester? Who is it?"

"Some kids. Good lads."

"What's the catch?"

"No catch. Never mind. Thanks for your help."

I sprung to my feet. Energised? You betcha. I paced off home, then paced back to take Emma by the hand.

"Who was that?" said Emma, smiling.

"Coach. Jackie."

"Who's Livia?"

"Woman he fancies."

"You didn't ask how he was."

"Yeah. He hates when I do that."

"Max."

"Next time I have a coaching emergency, I'll do some small talk first. Promise."

"Why did you choose him?"

We stopped. I turned and faced her. There was some subtext to the question that I couldn't work out. "Because he's top. Because he gets it."

"*What* does he get?"

"The way it could be."

Back in the house, Emma went to the cosy space and alternated between some mobile game and reading. She was letting me focus on the match. Of course, the more she did that, the more I wanted to give it all up for her.

For the second half I did small experiments with the Dutch team. Mostly ones that involved Depay. He was the one player I thought I wasn't using right. I moved him to the right to create overloads there. I tried him as a CAM and as a second striker. I tried dropping him into the centre of midfield with a big forward arrow. Finally, I put him back where I'd started him.

Then it was a case of throwing on some substitutes.

It was pretty scary. Most of the matches I'd managed had been with rolling subs. I could take players off and bring them back on. This was permanent. Mistakes would and could be punished.

The story goes that in the 1970 World Cup, with England beating West Germany 2–0, the manager took Bobby Charlton off. Charlton, a goalscoring midfielder of worldwide renown, had been keeping the Germans at bay. With him gone, they surged forward and went on to win. England were knocked out. The manager's hubris cost him his job.

(The story, by the way, isn't quite accurate. But as is often the case, the story's better than the truth.)

Still, I had to do something. There's a reason that when a manager doesn't make any substitutions he gets asked a billion questions about it. In the seventieth minute, I took three guys off and replaced them with guys who could do the same job. Fresh legs. More energy.

My breakthrough came in the seventy-fifth minute when a few chances fell our way in quick succession—Depay finally stuck one in the onion bag.

"Get in you slag!" I said, jumping to my feet. I did a tiny—and slow—victory lap around the coffee table, then returned to work.

While Emma eyed me from behind a lowered book, I shuffled things into a more defensive shape. When my opponent noticed, he went more attacking, and I instantly changed back to my most attacking setup. I was confident I'd dick him on counters. But the dude was cautious, and even though he was losing and his team weren't creating many chances, he pulled more men back to keep things tight.

Tight. I was starting to really fucking hate that word.

On the TV, the USA scored the jammiest goal in the history of jammy goals to make it 2–1. For five minutes my excitement ramped up to fever pitch again—one more goal in either game could see me meeting my objective! One goal to keep me in the World Cup!

But the real-life Dutch scored again and shut the game down. In my virtual match, my players kept attacking but couldn't carve out a good opening.

I won 1–0, but van Gaal won 3–1.

When it was all over, I stared at the TV for a couple of minutes. The curse had awarded me zero TINOs for my performance, which was harsh, but a lot better than having TINOs deducted. Still, I felt good. I'd won a World Cup knockout game! The only fly in the ointment was the late match. Argentina versus Australia. Would I be allowed to take part?

Or was my World Cup already over?

Once it was clear there wouldn't be extra time in the match, Emma started cooking. It didn't take long—some nice cuts of beef. Veggies. Sip of wine to help it on its way. Focusing on my table manners was a welcome distraction. Talking about Emma's life as a lawyer was a suitable calmative for my freewheeling mind.

GET READY

"Yes! I'm back in." Just in time, I pretended to look down at my phone like I'd had a text.

"Great!" said Emma, which seemed genuine. Though I'm sure she wouldn't have minded having me to herself for the rest of the evening. "Who are you?"

"Argentina. Oh my God! They're doing four-three-three. Australia are four-four-two. This is hilarious."

"Why?"

"I've been mocking these sixth-tier guys for using the most basic formations. Guess I've got egg on my face."

"Are you going to drop Messi?"

"Lol. He's in the team already. I don't get to choose. But imagine subbing him off in the first minute. I could spark riots in Buenos Aires. All right, I'm going in."

I didn't sub Messi off. In fact, most of my changes involved moving him around the pitch, trying to get a feel for the position where he'd be most useful. He was possibly the best player of all time, but he was ageing. I needed to set things up so that he wouldn't have to do much running but could still hurt the Socceroos.

In the end I shuffled one of my central midfielders into the DM slot, and put Messi in the centre. Let the kids do all the grunt work for him, give him the ball, and let him spray passes around.

With this 4-1-3-2, I was winning 1–0 at halftime, and in the second half brought on three superstar players and really went for it with a 4-1-2-3. I ended up winning 4–0, whereas the real team only beat an obdurate Aussie team 2–1.

I was awarded 127 TINOs. All or nothing!

So I was buzzing when I turned the TV off and clicked my laptop shut. I stretched massively and poured myself a bit more wine.

Emma was eyeing me. You know. With her *eyes*.

"All right," I said. "I'm all yours."

On Sunday morning all my aches and pains had melted away. In fact, I'd say that I had never felt more energetic than when I woke up. I'm sorry to say I had wasted a lot of that energy by the time Emma left.

She had to go home to watch the England match with family and friends. I walked her to the train station—it didn't even occur to me to drive her there—and while we waited we talked a load of shit about house-hunting and pirate tours and maybe finally doing a real date like real people. Real people. That became one of our phrases. Let's do X like real people.

We were both giddy, detached from the rest, anchored only to each other. The train was delayed by thirty minutes and it felt like three.

The first of Sunday's matches was France versus Poland. I was Poland, and knew that if I wasn't careful, France's superstar Kylian Mbappé would tear me a new one. Against a player with top speed, power, and perfect technique, you couldn't try funky formations. There absolutely had to be a right back. And there pretty much had to be a right mid. The real-life Polish coach went for 4-1-4-1, which made a lot of sense defensively, but generated nothing offensively. Loosening up might have given me five percent more in attack but would have made France fifteen percent more dangerous. It felt like trying to manage my way out of a boa constrictor. I hated being so defensive. Hated it.

I struggled with it until halftime. Then I called Henri.

"You have reached World Champion Henri Lyons."

"What are you the World Champion of?"

"Football."

"You didn't play in the last World Cup." I had a tiny panic. I *knew* that he didn't, but he had that way of talking that was so imperious I wondered if I'd somehow missed that he played for his national team. "Did you?"

"I am a native of France. That is the whole point of winning the tournament. We are all champions."

"Quick question for my online course. No big deal. Just tell me how to stop Mbappé without sacrificing offensive output."

"Why?"

"I'm playing a simulated match where I'm managing against France."

"You have my sympathies."

"Great. Tell me how to win."

I could hear him sweep his hair back, even though the gesture was totally silent. "Max. You cannot stop Mbappé, no more than you can stop the heat death of the universe. You cannot catch him, no more than you can catch the last dance of the last moth."

"The last what?"

"Moth."

"I'm playing four-one-four-one but I'm one–nil down and I'm out of options."

"So? Losing by only one goal to *this* France team is like being killed by mistake in an outbreak of revolutionary fervour. Yes, it's far from ideal for you, but for the wider world, it's a step in the right direction."

"I would like to win."

He sighed. "You have thought about football so much that you can no longer think about football. Defeat is inevitable. Accept it." He drank from some glass—ice cubes rattled around. "It will be France versus England in the next round."

"If England win."

"You will. I should like to watch the match with you, Max."

"Ugh. That will be incredibly stressful for me, Henri. I don't think I can take it."

He sloshed his drink around. "Please, Max."

I didn't like his tone. He suddenly sounded lonely. "Okay, let's do it. Think about where and whatnot. Maybe we can do a tiny party with Shona and Raffi and some friends."

I heard him stand up. "Yes! Great idea. I will begin planning immediately. Oh, and Max?"

"Yes?"

"Let France win. There's a good chap."

He hung up.

I didn't *let* France win, but I couldn't stop them. My final tactic involved trying to flood the right-hand side of the pitch. It didn't really achieve anything except to fatally weaken my left. My opponent didn't even change his formation to take advantage. As far as I could tell, the guy didn't do anything except copy the substitutions of the real-life French manager. It was like I wasn't even worth bothering with.

The whole match had been an exercise in futility. It went against my manifesto promise of always having a plan to win.

So what had I learned? Not much, and I got zero TINOs. But I thought it was significant that I'd managed Messi one day and tried to stop his heir apparent the next.

I moped around the house in a bit of a funk. If I was going out of the MUNDIAL game, I wanted to go down in a blaze of glory, a mad cavalry charge, cutting the red wire just as the timer hit :001. Not shuffling pawns around.

So imagine my relief when England versus Senegal neared kickoff and the words flashed up in my vision:

GET READY

I was England. It's hard to communicate how much fun I had. The first half I played it pretty straight. You might say professional. I flooded the midfield and stopped Senegal from progressing the ball. Easy. We raced to a 2–0 lead and at halftime I decided to spice things up a bit.

Off went some defensively minded players and on came Grealish, Maddison, and Trent, the best attacking right back in the world. I rubbed my hands together. This was going to be a slaughter!

While the real England team cruised to a 3–0 win, I spent the last ten minutes doing that terror sweat that comes with having made a terrible mistake. It was 2–2 and Senegal were taking the piss. Absolutely mullering us. I was almost frozen by the horror of what I'd done, and frankly was lucky to get to full-time. I splashed some water on my face, returned to a more balanced formation with fewer attacking players, and was relieved to get an extra time winner.

No TINOs, but maybe a valuable lesson: Don't get cocky, kid.

When I'd calmed down, I took stock.

I'd managed four knockout matches. I'd won three (including one in extra time) and lost one. I'd been awarded 127 TINOs, and earned four by shouting "TINO" when prompted. That, by the way, was a joke that was really fucking getting on my tits.

The rule that I had to do better than the real manager was harsh. Personally, I'd have been happy to match their efforts. Maybe the curse considered my job to be easier, since I wouldn't have to face the press after, and the hopes and dreams of a nation weren't riding on my shoulders.

The TINOs were going to be useful, but they weren't my main motivation anymore. The main thing was to make sure I was allowed to keep playing the game—I had the feeling it would kick me out if it felt I wasn't trying my best. Then there was the treasure trove of lessons I was learning. When would they be useful? I wasn't sure. Maybe never. Maybe soon.

I needed a break. A complete break. I turned the big TV on and found Henri's Netflix was already logged in. He was watching episode four of season two of *Emily in Paris*. It didn't seem like something he'd normally watch. Maybe he was homesick.

I turned the TV off and went to his bookcase. It was about fifty percent French, forty-nine percent English, and one percent German. I ran my fingers across the spines of the English ones. This was a good excuse to call him. "Hey, Henri," I said. "You've got a book here called *Catch-22*, but you don't have any of the earlier ones."

"What earlier ones?"

"For example, Catch-21."

Big pause. Stifling a smile? "I am busy watching Lars von Trier's masterwork, *Dogville*," he lied. "If you are looking for a book recommendation, yes, you will love *Catch-22*. Goodbye, Max."

I took it out to his back garden and read until it got too cold out there. It didn't take long to understand what catch-22 meant.

You can't get a football management job without experience, and without being a football manager you can't get experience.

Great book, but nah. I would keep attacking even if it meant moving side to side for a while. Side to side—disrupt enemy lines—then strike!

I found myself prowling around the ground floor, full of anticipation. My bones told me that my time was fast approaching. Something would happen at the end of the World Cup. I knew it. And I'd be ready.

TINOs: 2,960

Matches remaining: 12

37

DOUBLE DRIBBLE

Basketball glossary: *Double dribble. A rule interpreted on the side streets of Manchester to mean "don't dribble twice in one move or you get done."*

Manchester glossary: *To get done. To be punished.*

Monday, December 5.

The mood in the meeting room can best be described as disappointed excitement. Friday's result had been poor but the performance was the talk of the town. The lads were buzzing off the attention and keen to keep the vibe going. That'd mean getting six points in the week ahead.

Cutter showed his experience by quietly riding the wave. "Today, light sesh. Tomorrow a.m., light sesh and brief, then off to Manchester for the night game. No team bus, so don't leave any valuables in your cars. No offence, Max."

I was miles away. Thinking about Emma. About Henri. About Mbappé. Hoping for a quiet few days. (Spoiler alert: as if.) Everyone was looking at me; some response was needed. "Manchester is the home of the industrial revolution, the home of the nuclear age, the birthplace of the computer." This truth bomb dropped and caused an ear-splitting silence. "We also have the best chips."

I'd gone too far. Uproar.

After, Cutter pulled me aside. I was suddenly afraid he'd bollock me for taking control of his team after his sending off. But he never mentioned that, so I never knew if anyone told him or not. No, he wanted to suggest I keep my schedule clear on Wednesday in case my new friend Brad called with an opportunity. The subtext was very clear: there *would* be an opportunity. I nodded and walked away.

Huh. Interesting.

A club wanted me. Not one in tier six or Cutter would have blocked it. Something higher. League Two, maybe? Nobody poor or Brad wouldn't be making deals with them. Who had spare cash? Stockport. Salford. A step lower brought Wrexham into the mix. It didn't really matter—I wasn't interested in moving. I had a plan and was sticking to it. But any club smart enough to want me was smart enough to want James Yalley and other players I found.

What would Brad arrange? I was pretty sure I'd get a tour of the stadium, meet the potential manager, and start negotiations about a potential financial package. (Another spoiler alert: yes, yes, and yes. I didn't expect to be lured into a fucking Bond movie scene, but I'm getting ahead of myself.)

In football documentaries, I always saw players visiting interested clubs with their girlfriends, so I texted Emma to see if she wanted to skive off work on Wednesday and help me pretend to be a real boy.

Training was not intense and I mostly just kept my head down and did as I was told, but the one time I made a suggestion, people actually listened and thought about it. Incredible.

At Henri's gaff, I hit the phones pretty hard. My first call was to the Football Association to try to get on a coaching course that had already started. They said they'd get back to me. I also called my contact at Altrincham FC, plus James Yalley and Ziggy. I also called the *Northern Echo* and left a message for the guy who claimed to have interviewed me after the Kettering match.

Then I called Nice One. He was excited about the upcoming Broughton versus Chester under-fourteens match, but when I told him my latest plan, I think he was a bit disappointed in me.

There were two World Cup matches. First, I was Japan against Croatia. I won 2–0, and in football parlance, Croatia were lucky to get nil. In the second I was Brazil, but only beat South Korea by one goal.

The most interesting thing was getting a closer look at the Japanese breakout star, Kaoru Mitoma. He was a mystery winger who had been discovered playing for a university team and literally wrote his dissertation on how to dribble past players. The trick, he wrote, is to wait until they move and then go the other way. A dribble in two parts. A double dribble, you might say.

He was deadly. I thought I could learn a lot from him.

Tuesday, December 6.

There were two World Cup matches that day, but I only interacted with the MUNDIAL interface briefly. The first fixture kicked off just as the Darlo players set off for Manchester. And the second started during the match I was playing in. Both times I quickly tinkered with the formations and gave my focus to the real world. I did badly, no TINOs.

As Cutter had said, there was no team bus for the match against Curzon Ashton—I fretted I was costing Darlington too much with my goals and assists for the team to afford the bus. I carpooled with Junior and Doop in Smokes's car. Pretty good crowd, all things considered.

Smokes asked how I was getting on with my new free-kick technique. "Bad," I said. "You can stop asking. When I've perfected it, you'll be the first to know."

Junior asked if I'd be "doing more tactics if we needed it." I *reminded* him that I hadn't *done* any tactics and that our modified 4-4-2 would be perfectly fine against Curzon Ashton.

Doop made a joke about it always raining in Manchester, which was annoying because it's an insipid thing to say, factually untrue on a statistical basis, and in this one specific instance, totally accurate.

"Fuck," I said, as we hit the outskirts of greater Manchester. "That's torrential."

Torrential *begins* to describe it. It was beastly. Simply beastly! I like rain. I like playing football in rain. But this was a new level of rain. This was rain that had spent all its XP on bigger, colder, more invasive droplets.

We were already drenched from the warm-up, which in this case would be better described as the soak-up. In the dressing room, Cutter gave us our last instructions, then had to fuck off to the stands. This was the first of three games he was missing because of his red card. (What on *earth* had he said to the referee?) Same deal with Smokes and Tim. I thought it was good of Smokes to come even though he couldn't play. When I said that to him he looked blank. "What else would I do?"

Curzon Ashton were a decent team. Mid table. No great strengths and one big weakness—the fact that I was in no mood to play ninety minutes in that weather and had other things to be getting on with. There was a chance I was a CA 200 player. Until that night, I'd been keeping a lid on things—hiding my light under a bushel. When we got back onto the pitch I looked around the stadium. It was virtually deserted. If I really had access to God-mode, it was time to bust it out. My plan was to have the game won in a quarter of an hour and then make up an injury. "Bit of tweak in my hammy, Titan. Best if I come off, yeah?"

Then, after a quick shower, I'd go up to the stands and hang out with my friends.

What could go wrong?

Fast start needed then. Thirty seconds before kickoff, I told Doop and Glynn, our starting central midfielders, to take positions ten yards farther to the right. I told them to pass to me every time they got the ball or I'd go full murderhobo on them. They didn't know what that meant, but they understood what I wanted. And thank fuck, they obeyed. Although in retrospect, that might have contributed to me taking the whole God-mode thing to a bit of an extreme.

Now that my teammates actually sort of respected me as a player, in the first five minutes the ball came to me more than in most of the *halves* I'd played. I did tricks and skills to annoy my opponent, a generic skinhead type I'll call Goonhead for a few paragraphs and then never mention again. Once Goonhead was riled up, I told Glynn to play balls over his head for me to run onto.

That prompted five minutes of pure, gleeful mayhem. The defender's first instinct was always to come and stop me from doing skills, but then I'd splash past him and Jet Ski towards goal. It took him three tries to realise he should stop leaving his zone to harass me. The first time, I took a touch, then smashed the ball low and hard so that it would bounce in front of the goalie—if he even bothered trying to save it. He did try. The ball didn't bounce. It hit a patch of water and just kind of aquaplaned for about twelve yards. Comical. One–nil.

The second time, I kept going all the way to the byline where I pulled it back for our big lump of a striker, Gray. An open goal for him—he thumped the ball and several gallons of water into the net. Two–nil! The handful of plastic-coated Ashton fans behind the goal retreated like they were standing too close to a log flume.

The third time, I smacked the ball at goal from thirty yards out—the goalie saw it late and it smacked him on the nose. There was a delay while he got treatment, and Curzon's biggest caveman took the chance to yell at Goonhead. "Stop fucking fannying around trying to press him! You useless twat."

So that was fun, but Goonhead didn't like chasing my shadow and didn't like being told off by his captain. He spent the next five minutes trying to kick me, elbow me, and rile me up by saying things about my mother.

Wait till they go one way, then go the other way.

Now, one thing about me is that I don't really like using other people's material. And if I do, I want to put my own spin on it.

So my version of the double dribble . . . went a little something like this:

I was soaked to the atom. Humans are supposed to be sixty percent water. I was about ninety. At ninety-two, I'd probably burst. It was time to finish the job.

Doop spun the ball towards me—it spat water off like a mohawk haircut—I trapped it and accelerated. To top speed. I whizzed past Goonhead in a straight line. It would have been thrilling, had anyone been there to see it. When I was about ten yards past the guy, I stopped, did a skill to turn around, and moved back *towards the defender*. Dribbling back towards my own goal. When Goonhead realised I'd stopped playing properly and was simply out to humiliate him, something cracked.

I dropped my shoulder and he stuck a leg out to kick me, so I nutmegged him and gathered the ball on the other side. I did another jolly little feint, but now the fans on that side of the pitch were going feral, screaming blue murder at me, and his teammates were storming towards me. One of them would get me! I hit a long diagonal that led to nothing.

When the ball next went out of play, Goonhead stormed up to me. He had steam coming out of his ears—literally, it was that kind of weather. "Do that again I'll bury you." Good Manc accent. Local lad.

"I've been meaning to ask," I said. "You haven't played much recently. Now you're back in the team to face *me*." I chuckled. "Does your manager hate you?"

"You what?"

"You know what's funny? When you get subbed off, I'm going to let the new guy tackle me. You, no tackles from ten. Him, five from five. When your boss looks at the video, he's going to wonder what the *point* of you is. I hope you aren't pay-to-play."

"You're dead."

"How do you spell your surname?"

"You what?"

"You're going to be in my dissertation. It's called 'How to End a Career in Forty-Five Minutes or Less.'"

"Dead," he said, probably thinking I was talking about diss tracks.

Sure enough, next time the ball came to me, he sprinted and launched himself at me. Two-footed. Face distorted. Going for my shin. Leg breaker. Career ender.

Now, I *knew* it was coming. And I *saw* it coming. But holy shit, that moment haunted my nightmares for a long time to come.

I threw myself up and started to lift my right leg. As long as it wasn't planted on the ground when the guy hit me, nothing would break. Probably? My *intention* was to throw my leg backwards and up and flail around like a ragdoll. I'd scream, land safely, perhaps using the goon's face as a crash mat, and roll around for a bit. I was even thinking of doing something I'd seen a lot in the World Cup—a new innovation in the world of shithousery. It involved putting your hand up instead of rolling around. It signalled more authentically that you were really hurt.

But man. The guy's studs actually thumped into my shin—I hadn't started my hurdle in time to *completely* evade the brute. There was nothing fake about my cry of pain or the way I crumpled into a ball when I landed.

A melee ensued, and this time there were no handbags. My teammates were livid. Almost as livid as Curzon Ashton's lot. Caveman was on the scene in a flash, pushing people away from me, and once I was in a safe pocket of space, he grabbed someone by the throat. Blondie had someone in a headlock. Colin was leaning forward, fists clenched, ready for the actual fight to start so he could collect some teeth.

Our physio checked me out.

"Stretcher," I mumbled. "Get the stretcher. Quick."

The physio turned white and made the Lego-man-hands gesture that is used to summon the St John's Ambulance people. Then he came back and fussed over me.

"Just shut up for a second," I said. "Without being obvious, tell me what the ref's doing."

The physio gritted his teeth. "Max. Fuck's sake. Are you hurt or not?"

"Yes I'm fucking hurt," I hissed back. "But I'll live. The ref?"

Big sigh. "He's waiting for the sitch to cool off."

"Red card, do you think?"

"Yeah. Clearest red of all time. Now answer my fucking questions."

He went through his routine of checking for breaks and shit, and as soon as the guys started putting me on the stretcher, the ref showed the hoodlum the red card.

"Great," I said. "Tell Titan to replace me with Junior."

"What? We've got Webby on the bench."

"Mate," I said, putting my hands over my face as though I was sobbing. Part of the theatre.

"Fine. I'll tell him. But he won't listen."

The physio was right. Webby came on to replace me. Missed opportunity. Junior would have run riot. Apart from that, things had gone perfectly.

We were 2–0 up, playing against ten men. I'd get my appearance fee, plus a thousand pounds for scoring and assisting. And, even better, I'd earn 2 XP per minute from watching in the stands—the dry stands—compared to the one per minute I got for playing.

Better than perfect—if my shin was intact.

It was, though there was swelling and an already glowing bruise. The physio said I was millimetres away from a nasty break. He suggested that I stop prancing around like a twat winding everyone up. I asked if he was talking about football or just in general. He laughed, but quickly got serious. "Max, really. You were lucky. Really, really lucky. Buy-a-lottery-ticket lucky. Don't do that again until you've signed a long-term contract. Preferably with us."

I smiled at him. Not many people inside the club had actually said they liked having me there. "Yeah. That was dumb. Even for me." Unbidden, I remembered the moment I saw the knuckle-dragger launch his attack. Anywhere but on a football pitch and he'd have been in jail already. I shuddered.

"Don't go anywhere. Keep that iced."

"Nah," I said, shaking off my first, but not last, flashback from the tackle. "I'm off. I've got mates here. I'm going up to sit with them."

"Fucking hell, Max. Are you serious right now?" Turns out I was. He rubbed his temples and let out an animalistic groan. "I'm going to tell Cutter about this. You're supposed to listen to us. Here. Crutches. Use these for now and I'll check you again after the match." He pointed to my shin, my foot, and to my face in succession while he said, "Ice. Elevation. Prick."

So I was back on crutches. It took me a few seconds to remember how to move, but then I zoomed up into the stands and found James. As I went, a few heads turned to glare at me. Going into the heart of enemy territory was maybe pushing my luck a bit too far, but I suppose most people decided I couldn't have been the same person who was just stretchered off the pitch.

"Youngster!" I said.

"Mr. Best! Are you all right?" His eyes bulged at the crutches and the ice pack.

"Don't say my name too loud, buddy. I don't seem to be very popular round here for some reason. Am I all right? Not sure. Can you hold that in place, please? Just for a minute. Ah! That's the spot. Thanks. The physio said with these impacts sometimes nothing happens for a while, then the bone spontaneously breaks."

His eyes bulged even more. He swallowed. He was wondering if he might cause the break by holding the ice too close. "Is there any—? Oh. You are joking." His exhalation of relief made me laugh. "Mr. Best. Why are you like that?" He shook his head and as he did, his natural goofy smile returned. "You know Gavvo, though I do not believe you have met."

"Gavvo! My man!" I wedged a crutch into an armpit so I could bump him. He was my contact at Altrincham FC. The guy who had allowed James to train with his lads.

"Max," he said, with a big grin. "That was a hell of a show. Almost worth getting soaked to the gills for."

"You're under a roof," I said.

"That's no help when the rain comes horizontally. You went off in tears. We were worried sick."

"That was just me using my hands as a face umbrella," I said. "I'm surprised you even saw it in this weather."

"Oh, everyone saw it, and everyone saw your little . . ." He wiggled his fingers around, miming my double dribble move, which made me laugh and distracted me. If I'd been paying attention, I would have realised how ominous that statement was.

I changed the subject. "How's Youngster getting on? Is he behaving himself?"

"Oh," said Gavvo, cracking into his broadest smile yet. "He's a top lad. Trains well. Sponges up instructions. You got any more like him?"

I laughed. "Not yet, but I will. Youngster, are you enjoying it?"

"Yes, Mr. Best!"

"I was telling Youngster," said Gavvo, with care, "that we'd be interested in taking him on. As long as he doesn't copy any of your, ah, special moves."

"Oh?" I said. I gave him my full attention. "That could work. I'll come and check out the vibe first, if that's all right."

"Sure. You promised me a free kick clinic, anyway."

"Look who it is!" said a new voice. "Mister five goals in three games!"

"Ziggy! Mate!" I was so delighted I didn't correct him. I'd appeared twice as a sub, so my official record was five in five, with a measly two assists.

"Don't get up," said my first ever client. He was holding two beers in plastic cups. He saw me staring at them and looked guilty. "You dragged me outdoors in this tropical storm," he said. "I deserve a pint. I thought I'd be spending the night at a hospital waiting for news about you."

"If it was tropical," said Gavvo, taking the second beer, "the rain would be warm."

I'd taken Ziggy's seat, but he didn't mind. The stadium was far from full. I tried to guess the attendance, but could barely see the other side of the centre circle let alone count how many spectators were lining the pitch.

I had a great time. The kind of low-stakes normality I'd been craving. A brief moment of contentment before things *really* started to spiral.

Ziggy and Gavvo were a good hang. They were interested in my adventures. Ziggy was agog when I told him I'd been seeing more of Emma. James asked to see a picture of her and I told him he was too young.

I made him promise never to do a double dribble, and he said it was an inefficient play and he liked having his leg in two pieces.

"You mean one piece," I said.

"Tibia and fibula, Mr. Best," he said, with a big smile. He'd done me there. I showed him a pic of Emma. That shut him up.

Exchanging goss for goss, Ziggy told me that Jackie Reaper had some bee in his bonnet and FC United had been doing some weird new drills, and that Jackie had actually named the drill after me. He refused to elaborate.

The on-pitch action slowly changed from being a war to being a football match, at which point it reengaged me. "James, look at that," I said, and started pointing out things that Doop and Glynn were doing well, or badly. When I talked about the midfielders, James became still. Soaking it all up.

At halftime I learned that Ziggy was downbeat. As FC United's fifth-choice striker, he couldn't see where his next game was coming from. I gave him a little pep talk even though I didn't think he *really* needed one. When I'd done that, he shook my hand as if to say thanks, but he was actually giving me some cash.

The feel of the banknotes in my hand reminded me how poor I was. I'd started to ease into a mentality of knowing there'd be a few thousand pounds heading my way every month, and that if I ever needed a bit more I could just score another goal. But I'd come *so* close to having no income. With a shattered leg I'd be relying on the thirty-five quid a week from Ziggy and the forty-five from Raffi. Henri's eighty would kick in soon, but then again, in a month or so he'd want me to move out of his house or start paying rent. I stared at the colourful paper for a bit too long; it made Ziggy uncomfortable.

I found a way through the awkwardness. "I'm not sure if I was hallucinating, but I thought I saw a kid wearing a Best seventy-seven shirt this morning. I nearly crashed."

"Well, if you play like that every week, no wonder. When you turned back and dribbled that guy *again*, I nearly pissed myself laughing. What kid wouldn't love a player who can do that?"

"I shouldn't have done it."

"Probably not. But no one who saw it will ever forget it." Prophetic words, indeed. "Fuck it. I need another beer. Last one, I promise. You want?"

"Nah. Might need painkillers later."

"Have you heard the rumours?"

"What?" I said.

"Ian Evans is in the shit."

"Are you in some Chester fans' Facebook group?" I said, laughing at the absurdity of the idea.

"Jackie's connected to them over there. He hears things. They're only a few points above the relegation zone now." The mention of relegation made him speak more quietly. At the end of the season, teams in the relegation zone are demoted to a lower tier. It's bad. Sometimes clubs don't survive the process. Ziggy was right to be superstitious about it. "Chester can't score. They're in trouble. Evans Out is trending on Twitter. You know, in Chestershire."

"Cheshire," I said. I was excited, briefly. Evans out! Max Best in! But my performance at Shona's house had put the nail in that coffin. "Yeah, well. There's only a few more weeks for them to worry. In January, Henri will be able to play, and they'll sail out of danger."

"Jackie isn't so sure," mused Ziggy. "He thinks there's something wrong there. Something deeper."

"You don't need to be so mysterious," I laughed. "It goes no deeper than Ian Evans. They've got good players."

Just then I got a panicked phone call from Brad, the agent. Cutter must have called him. I assured Brad I hadn't broken my leg but that it had been a close call. Admitting that made me feel like I was going to be sick, so I hung up and swung myself to the nearest sink to splash water over my face. Ironic, given I'd worked so hard to get out of the rain.

Shortly after the start of the second half, I finally arrived at 300 XP. I instantly tried to buy Match Stats 2, and was actually quite surprised when the purchase went through.

The Match Overview now boasted even more data.

I could see each team's possession stats—who had the ball the most. In theory, possession would tell me at a glance who was dominating a game. Darlo were currently on 76% possession, which was very high.

On the newly unlocked Match Stats tab, I could see how many shots each team had attempted, plus how many were on and off target. Darlo were crushing that particular stat. Curzon hadn't had a single one so far. Then there was the number of corners, free kicks, throw-ins, fouls, offsides, and then three stats given as percentages: passes completed, tackles won, headers won. Finally, there were yellow and red cards. Useful stuff.

I also got the match attendance—which only appeared in the second half—plus details of the weather and referee. The attendance was

287, by far the lowest since I'd started playing, and the curse showed it had a sense of humour by describing the weather as "wet."

"There's only about three hundred people here," I said. "How can they afford to pay the players?"

Gavvo knew. "It's semi-pro, Max. They're not paid much. They train a couple of times a week. Try to stay fit. But they've all got day jobs."

Well, shit. I'd just taken the piss out of some hard-working Joe. On the other hand, he had tried to amputate my leg.

I shrugged. Beating him and getting him sent off was my job. Cutter wouldn't approve of me running back to dribble past him an extra time, but he'd love the rest.

All in all, Match Stats 2 was a step forward, and it made me feel good to know that underneath the weirdness of the MUNDIAL stuff, the curse was still working as I had grown to know and love.

Buying that perk unlocked a couple of others. Action Zones sounded exciting, but was only 300 XP. I wasn't sure what to make of that. Did that mean it was exactly as valuable as the one I'd just unlocked? Or that 300 was my new base price?

It also gave me the option of buying Bibliotekkers 1, a grotesquely named perk that would let me see the last twenty match reports from teams I was watching. Absolutely awesome, but at a cost of 1,000 XP it'd be fairly low on my list of priorities. When my TINOs matured, I planned to tuck into as many Attributes as poss.

The evening was a dream. I had played fifteen minutes of football, earning fifteen hundred pounds. That was what I used to be paid *per month*. Also, my team won and we kept the pressure up on King's Lynn. I spent time with my football mates, old and new, and made progress towards my goal of becoming a manager.

It came at a cost—a big, painful bruise—and something of a near-disaster in terms of injury. A reminder, if you will, that my financial situation was precarious. I couldn't afford a broken leg! So, no more double dribbles. No more verbals. No more risks. Get to ten league games for Darlington, then get out of playing completely. That was the sensible thing.

Football without emotion.

That's what I needed.

My resolution lasted about as long as you'd imagine.

38

THE ATTENTION GAME

It started with Emma ringing my doorbell at 7:30 a.m. She'd taken the day off work and didn't seem too worried about the consequences. I guessed that dreamy blondes got away with such things a bit more readily than the rest of us.

At 8:00, Brad arrived. He was surprised that Emma was coming with us, but delighted. He asked what her surname was because he saw some resemblance to a family he knew. "Weaver? Oh, that's not even close." That came with a chuckle and a look at his watch. "We need to hit the road."

"Any clue as to where we're going?" I said.

He frowned and paused tapping on his phone. When he wasn't driving, he was on WhatsApp or taking a call on his weirdly elongated in-ear headset. "Oh. You don't like surprises. That's fine. And I suppose it's better to do this now, before we get in the car. Do you have any objections to playing under a Black manager?" I became very still. He reacted to my reaction by raising his palms in surrender. "Max. It's a working-class sport. Some people are . . . I've found it's better to ask. I don't mean anything by it."

I processed what he'd said, then nodded. I turned to Emma and grabbed my house keys. "We're going to Sheffield."

She put on her coat. A sensibly cosy beige wool number with two huge wooden fasteners, plus a hood for if it rained. "Can we go to Plantology?"

"What's that?" I said.

"Really cool florist. They kill it on Instagram."

We were at the door and were surprised to see that Brad hadn't moved. Something had unnerved him, I think. "Come on, Brad. Let's see how much traffic we can miss."

In Brad's car, Emma asked me how I knew it was Sheffield.

"Forty percent of footballers are Black," I said. "But only four percent of managers."

"Damn," she said.

"Off the top of my head, there's one in the Premier League. He's in London so this isn't that. One's in charge of Burnley. Fits geographically but Burnley are crushing the Championship. Crushing it like there's no tomorrow. He seems to be an actual genius. God, I wish it was him. But it isn't. They'll be looking for players for next season in the Premier League. Top players from Belgium. Nigerian internationals. That sort of thing. No chance they'd be interested in me. Who else? There's Paul Ince. Former Man United player. Annoyed a lot of people by going to Liverpool, but I still like him. First Black England captain, if I remember that right. Not sure where he is."

"Reading," said Brad, who was a good driver so I didn't have to micromanage him like I did with Jackie and Henri.

"How are they doing?"

"Championship mid-table. He's doing a decent job, most people think."

"Who else is there? Just Craig Summers. He's at Sheffield Wednesday. They're top of League One. He's doing a mega job. From what I know, he's a tracksuit manager. His superpower is coaching. He's someone who'll improve his players and bring local kids into the first team. Wednesday have a big stadium and they're getting twenty thousand a match. That's enormous in the third tier; there are Premier League clubs who don't get so many. And the number's going up. I love it when numbers go up. So do the fans. It's exciting there. In fact, it's exciting times for football in Sheffield in general. The other team, United, are heading for the Premier League."

"You know your stuff, Max," said Brad.

"Tell me about you, Brad," said Emma, from the back.

"I can do that," I said. I'd been researching him. "I watched old clips of him as a player. He was a midfield schemer in the days when every tackle was like the one that I got last night."

"What?"

Oh, that's right. I hadn't told her. I would have if I needed to use crutches, but I'd woken up with no swelling. Probably best to downplay it. "Just a rough tackle. The guy got a red card. But in Brad's day you'd be lucky to even get a free kick! It's really something watching those clips. Brad wandering around those old turnip fields, socks down, no shinpads that I could see, trying through-balls, doing little hip wiggles to try to dribble past Scottish midfielders who ate tarmac for breakfast. What I saw was a guy trying a lot of low-percentage, high-outcome passes, a guy whose head didn't drop when something didn't go right."

Brad was glowing like I'd lit a candle inside him. "Thank you very much, Max. I have to say YouTube has not been kind to my playing career." He laughed like a maestro teasing a piano. "I could play a safe pass, too, but somehow none of those survived the digitisation process."

"I was impressed," I said. "Honestly. You reminded me of Bruno Fernandes. Man United and Portugal," I said, for Emma's benefit. "He's always attacking. Always trying something. Two hundred thousand pound a week. You were born in the wrong decade, mate."

"I liked playing in those days," he said. "It was the time of my life. But clubs always tried to rip me off. That hasn't changed. Clubs take liberties. They know what players are worth down to the penny but their day's not complete if they aren't shoving some garbage contract in someone's face. That's why I became an agent."

That was his cue to launch into a much-practiced spiel about his services. I didn't interrupt—I wanted to hear his pitch and compare it to his actions, and maybe learn a thing or two.

It was, honestly, pretty compelling. He seemed genuinely keen to extract full value for players while making sure their careers progressed. If a club wasn't right for a player, he wouldn't pursue the deal. As such, players liked and trusted him. It sounded an awful lot like the kind of brand I was trying to build for the agent side of my life.

When he finished, I asked what to expect from our time in Sheffield.

"We'll see their training session. They're starting late knowing you're coming." Holy shit! That was impressive. Brad had clout. "You can't do any contact work, but I thought you might take some free kicks. Meet Craig. See the facilities. The owner is very ambitious. They're looking for a site to build a new training compound. But even the ones they have are still a huge step up from Darlington. And the stadium, of course, is the jewel in the crown. Forty thousand all-seater. One of the best in the country. Famous. Historic. A fitting stage for a player of your talents." He sighed. "The fans there make a hell of a noise, let me tell you. They are going to fucking love *you*, Max Best."

"To know me is to love me," I said. "But Brad. What about your mate Dave Cutter? He shouldn't be happy about us doing this. But he doesn't seem to mind."

Brad made some calculation. To tell me, or not to tell me; that was the question. "If I arrange a move like this for you," said Brad, "I might take David to dinner. A very big dinner. As a thank you. Do you get me?"

"Yeah," I said. Me moving for free wasn't exactly in Darlington's best interests, but they weren't going to get anything anyway—I had batted away all talk of signing anything long-term. I'd become pretty convinced that Cutter was paid less than all the first team regulars. So why shouldn't he take a bit on the side? I tried to guess how much Brad would slip him. Five thousand pounds? Fifteen thousand? A decent chunk of change, that was for sure. One deal like that per year could make a lot of difference. "Yeah," I said again. "I get you."

When we got to the outskirts of Sheffield, Brad made a call. Whatever he heard led to us starting our tour at Hillsborough, Wednesday's famous stadium. Someone from the club was there to meet us. An older guy. He didn't introduce himself so I invented a backstory: he gave the stadium tours, remembered repeat visitors, told dad jokes, and was banned from his grandkid's football matches for threatening referees with petrol bombs. Motto: *I know where you live!*

"Max Best, I presume?" he said. He brought us into the belly of the beast, stupidly taking a shortcut through some admin section. He couldn't have expected a player to be so incredibly interested in the work that was done there and the software they were using. It created something of a stir when I took a chair next to an older lady and started peppering her with questions about ticketing and customer management. Eventually, Emma dragged me away and we went through well-equipped gyms and medical rooms and out onto the pitch.

Emma was virtually speechless. The size, the sense of history, the sounds. "Max," she said, hugging my arm.

"I know," I said.

The employee gave us the one-minute version of a Sheffield Wednesday history lesson. Named because the founders had a half-day on Wednesdays so that's when they played. Four times league champions. Three times FA Cup winners. A proud history of promoting youth players into the first team. Nicknamed The Owls. And, the guy said with a cheeky grin, they were the only football team in the world with a fanzine, named *War of the Monster Trucks*.

"What?" said Emma, laughing.

"In 1991, we beat Man United in the League Cup final. We were in the second tier then, so you can imagine how unlikely that was. It was a big, big deal for the club, and for football if you ask me. But instead of showing our celebrations, Yorkshire Television, which as you know is run by dirty Leeds fans, cut short the programme and broadcast a repeat of *War of the Monster Trucks*. Right, last stop, the dressing rooms."

Guess what we saw?

Two kits hanging up. Vertical blue and white stripes.

One: Best 77.

The other, and this is where Brad was waaaay more suited to being an agent than me: Weaver 77.

I smiled at him. The smooth prick! That's why he'd asked her family name. Amazing. This was next-level agenting. I had to take my hat off to him. And yeah. Seeing my name on the shirt. It was like a promise. If I signed some tiny little piece of paper I could play here. In this vast stadium. For one of the oldest football clubs in the world.

Brad tried to hurry us back out, but Emma had other ideas. "Wait there," she said, taking her shirt into the showers. There was a lot of rustling and unzipping and whatnot, all noises which I'd heard before. But Brad and the guy from the club were barely able to contain their excitement—she was taking her clothes off! Emma finally came back from around the corner . . . looking exactly the same as she had.

That only inflamed their imaginations even further. The poor guys. They thought they knew what they were missing. But they didn't.

We drove across town and caught the last ten minutes of the Sheffield Wednesday first team training session. It was eleven versus eleven but with frequent interventions from Craig Summers. The session looked absolutely top, but I'd been tricked once before, so I was cautious.

The training area itself, Middlewood Road, was two grass pitches and a 3G (third generation) artificial one. The 3G was inside a big circus tent thing. It looked like the underside of a memory foam pillow. In other words, it looked amazing. There was some activity over there. It felt, weirdly, like people were preparing a wedding inside it. There were caterers in posh uniforms and that kind of thing. I shrugged. Nothing to do with me.

I turned my attention to the players. The average CA of the first team was 120—way higher than the Darlo guys or anyone in my division. The reserves were much more variable, which made sense. Sheffield had invested heavily in the starting eleven and there was a big drop-off to the rest. That explained why they'd be interested in someone like me. I'd be free, except for some wages.

After the session, Summers brought his whole gang to a spot between the centre circle and the penalty box, and waved me, Brad, and Emma over.

"Brad," said Emma, as we approached the Sheffield Wednesday first team squad. "Is it bad that I'm here? I'm going to distract attention from Max."

"I think on balance it's a net positive," said Brad, which was unusually understated of him.

"Babes," I said, because for some reason I'd started calling her babes and she was doing the same to me. "They're footballers. They've seen women. They've never seen anything like me. Five minutes from now they'll have forgotten you exist."

"Want to bet?" she said.

"Absolutely. The Attention Game. Rules are self-explanatory. Loser pays a forfeit."

We walked to where the manager was—the squad fanned out a little bit to give us space. Emma was, inevitably, into an early lead in the battle for eyeballs.

Craig Summers was holding a clipboard and sort of indicated me with it. "Guys," he said, in what I thought was a London accent but could have been from anywhere south of the midlands. "This is Max Best and his, er . . ."

"Dream girl," I said, while Emma flushed.

Summers got a little sparkle in his eye. "I bet. So we've seen the clips, Max. A true number seven if ever there was one, and I hear you're a free-kick freak. We haven't scored a direct free kick this whole season. Want to show us your stuff?"

A few minutes earlier, Brad had told me to put my boots on, either from instinct or from some prearranged signal that I didn't notice. I was in my now-customary tracksuit bottoms, so there was nothing stopping me from taking a proper free kick. I probably should have warmed up a bit, but whatevs. Set pieces 20, blah blah blah.

I looked around at the squad. Some were interested in me. Most weren't. They were standing there because they had been told to stand there. These guys were top of the league. A great team, working as a unit. Did they want new blood to help them reach their targets? Or would they try to exclude me like the Darlo mob had done? As it stood, they were a whole lot more interested in Emma than me.

I mentally shrugged. Nothing would matter unless I scored from the free kick.

There was a ball there, and an empty goal in front of me.

I rolled the ball around under my studs, then bent to place it properly. "Who takes the dead balls in this gaff?" I said, pretending not to know every single thing about these players.

Summers pointed. "That'd be Kevvo. Young Damien there is starting to push him, though."

"Cool," I said. "Sorry about this, guys."

The one called Kevvo tilted his head. "Sorry about what?"

"About showing you how we do it in Manchester." I gave him a Maxy two-thumbs while his mates grabbed him by the shoulders going "oooh." Kevvo laughed. Good vibes here. Really good. I decided to treat them to some of my best material.

I went through a hilariously senseless pre-kick routine that was juuust on the verge of perhaps being real—three big steps to the left and four small ones to the right; two big paces back, one tiny one forward. All eyes were on me. With a ball at my feet, Emma had *no chance* in a battle for attention. I walked slowly towards the ball, and gently toe-poked it goalwards. It bounced approximately six hundred times, drooled over the goal line, and came to a rest two feet away from the net.

"Whoo!" I said, arms aloft.

Big laughs from the Wednesday players. Some anti-Manchester jokes.

Brad giggled nervously. "Max," he said. "We were hoping for something more . . . dramatic."

"Emma, sweetness," I said. "Did I score?"

"Yes?"

"So what's the problem?" Some of the Wednesday guys thought this was funny. Summers was frowning. He didn't get me; from his point of view this was my big break. A chance to skip a few divisions and play for a serious team. Why wasn't I taking it seriously? I helped him out by pointing at the empty goal. "Max Best thrives in the crucible of competition. Max Best needs a keeper."

"You told me *I* was a keeper," said Emma, deliciously. Half the nearby players went googly-eyed.

Summers got his phone out and called, I presumed, the goalkeeping coach. He chatted away, then turned to me. "Couple of minutes. Is that okay for Max Best?"

"Sure thing, gaffer."

"What's a number seven?" said Emma. At least seven guys sucked in some breath so they could explain.

"Cool your jets, boys," I said. "Leave the Maxsplaining to me. The numbers. It's simple, but complicated."

"Oh, boy," she said.

"In the old days . . . Well, I suppose in the old days there weren't any numbers. But when there were, they were from one to eleven. The goalkeeper was number one. Then the rest of the positions got their own numbers. What's the most basic formation?"

"Four-four-two," she said, causing another swathe of men to fall in love with her.

"Hands up everyone who found that sexy? That's too many hands. Don't be creepy, Sheffield. Sorry, babes. So the back four. You've got a right back and a left back. You notice I started with the right back?"

"So he's number two."

"Christ, you're so hot sometimes."

"Sometimes?"

"The left back is number three. The centre backs are four and five."

"Any particular order?"

"Who cares? They're just defenders. They're not important." That led to a lot of laughs in the ranks of the Wednesday squad. My sense of humour would go down well here. "Ah, here's our goalieshitlookatthisguy."

Along came a terrifying dude. Dean Casson. Six foot six. That's almost two metres tall. Then add his arms. They were, conservatively, another four metres. And he had good attributes: handling 16, jumping 16, and his CA was 125. This was a very, very serious goalkeeper. I briefly wondered if I'd bitten off more than I could chew. I mean, if I'd just hit some Beckhams into the top corner of the empty net, would Wednesday have offered me a juicy contract? Would I have taken it? Sure, if the amount was high enough. What would it cost to make me postpone my dream of becoming a manager? One hundred thousand a week would do it, that was for sure. There was some number between five hundred a week and fifty thousand a week where I would have no choice but to accept. I didn't want to leave Darlington yet, and I didn't even want to be a player, but I liked the idea that I might get an offer I couldn't refuse.

"Huh," I said.

"What about the midfield?" said Emma.

"One second," I said. I closed my eyes, took a few deep breaths, and tuned out Brad, Summers, and Sheffield. The universe was me, the ball, and the goalie, with a little bit of Emma. I placed a ball with the nozzle facing me, and wondered if I should start with a Beckham or a cannonball. Probably a Beckham, since that was the most beautiful and couldn't be replicated by accident. The football people watching would accept it as proof of my exceptional technique. "Two guys in central midfield. Six and eight. If you've got a defensive guy, he's the six. More attacking, he's the eight. Brad would have been an eight. James is a six. You'll meet him soon."

I blew some carbon dioxide out and eyed one patch of air about a yard above and to the right of the goal. That would be the spot the ball would head towards until the spin kicked in. I struck. Sure enough, my shot curled and dipped as though magnetically drawn to the *actual* target I'd chosen—one ball width below and inside the frame. The farthest point you could place a ball without it touching the post or crossbar. The most similar thing I can think of would be in basketball where someone shouts "Nothing but net!" My shot *sighed* into the goal, microns away from metal. Perfection.

Well, that tipped the Attention Game in my favour. There was a low buzz of admiration from the squad. I glanced at Brad—he was practically purring. Spending his agent fees already. What would I buy him? This year, a nice holiday. Next year, a nice island. Summers was wide-eyed. It was one thing seeing it on tape. It was another thing watching me from two yards away.

Casson, meanwhile, had been smiling and slapping his gloves and *doing*ing the crossbar to try to put me off. The manager had asked him to come and save some free kicks. And when I'd seemingly hit my first try miles over the bar, he'd relaxed. The moment the ball fizzed against the back of the net, he transformed. He became, frankly, insane. Insanely competitive. Okay, I'd scored against him, but he hadn't been trying. Try now, you smug prick!

Even from thirty yards away, I could sense the increased testosterone levels. I realised I was sort of snarling. I relaxed my jaw and gave some attention back to Emma. Firstly, because she deserved it. Second, because I knew that it would wind Casson up even more to see me casually chatting.

I got another ball and rolled it farther away from goal. The semicircle of players shuffled away obediently. "I'm a seven," I said to Emma. "You know where I play."

"Right midfield slash mystery winger," she said.

More swooning. I showed her my dimples, then it was concentrate o'clock. Casson wouldn't fall for the same trick again. But he didn't know what other tricks I had. Hmm.

I took an extra step back and positioned myself so that I was exactly in line with the ball. None of this curve shit. I ran up and wellied a cannonball with a theoretical endpoint a yard above the crossbar. It dipped at the last second. Casson had moved into position, just in case, but his last-second reflex save lacked the wrist strength to keep my shot out of the net.

BIG buzz from the players. A "holy shit" from Brad, and something even stronger from Summers.

The goalie, though, was not happy.

"The ball *dips*," I called out, helpfully. "Imagine the shot's like a rainbow," I said, miming a curve. I didn't think he could get more intense, but he did. He started prowling around, slapping his gloves and slapping himself on the head. "Wow. You try to help people. Where was I? I'm a seven. The me on the left is a number eleven."

Emma was frowning. "But wait. You missed something. You're not number seven. You're number seventy-seven."

"That's my *squad* number. There isn't always a correlation between the squad number and the role you play. Most sevens wouldn't want to wear seventy-seven because lower numbers are better."

"Why?"

"If your squad number is eleven or under, the manager thinks you're first choice. Number twelve is better than number twenty-four. Kevvo, the guy who used to take the free kicks here, is squad number eighteen. So just from that you know he's one of the top boys. If he was thirty-eight you'd be surprised to see him in the team. If he was fifty-eight, you'd assume he was shit."

"Wow."

"No offence to anyone who's wearing a high number here," I said to the watchers. "Where should I shoot this time?"

"Left?"

Left was tricky. If I did a Beckham, the ball would start in the middle of the goal and veer off. The goalie would be able to follow it. Or would he?

I ran at the ball at an angle, leaned, twisted my foot, and gave the ball more spin than I ever had before.

Casson watched it the whole way, sidestepped, sidestepped again, then at the last second he leaped, extended an arm, and diverted the ball over the crossbar.

"Holy shit!" I said.

"What?" said Emma.

"He fucking saved it. He's not supposed to save it." Casson got to his feet. He was snarling at me. "Do you mind?" I shouted. "I'm trying to be cocky over here."

He flipped me the bird, which drew some *ooohs* from the crowd.

But now that Casson was warmed up and hyper-focused, all eyes were on our battle. I'd smashed the Attention Game.

"Brad," said Emma. "I'm a bit warm. Can you hold my coat?" She unwrapped herself, taking her time, and peeled off her top to reveal she was wearing her Sheffield Wednesday jersey. It was *tight*. You know in cartoons when someone's mouth opens and his tongue rolls out?

Emma gave me a kind of blank, innocent look. "Oh, Max? Who's winning?"

To the outside world it seemed she was talking about me versus the keeper. I knew better.

"I'm winning, babes. I always win." I tried to give this statement some arrogant heat, but it made no dent in the crowd. Emma had soundly thrashed me. I shrugged. Sometimes losing felt good. At least I could win my other contest. "Right. No more making it easy for him. If he saves *this*, I'm off to live in a monastery."

I got a ball, positioned it with extreme care, and went through my little cannonball ritual. I fucking leathered it on a diagonal so that it would dip and he wouldn't be able to get a hand to it. But somehow he did. He diverted it onto the post, and it spun into the back of the net.

I felt no sense of triumph; the rebound could have gone anywhere. This guy was almost as good as me. He was CA 125. What did that make me? CA 140 maybe?

How did I feel about that?

Mostly fine. It felt good to know. Know that I had a limit. Know that I was right to pursue the manager thing. Being accidentally turned into a good player had never really sat right with me.

But yeah. There was some disappointment there. I wasn't completely against the idea of being a superstar. Of playing for a top club in the Champions League. Of scoring a hat trick for England at Wembley.

Well. This session wasn't exactly scientific. It wasn't conclusive. How about one more data point? I'd been working on that third free-kick type. The one that would bounce in front of the keeper and spit up. The one that would let my team score goals without Darlo having to pay me an assist bonus.

It might work here. Casson was tall and agile. He'd seen many players try Beckhams on him. He'd seen many try cannonballs. But he'd definitely not seen what I had tentatively named The Ace. I felt sure if I connected right, he'd dive along the ground, but the ball would spin way over his head.

The only problem was, I was far from mastering the technique. I was getting about two shots in twenty to obey me.

There was something in the air, though. Something that made me think that *this* time, it'd work.

With a slight grin, I got everything ready. I turned to Emma. "Last numbers. Nine is Henri. Ten can be a second striker or a more creative type who connects the midfield to the striker. Now, Emma. Watch carefully. This is new. No one's ever seen this before. Are you ready?"

I was grinning at her, but my grin faded. She was looking way up in the air. Now that I'd shut my gob, I heard that there was some thrumming noise. I followed her gaze. The noise came closer.

A helicopter was arriving. It wasn't a cute little civilian one, but a beefy, angular military-style attack chopper. The pilot was wearing one of those shiny wraparound jet fighter helmets. The windows were tinted black. The frame was matte black with a few markings painted in white. The downward pressure from the rotors was sending anything that wasn't nailed down flying. Emma let out a little squeak and grabbed onto me.

It became clear that the copter wanted to land on our pitch—right between me and Casson. If you wanted to get fanciful, you'd say it had been timed to put an end to our little competition. The rest of the players and coaches fled in something of a panic. I wanted to stay and so did Casson. But the flapping of Emma's hair made me sensible. I waved at Casson and pointed right. He nodded. We moved away on diagonals so that we converged. I offered him a handshake and tried to tell him he was top, but he couldn't hear what I was saying.

The blades of the rotor slowed, and Casson asked me to repeat myself.

I never did.

Stepping down from the helicopter was an old, distinguished-looking businessman with silver hair and a powerful body tucked into a killer suit. He strode forward with a smug look on his outrageously handsome face. Walking like he owned the place.

Someone slipped their hand under my arm. I glanced down. Emma was staring at the newcomer with wide eyes. She was looking at the older guy the way the Sheffield Wednesday players had been looking at *her*. "Oh, my," she said. "I guess we both lost the Attention Game. Looks like you've got some competition, Max. I wonder if we'll get to meet him?"

Yeah. Like there was any doubt about that.

39

THE DEVIL IS IN THE DETAIL

Brad rushed over with Emma's coat and helped her into it. "I don't know what's better," he said. "The guy's entrance or his suit."

Emma pulled the coat around her and rewarded Brad with a cute smile. "Who *is* that guy? Is it the owner?" She'd put him in the uncomfortable situation of admitting there was something about football he didn't know.

On cue, two giant, gleaming, silver Rolls Royces purred into view, coming to a stop by the edge of the grass. A guy in a black suit got out and looked around. Then he nodded and most of the other doors opened. A bunch of guys in more casual suits got out, along with one elderly guy who seemed to be wearing cheap blue pyjamas. "That's the owner," I said.

"How can you tell?" said Emma.

I glared at the helicopter. Fucking obnoxious piece of shit. "No one who cares about football would land on the pitch."

"The Rolls guy might not care, either. Maybe he just doesn't want to get his tyres dirty."

"That's the owner. I know because I know who the other guy is."

"Oh?" she giggled. "Can you introduce me?" When I didn't laugh, she grabbed the toggles of my hoodie and pulled one. "Can you at least find out who his tailor is?"

I was stupefied. "His tail-er?"

Emma looked at me like I'd grown horns.

I was busy staring at the chopper. Could I stick a banana in the tail pipe? When I thought that, the pilot's head snapped towards me. He, she, or it was still wearing the stupid space helmet. I think I took a couple of steps towards him; his head snapped right back to where it had started. The guy knew who I was and was scared of me. Good to know. *Weird* to know, but good to know.

Brad's phone pinged. "We need to hurry, Max. We've got a few minutes to talk to Summers, then we have to clear out. Something big's going down."

"We have to go in the tent, do we?" Old Nick and three minions had already gone in. Now the owner and his mob were following. I grimaced. "Of course. Of course I have to go in there."

"I mean, if you want to play for Sheffield Wednesday," said Brad, frowning. I was confounding him again. Like most people, he didn't get me. The feeling slipped off him. And *that* was the word I'd been looking for: slippery. It wasn't that he was two-faced or deceptive. He just didn't allow himself to get overly emotional or trapped in unwanted conversations. He slipped through. He wriggled out of them. Slippery has a negative connotation but to me, with Brad, it was positive. He was trying hard to be a positive person. "Max. They want you. I'd say they're desperate to sign you before other clubs realise there's an opportunity."

"Why not start a bidding war?" I said.

Brad shook his head. "You and Wednesday are a perfect match right now. You'd fit right into their team; they'd continue your development. We could get more elsewhere if money's the most important thing." He said it with no judgement.

"No, I agree with you. This seems like a good fit."

He smiled. "There will be numbers mentioned in there. But this is just their opening gambit. Try not to react! Do your best poker face. I'll get you a fair shake. Just listen and leave the talking to me. All right?"

"Sure, Brad. I'll go in there and not say a word." I scoffed and shook my head, knowing that I was about to step into some absolute fucking shitshow. Brad gave me another despairing look, then scampered away in that weirdly effeminate way of his.

"You're being weird," said Emma.

"I know."

"It's that guy, isn't it? I was only teasing you. He's hot but I wouldn't swap you for anyone."

I wasn't fully present. I was trying to work out why this confrontation was happening today. Was it because I'd slacked off on the MUNDIAL project? I hadn't made much effort to play the recent games. But I *couldn't*. Not without offending my teammates and threatening my career.

My career. That was it. Nick had been furious to discover I was suddenly a top player. He'd tried to stop me. This was his revenge for my defiance. This was the crisis. I realised I was grinding my teeth.

"Max, who is he?"

"He's nobody. He's a suit with connections."

"Are you in trouble?"

"No. *He* is."

"What's going on?"

I turned my full attention to her. Nick had obviously set this tent scenario up because I was coming to Sheffield today. But could he have known I'd invite Emma? Probably not. Or maybe he had a direct line into my head through the curse and today was the day *because* I'd invited Emma. That line of thinking brought up a lot of questions about free will and shit. Absolutely no interest in pondering that. Leave that to the taxi drivers. All that mattered was, would Emma be safe around Nick? Was this going to be a Spider-Man scenario where supervillains tried to get to me via my Mary Jane? What would I want if I were Mary Jane? To be safe? Or to be given a choice?

"I'm not sure what's going on," I said, truthfully. "But it's bound to be something absurd." I sighed. "Being selfish, I want you to come so I don't make a fool of myself like I normally do. But . . ."

She held out her hand. "Brad said to hurry."

I took it. She pulled me towards the tent. I pulled and spun her back to face me. I leaned in, ran my fingers through her hair, gripped the back of her head, and kissed her like it was the last time.

Just in case.

Inside was a surreal tableau. Underneath everything I'm about to describe was, of course, an artificial football pitch with all its markings and yes, even the goal nets and corner flags still in place. But in one large square area was the stuff that had given me wedding ceremony vibes: on the prosaic side, a lectern, a large screen connected to a laptop, and a couple of rows of chairs. To the left and to the right there were two premium recliner chair things. Obviously one was for Nick and one was for the owner of the football club. Status symbols. Mini thrones.

To one side was a vast, six-star hotel buffet. Dotted around were Greek plinths, and on each was a selection of beverages. In places where there was no practical furniture, there were massive plant pots—huge-leafed things I didn't know the names of, spectacular orchids in white and blue, white and blue roses, those plants that go *wooh*, and even a small, decrepit tree bearing one solitary lemon.

Behind the computer screen to the left was a freestanding poster proudly displaying a brand I didn't know: GOP, which came with a logo of a mighty frog and some writing in Thai.

The same to the right was a very generic business logo that could have been from any company in any country in the world. It was also based around three letters: O.N.E. Soccer.

Flowing over the screen was a giant wedding arch thing, with blue and white flowers intertwined.

Old Nick was sipping prosecco by one of the plinths, chatting handsomely to a guy who looked Thai. The elderly man in the blue pyjamas—also Thai—was being helped into one of the recliners. Nick's minions—three short guys who seemed to be from a different country every time I looked at them—were fussing around the laptop, checking brochures, saying, "Testing" into a Tony Robbins-style wraparound headset. For some reason, those little pricks wound me all the way up. The more I watched them, the more I became convinced they weren't real people. If Nick was a demon, they were imps. Sub-demons. I didn't care what the proper term was. I just wanted to pound their faces or throw holy water on them. Four more Thai guys—actual humans for sure—were milling around the halfway line taking awful shots at the distant goals, while two women were slumped into chairs looking bored to death already. Completing the scene were a dozen waiters and waitresses, plus a manager type who was only a few uniform iterations away from looking like a Death Star officer.

"Max," said Brad in an urgent whisper. I had, naturally, strode right into the middle of the VIP area. I turned towards the sound of his voice and was surprised to see he was quite far away, standing with Summers and Emma by a shitty little plastic table. I let out an amused chuckle as I walked over there; the first thing I did was grab the table and jiggle it.

"Of course it wobbles," I said, exasperated. The contrast between this little scene and the decadence of the rich people's area was a bit on the nose. A bit overdone, tbh.

"Craig is pressed for time," said Brad.

He was making me aware that I was inadvertently being rude. "Okay," I said, facing the Sheffield Wednesday manager.

"Max," he said, smiling at me. "We've watched your clips. It's a small sample size but sometimes things are clear. Really clear. You could do a job for us, we're sure. I have to be upfront with you, though, I'm not really a fan of the showboating." Ah. The first example of my dickery coming back to haunt me.

"You're a fan of me getting someone sent off. It's not like I'm Antony."

"Who's that?" said Emma.

"Guy who plays for Man United," I said. "His big party piece is to get the ball and spin around in a perfect circle. It's absolutely hilarious and completely pointless. It's like all those zips on your jacket. They're just for people to talk about. Which, you know, has its own value. But it's not a football purist kind of value. Do you know what I mean? It doesn't bring you closer to winning. Whereas everything I do on a football pitch is part of a narrative. At worst it's mathematical. Calculating. At best, it's part of an emotional journey I take the fans on. I don't expect everyone to understand me or my process. The life of a tortured artist is hard."

Summers rubbed his neck for a while, then exploded with laughter. "Fucking hell, Max. You could talk shit for Britain. Fuck me." He laughed some more, and slowly got serious. "Brad says I don't need to sell you on the history of the club."

"Playing for a club like this is beyond my wildest dreams," I said, surprised by my own authenticity.

"Well," said Summers, trying to subdue a proud little smile. "It doesn't have to be a dream. We understand you have an . . . unconventional contract. Which makes things easy. It's just a question of wages."

"No," I said.

"Excuse me?"

"You have to give Darlington something."

"Something? What kind of something?"

I shrugged, and took a mental photo of Brad's appalled face to laugh at later. "I don't really care what. Just something more than nothing. How much is a team bus? I don't know. Fifty thousand pounds would go a long way down there."

Summers smiled. "I think we can stretch to that, Max."

"I'm sure such a trivial amount won't affect Max's wages," said Brad, who tried to take control of the haggling.

Summers looked at his watch. He had somewhere to be. "Three thousand."

Emma spluttered. "Three thousand a month? To kick a ball around?"

Brad loved that. It gave him the chance to say, "Three thousand a *week*." Emma's jaw dropped. I frowned. Hadn't I discussed Henri's salary in front of her? "Of course," Brad added, "that's actually not very much for a player of Max's talents."

"It isn't?" said Summers, grinning hugely.

"Inflation. The cost-of-living crisis. Energy bills. Three thousand would barely heat Max's bedroom." Like my hypothetical property, Brad was just getting warmed up. It was clear he lived for these negotiations.

"Guys," I said. "Don't waste too much energy on the discussion. I'd like to know my worth, but it might soon be moot."

"Moot?" said Brad.

"Yeah. Moot." I was being called to the VIP area. By my own personal demons, maybe. Think what you want.

Emma snapped to attention. "Max! What are you thinking?"

"Emma," I said. "That's my secret." I winked at her. "I *never* think."

It was an epic line.

World-class posturing.

I left a dramatic pause.

There was absolutely no reaction of any kind. I was flabbergasted.

"*None* of you have seen *The Avengers*? It's literally the number one movie of all time. What is *happening*?" I sighed. "I'm just going over there for a minute. See if that guy is who I think he is. No big deal."

I sauntered over to the nearest plinth and picked up a prosecco. I smelled it, then took a massive swig. It hit nice. Real nice. I took the rest and a spare with me over to the laptop. The minions tried to intercept me.

"Aggression twenty," I said, eyes red and fiery, teeth gnashing. They chirped like fucking mad birds, then scattered to the winds. Their PowerPoint was on the laptop but not being transmitted onto the big screen just yet. I quickly flicked through the twenty-five slides, then went back and started again, this time slightly slower. When I finished, I looked over at Nick. He made eye contact with me for the first time. He smiled.

"It's time," he said, and the VIPs made their way to their seats. One of the four guys who'd been taking shots dribbled a ball to the VIP zone and threatened to blast it at one woman's face. His wife? His sister? He laughed as she flinched, then reacted to my glare with surprise and hostility; I found myself clenching my fists.

Slippery, Max. Be slippery.

It was one thing fighting Old Nick in whatever format this would take, but outright rage and actual physical violence was not going to help me achieve *any* of my goals. Also, Emma was watching.

Instead of pounding the guy to death, I collected the ball and made little circles with it under my right foot. Having something physical to do was calming.

The prick was the last to take his seat, at which point all the lights in the place dimmed, and new ones came on. Spotlights. Half pointed at me. Half at Nick. At least one light stayed on Nick at all times, which based on the lighting setup I'd seen was literally impossible. As the scene unfolded, I sensed Emma, Brad, and Summers edge closer to the VIP section, but once they were there, they didn't move. No one moved. It was like they *couldn't*.

"Ladies and gentlemen," Nick said. "Distinguished members of the Gop family. O.N.E. Soccer thanks you in the warmest possible terms for your tremendous hospitality." He gave a tiny bow. "Before we begin, let me introduce an old friend. You might say, an old sparring partner. Something of a prodigy." I wasn't sure if he said prodigy or protégé. Either would fit, I supposed, but I would have liked to know. "Introducing Max Best." We were there, standing before the wedding arch, like bride and groom. "Don't tell anyone I said this," he said in a stage whisper, "but you're looking at the future of football."

He was delighted by this line. And quite right, too. Everyone thought he was complimenting *me*. I decided to piss in his boots. "Am I?" I said, staring at the *real* future of football.

There was the tiniest moment of volcanic anger. Blink and you'd miss it. He composed himself. "Max Best. Football manager extraordinaire. How *is* your career in football management going, Max?"

I raised one eyebrow. "Well, I'm more of a player these days," I said, flicking the football up and doing some simple kick-ups. The Thai guys—brothers, I supposed—immediately became more interested, so I started bouncing the ball on my head. Like a genius. Like a performing seal. I'll let you choose. "By the way, I'm guessing you don't go by the same name anymore. What should I call you this time?"

His eyes were bouncing up and down, waiting for the ball to fall. His face contorted when he realised the ball would *not* fall. He tried to let the expression slip off his face but was only partly successful.

"Max! You've always called me Nick . . ." Then he added, so quietly only I could hear, "or some variant." Louder again. "Nick will do for an old friend. But as you *know*, amongst this circle I'm known as Zakan Nicolini." Za-kan, as in, za-can you believe it? "COULD YOU," he started, then laughed. "Could you please stop bouncing the ball?"

"Oh, sure." I headed the ball slightly sideways, then turned and wellied it towards one of the goals. The ball whizzed sixty yards and bounced up into the roof of the net. I glanced around—sure, it was dark over there, but everyone had seen it. The Thai guys, even the prick, were smitten. I smirked. "I forgot you're not interested in football, Nick."

His eyes flickered towards the Gops. That was a very definite point to me, even though I didn't know what the game was. He stepped to the left of me and put his right arm around my shoulders. He smelled of lemons. "I'm surprised, though, Max. You were always much more interested in becoming a football *manager*."

"My management career is on hold," I said. "As you *know*, I need to build a *reputation* in order to get a job. Hence my becoming a *player*."

He grinned. His teeth were huge. "Max! Why make things so complicated? All you need do is apply for a job. Who would turn you down?" His words sent shivers down my spine. Was he fucking with me? It didn't sound like it. It sounded like the truth. I'd gone so far around the houses in my quest to become a manager, I'd forgotten to try the single most simple thing. Seeing that his words had hit home, Nick continued. "Now, if you'll excuse me, I'm about to deliver a very important presentation." He tried to ease me away.

"Oh," I said, not budging. "I've got a better idea. Why don't we do it together?"

"Together?"

"Yes," I said. "You told me I needed to work on my public speaking skills. Remember?" He could hardly say no, so I pressed on. "And

I did a very good sermon in that church you go to. You weren't there that day, more's the pity. I was rather hoping to impress you. I'm not very good at public speaking," I said, in the vague direction of the Thai group. "But I'm succinct. I'll whizz through this presentation—there's only one slide that's important, anyway. And Nick can fill in the gaps."

"You are not familiar with the material," said one of the imps, in heavily accented English that modulated every time I heard it.

"Wait," said Nick, his smile enormous. And dangerous. "This could be quite entertaining. Go ahead, Max. Let's do it your way." He took a couple of steps away and folded his arms. While I talked, he looked from me to the Thais.

I looked at the Thai contingent. "You guys are the owners?" Some nods. "Do I need to simplify my English or does everyone understand everything?"

"We understand everything except who you are and why you're talking," said the one I'd taken a dislike to. Probably the oldest son. If I had to create a backstory for him, I'd say he was the guy who started all the aggro in his neighbourhood knowing that he had two bodyguards within shouting distance at all times.

Slippery, Max.

I pointed at the nearest imp. "Would you please send the signal from the laptop to the screen?"

He didn't want to move closer to me. "Press F-twelve," he said.

I did; it worked. "Thanks, bro. Help yourself to some piri piri chicken." The guy nodded happily, and started towards the buffet. A glance from Nick made him sit back down. We started on slide one. "Generic crap." I pressed the right arrow. "Crap. Crap." On the third *crap*, Nick let out a big laugh. Slide four came up. I looked at the Thai guys. "This should be the most obvious slide, but it's not. These twats are trying to buy Sheffield Wednesday from you. Is that right?"

Nick answered for them. "We're humble facilitators, Max. We match buyers and sellers. And the Gop family want to retain a significant holding. They love this club." He smiled in a way that set all my nerves jangling. "And so do we."

"Amazing," I said. "Since you don't know the first thing about football." The imps bristled, but once again a stern look was enough to quell them. "In fact, I'd say I've forgotten more about football than you know. Does that sound about right, Nick?"

He put his hands behind his back and took a kind of military stance. I wondered if he knew he was doing it. "I might have conceded the point, Max, until recently. But you know, since I watched you play I've become passionate about the sport. You might say you inflamed me."

So there it was. He was blaming *me* for *his* sloppiness. "You're welcome. But I must confess, this presentation is impressive." I laughed. "Wickedly impressive. You've learned a lot in a short time."

He grinned. "I didn't come up with this proposal. This is the brainchild of someone very much like yourself."

Oh-kay. That felt like confirmation that there were more people who'd been cursed with the Champion Manager interface. No bueno. I let it slip off me. Problem for another day. "It's strange, though. I heard the owners wanted to improve the facilities. I got the impression they were *good* owners. Committed. Long-term." I scratched my head. "It must be a fucking good proposal to make them want to give up control. So let's continue." I clicked through the next couple of slides. "Lies. Bullshit. *This* whole slide is pure fluff. The writer is clearly paid by the slide."

"It's thematic, Max," said Nick. "It pays off later."

I made a scoffing noise. With one more key press, I was looking at the Rosetta Stone to understanding this mystery. A diagram showing a connection between several football clubs. At the top of the page was the heading *Multi-Club Model*. In pride of place just underneath that was a big stadium. Below it, joined by a dotted line, was a medium-sized stadium. And below that were five tiny baby stadiums. It was all very cute. Very Goldilocks. "Slide seven. You might call it an organisation chart. We'll come back to this. I wonder how long Nick would have spent on it. Probably not long because it's the key to the whole scam. Slide eight, guff. Nine, bullshit. Ten, lies. It goes on like this till the end. How am I doing so far, Nick?"

"Not well. But you're right about being succinct." That line got a laugh. Fair enough.

"All right, let's zoom out a little bit." I clicked my head left and right like in a kung fu movie. I was getting riled up by the contents of slide seven. That was no good. Visible anger wasn't the right vibe, here. Slip, slip, slip, slip awaaay.

I thought about what I wanted to say. The right tone. The right words. I noticed that everyone was waiting for me. That was so *strange*.

Nick had done something to them, I was sure of it. But then there was also influence 20—since I'd been cursed, people had been listening to me. When I spoke from the heart, they responded. So I'd speak from the heart.

I cleared my throat.

"I'm from Manchester. I've never even been to Sheffield before. When I think about Sheffield Wednesday I only have romantic thoughts. There, Emma, I confess. I'm romantic; you got me." Some of the audience turned to see who I was talking to. "Sheffield Wednesday, though. Jesus Christ, it's ancient. What does it say on the stadium roof? 1867, isn't it? How many things are that old and still thriving? It's impossible to imagine all the fans who've been through those turnstiles. It's almost impossible to think of all the players. Nick told you one true thing, at least. I *would* like to be a manager. How many managers have there been since 1867? I can just imagine them in a line, with their changing fashions, their hats, their moustaches. They'd look at me with my hoodie and my trainers and my liberal philosophies and think I was the weirdest man they'd ever seen. But one chat about football and all that would evaporate. We'd disagree on the specifics. Which formation, how attacking, how many matches can you play in a week, how many bags of crisps before a match is too many? Yeah, we'd disagree. But we'd disagree over a pint. As friends. Because at heart, we'd all be on the same page. We'd all see football the same way, I'm sure of it."

I strolled up and down while I considered the next bit.

"What I mean is, the essentials. The fundamentals. Some philosophical things, maybe. Like: you've got to try to win but there's more important things than winning. So what's more important than winning? The health of the sport. If you love football, then football's more important than your club.

"What is football? In England, it's the pyramid. These pricks, these consultants, these investors, these fucking, what are they called? Hedge funds. You say the word pyramid and people like that think of the ancient times. Cities buried under dust. But English football is vibrant. It's bouncing. It's in a state of constant renewal." I went and touched one of the orchids. "This pyramid, our pyramid, is green and alive. The strong rise to the top and the weak are cast aside. And when a club wastes its resources, its nutrients, it withers, and when it's been fallow for long enough, the sun shines on it once more and it comes roaring back to life. Sheffield Wednesday has had a bad time, and now it's in rude health again. I love to see it. Storing energy in its roots, husbanding its water, ready to fucking bloom, mate."

I directed this last comment at Nick, who was regarding me with a princely smile. He was pressing his fingertips together. "I think we've gone far enough off topic, Max. How about you go back to Sunderland and let us continue with our day?"

He came at me.

I pointed to his throne. "How about you sit down and listen?" He reacted like he'd walked into an invisible wall. His nostrils flared. "By the way," I added. "And this is *really* off-topic, where's your bicycle?"

That absolutely floored him. He stared at me, almost blankly, but there was just the tiniest eye movement in the direction of the tent entrance.

Ah! The helicopter. He hadn't just chained his bike up at some train station and hopped into his chopper. He'd upgraded! I had a sudden burst of insight—when I used the curse, when I gained XP, when I acquired TINOs, Nick was growing stronger to an equal degree. Symbiotic. I needed him if I wanted to get to the top. But he needed me, too. Without me, he was little better than an imp.

He'd done well to bestow his gift on me. I would grind. I'd stand in the cold and the rain in dogged pursuit of progression. I could survive with less human contact than most, even going as far as to ask the sexiest woman alive to take second place to Holland versus the USA.

But his choice was fraught with danger. I don't mean him accidentally turning me into a good player. I mean the fact that I was exactly the type of person who would cut off my nose to spite my face.

I must have started grinning like a maniac or something because Nick became visibly less confident. I went into my screens and hovered my attention above the Retire button.

Would I really click it? If I did, presumably I'd revert to being average at all aspects of football. But I'd still have Emma. For a while. She wouldn't understand why I'd suddenly quit, so that was a risk. I'd need to throw myself into some new hobby. Announce my intention to become a world champion bonsai tree sculptor. Or maybe I'd focus on disabled football! The pay was shit, but I'd be above average as a manager in that world. I'd already proven *that* without the curse helping. Emma was going to be a hotshot lawyer, right? She could be the breadwinner while I turned strikers into defenders and defenders into flying wingers and all that.

Yes. I could do it. I could trigger the bomb and survive.

I didn't *want* to hit retire. But it'd hurt Nick a lot more than it'd hurt me. I'd do it if I had to.

My grin widened. I must have looked pretty sinister, because Nick backed down. "I had a long trip," said Nick. "Maybe I will sit down after all. Thanks for suggesting it, Max."

Slippery Nick.

I could be slippery, too. I went all the way from burn-it-all-down to diligent youth in half a heartbeat. "You're very welcome, Nick. Please do look after yourself. If anything happened to you, I'd be devastated."

He grimaced and looked away.

"Where was I?" I said. "Ah, yes. The pyramid. A team on an upward trajectory. Two teams, in fact. Yes, it's exciting times in Sheffield.

"Sheffield," I said, looking around as though I could see through the thick walls of whatever the tent was made from onto the streets around us. "Sheffield. Everyone knows Wednesday, and United have been in the Premier League recently, and should be again soon. But there's a third team. There's also Sheffield FC. The oldest club in the world! The actual oldest! No one says football was born in Sheffield. That honour probably goes to Manchester. I'll have to check that. But holy shit! What have we got here? Three of the five oldest football teams? It's historic! Football is woven into the threads of this city like a tapestry. Hundreds of years of success and failure, carved into the buildings, written into the music.

"Now," I said, turning back to the screen. "Slide seven of this proposal. Oh, boy. Let's take a good, hard look at this. On the top here, you have a football club. Below it, you have another club. Below *that* one, you have five, six, seven feeder clubs. It doesn't matter which club is yours, because this model kills *everyone*. But let's start from the bottom. This feeder here, Waffle FC, is in Belgium. They play in the Belgian league, division two or whatever, and recruit in their local area. They also get sent players from the . . . what do we call this? Multi-club HQ? They get sent players from the mothership. Then every year, Waffle FC send five players here." I moved my hand from the third level to the second. "Let's call this club, oh, I don't know, Sheffield Wednesday. But actually, that's a bit unwieldy. We're talking about the future of football, here, aren't we Nick? It isn't very 2045, if you know what I mean. So let's streamline it to Wednesday. Change the badge from an owl to a big W.

"Wednesday also get sent five players from a club in . . ." I leaned forward—the font was very faint—and couldn't believe my eyes. "Nigeria." I tried to glance at Emma, but with the spotlights I only saw her silhouette. Belgium. Nigeria. Those were exactly what I'd said in the car on the way here! Was Brad part of this? *Still*, no one made any move to stop my rant. "Five players from here, from there, from there. Great. These guys play reserve matches for Sheffield. They do well. They play first team matches. And the best ones get moved up to the top club. The only one that actually matters. The first level. Manchester City. Chelsea. Paris. Choose a city, choose a colour, they'll all be the same."

"It could be Sheffield at the top," said Nick, with an unattractive amount of petulance. He turned to the old man. "If they act fast."

I shook my head. "It's better to be at the top, but it's still shit. I don't see Wednesday making up the ground in time. No, they'll definitely end up in the middle." I picked up my prosecco and flung the rest down my throat. "You know what's been going through my head ever since I saw this slide? Sausage factory." I shook my head. "But this isn't a sausage factory. It's not even that dignified. This turns Sheffield Wednesday, formed 1867, into a sausage *assembly plant*. The meat comes from this club." I slapped one of the low-level clubs. "The outside thing. The sausage condom thing. What is it? Gelatine? The gelatine comes from here." I slapped another one. "The packaging comes from here. They all get sent to Sheffield. Some coaches here put the whole thing together and call it a football player. The ones that smell the best get sent to the mothership. Most will never play a meaningful game of football."

"Max!" said Nick, with heat. "That's a step too far. Stop heading down this fantastical path." He stood and paced around. "This model is healthy; everyone's doing it. It provides stability and certainty for everyone involved. We've had our differences, but you're one of the most talented young men I've ever met. Look at this slide. Really look at it! Any one of these clubs would be perfect for someone with your skills. A director of football." He pointed at the dotted lines, which I knew represented the flow of players. "Talent ID. Checking the coaches are improving the prospects. Monitoring the managers. Once you've got things rolling, you could even manage one of the teams yourself. I know you'd like that."

"How much?"

That threw him. "Excuse me?"

"If you're offering me a job, what's the salary?"

"This isn't the forum for such a discussion, Max," he said, all smiles again. He nodded towards Summers and Brad. "But take what they're offering and double it."

"They're already going to double it."

His smile doubled. "Then double that."

That would be over half a million a year. To do what? Scout players and manage a team? Almost my dream job. Almost.

"I'll think about it," I said. "I'll get my people to call your people. I have to say I'm not all that inclined to accept. You see, the most fun I've had recently was managing a disabled team. And after that it's probably managing eight talented kids against eleven average ones. Fair contests. Meaningful matches. Oh, not meaningful in a global sense. But absolutely the most important hour of those kids' weeks. There were stakes.

"And that's one of the many, many problems with this model. Let me walk you through it. In this model, in this brave new world, Sheffield We—sorry, *Wednesday*—are owned by Manchester City. So they can't play in the same division. That would be ludicrous, even for these guys. Look at Nick here. You think he could own two teams in the same league? You think he'd hesitate before ordering one team to lose to the other? No way. Be serious! So even in this dystopian nightmare where City own Wednesday and United own United and Chelsea own Birmingham, the owned and the owners wouldn't be allowed in the same division. But guess what? The top twenty teams own the next best twenty. So say goodbye to promotion and relegation! Say goodbye to the pyramid! To the very concept of competition! Bye bye Darlo! Bye bye Chester! And if you think that's not important, then fuck you. You shouldn't be in this room."

I'd gone slightly feral and forced myself to calm down. *Slippery! Emma watching!* I told myself to count to ten and got to, I don't know, three?

"So Wednesday now exists to collect players from down here and train them a bit before delivering them to their new masters up here. That is literally the only function of the club. Every year, forty-nine out of fifty players don't make it. They don't progress. They go home, having wasted their youth on a pipe dream. It takes years, but eventually in *this* part of Belgium and *this* part of Nigeria, Sheffield becomes synonymous with heartbreak and misery.

"And of the first ten players who *are* deemed good enough, who *do* make it to the top, still only one gets to play. So ninety percent of the *good* players are chewed up and spat out. No, that doesn't fit my metaphor. They aren't even chewed. They're just binned. Misery, misery, misery. This chart, this process, almost seems designed to inflict misery, doesn't it? Why would someone do that? Good question."

I won a brief staring contest with Nick.

"Now I want everyone here to take a look at this org chart and tell me which word is missing. Go on. Shout out. There's a word missing from this chart. I'll give you a clue. I've said it about fifty times."

I waited. The Thai guys leaned closer and tried to puzzle it out. The imps looked around, nervously. Nick had been amused by this interlude at first, but was growing increasingly angry. He was smouldering now. I wondered if Emma thought it was hot.

Finally, someone called out. "Sheffield!"

I shielded my eyes and saw that it was one of the waiters. Like everyone else, none of them had moved an inch while the lights were shining on me.

"That's right, mate. Sheffield." I let that word echo. As I'd been ranting, I'd started to realise who my true audience was. It should have been obvious, but it's easy in hindsight and when everything's laid out for you. I moved closer to the old man in the blue pyjamas. "Sheffield," I said, wistfully. "It's not on there. For one hundred and fifty years, getting on for two hundred, there has been a pathway from the streets outside this building to these pitches here. From Leppings Lane and . . . look, I don't know the names of the areas. But from all these places, these estates, these blocks of flats, there's always been the dream of playing for Wednesday. You've seen it! Dads taking their kids to the games. The kids dream of running out onto the pitch wearing the kit, making their dads proud. The dads dream of their kids playing. You don't own a football club. You own a dream factory. It's an endless loop, and all it takes is one talented little shit every few years to make it into the blue and white. You've heard them when some local kid runs onto the pitch as an eighty-eighth-minute sub. They fucking love it."

I slapped the screen.

"Turns out the endless loop has an end! What excuse would you give if anyone noticed, Nick? Not cost effective to train local kids? Cheaper to ship randos in from Belgium? The truth is, Mr. Gop, he's only interested in misery. He has zero interest in football. The club in the middle of this chart could be anywhere. Place? Community? A feeling of belonging? He wants that gone. The idea of severing the link between a hundred thousand people and the one thing they have in common, *that* excites Nick. That's catnip to him. And anyway, what would it *matter* if the team was made of local kids or international talents? The league will basically be a series of preseason friendlies. No promotion. No relegation. No stakes. No drama. No excitement. You're getting twenty thousand fans a match now because what you're doing means something. It has value. It's exciting. Even when it isn't exciting, it's real. It's honest." I tapped the screen. "This isn't football. This isn't sport. This is a process. It's sterile.

"I'm nearly done. So let's be completely clear about something. Twenty years from now, when Wednesday home matches are watched by two thousand people, and a group of former fans gets together and one of them asks, 'Hey, why did *you* stop going?', not a single one of them will point the blame at you, Mr. Gop. They'll all think you were a good owner. They'll blame whoever these pricks have lined up to replace you. I think it's very important that you know that not a single Sheffield Wednesday fan will put two and two together. This meeting's here instead of at the stadium to keep it secret, right? So don't worry about your name. Don't worry about your legacy." I moved close to the old guy. He returned my eye contact stronger than anyone I'd met since I got cursed. Our staring contest was epic. Sizzling. "But I'll know," I said. I jabbed my finger towards his nose. "And you'll know."

I stood back up and the lights went on. Nick glanced around, irritated. That hadn't been part of his plan.

"And you, you prick," I said, taking a few steps towards him. "You've learned enough about football to be dangerous. Hats off to you. You've proven you aren't as lazy and incompetent as you seem." I spread my arms wide. "But you still know fuck all! Yeah, you could take this model and piss people off. Make hundreds of thousands of people unhappy. But you don't get it. It won't be that long—twenty, twenty-five years, and this multi-club abomination will fold. No fan wants this. No fans, no club. And at some point, sooner than you think, there'll be a phoenix club. Sheffield Thursday. Fan owned. They'll start with 200 members. One by one, the faithful will leave Hillsborough and go and see what all the fuss is about. They'll hear their songs sung with gusto. They'll see people like them roaring on players like them. They'll think, hey, my son could play here. And that'll be that. You'll be fucked. Your creation will implode, and one day the fans will get the rights to the name and the badge. Wednesday will be reborn, an owl on the chest, fan-owned, safe from the likes of you forever, with the main word back in place: Sheffield."

I thought about giving him a double middle finger, but decided he wasn't worth it. I was about to leave when there was a burst of applause. It took me a second to locate its source, because like the rich twats I'd almost totally ignored the workers. But they were the only people from Sheffield who were present, and six or seven of them were clapping. I raised my fist in solidarity, gave Nick one final fuck-you glare, then strode towards the exit.

40

PLAY ON

Football glossary: *Play on. Continue the game. Your player was kicked, but you have the ball in an advantageous position. So play on!*

Saturday, December 10.

The first team gathered at Eastbourne and stayed indoors for as long as possible while our kit and bags were loaded onto the team bus. Indoors. Out of the cold, and boy was it cold. Our training pitches were under a foot of snow. We were heading south, far south, the deep south. Almost as far as *Bristol*. I tried to remember if I'd ever been farther from Manchester, and decided that no, Gloucester would be a new record.

Gloucester City. Good team. Just short of the playoff spots. Beat us and they'd move up to fifth or sixth.

The lads weren't talking about football, though. They were twenty weathermen, navigating fifteen different apps that they all swore by. *That's a good app for Darlington, but it doesn't know shit about the south. The south? We're not driving to Italy. It's still England, mate. I've got two apps; one for the summer. The winter one says Gloucester is buried. Buried, mate. You'll see.*

If the wisdom of the crowd is a real thing, then it seemed probable that our match wouldn't take place. We'd drive four hours to the home of everyone's fourth favourite cheese, the referee would arrive and declare the pitch unsafe, and we'd all pile back on the bus.

Football is about glory.

When the last bag was loaded, an infuriated Cutter barked at us to get onboard. We raced on like little kids, hopping over the snow, the snow is lava, piling into the doorway like the Marx Brothers. I got on last and Pat closed the doors behind me. The bus didn't seem much warmer than the outside world. That's because it wasn't. I checked the road ahead of us and glanced around at Cutter and the coaches. "Pat," I said. "Anyone asks you to go faster, send them to me."

"Ah, Max," he said. "I'm the captain of this vessel. Don't worry about me taking any risks. No chance. Not for all the tea in China." He peeled away. The bus slipped along, crunching snow underwheel. I had a bad feeling about this. Pat turned a fraction to check my face. "You go sit down, now. I'll steer you right."

Yeah, no. It wasn't Pat's driving that had me on edge. What was it?

I settled in next to Junior and tried to chill. Put one of my flea market earbuds in and realised it hadn't charged. Seething, I shoved it back into its case and jammed it into my backpack. Three, four, five thousand pounds a week. Just go to some team for a couple of years! Why the fuck not! Even Junior had a pair of expensive headphones.

I tapped him and he took them off. "Junior, mate. Is that logo upside down?"

"Huh? What?"

"Your Beats headphones. The logo seems wrong."

"Ah." He grinned. "They're not Beats. They're Peates." He waited. "Max, it's a knock-off."

"Oh!" A cheap imitation brand. "Oh, that's all right then."

He tutted and put them back on. I thought I heard a voice like a teacher, but on his tablet was an action movie. Weird.

A few minutes later, I got a text.

Emma: I put your photo on Insta. It's my fave. Let me know if you don't like it and I'll take it down. But I hope you let me keep it.

I sighed and tapped Junior again.
"What, Max?"
"You on Instagram?"
"Yeah. Who isn't?"
"Me. My girlfriend just put up some picture. Can you go there and show me?"

He tutted again. "Just sign up, Max. It's photos. It's not going to suck your brain out." I raised my eyebrows and pointed at his phone.

He paused his action movie, but I noticed the sound didn't pause. Huh. He took his phone out and went into Instagram. "What's her username? You don't know?"

"Type Emma Weaver." He did. It brought up a list of accounts. He started scrolling down and I said, "Whoa! Slow down there matey. It was the first one."

He laughed. "Max. You've been catfished. That's not a real account. That's like an AI generated girl. Did she ask for your bank details yet?"

"Click on it."

"Huh. Okay there's a picture of you. I notice you're not in the photo with her. That's suspish. Then there's, ah, hey. I need to be alone with these for a minute. Okay! Jesus. I'm *joking*."

"Gimme," I said.

He handed the phone over and I saw a photo of Emma and Gemma on a beach somewhere. It looked warm, but that might have been a filter. Maybe they were in Skegness. But maybe they were in Ibiza. Why not? Normal people had holidays abroad.

I pinched the screen to focus on Emma's face and drifted into my memories. Just after my outburst in the tent at Sheffield Wednesday's training ground.

I collected Emma on my way out and we walked past the Rolls Royces and onto the street. I knew enough about the layout of Sheffield to turn left and head towards the big stadium. There we bought tram tickets and hopped on one to the city centre. It seemed totally normal to make our own way home. It had the added benefit of not drawing attention to Brad and Summers. No need for their relationship with the club's owners to turn sour.

The tram accelerated away from Leppings Lane and trundled towards the city centre.

It took a while but Emma finally looked at me and said, "What just happened?"

I put my middle finger to the bridge of my nose and rubbed in a circle. "Good question." I took a minute to think of a possible explanation that would satisfy her curiosity and ideally put an end to all follow-ups. "I met Nick when I was working in the bank." That was good. A lie wrapped in truth. "Long story short, I helped him out once and he sort of latched onto me. He tried to bribe me. He's charming and everything, but he's a con man. A trickster. As soon as I saw him get off that helicopter, I was looking for the scam."

"Why did he let you stand there and wreck his deal?"

I shrugged. "People like that are arrogant. They always think they'll come out on top. And he's a showman. Loves drama. No, I get why *he* did it. I'm more interested in why no one else tried to shut me up."

"Well," she said, then bit her bottom lip. "It was pretty hot. Why interrupt a man in the throes of passion? Know what I mean? When the lights went out I was just . . . enchanted. And I wasn't the only one. I saw Brad run towards you like he was going to intervene, but then he changed his mind. Just like that." She snapped her fingers.

Enchanted. Ah. Okay. I went internal to ponder that. It seemed that Nick had subdued everyone to let me do my speech. No, that wasn't right. It was for *his* speech, and I'd interrupted him. But he'd waited till I was there. He must have known I'd do something like what I did. Or maybe it wasn't any kind of extra enchantment—maybe what happened was simply what happened when someone with influence 20 got on his soapbox.

Emma snapped me out of it. "But don't you want to play for Sheffield?"

I looked around the tram to see if anyone had heard. Leaning towards her, I whispered, "They don't like it when you call a team *Sheffield*."

"The con man did."

"Exactly." I leaned back and returned to a normal voice. "Would I like to play for Wednesday? Sure. I'd prefer to *manage* them. But er . . ." Thoughts that had bubbled up during my rant resurfaced. "Sometimes," I said, carefully, watching for her reaction, "sometimes I think I'd like to give it all up and manage a disabled team. Or do something totally different." I waved my hand around trying to think of an example. "Rescuing . . . swans . . . from trees. I don't know."

"As long as it's not becoming a butcher," she said. "Sausage skins are made of collagen." She shook her head at my ignorance of this basic fact of life. "Can you live off managing a disabled team? I thought it was all volunteers."

"It's not a lucrative career. I was thinking I might sponge off my rich lawyer girlfriend."

"You were thinking that, were you?"

"I was maybe thinking that?"

She gave me a weird look. I was convinced I'd blown it, blown the whole relationship, but she said, "You'll have to do the dishes."

"Deal." We shook hands. "Anyway," I continued, "I'll only be poor for a few more years. I've still got my clients. When James hits the Premier League, I'll buy us a dishwasher." I settled back and put my arm around her while the tram jiggled us around. "A dishwasher. A flash car. Holiday in Tahiti. And even," I said, punctuating the thought with a tiny gasp, "a nice suit."

Emma squirmed her head into the crook of my neck. "Forget the suit. Forget the car. My Max Best won't give up his dream so easily."

"I notice you didn't say forget Tahiti."

"Yeah, well," she said. "You can take a *break* from your dream. You have my permission to take a two-week break. Twice a year."

"Uh, Max?"

Junior was trying to pull his phone away. "Oh. Wait a second." I unpinched the screen so that Gemma was visible again.

"She's hot. Is she single?"

"She's seeing Henri Lyons. Fancy your chances?"

"Against him? Yeah!"

"Really?"

"Maybe not. He's got that accent. Anyway, he's a good guy. Helped me a lot."

I think Junior was giving examples of Henri's tips and tricks, but I was back in my memories.

We walked around Sheffield city centre for exactly thirty minutes. Emma's phone beeped.

"You set a timer?" I said, appalled.

She was unmoved. "Max. A deal's a deal. It's been half an hour and we didn't find it by, what did you call it? Kismet? Now be a big boy and ask a local for directions. Like we agreed."

I shook my head, mildly annoyed. I didn't want to ask for help, but she was right—a deal's a deal. So I looked around the busy street we were on, then burst into a massive smile. "Great, come on." I gripped her by the hand and we darted across to intercept an extremely beautiful woman. "Hi there," I said.

She was a Gemma type—tall, thin, long, wavy black hair—but much more my type of Gemma type. She had a coldness to her eyes and a hint of playfulness to her lips. She glanced from me to Emma to me to Emma. "Hi," she said, avoiding making any facial expression. Her eyes drifted to my hands—I was carrying my little boot bag and a Sheffield Wednesday shirt.

"Sorry to bother you. We're looking for Planetology."

"Plantology," said Emma.

"Well," I said with my cutest smile. "I'm looking for Planetology and she's looking for Plantology. I'd love directions to the nearest one."

The smile did the trick. The Gemma-type smiled back. "Planning your wedding in space? Plantology's great." She came next to me to point down the road and tell me where to go. But also, maybe a little bit, she came next to me to come next to me. "And then cross the street and it's there," she finished.

"Thanks," I said.

"Yeah thanks," said Emma, trying to pull me away.

"Do you play for Wednesday?" said the woman.

Emma let go of my hand. Danger!

"No," I said. "We just got a tour of the stadium. Didn't we, honeybunch? Pumplekins? Snuggles?"

Emma said something like "yeah, sure" then louder, she said, "Those guys look like they know a good place to eat. I'll go check with them."

And she wandered a few yards away and waved at a couple of handsome guys in stylish coats with nice hair. One had big designer glasses and the other a chunky, expensive-looking watch. They immediately began to fawn over her while she giggled excessively. Shameless.

The Gemma-type spoke. I checked her face—cold amusement. "I think your girlfriend is winning this game," she said.

"We're all winners if we all enjoy it," I said, watching her response carefully.

Her eyebrows raised a fraction and there was a little twitch of a smile. Her cold eyes heated up. "Enjoy your meal," she said. "I hope you like your new friends."

With that, she swished away magnificently. Holy shit.

I wandered over to Emma. No doubt she'd expect me to compete with these guys. "Honey," I said, butting into the conversation. "We might have to postpone the wedding."

That killed their conversation. "Why?" said Emma, genuinely annoyed. The news, though fictional, wound her up. Or maybe she thought I was breaking the rules of the game.

"Wednesday have increased their offer to eight thousand a week. But I've just heard Millwall are interested, too. Brad says he could get twenty there." I looked at the guys as though seeing them for the first time. "Oh, hi," I said, giving them handshakes. "You probably want autographs. I don't have a pen on me." I sort of exhaled noisily and stared at a particular lamppost. "Do you ever go into a room and forget why you went there?" I slapped my hips a few times. "Ah yes. The wedding flowers." I gave Emma a look of concern. "We might as well still go and choose them?"

She considered her response. "What is it the referees say? Play on."

"You cheated," said Emma, once we'd slipped away from the men.

"In what way?"

"Your star-player power. That's not fair. It's the Attention Game, not the Fame Game."

I laughed. "I'm not famous. Anyway, if we do it on looks alone, I've got no chance. Why were we playing the Attention Game anyway? I was only asking for directions."

"You know why."

"I simply thought she looked like Gemma and maybe you would want to be her friend."

"Max."

"Are we still friends?"

"No. Now let's go plan our wedding."

I came back to reality, back to the photo of Emma and Gemma on the beach. I wasn't sure I liked the thought of thousands of random men seeing my girlfriend in a bikini before me. I didn't want to think about it. I gave Junior his phone back and went to the front of the coach. Cutter and his assistants broke off their conversation to look at me. I held my hands up. "I've got questions for Spivvers."

The physio groaned. "Max! Again?"

"Have you got something better to do? Because I haven't."

"What's all this?" said Cutter.

"Max has started his coaching badges," said the physio. "And he's got to do first aid. And he's taking it very seriously."

"Too seriously?" said Cutter.

"You can't be too serious about first aid," said the physio.

"So what's the problem?" said Cutter.

Spivvers deflated. "Go on, Max. Fire away."

"Check my work," I said. I told him how to use a defibrillator, what to do if a player swallows his tongue, how to check for concussion, and ran through the A, B, C, D, E approach.

"Spot on," he said. "You're a good student."

"What else is in your course, Max?" said Cutter.

"I'm going through the introductory modules," I said. "Whizzing through, I should say. I did two weeks in one day. The meat of it is creating lesson plans. You know, this session aims to improve technique so we do this drill and that drill. My attitude as a coach is such and such. I'm just copy pasting from sessions I've seen. Your ones plus ones I saw from Jackie Reaper."

"Do you need to use our academy kids?" said Cutter. I must have looked surprised, because he added, "You know. For your inspections."

"This course is all online. But the next one, the UEFA C license, has a big practical component. If I can use the academy, yeah. That'd be top. Are you serious?"

"Of course, Max. We encourage all the players to do a badge. Not many are interested. Don't think ahead like you."

"Lucky them," I said, ominously.

"Now fuck off so we can gossip about you."

"Aye aye cap'n."

I shuffled back down the aisle of the bus. When Junior saw me coming, he quickly did something on his phone. Closing Instagram, the prick! Perving over my girl. Holy shit. I paused, holding onto one of the headrests. I looked out the side of the bus and saw the motorways were clear. They'd been gritted, or the sheer volume of traffic dealt with the snow. But beyond the roads, the white stuff lay thick everywhere.

Recent events came to mind. Me versus Nick. Me versus the future of football. It was going to be very hard to fight it alone. Scratch that. Impossible to fight it alone.

I glared at the back of the bus where the Cavemen were dicking around, being loud, playing cards, acting the maggot. When one of them saw me looking, the volume from that area halved. Even Captain Caveman himself bowed his head and pretended to be focused on the poker.

On the pitch, we were getting more and more effective. Off the pitch, they didn't exist.

I shuffled towards them.

Now, you probably remember there was a dude whose job it was to delay me from going down to the dressing room on my first morning at the club. He was extremely mediocre and his normal role was unused sub. I hadn't spoken to him, except to yell things like "Yes!" or "Man on!" or "One two!" during drills and training sessions. When he saw me looming over him, he visibly swallowed.

"Twatface!" I said. I did actually use his real name, but it's more satisfying to imagine it this way. "Twatface!" I said again, even more aggressively and just as fictionally. Yep, still satisfying.

"Yes, Best?"

"I'm ready to join the union. Sign me up."

He seemed confused by this entirely appropriate comment. Something clicked. "Oh. No, there isn't one."

"The PFA," I said, the way you'd point at the big yellow thing in the sky and say, "The sun."

"Yes," he said, waving a hand. "I know. But that's only for the leagues. The PFA doesn't cover non-league."

"The Professional Footballers Association doesn't cover non-league. Isn't everyone on this bus a *professional footballer?*"

"Not quite all, no. But you're right. We should be covered. But we're not."

"You've got to be joking."

"No, Max. I swear."

He was giving me big don't-shoot-the-messenger vibes. "And there's no union for non-league players? What the fuck."

Chumpy, for some inexplicable reason, decided I was being out of line. "So we have to stick up for each other."

I pushed away from Twatface and went to Chumpy. Clamped onto the headrest in front of his seat so I could menace him and point my cone of wrath into his stretchy face. "Right," I said. "So when are we going to start doing that?"

Chumpy's mouth opened and closed.

Once he'd retreated into a sullen silence, I stood there for a while thinking of the implications. When my fight with Nick next escalated, there wouldn't be any help for me from the players' union. I wasn't even sure what kind of help I'd need. But I crossed them off my mental list of potential allies. What did that leave? Almost nothing.

Well, shit.

I took a few steps back towards my seat. I passed Smokes, Paul Larkin, and Gray, the tall striker whose job was to be a battering ram for the team. Smokes pulled me into an empty seat.

"Max! Tommy Tactics! Did you see the Brazil game?"

See it? I managed it! "Yep."

"We couldn't believe they didn't win. They looked the best team in the tournament. What happened?"

"Well, they had eleven shots on target and Croatia scored from their only one," I said. "So mostly they were just unlucky. I actually liked Brazil's formation, but I played four-two-four instead."

"You played?"

Slip of the tongue . . . "I would have played four-two-four. We know Croatia have a great midfield. Let them have the centre. Give me a flat back four, no forward runs. Two DMs. So we've got six behind the ball at all times. Then four of the best attacking players in the world, spread out wide. And they don't have to defend. Croatia aren't pushing too many men forward in that scenario, let me tell you. But look, the real manager did it right. They were unlucky. That's football."

I'd earned 127 TINOs from that match. I'd been hyper-focused—phone off, no distractions—in case me losing TINOs meant some other cursed guy gained them. I wasn't just fighting to boost my own power—I was fighting to stop Nick's other protégés increasing theirs. First, because they were obviously dicks who were telling Nick how to turn football into a gated community where clubs like Darlo would be kept at arm's length. Second, because I needed to be Nick's top dog so that my threat to retire would keep him under control.

"What about Holland–Argentina?" said Larkin.

"That was weird," I said. "I didn't like what the Argentina manager did. He played five at the back so that he'd have a solid base and hope the forwards grabbed a goal. Me? I would have gone four-one-three-two and blown them away. Dominate all areas of the pitch. Don't let the Netherlands have a sniff while you keep pounding shots at them. Three–nil, job's a good 'un."

127 more TINOs, thank you very much.

In my version of the World Cup there would have been a mouth-watering semi-final between the two South American giants. Imagine that!

"What about today, Max?" said Smokes. "You going to dribble the wrong way and get your leg broke again?"

"Today?" I scoffed. "No chance. I don't know how to ski."

TINOs: 3,345

Matches remaining: 6

I went back to my seat and crashed back against it with a big sigh. I was unhappy. Anxious. Kind of stressed. What had I said to Shona that time? Stress is the time before you make a decision.

What did I need to decide?

I slapped Junior's arm again.

He inhaled and slowly took his headphones off. He paused the movie but it didn't pause the audio.

"What are you listening to?"

"*Plane*. Gerard Butler. Good, mindless action."

"Mate," I said. "You're listening to something and pretending to be watching that. It won't wash with me. I'm the greatest detective since Pikachu. Now fess up."

He became shifty and leaned in. "Motivational stuff. Okay? Self-help shit. Happy now?"

"No. Why are you ashamed of trying to improve yourself? Jesus. Anyway, listen." I made a little throat noise. "I need your Instagram again."

"Mate," he said.

"Mate," I explained.

He unlocked it and gave it to me. The first picture on Emma's Instagram was of me. She'd taken it in that florist, Plantology, when I'd gone so far internal I couldn't even see or hear.

The florist was tiny. I suppose I'd been expecting a giant shop, a tropicarium filled to the brim with plants and flowers from all over the world. Despite its size, as soon as we went in, Emma lost her mind, asking an assistant if she could take photos for her Insta and yeah, could the assistant help us plan our wedding? Some of the details Emma came up with were so specific that they could only have come from her actual wedding fantasies. When she said there'd be a castle with a drawbridge and we'd pull it up behind us to stop the paparazzi getting in, I had to turn away to stop myself from laughing and ruining her little adventure.

I ended up going to a window, putting my hand up on the old-fashioned wooden frame, and peering out into the world. The sun was trying to come out. The air was cold. Not much wind. Great football weather, if the pitch was safe.

Football. Football was eating itself. Clubs were choosing to move away from their own fans and their own traditions. Barely a week went by without some team changing their 150-year-old crest to some modern marketing-friendly logo. Spanish cup finals were held in Saudi Arabia. Big clubs bought talented young players and hoarded them like dragons hoarded gold, so much so that those clubs had created a whole new job for a guy just to remember all their names. This is only a slight exaggeration.

And the World Cup. I'd watched almost every game in Qatar, and it had been absolutely incredible. A masterpiece in storytelling, building nicely to a thrilling climax. But FIFA weren't happy to earn four billion dollars hosting the greatest tournament ever. They wanted more. More games, more dollars, more shots of the president sitting next to world leaders and trillionaires. The new proposal was 104 matches played by 48 teams over 39 days. Bloated. Half the matches would be meaningless. And they wanted to host it every two years instead of every four. More more more. Killing the goose that laid golden eggs.

So what Old Nick was doing was just one straw. For many fans, the camel's back had broken long ago. That's why FC United had been created. And for me, while there were teams like FC United and Darlington, there was still hope.

And there was still a route to the top. I could take control of Telford United and bring them to the Premier League.

But even at breakneck speed, that might take twenty years. Would the pyramid still *be* there in twenty years? There was talk that Bournemouth would soon be bought by a rich American. That would be the tenth Premier League team owned by Americans. Half. There's no relegation in American sports. Owning a sports franchise in the U.S.

is a license to print money, with no risk. Would they change the rules to align English football more with American sports? Why *wouldn't* they? Eliminating the chance that your team might be kicked out of the league would be entirely rational.

And it wasn't just Americans. If you were a nation state buying a club to increase your diplomatic clout, you needed your club on the biggest stage. And the few English guys who were left? You don't get to be a billionaire without killing a few billion fluffy mammals. They were as heartless as they come.

It seemed that Nick was right when he said I was looking at the future of football. Secret meetings of rich men surrounded by sumptuous food they didn't even pause to sniff, making decisions that would hurt millions of people in order to safeguard their investments and squeeze their bottom lines.

I sighed and felt the wood under my fingers.

There were twenty clubs in the Premier League. You needed fourteen votes to change something. If there wasn't currently a majority in favour of ending relegation, of lifting the drawbridge to the castle, there soon would be.

Once the bridge was up, that was that. The rest would slowly wither and die.

Resistance, I told myself, was futile.

I stood straighter and thought: *Fuck that.*

Six was the number.

Six votes could block changes to the Premier League that would harm the fans. Harm the sport. In England, anyway. I couldn't do anything about fucking FIFA. But I could get my hands on one of those votes. I could *be* that vote.

If I took Telford from the bottom of the National League North all the way to the Premier League, I'd have that power. I'd be in the secret meetings flicking *V*s at all the pricks. I'd hold them to ransom. "I'll vote against everything you propose from now till eternity unless you all get on social media and profess your love of relegation and the pyramid system." And even better, I thought to myself, my club would be there at the expense of one of the villains!

Nick must have thought he was punishing me for becoming a player.

But he'd simply lit a fire under my arse. My ambitions had just increased a million-fold.

I would jump behind the wheel of some shitty little fan-owned club, and drive it straight up the nearest cliff face into the professional leagues, through the Championship, and into the big one. Into those secret meetings, into every unscrupulous owner's nightmares.

And while I was doing it, I'd take a leaf out of Nick's book and transform my decrepit little vehicle into a fucking flying tank.

So I didn't have twenty years. So what? Flying tanks go fast, mate. Dead fast.

While I was deciding I needed to embark on a hostile takeover of English football, Emma had snuck into position and taken a photo of me.

I was there, one hand on the window frame, the sun hitting my skin just so. In my other hand I had my Wednesday kit and boot bag. My expression was what you can maybe imagine from my thoughts—steeling myself to fight future battles.

It became Emma's favourite photo of me.

Back on the bus with Junior's phone in my hand, I moved the picture and saw the caption. Emma had written, "Max, fresh from the fight."

Every time I read it I found a new meaning, and every new meaning felt true.

Me: I like it, too. Keep it.

Stress is the time before you make a decision. What was I going to do? Storm the castle. At what cost? Guerilla war didn't seem like the option that came with the most financial rewards. Fan-owned teams paid peanuts. I could make wheelbarrows of cash as a player, but not at Telford.

Okay, so I'd have to accept that my income would be low for a while until James got to a big club. I'd have to put up with shitty earphones and borrow money from Emma and my call centre suit would be my best suit for years to come.

I exhaled.

I could always play for a team like Sheffield Wednesday, build up a nest egg, drop down a few divisions and *then* start my management career. I shook my head. Far too long.

All right. Player-manager at a fan-owned club. Done. Side hustles to try to be less poor. Fine.

So now what? What about Darlington? What about January 31 and the whole Maxterplan?

I looked out the window. The snow was falling in clumps.

I slapped Junior. He paused his audiobook but not the movie.

"If this game today is called off, when will it be replayed?"

"Dunno. March or something." He waited for my follow-up question.

March or something. By the end of the transfer window, I wouldn't have played ten games. I wouldn't get a winner's medal. So if this match today was abandoned, there was no point staying at the club. I would stay only until a fan-owned club sacked their manager, at which point I'd hop in my car and apply in person. Based on what Nick had said, I'd definitely get the job. But that meant doing things his way. What about doing things *my* way?

"What do you think the odds of us playing today are? Like, really?"

"Fifty-fifty."

"Yeah. Me too. Thanks."

Junior went back to his motivational tapes. I bit my thumbnail.

Fifty-fifty. A coin toss. So why not let the universe decide, for once? If the game went ahead, I'd take it as a sign that I should follow the Maxterplan and stay at Darlington until January 31. Maybe there would be a way to leave that wasn't despicable.

And if the match didn't go ahead, the Maxterplan was dead in the water. So I'd take the next management job that fit my needs, whether it was next week or next year.

For now, I left things in the hands of the gods. By which I mean the referee and his assistants.

The pitch was hard and covered with a layer of snow, but the lines had been cleared and the ref thought we were good to go. Most players wore gloves. I didn't. I'd like to say it was because I was too big and tough, a real old-school hero. But I simply didn't have a pair and when I asked Junior if I could borrow his, he laughed.

So I stood around, teeth chattering, while the match went on around me. After five minutes, the snow started falling again. After a big flurry, the ref paused the match. The ground staff and all the players and coaches grabbed brooms and shovels and tried to brute force some of the snow off the pitch.

I say all the players, I mean almost all. I grabbed a puffy coat—I think it was the referee's—and stood in it and shivered. If this match didn't go ahead, it would have huge repercussions. Huge. The universe was flipping a coin.

Heads, do it the Max way.

Tails, do it the Nick way.

Helping to clear the pitch would mean putting my thumbs on the scale.

After about ten minutes of a lot of people working very hard so that the match could continue, the referee reappeared. He looked suspiciously like a man who had just had a lovely hot cup of tea and a few Hobnobs, and I hated him for it.

He went through an elaborate routine known as the pitch inspection. That involved him looking at the pitch and turning to the two managers. They and the eight hundred watching fans were agog.

I scampered forward, ready to learn my fate.

The ref cleared his throat. Like all refs, he loved a bit of attention. He stretched the moment out like he was announcing who was going home on *Love Island*. And the decision is . . .

"Play on."

41

THE KARMA BEFORE THE STORM

Saturday, December 10: Revenge fantasy minus eight days.

Henri: Are you still on the bus from Gloucester?

Me: Yeah. Still like 3 hours left. Did everyone you invited turn up?

Henri: Yes! And more! And early! Chester's match was snowed off. Yours is one of the only ones that took place in the whole country. I am trying not to take it personally.

Me: You know I'd be there if I could. England v France. Holy shit. What's the vibe?

Henri: There's a big buzz. I am the centre of attention. I am very happy.

Me: You shouldn't use your phone in a cinema.

Henri: Everyone is. It's Henri's rules today. I booked the screen. I can do what I want. At halftime I'm going to make everyone stay in their seats while I read aloud an inspiring work of narrative fiction.

Me: This is the bit where I'm supposed to ask to what you are referring?

Henri: The match report detailing your latest exploits has arrived. I get anything Bingo writes sent to my inbox; I'm still a subscriber. I will send the link. Oh and Max? Try not to be too smug.

From *The Northern Echo*:

Gloucester 2 Darlington 6: Best Shows Snow Mercy to Toothless Tigers

Darlington bounced back to the top of the table as Max Best was once again the star of the show in near-blizzard conditions. He scored four goals, including one straight from a corner, as Quakers beat Gloucester City 6–2.

The crushing win was even more comfortable than the scoreline suggested, and Darlington moved level on points with King's Lynn, whose match was postponed.

The 150 traveling fans, who set out despite the dire forecasts and England's World Cup quarter-final, were in good voice from the start and were rewarded with one of the finest team performances of the season.

"That was fantastic," said manager David Cutter, who watched from the stands in the second of his three-match suspension. "We had a tough match in midweek and didn't have a lot of recovery time. To do the double over Gloucester—no pun intended—is very satisfying because they're one of the best teams in the division. I have to say the lads done me proud today with their workrate and togetherness."

Blah blah blah. Then the bit about me:

Best set the stage for the rout after an early snow break. He played like a man who wanted the game to be won by halftime so he could slip into an early bath. His first goal came from a defensive mistake—Best latched onto a stray pass and thrashed the ball into the net with seemingly no backlift. His second was very similar, as Gloucester continued to try to play nice football from the defence to the midfield. Best knew exactly where every pass would go and was more than happy to punish any sloppiness. His third was scored direct from a corner in the 33rd minute, while his fourth involved tackling a defender, rounding the goalkeeper, retaining his balance and somehow slotting home from the tightest of angles.

Quakers will be keen to tie the 22-year-old to a long-term contract, but with rumours swirling of interest from big clubs, it would seem an uphill task.

Henri: I said not to be smug. I could hear you grinning from 200 miles away. Are you still doing your online course?

Me: Yes. I couldn't put much effort into Portugal vs Morocco because I was playing. I stuck Portugal in 4-4-2 and let them get on with it. Did the trick.

Henri: Max is using 4-4-2! Is this his blue period? Or is this maturity? Now pay attention. This is vital. Vital. You are currently pitting your wits against France, yes? Since you can't come to my soirée, I insist you allow us to win.

Me: No.

Henri: You know, it's strange. I tried to find such a course as the one you describe. It doesn't seem to exist. Isn't that strange, Max?

Me: Entertain your guests, bro. Don't celebrate too hard if you win. You promised me you'd go and check on Benny tomorrow.

Henri: I remember, Max. Do not distress yourself.

Ziggy: I can't stand this. France are going to win, aren't they?

Me: Yes.

Ziggy: Why though? We're just as good. It should be even. Why doesn't it feel even?

Me: We've fallen into France's trap. We should go on the front foot. Attack down their left.

Ziggy: But that's where Mbappé is!!

Me: Yeah. Their strength is their weakness. He doesn't defend. Fucking shove every attack down that side. Saka, Grealish, Bellingham. All the dribblers. Run at the left back nonstop. See what happens.

Ziggy: I wish you were in charge.

Me: No you don't. I'd go fucking mental. We'd lose big time. I don't know what to do about Mbappé. He terrifies me.

Ziggy: We'd go down punching though. This cautious shit is doing my head in.

Henri: Commiserations, Max. I hope you won in your game.

Me: I . . . did not. I still have a lot to learn. Congratulations, bro. France are in another World Cup final. You going to rent out the cinema again?

Henri: I don't think I'd be able to fill it.

Me: Book it! I'll be there! We can bring all the Broughton kids. They'll love it.

Henri: I'll think about it.

Sunday, December 11: revenge fantasy minus seven days.

Kisi: Max have you seen the video?

Me: No.

Kisi: Do you want me to send it?

Me: Kisi I am very busy and important. I don't know if you realise this but I am kind of a big deal now. I don't have time to type out my thoughts and feelings at length. From now on, please keep messages to five words or less.

Kisi: Click link it good.

I obeyed and a TikTok popped up. It was the Darlo fans at the Gloucester match debuting their new song. Imagine 150 men of all ages bouncing around, waving their arms, singing to the tune of "It's Magic" by Scottish pop-rock stars Pilot.

If you don't know it, the original lyrics go like this:
Oh oh oh it's magic
You know
Never believe it's not so.
And the Darlo lot were singing:
Oh oh oh it's Max Best
You know!
You'd never believe it's Darlo!!

Me: Thanks! Have you got your own chant yet?

Kisi: No! We don't play in front of fans.

Me: You will. And you will.

Kisi: How does it feel to have your own song?

Me: Totes normal. No biggie.

Kisi: You're lying right?

Me: Yeah. It's top.

Monday, December 12: revenge fantasy minus six days.

Nice One: Hi Max. This is Nice One. The kids loved the coach you found. I know you want to check him for yourself but he's good. Thumbs-up from us and I think Henri approved too. One small thing from the match that I thought you might want to see. Sending a video.

Me: There's no video.

Nice One: Oh oh right. Hang on. There.

Me: Still nothing.

Nice One: *bennywhynobennywhy.mp4*

It was a short clip. Broughton were playing some other team in their league. Nice One was zoomed in on his son, naturally, so I didn't get to see the formation or who else was in the lineup.

Benny seemed to be playing as a wide forward on the right, and he did a little move to dribble past the defender. He took the ball forward, did a skill to turn around, and went back at the defender again. He tricked his way past him and laughed, loud.

Oh, shit.

Oh shit oh shit oh shit.

Me: I'll talk to him.

Tuesday, December 13: revenge fantasy minus five days.

Emma: You didn't do your course because you were playing, right?

Me: No, I did both.

Emma: Oh. How? Were you Messi or the other one?

Me: I was Argentina again, but I only won 1–0. The real guys scored 3.

Emma: Oh no. So it's been the same rules since I was at your place?

Me: They make small changes every round. In the quarters I could choose victory conditions. Like option 1: Do better than the real manager with no restrictions. Option 2: get through to the next round, but you can only make one substitution.

Emma: Complicated.

Me: Yeah. And for the semis I didn't have to use the starting lineup the real manager used. I could pick anyone from the whole squad.

Emma: That's good. I wonder what the change will be for the final.

Me: They'll probably put me in a VR booth and make me stand on the touchline for 90 minutes waving at the players.

Emma: That'd be humiliating.

Me: Why?

Emma: You don't speak Spanish.

Me: Even I can learn how to shout "Pass to Messi."

Shona: Raffi made his debut! 85th-minute sub! 5 completed passes and a yellow card!

Me: Oh fuck! I didn't expect that so soon. Wow. Wow. Wowowow. All I can say is wow. And wowowow. A Chester legend is born! Was his dad there?

Shona: No. Too cold for him. He's already talking about getting a transfer down south. Somewhere warm.

Me: Lol. Tell Raffi I'm made up for him. Hope to see you both on Sunday!

Shona: We're not going to your revenge fantasy, Max. Raffi has been told to keep his head down.

Me: By whom?

Shona: By his wife.

Me: Oh. Okay. But tell him I'll be using a thrilling, all-action 4-3-3 formation.

Shona: Sure, Max. I'll do that. *Eye roll emoji.*

Wednesday, December 14: revenge fantasy minus four days.

Ziggy: Am I allowed to bet on football?

Me: No.

Ziggy: Everyone at FC United is convinced Morocco will beat France. Everyone! I want to put twenty quid on.

Me: You're allowed to bet on that one. Don't bet on club matches or which manager will be sacked or things like that.

Ziggy: K. Got you a treat. Say when.

Me: When.

He sent me a link to a video from the official FC United YouTube page. It was entitled "FCUM Take the Max Best Challenge."

It started with Jackie holding a phone in selfie pose with some men running around behind him.

"Y'all right? Jackie Reaper here taking training with FC United. Matches keep getting postponed so I'm on the three-G pitch trying to think of ways to keep the lads engaged. I've split the group into two. First eleven's been drilling with me, doing the Max Best Challenge. If you don't know who that is, don't worry: you will. Challenge is to drag the other team to one side of the pitch, switch the play, switch the play *back again*, and exploit the space. The other group is off over there practising four-three-three. They don't know they're about to be famous." Jackie grinned. "Famous last words. This could blow up in my face! Ah, sack it; I'm gonna post this whatever happens. It's not a challenge if it's easy."

There was a messy transition where we saw Jackie reach to end the recording, then we were watching mid-match from an elevated position.

Jackie turned the camera around to face himself, his breath visible, then pointed the lens at the pitch. "We've kicked off. See the shapes? It's just like Holland v USA in the World Cup. My lot are Holland. God I hope this works. It's bloody freezing up here! I can't feel my b—"

That snippet cut out, and then we were watching the training match again. The orange bibs had the ball and were passing left and right. They were spread out across the whole width of the pitch. The black bibs were way more narrow. They were shuffling and sliding all over, keeping their structure pretty easily.

Then there was a little period where the oranges zipped the ball around on the right-hand side—two sets of neat little triangles that drew their opponents into challenges and failed attempts to intercept. The oranges passed into midfield, and suddenly the game was wide open. One more pass to the left and the black bibs were sprinting back to try to recover their shape. The winger ran forward, looked up, and pulled the ball square.

It came to a striker, and he took a touch and rolled it even farther to the right. The right winger who had started the move controlled the ball and passed it into the goal.

It was almost a mirror image of the first Dutch goal in the game I'd watched.

"Get in!" yelled Jackie. After a couple of seconds, he started laughing. "Yes!" Selfie mode. "There you go, Maxy boy!" He laughed some more. He was flushed with pride. He leaned back and scratched his head vigorously. "Ah, yes. Come on. Come *on*. That was mint. Good lads. Good lads."

Thursday, December 15: revenge fantasy minus three days.

From *The Northern Echo*:

WORLD EXCLUSIVE: INTERVIEW WITH MYSTERY WINGER MAX BEST
by Bingo Williams

Nothing is conventional in the world of Max Best, Manchester's smoothest export since Boddingtons. After weeks of me pleading for an interview, he suddenly appears in the offices of the *Echo*, where his swagger and good looks cause quite a stir. He announces he'll consent to an interview under a set of conditions so specific that any hot-blooded reporter would immediately refuse. Yet I find myself agreeing and looking forward to the event more than any Christmas of my youth.

For once, I am the envy of my colleagues. I preen for days.

The time is set for Wednesday, just after lunch. The venue, adding to the strangeness, is not Blackwell Meadows, nor is it Darlington FC's training centre, nor is it a coffee shop. I have been instructed to meet Best in room 216 at Darlington College. Turning up on time, I am astonished to find the classroom has been emptied save for three desks—one alone under the blackboard, where I am instructed to sit. Two more are on the far side of the room. The layout is strangely confrontational, or perhaps it feels so because ten sullen youths are glaring at me.

This turns out to be a Media Studies class consisting entirely of young players from the Darlington FC Academy. Players, it seems, whom Max Best has taken under his wing. Once he enters, the mood transforms. The young men come alive. It might be an exaggeration to say they hang on his every word, but then again, it might not.

"Bingo," says Best, who luxuriates in the mouthfeel of my name. "Have you met the kids?"

"Uh, no," I stammer. If his intention is to put me on the back foot, it is working.

But it seems nothing of the sort was on his mind. Quite the opposite, in fact. He lambasts the students for not taking the opportunity to do some networking, reminding them that as footballers they need to use the media before it uses them. He finishes with the moving (for me) observation that I go to every match, home and away, and write clear and mostly accurate match reports in all kinds of weather—a wonderful and vital service for those who can't make the game. He finishes by proclaiming that I deserve to be considered an S-tier fan and treated as such. I don't know what this means and I'm too afraid to ask. But it seems to be positive—the young men are looking at me in a new way.

"Here's their teacher," says Best. "Miss Fox. That's F-O-X."

"Actually, it's Faulkes," she says. "Mr. Pest does like his little jokes."

"What, ah, what are we doing, Max?" I dare to ask.

"Interview." He glances at his phone. "I've got to get to my friend Longstaff's shop soon. I owe him money. I buy all my football equipment there. And most of my clothes. See this hoodie? Looks good on me, yes? Say yes."

"Yes."

"That's right. Guess how much it cost."

"A hundred pounds," I say.

He makes a buzzer noise. "No! It was 19 pounds. Can you believe that? It'd be 50 in Manchester. A hundred in London." He pulls a face. "Leave that in. That's good colour. All right. First question."

"Well," I say, startled. I am sitting down behind a desk and everyone else is standing around, waiting. "You beat Southport 2–0 on Tuesday. How do you feel about that?"

This question triggers an exodus—the cast of characters move to the distant desks and have a lively, but short, whispered discussion. They return and Best speaks. He seems to count items off on his fingers. "Good to get the win. Last match of manager's ban."

"Suspension," says Miss Faulkes.

"Yes! Better. Thanks. Er . . . good win. Suspension ends. Er . . ." The third finger. "Still in title race. Pleased for fans. Regret not dynamic. Feel free to expand all that."

"Regret not dynamic?" I say.

The gathering starts to move away, but Best makes a noise and they halt. "Just, you know. We'd like to attack and score goals but we had a long trip on the weekend and that takes it out of you, and we've got a game this Saturday. We want to give our all, but we need to be a bit more mathematical about it. Long-term thinking. Spread our energy out to maximise our points haul." Best is dragged away into a huddle, then pushed back into place. "All that's according to Cutter's instructions, of course. He's the brains of this operation."

"Right." A question I've thrown out as a simple icebreaker has turned into something weighty. The answer feels exceedingly curious, but I don't want to spend too long asking about football. I want to get to know the man himself. But where to even start? I check my notes. Every question seems deathly dull against this vibrant backdrop of energy and youth. Perhaps some of their spirit has rubbed off on me, because I find myself throwing my arms wide. "Where've you been?"

Best laughs. The group retreats, and this time I don't take it personally. He's letting the Media Studies students refine his responses. Why? Perhaps a future interviewer will dare to ask. When the group returns, Best does not count on his fingers. He becomes wistful. He transports himself somewhere, and I go part of the way with him. "It was the pandemic. All that time alone. Locked up. There was football on TV, thank God, but with no fans in the stadiums, what's the point? Better than nothing, yeah. I know the players hated it. Empty stadiums. Soulless, wasn't it? Did you go to Darlo games then?" I nod. "Must have been awful. The strange thing is, seeing it like that made me fall in love with football again. It's probably going to sound like your typical Manc arrogance, but I always thought I had something to offer."

"As a player?"

"No, as a manager. Or a director of football. Something like that. I've got a good brain on me. But I was always put off because clubs just want to squeeze more and more out of fans. Here's a new away kit. You bought that? Great. Here's the new home kit. Oh, and your season ticket's more expensive and we've charged your debit card for this cup match and if you complain you're never getting in again. Everyone reading this knows exactly what I mean. Clubs think fans have endless patience. Fans are inelastic. Nothing you can do will stop them coming. Then the pandemic hits and boom—empty stadiums. Directors are terrified. Vision of the future. So they start reengaging. Actually trying. And there's a point where I think, yeah, I want to get involved. I want to be part of this. But I don't know anyone. Who'd let me manage a team? Arrigo Sacchi joked that to be a jockey you have to be a horse first. So I dust off the old boots and go for a trial. The first one doesn't go well, but the second does. And here I am."

"Will you tell us about the first trial? Which club was it?"

"Ah. I'm saving that little snippet. There might be a perfect time to let it slip."

One of the young men is excited. He flicks his wrist, producing an explosive cracking sound. "I know when! Before you play that team!"

"Mr. Best, no!" cry the others, but they too are excited. "You gonna get the man sacked or what?"

"I have no ambitions in that direction," says Best, winking at the teacher. She pretends not to be amused.

"It seems impossible the manager in question didn't spot your talent," I suggest.

"Ah, but don't forget my bad attitude," says Best, apparently in earnest.

"The thing most readers want to know," I say, "is whether you will be staying at Darlington long-term."

This time the discussion on the far side of the room takes minutes. The entire group returns at funeral pace. Best pulls at the toggles of his hoodie. "It's like I say to my friend Longstaff—the one who owns the sports shop on Coniscliffe Road—if you love someone, you've got to let them go to Barnsley."

"Have you got an offer from Barnsley?"

"No, it was just an example. The truth is I'm happy here. I love the club and the fans and love making them happy and on Saturday we're going to Spennymoor and I'm going to put on a show." There is another huddle. Best returns to add, "If I'm selected."

I smile. "I suspect you will be. But there's very little chance the match will go ahead."

Best's demeanour changes in an alarming way. Now I see the assassin who spends the start of every match watching, calculating, triangulating. The bullfighter who puts scoring on hold to taunt his opponent a second time. "What do you mean?"

"The pitch has been under a tent for a week to protect it from the cold. The ground is still hard as rock." I find myself losing the will to speak. "There's basically no chance."

Best puts his hands on the desk and leans on them. His knuckles whiten. I fear he will flip the thing onto me. He bites his lip. This innocuous news—a postponed non-league match in the deep of winter—has come as a hammer blow. "We're done, Bingo. Print it all or print nothing. Miss Fox. Guys. Thanks."

And he strides out, taking all the air in the room with him.

Saturday, December 17: revenge fantasy minus one day.

It was not a good few days. The match *was* postponed. Most of the players were ecstatic—they could shop for Christmas presents and spend some festive time with their kids or girlfriends.

As for me, I wasn't sure how long I'd be staying in Darlington. My plan needed a lot of things to align perfectly, but now one tyre had a puncture and that was that. My race was over. What next? Wait for a manager to be sacked and see if Nick was true to his word that I only needed to apply for a job to get it. If so, there didn't seem to be much point playing more games. The money was good, but there was an ever-increasing risk of injury. I had earned a reputation as a piss-taker, and my opponents didn't like that.

Hold that thought—it was too early to end my playing career just yet. I'd tell Cutter that I'd play the home matches, but I'd skip training most days. And that if I didn't play the ninety minutes against Chester in mid-January he'd never see me again.

I decided I'd close some threads, just in case. I repaid Longstaff—he tried to refuse the money saying the interview had led to a mini boom in business. "Just before Crimbo, too," he said, all smiles. "I rehired one of me assistants!"

"Yeah, yeah," I said. "I didn't do it deliberately. Your name slipped out."

"You're such a bad liar! My name *and* address? I don't know how to thank you."

"If you want to thank me, tell me how much I owe you. And put those special shinpads on order." Just in case I felt like playing the odd match here and there.

Then, as far as I could think, there was one last thing. The stationers. The highlighter mystery.

The assistant looked up at me. "Help you?"

"I'm superstar football star Max Best. Have you got any merch with my face on? Mugs? Calendars? Lenticular pens?"

"I don't think so."

"Okay. Weird. Look, do you know this guy?" I showed her a pic of Henri.

"Yes, he used to come in."

"This will be weird but . . . do you know why?"

She rolled her eyes. "I do. He had a thing for Kate. Never asked her out, though."

I perked up. I hadn't expected such an easy ride. "Oh, top! Is she here?"

"No. She moved away. London, I think."

I had a think. I looked up the date of Henri's explosive interview. The one that had led to him being driven out of town. "Was it around

September when she left?"

"Oh. Huh. That's a thinker." She nodded slowly. "About then, yes."

"Did she speak French?"

"Don't think so."

"Like football?"

"She never mentioned it."

"Hey," I said. "That was helpful. Thanks."

So Henri's crush moved away, and to get her attention he spoke in riddles about a sport she didn't like to an obscure magazine in a language she didn't speak. A tale as old as time.

Nothing more to see here. Just Henri being Henri. Case closed. Move along.

The World Cup third-place playoff happened.

And was then instantly forgotten.

XP balance: 610

Debt repaid: 245/3,000

TINOs: 3,601

Matches remaining: 1

I went to bed that Saturday night feeling like a phase in my life was starting to wind down. I wasn't sure I'd done a very good job of being Max Best during my time in Darlington. But I certainly felt I'd done everything I could to prepare for the Broughton versus Chester match and the World Cup final that would follow it.

As you might have guessed, the next chapter is important. Stuff happened that Sunday. Big stuff.

The hardest part will probably be naming the chapter.

I'll probably call it "Chapter 42: Max Learns Humility."

Yeah. Let's go with that.

42
MAX BEST WINS IT ALL (PART 1 OF 1,000)

"How do you feel?"

"I feel good. I feel concentrated. I feel like I'm driving safely."

The fact that I didn't want to chat while driving was a minor source of friction in my relationship with Emma. Not that we'd driven together all that much. She made an exaggerated show of checking the road in front and behind. "It's seven o'clock on a Sunday morning. The road's quieter than one of your goal celebrations. I think you can spare a *little* concentration."

"Fine. Let me pull into the slow lane," I said, and indicated. I risked a glance; she was vexed. I flicked the indicator off, stayed in the fast lane, and smirked. She punched me. "Oh, *that's* safe."

"It's your big day. You've been planning this for weeks. How do you *feel*?"

I thrust my bottom lip out. "I'm fine. Henri's the one telling you it's a big deal, not me. All I'm doing is managing an under-fourteens match. It's as banal as football gets."

"In *Chester*, against the team that *rejected* you, and one of your players is the kid you've decided to secretly watch over like a *guardian angel*. Why do I believe Henri and not you?" We drove on for another mile or so. "The important thing is to win the match, right?"

"That's going to be one of many small wins. Yeah. Some small wins and one big one."

"What are they?"

"The small ones? Okay, win the match. Sure. But that's small potatoes. It doesn't mean anything. These kids want to be signed by a club."

"They're at a club."

"A serious club. So one win would be if I could persuade them to stop showboating."

"Which they learned from you."

"Yes. It's another win if the coach I chose turns out to be good. Another is any scouts that show up."

"Scouts?"

"I invited a few scouts. I told you."

"Pretty sure you didn't."

"Well, I did. If one shows up, that's a win. By the way, don't tell anyone."

"Why not?"

"If they know there are scouts, the kids might showboat more. Or they'll freeze. Nah. We'll let them enjoy their game and tell them after." I wasn't completely sure that was the best way to do it, but whatever. "So that's three small wins. Then it depends who shows up for the match and who comes to the cinema. If I can be charming with Shona, that's a win. If I can cheer Henri up, that's a win."

"Okay. And what's the big, big win?"

"Oh, that. The absolute best thing that could happen to me today is if I could make it so that I never have to come back to Chester ever again."

The bad weather had led to a change in venue. Instead of playing in Broughton, we'd be at Catholic High School in Handbridge, quite near Chester FC's stadium. Talk about losing home advantage! I followed the GPS to the school's car park. Emma and I got out. Her blonde hair flew everywhere in the wind, so she pulled a maroon beanie on.

"What?" she said.

"Why do you look good in everything?"

"I don't."

"How did you know Broughton play in maroon?"

"I didn't. It's just one of life's little wins." She lifted her hands like she'd score a goal. "Oh! One win for me!"

"No. No no no. We're not doing a winning competition. Even though I'd win." I checked the time. "We're early. I hear some matches being played. Let's go wander around." I hadn't picked up any XP from random games for quite a while. Every match I'd been to recently had been scheduled. We walked hand in hand towards the sound of football. "Oh, shit!" I said, letting go so I could surge ahead. "It's the Knights!"

The all-weather pitch had been split in half and the Chester Knights were playing on one side. I walked to the nearest line and found a spot. Big crowd today! I spent thirty seconds watching, fascinated, checking the Knights' player profiles. I was still only seeing three numbers for each attribute, 1, 10, or 20, but that was enough to check the ideas I'd had when I'd reorganised them. On the whole I thought I'd done pretty well, but there was still room for improvement. One of the players I hadn't used would be a good option on the left, for example, to be a counterweight to Johnny Winger.

I noticed someone waving at me. Mike Dean. He had been standing next to Terry, the Chester Knights coach, and now was doing a sort of walky-run around the pitch. What did he want? I really wasn't in the mood to talk to him.

While I was thinking that, something crashed into me and I very nearly toppled over.

"Mr. Best! Mr. Best!"

While Emma and some other spectators laughed, I looked down and saw I'd been aggressively koala-ed by Wilson, the striker slash nuisance-maker slash defender magnet. Some of the other players abandoned the game, too, and came to join the scene.

"Guys! What are you doing? There's a match! You're in a match! You *are* the match!"

"Mr. Best! Where've you been?" This was Zoe, the cyberpunk deaf girl I'd made captain.

"I've been kicking ass and taking names. What do you think? Now get back on the pitch. Holy moly. I didn't drive two hours for a group hug. I came to see you score six goals, each more beautiful than the last."

"We've already scored four," said Johnny Winger.

I scratched my head. "Hmm. What's six minus four?"

"Two," said a new player. The curse said he had good stamina and teamwork. Good midfielder. He was being used in defence.

"So," I said, brushing the kids back onto the pitch. "So give me two wondergoals, please."

Chesterkid, the goalie with the fading eyesight, had been the last to realise what was happening. He made it over and beamed at me. "Mr. Best! We saw you play for that club! You were on TikTok! You're a big star now! I wish it was for Chester. I took down my Neymar poster!"

I bent to give him a little hug, which was hard because Wilson was still clinging onto me. "You put that poster right back up, Mister. I love Neymar now."

"You do?" Big, magnified blinks.

"Yeah. Every time someone kicks me, I like Neymar a little bit more. Now get back in net, please. Goalies are important! Wilson, off you pop." Wilson refused to let go of me, so I picked him up and walked to the wide-left position that I'd put him in last time we'd met.

"He's playing right midfield," called Zoe.

I carried him to the correct spot. Once he was down, I rotated him to face the other team's goal. "Wilson. Concentrate now. Your team needs you. Okay?"

"Okay."

"Remember what I told you. Eye of the tiger!"

"You never said that."

"Well, remember what I did say. Whatever that was."

"Okay."

I apologised to the referee and the opposition and scampered off the pitch, choosing a point far away from Mike Dean. The match resumed before I'd even crossed the line. That was one thing I loved about pan-disability football—it was relentless.

"More fans," said Emma, when she finally caught up with me.

"They'll grow out of it," I said. "Trust me. Everyone in Chester over the age of fourteen thinks I'm a prick."

In case I was being a nuisance, I decided not to watch the rest of the Knights' match. I noticed Mike Dean was coming towards me again. He was like the Terminator, this guy! I tried to use a few people as a human shield to disguise the fact that I was sneaking away.

"Max," someone said, as I walked around the edge of the playing area. I was passing what I thought was a gaggle of parents but turned out to be a decent chunk of Chester's first team squad. "Centre of attention, as usual."

"Oh! Hi, Magnus. Guys. Er . . . this is Emma. Distant relation of Helen of Troy. Emma, this is Magnus. Player-coach. Sleeps on a bed of crystals. And we've got Aff. He's a left winger. Imagine a cross between me and someone who likes defending. Carl. He's one of those guys you see in movies. What are they called? Ah, yeah. Americans. Raffi Brown—my client and footballing soulmate. Ben. He's the reserve goalie but I think he's better than the first team guy. And Ryder. He's the defender Henri likes to fight with. Guys. Very surprised to see you lot here."

"Henri made them come," said Raffi, with a slight laugh.

"Yeah?" said Aff, in his Irish accent. "And who made *you*?"

"Shona," he said, simply.

"I thought she didn't want any part in this," I said.

Raffi shrugged. "Changed her mind, I guess."

"Hey," I said, holding my arms wide. "Everyone who got added to Wikipedia this week, give me a hug." I waited. "Raffi."

"Oh!"

We collided and slapped each other hard on the back. "You did it, mate."

"Yeah," he said, smiling with one half of his mouth.

"Never in doubt," said Ryder, also slapping Raffi on the back. "He's a natural."

"Tell me all about it later. I have to go and prepare something," I said, checking the time.

"Yeah," said Raffi. "Going to stick it to Ian Evans. We know."

Emma spoke up. "And you're okay with that?"

Ryder shook his head. "Of course not. We play for Chester. We want the Chester kids to win."

"Fat chance," said Emma, with a little heat. "Max has been perfecting his strategy for weeks. Four-three-three. Dynamic. Shapeshifting. Total football."

Ryder smiled. "I don't think Max wanted you to tell us his plan. We might tell the youth team manager."

"Tell him," said Emma, defiant. "Max doesn't care." She looked at me, and her face fell. "Oh, no. Have I made a mess?"

"No," I said, obviously lying. "Don't worry about it. But actually, Ryder, Mike Dean is just over there. Why don't you go and tell him? I think he'd be really interested . . . Emma, let's scoot."

"Did I say it right?" said Emma.

"You were perfect," I said, squeezing her tiny hand.

"What's total football?"

"It's where every player on a team can play any position. Your striker is comfortable at left back. Left back slips into right mid. Fluid. Whatever the team needs at any moment. Formations melt away. All that's left is football. Liquid football."

"Wow! These kids can do that?"

"Nobody can do that. It's ah . . . it's a destination that's always a few stops away. It's *shoot for the stars, land on the moon*. It's what Dutch people think about on those long winter nights."

She adjusted her beanie. "Is this what you and Henri sound like when you're alone?"

"Probably. I don't actually *listen* to him. I just wait for my turn to speak."

We were walking towards the far corner of the 3G pitch. Something made me turn and I stopped dead. Chester under-fourteens had started to arrive and were kicking balls around in an unstructured way. My gaze rested on Tyson, the flappy-armed little gobshite.

"What is it?"

"That kid. His dad is a sponsor."

"Oh. That's how he got in the team? No wonder you don't like the setup here."

"No, he got in the team on merit. He's really good. He just won't make it as a professional."

"Why not?"

"Not a team player. It's weird, though . . ." Tyson's player profile had changed. He'd added a point in CA, which wasn't much of a surprise given how much time had elapsed since I'd seen him play. He was now CA 5, which sounds shit, but to be fair, he was fourteen. A couple of attributes were green. But what really caught my attention, what really blew my mind, was that his teamwork was still 1. But it was red.

Red!

There was only one explanation. It had climbed to 2 (or more) and then fallen back.

"Max?"

I was pretty sure this was the first time I'd seen anyone's teamwork attribute change. Most of the attributes fluctuated or could be consciously improved, but some seemed fixed. I'd never seen green on bravery or teamwork. And I doubted I'd see any changes in influence, when I eventually unlocked that. That kind of thing seemed baked into someone's character. It seemed completely obvious to me that such attributes would never change. They *couldn't* change. But Tyson's had.

I tried to puzzle it out.

Chester versus Darlington. Had it been October? Two months ago, I'd come to town, made a big fuss about teamwork, and excluded Tyson. Sure, after I got fired he went back on the pitch and scored two goals. And maybe in front of everyone he'd bragged and he'd basked in his dad's pride. But deep down he'd known I was right. And in the weeks that followed, he'd really tried to be a better teammate. But then he'd backslid. Where had it gone wrong? His dad's negative influence? Lack of someone like me yelling at him to pass? He needed someone who'd yoink him out of the team if he wasn't *in* the team.

"Snookums?"

The situation infuriated me. I'd thought Tyson was a lost cause, but he wasn't. He was fourteen. He could *change*. If he could get to teamwork 7 or 8, he'd have a chance of a career. Fuck the Bulldog Brothers, fuck Spectrum, fuck Chester!

"Squeakbubble?"

Someone's hand was on my cheek, turning my face away from the grotesque spectacle of wasted talent and onto something a lot more desirable. "Your hands are really cold," I said.

"Talk to me," Emma said.

"Nah," I said, wrapping one of her hands in both of mine. "It's fine. Can't win 'em all. Let's go do what we came to do."

Broughton under-fourteens were doing some drills. Nothing too strenuous; they had a match in about twenty minutes. I'd arranged this little session to check on my new employee.

"That's the guy you chose?"

"Must be," I said. I'd advertised the position on that Jobsinfootball website and had quite a lot of responses. Lots of people wanted to coach young players. And young players wanted to be coached. If I couldn't make it as a manager, I'd take a setup like Broughton and turn it into a player farm. It'd just need a little seed money. Maybe Henri would chip in. Be my co-owner. We could grow it into a real football factory. Factory farming at first until I was rich, then a switch to organic when I could afford to have ethics.

We walked closer to the session. The coach, Jude, had an athletic build and a friendly, positive resting face. He was wearing glasses, which gave him an educated vibe. I was hoping he'd have a bit more steel to him than Chester FC's youth coach and my rival for the day, Spectrum. There was more to coaching kids than drills; I wanted someone who would stand up to unruly parents.

Jude's current drill involved six or seven plastic posts: red, yellow, or blue. The kids had to receive a pass then dribble towards the right colour. Or sometimes the *wrong* colour. I didn't exactly understand the rules, but that didn't matter. The kids did. There was a lot of laughter. Broughton's *actual* manager, Big Man, the guy with small ears and a beer belly, was watching and laughing, too. He must have been a bit bewildered that I'd chosen to hijack his club, but he seemed to accept that I had the interests of the kids at heart.

I sidled up to him. "Big Man. What do you think of the coach?"

"Max! Very good to see you again. Very good." He introduced himself to Emma, because I'd forgotten. "Jude? He's great. Thumbs-up. I hope he passes your test, whatever that is."

My test was simple—if I saw a kid's attribute turn green while he was coaching, that was that. Although now that I was here, I saw that Jude's name was hovering over his head, and underneath was a bunch of question marks. Same as with Jackie. Same as with the Darlo coaches. The curse was treating him like a coach. Even if he had 1 out of 20 for every coaching attribute, he was still better than me. And the kids were having fun—that was important, too.

This drill seemed like it'd improve skills I couldn't see. So I went over and interrupted. When the kids recognised me, there was subdued giddiness, especially from the ones who had defected from Chester: Benny, Future, Captain, the centre half, Bomber, the second centre half, and Sevenoaks, the right midfielder. Let's be clear—I could walk down any street in England and know that one hundred out of one hundred people would not recognise me. But in some very specific groups, I was the dog's. I was the bee's. I was the cat's.

"Guys," I said, "Calm the eff down. Selfies after the match. We don't have much time. Jude. Can you do a simple passing drill, please? I need to check something."

Jude's mouth went zigzaggy. Like everyone here, he'd watched my highlights on YouTube and TikTok, which were jaw-dropping and awe-inspiring, heavily edited as they were. But in addition, I was offering him regular work as a coach. I was the conduit to his dreams.

He pulled himself together and set up a rondo. Two-touch piggy-in-the-middle. Jude kept changing the rules, which as an outsider I found annoying, but the kids reacted to every change with renewed intensity. Great drill, good vibes, but I didn't see anything turn green. It'd been something of a long shot. What was I supposed to do? Keep him on probation for three months until the next time I saw him? Fuck that. The kids loved the sessions. Jude had come with the Henri and Big Man seal of approval. Absolutism hadn't ever done me any favours. This wasn't a hard decision. But there was one more thing I wanted to check.

"Top," I said to the kids, ending the session. "That's it. Go smash some shots or whatever. Then we'll do a team talk. Then we'll annihilate Chester."

Once the kids had sprinted off, I took Emma and Jude aside. "Jude. Imagine you're managing this team. Emma. Your son Gaz wants to play striker and take the penalties but Jude won't let him. Okay, go."

"Gaz?"

"Okay, go."

Jude was puzzled, but stepped into the part. "Miss Best, how can I help you?"

"That's *Mrs.* Best," said Emma, optimistically. Then she launched herself into the role. Jude stood firm. Gave his reasoning. Shut the conversation down politely. It didn't prove much, but it proved he knew the right thing to do.

"Jude, you're hired," I said.

He clenched his fists and did a tiny goal celebration. "Oh my God! Thank you. Thank you!"

I brought Big Man into the group and explained what I wanted. Jude would take training once a week, arranged and supervised by Big Man, and I'd pay Jude for two hours. At twenty-five pounds an hour, that would end up costing me about two hundred quid a month. Not much, really. Yeah, it wasn't exactly a great investment, but it'd get me some more data. It'd let me track the progress of a group of young players over time. I could do that if I was the manager of a club, but what if that didn't happen for a few years? I needed data ASAP.

And yeah, okay. Fine. You got me. This was also my penance for ruining Shona's party.

"Done and done," I said, fist-bumping both guys. I'd leave these kids' futures in their hands. Check on them in three months, maybe? Like a dentist?

"Interesting," said someone from a couple of feet away. I turned to see Mike Dean. He'd been spying on me! He was wearing a business shirt with the top buttons open. Who was he trying to seduce on a Sunday morning? "Who's financing this extra training?"

I frowned at him. I was still carrying some residual annoyance at the whole Tyson thing. "Darlington," I said.

He looked panicked. Like, genuinely. "Darlington are getting involved with Broughton?" Ha. That'd be megajustice—a rival club coming to Cheshire to pluck all the best talents. Didn't he know Darlo were too poor to hire a team bus for every away match?

"Darlington pay *me*. And I pay *Jude*."

MD relaxed, but not completely. He eyed Emma.

"This is Emma," I said. "You probably saw her on *Geordie Shore*." That got me an arm slap. "Emma, this is Mike Dean. Chester's managing director. We call him MD MD, or MD for short. He was the first guy to fire me as a football manager." MD sagged. I wanted to blast him with both barrels. *How can you fire me but not Ian Evans? You're dropping down the table like a stone, mate! Evans out! Best in!* But what was the point? Also: not in front of the children. Someone think of the children! "He was also the first person to pay me for my footy skills. Cash money. Yeah. And he dances when he's drunk. We had some good times. Well, it was nice to see you, Mike."

"Max, can I have a minute?"

"Nope. I've got to give a team talk."

"This is more important."

"Ah," I said, raising a finger and slicing the air with it. "Not this time. Nothing's more important than this. But look. I'll be around for a while. Come see me at halftime if you want."

"Won't you have another big team talk then?"

"Nah," I said. "We'll have won the game by then. Won't we, Emma?"

Her head bobbed like she'd just been switched on. "Max wants to try his four-three-three fantasy. Total left backs. Liquid players."

"Riiiiight," said MD, eyeing her in a new way.

"Dammit. Sorry, Max."

"Don't worry," said MD. "I already knew Max was planning four-three-three. For some reason, Chester FC's Instagram account was tagged by a team called Middleton Rangers. Max was using them to test his new tactical theories. They did one of those short videos about it. Inexplicably, they thought to include us in the post."

"I told them I'd be using it against you," I said. "They must have thought I wanted you to know. Ah, well."

The tiniest grin came to MD's face. "The deception is so obvious," he said. "That it has to be a double-cross. But the double-cross is even more obvious. Why would you keep talking about four-three-three if you were *going* to play it? But that's what you'd *want* us to think. So what that means is . . ." He made himself go cross-eyed—very useful skill!—and Emma laughed.

"Max. I'm not sure he's buying it."

"He's buying it. He's already bought it. It's in his pocket with a receipt for a line and a sinker."

"I'm too old for this, Max," said MD, walking away with multiple tiny shakes of the head.

"That couldn't have gone better," I said, delighted. "Okay. Time to inspire the next generation."

My team. The vehicle for my revenge. Broughton under-fourteens. Maroon tops, blue shorts. Goalie in green. Mostly CA 1, but with five good players who'd left Chester. Thanks to the outreach of Brother Benny, the entire squad had joined the cult of Max Best the Mystery Winger. Left unchecked, they'd spend their careers trying to nutmeg everyone, doing double dribbles, showing off in the most outlandish ways their talents would allow.

I stood on the edge of the penalty area with the goal behind me. The kids sat down in the D, forming a vague semicircle two or three deep. Three deep! Amazing. We had six subs! Chester only had two. Big Man, Jude, Emma, and some other people—parents, I guessed—shuffled forward to listen. I tried to tune the parents out. This had nothing to do with them, but I could hardly ask them to get lost while I indoctrinated their kids.

"First question," I said, and all conversation from the kids stopped. "Are we going to play this match on the full-size pitch?"

"Yes," said Big Man. "There's no other way. It's all a bit last minute. Your friend Mike arranged it. Pulled some strings."

"Absurd," I said. These fourteen-year-olds would play on the same size pitch as me, a bona fide physical freak slash footballing genius.

"But that just makes it easier to win. Second question. Dudes. Hombres. Amigos. Is it more important to you to be cool and top like me? Or to become a professional footballer?" I let that hang. No one seemed prepared to get so heavy so soon. "Guys, you can choose one thing. Play like me. Or become a pro. Choose. Choose one."

No one wanted to speak, so I pointed at one kid. The answer burped out from him. "Pro. I mean, you're top, but . . ."

Another one. "Yeah, pro."

Now that the ice was broken, they all agreed. "Benny?" I said.

"Yeah," he said. "I want to become a professional."

"Top. That's what I want for you, too. That's a healthy goal. Now, you all saw a clip of me taking the piss out of some chump. And you thought it was hilarious. You thought it was the single greatest moment in sporting history." The kids looked glum. They knew I was here to tell them not to play like that. "And you know what? Apart from Michael Smith versus Michael van Gerwen in the darts, you're right. What I did needs the balance and grace of a ballet dancer, the technical assurance of Johann Cruyff, and the fuck-you-this-is-my-pitch attitude of George Best. Er . . . no relation." The kids were agog. Even Emma was stunned. Plot twist! "Your parents probably want me to tell you not to do what I did. And guess what? I'm not going to do that. If you can play like me, you must be fucking incredible. Showing off is cool and awesome. That's my opinion."

There was a ball nearby. I flicked it up, bounced it on my head a few times, blindfolded myself with one hand, and turned and volleyed the ball into the goal behind me. The kids gasped.

"But listen. There are two moments that clip didn't show, one before; one after. There was the time *before* when the left back was kicking me, elbowing me, even pinching me, which was *really* fucking weird." The kids laughed. "I haven't been pinched—by a boy—since primary school." I stared into space, then shook the thought away. "Fucking bizarre. And he was saying things to wind me up. It didn't work—I was calm, but I felt he deserved to be shown up. Do you know what I mean?"

Lots of nods.

"But I saw this clip of Benny doing the same thing. And I'm not having a go, Benny mate. My first reaction was wow! Look at his technique! But then I felt a bit bad. It's just my opinion, but I don't think that kid deserved to be done like that. The little clip I saw, when you dribbled him the second time, he ignored it and got back into position. I don't know if he was upset later, but right there and then he had one thought—do my job for the team. Sound about right? And I fucking *love* players like that! I wouldn't go full Max Best on a player like that. No way. I'd nutmeg him. I'd beat him. That's my job, yeah? But nothing more. Not rubbing his nose in it. Not him."

I rubbed the bottom of *my* nose. It was starting to freeze up. Why don't they make gloves for noses?

"That was the before thing. The *after* thing was the guy I double dribbled tried to snap my leg in half. He nearly did as well. The physio said I was millimetres away from spending the rest of my life with this guy's boot sticking out of my shin. He told me to buy a lottery ticket—that's how lucky I was. If that oik had made a proper connection, I wouldn't be here. I'd be in a hospital today with one of those oxygen masks on. I'm not saying that to scare you, but one thing about being a professional is being available to play. If there's a fifty-fifty tackle and you get hurt, that's bad luck. If you're like me," I grinned, "dribbling around the pitch in a big circle saying 'nah nah nah NAH nah!' then you're going to get injured and what kind of teammate are you then? And yeah! Teammate! What I did just shows what my team is like. We don't get on. We're not friends. If my best mate Henri Lyons was running to the penalty spot, do you think I'd turn around and run back to my own half? No chance! I'd cross and he'd score and we'd both be happy. I think if you're in a good team you want to pass to your mates because that feels good. I wouldn't know. I've never been in an eleven-a-side team with ten people who liked me. That's why I always played five-a-side," I said, laughing at the horrible truth of the statement.

I took a step back and moved forward again. Just wanted to keep moving so my blood didn't turn to ice. "Oh! Another thing. I went to Sheffield Wednesday. They wanted to sign me. Guess what the first thing their manager said to me was?"

I really wanted another voice to come in, but no one wanted to break my flow. Emma sensed this and called out, "Who's the blonde and is she single?"

Lots of smiles.

"No, it wasn't that." I looked back at the Broughton kids. "He said, 'I don't like the showboating.'" I shrugged. Left a pause. "Guess who doesn't play for Sheffield Wednesday now?"

"You," said Benny. He'd been through a lot of emotions during my talk. I think he'd felt attacked at some points, but now he didn't. Now he felt sorry for me.

"Yeah. I'm *good enough*. But he's trying to build a proper team there. Passing team. Guys who care about teamwork. Do you get me? I'd love to play in that team. I'd fit in! That's what I want, too! But because I was dicking around, it might never happen."

I looked up at the sky, pretending to be regretful. "Yeah. Anyway. It's up to you. But I know you guys are into teamwork and work-rate and passing. That's why we've got six subs and Toxic FC over there have only got two. That's why I reckon you'll win today. Nice big artificial pitch, perfect for passing, against a team whose best player only ever dribbles. I mean, all I can say is lol. Next week you'll be back with Big Man and Jude and they'll take good care of you. So because I only get to see you now and then, I get to be preachy. Talk about the big picture. So here it goes. Don't make the mistakes that I've made. Respect yourself—don't sabotage your career. Respect your teammates—look for the pass, keep everyone involved, be positive. Respect your opponent—until they lose that respect." Cheeky grin. "Respect the referee, even if you *really* don't want to." Eye roll. "Because no ref, no game. And last but not least, respect the sport."

"What does that mean?" said the captain.

I smiled. "Good question. I have no idea. I just like the sound of my own voice." I checked my phone. Nearly time. The Knights had finished and cleared off, and the referee was over on the far side, checking the goal nets and corner flags. He'd come over here and do the same and then the match would start. It seemed all the spectators from that match were staying to watch this one, and more were arriving. I idly wondered if the curse would give me an attendance stat. "Right. Tactics. I've told those chumps we're playing four-three-three." I went into our tactics screen and set Broughton to 4-3-3.

Sevenoaks groaned. That was one formation he couldn't shine in. He didn't do well centrally.

I checked Chester's setup: 4-4-2 diamond. A good choice against 4-3-3. But one that played into my hands. I grinned. "So at every goal kick, every throw-in, as much as you can, stand in a 4-3-3 formation, okay? So here's the back four." I named them, but to everyone's surprise, I had the twelve-year-old Future as one of the two centre backs and one of the older CBs, Bomber, at right back. "Future's our passing outlet, okay? So I want him in the middle. He's going to pass to midfield. Captain, you'll have to win the headers for the both of you. Got it?"

"Yes, boss."

I named the midfield. Seven put his hand up. "You've got four midfielders there."

"Yeah," I said, with a dollop of sarcasm, suitable for talking to teenagers. "Because we're playing four-four-two. *Duh.* Pass pass pass. Let the ball do the work. Make Chester run around."

As I said that, I switched the formation. Of my five key players I had three in defence, plus Seven at right midfield, and Benny as a striker. He put his hand up. "You want us to pretend to be playing four-three-three. Okay. I'll do it. *We'll* do it. But will you tell us why?"

"Sure," I said. "One. Because it will help you win. Two. Because it's *funny.*"

As Emma and I walked to our technical area, I slowed to a near crawl. I had cursemail! An achievement. These had almost totally dried up since I'd become a player, to the point that I often forgot they existed.

New achievement: All Pacino

Increase the morale of one or more players on more than one occasion.

Reward: 1 XP

Morale! That was one of those hidden things I'd seen during the MUNDIAL matches. Based on what I'd seen in the World Cup, it didn't seem to make a *massive* difference, but higher morale was obviously better than lower. If I could use my pre-match and halftime speeches to boost morale, that was yet another tiny advantage.

I turned to see if the players looked visibly more motivated or whatever, and felt that there was more green in the player profiles. It took me a few seconds of scanning, but there it was! No fewer than three new green numbers. Benny and two of the Broughton originals had increased their teamwork attributes. My speech had increased morale AND improved an unimprovable attribute!

Wow. This opened up a lot of possibilities. If I scouted a fourteen-year-old with good attributes but a bad attitude, I could fix him! I could turn Tysons into Bennys!

I'd only been in town a few minutes and I'd already had several big wins.

43

MAX BEST WINS IT ALL (PART 2 OF 20)

My match overview screen read:

Broughton Under-fourteens versus Chester Under-fourteens

I had my in-vision clock, but for the sake of seeming like a real boy I suggested Emma set a thirty-five-minute timer.

"Thirty-five?" she said.

"Matches are seventy minutes in this league," I said. "They should make it shorter today because the pitch is so big, but you can't expect anyone in football to actually use their brain."

"Except you."

"Right. But it's good news. We've got loads of subs and we can roll them on and off. The plan is to pass the ball a lot and make Chester run. We'll overwhelm them in the second half of the second half. Which means I don't need to mess the kids about with mad tactics."

"Explain that bit to me," said Emma.

"Which bit?"

"People seem surprised that you'd choose four-four-two."

"Ah. That's because I'm a floating megabrain. They expect something weird from me. Something funky. Every match is a chance for me to show off. Why wouldn't I take it?"

"So why don't you?"

One side of my mouth lifted of its own accord. A pretty big part of the reason was that I only had access to three formations and I couldn't tweak them. Playing the MUNDIAL mini game had made me hungry to unlock every part of the curse. A month ago, my powers had seemed incredible. God-like. Now I felt feeble. I couldn't even drop a striker into midfield. "Emma! Because of what I've been saying. Why does no one believe me? This isn't about me. This is about my lifelong passion for Broughton. Four-four-two is the best formation to show what those little Broughton bastards can do. Remember the scouts? Sevenoaks can only play right midfield. So that rules out tons of formations. No, four-four-two is the best thing for them."

"So what's with the cloaks and daggers and mentioning four-three-three all the time?"

"That's partly for my own amusement. Henri called today my revenge fantasy. It's not, but I can have my little jokes. Winning's not *that* big a deal, but why not sort out the kids' futures *and* win? And it's like I said in my speech. You're allowed to take the piss if the other guy's a dick."

Emma looked Spectrum up and down. He was holding onto a clipboard. Clutching it to his chest. "Is he a dick?"

"He's a moderate dick. He's a good coach but he doesn't stand up to the parents so the net effect is negative. His team isn't fun. Notice they've only got two subs? That's shocking, really. Oh, and he called me names, the lily-livered soy boy. So yeah. His punishment is some low-level stress. I judge myself to be on the right side of history here."

"Oh, do you?"

"Yes. And by the way, all my shenanigans have made him give my most dangerous player a free ride."

"Benny?"

"No. Seven. He's the *me* in this team. If it stays like this in the second half, he'll receive passes under no pressure and drive forward. It's going to be carnage. Leaving him unmarked is like doing nothing to stop Mbappé."

"So you've learned a thing or two from the World Cup."

"I hope so. But to be fair, I've been doing this sort of thing for a while. Make space for the guys who can progress the ball. We're lucky today. We've got Future who can pass from defence to midfield. And we've got Seven who can dribble from midfield to attack. That's gold. I'm not sure what I learned from the World Cup. Probably hundreds of tiny little things. Do you know what I mean? Things you learn without knowing it."

The ref blew his whistle to start the match, and that in itself was interesting. I didn't get offered the Bench Boost and Triple Captain perks. Those were only supposed to trigger once per season, and this was explicitly the same league and the same season as last time I'd been here. No loopholes this time! I still had the Free Hit to boost our chances at a set piece, and I'd probably use it. I'd wait till the second half, though. I felt a narrative brewing . . .

I made some last-second tweaks to our tactics. I set every player to short passing. No forward runs. No through balls. Offside trap yes, pressing no. All I wanted was passing. Thousands of passes. Sterile possession. The kind of football I hated watching. But today it would lead somewhere. Somewhere spectacular . . .

The match soon fell into the pattern I'd expected—there were a lot of Chester players in the middle of the pitch getting in each other's way. They had to run wide, then return to base. My players had lots of time and space. It was all very comfortable.

Already starting to get bored, Emma asked me to point out the good players in the Chester team.

"Okay," I said. "See that guy there? He's called Henk. His mum is a piece of work. Very ambitious. Cut-throat. Great football brain, too."

"You're describing the mum a lot considering I asked about *him*."

I smiled. Maybe a *little* bit guiltily. "She's quite attractive. Henri was mad at me when I told her off. But her personality is important to understanding Henk. See he's playing as a defensive midfielder now? Look, there's the line of defenders, and there's Henk in front of them."

"Yes, I see it. He's like a moat in front of the castle."

"Floating megabrain Max Best says he's a centre back. But Mum thinks Henk will have a better career and make more money as a DM, so she's trying to turn him into one."

"Will it work?"

"No. But it's smart. I've been undercover in the football world for a while now, and she's one of the only people I've met who's thinking long-term like that. Okay. Then there's Sullivan. He's in the midfield there. He's good but he's scared of making mistakes because his dad will shout at him."

"That's horrible."

"Yes, it is. You'd be amazed how many people have told me it's just part of football culture and I should ignore it. Fuck *that*. Anyway, by playing safe all the time he guarantees he won't catch the eye of the scouts."

"But Henk's mum will?"

"Oh, yeah!"

"I don't like your enthusiasm."

"Talking of eye-catching, their final good player is that kid Tyson. You see him get the ball and dribble? Trying to take on the whole team. He's catastrophic for team spirit. It's harsh to say it but he's the reason no one wants to play for Chester."

Harsh, yes. Fair, yes. But it killed the conversation.

So we watched. On my new stats screen, we quickly shot up to 70% possession. Pass pass pass! I almost laughed at how boring I'd made the match.

Meanwhile, I rotated all my players in a constant whir. Everyone except the goalie. Benny came off. He looked at me, worried, wondering if he'd done something wrong. They all did. But five minutes later, they were back on. Rotation without judgement. The whole team relaxed.

The best players on the pitch, according to the match ratings, were Henk and Sevenoaks. They flitted between 8 and 9 out of 10. The two key strikers, Tyson and Benny, were both on 6. I'd noticed that most of a striker's match rating came down to how involved they were in creating goals.

Goals. For a while it seemed like this match could last infinity hours and not produce any. But as half-time approached, Captain made a mistake. He had an easy passing option to his right, but a mad compulsion to do something interesting hit him and he tried to chip the ball to the left, over Tyson. He made a mess of it.

Tyson couldn't believe his luck. He caught the ball on his chest, raced towards goal, and none of our defenders could get near him. The talented dipshit lashed the ball low into the corner. Good goal. Tyson ran around, arms aloft, celebrating on his own.

"Ugh," I said.

"Are we going to lose?"

I laughed. "No chance. But if any scouts *have* come, they'll be like 'Oooh, that was a good goal. Ooh, let me ask Max about Tyson. About Flappy Bird. About Gooseboy. Ooh, let's ignore the players who might actually be good.'"

"Why would they ask you about a Chester player?"

"Why wouldn't they? They know I was involved with the Chester youth setup in some way. They don't know about the whole fight-to-the-death thing."

Emma was restless. "We conceded a goal. Shouldn't we do something?"

"Like what?"

"Pump them up. Do a tactic. I don't know."

"Strange as it may seem, I'm not a youth football expert. But I think it's all right for them to have setbacks. Let them feel miserable for a minute."

"Max!"

"I'm serious. Captain shouldn't have tried that pass. This pain is good for him. You know, long term. Moving up the ranks shouldn't be *easy*. It just needs to be *possible*."

"Was he showing off?"

"I wouldn't call it that, no. They haven't done any of that."

She didn't know about the green attributes my stirring speech had provoked. "So that's another win? That and Jude?"

I grinned. "I suppose so!" I checked the match clock. "Nearly halftime, isn't it?"

"Oh! But we haven't even had a shot."

"I know. But Chester are running around way more than us. They'll pay for it in the second half."

"I'm bored! Where's my fearless football?"

I turned her towards me and put one hand on each shoulder. "Emma. This *is* fearless football. Not from the players, but from me. If this was a pro match, the fans would boo. I'm going to walk around at halftime and everyone will laugh at me. Everyone will have a smug comment. '*Oh, there's that guy who thinks he knows about football. Tommy Tactics? More like Freddie Fraud.*' And so on. I don't *want* to be losing, but I can use it. I'm trying to teach these kids something. Telling them a story about right and wrong. The team playing as a team are losing. The team playing as an individual are winning. Is Max mistaken? This moment of doubt now . . . that's powerful. When they turn it around, the lesson will stick."

Her lips curled deliciously. "These little outbursts. Your passion. It's pretty hot."

I grinned. "Do you want to go behind the bike sheds and do some winning?"

"Oops," she said, holding up her phone. It was beeping. "Halftime. What a shame."

Halftime. One–nil down.

The team came to the technical area to get instructions and take on liquids.

"Guys, gather round. Hurry up! One of the spectators did a murder last night and I've got fifteen minutes to solve the case."

"Halftime's only ten minutes, Max," said Big Man.

"Well, shit. I'll just say the butler did it. Okay. Big speech or little one? I'm thinking little one." Benny had his hand up. "What?"

"There's a girl watching. When I went to take a throw, she said, 'Why doesn't your manager give you instructions? Doesn't he like you?'" He rubbed his arm. "It sort of messed with my head."

I laughed. I laughed harder than I had for weeks. Benny's look of worry melted away and he grinned, too. "Benny. She's doing it because she knows you're dangerous. Ah, that's great. I'm glad she's here."

"Do you know her?"

"Yeah. I taught her to say that."

"Teach us that kind of thing!"

"Nah. I'm not into that anymore. It's funny but it's the wrong kind of funny. Unless maybe you deserve it, Benny mate?" He shook his head. "Okay listen. Feast your eyes upon the lifeless husk that is Chester FC. They're flat out. Lying down. They're *wrecked*. Look at us. Standing up. We're fresh. We've got legs. We could win a dance-off. Do you know the phrase *handbrake off*? Me and my assistant are turning our special keys. Keys to a weapon so powerful it needs two people to unlock it. Three, two, one, handbrake off. That means no more Mr. Nice Guy. New plan: mixed passing. Forward runs. Try through balls. Pressing. Goals goals goals. Captain, what is it? What's up?"

He looked pretty distressed. It hadn't really hit me how much it would mean for the defectors if they could beat Chester. "I messed up that pass. Gave them a goal. I'm sorry."

I wanted to tell him not to worry about it, and make a joke. But that probably wouldn't help him long-term. "There's different kinds of mistakes. Many lead to goals but no one thinks worse of you. Like if you slip or something. Mistakes are always bad if they're against the manager's instructions. I know what you were asked to do is boring. And I understand the compulsion to liven things up because I'd be the same as you. But I'm a winger; you're a centre back. You have to do what you're told all the time. It's not my idea of fun, but that's the role." I straightened and stretched. "Don't stress about it. But know that every manager you ever have is going to expect you to follow instructions." I imagined Captain's best possible future, being trained to shuffle and slide by an endless succession of Ian Evanses and Dave Cutters. Ah, well. Maybe he'd like it. "You know what is fun? Attacking. That's the team talk. Attack. If you're on the pitch thinking wait what's my job? Attack. That's your job. Hey, Benny. Have you got your phone? Your dad waits in the car when you play, right? Text him. Tell him I said he's allowed to watch the second half. No, I'm serious. He won't want to miss this. Okay, lads. Take it easy. Spend the rest of the break ranking my top ten goals."

Halftime. Seven minutes remaining.

I took Emma and started wandering down the edge of the pitch looking for social wins. I waved at Future's grandmother. I gave a double-finger-gun salute to a couple of the Knights parents I recognised. But before I could continue, I was intercepted from the right by James Yalley, Gavvo from Altrincham FC, and two men I didn't recognise. At the same time, Mike Dean arrived from the left. They all started talking at once.

"Whoa," I said. "Let's do it in age order. Youngster."

It took him a second to drag his attention away from Emma. "Oh. Reverse age order. I see. Yes, well. Mr. Gavins is here, as you can see. And these are the other scouts you invited. Wrexham and Tranmere." He said their real names, of course, but it's easier this way.

I shook hands with them and smiled at Emma. They had come! More wins! "Awesome. I'm ecstatic you came. This is Emma. Sixth in line to the Duchy of Monte Carlo."

"Fifth," she said. "Cousin Ludo died of gout."

"Of course. And guys, this is Mike Dean. Runs Chester." More handshakes and stuff. This was a really difficult industry to get things done quickly in.

Everyone wanted to say something, but Gavvo was quickest on the draw. "Max. Thanks for telling us about this. Couple of good players already." He looked at his notes. "Can we talk about Tyson?"

Subtract one win. "Yeah, at full-time. If you haven't seen the light."

"What do you mean?"

"Do you really want to sign a player with more shots than *attempted* passes?"

"He's got good balance. Good touch. Good eye for goal. Players are often selfish at this age."

"It's your call. I recommend you wait and see how he acts when things start to go wrong."

Mike Dean beamed. "Ah, but Max. Our boys are in total control! You haven't even had a shot! Something tells me the second half will be the Tyson show! What scout wouldn't be impressed?" He frowned. "Not that we want our best players to leave the club."

"I invited them to look at *my* guys, Mike. But maybe leaving would be good for Tyson. Change of scenery. Different input." I shrugged. I didn't care all that much. "So you want to talk about Benny now? Seven? Future?"

"Future?" smiled Tranmere. "He's quite short for a centre back."

"Yeah," I said, going off the guy in a flash. "You wouldn't see a centre back that short, I don't know, playing in the *World Cup final* later today."

Emma squeezed my palm. Trying to get me to calm down.

Tranmere raised a hand. "You're right. You're right. You think he'll be that good?"

Future had a PA of 99. "On talent, he could get to the Championship. He's the most talented kid here. You should be throwing yourselves at him." I looked around. Benny had PA 40. Captain and bomber were in the low 30s. Seven was 35. They wouldn't play to a very high level, but they could all run out for Chester one day. That would be an awesome moment for them and their families. "I've got four more. Make sure you stay for the second half. We'll put on a show."

I tried to move away but Gavvo and MD both tried to stop me. Gavvo was again first to shoot out a question. "What about Henk?"

Henk had PA 37 but had the appearance of having a much higher ceiling. He was tall and powerful for his age, great in the air, smooth and unruffled. "Yeah. Good player. A more obvious fit for your teams. How much are you willing to pay?"

"Pay?"

"You want to sign a top youth prospect. What do Chester get?"

Gavvo turned to Wrexham and made a face that said, "Can you believe this guy?"

Wrexham said, "They'll get a sell-on clause. If we take Henk and sell him later, Chester'll get five percent."

"Yeah," I said, checking the clock. These guys were burning my time talking about the wrong players. Big fail. "That plus twenty thousand pounds."

"What? That's crazy. No one would pay that."

"Nineteen," I said.

Gavvo laughed. "We bring him for a trial. If we end up inviting him into the programme, five thousand pounds."

"Eight thousand or after Darlo get promoted, I demolish Alty next season. Twice." I was starting to enjoy myself, but then I wondered what I was doing. "Fuck it. I don't care. Here's the MD. His mum's over there. The fit one. Just make sure Chester get something out of it."

"What about the other ones? The Broughton ones? Is there a fee for them, too?"

"No. I want them to land in the best environment I can arrange. You can donate some old kits and mannequins and shit if you want. We'll talk again later. I need to say hi to someone."

Halftime. Three minutes remaining.

While the scouts haggled with MD, Emma and I pottered off. James wasn't sure what to do, but decided to stay with Gavvo.

"Here's the Bulldog Brothers," I mumbled, as we passed Tyson's family. They'd added a third. As well as the two brothers, there was now a teenage version. Big and beefy but with a decent haircut and no tats. The older of the species saw me and turned to each other, laughing at some joke.

"So the plan is," said Emma, "that these guys are laughing now and you'll wipe that smile off their faces by the end."

"Yep. Ah! Now see that guy up ahead? Looks like an ostrich egg but actually it's a human being."

"His girlfriend is gorgeous."

"She's a physio here. Let's go have a quick—"

"Excuse me? Mr. Best?"

I turned, bewildered, to see that the third Bulldog had wiggled closer. He was just a yard away. What was it with people sneaking up on me? My first thought was that I should diffuse the situation peacefully with a Vulcan nerve pinch. Okay, that was a lie. My first thought was that I should punch him really hard, throw Emma over my shoulder, and sprint to safety.

All I could do was gawp at the guy, so Emma took over. "Can we help you?"

"Oh," he said. "I was wondering if I could have a selfie?"

"Do you follow her on Insta?" I said, trying to understand what was happening.

"Don't be a clown," said Emma. "He wants a selfie with *you*."

"What? Why?"

Wrong question. It unleashed a torrent. I guessed he didn't go to the same school as Tyson; he spoke much more bluntly. "When you was here! They was all laughing at you, said you was a disabled rando who thought he knew footy, and then it was all hey remember that weirdo? He signed for *Darlington*. And then it was check this out, he played against Whitby. And they was laughing because you was shit and they didn't even know your name on the PA."

"PA?" I said, startled.

"Public address," said Emma.

"Yeah!" said Baby Bulldog, as though we were agreeing with him. "And then you went psycho tackling your own player and they tried to laugh at *that* but you dribbled eighty yards and you sat two defenders *down* and I was like where's the joke, man? And then there was that mad free kick and every match you kept going mental and holy shit did you see it when you skanked that guy then said sack it let's do that again and mate you *scored* from a *corner*. It's like you're playing FIFA on cheat mode!" He nodded towards his family. "Those jokers stopped watching but I didn't. I keep telling everyone this guy's a legend and he coached my cuz and no one believes me, so I want a selfie so I can prove it."

All that came out in about eight seconds and I was twenty-eight seconds behind. "You want a selfie?" I said.

Emma pulled me towards the kid. "God sake, Max, pose for the selfie. Holy cow."

Second half.

Emma dragged me back to our technical area where I spent the first few minutes of the second half in a daze. What just happened?

One of my biggest enemies in football had a cousin who thought I was top? Were the Bulldogs over there right now bickering about whether I was a genius or a fraud? Or were that whole speech and the selfie part of a bigger prank?

The back of my neck felt hot and itchy. I rubbed it.

"Come on, Chester!"

I turned to face the sound. I couldn't see the face of the shouter, but I knew who it was.

I got my phone out and dialled.

"Max?"

"Kisi. What are you doing?"

"I'm watching my beloved Chester. You can't phone me during the match. You're supposed to be managing."

"Beloved Chester?"

She moved the phone away and yelled, "Chester, whoo!"

A man beside her repeated the shout. "Chester, whoo!" Mr. Yalley.

"Is your mum there, too? You should all be in church. God will smite you."

"James convinced Mum and Dad. Said we had to support you."

I rubbed my forehead with my free hand. "Right. Thanks. But you're cheering for the wrong fucking team!"

There was a bit of rustling on the line and I heard Mrs. Yalley. "Language, please, Mr. Best." More noise. She'd handed the phone back to Kisi.

"Kisi," I said, slowly. "I'm the manager of Broughton. We are playing against Chester. You are cheering for the wrong team. It's like if you were cheering for City against the Beth Heads."

"Well, that would be okay," she said. "I *am* a City player. Anyway," she added, "you were all Chester Chester Chester for ages. You can't blame me if I can't keep up with your moods. And another thing. Meghan taught me about football culture. I said I was a Darlo fan now because you were there and she said you can't change your team that's a big no-no. So I'm a Red Devil. I'm a Beth Head. I'm a Sandra Stan. And now I'm Chester. I have bonded with Chester boys under-fourteens. For life."

I exhaled. "Fine. Enjoy losing. Are you sticking around to watch the World Cup final with us?"

"Here in Chester? Where?"

"We've rented a cinema. Apparently watching footy on such a massive screen is top. James will love it. He can complain about the keystoning and that. Right. Stop mentally disintegrating my players. Stop cheering. Watch in sullen silence. Thank you very much."

I checked my tactics screens. Nothing needed a tweak. The match had taken on a radically different complexion—now, we were attacking relentlessly and Chester were on the back foot, pushed back so far all they could do was boot the ball away hoping for a breather. The breather never came. My boys were on one.

Captain was a rock. Tyson's dribbles kept smashing into him. Then a quick, simple pass and we were once again in full flow. Captain didn't look bored; he seemed to be having the time of his life.

I smiled at Emma. She smiled back.

This was a good setup. I could hang around with my girlfriend while managing the team and networking. I dialled again.

"Jackie! Nice to see you here. Are you coming to the World Cup final? I'll text you the details. So, Livia asked you out. I'm glad she finally plucked up the courage."

He sighed. "I asked *her*, Max."

"Oh, wow. I'm surprised. Question. Can you give Ziggy ten minutes in a match sometime soon?"

"Probably."

"Oh. That was easy. I feel he needs another kick. Another dose."

"Way ahead of you."

"Huh." Another win! "What do you think of my formation?"

I felt him shake his head. "Four-four-two? Max Best, King of Convention. It's true what they say, then."

"What's that?"

"You can teach a new dog old tricks."

I laughed. "Talking of. The Max Best Challenge. What the fuck?"

"It was your idea, Max. Shouldn't you be focusing on your team?"

"We're in control of the game, in case you hadn't noticed."

"I had noticed, actually. But I don't see what you changed to make this happen. You're very frustrating, Maxy boy."

"If you come to the final I'll explain it to you." I changed my tone. "And I'll pay you back what I owe."

"Oh." Brief pause. "All that goal bonus money starting to come in?"

"Yeah. Turns out," I said, "that I'm a pretty good player. If you'd spotted that . . . you could have signed me for FC United. The team you work for."

"Got to go, Max. I'm expecting a call from my mate who's into conspiracy theories. He wants to tell me the king's a flat lizard."

So I wouldn't get any answers from him today. "Ah. You don't want to confess on the phone. Got it. See you later."

I hung up.

"What did you mean by that?" asked Emma.

"I *always* feel that Jackie Reaper is up to something. But when I think it through, I was the one who went to FC United and I was the one who asked him to coach the Beth Heads. He never initiated anything. So why do I always feel that he did?"

"Max, I'm bored. Can we have a goal, please?"

"Absolutely," I said. I did some hand waving like I was casting a spell, then I pushed the energy I'd "summoned" onto the pitch.

Captain heads the ball down. He's winning all his duels today.

Future controls and looks up.

Future plays a pass to Sevenoaks.

He's in acres of space. He drives forward.

The left back makes a challenge. Sevenoaks skips around him.

He's clear! He pushes to the byline. He looks up and crosses low.

There's a scramble. The ball comes loose. Benny is sharpest.

GOOOOOAAAAALLLLL!

The equaliser!

It had been coming!

Emma squeaked. "How did you do that?"

"I didn't. That was coincidence. I promise I am not a witch."

Big Man and Jude came to celebrate with us. "Tidy finish," said the manager, which was about as effusive as he got.

"Did you see that skill?" said Jude, referring to the way Seven got past the defender. "I wonder who taught him that."

"Don't look at me," I said. "He was doing that kind of thing the first time I saw him. Maybe he learned it from Spectrum." While I was trying to give the Chester coach some credit, I noticed the first outbreak of flappy-arm-itis. Tyson was beginning his transformation into a man-goose. "Aaaand the sulking begins. Big Man, what's your record win against Chester?"

"Record win? We're yet to *record* a win."

"Oh, shit. I think I'm about to break the space-time continuum."

Two–one.

Three–one.

Kisi: Max! Stop it!

Four–one.

Jackie: Just so you know, there will be random drug tests after the match.

Five–one.

Nice One: I can honestly say I haven't enjoyed a single minute of my son's football career. Until now. This is a joy. Thank you.

Six–one.

Jackie: Stop! Stop! They're already dead!

Emma asked why I was laughing. I told her what Jackie had written.

"So we should stop scoring, then?"

"Huh? What?"

"Do they stop the game if the score gets too big?"

"Er . . . no. In America they have a thing called the Mercy Rule. Stops kids being humiliated."

"And that isn't a rule here?"

"No."

"So the only thing standing between these kids and utter humiliation . . . is your sense of morality."

"My sense of morality is telling me to thrash Chester so violently that somebody finally realises they have a big fucking problem. My morality says that's better for everyone, long-term."

"Yes, and that's fine. I understand that part. But the Chester kids look miserable."

"Yeah," I said, smiling at Tyson's body language. That didn't go down well with my girlfriend. I tried to see things from her point of view. "You're worried they'll all cry themselves to sleep tonight. You think I've done enough to prove my point." I wasn't sure that I had. Today, sure, MD, Spectrum, and the parents would be stunned. But six months from now, they'd look at the results and see won, won, won, lost, won, won. Six goals weren't enough to guarantee a long-term reaction.

"People are leaving," she said, pointing to the crowd. Little groups had started to detach from the hive and were heading off.

Okay, so maybe six goals were enough. "All right," I said. "I'll see what I can do."

Benny picked up a loose pass and dribbled into the penalty box. He waited for a defender to come, then rolled the ball sideways to himself. Nice trick! He was flattened by a second defender. A clumsy, tired, hapless defender.

Penalty kick, no complaints.

I held my hands up. "That wasn't me! I'm not a witch."

Emma laughed. "I know."

I took a couple of steps forward. "Future! Future! Take the pen."

He looked at me. Pointed to himself. *Me?*

"Yes! Hurry up."

He scurried forwards and asked Benny for the ball. Benny seemed confused and didn't hand it over until I went into the screens and made Future the official penalty taker. Benny blinked, but then crouched a little to give Future advice on where to shoot.

"Babes," I said. "I've put our tiniest player on the pen. He's a defender. He can barely kick the ball twelve yards. He's never taken a pen in his life. It's the best I can do. Okay?"

I hugged her and pulled her into me while the referee moved all the Chester players out of the D.

FREE HIT Y/N?

I had the option to boost Future's chance of scoring by ten percent.

I glanced over at Spectrum. At a sagging MD. At the thinning ranks of Chester FC parents and well-wishers.

I squeezed Emma again.

Help Future score? Or let Chester keep what little was left of their dignity?

This was *not* a hard decision.

44
MAX LOSES BIG (PART 3 OF 3)

At the final whistle, the kids ran around shaking hands with their defeated foes. I supposed I had to do the same with my equivalent, if only to be a role model. So I pottered over and offered a handshake to Spectrum. He took it in silence. The formalities have been observed!

While the Chester mob gathered their gear and trudged away, our kids ran over to the technical area to start the real celebrations.

"Go in the middle," I said, waving them back onto the pitch. "Go on, fuck off over there. Yes, I'm serious. Future? Good job. In the middle. Captain." I waved the captain over and bent to put a hand on his shoulder. "Big days. Special days. You'll know when. You gather your flock. Do a huddle. Tell them what you think."

I saw the whites of his eyes as he realised what I was asking of him. "I have to give a speech?"

"Yes. You're not at school. Okay, you're *at* a school but you're not *in* school. No one's grading you. I'm staying over here. This is between you and your mates. Say what you want. Stay positive, keep it short. All right?"

"Mr. Best. I really don't know what to say."

I formed a fist and pushed it against his chest. "Yeah you do. Off you pop."

I watched as he jogged into the middle of a lot of confused young men and started the huddle. The rest knew what to do—free arms found free shoulders like a graphical rendering of how water molecules combined.

Emma came beside me and took my arm. "What do you think he's saying?"

"He's probably telling them the seven reasons he's a Man United fan." I sensed the frown before I saw it. "That's an inside joke."

"Inside with who?"

"With them."

"Mr. Max?" I turned to see a cluster of parents hovering a respectful distance away.

"Er . . . yes?"

"Can we get a team photo? Please."

"You want a team photo after a routine seven–one win?"

"Oh. Er . . ."

Emma said, "He's fucking with you." The parent relaxed. Got the joke. "Of course we'll do some photos. Max, sort it out."

"Uh-uh," I said. "You're my assistant manager. You come, too. Big Man, Jude, come over here a sec. Team photo."

"But Max," said Big Man. "I didn't do anything. You be in this one. I'll do the next one. When I've earned it."

"No can do, buddy. You did more than me. I didn't tell those five Chester kids to quit, and I didn't tell them to come over to you. They did because they saw all the teams in the area and thought *yours* had the best atmosphere. You've created the best conditions for kids to grow. I painted the front door, but you built the house. Having said that," I said, rubbing my chin. Everyone waited for my next torrent of wisdom. "Having said that, I'm the best-looking, so I should go in the middle."

I didn't see Mike Dean and assumed whatever he had wanted to say he no longer wanted to say. Fine. As for me, I'd treasure the team photo, but I wanted to detach from the scene as fast as poss. Kids in Chester? That case was closed. Job done. Mission accomplished.

Emma and I drove to the cinema, where Henri and Gemma had taken over the foyer and turned it into a buffet. Lots of people came—the Yalleys. Jackie and Livia. Raffi, most of the same first team squad players as the morning, now with the addition of some wives and girlfriends. Including Shona. Ziggy couldn't come—he'd met a woman. If he could score on the pitch with the same frequency he scored off it . . .

Henri hadn't invited the Broughton kids. When I asked why, he mumbled something about not wanting to make jelly and custard, which is all he'd ever seen English kids eat. "I invited all the French children," he added.

"There aren't any," I said.

"Exactly. But if they were here they'd be able to name all the cheeses and possibly even the three different types of ham. Do you see all the ham, Max?"

"These hams are *different*?"

"*Mon dieu*. You are little better than an infant. Leave me! I must flamcray the smogrow." Or something like that. He was having fun, anyway. It was good to see.

I mingled and ate and mingled and drank and when there was half an hour until the World Cup final kicked off, I started to get really excited.

Excited not only to see a mouth-watering matchup, but for this whole MUNDIAL slog to be over. And to see how much a TINO was worth. I suspected one TINO would be worth at least one XP, because it was in Nick's interest for me to grow stronger.

What would I buy? I could maybe unlock three new attributes. Or buy seven new formations. What did I want? What would the next stage in my managerial career be? What skills would I need? The anticipation was making my heart pump faster. My fingertips were tingling.

I felt a tug on my arm. Emma and Gemma were there. Emma's chemical bond to me had vanished and now *they* were covalent. They would be friends long after Emma dumped me. I didn't mind it. If anything, I wished I had a similar friend for life. "Max," said Gemma. "We want to know the story."

"The story."

"Of the final!" said Emma. "The Shakespeare bit. If I have to sit through *another* football match . . . Two in a day. Ugh. At least we can try to get something out of it."

"Huh. Okay."

"Wait!" said Gemma. She gathered the nearby people to give me more of a crowd. I climbed a couple of steps on the staircase that led to the projection room and looked down on my tiny audience. Kisi and James were there, as was Aff and his partner. And Mike Dean! He'd snuck in at some point. I wondered how many hams *he'd* be able to identify. Maybe none. He didn't know the manager of his football club was a ham.

That was weak. I checked to see if anyone had read my thoughts. Emma was smirking at me. She knew *something* had happened. I wished I could spend some XP upgrading my ability to hide my microexpressions.

I spread my arms in a wide circle and intoned, "Beginner's guide to the World Cup final." Then added, "It's Argentina against France."

Henri interrupted me from behind a little suitcase that seemed to be full of spirits. "It's France against Argentina."

I closed my eyes and shook my head. I did another arm circle so that everyone knew where to look. "As most of you know, I'm all about teamwork. Teams that rely on the skill of one individual tend to crash and burn. They're like TV show pilots that get cancelled because the premise isn't strong enough." I tried not to look at MD. "But today's not an ensemble drama. It's a western. A gunfight. It's high noon. Mano a mano. Yeah, there's two incredible teams, but they are totally built around two incredible players. First, Argentina. Messi has been the best player in the world for . . . nearly twenty years? But he's never won the World Cup. If he can win it today, he'll cement his legacy and prove that he's the best who ever played the game. But twenty yards away, fingers twitching, is Kylian Mbappé. He's young, fast, fearless. Better-looking, too. He can do everything Messi can do, and more. He's already won the World Cup. This would be his second, and he's only twenty-three. That's absurd. So that's the story. The old hand versus the young gun. Evans versus Best," I added. I couldn't help myself.

"Who is going to win?" asked James.

"Ah. Great question. It might surprise you, but I actually know the answer." This time I did glance at MD, to check he was listening. He was. "You see, in a story, in a movie, it's the old guy who wins. His experience pays off in some way, or he sleeps with some woman who tells him the secret of beating the newcomer. Yeah. But movies are like that because old people buy more tickets. There's only one place an old guy wins: in fiction. Because in the real world, old people are just old. They do the same old things the same tired old way and if they win, it's blind luck. So what you do is, you fire the seventy-two-year-old mayor who refuses to let the rail company build a track to the town, and you replace him with a twenty-two-year-old who understands about trains and telegrams and can bring growth and prosperity. And maybe some high pressing and overlapping fullbacks."

Gemma groaned. "What the fuck are you talking about? Which one is the mayor? Messi?"

I smiled. "I'm just being a dick. Honestly, I have no clue who will win. It's two brilliant teams with two brilliant players. It's the most closely matched game I can ever remember. It's the perfect final. I just hope it doesn't go to penalties."

The crowd dispersed, and MD approached me. I sat on the stair and looked up at him. "Max," he said, shaking his head. "Great speech, as always. Was that you pitching your services? I fire Ian Evans and hire you? Is that it?"

"No chance," I said. "I told Emma this morning that my biggest goal for today was making it so I never had to come to Chester again."

He frowned and rotated the beer bottle he was holding. He sat next to me and took a swig. "No team at any age level has lost that badly since I took over. That hurt. When that tiny little one you call Future took that penalty . . . I knew he'd score. Players always score against their old teams, right? Seven–one. That hurts."

"Good."

His head snapped my way, but I kept my expression neutral. "I had to placate a lot of people after the match. Assure them it wouldn't happen again. My phone is blowing up. The board are on my case. My position is a lot more precarious than it was this morning." He waited for me to say "good" again. I didn't. He pursed his lips, but then there was a tiny smile. "It was amazing what you did with that team. The way they celebrated at the end was magical. But that eleven is basically the Chester team from the day you came. They never played that well before. How did you do it?"

I was pretty sure I'd already told him how to fix the under-fourteens but he had sided with his shitty employees instead of listening. I had no interest in going over old ground. "What do you want, Mike?"

He was quiet for a long time. The MUNDIAL game was trying to do something, but I suppressed it. It could wait a minute. MD finally spoke. "You got us five thousand pounds today."

"You seem pleased. It's peanuts. A clever manager would put Henk in the first team, give him ten matches against opposition that suited him. In short, make him look like the next big thing, then sell him for fifty K. But your manager didn't even turn up today." I had a lot more to say. I didn't say it.

We sat there for a while. Mike finally said, "I saw your Max Best Challenge video."

"Jackie chose the name."

"And I heard about what you did at Sheffield Wednesday."

I hadn't expected *that*. "How?"

"Your agent told David Cutter who told Ian Evans. They all talk. You joke about old guys not knowing about technology. You're dead wrong. Ian loves WhatsApp more than he loves his hair." He took another swig. "Max. Just tell me if the story is true."

"What's the story you heard?"

"They offered you a playing contract. Big money. Five figures." So Brad had exaggerated the tale! Ten thousand pounds a week! It made him look better, I suppose. "And instead of taking it you barged into a meeting of the owner and some investors and gave them a piece of your mind." A small smile played on his lips. "Is that about right?"

"Basically, yeah. I didn't *barge* into the meeting. It was right there. If you invite a vampire into your house he's allowed to do what he wants."

"Is that right? Well, people are saying you saved Sheffield Wednesday."

"What?"

"The owners decided not to sell. Took a closer look at the plans and didn't like what they found. They've bid on some land for their new training complex. If they were wavering, they're back. All the way back."

"Oh." I thought about it. I'd foiled one of Nick's plans, but I knew he'd simply turn his attention to some other club. It didn't feel like a big win, but it was better than a kick in the teeth. "I suppose I'll be getting my five-figure contract any day now."

He chuckled. "I doubt it. You might have pushed them into doing the right thing, but they're not going to want to have a forty-foot poster of you on the side of the stadium." Once he was finished stating the bleeding obvious, he wedged a fingernail between two teeth, presumably checking for ham. "It's not fun being on the receiving end of one of your outbursts. Believe me. The thing is, knowing that you did that reframes a lot of your actions. Ian said you're all about money. But then why turn down ten grand a week?"

"MD," I said. "Just to be honest and upfront here. I don't want you getting a false impression of my sacrifice. It wasn't ten grand. It was nine." I thought this was really funny, but he didn't even blink.

"It doesn't matter. It's a lot of money. When I asked you to do some scouting, you were ecstatic to be getting a couple of hundred from me. So if Ian's wrong about you being a money fiend, what else? You told me the youth setup was broken. Everyone said you were a fantasist. Today ended that debate. You brought us Raffi Brown and he's already made his debut, so anyone who says you can't spot a player doesn't have a leg to stand on. You're lighting the league up for Darlington so that's a black mark for anyone who doubted you as a player. And I just can't get over the joy on the faces of the Knights when they saw you again. And the Broughton lads. Nice One's son. That huddle at the end. What were they saying?"

"No clue. That's their inner sanctum. It's not for us to know."

MD gave me a strange look, but then stared at the beer again. "And you're hiring a coach for them! With your own money. No wonder they think the world of you."

"You're exaggerating. They think I'm cool and they trust me to tell them the truth. And most of all, they like me because I give them permission to do what they want to do." I stood up. I wanted to find a seat at the back of the cinema and get stuck into the MUNDIAL game. Earn some TINOs.

"What is it they want to do?"

I smiled. "To play football the Max Best way." It was an awesome exit line. I took two quick strides away, but MD wasn't thinking cinematically. Fucking amateurs!

"I should have made you director of football, shouldn't I?"

"Yeah." He looked so small, then, so sad, and I felt so sorry for him, that I decided to help him out. "Mike. You know what you have to do. Sack Ian Evans before January twenty-first. When you're interviewing the next guy, ask how many youth team players he's given debuts to. Ask how many youth team matches he's been to." I thought through what I'd learned in my time as a player. "Ask his opinion on hazing and what he does to build an inclusive culture. Ask what formation he'd play against three-five-two and four-five-one and if it's the same make him defend it. Does he let players give input into tactics? Can his assistant take over during a match or is he just a yes man?" I was suddenly tired; I waved my hand around. "Things like that."

"Max," he said, not looking at me. "Why the twenty-first?"

I sighed. He knew the answer. Why was he making me say it? "Because that's when Darlo are playing Chester. And that's when I'm going to do you one last favour. I'm going to run up the score to the point Chester are mentioned on the ten o'clock news. There will be a discussion on *talkSPORT*—what's the biggest sporting humiliation *you've* ever seen? I want the *Times* to run a think piece calling for the introduction of the Evans Rule—when the scoreline gets too overwhelming, the referee can stop the match. If you won't fire him, I'll make him quit. Because in his own way, the guy is as cancerous as those investors who wanted to kill Sheffield Wednesday."

I grabbed some drinks and went to hide at the back of the cinema. I finally opened the MUNDIAL screen and instantly regretted not doing it earlier. The final stage of the mini game was to be played without restriction. As with the semifinals, I could choose my starting lineup, captain, and formation. But now I could also choose which team I wanted to be.

France or Argentina. It was virtually impossible to say which team was better. The goalkeepers were similar, both had good defences, hardworking and talented midfielders, functional strikers. The main point of difference was the two star players. Messi or Mbappé? I liked and respected them both.

In the end I said if you can't beat them, join them. France had beaten me in every match of the MUNDIAL mini game. I hadn't found a way to stop Mbappé without leaving giant holes in the team. So fine. *Vive la France* and all that.

So, formation. Anything vaguely conservative would do. Keep it tight and let your star cause mayhem. That was how the real manager thought. It was boring but effective. I wasn't stupid enough to think I could do better. So . . . conservative.

There's a detective TV show where about thirty-eight minutes into every episode, while the hero is failing to solve the case, he sees the thing that helps him make a connection. Example: there's a red car and the detective says, "Of course! Ford! The killer couldn't af-*ford* his rent! The murderer is one of the tenants!" Or some shit like that. It's garbage. I love it. I looked around the cinema hoping for similar inspiration. Maybe the exit signs looked like a 4-4-2? Not really.

My eyes rested on Aff. The left winger. I quickly scanned the rest of his row. Seeing all the players there got my skin tingling. Here we go! Me on the right. Henri up front. Ryder in defence. James Yalley in the DM slot. Ziggy wasn't here, so we didn't have a second striker, but we had Raffi for midfield. Ben in goal, obvs. We had the bulk of a 4-1-4-1 right here in the cinema! Something about the thought froze me. The guys who had accepted Henri's invite, either to the morning matches or to this viewing, were top lads. No doubt about that. And they had talent to spare. These players could take a sixth-tier club to League Two. Two promotions in two seasons. Easy.

I daydreamed about that for a while, then remembered what I was actually supposed to be doing.

In my mental screens, I scanned the French squad and picked a team to suit 4-1-4-1, making sure all the little details were taken care of, like who should go up for corners and who would take the left-sided and right-sided set pieces. I took it seriously. I put all my current football knowledge into the task.

The work done, I relaxed and settled back to enjoy the first half of both matches.

Both were one-sided, dull affairs.

In my match, the halftime score was 0–0, but I was pleased with our domination. We had four shots against one for our opponents, and we were dominating possession, too. Twice the Argentines had been forced to take yellow cards to stop our attacks. It was going well.

Meanwhile, the real-world France were losing 2–0. They had been collectively shocking. Mbappé? Invisible. Messi? Majestic. Game over. Under the Evans Rule, I'd have stopped the contest.

The audience filed out of the screen and took positions in the foyer. Lots of chat. Mostly happy faces—it felt good to watch France lose on a screen that big! The more people I chatted to, the warmer I felt. The more at peace. Life wasn't half bad, sometimes.

Henri was downcast. Jackie Reaper, for some reason, was the one trying to cheer him up. It might have gone better if Livia wasn't by his side.

While that scene was playing out, Emma detached from her bestie long enough to give me some attention. I told her I was fine but would love to introduce her to some people. "To make me seem like a real boy." I started with Shona. Still trying to claw my reputation points back up to zero. It wasn't going all that well until I told her I'd remembered her Tupperware and had it in my car. That worked wonders.

The break was all too short. We drifted back into Screen 1 and retook our seats.

It was about the eightieth minute when everything went nuts. Henri, resigned to France losing, was doomscrolling Twitter more than watching the action. I couldn't blame him—France simply hadn't turned up. Giving Mbappé 4 out of 10 would have been generous.

"Max!" Henri screamed, leaping to his feet. I matched the move but my jump took me into a kung-fu stance. I, er . . . don't know kung fu. "Max! Telford have sacked their manager!"

"Holy shit! Oh!" I slipped out of my row and walked up and down the side of the cinema, holding my head, rubbing my face. This was it! This was the opportunity! Old Nick had basically promised me that I'd get any job I applied for. Well, here it was! I raced to the front, where the room had a little stage so they could host conferences. "Mute that!" I shouted. The projectionist obeyed. "Wow. Didn't expect that to work. Er . . . Emma! Emma!" I got down on one knee. "Babes. Will you Telford me?"

From the centre of a middle row, she tilted her head and popped a crisp into her mouth. "What?"

"Will you Telford me?"

"What does that involve?"

"Come with me to Telford. Right now."

Another crisp. Gemma gave her a dig and they giggled at each other. Emma remembered I was there. "Why?"

"I'm going to apply for and accept the position of manager."

"You're inviting me to Telford? Where is it?"

"Down south somewhere. What does it matter? I'll be the manager. Hey," I said, standing, looking for Mike Dean—he seemed the most likely to know the answer to my next question. I didn't spot him, so I opened it up. "Football dudes. What colour do Telford play in?"

"Black and white," said Ben Cavanagh.

"Max Best's black and white army!" I chanted. "Max Best's black and white army!" Kisi joined in on the second round, but no one else. Partly because almost everyone was affiliated to Chester, but also because they were gaping at the big screen.

The sound came back on. I turned and saw why—France had a penalty. I rushed from the stage to a seat. The ref finished checking the hundreds of things they feel they need to check. Mbappé approached the ball, hesitated, and smacked it into the left of the goal. Two–one!

Fun, but France were toast. They had no chance. I wanted to start my career, finally. I snuck into the middle of the theatre. "Emma," I whispered. "You coming?"

"Yes," she said. "After the match."

"You hate football," I reminded her. "This is torture for you."

"Nope. It just got good."

"It's not that gerrr holy shiiiiit!"

Henri cried out. Gemma shrieked. The place went nuts.

France had won the ball, played it to the left, hit a hopeful lob in the direction of Mbappé, and he'd—stupidly—tried a first-time shot from miles out. He could have dribbled closer! But guess what? The guy knew how to play. Hitting it so early took the keeper by surprise. The ball thumped into the bottom right. Two–two!

Henri went tonto. He was riding his cinema seat like it was a rodeo bull.

"Okay," I said. "We can wait till it's over."

The room was abuzz.

Jackie Reaper was watching like his hands were glued to his head. Mr. and Mrs. Yalley were turned away from the screen. Mr. Yalley kept dabbing his neck with a handkerchief. Aff, the Irishman, kept saying, "But I don't care who wins. Why am I so stressed?" Shona kept leaving because the noise was too much for baby Serina, but then running back in to see the latest wild twist.

The final had hit the heights.

Messi had scored. Mbappé had scored twice. France were alive. Football as chess with men, a highly structured, regimented, turn-based strategy, was out of the window. This game was untethered. Wild. Players were running everywhere, seemingly at random, with one thought and one thought alone: win.

France had a ninety-third-minute attack. Close! Argentina got the ball to Messi in the sixth minute of injury time and you'd have bet your house on him scoring. The French keeper tipped it over the bar. Full-time and I was exhausted. The last twenty minutes had been so intense.

I had just enough mental capacity to check my MUNDIAL—it was 0–0 and, like the real match, heading for extra time. I threw on a load of subs to keep things fresh.

I went to the bathroom. Emma and Gemma went, too. The timing turned out to be important.

Extra time had already started when I snuck back in. For the first time, the projectionist turned the house lights down. The match was so good that it deserved the full cinematic treatment. What would happen next? Who knew? The cameras found Messi and Mbappé. They seemed to know.

I leaned back and drank it in. The noise was incredible. The commentators were high on the drama.

Gemma was back, somewhere in the theatre. As the thirty minutes of extra time unfolded, she screamed every time there was an attack. As Argentina restored their grip on the contest, Henri was as loud as the surround-sound system. "No, don't do that!" "Why are you offside, you lazy shit?" and when Messi scored in the 108th minute, he switched to French.

The winning goal deserves its own chapter, but suffice to say that I was taken by how almost everyone played the situation perfectly—the goalkeeper made a great save and a defender took up a position and very nearly kept the ball from crossing the line. But Messi did it. It was over. At last!

I started to think about Telford United.

But the French were still playing. Why were they still playing? Didn't they know it was over?

They had a corner. The ball travelled to Mbappé. He shot for the top-right corner—someone handballed it! I couldn't believe what I was seeing. Mbappé had another penalty! To equalise, with mere minutes remaining. Henri was not yelling now. I tried to spot him in the darkened room, and I saw one shape that was more slumped than the others. It must have been him.

Mbappé scored, becoming only the second player in history to score a hat trick in a World Cup final. The young gun, the old master, what happens when *both* win?

I realised this wasn't a western—it was a *Fast and Furious* movie and the stars had contracts that said they couldn't lose fights. In those movies, fights had to be ended by some improbable outside event.

The last thirty seconds of the match were the closest I hope to ever come to an out-of-body experience. I was fixed in place. Was I breathing? Not sure. My MUNDIAL match ended, still 0–0. I was supposed to choose penalty takers. But all I could do was watch, and what I was seeing was unreal. Totally incomprehensible.

A lofted pass over the Argentina defence fell to a French player—he absolutely wellied it, but the goalie stuck out a leg and it rebounded to safety. Incredible! One guy nearly won the World Cup! The other guy single-handedly saved it! The ball was cleared to the midfield, where an Argentine guy took it, turned, and suddenly they were on the attack! French players steamed back, but the cross came in—it was perfect!—onto the head of the striker—but it went wide!

The only person not screaming was baby Serina.

The referee blew the final whistle. My pulse came down to a healthy level. A coin toss meant the penalty shoot-out would take place against a backdrop of Argentina fans. Big advantage for Messi and his men. In my MUNDIAL game, France won that toss and shot into their fans.

And that was the difference, perhaps. My fictional French team won, but the real one lost. Mbappé and Messi scored *their* penalties. Then all they could do was watch, fingers crossed.

I got cursemail. I couldn't deal with it right then and there.

It took a minute for the house lights to come back on. Nobody moved for a while, then we started to file out into the foyer.

As the host and only Frenchman, Henri became the sun around which we orbited. He seemed to be philosophical about the defeat, and effusive in his praise for Messi. Emma made eye contact with me—time to go?

I grabbed a glass and knife and stood on the nearest chair. *Ding ding ding.* "Attention, *s'il vous plait!*" People rotated to face me. "I just want to thank our gracious and charming host, Henri Lyons, for booking this cinema and giving us all a wonderful experience. I know I'll never forget that last forty minutes. To Henri!" I raised the glass and so did anyone else who was currently carrying one.

I stepped down.

"Max?" said Mike Dean, emerging from the bathroom. His voice cut through. The crowd parted between us, then took on the shape of a circle. "I thought you'd gone."

"Still here," I said, smiling. "Not for long." I was about to leave Chester with a big bag full of tiny wins.

"I heard someone say," he declaimed, with a dramatic nose-pinch, "you were going to apply for the Telford United position."

He must have been at the buffet when Henri had told me the news, and he must have thought I'd driven off when the house lights were dimmed. "Yep! Heading there right now."

"It's Sunday! There's no one around."

"Someone fired the manager today. *Someone's* there. If I can't find anyone, I'll check into a hotel. I'll be at the ground at seven a.m. Hopefully be the manager by quarter past."

He gestured. "They're fifteen points from safety. They'll be relegated for sure."

"It's three points for a win. Fifteen points is five wins. We'll be ahead of Chester by the end of January. I haven't checked the maths but if it's possible, I'll be gunning for the playoffs. If not, we'll start building for next season. James! Where's James? James, want to be my starting DM by the end of the season?"

He grinned. "Manager Best, I would like that. But I will have to discuss your offer with my agent."

I gave him a fist bump. "Telford United are pleased to announce the signing of the league's best right winger and non-league's best defensive midfielder. Please do not choke on our exhaust fumes." I smiled and took a step forward. The exit was behind Mike Dean.

He took a step to block me. "Max, wait. I thought you were a big-shot player now. I thought you would get a huge contract at a big club. What kind of money can Telford pay? Did they get a rich owner?"

"They're fan-owned. I assume they'll pay peanuts." I took a step to the right, just to see what he'd do. Sure enough, he matched me.

"But if Telford can afford you, so can we."

My smile faded. "Chester does not have a managerial vacancy, MD. Unless you've finally seen sense."

"I won't sack Ian Evans."

"Then what are you *doing*?" I was annoyed now. It felt like he was trying to delay me from getting to Telford. Had he been on the phone to a mate? Trying to make sure his friend got the job before me?

He put his palms out, waist high. The way you might do with a crazy person. "When I thought you'd driven off I got desperate. I tried to call but your phone is off." He took in a breath. "We need you."

I tried to parse what he was saying. "Not to be a *manager*. Not to be a *player*, because there's no way I'd play for Evans. So what? What do you need?"

"Fix the youth setup."

"Mike!" I yelled. "It can't be fixed while Ian Evans is there! Jesus Christ, man. Will you please listen to me? The twelves feed into the fourteens, who feed into the sixteens, who feed into the eighteens, who need to get chances in the first team. If you block *any* step, the whole thing fails. You can't fix a youth system at a club where young players can't progress!"

"Then be our head scout. Head of recruitment."

"I'll be that at Telford. And I'll get to put the players I find into the team and give them enough game time to reach their potential. I'll have total control, Mike. I'll be able to do things my way. Here? I'd need to find Ian Evans-shaped players. Would he put James into the team? Would he fuck! And that's the joke. Unless Mo Salah is shopping at Cheshire Oaks, James is the most talented player in this *county* right now! Mike! Telford will give me the chance to flex all my muscles. All you have to offer me is Ian Evans."

"You're not ready to be a manager," he said. "You can be immature and abrasive. Parents will put up with it when they see their kids so happy and energised. But think about dealing with players. Sponsors. The board. The media. You're talking about carrying a whole club on your shoulders. It's too much, Max. Too much, too soon. Take an intermediate step."

"You're probably right," I said, done with this conversation. I looked around. Most of my friends and clients were here. I tried to read their eyes, tried to see if anyone thought I was being a dick. It didn't feel like that. "But I'm going anyway. I'll send you a postcard from the Premier League."

"But Max!" MD whined. "If there were three games left of the season and we needed six points to be safe, wouldn't you play for us, then?"

"If I was choosing the team, yes." He shook his head and looked at the fluorescent ceiling lights. "Fine," I admitted. "Yes, I'd make sure you stayed up. But I can only play for two teams in one season. Darlington and Telford makes two. So that's not an option."

"It is," he said, "if you don't go. If you take a job with us. Look, I . . . can we talk in private, please?"

"Nope."

I'd forced him into a place where he had to make a very public pitch. What he said next would tell me how serious he was. "Ian's contract runs out in six months. We have a succession plan. A young, dynamic, forward-thinking manager. You'll like him. He'll promote youth players. He'll take your advice on how to use players. You can do almost everything you can do at Telford, here! With your friends. Your clients. Perfect conditions to achieve your goals while growing as a person."

"What job are you offering me, Mike?"

He looked away. "Director of football."

There were gasps, especially from the footballers in the audience. This was more mind-blowing to them than me becoming player-manager of a struggling team. I'd be in charge of virtually every aspect of the club. Scouting, recruitment, contracts, the youth teams. Ryder, Aff, Ben—their futures would be in my hands. I'd be in charge. In charge of everything except the first team.

"Okay, I accept. First order of business. I order you to sack Ian Evans."

I lost some of the spectators, then. That was the immature Max everyone kept talking about.

"That's not on the table. We don't sack people at the drop of a hat. When a sacking is justified, you won't have any complaints about my speed." He seemed to be thinking of one person in particular.

"You mean Spectrum? I wouldn't fire him," I said. MD's eyes widened. I shook my head. If he'd offered the job to me at halftime, I think I'd have bitten his hand off. But now . . . now there was a fantastic job waiting for me. Player-manager at a fan-owned club. With the club being as small as it was, I'd be the de facto director of football, too, there. The main difference being that I'd get to pick the team. The role at Telford was more than I'd ever dreamed of.

I took a breath and was about to refuse when Henri pulled at my sleeve. He was smiling. "We could play together. This season."

"Do you think it's immature that I would refuse to play for Evans?"

He shrugged. "It is your right given your position. But you'd still train, no? Would you train? What about friendlies? What about the final day of the season? A win needed to save Chester. 'Up steps Max Best with the free kick. Henri Lyons rises above all! Chester have done it!'"

I thought about the 4-1-4-1 formation made up of players from Chester. With James and Ziggy on board, we'd have a hell of a squad. Hell, with a bit of scouting I could create a powerhouse team that even a hack like Evans could have led to the title.

Shona stepped closer. She was holding her daughter. "You're wrong about Ian Evans. He's a good man. A kind man. It sounds like you'd only need to work with him for six months. Six months! If you can't do that, that says more about you than it does about him."

"Shona," complained Raffi.

"That's all right, Raffi. She's right. When she says it like that, she's right." I bit a fingernail while everyone watched. It was surreal.

Emma came up to me. Little arm rub. Smile. "What do the choices mean?"

"At Telford I'd be like Mbappé. Star player. Everything goes through me. The Chester gig would be like being Messi. A little bit removed, pulling the strings."

"You want to be more involved."

"Both sound fun. But yes. I want to manage."

Her lips curled. "There's plenty of time for that. I'm sure you can find some way to satisfy that particular urge."

She didn't know about my ambition of taking a team all the way to the top as fast as possible. As director of football, could I create a team so dominant that any manager would lead them to promotion? It was an added layer of risk. Trusting someone else could set me back a year or two.

I looked at MD. I knew where the first team needed improving. I could fix the youth team in ten minutes. "Mike, Tyson has to go. Sullivan has to go." MD expressed unhappiness, but nodded. "That's the fourteens fixed. Didn't take long. Any talented older kids we'll have to loan out to other clubs to get some first-team minutes. That's humiliating." I bit my nails some more. "I suppose this way I'd be able to play a couple more games for Darlo. Have a proper goodbye instead of fucking off one random Sunday." I sensed that I was tilting towards Chester. But why? At Telford, I'd be able to do what I really loved—manage games.

MD seemed to read my mind. "You'll be able to take control over the Knights and the boys' teams, whenever you want! To keep your hand in."

I nodded. The kids. Yeah. Maybe. Every now and then.

Kisi tutted. "Oh, now he's going back to Chester!" She laughed. "Make up your mind!"

I opened my mouth to hit her with some witticism, but a thought struck me. A way to make the next six months more bearable. Keep me busy. Keep me energised.

"Mike, I'll do it." He stood straighter, until I added, "For two hundred thousand pounds."

His mouth dropped open. He looked around for help. Henri volunteered. "Is that to be your transfer fee, Max?"

"What? No. If I can't manage the first team, I'll create a different first team. I'll sign for Chester as a player, for emergencies only. I'll be director of football. Piece of piss. And I'll also create and manage Chester's first-ever official women's team. Two hundred K should be enough to get us off the ground."

Kisi yelped and raced over to hug me. "Make me your first signing!"

"We can't afford players of your class." I smiled. "Not yet." I grinned at Emma, at Jackie, Livia, and the first-team players. Henri sidled up to me and put his arm around my shoulders. I copied the gesture. "And Mike," I said. "One last demand." He peered at me nervously. "I want your parking space."

45

EPILOGUE

I was mashed. Decision fatigue. Overstimulation. Too much football. Too much progress.

Or maybe just too much champagne.

Emma took the car keys and I fell into the passenger seat.

She concentrated until we got onto the M56. Those ten minutes were good for me. Regenerative.

My car's heating was having one of those days when it didn't want to work too hard. Emma had her Broughton beanie on. Blonde hair poked out. She pushed a few strands away and glanced at me. "Sometimes I really like you," she said. I smiled and waited for her to explain. She didn't. That was top.

A while later, the conversation resumed.

"So," she said. "You lost."

"I did?"

"You said the biggest win would be if you never had to set foot in Chester again."

"Yeah," I said, with a smile. "I did say that. Feels like a win, though. I've finally got a job where I can make a difference. Do things my way."

"I'm glad."

"If it works out."

"What?"

I leaned forward, then squirmed back. I felt guilty. I had to tell her my secret. I'm sure I had a cheeky grin on my face. "After the whole, you know, scene . . . MD came over. A bit sheepishly. The idea of me racing off to Telford made him speak out of turn. Jump the gun. He said there was one minor hurdle. Little more than a technicality. But since he's creating a new position, it'll need to be approved by the owners. That's the fans. He'll have to get the board on board."

"And?"

"The board comprises seven fans. Members. They oversee Mike Dean. I'll have to meet them and charm them."

"Oh."

"I know one of the seven. No chance that prick'll vote for me. But there's no reason the others won't. I'm a million-pound player and all that. Also, not many people know this, Emma, but I can be *quite* charming. Anyway, if I can't persuade four fans that I know what I'm doing, none of this would work anyway."

Her fingers twitched on the steering wheel. "One thing I *didn't* like. Are you really going to kick those two kids out?"

"No. Not right away. They're Chester fans. I'll give them a chance. When I said that, I was testing MD. How far's he willing to go? His limit is somewhere between cutting two kids and firing a failing manager. That's fine . . . for now. But look. In this job I'll have to do some shitty things to good people."

"And what about Darlington?"

"I'll stay for the time being. Once I've met the board and they've made their decision, I'll tell Cutter." That didn't sound right. "Or maybe I should talk to him already in case word leaks out."

"That would be the mature thing to do."

I glanced at her. Tried to read her lips. "Do you think I'm immature?"

"I think you're more mature than most twenty-two-year-old men."

That pleased me. It was days until I realised she'd tricked me into thinking it was a compliment.

She shifted gear, literally and conversationally. "What was the last thing that helped you make your mind up? It wasn't managing a women's team."

I frowned. "It was you and Gemma."

"The fact that we'll be able to do double dates all the time?"

"No, I don't mean that. But that might be nice. In moderation . . . No, I was thinking of your relationship. You're such good friends. I don't have that. I don't have a real friend."

Emma opened her mouth, but chose to keep her thoughts to herself.

"As director of football, I might have to fine Henri. One day I'll sell Raffi. I might decide the whole club has to play four-three-three and that'll be the end of Aff. I'll be a fucking nonstop pain in the arse for Mike Dean. Do you get what I'm saying? There's no way I'll still be friends with *all* these guys when I'm an old man." I rubbed my hands together and studied the folds in my skin. Being an old man was many years away. "But one. I can save football and have one friend, right?"

"What did you say?"

"I can save Chester and have one friend, can't I?"

"Of course you can. Why not?"

I thought about it. About my failings as a person. "Oh . . ."

"What?"

"I forgot to give Shona her Tupperware. Fucking hell, Max."

She patted my hand. "I did it."

"You did? Wow." My little moment of melancholy was gone. I smiled at her. "Sometimes I really like you."

I opened my cursemail.

Quadrennial Assigned TINO Accumulator/Reducer

VERSION COPA MUNDIAL

– COMPLETED –

TINOs gained: 3,728

Converting TINOs into Experience Points . . .

At the bottom of my vision was a loading bar. As it progressed, sometimes quickly, sometimes not at all, the curse told me what it was working on.

Assessing multipliers . . .

Adding World Cup final victory bonus.

Minutes watched bonus . . . applied.

Entertainment bonus . . . applied.

Funky formation bonus . . . denied.

TINOs spotted . . . majority.

TINOs celebrated . . . most.

Applying deduction for lack of interest in the third-place playoff.

Applying penalty for mocking the fashion choices of talented FIFA executives.

The loading bar hit 99% and stayed there for ages. I thought it had crashed. Would it stay in my vision forever? How could I reboot it? Turn myself off and on?

The wait gave me time to reflect on the whole MUNDIAL farce. I'd watched most of the matches from Qatar and answered trivia questions or managed the teams. Why? Obviously it was a test. But a test of what? What was it preparing me for? Had it all been worth it?

Process complete.

Your multiplier: 1.

Converting TINOs into Experience Points.

You have been awarded: 3,728 experience points.

XP balance: 4,465

Thank you for playing COPA MUNDIAL.

Given how much time I'd put in, I'd have earned more XP by going to watch park football instead of doing the MUNDIAL thing. But somehow the time spent didn't seem like a waste. In a way I couldn't put my finger on, I felt more complete.

One thought that had been nagging at me was the timing of the perk. It had arrived when I was talking to James, and I'd spent more time with him than I'd planned. I'd also spent more time with Longstaff and Junior. I'd reconnected with Jackie and had an excuse to call Henri when I suspected he was feeling down. I could have done all that without the mini game, but I wouldn't have. It had given me a little shove in the direction of connection.

And the effort had earned me *some* XP.

Time for some retail therapy! I went to the curse shop and saw all the things I had available—formations, statistics upgrades, attributes, and the mysterious perk called Playdar.

I exited the shop and blinked—the entire MUNDIAL interface was gone.

That saddened me in some small way. It had been a big part of my life and now it was just . . . not there.

I shook it off. Things change. So, what to buy? The formation I would use with the women's team depended on which players I could find, but I'd almost certainly start with 4-4-2. Loading up on new formations could wait a few weeks.

As DoF, I'd *surely* be able to get access to real-life scouting data, maybe even a subscription to that scouting platform paid for by the club. Which lessened the benefit of buying a statistics upgrade.

One thing was for sure: I'd get a lot of use out of any attribute perks I bought. That was a slam-dunk investment.

But what of Playdar? I read and re-read the description.

Playdar. 8,000 XP. This perk directs you to the most talented footballer not in your database who is currently playing football within a certain radius. Can be upgraded.

I hated when the curse was vague like this. Certain radius? Could mean anything. Most talented? Did that mean CA or PA? There was only one way to find out, really, and that was to buy it.

I expected I'd be underwhelmed at first, have a major case of buyer's remorse. Then over time I'd realise it was a top perk and be thankful I bought it.

There were two major factors in this decision. One was the fact that I was over halfway to being able to afford it. I wasn't sure I'd have the discipline to save up for months to buy it without buying every formation and attribute perk as soon as I could. I'd always find some excuse where I needed the shiny new object. So it was sort of a now or never situation.

Two, as DoF I'd be immersed in football and XP would surely come thick and fast. Especially if I paused my playing career for the rest of this season. That would free up two match days a week. I wondered if a director of football would get free tickets to watch teams like Newcastle? Probably, right? So that would be 630 XP.

I'd mostly made my mind up, but then remembered I had an assistant.

"Emma. If you were me, you'd need to scout loads of players, right? I'll be scouting an entire *squad* of women."

"That seems like a zany 1990s comedy."

"And I'll be looking at loads of boys to restock the youth teams. And the men's team have a couple of weak spots. Could use a left back. And so on, right? So imagine I had money for an assistant. Would I want him to be able to find hot prospects, or to give me more detailed info about individual players?"

"I don't get it."

"Let's say he was with us this morning watching Chester. Option one. He'd point to Tyson and say, 'He's the best one.' Or option two. He'd point to Henk and say, 'He's got good passing but bad leadership.' That's . . . that's the choice."

She pushed her bottom lip out. "But that's not hard, is it? The first one. Find the best players. You need to find lots, quickly. They're all going to have flaws, aren't they? If Henk has bad leadership, does that mean you wouldn't sign him? Doesn't it simply mean you wouldn't make him captain?"

Yeah. That seemed right. Buying Playdar was risky compared to unlocking attributes, but I was more than halfway there, and the payoff was potentially much greater. I fancied a quick break from football, but then I'd be grinding hard. Playdar was too intriguing not to aim for.

I closed the shop.

I got a text.

"Emma, babes. What is FWIW?"

"For what it's worth."

"Ah, yeah."

Jackie: FWIW I think you made the right choice. Chester's lucky to have you.

That was nice. Thoughtful.

"BTW is by the way, right?"
"Right."

Jackie: BTW. Now that I think about it, it's good Ziggy didn't sign for FC United long-term. You'll be able to bring him to Chester next season. And James. The next manager's going to have a decent team. Isn't he?

There was no smiley face. No party horn emoji. But I felt him smirking at me.

"That fuck!" I said, slapping the dashboard. Emma's eyes widened and the car slowed a little. "Sorry," I said. "I'm calm. It's all good. I just realised I've been played. And how I've been played. And who MD has got lined up to be the next Chester manager."

"Oh," she said, worried. "Is it bad?"

"No," I said. "It's top." I realised what it all meant and let out a tiny, orgasmic groan. "Oh! With him in charge, we'll win the league next season. For sure. He *gets* it. Oh, that was the only cloud on the horizon. Now it's gone. Whoo! Yeah, we'll win and he'll develop my players. Oh, fuck. To think I nearly went to Telford. This is much better." Suddenly I was laughing. Laughing hard.

"What?" said Emma, laughing because I was.

"It's all top, but the toppest of all? I'll be his boss."

I finished wiping the joy from my eyes and sighed. "Best day ever," I said.

I sensed Emma doing something weird with her face, but by the time I turned, she was normal. "Maybe now's a good time to ask, then."

"Oh, shit."

She smiled. "Nothing bad. I understand if it's too early for you but . . . do you want to come to Christmas dinner? With my mum and dad."

For some reason I thought of Beth. When we'd started our fling or whatever the word for it was, I'd been scared she'd get clingy. I was afraid of commitment, big time. If she'd invited me to meet her parents I would have run a mile. Now, I was more alive. More social. More willing to meet people. To connect. "Like a real boy."

"What?"

"I didn't say anything. Um . . . yes. Let's do it. I'd like to meet your dad."

"You already have."

That was a thinker. Of course I hadn't. "Oh!" I imploded into a tiny ball of shame. "Your knight in shining armour. Why didn't you tell me?"

"I thought you were pretending not to get it. I thought it was a weird prank."

An older guy who'd paid her way through university. Duh! "Fuck me. That's the stupidest thing I've ever done."

"I doubt it. Well, great. Christmas with Max Best. I'll let them know!"

A road sign showed the distance until Manchester. We'd drive around and head to Leeds, then turn towards Darlo. "Hey, since we're doing family Christmas and stuff. And seeing as Manchester's right there . . ." I double-checked I wanted to finish the thought. I did. "Let's go see my mum."

"Oh! Yes! Of course. But it's Sunday night. Will they let you in? Don't they have rules about visiting times?"

"Emma," I said. "I'm a twenty-two-year-old director of football." I leaned back, looked out of the window at the world I was about to conquer. "I make my own rules."

Senior Management Stats

None

Your Status

Your Reputation in England: Unknown

Your World Reputation: Unknown

XP balance: 4,465

Playing Stats

Darlington FC 22/23

Squad number: 77

TED STEEL

Appearances: 5 starts, 2 matches as sub

Goals: 9

Assists: 3

Man of the Match Awards: 4

Yellow Cards: 0

Red Cards: 0

Average Rating out of 10 (As estimated by Max Best): 11

ABOUT THE AUTHOR

Ted Steel is the author of the Player Manager series, which features a charming but secretive main character. He also wrote *Nerves of Steel*, a LitRPG featuring a charming but secretive main character. When asked to provide a bit of color for his biography, Steel was charming but . . . secretive. Learn more at www.ted-steel.com.

DISCOVER
STORIES UNBOUND

PodiumAudio.com

www.ingramcontent.com/pod-product-compliance
Ingram Content Group UK Ltd.
Pitfield, Milton Keynes, MK11 3LW, UK
UKHW041433180426
11947UKWH00007B/406